PRAISE FOR THESE TALENTED

AUTHORS

DIANA PALMER

"Simmering with leashed sensuality, pulsating with passion restrained, and seething with a sexuality ruthlessly suppressed, *Rogue Stallion* generates enough electricity to light up a Montana city."
—*Affaire de Coeur*

"Nobody tops Diana Palmer...I love her stories."
—*New York Times* bestselling author
Jayne Ann Krentz

JACKIE MERRITT

"With masterful use of emotions, Jackie Merritt brings her marvelous storytelling abilities to *The Widow and the Rodeo Man*."
—*Romantic Times Magazine*

"Jackie Merritt knows just how to set every reader's heart on fire."
—*Romantic Times Magazine*

MYRNA TEMTE

"*Sleeping with the Enemy* is a tremendous romance story.... Kudos to marvelous Myrna Temte for doing such a great job by capturing the heart and soul of the Native American people."
—*Affaire de Coeur*

"Myrna Temte just gets better and better...."
—*Romantic Times Magazine*

Diana Palmer

With over 35 million copies of her books in print, bestselling, award-winning Diana Palmer is one of North America's most beloved authors. She got her start in writing as a newspaper reporter and published her first romance novel for Silhouette Books in 1982. In 1993 she celebrated the publication of her fiftieth novel for Silhouette Books. *Affaire de Coeur* lists her as one of the top ten romance authors in the country. She is the recipient of eleven national bestseller awards and numerous readers' choice awards. Her fans the world over treasure her sensual and charming stories.

Jackie Merritt

An accountant for many years, Jackie has happily traded numbers for words. Next to her family, books are her greatest joy. She started writing in 1987 and her efforts paid off only a year later with the publication of her first novel. She recently gave up her permanent home in Las Vegas, Nevada, in favor of one that can be moved—on a daily basis, if need be. She and her husband are traveling in a large, comfortable recreational vehicle, and Jackie plans to soak up the atmosphere of the western states where she sets most of her books.

Myrna Temte

Myrna grew up in Montana and attended college in Wyoming. She currently resides with her husband in Washington State. Known for her highly emotional, compelling stories, Myrna has developed a loyal reader following. Though always a "readaholic," Myrna never dreamed of becoming an author. But once she started reading romances, she soon became hooked, both as a reader and a writer. Now this bestselling author is also a two-time finalist for the prestigious Romance Writers of America RITA Award.

DIANA PALMER

JACKIE MERRITT

MYRNA TEMTE

MAVERICK

Hearts

Silhouette Books

Published by Silhouette Books

America's Publisher of Contemporary Romance

Special thanks and acknowledgment are given to Diana Palmer, Jackie Merritt and Myrna Temte for their contributions to MAVERICK HEARTS.

 SILHOUETTE BOOKS

ISBN 0-373-65210-0

MAVERICK HEARTS

Copyright © 1999 by Harlequin Books S.A.

The publisher acknowledges the copyright holders of the individual works as follows:

ROGUE STALLION
Copyright © 1994 by Harlequin Books S.A.

THE WIDOW AND THE RODEO MAN
Copyright © 1994 by Harlequin Books S.A.

SLEEPING WITH THE ENEMY
Copyright © 1994 by Harlequin Books S.A.

Printed in U.S.A.

CONTENTS

ROGUE STALLION
by Diana Palmer

One

There was a lull in Sheriff Judd Hensley's office, broken only by the soft whir of the fan. It sometimes amused visitors from back East that springtime in Whitehorn, Montana, was every bit as unpredictable as spring in the southeastern part of America, and that the weather could be quite warm. But the man sitting across the desk from Hensley was neither visitor nor was he amused. His dark, handsome face was wearing a brooding scowl, and he was glaring at his superior.

"Why can't the city police investigate? They have two detectives. I'm the only special investigator in the sheriff's department, and I'm overworked as it is," Sterling McCallum said, trying once more.

Hensley toyed with a pen, twirling it on the desk absently while he thought. He was about the same build as McCallum, rugged and quiet. He didn't say much. When he did, the words meant something.

He looked up from the desk. "I know that," he said. "But right now, you're the one who deserves a little aggravation."

McCallum crossed his long legs and leaned back with a rough sigh. His black boots had a flawless shine, a legacy from his years in the U.S. Navy as a career officer. He had an ex-military mind-set that often put him at odds with his boss, especially since he'd mustered out with the rank of captain. He was much more used to giving orders than to taking them.

In the navy, the expected answer to any charge of dereliction of duty, regardless of innocence or guilt, was, "No excuse, sir." It was still hard for McCallum to get used to defending his actions. "I did what the situation called for," he said tersely. "When someone tries to pull a gun on me, I get twitchy."

"That was only bravado," Hensley pointed out, "and you knocked out one of his teeth. The department has to pay for it. The county commission climbed all over me and I didn't like it." He leaned forward with his hands clasped and gave the younger man a steady look. "Now you're the one with the problems. Dugin Kincaid found an abandoned baby on his doorstep."

"Maybe it's his," McCallum said with smiling sarcasm. Dugin was a pale imitation of his rancher father, Jeremiah. The thought of him with a woman amused McCallum.

"As I was saying," the sheriff continued without reacting to the comment, "the baby was found outside the city limits— hence our involvement—and its parents have to be found. You're not working on anything that pressing. You can take this case. I want you to talk with Jessica Larson at the social-welfare office."

McCallum groaned. "Why don't you just shoot me?"

"Now, there's no need to be like that," Hensley said, surprised. "She's a nice woman," he said. "Why, her dad was a fine doctor...."

His voice trailed off abruptly. McCallum remembered that Hensley's son had died in a hunting accident. Jessica's father had tried everything to save the boy, but it had been impossible. Hensley's wife, Tracy, divorced him a year after the funeral. That had happened years ago, long before McCallum left the service.

"Anyway, Jessica is one of the best social workers in the department," Hensley continued.

"She's the head of the department now, and a royal pain in the neck since her promotion," McCallum shot right back. "She's Little Miss Sunshine, spreading smiles of joy wherever she goes." His black eyes, a legacy from a Crow ancestor, glittered angrily. "She can't separate governmental responsibility from bleeding-heart activism."

"I wonder if it's fair to punish her by sticking her with you?" Hensley asked himself aloud. He threw up his hands. "Well, you'll just have to grin and bear it. I can't sit here

arguing with you all day. This is my department. I'm the sheriff. See this?'' He pointed at the badge on his uniform.

"Needs polishing," McCallum noted.

Hensley's eyes narrowed. He stood up. "Get out of here before I forget you work for me."

McCallum unfolded his six-foot-plus length from the chair and stood up. He was just a hair taller than the sheriff, and he looked casual in his jeans and knit shirt and denim jacket. But when the jacket fell open, the butt of his .45 automatic was revealed, giving bystanders a hint of the sort of work he did. He was a plainclothes detective, although only outsiders were fooled by his casual attire. Most everyone in Whitehorn knew that McCallum was as conservative and military as the shine on his black boots indicated.

"Don't shoot anybody," Hensley told him. "And next time a man threatens to shoot you, check for a gun and disarm him before you hit him, please?'' Hensley's eyes went to the huge silver-and-turquoise ring that McCallum wore on the middle finger of his right hand. "That ring is so heavy it's a miracle you didn't break his jaw."

McCallum held up his left hand, which was ringless. "This is the hand I hit him with."

"He said it felt like a baseball bat."

"I won't tell you where he hit *me* before he started ranting about shooting," the detective replied, turning to the door. "And if I didn't work for you, a loose tooth would have been the least of his complaints."

"Jessica Larson is expecting you over at the social-services office," Hensley called.

McCallum, to his credit, didn't slam the door.

Jessica Larson was fielding paperwork and phone calls with a calmness that she didn't feel at all. She'd become adept at presenting an unflappable appearance while having hysterics. Since her promotion to social-services director, she'd learned that she could eat at her desk during the day and forgo any private life after work at night. She also realized why her pre-

decessor had taken an early retirement. A lot of people came into this office to get help.

Like most of the rest of the country, Montana was having a hard time with the economy. Even though gambling had been legalized, adding a little more money to the state's strained coffers, it was harder and harder for many local citizens to make ends meet. Ranches went under all the time these days, forced into receivership or eaten up by big corporations. Manual labor, once a valuable commodity in the agricultural sector, was now a burden on the system when those workers lost jobs. They were unskilled and unemployable in any of the new, high-tech markets. Even secretaries had to use computers these days. So did policemen.

The perfunctory knock on her office door was emphasized by her secretary's high-pitched, "But she's busy...!"

"It's all right, Candy," Jessica called to the harassed young blonde. "I'm expecting McCallum." She didn't add that she hadn't expected him a half hour early. She tried to think of Sterling McCallum as a force of nature. He was like a wild stallion, a rogue stallion who traveled alone and made his own rules. Secretly, she was awed by him. He made her wish that she was a gorgeous model with curves in all the right places and a beautiful face—maybe with blond hair instead of brown. At least she was able to replace her big-rimmed glasses with contacts, which helped her appearance. But when she had allergies, she had to wear the glasses...like right now.

McCallum didn't wait for her to ask him to sit down. He took the chair beside her desk and crossed one long leg over the other.

"Let's have it," he said without preamble, looking unutterably bored.

Her eyes slid over his thick dark hair, so conventionally cut, down to his equally dark eyebrows and eyes in an olive-tan face. He had big ears and big hands and big feet, although there was nothing remotely clumsy about him. He had a nose with a crook in it, probably from being broken, and a mouth that she dreamed about: very wide and sexy and definite. Broad shoul-

ders tapered to a broad chest and narrow hips like a rodeo rider's. His stomach was flat and he had long, muscular legs. He was so masculine that he made her ache. She was twenty-five, a mature woman and only about ten years younger than he was, but he made her feel childish sometimes, and inadequate—as a professional and as a woman.

"Hero worship again, Jessica?" he chided, amused by her soft blush.

"Don't tease. This is serious," she chided gently in turn.

He shrugged and sighed. "Okay. What have you done with the child?"

"Jennifer," she told him.

He glowered. "The abandoned baby."

She gave up. He wouldn't allow anyone to become personalized in his company. Boys he had to pick up were juvenile delinquents. Abandoned babies were exactly that. No names. No identity. No complications in his ordered, uncluttered life. He let no one close to him. He had no friends, no family, no connections. Jessica felt painfully sorry for him, although she tried not to let it show. He was so alone and so vulnerable under that tough exterior that he must imagine was his best protection from being wounded. His childhood was no secret to anyone in Whitehorn. Everyone knew that his mother had been an alcoholic and that, after her arrest and subsequent death, he had been shunted from foster home to foster home. His only real value had been as an extra hand on one ranch or another, an outsider always looking in through a cloudy window at what home life might have been under other circumstances.

"You're doing it again," he muttered irritably.

Her slender eyebrows lifted over soft brown eyes. "What?" she asked.

"Pigeonholing me," he said. "Poor orphan, tossed from pillar to post..."

"I wish you'd stop reading my mind," she told him. "It's very disconcerting."

"I wish you'd stop bleeding all over me," he returned. "I

don't need pity. I'm content with my life, just as it is. I had a rough time. So what? Plenty of people do. I'm here to talk about a case, Jessica, and it isn't mine.''

She smiled self-consciously. ''All right, McCallum,'' she said agreeably, reaching for a file. ''The baby was taken to Whitehorn Memorial and checked over. She's perfectly healthy, clean and well-cared for, barely two weeks old. They're keeping her for observation overnight and then it will be up to the juvenile authorities to make arrangements about her care until her parents are located. I'm going over to see her in the morning. I'd like you to come with me.''

''I don't need to see it—''

''*Her,*'' she corrected. ''Baby Jennifer.''

''—to start searching for its parents,'' he concluded without missing a beat.

''Her parents,'' Jessica corrected calmly.

His dark eyes didn't blink. ''Was there anything else?''

''I'll leave here about nine,'' Jessica continued. ''You can ride with me.''

His eyes widened. ''In that glorified yellow tank you drive?''

''It's a pickup truck!'' she exclaimed defensively. ''And it's very necessary, considering where I live!''

He refused to think about her cabin in the middle of nowhere, across a creek that flooded with every cloudburst. It wasn't his place to worry about her just because she had no family. In that aspect of their lives they were very much alike. In other ways...

He stood up. ''You can ride with me,'' he said, giving in with noticeable impatience.

''I hate riding around in a patrol car,'' she muttered.

''It doesn't have a sign on it. It's a plainclothes car.''

''Of course it is, with those plain hubcaps, no white sidewalls, fifteen antennas sticking out of it and a spotlight. It doesn't need a sign, does it? Anyone who isn't blind would recognize it as an unmarked patrol car!''

''It beats driving a yellow tank,'' he pointed out.

She stood up, too, feeling at a disadvantage when she didn't.

But he was still much taller than she was. She pushed at a wisp of brown hair that had escaped from the bun on top of her head. Her beige suit emphasized her slender build, devoid as it was of any really noticeable curves.

"Why do you screw your hair up like that?" he asked curiously.

"It falls in my face when I'm trying to work," she said, indicating the stack of files on her desk. "Besides Candy, I only have two caseworkers, and they're trying to take away one of them because of new budget cuts. I'm already working Saturdays trying to catch up, and they've just complained about the amount of overtime I do."

"That sounds familiar."

"I know," she said cheerily. "Everyone has to work around tight budgets these days. It's one of the joys of public service."

"Why don't you get married and let some strong man support you?" he taunted.

She tilted her chin saucily. "Are you proposing to me, Deputy?" she asked with a wicked smile. "Has someone been tantalizing you with stories of my homemade bread?"

He'd meant it sarcastically, but she'd turned the tables on him neatly. He gave in with a reluctant grin.

"I'm not the marrying kind," he said. "I don't want a wife and kids."

Her bright expression dimmed a little, but remnants of the smile lingered. "Not everyone does," she said agreeably. The loud interruption of the telephone ringing in the outer office caught her attention, followed by the insistent buzz of the intercom. She turned back to her desk. "Thanks for stopping by. I'll see you in the morning, then," she added as she lifted the receiver. "Yes, Candy," she said.

McCallum's eyes slid quietly over her bowed head. After a minute, he turned and walked out, closing the door gently behind him. He did it without a goodbye. Early in his life, he'd learned not to look back.

The house where McCallum lived was at the end of a wide, dead-end street. His neighbors never intruded, but it got back

to him that they felt more secure having a law-enforcement officer in the neighborhood. He sat on his front porch sometimes with a beer and looked at the beauty of his surroundings while watching the children ride by on bicycles. He watched as a stranger watches, learning which children belonged at which houses. He saw affection from some parents and amazing indifference from others. He saw sadness and joy. But he saw it from a distance. His own life held no highs or lows. He was answerable to no one, free to do whatever he pleased with no interference.

He'd had the flu last winter. He'd lain in his bed for over twenty-four hours, burning with fever, unable to cook or even get into the kitchen. Not until he missed work did anyone come looking for him. The incident had punctuated how alone he really was.

He hadn't been alone long. Jessica had hotfooted it over to look after him, ignoring his ranting and raving about not wanting any woman cluttering up his house. She'd fed him and cleaned for him in between doing her own job, and only left when he proved to her that he could get out of bed. Because of the experience, he'd been ruder than ever to her. When he'd gone back to work, she'd taken a pot of chicken soup to the office, enough that he could share it with the other men on his shift. It had been uncomfortable when they'd teased him about Jessica's nurturing, and he'd taken out that irritation on her.

He hadn't even thanked her for her trouble, he recalled. No matter how rude he was she kept coming back, like a friendly little elf who only wanted to make him happy. She was his one soft spot, although, thank God, she didn't know it. He was curt with her because he had to keep her from knowing about his weakness for her. He had been doing a good job; when she looked at him these days, she never met his eyes.

He sipped his beer, glowering at the memories. His free hand dropped to the head of his big brown-and-black Doberman. He'd had the dog for almost a year. He'd found Mack tied in a croker sack, yipping helplessly in the shallows of a nearby

river. Having rescued the dog, he couldn't find anyone who was willing to take it, and he hadn't had the heart to shoot it. There was no agency in Whitehorn to care for abandoned or stray animals. The only alternative was to adopt the pup, and he had.

At first Mack had been a trial to him. But once he housebroke the dog and it began to follow him around the house—and later, to work—he grew reluctantly fond of it. Now Mack was part of his life. They were inseparable, especially on hunting and fishing trips. If he had a family at all, McCallum thought, it was Mack.

He sat back, just enjoying the beauty of Whitehorn. The sun set; the children went inside. And still McCallum sat, thinking and listening to the hum of the quiet springtime night.

Finally, he got up. It was after eleven. He'd just gone inside and was turning out the lights when the phone rang.

"It's Hensley," the sheriff announced over the phone. "We've got a 10-16 at the Miles place, a real hummer. It's outside the city police's jurisdiction, so it either has to be you or a deputy."

"It won't do any good to go, you know," McCallum said. "Jerry Miles beats Ellen up twice a month, but she never presses charges. Last time he beat up their twelve-year-old son, and even then—"

"I know."

"I'll go anyway," McCallum said. "It's a hell of a shame we can't lock him up without her having to press charges. She's afraid of him. If she left him, he'd probably go after her, and God knows what he'd do. I've seen it happen. So have you. Everybody says leave him. Nobody says they'll take care of her when he comes looking for her with a gun."

"We have to keep hoping that she'll get help."

"Jessica has tried," McCallum admitted, "but nothing changes. You can't help people until they're ready to accept it, and the consequences of accepting it."

"I heard that."

McCallum drove out to the Miles home. It was three miles out of Whitehorn, in the rolling, wide-open countryside.

He didn't put on the siren. He drove up into the yard and cut the lights. Then he got out, unfastening the loop that held his pistol in place in the holster on his hip, just in case. One of Whitehorn's policemen had been shot and killed trying to break up a domestic dispute some years ago.

There was no noise coming from inside. The night was ominously quiet. McCallum's keen eyes scanned the area and suddenly noticed a yellow truck parked just behind the house, on a dirt road that ran behind it and parallel to the main highway.

Jessica was in there!

He quickened his steps, went up on the front porch and knocked at the door.

"Police," he announced. "Open up!"

There was a pause. His hand went to the pistol and he stood just to the side of the doorway, waiting.

The main door opened quite suddenly, and a tired-looking Jessica Larson smiled at him through a torn screen. "It's all right," she said, opening the screen door for him. "He's passed out on the bed. Ellen and Chad are all right."

McCallum walked into the living room, feeling uncomfortable as he looked at the two people whose lives were as much in ruin as the broken, cheap lamp on the floor. The sofa was stained and the rug on the wood floor had frayed edges. There were old, faded curtains at the windows and a small television still blaring out a game show. Ellen sat on the sofa with red-rimmed eyes, her arm around Chad, who was crying. He had a bruise on one cheek.

"How much longer are you going to let the boy suffer like this, Ellen?" McCallum asked quietly.

She stared at him from dull eyes. "Mister, if I send my husband to jail, he says he'll kill me," she announced. "I think he will. Last time I tried to run away, he shot our dog."

"He's sick, Ellen," Jessica added gently. Her glance in the direction of the bedroom had an odd, frightened edge to it.

"He's very sick. Alcoholism can destroy his body, you know. It can kill him."

"Yes, ma'am, I know that. He's a big man, though," the woman continued in a lackluster voice, absently smoothing her son's hair. "He loves me. He says so. He's always sorry, after."

"He's not sorry," McCallum said, his voice deep and steady. "He enjoys watching you cry. He likes making you afraid of him. He gets off on it."

"McCallum!" Jessica said sharply.

He ignored her. He knelt in front of Ellen and stared at her levelly. "Listen to me. My mother was an alcoholic. She used a bottle on me once, and laughed when she broke my arm with it. She said she was sorry, too, after she sobered up, but the day she broke my arm, I stopped believing it. I called the police and they locked her up. And the beatings stopped. For good."

Ellen wiped at her eyes. "Weren't you sorry? I mean, she was your mother. You're supposed to love your mother."

"You don't beat the hell out of people you love," he said coldly. "And you know that. Are you going to keep making excuses for him until he kills your son?"

She gasped, clasping the boy close. "But he won't!" she said huskily. "Oh, no, I know he won't! He loves Chad. He loves me, too. He just drinks so much that he forgets he loves us, that's all."

"If he hurts the child, you'll go to jail as an accessory," McCallum told her. He said it without feeling, without remorse. He said it deliberately. "I swear to God you will. I'll arrest you myself."

Ellen paled. The hands holding her son contracted. "Chad doesn't want to see his daddy go to jail," she said firmly. "Do you, Son?"

Chad lifted his head from her shoulder and looked straight at McCallum. "Yes, sir, I do," he said in a choked voice. "I don't want him to hit my mama anymore. I tried to stop him and he did this." He pointed to his eye.

McCallum looked back at Ellen. There was accusation and

cold anger in his dark eyes. They seemed to see right through her.

She shivered. "He'll hurt us if I let you take him to jail," she said, admitting the truth at last. "I'm scared of him. I'm so scared!"

Jessica stepped forward. "There's a shelter for battered women," she replied. "I'll make sure you get there. You'll be protected. He won't come after you or Chad, and even if he tries, he can be arrested for that, too."

Ellen bit her lower lip. "He's my *husband*," she said with emphasis. "The good book says that when you take a vow, you don't ever break it."

McCallum's chin lifted. "The same book says that when a man marries a woman, he cherishes her. It doesn't say one damned thing about being permitted to beat her, does it?"

She hesitated, but only for a minute. "I have an aunt in Lexington, Kentucky. She'd let me and Chad live with her, I know she would. I could go there. He doesn't know about my aunt. He'd never find us."

"Is that what you want?" Jessica asked.

The woman hesitated. Her weary eyes glanced around the room, taking measure of the destruction. She felt as abused as the broken lamp, as the sagging sofa with its torn fabric. Her gaze rested finally on her son and she looked, really looked, at him. No child of twelve should have eyes like that. She'd been thinking only of her own safety, of her vows to her husband, not of the one person whose future should have mattered to her. She touched Chad's hair gently.

"It's all right, Son," she said. "It's gonna be all right. I'll get you out of here." She glanced away from his wet eyes to McCallum. Her head jerked toward the bedroom. "I have to get away. I can't press charges against him...."

"Don't worry about it," McCallum said. "He'll sleep for a long time and then he won't know where to look for you. By the time he thinks about trying, he'll be drunk again. The minute he gets behind a wheel, I'll have him before a judge. With three prior DWI convictions, he'll spend some time in jail."

"All right." She got uneasily to her feet. "I'll have to get my things...." Her eyes darted nervously to the bedroom.

McCallum walked to the doorway and stood there. He didn't say a word, but she knew what his actions meant. If her husband woke up while she was packing, McCallum would deal with him.

She smiled gratefully and went hesitantly into the dimly lit bedroom, where her husband was passed out on the bed. Jessica didn't offer to go with her. She sat very still on the sofa, looking around her with a kind of subdued fear that piqued McCallum's curiosity.

Jessica drove her own truck to the bus station, parking it next to the unmarked car in which McCallum had put Chad and his mother. It was acting up again, and she tried to recrank it but it refused to start.

They saw the mother and son onto the bus and stood together until it vanished into the distance.

McCallum glanced at his watch. It was after midnight, but he was wound up and not at all sleepy.

Jessica mistook the obvious gesture for an indication that he wanted to get going. "Thanks for your help," she told him. "I'd better get back home. Could you take me? My truck's on the blink again."

"Sure. I'll send someone over in the morning to fix the truck and deliver it to your office. I'm sure you can get a ride to work."

"Yes, I can. Thanks," she said, relieved.

He caught her arm and shepherded her into the depot, which was open all night. There was a small coffee concession, where an old man sold coffee and doughnuts and soft drinks.

Jessica was dumbfounded. Usually McCallum couldn't wait to get away from her. His wanting to have coffee with her was an historic occasion, and she didn't quite know what to expect.

Two

McCallum helped her into a small booth and came back with two mugs of steaming coffee.

"What if I didn't drink coffee?" she asked.

He smiled faintly. "I've never seen you without a cup at your elbow," he remarked. "No cream, either. Sugar?"

She shook her head. "I live on the caffeine, not the taste." She cupped her hands around the hot cup and looked at him across the table. "You don't like my company enough to take me out for coffee unless you want something. What is it?"

He was shocked. Did she really have such a low self-image? His dark eyes narrowed on her face, and he couldn't decide why she looked so different. She wasn't wearing makeup—probably she'd been in too big a hurry to get to Ellen's house to bother. And her infrequently worn, big-lensed glasses were perched jauntily on her nose. But it was more than that. Then he realized what the difference was. Her hair—her long, glorious, sable-colored hair—was falling in thick waves around her shoulders and halfway down her back. His fingers itched to bury themselves in it, and the very idea made his eyebrows fly up in surprise.

"I don't read minds," she said politely.

"What?" He frowned, then remembered her question. "I wanted to ask you something."

She nodded resignedly and sipped at her coffee.

He leaned back against the dark red vinyl of the booth, studying her oval face and her big brown eyes behind the round lenses for longer than he meant to. "How is it you wound up in that house during a domestic dispute?"

"Oh. That."

He glared at her. "Don't make light of it," he said shortly.

"More cops have been hurt during family quarrels than in shoot-outs."

"Yes, I know, I do read statistics. Ellen called me and I went. That's all."

One eye narrowed. "Next time," he said slowly, "you phone me first, before you walk into something like that. Do you understand me?"

"But I was in no danger," she began.

"The man weighs two-fifty if he weighs a pound," he said shortly. "You're what—a hundred and twenty sopping wet?"

"I'm not helpless!" She laughed nervously. It wouldn't do to let him know the terror she'd felt when Ellen had called her, crying hysterically, begging her to come. It had taken all her courage to walk into that house.

"Do you have martial-arts training?"

She hesitated and then shook her head irritably.

"Do you carry a piece?"

"What would I do with a loaded gun?" she exclaimed. "I'd shoot my leg off!"

The scowl got worse. "Then how did you expect to handle a drunken man who outweighs you by over a hundred pounds and was bent on proving his strength to anyone who came within swinging range?"

She nibbled her lower lip and stared into her coffee. "Because Ellen begged me to. It's my job."

"No, it's not," he said firmly. "Your job is to help people who are down on their luck and to rescue kids from abusive environments. It doesn't include trying to do a policeman's work."

His eyes were unblinking. He had a stare that made her want to back up two steps. She imagined it worked very well on lawbreakers.

She let out a weary breath. "Okay," she said, holding up a slender, ringless hand. "I let my emotions get the best of me. I did something stupid and, fortunately, I didn't get hurt."

"Big of you to admit it," he drawled.

"You're a pain, McCallum," she told him bluntly.

"Funny you should mention it," he replied. "I made the same complaint about you to Hensley only this morning."

"Oh, I know you don't approve of me," she agreed. "You think social workers should be like you—all-business, treating people as though they were statistics, not getting emotionally involved—"

"Bingo!" he said immediately.

She put her coffee cup down gently. "A hundred years ago, most of the country south of here belonged to the Crow," she said, looking pointedly at him, because she knew about his ancestry. "They had a social system that was one of the most efficient ever devised. No one valued personal property above the needs of the group. Gifts were given annually among the whole tribe. When a man killed a deer, regardless of his own need, the meat was given away. To claim it for himself was unthinkable. Arguments were settled by gift giving. Each person cared about every other person in the village, and people were accepted for what they were. And no one was so solitary that he or she didn't belong, in some way, to every family."

He leaned forward. "With the pointed exception of Crazy Horse, who kept to himself almost exclusively."

She nodded. "With his exception."

"Someone told you that I had a Crow ancestor," he guessed accurately.

She shrugged. "In Whitehorn, everyone knows everyone else's business. Well, mostly, anyway," she added, because she was pretty sure that he didn't know about her own emotional scars. The incident had been hushed up because of the nature of the crime, and because there'd been a minor involved. It was just as well. Jessica couldn't have a permanent relationship with a man, even if she would have given most of a leg to have one with McCallum. He was perfect for her in every way.

"I'm more French Canadian in my ancestry than Crow." He studied her own face with quiet curiosity. She had a pretty mouth, like a little bow, and her nose was straight. Her big, dark eyes with their long, curly lashes were her finest feature. Even glasses didn't disguise their beauty.

"Are you nearsighted or farsighted?" he asked abruptly.

"Nearsighted." She adjusted her glasses self-consciously. "I usually wear contacts, but my eyes itch lately from all the grass cuttings. I'm blind as a bat without these. I couldn't even cross a street if I lost them."

His eyes fell to her hands. They were slightly tanned, long-fingered, with oval nails. Very pretty.

"Are you going to arrest Ellen's husband?" she asked suddenly.

He pursed his lips. "Now what do you think?"

"We didn't get Ellen to press charges," she reminded him.

"We couldn't have. If she had, she'd have to come back and face him in court. She's afraid that he might kill her. He's threatened to," he reminded her. "But as it is, he won't know where to look for her, and even if he did, it won't matter."

"What do you mean?" she asked curiously.

His eyes took on a faint glitter, like a stormy night sky. "He gets drunk every night. He's got three previous convictions on DWI and he likes to mix it up in taverns. He'll step over the line and I'll have him behind bars, without Ellen's help. This time I'll make sure the charges stick. Drunkenness is no excuse for brutality."

She was remembering what he'd said to Ellen about his own mother breaking his arm with a bottle when he was a little boy.

She reached out without thinking and gently touched the long sleeve of his blue-patterned Western shirt. "Which arm was it?" she asked quietly.

The compassion in her voice hurt him. He'd never known it in his youth. Even now, he wasn't used to people caring about him in any way. Jessica did, and he didn't want her to. He didn't trust anyone close to him. Years of abuse had made him suspicious of any overture, no matter how well meant.

He jerked his arm away. "What you heard wasn't something you were meant to hear," he said icily. "You had no business being in the house in the first place."

She cupped her mug in her hands and smiled. The words didn't sting her. She'd learned long ago not to take verbal abuse

personally. Most children who'd been hurt reacted that way to kindness. They couldn't trust anymore, because the people they loved most had betrayed them in one way or another. His was the same story she'd heard a hundred times before. It never got easier to listen to.

But there was a big difference between anger and hostility. Anger was normal, healthy. Hostility was more habit than anything else, and it stemmed from low esteem, feelings of inadequacy. It was impersonal, unlike aggression, which was intended to hurt. A good social worker quickly learned the difference, and how not to take verbal outpourings seriously. McCallum was something of a psychologist himself. He probably understood himself very well by now.

"I didn't mean to snap," he said curtly.

She only smiled at him, her eyes warm and gentle. "I know. I've spent the past three years working with abused children."

He cursed under his breath. He was overly defensive with her because she knew too much about people like him, and it made him feel naked. He knew that he must hurt her sometimes with his roughness, but damn it, she never fought back or made sarcastic comments. She just sat there with that serene expression on her face. He wondered if she ever gave way to blazing temper or passion. Both were part and parcel of his tempestuous nature, although he usually managed to control them. Years of self-discipline had helped.

"You don't like being touched, do you?" she asked suddenly.

"Don't presume, ever, to psychoanalyze me," he replied bluntly. "I'm not one of your clients."

"Wasn't there any social worker who tried to help you?" she asked.

"They helped me," he retorted. "I had homes. Several of them, in fact, mostly on ranches."

Her hands tightened on the cup. "Weren't you loved?"

His eyes flashed like glowing coals. "If you mean have I had women, yes," he said with deliberate cruelty. "Plenty of them!"

Jessica surrendered the field. She should have known better than to pry. She didn't want to hear anything about his intimate conquests. The thought of him...like that...was too disturbing. She finished her coffee and dragged a dollar bill out of her pocket to pay for it.

"I'll take care of it," he said carelessly.

She looked at him. "No, you won't," she said quietly. "I pay my own way. Always."

She got up and paid the old man behind the counter, and walked out of the concession ahead of McCallum.

She was already unlocking her pickup truck when he got outside. Even if it wouldn't start, she needed her sweater. She got it out and locked it up again.

"You actually lock that thing?" he asked sarcastically. "My God, anyone who stole it would be doing you a favor."

"I can't afford theft insurance," she said simply. "Keeping my family home takes all my spare cash."

He remembered where she lived, across the creek on the outskirts of town, with a huge tract of land—hundreds of acres. She played at raising cattle on it, and she had a hired hand who looked after things for her. Jessica loved cattle, although she knew nothing about raising them. But prices were down and it wasn't easy. He knew that she was fighting a losing battle, trying to keep the place.

"Why not just sell out and move into one of the new apartment complexes?"

She turned and looked up at him. He was taller up close. "Why, because it's my home. My heritage," she said. "It was one of the first homes built in Whitehorn, over a hundred years ago. I can't sell it."

"Heritage is right here," he said abruptly, placing his hand against her shoulder and collarbone, in the general area of her heart.

The contact shocked her. She moved back, but the truck was in the way.

He smiled quizzically. "What are you so nervous about?" he asked lazily. "This isn't intimate."

She was flushed. The dark eyes that looked up into his were a little frightened.

He stared at her until images began to suggest themselves, and still he didn't move his hand. "You've had to go a lot of places alone, to interview people who wanted assistance," he began. "At least one or two of those places must have had men very much like Ellen's husband—men who were drunk or who thought that a woman coming into a house alone must be asking for it. And when you were younger, you wouldn't have expected…" She caught her breath and his chin lifted. "Yes," he said slowly, almost to himself. "That's it. That's why you're so jumpy around men. I noticed it at Ellen's house. You were concerned for her, but that wasn't altogether why you kept staring so nervously toward the bedroom."

She bit her lower lip and looked at his chest instead of his eyes. His pearl-button shirt was open down past his collarbone, and she could see a thick, black mat of curling hair inside. He was the most aggressively masculine man she'd ever known, and God only knew why she wasn't afraid of him when most men frightened her.

"You won't talk, will you?" he asked above her head.

"McCallum…" She caught his big hand, feeling its strength and warmth. She told herself to push it away, but her fingers couldn't seem to do what her brain was telling them.

His breathing changed, suddenly and audibly. His warm breath stirred the hair at her temple. "But despite whatever happened to you," he continued as if she hadn't spoken, "you're not afraid of me."

"You must let me go now." She spoke quietly. Her hand went flat against his shirtfront. She knew at once that it was a mistake when she felt the warm strength of his body and the cushy softness of the thick hair under the shirt. The feel of him shocked her. "My…goodness, you're—you're furry," she said with a nervous laugh.

"Furry." He deliberately unsnapped two pearly buttons and drew the fabric from under her flattened hand. He guided her

cold fingers over the thick pelt that covered him from his collarbone down, and pressed them over the hard nipple.

She opened her mouth to protest, but his body fascinated her. She'd never seen a man like this at close range, much less touched one. He smelled of soap and faint cologne. He drowned her in images, in sensations, in smells. Her fascinated eyes widened as she gave way to her curiosity and began to stroke him hesitantly.

He shivered. Her gaze shot up to his hard face, but his expression was unreadable—except for the faint, unnerving glitter of his eyes.

"A man's nipple is as sensitive as a woman's," he explained quietly. "It excites me when you trace it like that."

The soft words brought her abruptly to her senses. She was making love to a man on a public street in front of the bus depot. With a soft groan, she dragged her hand away from him and bit her lower lip until she tasted blood.

"What a horrified expression," he murmured as he refastened his shirt. "Does it shock you that you can feel like a woman? Or don't you think I know that you hide your own emotions in the job? All this empathy you pour out on your clients is no more than a shield behind which you hide your own needs, your own desires."

Her face tightened. "Don't *you* psychoanalyze *me!*" she gasped, throwing his earlier words right back at him.

"If I'm locked up inside, so are you, honey," he drawled, watching her react to the blunt remark.

"My personal life is my own business, and don't you call me honey!"

She started to turn, but he caught her by the upper arms and turned her back around. His eyes were merciless, predatory.

"Were you raped?" he asked bluntly.

"No!" she said angrily, glaring at him. "And that's all you need to know, McCallum!"

His hands on her arms relaxed, became caressing. He scowled down at her, searching for the right words.

"Let me go!"

"No."

He reached around her and relocked the truck. He helped her into his car without asking if she was ready to come with him, started it and drove straight to his house.

She was numb with surprise. But she came out of her stupor when he pulled the car into his driveway and turned off the engine and lights. "Oh, I can't," she began quickly. "I have to go home!"

Ignoring her protest, he got out and opened the door for her. She let him extricate her and lead her up onto his porch. Mack barked from inside, but once Sterling let them in and turned on the lights, he calmed the big dog easily.

"You know Mack," he told Jessica. "While you're getting reacquainted, I'll make another pot of coffee. If you need to wash your face, bathroom's there," he added, gesturing toward a room between the living room and the kitchen.

Mack growled at Jessica. She would try becoming his friend later, but right now she wanted to bathe her hot face. She couldn't really imagine why she'd allowed McCallum to bring her here, when it was certainly going to destroy her reputation if anyone saw her alone with him after midnight.

By the time she got back to the living room, he had hot coffee on the coffee table, in fairly disreputable black mugs with faded emblems on them.

"I don't have china," he said when she tried to read the writing on hers.

"Neither do I," she confessed. "Except, I do have two place settings of Havilland, but it's cracked. It was my great-aunt's." She looked at him over her coffee cup. "I shouldn't be here."

"Because it's late and we're alone?"

She nodded.

"I'm a cop."

"Well...yes."

"Your reputation won't suffer," he said, leaning back to cross his long legs. "If there's one thing I'm not, it's a womanizer, and everyone knows it. I don't have women."

"You said you did," she muttered.

He looked toward her with wise, amused eyes. "*Did,* yes. Not since I came back here. Small towns are hotbeds of gossip, and I've been the subject of it enough in my life. I won't risk becoming a household word again just to satisfy an infrequent ache."

She drank her coffee quickly, trying to hide how much his words embarrassed her, as well as the reference to gossip. She had her own skeletons, about which he apparently knew nothing. It had been a long time ago, after all, and most of the people who knew about Jessica's past had moved away or died. Sheriff Judd Hensley knew, but he wasn't likely to volunteer information to McCallum. Judd was tight-lipped, and he'd been Jessica's foremost ally at a time when she'd needed one desperately.

After a minute, Sterling put down his coffee cup and took hers away from her, setting it neatly in line with his. He leaned back on the sofa, his body turned toward hers.

"Tell me."

She clasped her hands tightly in her lap. "I've never talked about it," she said shortly. "He's dead, anyway, so what good would it do now?"

"I want to know."

"Why?"

His broad shoulders rose and fell. "Who else is there? You don't have any family, Jessica, and I know for a fact you don't have even one friend. Who do you talk to?"

"I talk to God!"

He smiled. "Well, He's probably pretty busy right now, so why don't you tell me?"

She pushed back her long hair. Her eyes sought the framed print of a stag in an autumn forest on the opposite wall. "I can't."

"Have you told anyone?"

Her slender shoulders hunched forward and she dropped her face into her hands with a heavy sigh. "I told my supervisor. My parents were dead by then, and I was living alone."

"Come on," he coaxed. "I may not be your idea of the

perfect confidant, but I'll never repeat a word of it. Talking is therapeutic, or so they tell me.''

His tone was unexpectedly tender. She glanced at him, grimaced at the patience she saw there—as if he were willing to wait all night if he had to. She might as well tell him a little of what had happened, she supposed.

''I was twenty,'' she said. ''Grass green and sheltered. I knew nothing about men. I was sent out as a caseworker to a house where a man had badly beaten his wife and little daughter. I was going to question his wife one more time after she suddenly withdrew the charges. I went there to find out why, but she wasn't at home and he blamed me for his having been accused. I'd encouraged his wife and daughter to report what happened. He hit me until I couldn't stand up, and then he stripped me....'' She paused, then forced the rest of it out. ''He didn't rape me, although I suppose he would have if his brother-in-law hadn't driven up. He was arrested and charged, but he plea-bargained his way to a reduced sentence.''

''He wasn't charged with attempted rape?''

''One of the more powerful city councilmen was his brother,'' she told him. She left out the black torment of those weeks. ''He was killed in a car wreck after being parolled, and the councilman moved away.''

''So he got away with it,'' McCallum murmured angrily. He smoothed his hand over his hair and stared out the dark window. ''I thought you'd led a sheltered, pampered life.''

''I did. Up to a point. My best friend had parents who drank too much. There were never any charges, and she hid her bruises really well. She's the reason I went into social work.'' She smiled bitterly. ''It's amazing how much damage liquor does in our society, isn't it?''

He couldn't deny that. ''Does your friend live here?''

She shook her head. ''She lives in England with her husband. We lost touch years ago.''

''Why in God's name didn't you give up your job when you were attacked?''

''Because I do a lot of good,'' she replied quietly. ''After it

happened, I thought about quitting. It was only when the man's wife came to me and apologized for what he'd done, and thanked me for trying to help, that I realized I had at least accomplished something. She took her daughter and went to live with her mother.

"I cared too much about the children to quit. I still do. It taught me a lesson. Now, when I send caseworkers out, I always send them in pairs, even if it takes more time to work cases. Some children have no advocates except us."

"God knows, someone needs to care about them," he replied quietly. "Kids get a rough shake in this world."

She nodded and finished her coffee. Her eyes were curious, roaming around the room. There were hunting prints on the walls, but no photographs, no mementos. Everything that was personal had something military or work-related stamped on it. Like the mugs with the police insignias.

"What are you looking for? Sentiment?" he chided. "You won't find it here. I'm not a sentimental man."

"You're a caring one, in your way," she returned. "You were kind to Ellen and Chad."

"Taking care of emotionally wounded people goes with the job," he reminded her. He picked up his coffee cup and sipped the black liquid. His dark eyes searched hers. "I'll remind you again that I don't need hero worship from a social worker with a stunted libido."

"Why, McCallum, I didn't know you knew such big words," she murmured demurely. "Do you read dictionaries in your spare time? I thought you spent it polishing your pistol."

He chuckled with reserved pleasure. His deep voice sounded different when he laughed, probably because the sound was so rare, she mused.

"What do you do with yours?" he asked.

"I do housework," she said. "And read over case files. I can't sit around and do nothing. I have to stay busy."

He finished his coffee and got up. "Want another cup?" he asked.

She shook her head and stood up, too. "I have to get home. Tomorrow's another workday."

"Let me open the latch for Mack so that he has access to the backyard and I'll take you over there."

"Won't he run off?" she asked.

"He's got a fenced-in area and his own entrance," he replied. "I keep it latched to make sure the neighbor's damned cat stays out of the house. It walks in and helps itself to his dog food when I'm not home. It climbs right over the fence!"

Jessica had to smother a laugh, he sounded so disgusted. She moved toward the dog, who suddenly growled up at her.

She stopped dead. He was a big dog, and pretty menacing at close range.

"Sorry," McCallum said, tugging Mack toward his exit in the door. "He's not used to women."

"He's big, isn't he?" she asked, avoiding any further comment.

"Big enough. He eats like a horse." He took his car keys out of his pocket and locked up behind her while she got into the car.

They drove back toward her place. The night sky was dark, but full of stars. The sky went on forever in this part of the country, and Jessica could understand how McCallum would return here. She herself could never really leave. Her heart would always yearn for home in Montana.

When they got to her cabin, there was a single lighted window, and her big tomcat was outlined in it.

"That's Meriwether," she told him. "He wandered up here a couple of years ago and I let him stay. He's an orange tabby with battle-scarred ears."

"I hate cats," he murmured as he stopped the car at her front door.

"That doesn't surprise me, McCallum. What surprises me is that you have a pet at all—and that you even allow a stray cat on your property."

"Sarcasm is not your style, Miss Larson," he chided.

"How do you know? Other than the time you were sick, you only see me at work."

He pursed his lips and smiled faintly. "It's safer that way. You lonely spinsters are dangerous."

"Not me. I intend to be a lonely spinster for life," she said firmly. "Marriage isn't in my plans."

He scowled. "Don't you want kids?"

She opened her purse and took out her house key. "I like my life exactly as it is. Thanks for the lift. And the shoulder." She glanced at him a little self-consciously.

"I'm a clam," he said. "I don't broadcast secrets; my own or anyone else's."

"That must be why you're still working for Judd Hensley. He's the same way."

"He knew about your problem, I gather?"

She nodded. "He's been sheriff here for a long time. He and his wife were good friends of my parents. I'm sorry about their divorce. He's a lonely man these days."

"Loneliness isn't a disease," he muttered. "Despite the fact that you women like to treat it like one."

"Still upset about my bringing you that pot of soup, aren't you?" she asked him. "Well, you were sick and nobody else was going to feed and look after you. I'm a social worker. I like taking care of the underprivileged."

"I am *not* underprivileged."

"You were sick and alone."

"I wouldn't have starved."

"You didn't have any food in the house," she countered. "What did you plan to do, eat your dog?"

He made a face. "Considering some of the things *he* eats, God forbid!"

"Well, I wouldn't eat Meriwether even if I really were starving."

He glanced at the cat in the window. "I don't blame you. Anything that ugly should be buried, not eaten."

She made a sound deep in her throat and opened the car door.

"Go ahead," he invited. "Tell me he's not ugly."

"I wouldn't give you the satisfaction of arguing," she said smugly. "Good night."

"Lock that door."

She glowered at him. "I'm twenty-five years old." She pointed at her head. "This works."

"No kidding!"

She made a dismissive gesture with her hand and walked up onto the porch. She didn't look back, even when he beeped the horn as he drove away.

Three

Jessica unlocked her front door and walked into the familiar confines of the big cabin. A long hall led to the kitchen, past a spare bedroom. The floor, heart of pine, was scattered with worn throw rugs. The living and dining areas were in one room at the front. At the end of the hall near the kitchen was an elegant old bathroom. The plumbing drove her crazy in the winters—which were almost unsurvivable in this house—and the summers were hotter than blazes. She had no air-conditioning and the heating system was unreliable. She had to supplement it with fireplaces and scattered kerosene heaters. Probably one day she'd burn the whole place down around her ears trying to keep warm, but except for the infrequent cold, she remained healthy. She dreamed of a house that was livable year-round.

A soft meow came from the parlor, and Meriwether came trotting out to greet her. The huge tabby was marmalade colored. He'd been a stray when she found him, a pitiful half-grown scrap of fur with fleas and a stubby tail. She'd cleaned him up and brought him in, and they'd been inseparable ever since. But he hated men. He was a particularly big cat, with sharp claws, and he had to be locked up when the infrequent repairman was called to the house. He spat and hissed at them, and he'd even attacked the man who read the water meter. Now the poor fellow wouldn't come into the yard unless he knew Meriwether was safely locked in the house.

"Well, hello," she said, smiling as he wrapped himself around her ankle. "Want to hear all about the time I had?"

He made a soft sound. She scooped him up under one arm and started up the staircase. "Let me tell you, I've had better nights."

Later, with Meriwether curled up beside her, his big head on her shoulder, she slept, but the old nightmare came back, resurrected probably by the violence she'd seen and heard. She woke in a cold sweat, crying out in the darkness. It was a relief to find herself safe, here in her own house. Meriwether opened his eyes and looked at her when she turned on the light.

"Never mind. Go back to sleep," she told him gently. "I think I'll just read for a while."

She picked up a favorite romance novel from her shelf and settled back to read it. She liked these old ones best, the ones that belonged to a different world and always delivered a happy ending. Soon she was caught up in the novel and reality thankfully vanished for a little while.

At nine o'clock sharp the next morning, McCallum showed up in Jessica's office. He was wearing beige jeans and a sports jacket over his short-sleeved shirt this morning. No tie. He seemed to hate them; at least, Jessica had yet to see him dressed in one.

She was wearing a gray suit with a loose jacket. Her hair was severely confined on top of her head and she had on just a light touch of makeup. Watching her gather her briefcase, McCallum thought absently that he much preferred the tired woman of the night before, with her glorious hair loose around her shoulders.

"We'll go in my car," he said when they reached the parking lot, putting his sunglasses over his eyes. They gave him an even more threatening demeanor.

"I have to go on to another appointment, so I'll take my truck, now that it's been fixed, thanks to you...."

He opened the passenger door of the patrol car and stood there without saying a word.

She hesitated for a minute, then let him help her into the car. "Are you deliberately intimidating, or does it just come naturally?" she asked when they were on the way to the hospital.

"I spent years ordering noncoms around," he said easily.

"Old habits are hard to break. Plays hell at work sometimes. I keep forgetting that Hensley outranks me."

That sounded like humor, but she'd had no sleep to speak of and she felt out of sorts. She clasped her briefcase closer, glancing out the window at the landscape. Montana was beautiful in spring. The area around Whitehorn was uncluttered, with rolling hills that ran forever to the horizon and that later in the year would be rich with grain crops. Occasional herds of cattle dotted the horizon. There were cottonwood and willow trees along the streams, but mostly the country was wide open. It was home. She loved it.

She especially loved Whitehorn. With its wide streets and multitude of trees, the town reminded her of Billings—which had quiet neighborhoods and a spread-out city center, with a refinery right within the city limits. The railroad cut through Billings, just as it did here in Whitehorn. It was necessary for transportation, because mining was big business in southern Montana.

The Whitehorn hospital was surrounded by cottonwood trees. Its grounds were nicely landscaped and there was a statue of Lewis and Clark out front. William Clark's autograph in stone at Pompey's Pillar, near Hardin, Montana, still drew photographers. The Lewis and Clark expedition had come right through Whitehorn.

Jessica introduced herself and McCallum to the ward nurse, and they were taken to the nursery.

Baby Jennifer, or Jenny as she was called, was in a crib there. She looked very pretty, with big blue eyes and a tiny tuft of blond hair on top of her head. She looked up at her visitors without a change of expression, although her eyes were alert and intelligent.

Jessica looked at her hungrily. She put down her briefcase and with a questioning glance at the nurse, who nodded, she picked the baby up and held her close.

"Little angel," she whispered, smiling so sadly that the man at her side scowled. She touched the tiny hand and felt it curl around her finger. She blinked back tears. She would never

have a baby. She would never know the joy of feeling it grow in her body, watching its birth, nourishing it at her breast....

She made a sound and McCallum moved between her and the nurse with magnificent carelessness. "I want to see any articles of clothing that were found on or with the child," he said courteously.

The nurse, diverted, produced a small bundle. He unfastened it. There was one blanket, a worn pink one—probably home-made, judging by the hand-sewn border—with no label. There was a tiny gown, a pretty lacy thing with a foreign label, the sort that might be found at a fancy garage sale. There were some hand-knitted booties and a bottle. The bottle was a com-mon plastic one with nothing outstanding about it. He sighed angrily. No clues here.

"Oh, yes, there's one more thing, Detective," the nurse said suddenly. She produced a small brooch, a pink cameo. "This was attached to the gown. Odd, isn't it, to put something so valuable on a baby? This looks like real gold."

McCallum touched it, turned it over. It was gold, all right, and very old. That was someone's heirloom. It might be the very clue he needed to track down the baby's parents.

He fished out a plastic bag and dropped the cameo into it, fastening it and sticking it in his inside jacket pocket. It was too small to search for prints, and it had been handled by too many people to be of value in that respect. Hensley had checked all these things yesterday when the baby was found. The bottle had been wiped clean of prints, although not by anybody at the Kincaid home. Apparently the child's parents weren't anxious to be found. The puzzling thing was that brooch. Why wipe fingerprints off and then include a probably identifiable piece of heirloom jewelry?

He was still frowning when he turned back to Jessica. She was just putting the child into its crib and straightening. The look on her face was all too easy to read, but she quickly con-cealed her thoughts with a businesslike expression.

"We'll have to settle her with a child-care provider until the court determines placement," Jessica told the nurse. "I'll take

care of that immediately when I get back to the office. I'll need to speak to the attending physician as well.''

"Of course, Miss Larson. If you'll come with me?''

McCallum fell into step beside her, down the long hall to Dr. Henderson's office. They spoke with him about the child's condition and were satisfied that she could be released the next morning.

"I'll send over the necessary forms,'' Jessica assured him, shaking hands.

"Pity, isn't it?'' the doctor said sadly. "Throwing away a baby, like a used paper plate.''

"She wasn't exactly thrown away,'' Jessica reminded him. "At least she was left where people would find her. We've had babies who weren't so fortunate.''

McCallum pursed his lips. "Has anyone called to check on the baby?'' he asked suddenly.

"Why, yes,'' the doctor replied curiously. "As a matter of fact, a woman from *The Whitehorn Journal* office called. She wanted to do a story, but I said she must first check with you.''

McCallum lifted an eyebrow. "*The Whitehorn Journal* doesn't have a woman reporter.''

He frowned. "I understood her to say the *Journal*. I may have been mistaken.''

"I doubt it,'' McCallum said thoughtfully. "It was probably the child's mother, making sure the baby had been found.''

"If she calls again, I'll get in touch with you.''

"Thanks,'' McCallum said.

He and Jessica walked back down the hall toward the hospital exit. He glanced down at her. "How old are you?''

She started. "I'm twenty-five,'' she said. "Why?''

He looked ahead instead of at her, his hands stuck deep in his jean pockets. "These modern attitudes may work for some women, but they won't work for you. Why don't you get married and have babies of your own, instead of mooning over someone else's?''

She didn't answer him. Rage boiled up inside her, quickening her steps as she made her way out the door toward his car.

He held the door open for her. She didn't even bother to comment on the courtesy or question it, she was so angry. He had no right to make such remarks to her. Her private life was none of his business!

He got in beside her, but he didn't start the engine. He turned toward her, his keen eyes cutting into her face. "You cried," he said shortly.

She grasped her briefcase like a lifeline, staring straight ahead, ignoring him.

He hit the steering wheel with his hand in impotent anger. He shouldn't let her get to him this way.

"How can you be in law enforcement with a temper like that?" she demanded icily.

He stared at her levelly. "I don't hit people."

"You do, too!" she raged. "You hit that man who threatened to pull a gun on you. I heard all about it!"

"Did you hear that *he* kicked me in the... Well, never mind, but he damned near unmanned me before I laid a finger on him!" he said harshly.

She clutched the briefcase like a shield. "McCallum, you are crude! Crude and absolutely insensitive!"

"Crude? Insensitive?" he exclaimed shortly. He glared at her. "If you think that's crude, suppose I give you the slang term for it then?" he added with a cold smile, and he told her, graphically, what the man had done.

She was breathing through her nostrils. Her eyes were like brown coals, and she was livid.

"Your hand is itching, isn't it?" he taunted. "You want to slap me, but you can't quite work up the nerve."

"You have no right to talk to me like this!"

"How did you ever get into this line of work?" he demanded. "You're a bleeding-heart liberal with more pity than purpose in your life. If you'd take down that hair—" he pulled some pins from her bun "—and keep on those contact lenses, you might even find a man who'd marry you. Then you wouldn't have to spend your life burying your own needs in a

job that's little more than a substitute for an adult relationship with a man!''

"You...!'' The impact of the briefcase hitting his shoulder shocked him speechless. She hit him again before he could recover. The leather briefcase was heavy, but it was the shock of the attack that left him frozen in his seat when she tumbled out of the car and slammed the door furiously behind her.

She started off down the street with her hair hanging in unruly strands from its once-neat bun and her jacket askew. She looked dignified even in her pathetic state, and she didn't look back once.

Four

She made it two blocks before her feet gave out. Thank goodness for the Chamber of Commerce, she thought, taking advantage of the strategically placed bench near the curb bearing that agency's compliments. The late April sun was hot, and her suit, though light, was smothering her. The high heels she was wearing with it were killing her. She took off the right one, grimaced and rubbed her hose-clad foot.

She was suddenly aware of the unmarked patrol car that cruised to the curb and stopped.

McCallum got out without any rush and sat down beside her on the bench.

"You are the most difficult man I've ever met," she told him bluntly. "I don't understand why you feel compelled to make me so miserable, when all I've ever wanted to do was be kind to you!"

He leaned back, his eyes hidden behind dark sunglasses, and crossed his long legs. "I don't need kindness and I don't like your kind of woman."

"I know that," she said. "It shows. But I haven't done a thing to you."

He took off his sunglasses and turned his face toward her. It was as unreadable as stone, and about that warm. How could he tell her that her nurturing attitude made him want to scream? He needed a woman and she had a delectable body, but despite her response to him that night in front of the bus station, she backed away from him the minute he came too close. He wasn't conceited, yet he knew he was a physically dynamic, handsome man. Women usually ran after him, not the reverse. Jessica was the exception, and perhaps it was just as well. He wasn't a man with commitment on his mind.

"We're supposed to be working on a case together," he reminded her.

"I don't work on cases with men who talk to me as if I were a hooker," she shot back with cold dark eyes. "I don't have to take that sort of language from you. And I'll remind you that you're supposed to be upholding the law, not verbally breaking it. Or is using foul language in front of a woman no longer on the books as a misdemeanor in Whitehorn?"

He moved uncomfortably on the bench, because it *was* a misdemeanor. She'd knocked him off balance and he'd reacted like an idiot. He didn't like admitting it. "It wasn't foul language. It was explicit," he defended himself.

"Splitting hairs!"

"All right, I was out of line!" He shifted his long legs. "You get under my skin," he said irritably. "Haven't you noticed?"

"It's hard to miss," she conceded. "If I'm such a trial to you, Detective, there are other caseworkers in my office...."

He turned his head toward her. "Hensley said I work with you. So I work with you."

She reached down and put her shoe back on, unwittingly calling his attention to her long, elegant legs in silky hose.

"That doesn't mean we have to hang out together," she informed him. "We can talk over the phone when necessary."

"I don't like telephones."

Her eyes met his, exasperated. "Have you ever thought of making a list of your dislikes and just handing it to people?" she asked. "Better yet, you might consider a list of things you *do* like. It would be shorter."

He glowered at her. "I never planned to wind up being a hick cop in a hick town working with a woman who thinks a meaningful relationship has something to do with owning a cat."

"I can't imagine why you don't go back into the service, where you felt at home!"

"Made too many enemies." He bit off the words. "I don't fit in there, either, anymore. Everything's changing. New regulations, policies..."

"Did you ever think of becoming a diplomat?" she said with veiled sarcasm.

"No chance of that," he murmured heavily, then sighed. "I should have studied anthropology, I guess."

Her bad temper dissipated like clouds in sunlight. She could picture it. She laughed.

"Oh, hell, don't do that," he said shortly. "I didn't mean to be funny."

"I don't imagine so. Is your lack of diplomacy why you're not in the service anymore?"

He shook his head. "It didn't help my career. But the real problem was the new political climate. I'm no bigot, but I'm not politically correct when it comes to bending over backwards to please special-interest groups. If I don't like something, I can't pretend that I do. I didn't want to end up stationed in a microwavable room in Moscow, listening to people's conversations."

She frowned. "I thought you were in the navy? You know…sailing around in ships and stuff."

His dark eyes narrowed. "I didn't serve on a ship. I was in Naval Intelligence."

"Oh." She hadn't realized that. His past took on a whole new dimension in her eyes. "Then how in the world did you end up here?"

"I had to live someplace. I hate cities, and this is as close to a home as I've ever known," he said simply. "The last place I lived was with an elderly couple over near the county line. They're dead now, but they left me a little property in the Bighorn Mountains. Who knows, I may build a house there one day. Just for me and Mack."

"I don't think I like dogs."

"And I hate cats," he said at once.

"Why doesn't that surprise me?"

His eyebrow jumped. He put his sunglasses back on and got to his feet. He looked marvelously fit, all muscular strength and height, a man in the prime of his life. "I'll run you back to

your office. I want to go out to the Kincaid place and have a talk with Jeremiah.''

She stood up, holding her briefcase beside her. ''I can walk. It's only another block or so.''

''Five blocks, and it's midday,'' he reminded her. ''Come on. I won't make any more questionable remarks.''

''I'd like that sworn to,'' she muttered as she let him open the door for her.

''You're a hot-tempered little thing, aren't you?'' he asked abruptly.

''I defend myself,'' she conceded. ''I don't know about the 'little' part.''

He got in beside her and started the engine. Five minutes later she was back in the parking lot at her office. She was strangely reluctant to get out of the car, though. It was as though something had shifted between them, after weeks of working fairly comfortably with each other. He'd said 'the last place he lived,' and he'd mentioned an elderly couple, not parents.

''May I ask you something personal?'' she said.

He looked straight at her, without removing his sunglasses. ''No.''

She was used to abruptness and even verbal abuse from clients, but McCallum set new records for it. He was the touchiest man she'd ever met.

''Okay,'' she said, clutching her briefcase as she opened the door. She looked over her shoulder. ''Oh, I'm, uh, sorry about hitting you with this thing. I didn't hurt you, did I?''

''I've been shot a couple of times,'' he mentioned, just to make sure she got the idea that a bash with a briefcase wasn't going to do much damage.

''Poor old bullets,'' she muttered.

His face went clean of all expression, but his chest convulsed a time or two.

She got out of the car and slammed the door. She walked around to the driver's side and bent down. ''I accept your apology.''

"I didn't make any damned apology," he shot right back.

"I'm sure you meant to. I expect you were raised to be a gentleman, it's just that you've forgotten how."

The sunglasses glittered. She moved back a little.

"Don't you have anything to do? What the hell do they pay you for, and don't tell me it's for stand-up comedy."

"Actually, I'm doing a brain-surgery-by-mail course," she said pertly. "You're first on my list of potential patients."

"God forbid." He slipped the car into gear.

"Wait a minute," she said. "Are you going to tell anyone about the brooch you found?"

"No," he replied impatiently. "That brooch is my ace in the hole. I don't want it publicized in case someone comes to claim the baby. I'll mention it to selected people when it comes in useful."

"Oh, I see," she said at once. "You can rule out impostors. If they don't know about the brooch, they're not the baby's mother."

"Smart lady. Don't mention it to anyone."

"I wouldn't think of it. You'll let me know what you find out at the Kincaids', won't you?" she asked.

"Sure. But don't expect miracles. I don't think Dugin's the father, and I don't think we're going to find the baby's mother or any other relatives."

"The baby is blond," she said thoughtfully. "And so is Dugin."

"A lot of men in this community are blond. Besides, have you forgotten that Dugin is engaged to Mary Jo Plummer? With a dish like that wearing his ring, he isn't likely to be running around making other women pregnant."

"And he could afford to send it away if it was his, or have it adopted," she agreed. "Funny, though, isn't it, for someone to leave a baby on his doorstep? What did his father say?"

"Jeremiah wasn't there, according to Hensley. He'd been away and so Dugin called the law."

"That isn't like the Jeremiah Kincaid I know," she mused.

"It would be more in character for him to start yelling his head off and accusing Dugin of fathering it."

"So I've heard."

He didn't say another word. Under that rough exterior, there had to be a heart somewhere. She kept thinking she might excavate it one day, but he was a hard case.

He gave her a curt nod, his mind already on the chore ahead. Dismissing her from his mind, he picked up the mike from his police radio and gave his position and his call letters and signed off. Without even a wave, he sped out of the parking lot.

She watched him until he was out of sight. She was feeling oddly vulnerable. There was a curious warm glow inside her as she went back into the office. She wished she understood her own reactions to the man. McCallum confused and delighted her. Of course, he also made her homicidal.

McCallum went out to the Kincaid ranch the next day, with the brooch in hand. He had some suspicions about that brooch, and it would be just as well to find out if anyone at the ranch recognized it.

When he drove up, the door was opened by Jeremiah himself. He was tall and silver haired, a handsome man in his late sixties. His son was nothing like him, in temperament or looks. Jeremiah had a face that a movie star would have envied.

"Come on in, McCallum, I've been expecting you," Jeremiah said cordially. "Can I pour you a whiskey?"

Characteristically, the man thought everyone shared his own fondness for Old Grandad. McCallum, when he drank, which was rarely, liked the smoothness of scotch whiskey.

"No, thanks. I'm working," McCallum replied.

"You cops." Jeremiah shook his head and poured himself a drink. "Now," he said, when they were seated on the elegant living room furniture, "how can I help you?"

McCallum pulled the brooch, in its plastic bag, out of his pocket and tossed it to the older man. Jeremiah stared at it for a long moment, one finger touching it lightly, reflectively. Then his head lifted.

"Nope," he told McCallum without any expression. "Never saw this before. If it was something that belonged to anyone in this family, you'd better believe I'd recognize it," he added.

He tossed it back to McCallum and lifted his glass to his lips. "What else can I tell you?"

"Was there anything on the baby that wasn't turned in when Sheriff Hensley came?" McCallum persisted.

"Not that I'm aware of," the other man said pleasantly. "Of course, I wasn't home at the time, you know. I didn't find out what had happened until the baby had been taken away. Hell of a thing, isn't it, for a mother to desert her child like that!"

"I didn't say it was deserted by its mother," McCallum replied slowly.

Jeremiah laughed, a little too loudly. "Well, it's hardly likely that the baby's father would have custody, is it? Even in these modern times, most men don't know what to do with a baby!"

"Apparently, some men still don't know how to prevent one, either."

Jeremiah grunted. "Maybe so." He glanced at the younger man. "It isn't Dugin's. I know there's been talk, but I asked the boy straight out. He said that since he got engaged to Mary Jo last year, there hasn't been any other woman."

"And you believe him?"

Jeremiah cleared his throat. "Dugin's sort of slow in that department. Takes a real woman to, uh, help him. That's why he's waited so late in life to marry. Mary Jo's a sweet little thing, but she's a firecracker, too. Caught her kissing him one afternoon out in the barn, and by God if they didn't almost go at it right there, standing up, in front of the whole world! She's something, isn't she, for a children's librarian."

McCallum's eyes were on the lean hands holding the glass of whiskey. They were restless, nervous. Jeremiah was edgy. He hid it well, but not with complete success.

"It sounds as though they'll have a good marriage."

"I think so. She's close to his age, and they sure enjoy being together. Pity about your boss's marriage," he added with a shrug, "but his wife always was too brainy for a man like that.

I mean, after all, a cop isn't exactly an Ivy League boy." He noticed the look on McCallum's face and cleared his throat. "Sorry. No offense meant."

"None taken," Sterling replied. He got to his feet. "If you think of anything that might help us, don't hesitate to call."

"Sure, sure. Look, that crack I made about cops not having much education..."

"I took my baccalaureate degree in science while I was in the navy," he told Jeremiah evenly. "The last few years before I mustered out, I worked in Naval Intelligence."

Jeremiah was surprised. "With that sort of background, why are you working for the sheriff's department?"

"Maybe I just like small towns. And I did grow up here."

"But, man, you could starve on what you make in law enforcement!"

"Do you think so?" McCallum asked with a smile. "Thanks for your time, Mr. Kincaid."

He shook hands with the man and left, thinking privately that he'd rather work for peanuts in law enforcement than live the sort of aimless existence that Jeremiah Kincaid did. The man might have silver hair, but he was a playboy of the first order. He was hardly ever at home, and Dugin certainly wasn't up to the chore of taking care of a spread that size.

Speaking of Dugin... McCallum spotted him near the tool-shed, talking to a younger man, and walked toward him.

Dugin shaded his eyes against the sun. He was tall and fair, in his forties, and he was mild-mannered and unassuming. He'd always seemed younger than he was. Perhaps it was because his father had always overshadowed him. Dugin still lived at home and did most everything his father told him to. He smiled and held out his hand when McCallum reached him.

"Nice day, isn't it?" Dugin asked. "What can I do for you, Deputy? And how's the kid?"

"She's fine. They're placing her in care until the case comes up. Listen, do you know anything that you haven't told the sheriff? Was there anything else with the baby that wasn't turned in?"

Dugin thought for a minute and shook his head. "Not a thing. It isn't my kid," he added solemnly. "I hear there's been some talk around Whitehorn about my being the father, but I'm telling you, I don't know anything. I wouldn't risk losing Mary Jo for any other woman, Deputy. Just between us," he added wryly, "I wouldn't have the energy."

McCallum chuckled. "Okay. Thanks."

"Keep in touch with us about the case, will you?" Dugin asked. "Even though it's not my child, I'd still like to know how things come out."

"Sure."

McCallum walked slowly back to his patrol car, wondering all the way why the baby had been left here, and with Dugin. There had to be a clue. He should have shown that cameo to Dugin, but if Jeremiah didn't recognize it, there was little point in showing it to his son. As Jeremiah had suggested, if it were a family heirloom, he would have recognized it immediately.

It was a lazy day, after that. McCallum was drinking coffee in the Hip Hop Café with his mind only vaguely on baby Jennifer and her missing parents. He was aware of faint interest from some of the other diners when his portable walkie-talkie made static as it picked up a call. Even though most people in Whitehorn knew him, he still drew some curiosity from tourists passing through. He was a good-looking man with a solid, muscular physique that wasn't overdone or exaggerated. He looked powerful, especially with the gun in its holster visible under his lightweight summer jacket.

The call that came over the radio made him scowl. He'd had enough of Jessica Larson the day before, but here she was after him again. Apparently there was a domestic disturbance at the Colson home, where a young boy lived with his father and grandmother.

Sterling went out to the car to answer the call, muttering all the way and as he sat down and jerked up the mike.

"Why is Miss Larson going?" he demanded.

"I don't know, K-236," the dispatcher drawled, using his

call letters instead of his name. "And even if I did, I wouldn't tell you on an open channel."

"I'll see that you get a Christmas present for being such a good boy," McCallum drawled back.

There was an unidentified laugh as McCallum hung up and drove to the small cottagelike Colson house on a dirt road just out of town.

He got there before Jessica did. If there was a fight going on here, it wasn't anything obvious. Terrance Colson was sitting on the porch cleaning his rifle while his mother fed her chickens out back in the fenced-in compound. The boy, Keith, was nowhere in sight. Terrance was red-faced and seemed to have trouble holding the rifle still.

"Afternoon, McCallum!" Terrance called pleasantly. "What can I do for you?"

McCallum walked up on the porch, shook hands with the man and sat down on one of the chairs. "We had a report, but it must have been some crank," he said, looking around.

"Report of what?" Terrance asked curiously.

Before McCallum could answer, Jessica came driving up in her rickety yellow truck. She shut it off, but it kept running for a few seconds, knocking like crazy. That fan belt sounded as if it were still slipping, too. He'd noticed it the night at the bus station.

She got out, almost dropping her shoulder bag in the dirt, and approached the house. McCallum wondered just how many of those shapeless suits she owned. This one was green, and just as unnoticeable as the others. Her hair was up in a bun again. She looked the soul of business.

"Well, hello, Miss Larson," Terrance called. "We seem to be having a party today!"

She stopped at the steps and glanced around, frowning. "We had a call at the office..." she faltered for a moment "...about a terrible fight going on out here. I was requested to come and talk to you."

Terrance looked around pointedly, calling her attention to the peaceful surroundings. "What fight?"

She sighed. "An unnecessary call, I suppose," she said with a smile. "I'm sorry. But as I'm here already, do you think I might talk to Keith for a minute? He told his counselor at school that he'd like to talk to me when I had time."

Terrance stared at her without blinking. "Funny, he never said anything to me about it. And he's not here right now. He's out fishing."

"Do you think I could find him?" she asked persistently.

"He goes way back in the woods," he said quickly. "It's not a good time. He came home in a real bad mood. Best to leave him alone until he cools down."

She shrugged. "As you wish. But do tell him that I'll be glad to listen any time he wants to talk about those school problems." She didn't add that she wondered why he couldn't tell them to the counselor, who was a good psychologist.

"I'll tell him," Terrance said curtly.

"Good day then." She smiled at Terrance, nodded at McCallum and went to climb back into her truck.

McCallum said his own goodbye, wondering why Mrs. Colson never came out of the chicken pen to say hello the whole time he was there. And Terrance's expression had hardened when he'd mentioned the boy. Odd.

He climbed into the patrol car and gave his call sign and location, announcing that he was back in service again. He followed after Jessica's sluggish truck and wondered if she was going to make it back into town.

When she parked her car at the office, he drove in behind her. The squealing of her fan belt was louder than ever. She really would have to do something about it when she had time.

"Your fan belt is loose," he told her firmly. "It's going to break one day and you'll be stranded."

"I know. I'm not totally stupid."

He got out of the car and walked with her to the office, not making a comment back, as he usually did. He seemed deep in thought. "Something funny's going on out at that place," he said suddenly. "Old Mrs. Colson hiding out with the chickens,

Keith nowhere in sight, Terrance cleaning his gun, but without any gun oil...."

"You have a very suspicious mind," she accused gently. "For heaven's sake, do you always go looking for trouble? I'm delighted that there wasn't anything to it. I know the family, and they're good people. It's Keith who gives them fits. He's been into one bout of trouble after another at school since he was in the fifth grade. He's a junior now, and still getting into fights and breaking rules. He was picked up with another boy for shoplifting, although Keith swore he was innocent and the officers involved believed him. I've been trying to help the family as much as possible. Terrance lost his job at the manufacturing company that shut down last fall, and Milly is trying to make a little money by taking in ironing and doing alterations for the dry cleaners. The Colsons are hurting, but they're too proud to let me help much."

He frowned thoughtfully. "Isn't that the way of it?" he asked quietly. "The people who need help most never ask for it. On the other hand, plenty who don't deserve it get it."

She glowered up at him. "You're so cynical, McCallum! Don't you believe anybody can be basically good?"

"No."

She laughed and shook her head. "I give up. You're a hopeless case."

"I'm in law enforcement," he pointed out. "What we see doesn't lead us to look for the best in people."

"Neither does what I see, but I still try to believe in basic goodness," she replied.

He looked down at her for a long moment, letting his eyes linger on her soft mouth and straight nose before they lifted to catch her eyes.

"No, you don't," he said abruptly. "How can you still believe? What happens is that you just close your eyes to the ugliness. That's what most people do. They don't want to know that human beings can do such hideous things. Murder and robbery and beatings are so unthinkable that people pretend it

can't occur. Then some terrible crime happens to them personally, and they have to believe it.''

"You don't close your eyes to it," she said earnestly. "In fact, you look for it everywhere, even when you have to dig to find it. You have to try to rise above the ugliness.''

His eyes darkened. He turned away. "I work for a living," he said lazily. "I haven't got time to stand around here socializing with you. Get that fan belt seen to.''

She looked after him. "My goodness, do I really need a big, strong man to tell me how to take care of myself?''

"Yes.''

He got into his car, leaving her aghast, and drove off.

Five

For several days, McCallum scoured the area for any clues as to the identity of the baby called Jennifer. He checked at every clinic and doctor's office in the area, as well as the local hospital and those in the surrounding counties. But every child's parents were accounted for. There were no leftover babies at any of the medical facilities. Which meant that the baby had probably been born at home, and a midwife had attended the birth. There were plenty of old women in the community who knew how to deliver a baby, and McCallum knew that he could spend years searching for the right person. Prospects looked dismal.

He was just leaving the office for lunch when Jessica Larson walked up to him on the street.

"I need to get your opinion on something," she said, and without preamble, caught his big, lean hand in hers and began to drag him off toward a parked car nearby.

"Now, hold it," he growled, hating and loving the feel of her soft hand in his.

"Don't grumble," she chided. "It won't hurt a bit. I just want you to talk to these young people for me before they make a big mistake." She paused at the beat-up old Chevy, where two teenagers sat guiltily in the front seat. They didn't look old enough to be out of school.

"This is Deputy McCallum," Jessica told the teens. "Ben and Amy want to get married," she explained to him. "Their parents are against it. Ben is seventeen and Amy is sixteen. I've told them that any marriage they make can be legally annulled by her parents because she's under age. Will you tell them that, too?"

He wasn't sure about the statutes on marriageable age in

Montana, having never had occasion or reason to look them up. But he was pretty sure the girl was under the age of consent, and he knew what Jessica wanted him to say. He could bluff when he had to.

"She's absolutely right," he told them. "A minor can't legally marry without written permission from a parent. It would be terrible for you to have to—"

"She's pregnant," Ben mumbled, red-faced, and looked away. "I tried to get her to have it… Well, to not have it, really. She won't listen. She says we have to get married or her folks'll kill her."

Jessica hadn't counted on that complication. She stood there, stunned.

McCallum squatted down beside the car and looked at Amy, who was obviously upset. "Why don't we start at the beginning?" he asked her gently. "These are big decisions that need thought."

While Jessica looked on, stunned by the tenderness in McCallum's deep voice, Amy began to warm to him. "I don't know if I'm pregnant, really," she confessed slowly. "I think I am."

"Shouldn't you find out for sure, before you wind up in a marriage neither of you is ready for?" he asked evenly.

"Yes, sir."

"Then the obvious next step is to see a doctor, isn't it?"

She grimaced. "My dad'll kill me."

"I'll speak to your parents," Jessica promised her. "They won't kill you. They're good people, and they love you. You're their only child."

"I'd just love to have a baby," Amy said dreamily, looking at Ben with fantasy-filled eyes that didn't even see his desperation, his fear. "We can have a house of our own, and I can get a job…."

McCallum looked hard at Jessica.

"Let's go over to your parents' house, Amy," she said. She had McCallum firmly by the hand again, and she wasn't about

to let go. "I'm sure Deputy McCallum won't mind coming with us," she added, daring him to say no.

He gave up plans for a hamburger and fries and told his stomach to shut up. Resignedly, he helped Jessica into his car, and they followed the teens to Amy's house.

"It wasn't so bad, was it?" Jessica commented after the ordeal was finally over. "She'll see a doctor and then get counseling if she needs it. And there won't be a rushed marriage with no hope of success. They didn't even blame Ben too much."

"Why should they?" he muttered as he negotiated a right turn. "She's the one with dreams of babies and happy ever after, not him. He just wants to finish high school and go on to veterinary college."

"Ah, the man's eternal argument. 'Eve tempted me with the apple.'"

He glanced at her musingly. "Most women can lead a man straight to bed with very little conscious effort. Especially a young man."

She lifted her eyebrows. "Don't look at me. I've never led anyone to my bed with conscious effort or without it." She stemmed the memories that thoughts of intimacy resurrected.

"Have you wanted to?"

The question, coming from such an impersonal sort of man, surprised her. "Why…no."

"Have you let the opportunity present itself?" he persisted.

She straightened her skirt unnecessarily. "I'm sorry I made you miss your lunch."

He let the subject go. "How do you know you did?"

"Oh, you always go to lunch at eleven-thirty," she remarked. "I see you crossing over to the café from my office."

He chuckled softly, and it wasn't until she saw the speculation on his face that she realized why.

"I wasn't…watching you, for God's sake!" she blurted out, reddening.

"Really?" he teased. "You mean I've mistaken that hero worship in your eyes all this time?"

Her dark eyes glared at him. "You are very conceited."

"Made so by a very expressive young face," he countered. He glanced at her while they paused at a stop sign. "Don't build a pedestal under me, Jessie," he said, using a nickname for her for the first time. "I'm not tame enough for a woman like you."

She gaped at him. "If you think that I...!"

Incredibly, he caught the back of her head with a steely hand and leaned over her with slow, quiet intent. His dark eyes fell to her shocked mouth and he tugged gently until her mouth was a fraction below his. She could taste his minty breath, feel the heat of his mouth threatening her lips. She could feel the restrained passion in his long, fit body as it loomed over to hers.

"You're afraid of me," he whispered into her mouth. "And it has nothing to do with that bad experience you had. It isn't the kind of fear that causes nightmares. It's the kind that makes your body swell hard with desire."

While she was absorbing the muted shock the words produced, his mouth lowered to touch and tease her soft lips in tender, biting kisses that made her muscles go rigid with sensation. Her hand caught at his shirt, searching for something to hold on to while she spun out of reality altogether. Her nails bit into his chest.

He groaned under his breath. "You'd be a handful," he whispered. "And if you were a different sort of woman, I'd accept with open arms the invitation you're making me right now."

"What...invitation?"

His nose rubbed against hers. "This one."

He brought his mouth down over her parted lips with real intent, feeling them open and shiver convulsively as he deepened the pressure. She whimpered, and the sound shot through him like fire. He abruptly drew back.

His breathing was a little quick, but his expression showed none of the turmoil that kissing her had aroused in him.

She was slower to recover. Her face was flushed, and her mouth was red, swollen from the hard pressure of his lips. She looked at him with wide-eyed surprise.

"You're like a little violet under a doorstep," he commented quietly. "A lovely surprise waiting to be discovered."

She couldn't find the words to express what she felt.

He touched her soft mouth. "Don't worry about it. Someday the right man will come along. I'm not him."

"Why did you do that?" she whispered in a choked voice.

"Because you wanted me to, Jessica," he drawled. "You've watched me for months, wondering how it would feel if I kissed you. Okay. Now you know."

Her eyes darkened with something like pain. She averted them.

"What did you expect?" he mused, pulling the car back out into the road. "I'm not a teenager on his first date. I know exactly what to do with a woman. But you're off-limits, sweetheart. I don't make promises I can't keep."

"I haven't asked you to marry me, have I?" she asked, bouncing back.

He smiled appreciatively. "Not yet."

"And you can hold your breath until I do." She pushed back a disheveled strand of hair. "I'm not getting mixed up with you."

"You like kissing me."

She glared at him. "I like kissing my cat, too, McCallum," she said maliciously.

"Ouch!"

She nodded her head curtly. "Now how arrogant do you feel?"

He chuckled. "Well, as one of my history professors was fond of saying, I've always felt that arrogance was a very admirable quality in a man."

She rolled her eyes.

He drove back into town, but he didn't stop at her office. He kept going until he reached the Hip Hop Café, a small restau-

rant on the southeast corner of Amity Lane and Center.

She glanced at him uncertainly.

"If I haven't eaten, I know you haven't," he explained.

"All right. But I pay for my own food."

His eyes slowly wandered over her face. "I like independence," he said unexpectedly.

"Do I care?" she asked with mock surprise.

He smiled. "Fix your lipstick before we go inside, or everyone's going to know what we've been doing."

She wouldn't blush, she wouldn't blush, she wouldn't...!

All the same, her cheeks were pink in the compact mirror she used as she reapplied her lipstick and powdered her nose.

McCallum had taken the time to wipe the traces of pink off his own firm mouth with his handkerchief.

"Next time, I'll get rid of that lipstick before I start," he murmured.

"Oh, you'd be so lucky!" she hissed.

He lifted an eyebrow over wise, soft eyes. "Or you would. It gets better, the deeper you go. You cried out, and I hadn't even touched you. Imagine, Jessica, how it would feel if I did."

She was out of the car before he finished speaking. She should go back to her office and leave him standing there. He was wicked to tease her about something she couldn't control. It didn't occur to her that he might be overcompensating for the desire he'd felt with her. Experienced he might be, but it had been a while since he'd had a woman and Jessica went right to his head. He hadn't realized it was going to be so fulfilling to kiss her. And it seemed to be addictive, because it was all he could think about.

"I won't let you torment me," she said, walking ahead of him to the door. "And before we go any farther, you'd better remember that Whitehorn isn't that big. Everybody knows everybody else's business. If I go in there with you, people are going to talk about us."

He had one hand in his pocket, the other on the door handle. He searched her eyes. "I know," he said quietly. He opened

the door deliberately.

It was a quiet, companionable lunch. There were a few interested looks, including a sad one from a young waitress who had a hopeless crush on McCallum. But people were discreet enough not to stare at them.

"After all, we could be talking over a case," Jessica said.

He frowned at her. "Does it really matter?" he asked. "You're very sensitive to gossip. Why?"

She shrugged, averting her eyes. "Nobody likes being talked about."

"I don't know that I ever have been since I've come back," he said idly. He sipped his coffee. "And with your spotless reputation, it's hardly likely to think that you have," he added with a chuckle.

She picked up her coffee cup, steadying it with her other hand. "Thank you for helping me with Amy and Ben."

"Did I have a choice? I wonder if there isn't a law against deputy sheriffs being kidnapped by overconscientious social workers. And while we're on the subject of laws, that one about under-age marriages is one I'll have to look up or ask Hensley about. I've never had cause to use it before."

"You may again. We've had several cases like Amy and Ben over the years."

"What if she is pregnant?" he asked.

"Then she'll have choices and people to help her make them."

He glared at her.

"I know that look," she said softly. "I even understand it. But you have to consider that sometimes what's best for a young girl isn't necessarily what you feel is right."

"What if I lost my head one dark night and got you pregnant, Jessica?" He leaned back, his eyes narrowed. "What would you do in Amy's place?"

The color that rushed into her face was a revelation. She spilled a bit of coffee onto the table.

"Well, well," he murmured softly.

She put the cup down and mopped up the coffee with napkins. "You love shocking me, don't you?"

"Never mind the shock. Answer me. What would you do?"

She bit her lower lip. "The correct thing…"

He caught her hand and held it tight in his. "Not the correct thing, or the sensible thing, or even the decent thing. What would *you* do?" he asked evenly.

"Oh, I'd keep it," she said, angry at being pushed into answering a question that would not, could not, ever arise. It hurt her to remember how barren she was. "I'm just brimming over with motherly instincts, old-fashioned morality and an overworked sense of duty. But what I'm trying to make you see is that regardless of my opinion, I have no right to force my personal sense of right and wrong on the rest of the world!"

He forgot the social issue in the heat of the moment, as he allowed himself to wonder how it would feel to create a child with Jessica. It made him feel…odd.

Jessica saw the speculation in his eyes and all her old inadequacies came rushing back. "McCallum," she began, wondering whether or not to tell him about her condition.

His fingers linked with hers, his thumb smoothing over them. "You're twenty-five, aren't you? I'm ten years older."

"Yes, I know. McCallum…"

His eyes lifted to catch hers. "My first name is Sterling," he said.

"That's an unusual name. Was it in your family?"

He shrugged. "My mother never said." Memories of his mother filled his mind. He withdrew, mentally and physically. He pulled his hand slowly away from Jessica's. "Maybe it was the name of her favorite brand of gin, who knows?"

She grimaced, hating that pain in his eyes. She wanted to soothe him, to comfort him.

He looked up and saw the expression on her face. It made him furious.

"I don't need pity," he said through gritted teeth.

"Is that how I looked? I'm sorry. It disturbs me to see how badly your past has affected you, that's all." She smiled. "I

know. I'm a hopeless do-gooder. But think, McCallum—if you'd had someone who really cared what happened to you, wouldn't it have changed your whole life?''

He averted his eyes. ''Facts are facts. We can't go back and change the past.''

''I know that. If we could, think how many people would leap at the chance.''

''True,'' he agreed.

She studied him over her cup. ''This town must hold some bad memories for you. Why did you come back after all these years?''

''I got tired of my job,'' he replied. ''I can't even talk about it, do you know? It was all classified. Let's just say that I got into a situation I couldn't handle for the first time in my life, and I got out. I don't regret it. I manage better here than I ever dreamed I would. I'm not rich, but I'm comfortable, and I like my job and the people I work with. Besides,'' he added, ''the memories weren't all bad. I have a few good ones tucked away. They keep me going when I need them.''

''And was there ever a special woman?'' she asked, deliberately not looking at him.

He cocked an eyebrow. ''*Women,* plural,'' he replied. ''Not just one woman. They all knew the score. I made sure of it and I'm a loner. I don't want to change.''

Jessica felt a vague disappointment.

''Were you hoping?'' he taunted.

She glared at him. ''For what? You, with a bow around your neck on Christmas morning? It's a long time until Christmas, McCallum, and you'd look silly in gift wrapping.''

''Probably so.'' He studied her. ''I wonder how you'd look in a long red stocking?''

''Dead, because that's the only way I'd ever end up in one. Heavens, look at the time! I've got my desk stacked halfway to the ceiling. I have to go!''

''So do I,'' he agreed. ''The days are never long enough to cope with all the paperwork, even in my job.''

''In everyone's job. God knows how many trees die every

day to satisfy bureaucrats. Know what I think they do with all those triplicate copies? I think they make confetti and store it for parades.''

''I wouldn't doubt it.'' He pushed away his empty cup, stood up, laid a bill on the table, picked up the check and walked to the counter with it.

Jessica dug out a five-dollar bill and paid her share.

''Late lunch, huh, McCallum?'' the waitress asked with an inviting smile.

''Yeah.'' He smiled back at her. ''Thanks, Daisy.''

She colored prettily. She was barely twenty, redheaded, cute and totally infatuated with McCallum.

He opened the door for Jessica and walked her back to his car.

''Thanks for your help,'' she told him with genuine appreciation. ''Those kids needed more of a talking to than I could give them. There's something about a uniform...'' she added with a gleam in her eyes. Of course she was kidding; McCallum, a plainclothesman, wasn't wearing a uniform.

''Tell me about it.'' He'd already discovered that uniforms attracted women. It was something most career law-enforcement officers learned how to deal with early.

''Have you found out anything about Jennifer?'' she asked on the way back to her office.

He detailed the bits and pieces he'd been following up. ''But with no luck. Do you know any midwives around the community?'' he asked. ''Someone who would be able to deliver a child and could do it without telling half the world?''

Jessica pursed her lips. ''One or two women come to mind. I'll look into it.''

''Thanks.''

He stopped at her office and waited, with the car idling, for her to get out.

''I'll let you know how things go with Amy,'' she offered.

He looked at her with an expression that bordered on dislike. It had flattered him that she kept asking for his help, and she seemed to like his company. But he liked kissing her too much,

and that made him irritable. He didn't want a social worker to move into his life. He was weakening toward her, and he couldn't afford that. "I don't remember asking for a follow-up report," he said, deliberately being difficult.

It didn't faze Jessica, who was used to him. His bad humor bounced off her. That kiss hadn't, of course, but she had to remember that he was a loner and keep things in perspective. She could mark that lapse down to experience. She knew she wouldn't forget it anytime soon, but she had to keep her eyes off McCallum.

"You're so cynical, McCallum," she said heavily. "Haven't you ever heard that old saying about no man being an island?"

"I read John Donne in college," he replied. "I can be an island if I please."

She pursed her lips again, surveying him with marked interest. "If you really were an island, you'd have barbed wire strung around the trees and land mines on the beaches."

She went inside, aware of the deep masculine laughter she left behind her.

The abandoned baby, Jennifer, had been placed in care, and Jessica couldn't help going to see her. She was living temporarily as a ward of the court with a local family that seemed to thrive on anyone's needful children.

"We can't have any of our own, you see," Mabel Darren said with a grin. She was in her mid-thirties, dark and bubbly, and it didn't take a clairvoyant to know that she loved children. She had six of them, all from broken homes or orphaned, ranging in age from a toddler to a teen.

The house was littered, but clean. The social-services office had to check it out periodically to comply with various regulations, but there had never been any question of the Darrens' ability to provide for their charges. And if ever children were loved, these underprivileged ones were.

"Isn't she a little angel?" Mabel asked when Jessica had the sweet-smelling infant in her arms.

"Oh, yes," Jessica said, feeling a terrible pain as she cuddled

the child. She would never know the joy of childbirth, much less that of watching a baby grow to adulthood. She would be alone all her life.

Mabel would have understood, but Jessica could never bring herself to discuss her anguish with anyone. She carried Jennifer to the rocking chair and sat down with her, oblivious to the many other duties that were supposed to be demanding her attention.

The older woman just smiled. "It's time for her bottle. Would you like to feed her while you're here? Then I could get on with my dirty dishes," she added. She knew already that if she could make Jessica think she was helping, the social worker was much more likely to do what she really wanted to.

"If it would help," Jessica said. Her soft, dark eyes were on the baby's face and she touched the tiny head, the hands, the face with fingers that trembled. She'd never known such a profound hunger in her life, and tears stung her eyes.

As if the baby sensed her pain, her big eyes opened and she stared up at Jessica, unblinking. She made a soft gurgling noise in her throat. With a muffled cry, Jessica cuddled Jennifer close and started the chair rocking. At that moment, she would have given anything—anything!—for this tiny precious thing to be her very own.

Mabel's footsteps signaled her approach. Jessica composed herself just before the other woman reappeared with a bottle. She managed to feed the baby and carry on a pleasant conversation with Mabel, apparently unruffled by the experience. But deep inside, she was devastated. Something about Jennifer accentuated all the terrible feelings of inadequacy and made her child hungry. She'd never wanted anything as much as she wanted the abandoned infant.

After she fed the baby, she went back to the office, where she was broody and quiet for the rest of the day. She was so silent that Bess, who worked in the outer office, stuck her auburn head in the door to inquire if her boss was sick.

"No, I'm all right, but thanks," Jessica said dully. "It's been a long day, that's all."

"Well, you got to have lunch with Sterling McCallum," Bess mused. "I wouldn't call that tedious. I dress up, I wear sexy perfume, but he never gives me a second look. Is he really that formidable and businesslike *all* the time?" she asked with a keen stare.

Jessica's well-schooled features gave nothing away. She smiled serenely. "If I ever find out, you'll be the first to know. It was a business lunch, Bess, not a date," she added.

"Oh, you stick-in-the-mud," she muttered. "A gorgeous man like that, and all you want to talk about is work! I'd have him on his back in the front seat so fast…!"

Shocking images presented themselves, but with Jessica, not Bess, imprisoning Sterling McCallum on the seat of his car. She had to stop thinking of him in those terms! "Really, Bess!" she muttered.

"Jessica, you do know what century this is?" Bess asked gently. "You know, the nineties, uninhibited sex?"

"AIDS?" Jessica added.

Bess made a soft sound. "Well, I didn't mean that you don't have to be careful. But McCallum strikes me as the sort of man who would be. I'll bet he's always properly equipped."

Jessica's face had gone scarlet and she stood up abruptly.

"I'm just leaving for home!" Bess said quickly, all too aware that she'd overstepped the mark. "See you tomorrow!"

She closed the door and ran for it. Jessica was even-tempered most of the time, but she, too, could be formidable when she lost her cool.

Jessica restrained a laugh at the speed with which Bess took to her heels. It was just as well not to let employees get too complacent, she decided, as she opened another file and went back to work.

It was after dark and pouring rain when she decided to go home. Meriwether would be wanting his supper, and she was hungry enough herself. The work would still be here, waiting, in the morning. But it had taken her mind off Baby Jennifer, which was a good thing.

She locked up the office and got into her yellow pickup as quickly as possible. Her umbrella, as usual, was at home. She had one in the office, too, but she'd forgotten it. She was wet enough without trying to go back and get it. She fumbled the key into the ignition, locked her door and started the vehicle.

The engine made the most ghastly squealing noise. It didn't help to remember McCallum's grim warning about trouble ahead if she didn't get it seen to.

But the mechanic's shop was closed, and so were all the service stations. The convenience store was open, and it had self-service gas pumps, but nobody who worked inside would know how to replace a fan belt. In fact, Tammie Jane was working the counter tonight, and the most complicated thing she knew how to do was change her nail polish.

With a long sigh, Jessica pulled the truck out onto the highway and said a silent prayer that she would be able to make it home before the belt broke. The squeal that usually vanished when she went faster only got worse tonight.

The windshield wipers were inadequate, too. A big leaf had gotten caught in the one on the driver's side, smearing the water rather than removing it. Jessica groaned out loud at her bad luck. It had been a horrible day altogether, and not just because of the predicament she was in now.

She pulled onto the dirt road that led to her home. The rain was coming down harder. She had no idea how long it had been pouring, because she'd been so engrossed in her work. Now she saw the creek ahead and wondered if she'd even be able to get across it. The water was very high. This was an old and worrying problem.

She gunned the engine and shot across, barely missing another struggling motorist, her elderly CB-radio-fanatic neighbor. He waved to her as he went past, but she was too occupied with trying to see ahead to really look at him. She almost made it up the hill, but at that very moment, the fan belt decided to give up the ghost. It snapped and the engine raced, but nothing happened. The truck slid back to the bottom of the hill beside the wide, rising creek, and the engine went dead.

Six

Jessica sat in the truck without moving, muttering under her breath. She hoped that her eccentric neighbor had noticed her plight and alerted someone in town on his CB radio, but whether or not he'd seen her slide back down the hill was anyone's guess.

She decided after a few minutes that she was going to be stranded unless she did something. The creek was rising steadily. She was terrified of floods. If she didn't get up that hill, God only knew what might happen to her when the water rose higher. The rain showed no sign of slackening.

She opened the door and got out, becoming soaked within the first couple of minutes. She made a rough sound in her throat and let out an equally rough word to go with it. Stupid old truck! She should have listened to McCallum.

She managed to get the hood up, but it did no good. There was no source of light except the few patches of sky on the horizon that weren't black as thunder. She didn't even have a flashlight. Well, she had one—but the battery was dead. She'd meant to replace it....

The deep drone of an engine caught her attention. She turned, blinded by headlights, hoping against hope that it was her elderly neighbor. He could give her a ride home, at least.

A huge red-and-black Bronco with antennas all over it and a bar of lights on top swept up beside her and stopped. She recognized it from McCallum's house. It had been sitting in the garage next to the patrol car he used when he was on call at night. He got out of it, wearing a yellow rain slicker. The rain seemed to slacken as he approached her.

"Nice wheels," she commented.

"I like it," he replied. "Fan belt broke, huh?"

She glowered, shivering in the rain. "Terrific guess."

"No help here, until I can get a new belt and put it on for you. Nothing's open this late." He closed the hood and marched her around to the passenger side of the Bronco. "Climb in."

He helped her into the big vehicle and she sat, shivering, on the vinyl seat while, with the four-wheel drive in operation, he drove effortlessly up the muddy hill and on to her cabin.

"What were you doing out at this time of night anyway?" he asked.

"Trying to get stranded in the rain," she told him.

He glared at her.

"I was working late." She sneezed.

"Get in there and take a bath."

"I had planned to. Have you…had supper?" she added, without looking at him.

"Not yet."

She touched the door handle. "I have a pot of soup in the refrigerator. I could make some cornbread to go with it."

"If you could make some coffee, I'd be delighted to join you. I'd just got off duty when I monitored a call about a stranded motorist."

She grinned, because she knew which motorist he meant. "Done." She got out and left him to follow.

The minute he walked in the door, Meriwether, having come to meet his mistress, bristled and began spitting viciously at the newcomer.

"I like you, too, pal," McCallum muttered as he and the cat had a glaring contest.

"Meri, behave yourself!" Jessica fussed.

"If you'll show me what the soup's in, I'll start heating it while you're in the shower," he offered.

She led him into the kitchen, dripping everywhere, and got out the big pot of soup while he hung up his drenched slicker.

"I'll make the cornbread when I get back. You could preheat the oven," she added, and told him what temperature to set it.

"Okay. Where's the coffee?"

She showed him the filters and coffee and how to work the pot. Then she rushed down the hall to the bathroom.

Ten minutes later, clean and presentable in a sweatshirt and jeans, with her hair hanging in damp strands down her back, she joined him in the kitchen.

"You'll catch a cold," he murmured, glancing at her from his seat at the table with a steaming cup of black coffee. "Sit down for a minute and I'll pour you a cup."

"I'll make the cornbread first," she said. "It won't take a minute."

And it didn't. She put it in the preheated oven to bake and then sat down across from McCallum to sip her coffee. He was wearing a brown plaid shirt with jeans and boots. He always looked clean and neat, even when he was drenched, she thought, and wondered if his military training had a lot to do with it.

"Do you always keep your house this hot?" he asked, unfastening the top buttons of his shirt.

"I don't have air-conditioning," she explained apologetically. "But I can turn on the fan."

"Are you cool?"

She shook her head. "I'm rather cold-blooded, I'm afraid. But if you're too hot..."

"Leave it. It's probably the coffee." He leaned back. The action pulled his shirt away from his chest and she got a glimpse of the thick mat of curling black hair that covered it.

She averted her eyes in the direction of the stove and watched it fanatically, not daring to look at him again. He was devastating like that, so attractive physically that he made her toes curl.

He saw the look he was getting. It made his heart race. She was certainly less sophisticated than most women he knew, but she still made him hungry in a new and odd sort of way.

"You said you monitored a stranded motorist's call?" she asked curiously.

"Yes. Your neighbor called the office on his mobile unit, and when I heard where the stranded motorist was, I told Dis-

patch that I'd respond." He grinned at her. "I knew who it was and what was wrong before I got here."

She took an audible breath. "Well, it might have been something besides the fan belt," she said.

"You're stubborn."

"I meant to have it checked," she defended herself. "I got busy."

"Next time you'll know better, won't you?"

"I hate it when you use that tone," she muttered. "I'm not brain dead just because I'm a woman!"

His eyebrows raised. "Did I imply that you were?"

"You have an attitude...."

"So do you," he shot back. "Defensive and standoffish. I'd have told a man no differently than I told you that your fan belt needed replacing. The difference is that a man would have listened."

She put her coffee cup down hard and opened her mouth to speak just as the beeper on the oven's timer went off.

He got up with her and took the soup off the burner while she checked the cornbread in the oven. It was nicely browned, just right.

She was silent while she dished up the abbreviated meal, and while they ate it.

"You're a good cook, Jessie," he commented when he'd finished his second helping. "Who taught you?"

"My grandmother," she said. "My mother was not a good cook. She tried, God bless her, but we never gained weight around here." She pushed back her bowl. "You're handy enough in a kitchen yourself."

"Had to be," he said simply. "My mother was never sober enough to cook. If I hadn't learned, we'd both have starved. Not that she ate much. She drank most of her meals."

"You sound so bitter," she said gently.

"I *am* bitter," he shot back. He crossed his long legs, brushing at a smudge of mud on one polished black boot. "She robbed me of my childhood." His eyes sought hers. "Isn't that

what most victims of child abuse tell you—that what they mourn most is the loss of childhood?''

She nodded. ''That's the worst of it. The pain and bitterness go on for a long time, even after therapy. You can't remake the past, McCallum. The scars don't go away, even if the patient can be made to restructure the way he or she thinks about the experience.''

He turned his coffee cup around, his eyes on the white china soup bowl, now empty. ''I never did what young boys usually get to do—play sports, join the Boy Scouts, go on trips, go to parties... From the time I was old enough, I did nothing except look after my mother, night after drunken night.'' His lean hand contracted absently on the bowl. ''I used to hope she'd die.''

''That's very normal,'' she assured him.

His broad shoulders rose and fell. ''She did die, though in jail. I had her arrested when it all got too much after she attacked me one night. She was convicted of child abuse, sent to jail, and she died there when I was in my early teens. I was put to work as a hired hand for any family that would take me in. I had a room in the bunkhouse or in the barn, never with the family. I spent most of my life as an outsider looking in, until I was old enough to join the service. The uniform gave me a little self-esteem. As I grew older, I learned that my situation wasn't all that rare.''

''Sadly, it isn't,'' she told him. ''Sterling, what about your father?''

Her use of his first name made him feel warm inside. He smiled at her. ''What about him?''

''Did he die?''

''Beats me,'' he said quietly. ''I never found out who he was. I'm not sure she knew.''

The implications of that statement were devastating. She winced.

''Feeling sorry for me all over again?'' he murmured gently. ''I don't need pity, Jessie. I've come to grips with it over the years. Plenty of people had it worse.''

She traced the rim of her coffee cup soberly. "I'm sorry that it was that way for you."

"Different from your childhood, I imagine."

"Oh, yes. I was loved and wanted, and petted. I don't suppose I had a single bad experience in my whole childhood."

"They say we carry our childhoods around with us, like luggage. I'll have to worry about not being too rough on my kids. You'll be just the opposite."

She felt sick inside, and tried not to show it. "Have you managed to find out anything else about little Jenny?" she asked, changing the subject.

"Nothing except dead ends," he had to admit. "I did find one new lead, but it didn't work out. How about you? Anything on the midwives?"

"I've spoken to two, but they say they don't know anything." She twirled her spoon on the tablecloth. "I'm not sure they'd tell me if they did," she added, looking up. "Sometimes they get in trouble for helping with deliveries, especially if something goes wrong. What if the mother died giving birth, Sterling?"

"That's a thought." His lips pursed. "I might check into any recent deaths involving childbirth."

"It might not lead to anything at all, but someone has to know about her. I mean, she didn't come from under a cabbage leaf."

He chuckled. "I don't think so."

She liked the sound of his laughter. She smiled as she got up to put the dishes in the sink.

"No dishwasher?" he teased as he helped.

"Of course I have a dishwasher—myself." She smiled at him. "I'll put these in to soak and do them later."

"Do them now, while I'm here to help you."

She did, because it would keep him here that much longer. She enjoyed his company far too much. She filled the sink with soapy water, while outside the rain continued steadily, broken occasionally by a rumble of thunder. "Were you always so

bossy?'' she asked as she washed a plate and handed it to him to be rinsed.

"I suppose so,'' he confessed. ''That's force of habit. I was the highest-ranking officer in my group.''

"What did you do in Naval Intelligence?''

He put the plate in the dish drainer and leaned toward her. ''That's classified,'' he whispered.

''Well, excuse me for asking!'' she teased.

His dark eyes searched hers. ''I like the way you look when you smile,'' he commented absently. ''It lights up your whole face.''

''You hardly ever smile.''

''I do when I'm with you. Haven't you noticed?''

She laughed self-consciously. ''Yes, but I thought it was because you find me tedious.'' She washed another few dishes and passed them to him.

He rinsed them and then began drying, because there were none left to be washed. ''I find you disturbing,'' he corrected quietly.

She let the water out of the sink and took a second cloth, helping to dry the few dishes. ''Because I'm forever dragging you into awkward situations?''

''Not quite.''

They finished drying the dishes and Jessica put them away. She hung up the kitchen towels. Lightning flashed outside the window, followed by a renewal of pelting rain and a deep, vibrating rumble of thunder.

''Are you afraid of thunderstorms?'' he asked her.

''A little.''

He moved closer, his face filling her whole line of vision. ''Are you afraid of me?'' he continued.

Her eyes slid over his face, lingering on his firm mouth and chin. ''That would depend on what you wanted from me,'' she countered bluntly.

''That's forthright enough,'' he said. ''All right, cards on the table. Suppose I want you sexually?''

She didn't drop her eyes. ''I don't want sex.''

His gaze narrowed. "Because of what happened to you?" he guessed.

"Not entirely." She stared at the opening in his shirt, feeling her heartbeat increase as the clean cologne-and-soap scent of his body drifted into her nostrils. "It's mainly a matter of morality, I guess. And I'm not equipped for casual affairs, either. This is a small town. I...don't like gossip. I've always tried to live in such a way that people wouldn't think less of me."

"I see," he said slowly.

She shifted her shoulders. "No, you don't. You've been away so long maybe you've forgotten what it's really like." Her eyes were faintly pleading. "I like my life the way it is. I don't want to complicate it. I'm sorry."

His lean hands caught her waist gently and brought her against the length of his body. He stopped her instinctive withdrawal.

"Hush," he whispered. "Be still."

"What are...you doing?"

"I'm showing you that it's too late," he replied. His big hands smoothed her back up to her shoulder blades. "You want me. I want you. We can slow it down, but we can't stop it. Deep inside, you don't want to stop me." His gaze dropped to her soft mouth, and he watched her lips part. "You've been handled brutally. But you've never been touched with tenderness. I'm going to show you how it feels."

"I'm not sure that I want to know," she whispered.

He bent toward her. "Let's see."

Her fingers went up to touch his lips, staying their downward movement. Her eyes were wide and soft and faintly pleading. "Don't...hurt me," she said.

He moved her hand to his shirtfront and scowled. "Do you think I want to?"

"No, I don't mean physically. I mean..." She searched for words. "Sterling, I can't play games. I'm much too intense. It would be better if we were just friends."

He tilted her chin up and held her eyes. "Think about what you're saying," he said gently. "I know about your past. I

know that you've been assaulted, that you don't date anyone. I even know that you're half-afraid of me. Considering all that, do you think I'm the sort of man who would tease you?''

She looked perplexed. Her hand had moved somehow into the opening where the buttons were unfastened. She felt the curly tangle of thick chest hair over warm, hard muscle. It was difficult to concentrate when all she wanted to do was touch him, test his maleness.

''Well, no,'' she confessed.

''I don't play games with women,'' he said flatly. ''I'm straightforward. Sometimes too much so. I want you, but I'd never force you or put you in a position where you couldn't say no.'' He laughed mirthlessly. ''Or don't you realize that I've been in that position myself?''

Her brows jerked together as she tried to puzzle out what he was saying.

''When one of my foster mothers got drunk enough,'' he said slowly, bitterly, ''anything male would do. She tried to seduce me one night.''

Her heart ached for him. What a distasteful, sickening experience it would have been for a young boy. ''Oh, Sterling!'' she said sadly.

The distaste dominated his expression. ''I knocked her out of the bed and left the house. The next morning, we had it out. I told her exactly what would happen if she ever tried it again. I was almost as big then as I am now, you see. She couldn't force me.'' His hands let her go and he moved away.

She'd come across the same situation so many times, with so many families. It was amazing how many children suffered such traumas and never told, because of the shock and shame.

She moved closer to him, but she didn't touch him. She knew very well that abused children had real problems about being touched by other people sometimes—especially when something reminded them of the episodes—unless it was through their own choice. The scars were long lasting.

''You never told anyone,'' she guessed.

He wouldn't look at her. ''No.''

"Not even your caseworker?"

He shrugged. "He was the sort who wouldn't have believed me. And I had too much pride to beg for credibility."

She mourned the help he could have gotten from someone with a little more compassion.

"I've never told anyone," he continued, glancing down at her. "Amazing that I could tell you."

"Not really," she said, smiling. "I think you could tell me anything."

His face tautened. It was true. He would never balk at divulging his darkest secrets to this woman, because she had an open, loving heart. She wouldn't ridicule or judge, and she wouldn't repeat anything he said.

"I think I must have that sort of face," she continued, tongue-in-cheek, "because total strangers come up and talk to me about the most shocking things. I actually had a man ask me what to do about impotence."

He chuckled, his bad memories temporarily driven away. "And what did you tell him?"

"That a doctor would be a more sensible choice for asking advice," she returned. Her eyes searched his dark, hard face. "Sex was really hard for you the first time, wasn't it?" she asked bluntly.

Again his face tautened. "Yes."

She glanced away, folding her arms over her breasts. "I wasn't a child when I had my bad experience, but it made the thought of intimacy frightening to me. I'm realistic enough to know that it would be different with someone I cared about, but all I can see is the way he was. He reminded me of an animal."

"Do I?"

She turned quickly. "Don't be absurd!"

One eyebrow quirked. "Well, that's something."

She went back to him, looking up solemnly into his face. "I find *you* very disturbing," she confessed. "Physically, I mean. I guess that's why I shy away from you sometimes."

He traced her smooth cheek with a steely forefinger. "I don't think I've ever known anyone as honest as you."

"I hate lies. Don't you?"

"I hear enough of them. Nobody I've ever arrested has been guilty. It was a frame-up, or they didn't mean to, or somebody talked them into it."

"I know what you mean."

The exploring finger reached her mouth and traced its soft bow shape gently. His jaw tightened. She could hear the heavy breath that passed through his nostrils as his eyes began to darken and narrow.

"Why don't you unfasten my shirt and put your hands on me?" he asked huskily.

Her face colored vividly. "I don't know if that would be a good idea."

"It's the best one I've had tonight," he assured her. "No games. Honest. I want to make love to you a little, that's all. I won't let it go too far."

She put her hands against his shirtfront, torn between what she wanted to do and what was sensible.

"It's hard for me, with women," he said roughly. "Does that reassure you any?"

She smiled gently. "Will it make you angry if I confess that it does?"

He bent and his smiling mouth brushed against hers. "Probably. Open your mouth."

She obeyed him like a sleepwalker, but he soon brought every single nerve she had singing to life. Her hands slid under the shirt and over the thick tangle of hair that covered him, past male nipples that hardened at her touch. He moaned softly and pulled her closer. She sighed into his mouth as he deepened the kiss and made her knees go weak with the passion he kindled in her slender body.

"It isn't enough," he said in a strained tone. He bent and lifted her, his gaze reassuring as she opened startled eyes. "I want to lie down with you," he whispered as he carried her to the sofa. "I have to get closer, Jessie. Closer than this."

"It's dangerous," she managed through swollen lips.

"Life is dangerous." He put her down on the sofa, full length, and stretched out alongside her. "I won't hurt you. I swear to God, I won't. All it will take is one word, when you want me to stop."

His mouth traced hers. "And what...if I can't say it?" she whispered brokenly.

"I'll say it for you...."

He kissed her until she trembled, but even then he didn't touch her intimately or attempt to carry their lovemaking to greater depths. He lifted his head and looked down at her with tenderness and bridled passion. With her long hair loose around her face and her lips swollen from his kisses, her dark eyes wide and soft and dazed, he thought he'd never seen anything so beautiful in all his life.

"Are you stopping?" she whispered unsteadily.

"I think I should," he mused, managing to project a self-assurance he didn't really feel. His lower body ached.

"But we haven't done anything except kiss each other...." She stopped abruptly when she realized what she was saying.

He chuckled wickedly. "Jessie, if I push up that sweatshirt, we're both going to be in trouble. Because, frankly, it shows that you aren't wearing anything under it."

She followed his interested gaze and saw two hard peaks outlined vividly against the soft material. Scarlet faced, she got to her feet. "Well!"

He sat back on the sofa, watching her with smug, delighted eyes. She aroused an odd protectiveness in him that he'd never felt with another woman. She was unique in his shattered life. He wanted her, but it went far beyond desire.

"Don't be embarrassed," he said gently. "I didn't say it with any cruel intent. It delights me that you can want me, Jessie." He hesitated. "It delights me that I can want you. I wasn't sure..."

She searched his hard face. "Yes?" she prompted gently.

He got up and went to her slowly, secrets in his eyes.

She pushed back the glorious cloud of her hair and then

reached up to touch his sculptured cheek. "Tell me," she coaxed.

He brought her hand to his lips. "I exaggerated when I told you there had been a parade of women through my bed," he said quietly.

Her eyes were solemn, steady, questioning.

His shoulders moved restlessly. He looked tormented. He tried to tell her, but the words wouldn't come.

Her fingers traced his hard mouth. "It's all right." She pulled his head down and kissed his eyes closed. He shivered. "My dear," she whispered. Her mouth traced his and softly kissed his lips, feeling them open and press down, responding with a sudden feverish need. He pulled her close and increased the pressure, groaning as she gave in to him without a single protest.

He let her go slowly, his tall, fit body taut with desire and need as he looked down at her hungrily.

"I've never been with anyone like you," he said flatly. "Because of the way I grew up, I always equated sex with a certain kind of woman," he said huskily. "So that's where I went, when I had to have it." He sighed heavily. "Not that I was ever careless, Jessie."

She bit her lip, trying not to remember Bess's taunt.

"What is it?" he asked suspiciously.

"I can't tell you. You'll get conceited."

His eyebrows arched. He cocked his head. "Come on."

"A girl I know made the comment that she thought you'd be absolute heaven to make love with, and that she'd bet you were always prepared."

He chuckled softly. "Did she? Who?"

"I'll never tell!"

He pursed his lips, amused. "As it happens, she was right." He bent and brushed her mouth with his. "On both counts," he whispered and nipped her lower lip.

She smiled under his lips. "I know. About the first count anyway."

"You can take my word for the other. How about supper tomorrow night?"

She stared at him blankly. "What?"

"I want to take you out on a date," he explained. "One of those things where a man and a woman spend time together, and at the end of the evening, do what we've already done."

"Oh."

His eyebrow lifted as he fastened his shirt. "Well?"

Her face lit up. "I'd love to!"

He smiled. "So would I. Thanks for supper." He moved to the door and glanced back. She was ruffled and flustered. He liked knowing that he'd made her that way. "I'll send the mechanic over first thing in the morning to see about that fan belt. And I'll come and drive you to work."

"You don't have to," she declared breathlessly.

"I want to." The way he said it projected other images, exciting ones. She laughed inanely, captivated by the look on his dark face.

"I'd better go," he murmured dryly. "Good night, Jessie."

"Good night."

He closed the door gently behind him. "Lock it!" he added from outside.

She rushed forward and threw the lock into place. A minute later she heard deep laughter and the sound of his booted feet going down the steps.

Seven

The restaurant was crowded, and heads turned from all directions when Jessica, in a neat-fitting burgundy dress with her hair loose around her shoulders, walked in with McCallum, who was wearing slacks and a sports coat.

"I told you people would notice that we're together," she said under her breath as they were seated.

"I didn't mind the last time, and I don't mind now," he murmured, smiling. "Do you?"

She smiled back. "Not at all."

The waitress brought menus, poured water into glasses and went away to give them time to decide what to order.

"Why…Miss Larson!"

Jessica looked up. Bess, one of her caseworkers, and a good-looking young man who worked in the bank had paused by their table.

"Hello, Bess," Jessica said, smiling. "How are you?"

"Fine! Don't you look nice? Hi, McCallum," she added, letting her blue eyes sweep over him in pure flirtation. "You look nice, too!"

"Thanks."

"Bess, the waitress is gesturing to us," the young man prompted. He was giving McCallum a nervous look. Probably it was the fact that McCallum was in law enforcement that disturbed him. Lawmen were set apart from the rest of the world, Jessica had discovered over the years. But it could have been the way Bess was looking at the older man. Jessica had to admit that McCallum was sensuous and handsome enough to fit any woman's dream. Compared to him, Bess's date seemed very young, and he was undoubtedly jealous.

"Oh, sure, Steve. Good to see you both!" she said breezily, leading him away.

"She thinks you're a hunk," Jessica said without thinking, then bit her lip.

His eyebrows lifted. "So?" Now he knew who'd made the comment she'd related at her cabin.

"She's very young, of course," she added mischievously.

"No, she isn't," he countered. "In fact, she's only a year younger than you. Nice figure, too."

Jessica fought down an unfamiliar twinge of jealousy. She fumbled with her silverware. Nobody disturbed her like McCallum did.

He reached across the table and caught her hand in his, sending thrills of pleasure up her arm that made her heart race. "I didn't mean it like that. Jessie, if I were interested in your co-worker, why would I spend half my free time thinking about you?"

She smiled at him, thrown off balance by the look in his dark eyes. "Do you?" she asked. Her hand slipped and almost overturned her water glass. He righted it quickly, smiling patiently at her clumsiness. It wasn't like her to do such things.

"Hold tight, and I'll protect you from overturning things," he said, clasping her cold fingers in his. "We'll muddle through together. In my own way, I've got as many hang-ups and inhibitions as you have. But if we try, we can sort it out."

"Sort what out?" she echoed curiously.

He frowned. "Do you think I make a habit of taking women out? I'm thirty-five years old, and since I've been back here, I've lived like a hermit. I'm hungry for a woman...."

This time the glass went over. He called the waitress, who managed to clear away the water with no effort at all. She smiled indulgently at an embarrassed Jessica, who was abjectly apologetic.

She took their order and left. Across the restaurant, Bess was giggling. Jessica looked at Sterling McCallum and knew in that moment that she loved him. She also knew that she could never marry him. He might not realize it now, but he'd want children

one day. He was the sort of man who needed children to love and take care of. He'd make a good husband. Of course, marriage was obviously the last thing on his mind at the moment.

"Good God, woman," he muttered, shaking his head with indulgent amusement. "Will you just let me finish a sentence before you react like that? I don't have plans to ravish you. Okay? Now, move that glass aside before we have another mishap."

"I'm sorry. I'm just all thumbs."

"And I keep putting my foot in my mouth," he said ruefully. "What I was going to say, before the great water glass flood," he added with a grin at her flush, "was that it's time I started going out more. I like you. We'll keep it low-key."

She looked at the big, lean hand holding hers so gently. Her fingers moved over the back of it, tracing, savoring its strength and masculinity. "I like your hands," she said absently. "They're very sensitive, for such masculine ones." She thought about how they might feel on bare, soft skin and her lips parted as she exhaled with unexpected force.

His thumb eased into the damp palm of her hand and began to caress it, making her heart race all over again. "Yours are beautiful," he said, and the memory of how her hands felt on his chest was still in his gaze when he looked up.

She was holding her breath. She looked into his eyes, and neither of them smiled. It was like lightning striking. She could see what he was thinking. It was all there in his dark gaze— the need and the hunger and the ardent passion he felt for her.

"Uh, excuse me?"

They both looked up blankly as the waitress, smiling wryly, waited for them to move their hands so she could put the plates down.

"Sorry," Sterling mumbled.

The waitress didn't say a word, but her expression spoke volumes.

"I think we're becoming obvious," he remarked to Jessica as he picked up his fork, trying not to look around at the interested glances they were getting from Bess and Steve.

"Yes." She sounded pained, and looked even more uncomfortable.

"Jessie?"

"Hmm?" She looked up.

He leaned forward. "I'm dying of frustrated passion here. Eat fast, could you?"

She burst out laughing. It broke the tension and got them through the rest of the meal.

But once he paid the check and they went out to the parking lot and got into the Bronco, he didn't take her straight home. He drove a little way past the cabin and pulled down a long, dark trail into the woods.

He locked his door, unfastened his seatbelt and then reached across her wordlessly to lock her own door and release her seatbelt as well.

His eyes in the darkness held a faint glitter. She could feel the quick, harsh rush of his breath on her forehead. She didn't protest. Her arms reached around his neck as he pulled her across his lap. When his mouth lowered, hers was ready, waiting.

They melted together, so hungry for each other that nothing else seemed to matter.

She'd never experienced kisses that weren't complete in themselves. He made her want more, much more. Every soft stroke of his hands against her back was arousing, even through the layers of fabric. The brush of his lips on hers didn't satisfy, it taunted and teased. He nibbled at the outside curves of her mouth with brief little touches that made her heart run wild. She clung to him, hoping that he might deepen the kiss on his own account, but he seemed to be waiting.

She reached up, finally, driven to the outskirts of desperation by the teasing that went on and on until she was taut as drawn rope with unsatisfied needs.

"Please!" she whispered brokenly, trying to pull his head down.

"It isn't enough, is it?" he asked calmly. "I hoped it might not be. Open your mouth, Jessica," he whispered against her

lips as he shifted her even closer to his broad, warm chest. "And I'll show you just how hungry a kiss can make you feel."

It was devastating. She felt her breath become suspended, like her mind, as his lips fitted themselves to hers and began to move in slow, teasing touches that quickly grew harder and rougher and deeper. By the time his tongue probed at her lips, they opened eagerly for him. When his tongue went deep into her mouth, she arched up against him and groaned out loud.

Her response kindled a growing hunger in him. It had been a long time for him, and the helpless twisting motions of her breasts against him made him want to rip open her dress and take them in his hands and his mouth.

Without thinking of consequences, he made her open her mouth even farther under the crush of his, and his lean hand dropped to her bodice, teasing her breasts through the cloth until he felt the nipples become hard. Only then did he smooth the firm warmth of one and begin to caress it with his fingertips. When he caught the nipple deliberately in his thumb and forefinger, she cried out. He lifted his head to see why. As he'd suspected, it wasn't out of fear or pain.

She lay there, just watching him as he caressed her. He increased the gentle pressure of his fingers and she gasped as she looked into his eyes. A slow flush spread over her high cheekbones in the dimly lit interior.

He didn't say a word. He simply sat there, holding her and looking down into her shadowed eyes. It was hard to breathe. Her body was soft in his arms and that pretty burgundy dress had buttons down the front. His eyes went past the hand that now lay possessively on her breast and he calculated how easy it would be to open the buttons and bare her breasts to his hungry mouth. But she was trembling, and his body was getting quickly out of control. Besides that, it was too soon for that sort of intimacy. He had to give her time to get used to the idea before he tried to further their relationship. It was important not to frighten her so that she backed away from him.

He moved his hand up and pushed back her disheveled hair

with a soft smile. "Sorry," he murmured dryly. "I guess I let it go a little too far."

"It was my fault, too. You're...you're very potent," she said after a minute, feeling the swelling of her mouth from his hard kisses and the tingling of her breast where his hand had toyed with it. She still couldn't imagine that she'd really let him do that. But, oddly, she didn't feel embarrassed about it. It seemed somehow proper for McCallum to touch her like that, as if she belonged to him already.

He grinned at her expression. "You're potent yourself. And that being the case, I think I'd better get you home."

She fingered his collar. "Okay." Her hands traced down to his tie and the top button of his shirt.

"No," he said gently, staying her fingers. "I like having you touch me there too much," he murmured dryly. "Let's not tempt fate twice in one night."

She was a little disappointed, even though she knew he was right. It *was* too soon. But her eyes mirrored more than one emotion.

He watched those expressions chase across her face, his eyes tender, full of secrets. "How did you get under my skin?" he wondered absently.

She glowed with pleasure. "Have I?"

"Right down to the bone, when I wasn't looking. I don't know if I like it." He studied her for a long moment. "Trust comes hard to me. Don't ever lie to me, Jessica," he said unexpectedly. "I can forgive anything except that. I've been sold out once too often in the past. The scars go deep and they came from painful lessons. I can't bear lies."

She thought about being barren, and wondered if this would be the right time to tell him. But it wasn't a lie, was it? It was a secret, one she would get around to, if it ever became necessary to tell him. But right now they were just dating, just friends. She was overreacting. She smiled. "Okay. I promise that I'll never deliberately lie to you." That got her around the difficult hurdle of her condition. She wasn't lying. She just

wasn't confessing. It was middle ground, and not really dishonest. Of course it wasn't.

He let go of her hand and started the vehicle, turning on the lights. He glanced sideways at her as he pulled the Bronco out into the road and drove back to her cabin. She might be afraid, but there was desire in her as well. She wanted him. He had to keep that in mind and not give up hope.

He stopped at her front steps. "I want to take you out from time to time," he said firmly. "We can go out to eat—as my budget allows," he added with a grin, "and to movies. And I'd like to take you fishing and deer tracking with me this fall."

"Oh, I'd enjoy that." She looked surprised and delighted. The radiance of her face made her so stunning that he lost his train of thought for a minute.

He frowned. "Just don't go shopping for wedding bands and putting announcements in the local paper," he said firmly. He held up a hand when she started, flustered, to protest. "There's no use arguing about it, my mind's made up. I do know that you make wonderful homemade bread, and that's a point in your favor, but you mustn't rush me."

Her eyes brightened with wicked pleasure. "Oh, I wouldn't dream of it," she said, entering into the spirit of the thing. "I never try to rush men into marriage."

He chuckled. "Okay. Now you stick to that. I don't like most people," he mused. "But I like you."

"I like you, too."

"In between hero worshipping me," he added outrageously.

She looked him over with a long sigh. "Can I help it if you're the stuff dreams are made of?"

"Pull the other one. I'll see you tomorrow."

"That reminds me, there's a young man in juvenile detention that I'd like you to talk to for me," she said. "He's on a rocky path. Maybe you can turn him around."

He rolled his eyes upward. "Not again!"

"You know you don't mind," she chided. "I'll phone you from the office tomorrow."

"All right." He watched her get out of the Bronco. "Lock your doors."

His concern made her tingle. She grinned at him over her shoulder. "I always do. Thanks for supper."

"I enjoyed it."

"So did I." She wanted to, but she didn't look back as she unlocked the door. She was inside before she heard him drive off. She was sure that her feet didn't touch the floor for the rest of the night. And her dreams were sweet.

In the days and weeks that followed, Jessica and McCallum saw a lot of one another. He kissed her, but it was always absently, tenderly. He'd drawn back from the intensity of the kisses they'd shared the first night he took her out. Now, they talked about things. They discovered much that they had in common, and life took on a new beauty for Jessica.

Just when she thought things couldn't get any better, she walked into the Hip Hop Café and came face-to-face with a nightmare—Sam Jackson.

The sandy-haired man turned and looked at her with cold, contemptuous eyes. He was the brother of the man who'd attacked her and who had later been killed. He was shorter and stockier, but the heavy facial features and small eyes were much the same.

"Hello, Jessica Larson," he said, blocking her path so that she was trapped between the wall and him. "I was passing through and thought I might look you up while I was in town. I wanted to see how my brother's murderer was getting along."

She clutched her purse in hands that trembled. She knew her face was white. Her eyes were huge as she looked at him with terror. He had been the most vocal person in court during the trial, making remarks about her and to her that still hurt.

"I didn't kill your brother. It wasn't my fault," she insisted.

"If you hadn't gone out there and meddled, it never would have happened," he accused. His voice, like his eyes, was full of hate. "You killed him, all right."

"He died in a car wreck," she reminded him with as much

poise as she could manage. "It was not my fault that he attacked me!" She carefully kept her voice down so that she wouldn't be overheard.

"You went out there alone, knowing he'd be on his own because you'd tried to get his wife to leave him," he returned. "A woman who goes to a man's house by herself when he's alone is asking for it."

"I didn't know that he was alone!"

"You wanted him. That's why you convinced his wife to leave him."

The man's attitude hadn't changed, it had only intensified. He'd been unable from the beginning to believe his brother could have beaten not only his wife, but his little girl as well. To keep from accepting the truth, he'd blamed it all on Jessica. His brother had been the most repulsive human being she'd ever known. She looked at him levelly. "That's not true," she corrected. "And you know it. You won't admit it, but you know that your brother was on drugs and you know what he did because of it. You also know that I had nothing to do with his death."

"Like hell you didn't," he said with venom. "You had him arrested! That damned trial destroyed my family, humiliated us beyond belief. Then you just walked away. You walked off and forgot the tragedy you'd caused!"

Her whole body clenched at the remembered agony. "I felt for all of you," she argued. "I didn't want to hurt you, but nothing I did was strictly on my own behalf. I wanted to help his daughter, your niece! Didn't any of you think about her?"

He couldn't speak for a minute. "He never meant to hurt her. He said so. Anyway, she's all right," he muttered. "Kids get over things."

Her eyes looked straight into his. "No, they don't get over things like that. Even I never got over what your brother did to me. I paid and I'm still paying."

"Women like you are trash," he said scornfully. "And before I'm through, everyone around here is going to know it."

"What do you mean?"

He smiled. "I mean I'm going to stick around for a few days and let people know just what sort of social worker they've got here. Maybe during the last few years, some of them have forgotten...."

"If you try to start trouble—" she began.

"You'll what?" he asked smugly. "Sue me for defamation of character? Go ahead. It took everything we had in legal fees to defend my brother. I don't have any money. Sue me. You can't get blood out of a rock."

She tried to breathe normally, but couldn't. "How is Clarisse?" she asked, mentioning the daughter of the man who'd assaulted her so many years before.

"She's in college," he said, "working her way through."

"Is she all right?"

He shifted irritably. "I guess. We hear about her through a mutual cousin. She and her mother washed their hands of us years ago."

Jessica didn't say another word. She'd been planning to eat, but her appetite was gone.

"Excuse me, I have to get back to work," she said. She turned around and left the café. She hardly felt anything all the way to her office. She'd honestly thought the past was dead. Now here it was again, staring her in the face. She'd done nothing wrong, but it seemed that she was doomed to pay over and over again for a crime that had been committed against her, not by her.

It was a cruel wind that had blown Sam Jackson into town, she thought bitterly. But if he was only passing through, perhaps he wouldn't stay long. She'd stick close to the office for a couple of days, she decided, and not make a target of herself.

But that was easier said than done. Apparently Sam had found out where her office was, because he passed by it three times that day. The next morning, when Jessica went into work, it was to find him sitting in the Hip Hop Café where she usually had coffee. She went on to the office and asked Bess if she'd mind bringing her a coffee when she went across the street.

"Who is that fat man?" Bess asked when she came back. "Does he really know you?"

Jessica's heart stopped. "Did he ask you about me?"

"Oh, no," Bess said carelessly. She put a plastic cup of coffee in front of Jessica. "He didn't say anything to me, but he was talking to some other people about you." She hesitated, wondering if she should continue.

"Some people?" Jessica prompted.

"Sterling McCallum was one of them," the caseworker added slowly.

Jessica didn't have to ask if what the man had said was derogatory. It was obvious from the expression on her face that it was.

"He said his brother died because of you," Bess continued reluctantly. "That you led him on and then threw him over after you'd gotten his wife out of the way."

Jessica sat down heavily. "I see. So I'm a femme fatale."

"Nobody who knows you would believe such a thing!" Bess scoffed. "He was a client, wasn't he? Or rather, his brother was. Honest to God, Jessica, I knew there had to be some reason why you always insist that Candy and Brenda go out on cases together instead of alone. His brother was the reason, wasn't he?"

Jessica nodded. "But that isn't how he's telling it. New people in the community might believe him, though," she added, trying not to remember that several old-timers still believed that Jessica had been running after the man, too.

"Tell him to get lost," the other woman said. "Or threaten to have him arrested for slander. I'll bet McCallum would do it for you. After all, you two are looking cozy these days."

"We're just friends," Jessica said with emphasis. "Nothing more. And Sterling might believe him. He's been away from Whitehorn for a long time, and he doesn't really know me very well." She didn't add that McCallum had such bad experiences in the past that it might be all too easy for him to believe what Sam Jackson was telling him. She was afraid of the damage that might be done to their fragile relationship.

"Don't worry," Bess was saying. "McCallum will give him his walking papers."

"Do you think so?" Jessica took a sip of her coffee. "We'd better get to work."

She half expected McCallum to come storming into the office demanding explanations. But he didn't. Nothing was said at all, by him or by anyone else. Life went on as usual, and by the end of the day, she'd relaxed. She'd overreacted to Sam's presence in Whitehorn. It would be all right. He was probably on his way out of town even now.

McCallum was drinking a beer. He hardly ever had anything even slightly alcoholic. His mother had taught him well what alcohol could do. Therefore, he was always on guard against overindulgence.

That being the case, it was only one beer. He was off duty and not on call. Before he'd met the newcomer in the café that morning, he might have taken Jessica to a movie. Now he felt sick inside. She'd never told him the things he'd learned from Sam Jackson.

Jessica was a pretty woman when she dressed up. She'd been interning at the social-services office, Sam Jackson had told him, when she'd gone out to see his brother Fred. Fred's wife had become jealous of the way Jessica was out there all the time, and she'd left him. Jessica teased and flirted with him, and then, when things got out of hand and the poor man was maddened with passion, she'd yelled rape and had him arrested. The man had hardly touched her. He'd gone to jail for attempted rape, got out on parole six months later and was killed in a horrible car wreck. His wife and child had been lost to him, he was disgraced and it was all Jessica's fault. Everybody believed her wild lies.

Sam Jackson was no fly-by-night con man. He'd been a respected councilman in Whitehorn for many years and was still known locally. McCallum had asked another old-timer, who'd verified that Jessica had had Jackson's brother arrested for sexual assault. It had been a closed hearing, very hushed up, and

a bit of gossip was all that managed to escape the tight-lipped sheriff, Judd Hensley, and the attorneys and judge in the case. But people knew it was Jessica who had been involved, and the rumors had flown for weeks, even after Fred Jackson's family left town and he was sent to jail for attempted rape.

The old man had shaken his head as he recalled the incident. Women always said no when they meant yes, he assured McCallum, and several people thought that Jessica had only gotten what she'd asked for, going out to a man's house alone. Women had too goldarned much freedom, the old-timer said. If they'd never gotten the vote, life would have been better all around.

McCallum didn't hear the sexism in the remark; he was too outraged over what he'd learned about Jessica. So that shy, retiring pose was just that—an act. She'd played him for an absolute fool. No woman could be trusted. Hadn't he learned from his mother how treacherous they could be? His mother had smiled so sweetly when people came, infrequently, to the house. She'd lied with a straight face when a neighbor had asked questions about all the yelling and smashing of glass the night before. Nothing had happened except that she'd dropped a vase, she'd insisted, and she'd cried out because it startled her.

Actually, she'd been raving mad from too much alcohol and had been chasing her son around the house with an empty gin bottle. That was the night she'd broken his arm. She'd managed to convince the local doctor, the elderly practitioner who'd preceeded Jessica's father, that he'd slipped and fallen on a rain-wet porch. She'd tried to coax him to set it and say nothing out of loyalty to the family. But Sterling had told. His mother had hurt him. She'd lied deliberately about their home life. She'd pretended to love him, until she drank. And then she was like another person, a brutal and unfeeling one who only wanted to hurt him. He'd never trusted another woman since.

Until Jessica. She was the one exception. He'd grown close to her during their meetings, and he wanted her in every way there was. He valued her friendship, her company. But she'd

lied to him, by omission. She hadn't told him the truth about her past.

There was one other truth Sam Jackson had imparted to him, an even worse one. In the course of the trial, it had come out that the doctor who had examined Jessica found a blockage in her fallopian tubes that would make it difficult, if not impossible, for her to get pregnant.

She knew that Sterling was interested in her, that he would probably want children. Yet she'd made sure that she never told him that one terrible fact about herself. She could not give him a child. Yet she'd never stopped going out with him, and she knew that he was growing involved with her. It was a lie by omission, but still a lie. It was the one thing, he confessed to himself, that he could never forgive.

He was only grateful that he'd found her out in time, before he'd made an utter fool of himself.

Eight

Unfortunately, it was impossible for Jessica not to notice that McCallum's attitude toward her had changed since Sam Jackson's advent into town. He didn't call her that evening or the next day. And when she was contacted by the sheriff's office because the child of one of her client families—Keith Colson—was picked up for shoplifting, she wondered if he would have.

She went to the sheriff's office as quickly as she could. McCallum was there as arresting officer. He was polite and not hateful, but he was so distant that Jessica hardly knew what to say to him.

She sat down in a chair beside the lanky boy in the interrogation room and laid her purse on the table.

"Why did you do it, Keith?" she asked gently.

He shrugged and averted his eyes. "I don't know."

"You were caught in the act," she pressed, aware of McCallum standing quietly behind her, waiting. "The store owner saw you pick up several packages of cigarettes and stick them in your pockets. He said you even looked into the camera while you were doing it. You didn't try to hide what you were doing."

Keith moved restlessly in the chair. "I did it, okay? How about locking me up now?" he added to McCallum. "This time I wasn't an accomplice. This time I'm the—what do you call it?—perpetrator. That means I do time, right? When are you going to lock me up?"

McCallum was scowling. Something wasn't right here. The boy looked hunted, afraid, but not because he'd been caught shoplifting. He'd waited patiently for McCallum to show up and arrest him, and he'd climbed into the back of the patrol car

almost eagerly. There was one other disturbing thing: a fading bruise, a big one, was visible beside his eye.

"I can't do that yet," McCallum said. "We've called the juvenile authorities. You're under age, so you'll have to be turned over to them."

"Juvenile? Not *again!* But I wasn't an accomplice, you know I did it. I did it all by myself! I shouldn't have to go back home this time!"

McCallum hitched up his slacks and sat down on the edge of the table, facing the boy. "Why don't you tell me the truth?" he invited quietly. "I can't help you if I don't know what's going on."

Keith looked as if he wanted to say something, as if it was eating him up inside not to. But at the last minute, his eyes lowered and he shrugged.

"Nothing to tell," he said gruffly. He glanced at McCallum. "There's a chance that they might keep me, isn't there? At the juvenile hall, I mean?"

McCallum scowled. "No. You'll be sent home after they've done the paperwork and your hearing's scheduled."

Keith's face fell. He sighed and wouldn't say another word. McCallum could remember seeing that particular expression on a youngster's face only once before. It had been on his own face, the night the doctor set the arm his mother had broken. He had to get to the bottom of Keith's situation, and he knew he couldn't do that by talking to Keith or any of his family. There had to be another way, a better way. Perhaps he could talk to some people at Keith's school. Someone there might know more than he did and be able to shed some light on the situation for him.

Jessica went out to see Keith's father and grandmother. She'd hoped McCallum might offer to go with her, but he left as soon as Keith was delivered to the juvenile officer. It was all too obvious that he found Jessica's company distasteful, probably because Sam Jackson had been filling his head full of half-truths. If he'd only come out and accuse her of something, she

could defend herself. But how could she make any sort of defense against words that were left unspoken?

Terrance Colson was not surprised to hear that his son was in trouble with the law.

"I knew the boy was up to no good," he told Jessica blithely. "Takes after his mother, you know. She ran off with a salesman and dumped him on me and his grandmother years ago. Never wanted him in the first place." He sounded as if he felt the same way. "God knows I've done my best for him, but he never appreciates anything at all. He's always talking back, making trouble. I'm not surprised that he stole things, no, sir."

"Did you know that he smoked?" Jessica asked deliberately, curious because the boy's grandmother stayed conspicuously out of sight and never even came out to the porch, when Jessica knew she'd heard the truck drive up.

"Sure I knew he smoked," Terrance said evenly. "I won't give him money to throw away on cigarettes. That's probably why he stole them."

That was a lie. Jessica knew it was, because McCallum had offered the boy a cigarette in the sheriff's office and he'd refused it with a grimace. He'd said that he didn't like cigarettes, although he quickly corrected that and said that he just didn't want one at the moment. But there were no nicotine stains on his fingers, and he certainly didn't smell of tobacco.

"You tell them to send him home, now, as soon as they get finished with him," Terrance told Jessica firmly. "I got work to do around here and he's needed. They can't lock him up."

"They won't," she assured him. "But he won't tell us anything. Not even why he did it."

"Because he needed cigarettes, that's why," the man said unconvincingly.

Jessica understood why McCallum had been suspicious. The longer she talked to the boy's father, the more curious she became about the situation. She asked a few more questions, but he was as unforthcoming as Keith himself had been. Eventually, she got up to leave.

"I'd like to say hello to Mrs. Colson," she began.

"Oh, she's too busy to come out," he said with careful indifference. "I'll give her your regards, though."

"Yes. You do that." Jessica smiled and held out her hand deliberately. As Terrance reluctantly took it, she saw small bruises on his knuckles. He was right-handed. If he hit someone, it would be with the hand she was holding.

She didn't remark on the bruises. She left the porch, forming a theory that was very disturbing. She wished that she and McCallum were on better terms, because she was going to need his help. She was sorry she hadn't listened to him sooner. If she had, perhaps Keith wouldn't have another shoplifting charge on his record.

When she got back to her office, she called the sheriff's office and asked them to have McCallum drop by. Once, he would have stopped in the middle of whatever he was doing to oblige her. But today it was almost quitting time before he put in a belated appearance. And he didn't look happy about being summoned, either.

She had to pretend that it didn't matter, that she wasn't bothered that he was staring holes through her with those angry dark eyes. She forced a cool smile to her lips and invited him to sit down.

"I've had a long talk with Keith's father," she said at once. "He says that Keith smokes and that's why he took the cigarettes."

"Bull," he said curtly.

"I know. I didn't notice any nicotine stains on Keith's fingers. But I did notice some bruises on Terrance's knuckles and a fading bruise near Keith's eye," she added.

He lifted an eyebrow. "Observant, aren't you?" he asked with thinly veiled sarcasm. "You were the one who said there was nothing wrong at Keith's home, as I recall."

She sat back heavily in her chair. "Yes, I was. I should have listened to you. The thing is, what can we do about it? His father isn't going to admit that he's hitting him, and Keith is too loyal to tell anyone about it. I even thought about talking to old Mrs. Colson, but Terrance won't let me near her."

"Unless Keith volunteers the information, we have no case," McCallum replied. "The district attorney isn't likely to ask a judge to issue an arrest warrant on anyone's hunch."

She grimaced. "I know." She laced her fingers together. "Meanwhile, Keith's desperate to get away from home, even to the extent of landing himself in jail to accomplish it. He won't stop until he does."

"I know that."

"Then do something!" she insisted.

"What do you have in mind?"

She threw up her hands. "How do I know? I'm not in law enforcement."

His dark eyes narrowed accusingly on her face. "No. You're in social work. And you take your job very seriously, don't you?"

It was a pointed remark, unmistakable. She sat up straight, with her hands locked together on her cluttered desk, and stared at him levelly. "Go ahead," she invited. "Get it off your chest."

"All right," he said without raising his voice. "You can't have a child of your own."

She'd expected to be confronted with some of the old gossip, with anything except this. Her face paled. She couldn't even explain it to him. Her eyes fell.

The guilt told him all he needed to know. "Did you ever plan to tell me?" he asked icily. "Or wasn't it any of my business?"

She stared at the small print on a bottle of correction fluid until she had it memorized. "I thought...we weren't serious about each other, so it...wasn't necessary to tell you."

He didn't want her to know how serious he'd started to feel about her. It made him too vulnerable. He crossed one long leg over the other.

"And how about the court trial?" he added. "Weren't you going to mention anything about it, either?"

Her weary eyes lifted to his. "You must surely realize that

Sam Jackson isn't anyone's idea of an unbiased observer. It was his brother. Naturally, he'd think it was all my fault.''

"Wasn't it?'' he asked coldly. "You did go out to the man's house all alone, didn't you?''

That remark was a slap in the face. She got to her feet, her eyes glittering. "I don't have to defend a decision I made years ago to you,'' she said coolly. "You have no right to accuse me of anything.''

"I wasn't aware that I had,'' he returned. "Do you feel guilty about what happened to Jackson's brother?''

Her expression hardened to steel. "I have nothing to feel guilty about,'' she said with as much pride as she could manage. "Given the same circumstances, I'd do exactly what I did again and I'd take the consequences.''

He scowled at her. "Including costing a man his family, subjecting him to public humiliation and eventually to what amounted to suicide?''

So that was what Sam had been telling people. That Jessica had driven the man to his death.

She sat back down. "If you care about people,'' she said quietly, "you believe them. If you don't, all the words in the world won't change anything. Sam should have been a lawyer. He really has a gift for influencing opinion. He's certainly tarred and feathered me in only two days.''

"The truth usually comes out, doesn't it?'' he countered.

She didn't flinch. "You don't know the truth. Not that it matters anymore.'' She was heartsick. She pulled her files toward her. "If you'll excuse me, Deputy McCallum, I've already got a day's work left to finish. I'll have another talk with Keith when the juvenile officers bring him back to the sheriff's office.''

"You do that.'' He got up, furious because she wouldn't offer him any explanation, any apology for keeping him in the dark. "You might have told me the truth in the beginning,'' he added angrily.

She opened a file. "We all have our scars. Mine are such that it hurts to take them out and look at them.'' She lifted

wounded dark eyes to his. "I can't ever have babies," she said stiffly. "Now you know. Ordinarily, you wouldn't have, because I never had any intention of letting our relationship go that far. You were the one who kept pushing your way into my life. If you had just let me alone…!" She stopped, biting her lower lip to stifle the painful words. She turned a sheet of paper over deftly. "Sam Jackson's brother got what he deserved, McCallum. And that's the last thing I'll ever say about it."

He stood watching her for a minute before he finally turned and went out. He walked aimlessly into the outer office. She was right. He was the one who'd pursued her, not the reverse. All the same, she might have told him the truth.

"Hi, McCallum," Bess called to him from her desk, smiling sweetly.

He paused on his way out and smiled back. "Hi, yourself."

She gave him a look that could have melted ice. "I guess you and Jessica are too thick for me to try my luck, hmm?" she asked with a mock sigh.

He lifted his chin and his dark eyes shimmered as he looked at her. "Jessica and I are friends," he said, refusing to admit that they were hardly even that anymore. "That's all."

"Well, in that case, why don't you come over for supper tonight and I'll feed you some of my homemade spaghetti?" she asked softly. "Then we can watch that new movie on cable. You know, the one with all the warnings on it?" she added suggestively.

She was pretty and young and obviously had no hang-ups about being a woman. He pursed his lips. It had been a long, dry spell, although something in him resisted dating a woman so close to Jessica. On the other hand, he told himself, Jessica had lied to him, and what was it to her if he dated one of her employees?

"What time?" he asked gruffly.

She brightened. "Six, sharp. I live next door to Truman Haynes. You know where his house is, don't you?" He nodded. "Well, I rent his furnished cottage. It's very cozy, and old Truman goes to bed real early."

"Does he, now?" he mused.

She grinned. "Yes, indeed!"

"Then I'll see you at six." He winked and walked out, still feeling a twinge of guilt.

Bess stuck her head into Jessica's office just before she left. "McCallum said that you and he were just good friends, and you keep saying the same thing," she began, "so is it all right if I try my luck with him?"

Jessica was dumbfounded, but she was adept at hiding her deepest feelings. She forced a smile. "Why, of course."

Bess let out a sigh of relief. "Thank goodness! I invited him over for supper. I didn't want to step on your toes, but he is so sexy! Thanks, Jessica! See you tomorrow!"

She closed the door quickly, and a minute later, Jessica heard her go out. It was like a door closing on life itself. She hesitated just briefly before she turned her eyes back to the file she was working on. The print was so blurred that she could hardly read it.

Whitehorn was small and, as in most small towns, everyone knew immediately about McCallum's supper with Bess. They didn't know that nothing had happened, however, because Bess made enough innuendos to suggest that it had been the hottest date of her life. Jessica was hard-pressed not to snap at her employee, but she couldn't let anyone know how humiliating and painful the experience was to her. She had her pride, if nothing else.

Sam Jackson heard about the date and laughed heartily. Originally he'd planned to spend only one night in Whitehorn, but he was enjoying himself too much to leave in a rush. A week later, he was still in residence at the small motel and having breakfast every morning at the café across from Jessica's office.

Jessica was near breaking point. People were gossiping about her all over again. She became impatient with her caseworkers and even with clients, which was unlike her. She couldn't do anything about Sam Jackson, and certainly McCallum wasn't going to. He seemed to like the man. And he seemed to like

Bess as well, because he began to stop by the office every day to take her to lunch.

"I'm leaving now," Bess said at noon on Friday. She hesitated, and from the corner of her eye, Jessica saw her looking at her in concern. No wonder since even to her own eyes she looked pale and drawn. In fact, she was hardly eating anything and was on the verge of moving out of town. Desperation had cost her the cool reason she'd always prided herself on.

"Have a nice lunch," she told Bess, refusing to look up because she knew Sterling McCallum was standing in the outer office, waiting.

Bess still hesitated. She felt so guilty she couldn't stand herself lately. It was painfully obvious how her boss felt about Sterling McCallum. It was even more obvious now that McCallum was taking Bess out. She hated being caught between the two of them, and it was shocking to see how Jessica was being affected by it. Bess had a few bad moments remembering how she'd embroidered those dates with McCallum to make everyone in the office think they had a hot relationship going.

Jessica was unfailingly polite, but she treated Bess like a stranger now. It was painful to have the old, pleasant friendliness apparently gone for good. Jessica never looked into her eyes. She treated her like a piece of furniture, and it really hurt. Bess couldn't even blame her. She'd asked for permission to go out with McCallum, but she'd known even when Jessica gave it that the other woman cared deeply about him. She was ashamed of herself for putting her own infatuation with McCallum over Jessica's feelings. Not that it had done her any good. McCallum was fine company, and once he'd kissed her with absent affection, but he couldn't have made it more obvious that he enjoyed being with her only in a casual way. On the other hand, when he looked at Jessica there was real pain in his eyes.

"Can't I bring you back something?" Bess asked abruptly. "Jessica, you look so—"

"I'm fine," Jessica said shortly. "I have a virus and I've lost my appetite, that's all. Please go ahead."

Bess grimaced as she closed the door, and the concern was still on her face when she joined McCallum.

He'd seen Jessica, too, in that brief time while her office door was open. He'd wanted to show her that he didn't care, that he could date other women with complete indifference to her feelings. But it was backfiring on him. He felt sick as he realized how humiliated she must be, to have him dating one of her own co-workers. It wasn't her fault that she couldn't bear a child, after all, and she was right—he'd never acted as if he had any kind of permanent relationship in mind for the two of them. He was still trying to find reasons to keep her at arm's length, he admitted finally. He was afraid to trust her, afraid of being hurt if he gave his heart completely. He'd believed Sam Jackson because he'd wanted to. But now, as he thought about it rationally, he wondered at his own gullibility. Was he really so desperate to have Jessica out of his life that he'd believe a total stranger, a biased total stranger, before he'd even ask Jessica for her version of what had happened?

Sam Jackson had been having lunch in the café, too, and stopped by McCallum's table to exchange pleasantries with him and Bess. Sheriff Hensley drove by in the patrol car and saw them in the window. Later that afternoon, he invited McCallum into his office and closed the door.

"I heard Sam Jackson's been in town six days," he said quietly. "What's his business here?"

"He's just passing through," McCallum said.

"And...?"

McCallum was puzzled. It wasn't like his boss to be so interested in strangers who visited town. "And he's just passing the time of day as well, I guess."

Hensley folded his hands together on his desk and toyed with a paper clip. "He's the sort who holds grudges." He looked up. "I've heard some talk I don't like. It was a closed trial, but a lot of gossip got out anyway. Fred's wife and daughter left town as soon as the verdict was read, but Jessica had nowhere to go except here. Fred, of course, gave her a rough time of it."

"Maybe he had reason to," McCallum ventured curtly.

Hensley put the paper clip down deliberately. "You listen to me," he said coldly. "Jessica did nothing except try to help his wife and child. Fred was a cocaine addict. He liked to bring his friends home at night while his wife was working at the hospital. One night he was so high that he beat his daughter and she ran away. It was Jessica who took her in and comforted her. It was Jessica who made her mother face the fact that she was married to an addict and that she had to get help for them. Jessica was told—probably by your buddy Sam—that Fred had forced Clarisse, his daughter, to go back home with him. That's why she went out there that day. He attacked Jessica instead, and she barely got away in time."

McCallum didn't say a word. His complexion paled, just a little.

"For her pains, because the court trial was in the judge's chambers, and not publicized for Clarisse's sake, Jessica took the brunt of the gossip. All anyone heard was that Jessica had almost gotten raped. It was the talk of the town. Everywhere she went, thanks to Sam Jackson, she was pointed out and ridiculed as the girl who'd led poor Fred on and then yelled rape. She took it, for Clarisse's sake, until her mother could get another job and they could leave town while Fred was safely in jail."

"He didn't tell me that," McCallum said dully.

"Sam Jackson hated Jessica. He was on the city council. He had influence and he used it. But time passed and Sam left town. It didn't end there, however. Fred got out of jail in six months and came after Jessica. He was killed in a wreck, all right," the sheriff stated. "He was out for vengeance the day he was paroled and was chasing Jessica in his car, high as a March kite, until he ran off a cliff in the process. He would have killed her if he hadn't."

McCallum felt cold chills down his spine. He could picture the scene all too easily.

"Jessica survived," Hensley continued curtly, and McCallum barely registered the odd phrasing. "She held her head

up, and those of us who knew the truth couldn't have admired her more. She's suffered enough. I didn't realize Sam Jackson was even in town until I happened to see him this morning, but he won't be here any longer. I'm going to give him a personal escort to the county line right now.'' He stood up, grabbing his hat. ''And for what it's worth, I think you're petty to start dating Bess right under Jessica's nose, on top of everything else. She doesn't deserve that.''

McCallum got to his feet, too. ''I'd like a word with Jackson before you boot him out of town.''

Hensley recognized the deputy's expression too well to agree to what McCallum was really suggesting.

''You believed him without questioning what he said,'' Hensley reminded him. ''If there's fault, it's as much yours as his. You aren't to go near him.''

McCallum's thin lips pressed together angrily. ''He had no business coming here to spread more lies about her.''

''You had no business listening to them,'' came the merciless reply. ''Learn from the experience. There are always two sides to every story. You've got enough work to do. Why don't you go out there and act like a deputy sheriff?''

McCallum reached for his own hat. ''I don't feel much like one right now,'' he said. ''I've been a fool.''

''Hard times teach hard lessons, but they stay with us. Jessica isn't judgmental, even if you are.''

McCallum didn't say another word, but he had his reservations. He'd hurt her too much. He knew before he even asked that she might forgive him, but that she'd never forget the things he'd said to her.

Nine

Sam Jackson left town with the sheriff's car following him every inch of the way to the county line. He'd had to do some fast talking just to keep an irritated Hensley from arresting him for vagrancy. But his bitter hatred of Jessica hadn't abated, and he hoped he'd done her some damage. His poor brother, he told himself, had deserved some sort of revenge. Perhaps now he could rest in peace.

McCallum didn't go near Jessica's office, for fear that Bess might make another play for him and complicate things all over again. He did go to Jessica's house the next afternoon, hat in hand, to apologize.

She met him at the door in a pair of worn jeans and a T-shirt, her hair in a ponytail and her glasses perched on her nose. It was a beautiful day, and the Montana air sparkled. The world was in bloom, and the Whitehorn area had never been more beautiful under the wide blue sky.

"Yes?" Jessica asked politely, as if he were a stranger.

He felt uncomfortable. He wasn't used to making apologies. "I suppose you know why I'm here," he said stiffly.

She stripped off her gardening gloves. "It's about Keith, I guess," she replied matter-of-factly, without any attempt at dissembling.

He frowned. "No. We persuaded the authorities to keep Keith for a few days at the juvenile hall while we did some investigating. I haven't come about that."

"Oh." Her eyes held no expression at all. "Then what do you want?"

He propped one foot on the lowest step and stared at the spotless shine of his black boot. "I came to apologize."

"I can't imagine why."

He looked up in time to catch the bitterness that touched her face just for an instant. "What?"

"I'm a liar and a temptress and a murderess, according to Sam Jackson," she said heavily. "From what everyone says, you were hanging on to every word he said. So why should you want to apologize to me?"

He drew in a breath and shifted his hat from one hand to the other. "Hensley told me all of it."

"And that's why you're here." She sounded weary, resigned. "I might have known it wasn't because you came to your senses," she said without inflection in her voice. "You preferred Sam Jackson's version of the truth, even after I reminded you that he was biased."

"You told me a half-truth from the beginning!"

"Don't you raise your voice to me!" she said angrily, punching her glasses up onto her nose when they started to slip down. "I didn't want to remember it, can't you understand? I hate having to remember. Clarisse was the real victim, a lot more than I was. I just happened to be stupid enough to go out there alone, trying to protect her. And believe me, it wasn't to tempt Fred! The only thing I was thinking about was how to spare Clarisse any more anguish!"

"I know that now." He groaned silently. "Why didn't you tell me?"

"Why should you have expected me to?" she replied, puzzled. "I don't know very much about you, except that your mother drank and was cruel to you and that you had a very nasty time of it in foster care."

He hesitated, searching her eyes.

"You've told me very little about yourself," she said. "I only know bits and pieces, mostly what I've heard from other people. But you expected me to tell you things I haven't told anyone my whole life. Why should you expect something from me that you're not willing to give in return?"

That gave him food for thought. He ran a hand through his hair. "I don't suppose I should have."

"And it's all past history now," she added. "You're dating

Bess. I don't trespass on other women's territory. Not ever. Bess even asked if I had anything going with you before she invited you to supper. I told her no," she added firmly.

There was a sudden faint flush high on his cheekbones, because he remembered telling Bess the same thing. But it wasn't true, then or now. "Listen—" he began.

"No, you listen. I appreciate the meals we had together and the help you gave me on cases. I hope we can work together amicably in the future. But as you have reason to know, I have nothing to offer a man on any permanent basis."

He moved closer, his eyes narrowed with concern. "Being barren isn't the end of the world," he said quietly.

She moved back and folded her arms over her chest, stopping him where he stood. "You thought so. You even said so," she reminded him.

His teeth ground together. "I was half out of my mind! It upset me that you could keep something so important to yourself. That was why I got uptight. It isn't that I couldn't learn to live with it...."

"But you don't have to. Nobody has to live with it except me," she said quietly. "I'm sure that Bess has no such drawbacks, and she has the advantage of being completely without inhibitions. She's sweet and young, and she adores you," she said through tight lips. "You're a very lucky man."

"Lucky," he echoed with growing bitterness.

"Now, if you'll excuse me," she said with a bright smile, pulling her gloves back on, "I have to finish weeding my garden. Thanks for stopping by."

"Just like that?" he burst out angrily. "I hadn't finished."

She brushed dirt off the palm of one glove. "What is there left to say?" she asked with calm curiosity.

He studied her impassive face. She had her emotions under impeccable control, but beneath the surface, he perceived pain and a deep wounding that wasn't likely to be assuaged by any apology, however well meant. He was going to have to win back her trust and respect. That wasn't going to happen overnight. And he didn't expect her to make it easy for him.

He rammed his hat back onto his head. "Nothing, I guess," he agreed, nodding. "I said it all, one way or another, when I jumped down your throat without knowing the truth."

"Sam can be very convincing," she replied. She averted her face. "He turned the whole town against me for a while. You can't imagine how vicious the gossip was," she added involuntarily. "I still hate being talked about."

Jessica didn't add that he'd helped gossip along by dating Bess, so that his rejection of her was made public. But he knew that already. It must have added insult to injury to have his new romantic interest and Sam's renewed accusations being discussed at every lunch counter in town. He understood now, as he hadn't before, why she'd worried so much about being seen in public with him.

"How about Jennifer?" she added suddenly, interrupting his gloomy thoughts. "Any news on her parents?"

"No luck yet," he replied. "But I think I may be on to something with Keith."

"I hope so," she said. "I feel terrible that I didn't suspect something before this."

"None of us is perfect, Jessica," he said, his voice deep and slow and full of regret. His dark eyes searched hers in silence, until she averted her own to ward off the flash of electricity that persisted between the two of them. "I'll let you know what I find out."

She nodded, but didn't reply. She just walked away from him.

He talked to a school official about Keith, and discovered that the boy had been an excellent student until about the time his father lost his job.

"He was never a problem," the counselor told him. "But he let slip something once about his father liking liquor a little too much when he was upset. Things seemed to go badly for Terrance after his wife left, you know. Losing his job must be the last straw."

"I'm sure it's unpleasant for him to have to depend on public

assistance," McCallum agreed. "But taking it out on his child isn't the answer."

"People drink and lose control," the counselor said. "More and more of them, in these pressured economic times. They're usually sorry, too late. I'll try to talk to Keith again, if you like. But I can't promise anything. He's very loyal to his father."

"Most kids are," McCallum said curtly. He was remembering how he'd protected his brutal mother, right up until the night she'd broken his arm with the bottle. He'd made excuse after excuse for her behavior, just as Keith was probably doing now.

He contacted the juvenile officer and had a long conversation with him, but the man couldn't tell him any more than he already knew. Keith hadn't reached the end of his rope yet, and until he did, there was little anyone could do for him.

McCallum did get a break, a small one, in the abandoned-baby case. It seemed that a local midwife did remember hearing an old woman from out of town talk about delivering a child in a clandestine manner for a frightened young woman. It wasn't much to go on, but anything would help.

McCallum decided that it might be a good idea to share that tidbit with Jessica. He dreaded having to see Bess again, after the way he'd led her on.

But it turned out not to be the ordeal he'd expected. Bess was just coming back from the small kitchen with a cup of coffee when he walked into the office. She moved closer and grinned at him.

"Hi, stranger!" she said with a friendly smile. "How about some coffee?"

"Not just now, thanks." He smiled ruefully. "Bess, there's something I need to tell you."

"No, there isn't," she said with a sigh. "I'd already figured it all out, you know. I never meant to step on Jessica's toes, but I had a major crush on you that I had to get out of my system." She gave him a sheepish glance. "I didn't realize how painful it was going to be, trying to work here after I'd all but stabbed Jessica in the back. No one in the office will speak to

me, and Jessica's very polite, but she isn't friendly like she used to be. Nothing is the same anymore."

"I'm sorry about that," he said, knowing it was as much his fault as hers.

She shrugged and moved a little closer. "Still friends?" she asked hesitantly.

"Of course," he replied gently. He bent and kissed her lightly on the cheek.

Jessica, who'd come into the outer office to ask Bess to make a phone call for her, got an eyeful of what looked like a tender scene and froze in place.

"Jessica," McCallum said roughly as he lifted his head and saw her.

Bess turned in time to watch her boss disappear back into her own office, her back straight and dignified.

"Well, that was probably the last straw," Bess groaned. "I was going to talk to her today and apologize."

"So was I," he replied. "She didn't deserve to be hurt any more, after what Sam Jackson did to her."

"I hope it's not too late to undo the damage," Bess added. Then she realized how false a picture she'd given everyone about her dates with McCallum, and she felt even worse. She'd embroidered them to make herself look like a femme fatale, because McCallum hadn't been at all loverlike. But her wild stories had backfired in the worst way. In admitting that she'd lied, she'd make herself look like a conceited idiot. Jessica was cool enough to her already. She hated the thought of compounding the problem with confessions of guilt.

"There's nothing to undo," McCallum replied innocently. "I did enjoy your cooking," he added gently.

"I'm glad." She hesitated nervously. She might as well tell him how she'd blown up their friendship, while there was still time. "McCallum, there's just one little thing—"

"Later," he said, patting her absently on the shoulder. "I've got to talk to Jessica about a case."

"Okay." She was glad of the reprieve. Not that she didn't still have to confess her half-truths to Jessica.

He knocked briefly on Jessica's door and walked in. She looked up from her paperwork. Nothing of her inner torment showed on her unlined face, and she even smiled pleasantly at him.

"Come in, Deputy," she invited. "What can I do for you?"

He closed the door and sat down across from her. "You can tell me that I haven't ruined everything between us," he said bluntly.

She looked at him with studied curiosity. "We're still friends," she assured him. "I don't hold grudges."

His jaw clenched. "You know that wasn't what I meant."

She put down the file she'd been reading and crossed her hands on it. "What can I do for you?" she asked pleasantly.

Her bland expression told him that he couldn't force his way back into her life. He couldn't make her want him, as she might have before things went wrong between them. She was going to draw back into her shell for protection, and it would take dynamite to get her out of it this time. He doubted if he could even get her to go out for a meal with him ever again, because she wouldn't want gossip about them to start up a second time. He'd never felt so helpless. Trust, once sacrificed, was hard to regain.

"What about Keith?" she asked. "I presume that's why you came?"

"Yes," he confirmed untruthfully. He sat back in the chair and told her about the talk he'd had with the school counselor. "But there's nothing we can do until I have some concrete reason to bring his father in for questioning. And Keith is holding out. The juvenile authorities can't dig anything out of him." He crossed his long legs. "On the other hand, we may have a break in the Baby Jennifer case."

She started. It wasn't pleasant to hear him say that. She'd become so involved with the tiny infant that a part of her hoped the mother would never be found. She was shocked at her own wild thoughts.

"Have you?" she asked numbly.

"A midwife knows of an old woman who helped a fright-

ened young woman give birth. I'm trying to track her down. It may be our first real lead to the mother.''

"And if you find her, then what?'' she asked intently. "She deserted her own little baby. What sort of mother would do that? Surely to God the courts won't want to give the child back to her!''

He'd never seen Jessica so visibly upset. He knew she'd allowed herself to become attached to the infant, but he hadn't realized to what extent until now.

"I'm sure it won't come to that,'' he said slowly. "Jessica, you aren't having any ideas about taking the baby yourself?'' he added abruptly.

She glared at him. "What if I do? What can a court-appointed guardian do that I can't? I can manage free time to devote to a child, I make a good salary—''

"You can't offer her a settled, secure home with two parents,'' he said curtly. "This isn't the big city. Here in White-horn the judge will give prior consideration to a married couple, not a single parent.''

"That's unfair!''

"I'm not arguing with that,'' he said. "I'm just telling you what to expect. You know the judges around here as well as I do—probably better, because you have more dealings with them. Most of them have pretty fixed ideas about family life.''

"The world is changing.''

"Not here, it isn't,'' he reminded her. "Here we're in a time capsule and nothing very much changes.''

She started to argue again and stopped on a held breath. He was right. She might not like it, but she had to accept it. A single woman wasn't going to get custody of an abandoned baby in Whitehorn, Montana, no matter how great a character she had.

She faced the loss of little Jennifer with quiet desperation. Fate was unfair, she was thinking. Her whole life seemed to be one tragedy after another. She put her head in her hands and sighed wearily.

"She'll be better off in a settled home," he mumbled. He hated seeing her suffer. "You know she will."

She sat up again after a minute, resignation in her demeanor. "Well, I won't stop seeing her until they place her," she said doggedly.

"No one's asked you to."

She glared at him. "She wouldn't get to you, would she, Deputy?" she asked with bitter anger. "You can walk away from anyone and never look back. No one touches you."

"You did," he said gruffly.

"Oh, I'm sure Bess got a lot further than I did," she said, her jealousy rising to the surface. "After all, she doesn't have any hang-ups and she thinks you're God's gift to women."

"You don't understand."

"I understand everything," she said bluntly. "You wanted to make sure that no one in town connected you with the object of so much scandal. Didn't you tell me once that you hated gossip because people talked about you so much when you were a boy? That's really why you started taking Bess out, isn't it? The fact that she was infatuated with you was just a bonus."

He scowled. "That wasn't why—"

She stood up, looking totally unapproachable. "Everyone knows now that Bess is your girlfriend. You're safe, McCallum," she added proudly. "No one is going to pair you off with me ever again. So let well enough alone, please."

He stood up, too, feeling frustrated and half-mad with restrained anger. "I'd been lied to one time too many," he said harshly. "Trust comes hard to me."

"It does to me, too," she replied in a restrained tone. "You betrayed mine by turning your back on me the first chance you got. You believed Sam instead of me. You wouldn't even come to me for an explanation."

His face tautened to steel. He had no defense. There simply was none.

"You needn't look so torn, McCallum. It doesn't matter anyway. We both know it was a flash in the pan and nothing more.

You can't trust women and I'm not casual enough for affairs. Neither of us would have considered marriage. What was left?''

His dark eyes swept over her with quiet appreciation of her slender, graceful body. ''I might have shown you, if you'd given me half a chance.''

She lifted her chin. ''I told you, I'm not the type for casual affairs.''

''It wouldn't have been casual, or an affair,'' he returned. ''I'm not a loner by choice. I'm by myself because I never found a woman I liked. Wanted, sure. But there has to be more to a relationship than a few nights in bed. I felt...more than desire for you.''

''But not enough,'' she said, almost choking on the words. ''Not nearly enough to make up for what I...am.''

His face contracted. ''For God's sake, you're a woman! Being barren doesn't change anything!''

She turned away. The pain was almost physical. ''Please go,'' she said in a choked tone. She sat back down behind her desk with the air of an exhausted runner. She looked older, totally drained. ''Please, just go.''

He rammed his hands into his pockets and glared at her. ''You won't give an inch. How do you expect to go through life in that sewn-up mental state? I made a mistake, okay? I'm not perfect. I don't walk around with a halo above my head. Why can't you forget?''

Her eyes were vulnerable for just an instant. ''Because it hurt so much to have you turn away from me,'' she confessed huskily. ''I'm not going to let you hurt me again.''

His firm lips parted. ''Jessica, we learn from our mistakes. That's what life is all about.''

''Mistakes are what *my* life is all about,'' she said, laughing harshly. She rubbed her hand over her forehead. ''And there are still things you don't know. I was a fool, McCallum, and it was your fault because you wouldn't take no for an answer. Why did you have to interfere? I was happy alone, I was resigned to it....''

''Why did you keep trying to take care of me?'' he shot back.

She had to admit she'd gone out of her way in that respect. She glanced up and then quickly back down to her desk. "Temporary insanity," she pleaded. "You had no one, and neither did I. I wanted to be your friend."

"Friends forgive each other."

She gnawed her lower lip. She couldn't tell him that it was far more than friendship she'd wanted from him. But she had secrets, still, that she could never share with him. She couldn't tell him the rest, even now. His fling with Bess had spared her the fatal weakness of giving in to him, of yielding to a hopeless affair. If it had gone that far, she corrected. Because it was highly doubtful that it would have.

"What are you keeping back?" he asked. "What other dark skeletons are hiding in your closet?"

She pushed her hair back from her wan face. "None that you need to know about, McCallum," she said, leaning back. She forced a smile. "Why don't you take Bess to lunch?"

"Bess and I are friends," he said. "That's all. And I've caused enough trouble around here. I understand that you're barely speaking to her. That's my fault, not hers."

She glared at him. "Bess is a professional who reports to me, and how I treat her is my business."

"I know that," he replied. "But she's feeling guilty enough. So am I."

Her eyebrows lifted. "About what?"

"Neither of us made your life any easier," he said. "I didn't know what happened to you. But even if you'd been all that Sam Jackson accused you of being, I had no right to subject you to even more gossip. Bess knows why I took her out. I could have caused her as much pain as I caused you. I have to live with that, too. Fortunately, she was no more serious than I was."

"That isn't what she told us," Jessica said through her teeth.

He stared at her with dawning horror. What stories had Bess told to produce such antagonism from Jessica, to make her look so outraged?

He scowled. "Jessica, nothing happened. We had a few meals together and I kissed her, once. That's all."

"It's gentlemanly of you to defend her," she said, stone faced. "But I'm not a child. You don't have to lie to protect her."

"I'm not lying!"

She pulled the file open and spread out the papers in it. "I'd like to know what you find out about that midwife," she said. "And about Keith, if the juvenile authorities get any results."

He stared at her for a long moment. "Tit for tat, Jessica?" he asked quietly. "I wouldn't believe you, so now you won't believe me?"

She met his eyes evenly. "That has nothing to do with it. I think you're being gallant, for Bess's sake," she replied. "It's kind of you, but unnecessary. Nothing you do with Bess or anyone else is my business."

He wouldn't have touched that line with a gloved hand. He stared at her for a long moment, searching for the right words. But he couldn't find any that would fit the situation.

He found plenty, however, when he closed Jessica's door and stood over Bess, who'd been waiting for him to finish.

"What did you tell her?" he asked bluntly.

She grimaced. "I embroidered it a little, to save face," she protested. "I thought we were going to be a hot item and it hurt my feelings that you didn't even want to kiss me. I'm sorry! I didn't know how hard Jessica was going to take it, or I'd never have made up those terrible lies about us."

He grimaced. "How terrible?"

She flushed. She couldn't, she just couldn't, admit that! "I'll tell her the truth," she promised. "I'll tell her all of it, honest I will. Please don't be mad."

"Mad." He shook his head, walking toward the door. "I must be mad," he said to himself, "to have painted myself into this sort of corner. Or maybe I just have a talent for creating my own self-destruction."

He kept walking.

Ten

The last words McCallum spoke to Bess might have been prophetic. He was thinking about Jessica when he shouldn't have been, and he walked into a convenience store outside town not noticing the ominous silence in the place and the frightened look on the young female clerk's face.

It seemed to happen in slow motion. A man in a faded denim jacket turned with a revolver in his hand. As McCallum reached for his own gun, the man fired. There was an impact, as if he'd been hit with a fist on his upper arm. It spun him backwards. A fraction of a second later, he heard the loud pop, like a firecracker going off. In that one long minute while he tried to react, the perpetrator forgot his quarry—Tammie Jane, the terrified young clerk—and ran out the door like a wild man.

"You've been shot! Oh, my goodness, what shall I do?" Tammie Jane burst out. She ran to McCallum, her own danger forgotten in her concern for him.

"It's not so bad," he said, gritting his teeth as he pulled out a handkerchief to stem the surging, rhythmic flow of blood. "Nothing broken, at least, but it looks as if the bullet may have…clipped an artery." He wound the handkerchief tighter and put pressure over the wound despite the pain it caused. "Are you all right?"

"Sure! He came in and asked for some cigarettes, and when I turned to get them, he pulled out that gun. Gosh, I was scared! He'd just told me to empty the cash register when you walked in."

"I walked in on it like a raw recruit," he added ruefully. "My God, I don't know where my mind was. I didn't even get off a shot."

"You're losing a lot of blood. I'd better call for an ambulance—"

"No need. I'll call the dispatcher on my radio." He made his way out to his patrol car, weaving a little. He was losing blood at a rapid rate and his head was spinning. He raised the dispatcher, gave his location and succinctly outlined the situation, adding a terse description of the suspect and asking for an all-points bulletin.

"Stay put. We'll send the ambulance," the dispatcher said, and signed off. The radio blared with sudden activity as she first called an ambulance and then broadcast a BOLO—a "be on the lookout for" bulletin—on the municipal frequency.

The clerk came out of the store with a hand towel and passed it to McCallum. His handkerchief was already soaked.

"I don't know how to make a tourniquet, but I'll try if you'll tell me how," Tammie Jane volunteered worriedly. Blood from his wound was pooling on the pavement, as McCallum was holding his arm outside the car.

He leaned back against the seat, his hand still pressing hard on the wound. "Thanks, but the ambulance will be here any minute. I can hear the siren."

It was fortunate that Whitehorn was a small town. Barely two minutes later, the ambulance sped up and two paramedics got out, assessed the situation and efficiently loaded a dazed McCallum onto a stretcher and into the ambulance.

He was still conscious when they got to the hospital, but weak from loss of blood. They had him stabilized and the blood flow stemmed before they pulled up at the emergency-room entrance.

He grinned sheepishly as they unloaded him and rolled him into the hospital. "Hell of a thing to happen to a law-enforcement officer. I got caught with my eyes closed, I guess."

"Thank your lucky stars he was a bad shot," one of them said with an answering smile. "That's only a flesh wound, but it hit an artery. You'd have bled to death if you'd taken your time about calling us."

"I'm beginning to believe it."

They wheeled him into a cubicle and called for the resident physician who was covering the emergency room.

Jessica had had a long morning, and her calendar was full of return calls to make. McCallum had shaken her pretty badly about Baby Jennifer. She hadn't been facing facts at all while she was spinning cozy daydreams about herself and the baby together in her cozy cottage.

Now she was looking into a cold, lonely future with nothing except old age at the end of it. From the bright, flaming promise of her good times with McCallum, all that was left were ashes.

She took off her glasses and rubbed her tired eyes. She'd just about given up wearing the contact lenses now that she wasn't seeing McCallum anymore. She didn't care how she looked, except in a business sense. She dressed for the job, but there was no reason to dress up for a man now. She couldn't remember ever in her life feeling so low, and there had been plenty of heartaches before this one. It seemed as if nothing would go right for her.

The telephone in the outer office rang noisily, but Jessica paid it very little attention. She was halfheartedly going through her calendar when Bess suddenly opened Jessica's office door and came in, pale and unsettled.

"Sterling McCallum's been shot," she blurted out, and was immediately sorry when she saw the impact the words had on Jessica, who stumbled to her feet, aghast.

"Shot?" she echoed helplessly. "McCallum? Is he all right?"

"That was Sandy. She's a friend of mine who works at the hospital. She just went on duty. She said he was in the recovery room when she got to the hospital. Apparently it happened a couple of hours ago. Goodness, wouldn't you think *someone* would have called us before now? Or that it would have been on the radio? Oh, what am I saying? We don't even listen to the local station."

"Does Sandy know how bad he is?" Jessica asked, shaken.

"She didn't take time to find out. She called me first." She

didn't add that it was because Sandy thought, like most people did, that McCallum and Bess were a couple. "All she knew was that he'd been shot and had just come out of emergency surgery."

"Cancel my afternoon appointments," Jessica said as she gathered up her purse. "I'll finish this paperwork when I get back, but I don't know when that will be."

"Do you want me to drive you?" Bess offered.

Jessica was fumbling in her purse for the keys to her truck. "No. I can drive myself."

Bess got in front of her in time to prevent her from rushing out the door. "I lied about Sterling and me," she said bluntly, flushing. "It wasn't true. He didn't want anything to do with me and I was piqued, so I made up a lot of stuff. Don't blame him. He didn't even know I did it."

Jessica hesitated. She wanted to believe it, oh, so much! But did she dare?

"Honest," Bess said, and her eyes met Jessica's evenly, with no trace of subterfuge. "Nothing happened."

"Thanks," Jessica said, and forced a smile. Then she was out the door, running. If he died... But she wouldn't think about that. She had to remember that to stay calm, and that they hadn't said he was in critical condition. She had to believe that he would be all right.

It seemed to take forever to get to the hospital, and when she did, she couldn't find a parking space. She had to drive around, wasting precious time, until someone left the small parking area reserved for visitors. There had been a flu outbreak and the hospital was unusually crowded.

She ran, breathless, into the emergency room. She paused at the desk to ask the clerk where McCallum was.

"Deputy McCallum is in the recovery room three doors down," the clerk told her. "Wait, you can't go in there...!"

Jessica got past a nurse who tried to stop her and pushed into the room, stopping at the sight of a pale, drawn McCallum lying flat on his back, his chest bare and a thick bandage wrapped around his upper arm. There were tubes leading to

both forearms, blood being pumped through one and some sort of clear liquid through the other.

The medical team looked up, surprised at Jessica's sudden entrance and white face.

"Are you a relative?" one of them—probably the doctor—asked.

"No," McCallum said drowsily.

"Yes," Jessica said, at the same time.

The man blinked.

"He hasn't got anyone else to look after him," Jessica said stubbornly, moving to McCallum's side. She put her hand over one of his on the table.

"I don't need looking after," he muttered, hating having Jessica see him in such a vulnerable position. He was groggy from the aftereffects of the anesthetic they'd given him while they removed the bullet and repaired the damage it had done.

"Well, actually, you do, for twenty-four hours at least," the doctor replied with a grin. "We're going to admit him overnight," he told Jessica. "He's lost a lot of blood and he's weak. We want to pump some antibiotics into him, too, to prevent infection in that wound. He's going to have a sore arm and some fever for a few days."

"And he can't work, right?" she prompted.

McCallum muttered something.

"Right," the doctor agreed.

"I'll stay with him tonight in case he needs anything," Jessica volunteered.

McCallum turned his head and looked up at her with narrow, drowsy dark eyes. "Sackcloth and ashes, is it?" he asked in a rough approximation of his usual forceful tones.

"I'm not doing penance," she countered. "I'm helping out a friend."

For the first time, his eyes focused enough to allow him to see her face clearly. She was shaken, and there was genuine fear in her eyes when she looked at him. Probably someone had mentioned the shooting without telling her that it was rel-

atively minor. She looked as if she'd expected to find him dead or shot to pieces.

"I'm all right," he told her. "I've been shot before, and worse than this. It's nothing."

"Nothing!" she scoffed.

"A little bitty flesh wound," he agreed.

"Torn ligament, severed artery that we had to sew up, extensive loss of blood..." the doctor was saying.

"Compared to the last time I was shot, it's nothing," McCallum insisted drowsily. "God, what did you give me? I can't keep my eyes open."

"No need to," the doctor agreed, patting him gently on his good shoulder. "You rest now, Deputy. You'll sleep for a while and then you'll have the great-grandfather of a painful arm. But we can give you something to counteract that."

"Don't need any more...painkillers." He yawned and his eyes closed. "Go home, Jessica. I don't need you, either."

"Yes, you do," she said stubbornly. She looked around her, realizing how crazy she'd been to push her way in. She flushed. "Sorry about this," she said, backing toward the door. "I didn't know how badly he was hurt. I was afraid it was a lot worse than this."

"It's all right," the doctor said gently. He smiled. "We'll take him to his room and you can sit with him there, if you like. He'll be fine."

She nodded gratefully, clutching her purse like a life jacket. She slipped out of the room and went to sit down heavily in a chair in the waiting room. Her heart was still racing and she felt sick. Just that quickly, McCallum could have been dead. She'd forgotten how uncertain life was, how risky his job was. Now she was face-to-face with her own insecurities and she was handling them badly.

When they wheeled him to a semiprivate room, she went along. The other half of the room was temporarily empty, so she wouldn't have to contend with another patient and a roomful of visitors. That was a relief.

She noticed that there was a telephone, and when McCallum

had been settled properly and the medical team had left, she dialed her office and told Candy his condition and that she wouldn't be back, before asking to be transferred to Bess.

"Can I bring you anything?" Bess offered.

"No, thank you. I'm fine." She didn't want Bess here. She wanted McCallum all to herself, with no intrusions. It was selfish, but she'd had a bad fright. She wanted time to reassure herself that he was all right, that he wasn't going to die.

"Then call us if you need us," Bess said. "I talked to Sandy again and told her the truth, so she won't, well, say anything to you about me and Sterling McCallum. I'm glad he's going to be okay, Jessica."

"So am I," she agreed. She hung up and pulled a chair near the bed. She'd noticed a strange look from one of the nurses earlier. That had probably been Bess's friend.

McCallum was sleeping now, his expression clear of its usual scowl. He looked younger, vulnerable. She grimaced as she looked at his poor arm and thought how painful it must have been. She didn't even know if they'd caught the man who'd shot him. Presumably they were combing the area for him.

A few minutes later, Sheriff Hensley and one of the other deputies stopped by the room to see him. Hensley had gone by McCallum's house to feed Mack and get McCallum a change of clothing. The shirt he'd been wearing earlier was torn and covered in blood. McCallum was still sleeping off the anesthesia.

"Have you caught the man who did it?" Jessica asked.

Hensley shook his head irritably. "Not yet. But we will," he said gruffly. "I wouldn't have had this happen for the world. McCallum's a good man. On the salary the job pays, we don't get a lot of men of his caliber."

Jessica had never questioned a man of McCallum's education and background working in such a notoriously low-paying job. "I wonder why he does a lot of things," she mused, watching the still, quiet face of the unconscious man. "He's very secretive."

"So are you."

She grimaced. "Well, everyone's entitled to a skeleton or two," she reminded him.

He shrugged. "Plenty of us have them. Tell him I fed his dog, and brought those things by for him. I'll be back tomorrow. Are they going to try to keep him overnight?"

"Yes," she said definitely. "I'll stay with him. He won't leave unless he knocks me out."

"Harris here can stay with you if you think you'll need him," Hensley said with a rare smile.

Jessica glanced at the pleasant young deputy. "Thanks, but the doctor has this big hypodermic syringe...."

"Good point." Hensley took another look at McCallum, who was sleeping peacefully. "Tell him we're on the trail of his assailant. We're pretty sure who it is, from the description. We're watching the suspect's grandmother's house. It's the one place he's sure to run when he thinks it's safe."

Jessica nodded. "That's one advantage of small towns, isn't it?" she mused. "At least we generally know who the scoundrels are and where to find them."

"It makes police work a little easier. The police are helping us. McCallum's well liked."

"Yes." She looked up. "Thanks for getting Sam Jackson off my back."

He smiled. "Neighbors help each other. Maybe you'll do me a favor one day."

"You just ask."

"Well, a loaf of that homemade raisin bread wouldn't exactly insult me," he volunteered.

"When I get McCallum out of here, raisin bread will be my first priority," she promised him.

The way she worded it amused him, but it shocked her that she should feel proprietorial about McCallum, who'd given her no rights over him at all. She'd simply walked in and taken charge, and he wasn't going to like it. But she knew what he'd do if she left—go home this very night and back to work in the morning. He didn't believe in mollycoddling himself. No, she couldn't leave. She had to keep him here overnight and

then make sure that he rested as the doctor had told him to. But how was she going to accomplish that?

She was still worrying about the problem when he woke up, after dark, and winced when he tried to stretch. They had a hospital gown on him, and the touch of the soft cotton fabric seemed to irritate him. He tried to pull it off.

Jessica got up and restrained his hand. They still had tubes in him, the steady drips going at a lazy speed.

"No, you mustn't," she said gently, bending over him.

His eyes opened. He stared at her and then looked around and frowned. "I'm still here?"

She nodded. "They want you to stay until tomorrow. You're very weak and they haven't finished the transfusion."

He let out a long, drowsy breath. "I feel terrible. What have they done to me?"

"They stitched you up, I think," she said. "Then they gave you something to make you rest."

He looked up at her again, puzzled. "What are you doing here? It's dark."

"I'm staying tonight, too," she said flatly. Her eyes dared him to argue with her.

"What for?"

"In case you need anything. Especially in case you try to leave," she added. "You're staying right there, McCallum. If you make one move to get up, I'll call the nurse and she'll call the doctor, and they'll fill you so full of painkillers that you'll sleep until Sunday."

He glared at her. "Threats," he said, "will not affect me."

"These aren't threats," she replied calmly. "I asked the doctor, and he said he'd be glad to knock you out anytime I asked him to if you tried to leave."

"Damn!" He lifted both hands and glared at the needles. "How did I get into this mess?"

"You let a man shoot you," she reminded him.

"I didn't let him," he said gruffly. "I walked in without looking while he was trying to rob the store. I didn't even see the gun until the bullet hit me. A police special, no less!" he

added furiously. "It was a .38. No wonder it did so much damage!"

"I'm very glad he can't shoot straight," she said.

"Yes. So am I. He was scared—that's probably why he missed any vital areas. He fired wildly." His eyes closed and his face tightened as he moved. "I hope I get five minutes alone with him when they catch him. Have you heard from Hensley?"

"He and Deputy Harris came by to see you while you were asleep. They think they know who it was. They're staking out one of his relative's houses."

"Good."

"Didn't you know the place was being robbed? Wasn't that why you went in?" she persisted.

"I went in because I wanted a cup of coffee," he said with a rueful smile. "I don't think I'll ever want another one after this. Or if I do, I'll make it at home."

"I could ask the nurse if you can have one now," she offered.

"No, thanks. I'll manage." He hesitated. "Do they have a male nurse on this floor?"

"Yes."

"Could you ask him to step in here, please?"

She didn't have to ask why. She went out to find the nurse and sent him in. She waited until she saw him come out again before she rejoined McCallum.

"Damned tubes and poles and machines," he was muttering. He looked exhausted, lying there among the paraphernalia around the bed. He turned his head and looked at her, seeing the lines in her face, the lack of makeup, the pallor. "Go home."

"I won't," she said firmly. She sat back down in the chair beside his bed. "I'll leave the hospital when you do. Not before."

His eyebrows lifted. "Have I asked you to be responsible for me?" he asked irritably.

"Somebody has to," she told him. "You don't have anybody else."

"Hensley would sit with me if I asked him, or any of the deputies."

"But you wouldn't ask them," she replied. "And the minute I walk out the door, you'll discharge yourself and go home."

"I need to go home. What about Mack?" He groaned. "He'll have to go without his supper."

"Sheriff Hensley has already fed him. He also brought you a change of clothing."

That seemed to relax him. "Nice of him," he commented. "Who'll feed Mack tomorrow morning and let him out?"

"I guess we'll have to ask the sheriff to go again. I'd offer, but that dog doesn't like women. I don't really want to go into your house when you aren't there. He growls at me."

"Your cat growls at me. It didn't stop me from going to your house."

"Meriwether couldn't do too much damage to you. But Mack is a big dog with very sharp teeth."

His eyes searched hers. "Afraid of him?"

"I guess maybe I'm afraid of being chewed up," she said evasively.

"Okay. Hand me the phone."

She did, and helped him push the right buttons. He phoned Hensley and thanked him, then asked him about feeding Mack in the morning. Hensley already knew McCallum kept a spare key in his desk and had used it once already. He readily agreed to take care of Mack.

"That's a load off my mind," McCallum said when he finished and lay back against the pillows. He flexed his shoulder and then frowned. "Do I smell something?"

As he said that, the door opened and a nurse came in bearing two trays. "Dinnertime," she said cheerfully, arranging them on the table. "I brought one for you, too, Miss Larson," she added. "You haven't even had coffee since you've been here."

"That's so nice of you!" Jessica said. "Thank you!"

"It's our pleasure. Make sure he eats," she added to Jessica

on her way out. "He'll need all the protein he can get to help replenish that lost blood."

"I'll do that," Jessica promised.

She lifted the tops off the dishes on one tray while McCallum made terrible faces.

"I hate liver," he told her. "I'm not eating it."

She didn't answer him. She cut the meat into small, bite-sized pieces and proceeded to present them at his lips. He glared at her, but after a minute of stubborn resistance, opened his mouth and let her put the morsels in, one at a time.

"Outrageous, treating a grown man like this," he muttered. But she noticed that he didn't refuse to eat, as he easily could have. In fact, he didn't lodge a single protest even when she followed the liver with vegetables and, finally, vanilla pudding.

It was intimate, doing this for him. She hadn't considered her actions at all, but now she realized that they could be misconstrued by a large number of people, starting with McCallum. She was acting like a lovesick idiot. What must he have thought when she came bursting into the recovery room where he was lying, forcing her way into his life like this?

She fed him the last of the pudding and, with a worried look, moved the tray to the other table.

"Now eat your own dinner before it gets cold," he insisted. "If you're determined to stay here all night, you need something to keep you going."

"I'm not really hungry...."

"Neither was I," he said with a cutting smile. "But *I* didn't have any choice. Now do you pick up that fork, or do I climb out of this bed and pick it up for you?"

His hand went to the sheet. With a resigned sigh, she uncovered her own plate and took it, and her fork, back to her chair. She didn't like liver any more than he did, but she ate it. At least it was filling.

He watched her until she cleared her plate and finished the last drop of her coffee. "Wasn't that good?" he taunted.

"I hate liver," she muttered.

"So do I, but that didn't save me." He grinned at her. "Turnabout is fair play."

She sighed, standing to replace her plate on the tray. She hadn't touched her pudding.

"Aren't you going to eat that?" he asked.

"I like chocolate," she muttered. "I hate vanilla."

"I don't." His eyes twinkled. "Want to feed it to me?"

Her blush was caused more by the silky soft tone of his voice than by the words. She couldn't help it.

"If you like," she said hesitantly.

"Come on, then."

She got the pudding and approached the bed. But when she started to open the lid, he caught her hand and tugged until she bent forward.

"Sterling!" she protested weakly.

"Humor me," he whispered, reaching up to cup her chin in his lean hand and pull her face down. "I'm a sick man. I need pampering."

"But—"

"I want to kiss you," he whispered at her lips. "You can't imagine how much. Just a little closer, Jessie. Just another inch…"

She sighed against his hard mouth as she moved that tiny distance and let her lips cover his. He made a soft sound and, despite the tubes attached to his arm, his hand snaked behind her head to increase the pressure of his mouth. She stiffened, but it was already too late to save herself. The warm insistence of the kiss worked its way through all her doubts, fears and reservations and touched her very soul. She sighed and gave in to the need to reassure herself that he was alive. Her own mouth opened without coyness and she felt the shock that ran through him before he groaned and deepened the kiss.

The sound of a tray rattling outside the room brought her head up. He looked somber and his eyes were narrow and hot.

"Coward," he taunted.

Her lips felt swollen. She pulled gently back from him and stood up, her knees threatening to give way. He had an effect

on her body that no other man ever had. There were so many
reasons why she shouldn't allow this feeling between them to
grow. But other than disappointment, there was no other emotion left in her at the moment. That, and a raging pleasure that
turned quickly to frustration.

Eleven

The nurse came in to remove the dishes, and somehow Jessica managed to look calm and pleasant. But inside, her whole being was churning with sensation. She looked at Sterling and her mouth tingled in memory.

She was wondering how she was going to manage the situation, but then the doctor came in on his rounds and ordered a sedative for the patient. It was administered at once, and McCallum glowered as the nurse finished checking his vital signs and the technicians came back to get some samples they needed for the lab. It was fifteen minutes before they left him alone with Jessica. And by then, the shot was beginning to take effect.

"Hell of a thing, the way they treat people here," he murmured as his eyelids began to droop. "I wanted to talk to you."

"You can talk tomorrow. Now go to sleep. You'll feel better in the morning."

"Think so?" he asked drowsily. "I'm not sure about that."

He shifted and a long sigh passed his lips. Only seconds later, he was dozing. Jessica settled in her chair with a new paperback she'd tucked into her purse after a brief stop at the bookstore on her way to lunch. She must have had some sort of premonition, she mused. And unlike McCallum, she didn't have to worry about her pet. Meriwether had plenty of water and cat food waiting for him, and a litter box when he needed it. He might be lonely, but he wouldn't need looking after. She opened the book.

But the book wasn't half as interesting as McCallum. She finally put it aside and sat looking at him, wishing that her life had been different, that she had something to offer such a man. He was a delight to her eyes, to her mind, her heart, her body.

She couldn't have imagined anyone more perfect. He liked her, that was obvious, and he was attracted to her. But for his own sake, she had to stop things from progressing any further than liking. Her own weakness was going to be her worst enemy, especially while he was briefly vulnerable and needed her. She had to be sure that she didn't let his depleted state go to her head. Above all, she had to keep her longings under control.

Eventually, she tried to sleep. But the night was long and uncomfortable as she tried to curl up in the padded chair. In the morning, McCallum was awake before she was, and she opened her eyes to find him propped up in bed watching her.

"You don't snore," he commented with a gentle smile.

"Neither do you," she returned.

"Fortunate for us both, isn't it?"

She sat up, winced and stretched. Her hair had come down in the night and it fell around her shoulders in a thick cloud. She pushed it back from her face and readjusted her glasses.

"Why don't you wear your contact lenses?" he asked curiously. "And before you fly at me, I don't mean you look better with them or anything. I just wondered why you'd stopped putting them in."

She stood up. "It didn't seem worth the effort anymore," she said. "And they're not as comfortable as these." She touched the big frames with her forefinger. She smiled. "And they're a lot of trouble. Maybe I'm just lazy."

He smiled. "Not you, Jessie."

"How do you feel?"

"Sore." He moved his shoulder with a groan. "It's going to be a few days before I feel like much, I guess."

"Good! That means you won't try to go back to work!"

He glowered at her. "I didn't say that."

"But you meant it, didn't you?" she pressed with a wicked grin.

He laid his head back against the pillow. "I guess so." He studied her possessively. "Are you coming home with me?"

Her heart jumped up into her throat. "What?"

"How do you expect to keep me at home if you don't?" he

asked persuasively. "Left on my own, I'm sure I'd go right back to the office."

There was a hint of cunning in his eyes, and she didn't trust the innocent expression on his face. He had something in mind, and she didn't want to explore any possibilities just now.

"You could promise not to," she offered.

"I could lie, too."

"I have a job," she protested.

"Today is Friday. Tomorrow is Saturday. What do you do that someone else can't do as well for one day?"

"Well, nothing, really," she said. She hesitated. "People might talk...."

"Who gives a damn?" he said flatly. "We've both weathered our share of gossip. To hell with it. Come home with me. I need you."

Those three words made her whole body tingle with delight. She stared at him with darkening eyes, with a faint flush on her cheekbones that betrayed how much the statement affected her.

"I need you," he repeated quietly.

"All right."

"Just like that?"

She smiled. "Just like that. But only for today," she added.

His eyebrows rose. "Why, Jessica, did you think I was inviting you to spend the night with me?"

She glowered back. "You stop that. I'm just going to take care of you."

He beamed. "What a delightful prospect."

Her jaws tightened. "You know what I mean, and it isn't that!"

"I know what I wish you meant," he teased softly.

"You're going to be a handful, aren't you?" she asked with resignation.

"I'll try not to cause you a lot of trouble." He studied her long and intently. "Besides, how difficult can it be?" He indicated his shoulder. "I'm not in any shape for what you're most concerned about. Long, intimate sessions on my sofa will

have to wait until I'm properly fit again, Jessica," he added in a soft, wicked tone. "Sorry if that disappoints you."

She turned away to keep him from seeing the flush on her cheeks. "Well, if you're going to leave today, I'd better see if the doctor agrees that you can. I'll go and check at the nurses' station."

"You tell them that even if he says I can't, I'm going home," he informed her.

She didn't argue. It wouldn't really do any good.

By noon, they'd discharged him, and Jessica, after stopping by her house to change clothes and feed her cat, drove him to his house. It disturbed her a little to have her pickup truck sitting in his driveway, but there wasn't a lot she could do about it. He wasn't able to cook or clean, and there was no one else she could ask to do it—except possibly Bess, and that was out of the question.

She hesitated when he unlocked the door and Mack growled at the sight of her.

"Stop that," McCallum snapped at the dog.

Mack stopped at once, eagerly greeting his master.

McCallum petted him and motioned Jessica into the house before he dropped heavily into his favorite armchair.

"It's good to be home," he remarked.

"How about something to eat?" she asked. "You didn't stay long enough to have lunch."

"I wasn't hungry then. There's a pizza in the freezer and some bacon and eggs in the fridge."

"Any flour?"

He glared at her. "What the hell would I want with flour?"

She threw up her hands. It wasn't a question she should have asked a bachelor who liked frozen pizza.

"So much for hopes of quiche," she said half to herself as she put down her purse and walked toward the kitchen.

"Real men don't eat quiche," he called after her.

"You would if you had any flour," she muttered. "But I guess it's going to be bacon and eggs."

"We could order a pizza from the place downtown."

"I don't want pizza. And you need something healthy."

"I won't eat tofu and bean sprouts."

She was searching through the refrigerator and vegetable bins. There were three potatoes and a frozen pizza, four eggs of doubtful age, a slice of moldy bacon and a loaf of green bread.

"Don't you ever clean things out in here?" she called.

He shrugged, then winced as the movement hurt his shoulder. "When I get time," he told her.

She came back and reached for her purse. "Please don't try to go to work while I'm gone."

"Where, exactly, are you going?"

"To get some provisions," she said. "Some *edible* provisions. You couldn't feed a dedicated buzzard on what's in your kitchen."

He chuckled and reached for his wallet. He handed her a twenty-dollar bill. "All right. If you're determined, go spend that."

"I'll need to stop by my office, too."

"Whatever."

She hesitated in the doorway, indecision on her face.

"If you'd rather I sent Bess over—"

"Bess was a pleasant companion," he replied. "She was never anything more, regardless of what she might have told you."

"Okay." She went out and closed the door behind her.

She stopped by the office just long enough to delegate some chores and answer everyone's concerns about McCallum. Bess was interested, but not overly so, and she smiled reassuringly at Jessica before she told her to wish him well.

After that, Jessica went shopping. When she got back to McCallum's house, he was sprawled on the sofa in his sock feet with a can of beer in his hand, watching a movie.

"What did you buy?" he asked as she carried two plastic sacks into the kitchen.

"Everything you were out of." She handed him back two dollars and some change.

He glanced at the grocery bags. "What are you going to cook me?"

"Country-fried cubed steak, gravy, biscuits and mashed potatoes."

"Feel my pulse. I think I've just died and gone to heaven. Did I hear you right? I haven't had that since it was a special at the café last month."

"I hope it's something you like."

"'Like' doesn't begin to describe how I feel about it. Try 'overwhelmed with delight.' But to answer your question, yes, I like it."

"It's loaded with cholesterol and calories," she added, "but I can cut down on the grease."

"Not on my account." He chuckled. "I love unwholesome food."

She prepared the meal in between glimpses of the movie he was watching. It was a thriller, an old police drama set back in the thirties, and she enjoyed it as much as he did. Later, they ate in front of the television and watched a nature special about the rain forest.

"That's a good omen," he said when they'd finished and she was collecting the plates.

"What is?"

"We like the same television programs. Not to mention the same food."

"Most people like nature specials."

"One woman I dated only watched wrestling," he commented.

She stacked the plates and picked them up. "I don't want to hear about your other dates."

"Why not?" he asked calculatingly. "I thought you only wanted to be friends with me."

She stopped, searching for words. But she couldn't quite find the right ones, so she beat it back to the kitchen and busied herself washing dishes. Mack sat near her on the floor, watching

her without hostility. It was the first time since she'd been in the house that he didn't growl at her.

She put away the dishcloth and cleaned up the kitchen. There was enough food left for McCallum to have for supper. She put it on a platter and covered it, so that he could heat it up later.

He'd turned off the television when she came back into the living room. He was lying full length on the sofa with his eyes closed, but he opened them when he heard her step. His dark eyes slid up and down her body, over the simple blue dress that clung to her slender body. The expression in them made her pulse race.

"I should...go home." Her voice faltered.

He didn't say a word. His hand went to his shirt and slowly, sensually, unfastened it. He moved it aside, giving her a provocative view of his broad, hair-roughened chest.

"I have things to do," she continued. She couldn't quite drag her eyes away from those hard, bronzed muscles.

He held out his good arm, watching her in a silence that promised pleasures beyond description.

She knew the risks. She'd known them from the first time she saw him. Up until now, they'd weighed against her. But the realization of how close he'd come to death shifted the scales.

She went to him, letting him draw her down against him, so that she was stretched out beside him on the long sofa, pressed close against his hard, warm body.

"Relax," he said gently, easing her onto her back and grimacing as he moved to loom over her. "I'm not stupid enough to start something I can't finish."

"Are you sure?" she asked a little worriedly, because the minute her hips tilted into his, she felt the instant response of his body.

"Not really." He groaned and laughed softly in the same breath, shifting her away slightly. "But let's pretend that I am. I like you in this dress, Jessie. It fits in all the right places. But

I don't like the way it fastens. Too damned many buttons and hooks in back.... Ah, that's better.''

"McCallum!" she cried as the bodice began to slip. She made a grab for it, but his fingers intercepted the wild movement.

"What are you afraid of?" he murmured softly, smiling down at her. "It won't hurt."

She bit her lower lip. "I...can't let you look at me," she said, lowering her eyes to the hard throbbing of his pulse in his neck.

He frowned. "Now, or ever?" he asked with a patience he didn't feel.

"E-ever," she clarified. She pulled the bodice closer. "Let me up, please, I want to...McCallum!"

Even with a bullet wound, he was stronger and quicker than she was. The dress was suddenly around her waist, and he was looking at her body in the wispy nylon bra with its strategically placed lace. But it wasn't her breasts that had his attention.

She closed her eyes and shivered with pain. "I tried to stop you," she said harshly, biting back tears. "Now, will you let me go!"

"My God." The way he spoke was reverent. But there was no revulsion, either in the words or in his face. There was only pain, for what she must have suffered.

"Oh, please," she whispered, humiliated.

"There's no need to look like that," he said quietly. "Lie still. I'm going to take you out of this dress."

"No...!"

He caught her flailing hand and brought it to his mouth, kissing the palm gently. His dark eyes met her wild ones. "You need to be made love to," he said softly. "More than you realize. You're not hideous, Jessica. The scars aren't that bad."

She fought tears and lost. They fell, hot and profuse, pouring down her cheeks. Her hand relaxed its hold on her dress and she lay still, letting him smooth away it and her half-slip and pantyhose until she lay there in only her briefs and bra.

He bent and she felt with wonder the touch of his mouth as

it traced the thin white lines from her breasts down her belly to where they intersected just below her naval.

His big, lean hand held her hip while he caressed her with his mouth, his thumb edging under the lace of the briefs to touch her almost, but not quite, intimately. She caught her breath at the sensations he was teaching her and arched involuntarily toward the pleasure.

"You crazy woman," he breathed as he lifted his head and looked down into her dazed, hungry eyes. "Why didn't you tell me?"

"I thought... They're so ugly."

He only smiled. He bent and his mouth brushed lazily over hers, parting her lips, teasing, tasting. And while he held her in thrall, his hand went behind her to find the single catch. He freed it and lazily tugged the bra away from her firm, high breasts.

She didn't protest. His eyes on her gave her the purest delight she'd ever known. She gazed up at him with rapt wonder while he looked and looked until her nipples grew hard and began to ache.

Then, finally, he began to touch them, and she shivered with sensations she'd never known. Her lips parted as she tried to catch her breath.

He chuckled with appreciation and triumph. "All that time wasted," he murmured. "They're very sensitive, aren't they?" he added when she jerked at the faint brush of his fingertips. He took the hardness between his thumb and forefinger and pressed it gently, and she cried out. But it wasn't because he was hurting her. She was responsive to a shocking degree. That embarrassed her, because he was watching her like a hawk, and she tried to push his hand away.

"Shh," he whispered gently. "Don't fight it. This is for you. But when you're a little more confident, I'm going to let you do the same thing to me and watch how it excites me. I'm just as susceptible as you are, just as hungry."

"You're...watching me," she got out.

"Oh, yes," he agreed quietly. "Can you imagine how it

makes me feel, to see the pleasure my touch gives you?'' His fingers contracted and she shivered. ''My God, I couldn't get my head through a doorway right now, do you know that? You make me feel like ten times the man I am.''

He bent and put his mouth where his fingers had been. She whimpered at first and pushed against him frantically.

He lifted his head and looked into her eyes, seeing the fear.

''Tell me,'' he said softly.

''He...bit me there,'' she managed hoarsely.

He scowled. His eyes went to her body and found the tiny scars. His expression hardened to steel as he touched them lightly.

''I won't bite you,'' he said deeply. ''I promise you, it won't hurt. Can you trust me enough to let me put my mouth on you here?''

She searched his face. He wasn't a cruel man. She knew already that he was protective toward her. She let herself relax into the soft cushions of the sofa and her hands dropped to his shoulders, lingering there, tremulous.

''Good,'' he whispered. He bent again, slowly. This time it was his tongue she felt, soothing and warm, and then the whispery press of his lips moving on soft skin. The sensations were a little frightening, because they seemed to come out of nowhere and cause reactions not only in her breasts, but much lower.

His hand slid down her body and slowly trespassed under the elastic.

She should protest this, she should tell him to...stop!

He felt her nails bite into him, heard her moans grow, felt her body tauten almost to pain.

He lifted his head and stopped. Her face was gloriously flushed, her eyes shy and hungry and frustrated. She looked at him with wonder.

''Your body is capable of more pleasure than you know,'' he said gently. ''I won't hurt you.''

She arched back faintly, involuntarily asking for more, but

he moved away. He wasn't touching her now. He was propped just over her, watching her face, her body.

"Why did you stop?" she whispered helplessly.

"Because it's like shooting fish in a barrel," he said simply. "You've just discovered passion for the first time in your life. I want to be sure that it's me, and not just new sensations, that are motivating you. The next step isn't so easy to pull back from, Jessie," he added solemnly. "And I don't know if I can make love completely with my shoulder in this fix."

She blinked, as if she hadn't actually realized how involved they were becoming.

His eyes dropped to her taut breasts and down her long, elegant legs before they moved back up to meet her shy gaze. He didn't smile even then. "I didn't really understand before," he said. "You were involved in the crash that killed Fred, weren't you? You were damaged internally in the wreck."

She nodded. "Fred was released because of a technicality six months after he went to prison. He blamed me for all his trouble, so he got drunk and laid in wait for me one night when I was working late. He chased me and ran me off the road. I was hurt. But he was killed." She shivered, remembering that nightmare ride. "They had to remove an ovary and one of my Fallopian tubes. Even before the accident the doctors thought I'd be unlikely to get pregnant, and now... Well, it would be a long shot."

His face didn't change, his expression didn't waver. He didn't say a word.

She grimaced. "You need children, Sterling," she said in a raw whisper, her eyes mirroring the pain in the words. "A wife who loves you, and a home." Her gaze fell to his broad, bare chest and her hands itched to touch him.

"And you think that puts you out of the running?" he asked.

"Doesn't it?"

His fingers pressed down gently over her belly, and his hand was so big that it almost covered her stomach completely. "You're empty here," he said, holding her gaze. "But I'm empty here."

His hand moved to his chest, where his heart was, before it dropped back down beside her to support him. "I've never been loved," he said flatly. "I've been wanted, for various reasons. But my life has been conspicuously lacking in anyone who wanted to look after me."

"Bess did," Jessica recalled painfully.

He touched her mouth with his fingertips. "Bess is young and unsettled and looking for something that she hasn't found yet. I'm fond of her. But I never felt desire for her. It's hard to explain," he added with a humorless laugh, "but for me, desire and friendship don't usually go together."

She searched his face. "They didn't, with Bess?"

"That's right. Not with *Bess*."

He emphasized the name, looking at her with more than idle curiosity.

"With...anyone else?"

He nodded.

Obviously, she was going to have to drag it out of him, but she had to know. "With...me?" she asked, throwing caution to the winds.

"Yes," he said quietly. "With you."

She didn't know how to answer him. Her body felt hot all over at the look he was giving her. She'd never known passion until now, and it was overwhelming her. She wanted him, desired him, ached for him. She wanted to solve all the mysteries with him. The inhibitions she'd always felt before were conspicuously absent.

She felt her breasts tightening as she stared at the hair-matted expanse of his muscular chest.

"Are you surprised that you can feel desire, after all you've been through?" he asked gently.

"Yes."

"But then, strong emotions can overcome fear, can't they?" He bent, nuzzling his face against her bare breasts, savoring the softness of her skin against his. "Jessie, if my arm didn't throb like blazing hell, I'd have you right here," he breathed. "I ache all over from wanting you."

"So do I," she confessed. She slid her arms around his neck and pressed her body completely against his, shivering a little when she felt the extent of his arousal.

He felt her stiffen and his hands were gentle at her back. "Lie still," he whispered. "It's all right. You're in no danger at all."

"I never dreamed that I could feel like this," she whispered into his throat, where her face was pressed. "That I could want like this." Her breasts moved against the thick hair that covered his chest and she moaned at the sensations she felt.

His lean hand slipped to the base of her spine and one long leg moved, so that he could draw her intimately close, letting her feel him in an embrace they'd never shared.

Her intake of breath was audible and she moaned harshly. So did he, pushing against her roughly for one long, exquisite minute until he came to his senses and rolled away from her. He got unsteadily to his feet with a rough groan.

"Good God, I'm losing it!" he growled. He made it to the window and stared out, gripping the sash. He fought to breathe, straining against the throbbing pain of his need for her.

She lay still for a minute, catching her own breath, before she sat up and quickly got back into her clothes. Her long hair fell all around her shoulders in tangles, but she couldn't find the pins he'd removed that had held it in place.

He turned finally and stared at her with his hands deep in his pockets. He was pale and his shoulder hurt.

"They're in my pocket," he told her, smiling gently at her flush. "Embarrassed, now that we've come to our senses?"

She lifted her eyes to his. "No," she said. "I don't really think I can be embarrassed with you. I—" she smiled gently "—I loved what you did to me."

Twelve

For a minute, he didn't seem to breathe at all. Then his eyes began to soften and a faint smile tugged at the corners of his mouth.

"In that case," he said, "we might do it again from time to time."

She smiled, too. "Yes."

He couldn't remember when he'd felt so warm and safe and happy. Just looking at Jessica produced those feelings. Touching her made him feel whole.

"I should go," she said reluctantly. "Meriwether will need his food and water changed, and I have other chores to do."

He thought about how the house was going to feel when she left, and it wasn't very pleasant. He'd been alone all his life and he was used to it. It had never bothered him before, but suddenly, it did. He frowned as he studied her, wondering at the depth of his feelings, at his need to be near her all the time. Once he would have fought that, but something had rearranged his priorities...perhaps getting shot.

"Okay," he said after a minute. "Let me feed Mack and we'll go."

Her heart flew up. "*We'll* go.... You're coming home with me?"

He nodded.

Her lips parted as she looked at him and realized that he didn't want to be separated from her any more than she wanted to be apart from him.

"Did you think it was one-sided?" he asked, moving toward her. "Didn't it occur to you that in order for something to be this explosive, it has to be shared?"

Her expression mirrored her sense of wonder. So did his. He

pulled her against him, wincing a little when the movement tugged at his stitches, and bent his head. He kissed her with slow, aching hunger, feeling her instant response with delight.

"If I go home with you, people will really talk about us," he whispered against her mouth. "Aren't you worried?"

"No," she said with a smile. "Kiss me...."

He did, thoroughly, and she returned it with the same hunger. After a minute, he had to step back from her. His chest rose and fell heavily as he searched her eyes.

"Do you have a double bed?" he asked.

"Yes." She flushed and then laughed at her own embarrassment. That part of their relationship was something she'd have to adjust to, but she wasn't too worried about being able to accomplish it.

He touched her mouth with aching tenderness. "I was teasing," he chided. "I can't stay, as much as I want to. But I'll stay until bedtime."

"You could sleep on the sofa," she offered.

"I know that. I'll have one of the guys pick me up and drive me home. I don't want you alone on the roads late at night." He gently touched her cheek, which was flushed at his concern for her. "It's going to be rough. I don't want to be apart from you anymore, even at night. Especially at night," he said with a rough laugh.

"Yes, I know. I feel the same way." With her fingertips, she traced his thick eyebrows and then his closed eyelids, his cheeks, his mouth. "It's...unexpected. What are we going to do now?"

"Get married as soon as we can," he said simply. He smiled reluctantly at her expression. "Don't faint on me, Jessie."

"But you don't want to get married," she protested. "You said you never wanted to."

"Honey, do you think we could live together in Whitehorn without raising eyebrows?" he asked gently. He smiled. "Besides that, when my shoulder heals, I'm going to have you. It's inevitable. We want each other too badly to abstain for much longer. Let's do this thing properly, by the book."

She traced a pattern in the thick tangle of hair on his broad chest. All her dreams hadn't prepared her for the reality of this. She could hardly believe it. "Marriage," she whispered with aching hunger. She lifted her eyes to his lean, hard face. "Someone of my own," she added involuntarily.

"There's that, too. Belonging to another person." He brought her hand to his lips. His teeth nipped the soft palm and she laughed. The glitter in his eyes grew. "You've never had a man, have you? Except for that one bad experience, you're untouched."

"Not anymore," she murmured demurely. "I've been all but ravished today."

He chuckled. "If you think that was ravishment, you've got a lot to learn."

She searched his eyes and sadness overlaid her joy. "It's a lovely dream. But it isn't realistic. It will matter to you one day, not being able to have a child of your own."

He touched her mouth and his face became as serious as hers. "Jessie, if you could have a child with another man, but not with me, would you marry him?"

She looked confused for a minute. "Well, no," she said. "Why?"

"Because I lo...because I care for you," she corrected.

He pulled her close. "You're not getting away with that," he said. "Tell me. Say the words."

She gnawed at her lower lip, hesitating.

"All the way, Jessie," he coaxed. "Say it."

"You won't," she said accusingly.

"I don't need to," he asserted. "If sex was all I wanted from you, I could have seduced you long ago. If it isn't just for the sake of sex, what other reason would I have for wanting to marry you?"

He hadn't said it, but she looked at him and realized with a start that he was telling her he loved her with everything except words. He couldn't bear to be parted from her, he wanted to marry her even though she couldn't give him a child....

"Of course I love you," she whispered softly. "I've loved you from the first time I saw you, but I never dared to hope—"

The last of the sentence was lost under the soft, slow crush of his mouth on her lips. He drew her close and kissed her with tenderness and passion, savoring her mouth until he had to lift his head to breathe. Yes, it was there, in her eyes, in her face; she loved him, all right. He began to smile and couldn't stop.

"You're surprisingly conventional," she mused, staring at him with loving eyes.

"Depressingly so, in some ways. I want the trimmings. I've never had much tradition in my life, but it starts now. We get engaged, then we get married, in church, and you wear a white gown and a veil for me to lift up when I kiss you."

She sighed. "It sounds lovely."

"It's probably Victorian." He chuckled. "Abstinence until the event and all. But a little tradition can be beautiful. All that separates people from animals, I read once, is a sense of nobility and honor. These days people want instant satisfaction. They don't believe in self-denial or self-sacrifice, or patience. I do. Those old virtues had worth."

"Indeed they did. I'm just as old-fashioned at heart as you are," she said gently. "I believe in forever, Sterling."

He drew her close and held her, hard. "So do I. We'll have differences, but if we compromise and work at it, we can have a long and happy life together." He kissed her forehead with breathless tenderness, grimacing, because holding her pulled the stitches and made his arm throb. But it was a sweet pain, for all that.

"My job..." she began.

He smoothed her hair away from her face. "I work. You work. We won't have to worry about someone staying home with a child."

Her face contorted.

"Don't," he said gently. He scowled with concern. "Don't. We'll be happy together, I promise you we will. It's all right."

She had to fight down the tears. She pressed against him and closed her eyes. She would never stop regretting her condition.

But perhaps Sterling was right. There would be compensations. First and foremost would be having this man love her as she loved him.

It took several weeks for McCallum's arm to heal completely, but they announced their wedding plans almost immediately. No one was really surprised, especially not Bess.

"When I saw how you looked at him that day, it didn't surprise me when I heard the news," Bess said with a grin. "I'm happy for both of you, honestly. I hope I get that lucky someday."

"Thanks," Jessica said warmly.

The office staff gave her an engagement party, complete with necessary household goods to start out—even though she'd accumulated a lot of her own. It was the thought that counted, and theirs were warm and pleasant.

An invitation to the wedding of Mary Jo and Dugin was forthcoming. It would take place in late June, about a month before Jessica and Sterling's. They decided to go together.

Meanwhile, another problem cropped up quite unexpectedly. Keith Colson had finally done something that landed him in the purview of the county sheriff and not the juvenile authorities. He held up a small car dealership out in the country.

The pistol he used was not loaded, and he didn't even run. They picked him up not far away, walking down a lonely highway with his sack of money. He even smiled at the sheriff's deputy—not McCallum—who arrested him.

He was brought into the sheriff's office for questioning, with new marks on his face.

This time McCallum wasn't willing to listen to evasions. He sat Keith down in the interrogation room and leaned forward intently.

"I've been too involved in my own life lately to see what was going on around me," he told Keith. "I meant to check on you again when the juvenile authorities released you, but I got shot and I've been pretty well slowed down. Now, however, I'm going to get to the root of this problem before you end up

in federal prison.'' He looked the boy straight in the eye. ''Your father is beating you.'' He watched Keith's eyes dilate. ''And probably hitting your grandmother, too. You're going to tell me right now exactly what he's done to you.''

Keith gaped at him. He couldn't find words. He shifted nervously in the chair. ''Listen, it's not that—''

''Loyalty is stupid after a certain point,'' McCallum said shortly. ''I was loyal to my mother, but when she broke my arm, I decided that my own survival was more important than the family's dark secret.''

Keith's expression changed. ''Your mother broke your arm?''

McCallum nodded curtly. ''She was an alcoholic. She couldn't admit that she had a problem and she couldn't stop. It just got worse, until finally I realized that if she really cared about me, she'd have done something to help herself. She wouldn't, so I had to. I had her arrested. It was painful and there was a lot of gossip. Afterwards, I had no place to go, so I got shuffled around the county, to whichever farm needed an extra hand in exchange for bed and board. She died of a heart attack in jail when I was in my early teens. I had a hell of a life. But even then it was better than having to fend her off when she came at me with bottles or knives or whatever weapon she could lay her hand on.''

Keith seemed to grow taller. He let out a long sigh and rubbed the arms of the old wooden chair. ''You know all about it then.''

''Living with an alcoholic, you mean? Yes, I know all about it. So you won't fool me anymore. You might as well come clean. Protecting your father isn't worth getting a criminal record that will follow you all your life. You can't run away from the problem by getting thrown in jail, son. In fact, you'll find people worse than your father there.''

Keith leaned forward and dangled his hands between his knees. ''He says it's because he lost his job and nobody else will hire him, at his age. But I don't believe it anymore. He hits my grandma, you see. Mostly he hits her, and I can't stand

that, so I try to stop him. But he hits me when I interfere. Last time I landed a couple of shots, but he's bigger than I am. Whenever he sobers up, he says he'll quit. He always says he'll quit, that it will get better.'' He shook his head and smiled with a cynicism beyond his years. ''Only it doesn't. And I'm scared he'll really hurt Grandma one day. But if I left, she could, too. She only stays to try and make some sort of home for me, and cook and clean for us. She can't talk to him. Neither can I. He just doesn't hear us.''

''He'll hear me,'' McCallum said, rising.

''What will you do?'' Keith asked miserably.

''I'll pick him up for assault and battery, and you'll sign a warrant,'' he told the boy. ''He may go to jail, but they'll help him and he'll dry out. Meanwhile, we'll place you in a foster home. Your grandmother is too old to look out for you, and she's got a sister in Montana who'd enjoy her company.''

''Miss Larson told you, I guess,'' he mused, smiling sheepishly.

''Yes. Jessica and I are getting married.''

''I heard. She's a nice lady.''

''I think so.''

''You won't hurt my dad?''

''Of course not.''

The boy got to his feet. ''There's this robbery charge....''

''I'll talk to Bill Murray,'' McCallum said. ''When he knows the circumstances, he won't press charges. The money was all recovered and he knows the gun wasn't loaded. He's a kind man, and not vindictive.''

''I'll write him a note and tell him how sorry I am. I didn't want to do it, but I couldn't turn Dad in,'' he added, pleading for understanding.

McCallum clapped him on the back. ''Son, life is full of things we can't do that we have to do. You'll learn that the hard part is living with them afterward. Come on. Let's go see the magistrate.''

A warrant was sworn out and signed, and McCallum went to serve it. He felt sorry for Terrance Colson, but sorrier for

the boy and his grandmother, who were practically being held hostage by the man.

He found Terrance sitting on his front porch, and obviously not expecting company, since he had a bottle of whiskey in one hand.

"What the hell do you want?" he demanded belligerently. "If it's that damned boy again, you can lock him up and throw away the key. I've had it with him!"

"He's had it with you, too, Terrance," McCallum replied, coming up onto the porch. "This is a warrant for your arrest, for assault and battery. Keith signed it."

"A…what?"

He stumbled to his feet, only to have McCallum grab him and whirl him around to face the wall, pinning him there while he cuffed him efficiently.

"You can't do this to me," Terrance yelled, adding a few choice profanities to emphasize his anger.

The door opened timidly and little Mrs. Colson peered out. Her eyes were red and there was bad bruises on one cheek and around her mouth.

"Are you…gonna take him off?" she asked McCallum.

He had to fight for control at the sight of the bruises on that small, withered face. "Yes, ma'am," he said quietly. "He won't be home for a while. The very least that will happen to him is that he'll be sent off to dry out."

She slumped against the door facing. "Oh, thank God," she breathed, her voice choked. Tears streamed down her face. "Oh, thank God. I've always been too weak and afraid to fight back, and Terrance takes after his daddy—"

Terrance glared at her. "You shut your mouth…!"

McCallum jerked him forward. "Let's go," he said tersely. "Mrs. Colson, Jessica will be out this afternoon to talk to you when I tell her what's happened. I have an idea about where we can place Keith, but we'll talk about that later. Are you all right? Do you need me to take you to the doctor?"

"No, thank you, sir," she replied. "If you'll just carry him off, that's all I need. That's all I need, yes, sir."

Terrance yelled wild, drunken threats at her, which made McCallum even angrier. But he was a trained law-enforcement officer, and didn't allow his fury to show. He was polite to Terrance, easing him into the patrol car with a minimum of fuss. He called goodbye to Mrs. Colson and took Terrance off to jail.

Later, Jessica went with Sterling and Keith to talk to Mrs. Colson.

"This is short notice, but I called Maris Wyler before I came out here. She needs a good hand out at her ranch, and when I explained the circumstances, she said she'd be happy to have Keith if he wanted to come."

"Do I ever!" Keith interjected. "Imagine, Gram, a real ranch! I'll learn cowboying!"

"If that's what you want, Son," Mrs. Colson said gently. "Heaven knows, it's about time you had some pleasure in life. I know how you love animals. I reckon you'll fit right in on a ranch. It's very nice of Maris to let you come."

"She's a good woman. She'll take care of Keith, and he'll be somewhere he's really needed," McCallum told the old woman. "He and I have had a long talk about it. The judge has offered to let him plead to a lesser charge in exchange for a probationary sentence in Maris's custody. He'll have a chance to change his whole life and get back on the right track. She's even going to arrange for the homebound teacher to come out and give him his lessons so he won't have to go to school and face the inevitable taunting of the other students."

Mrs. Colson just nodded. "That would be best, Keith," she told her grandson. "I tried to help you as much as I could, but I couldn't fight your father when he was drinking."

"It's all right, Gram," Keith said gently. "You did all you could. I wish you could stay."

"I do, too, but this is your father's house and I could never stay here again."

"Yeah, neither could I," Keith replied. "It wouldn't ever be the same again, even if he does dry out. He talked about mov-

ing, and maybe he will. But I won't go with him. The way he's gotten, I'm not sure he wants to change. I'm not sure he can.''

"The state will give him the opportunity to try," McCallum told them. "But the rest is up to him. If you want to see him, I can arrange it."

Keith actually shivered. "No, thanks," he said with a laugh. "When can I go and see this lady who says she'll take me in?"

"Right now, I guess," McCallum said with a grin. "We'll take Jessica with us, in case we need backup."

Keith frowned. "This sounds serious."

"Maris is a character," he replied. "But she's fair and she has a kind heart. You'll do fine. Just don't get on the wrong side of her."

"What he means," Jessica said, with a pointed glance at McCallum, "is that Maris is a strong and capable woman who can run a ranch all by herself."

McCallum started to open his mouth.

"You can shut up," Jessica interrupted him deftly. "And you'd better not swagger in front of Maris, or she'll cut you off at the ankles. She isn't the forgiving, long-suffering angel of mercy that I am."

"And not half as modest." McCallum grinned.

Jessica made a face at him, but love gleamed out of her soft brown cycs—and his, too. They had a hard time separating work from their private lives, but they managed it. They lived in each others' pockets, except at night. The whole town looked at them with kind indulgence, because they were so obviously in love that it touched people's hearts.

Even old Mrs. Colson smiled at the way they played. It took her back fifty years to her own girlhood and her late husband.

"Well, we'd better be on our way. I'll drive you to the bus station when you're packed and ready to leave," McCallum told her. "And if there's anything we can do, please let us know."

"All I need is to leave here," she replied, touching her swollen cheek gingerly. "Thank you for trying to help me, Son,"

she told Keith. "You were the only reason I stayed at all. I was scared of what he'd do to you if I left."

"I kept trying to find ways to get out," Keith confessed, "so that you could leave. But they kept sending me home again."

"Well, nobody's perfect, not even the criminal-justice system," McCallum said, tongue-in-cheek.

They left Mrs. Colson with an ice bag on her cheek and drove to the No Bull Ranch. Maris Wyler came out to meet them.

She was tall and lean, very tan from working outdoors, her long golden hair pulled back into a ponytail. She wore jeans and boots and a faded long-sleeved shirt, but she looked oddly elegant even in that rig.

"You're Keith. I'm Maris," she said forthrightly, introducing herself to the boy with a smile and a firm handshake. "Ever work with cattle?"

"No, ma'am," Keith shook his head.

"Well, you'll learn quickly. I can sure use a hand out here. I hope you like the work."

"I think I will," he said.

"That's good, 'cause there's plenty of it." Maris replied with a grin.

"He'll be fine here," Maris assured Jessica.

"I knew that already," Jessica replied. "Thanks, Maris. I hope someone does something as kind for you one day."

"No problem. Come on, Keith, grab your gear and let's get you settled. So long, McCallum, Jessica. Feel free to come out and see him whenever you like. Just call first and make sure we're home."

"I will," Jessica replied.

She watched the two walk off toward the neat, new bunkhouse. The ranch, originally called the Circle W, had been in Maris's husband's family for years. Ray hadn't been the sort of man a woman like Maris deserved. He was a heavy drinker like Keith's father, as well as a gambler and womanizer. Nobody had been surprised when he'd recently come to a bad end—running his pickup into a cement bunker on the highway

in a drunken state one night. Maris had been doing all the work on the ranch for years while her lazy husband spent money on foolish schemes and chased the rodeo. It was poetic justice that she ended up with the ranch.

"Hensley's always been a little sweet on her, you know," McCallum confided to Jessica as he drove them back to her place. "It was hard for him to tell her about Ray's death."

"Really? My goodness, she's nothing like his ex-wife."

"Men don't always fall for the same type of woman," he teased. "He called her for me when I approached him about someplace for Keith to go, besides into foster care."

"I'm glad Maris was willing," she said quietly. "Keith's not a bad boy, but he could have ended up in prison so easily, trying to get away from his father."

"It's a hell of a world for kids sometimes," he said.

She straightened the long denim skirt she was wearing with a plaid shirt and boots. "Yes."

He reached over and clasped her hand tightly in his. "I've been thinking."

"Have you? Did it hurt?" she teased.

He chuckled. "Not nice."

"Sorry. I'll behave. What were you thinking?"

His grip eased and he slipped his fingers in between hers. "That Baby Jennifer needs a home and we need a baby."

Thirteen

Jessica had thought about that a lot—that Baby Jennifer needed someone to love her and take care of her. McCallum had been firm about the improbability of a court awarding the baby's care to a single woman. But that situation had changed. She and McCallum were engaged, soon to be married. There was every reason in the world to believe that, under the circumstances, a judge might be willing to let them have custody.

She caught her breath audibly. Bubbles of joy burst inside her. "Oh, Sterling, do you think…!"

His hand grasped hers. "I don't know, but it's worth a try. She's a pretty, sweet baby. And I agree with you—I think our lives would be enriched by having a child to love and raise. There's more to being a mother and father than just biology. It takes love and sacrifice and day-to-day living to manage that." He glanced at her gently. "You aren't the sort of woman who will ever be happy without a baby."

She smiled sadly. "I would have loved to have yours."

"So would I," he replied, his tone as tender as his eyes, which briefly searched hers. "But this is the next best thing. What do you think? Do you want to petition the court for permission to adopt her?"

"Yes!"

He chuckled. "That didn't take much thought."

"Oh, yes, it did. I've thought of nothing else since she was found."

"The judge may say no," he cautioned.

"He may say yes."

He just shook his head. That unshakable optimism touched him, especially in view of all the tragedy Jessica had had in

her life. She was amazing. A miracle. He loved her more every day.

"All right, then," he replied. "We'll get a lawyer and fill out the papers."

"Today," she added.

He smiled. "Today."

The wedding of Mary Jo Plumber and Dugin Kincaid was the social event of the decade in Whitehorn. It had all the elements of a Cinderella wedding, except that Mary Jo was a bit past the girlish stage. Nevertheless, she had a designer dress that any princess would have envied. It had a keyhole neckline and a full skirt with yards and yards of satin and imported Belgian lace. The veil trailed back over the long train in a symphony of grace. It was the sort of dress that every young girl dreams of wearing, and Jessica was no exception. She would have loved to have worn that wedding gown.

But being the practical woman she was, she realized that she and Sterling would have to pinch pennies a bit, so an expensive dress was out of the question. It didn't matter, though, she thought as she looked at her handsome fiancé in his dark suit, white shirt and sedate red tie. If she had to be married in a pillowcase with armholes, that would be all right. She loved him so much that nothing else mattered.

The Kincaid ranch had been chosen for the cermony, rather than any of the small Whitehorn churches. Since it was late June, the weather allowed for an outside wedding, and that was what the Kincaids had planned.

There was a canopy, decorated with orchids that Jeremiah had ordered flown in from Hawaii for the occasion. There were pots of flowers everywhere, and the swimming pool was filled to capacity with floating gardenias. Their scent was delicious.

For the wedding ceremony, chairs had been lined up in front of a lavishly decorated altar flanked by candelabra. No expense had been spared. The reception was being held on the patio of the enormous ranch house, and caterers were already busy setting up tables.

The enormous manicured lawn behind the house was filled to capacity as Mary Jo walked down the aisle toward her husband-to-be. Dugin looked vaguely uncomfortable in his suit, frequently glancing toward his father as if he needed Jeremiah's permission even to get married. It was typical of the way he always bowed to his father's wishes. Dugin had spent most of his life seeking Jeremiah's approval, in one way or another. He'd always been a disappointment to Jeremiah, nevertheless.

The grand piano, brought outside from the living room, was exquisitely played by a local church organist. The wedding march echoed in pure, sweet notes across the lawn, and Mary Jo looked ten years younger in her finery.

She stopped beside Dugin and smiled at him demurely through her veil. Jessica noticed that her hand trembled just before Dugin grasped it, and she was breathing rather quickly. Naturally, she would be nervous, because it was her first marriage. Mary Jo was no spring chicken. Probably she'd never dreamed that she, a children's librarian, would end up married to the son of the richest man in Whitehorn. It was truly a fairy-tale occasion.

The minister presiding at the brief ceremony performed his duties with solemn dignity. Watching the wedding, Jessica thought dreamily of her own forthcoming marriage to Sterling. She lifted her eyes to his when the minister pronounced Dugin and Mary Jo man and wife, and the love in them made McCallum lose track of everything except her radiance.

"I never dreamed of being so happy," she whispered to him, while shouts of glee went up after Dugin had kissed his bride.

"Neither did I," McCallum replied with breathless delight. He touched her face lightly. "You'll be a beautiful bride, Jessie."

"Mary Jo looks gorgeous, doesn't she?" she asked, glancing at the bride. "So pretty—"

A curdling scream cut her off. Everyone else stopped talking, too, and the sudden silence of the bridal party seemed deafening as the scream heightened in pitch and loudness.

"What is it?" someone cried.

McCallum turned instantly, his professional demeanor snapping into place as a woman wearing a caterer's uniform came running toward the crowd.

"It's a man," she cried hysterically. "He's dead, he's dead!"

McCallum moved Jessica gently aside and went to the woman. "Calm down," he said soothingly. "Where is he?"

"Over there," she whimpered. "Behind the oak trees. He's dead...!"

Jeremiah and Dugin Kincaid went with McCallum and a stiff-lipped Sheriff Hensley to a point just beyond the big oaks. A man in a suit was lying faceup on the ground. His eyes were open, staring sightlessly at the blue sky. He had a knife—the kind meat was carved with—sticking out from under his rib cage.

Hensley and McCallum knelt by the body.

Hensley felt around the ears and checked the nails. "Rigor hasn't set in," he stated calmly. "He hasn't been dead long. Skin's not cold." He lifted his head. "Nobody leaves! Lock that front gate and make sure nobody gets out of here," he told McCallum.

"They'll have to get over me first. I'll radio for the coroner and an ambulance."

"Get Bill out here with that fingerprint kit," Hensley added quietly. "If there's a print on that knife, I don't want it smudged. See if someone in the kitchen has some plastic bags."

"On my way," McCallum said. He motioned for another guest who was a deputy to help him, and stopped to explain to Jessica what had happened. "I'll be back as soon as I can," he added.

"Is it anyone we know?" she asked worriedly.

"No," he replied. "I haven't seen him before, and I've been in Whitehorn long enough to recognize a face even if I can't put a name with it. He's a stranger. God knows why he ended up like this." He touched her shoulder. "Try to help us keep people away from there until we get the forensic evidence in

hand. It might be the difference between catching the killer or not.''

''I'll do what I can.''

He nodded and went off to follow the sheriff's orders. The manner in which the man had been killed was disturbing, although he didn't mention that to Jessica. The stabbing was precise enough to indicate that the killer was experienced. It also indicated that the fatal wound had struck in a most efficient manner—underhanded, not overhanded, and with deadly accuracy. McCallum had investigated murders before. He knew that such proficiency denoted skill. He was hoping against hope that this murder didn't indicate a professional killer was on the loose in Whitehorn.

Two hours later, the forensic evidence was bagged, the medical examiner and the coroner had done their parts and the body had been taken away by ambulance for autopsy at the state crime lab. Hensley had concurred with McCallum's deductions, but that brought them no closer to identifying the killer.

The guests were all closely questioned, but everyone's story seemed to check out. Most troubling was that not one of the guests recognized the murdered man. He was a total stranger, which raised some disquieting questions.

Hensley had to let people go in the end. Mary Jo and Dugin were remarkably patient and understanding about the disruption to what should have been the most memorable day of their lives.

''Imagine that, a murder at my wedding!'' Mary Jo said nervously. ''What is the world coming to!''

Dugin had his arm around her. ''Now, now, honey, let's try not to let it spoil our day.''

She looked up at him tearfully. ''But it has, don't you see? Oh, why did he have to come here?'' She took a steadying breath and lowered her eyes. ''After all, nobody even knows who he is!''

''We'll find out,'' the sheriff said solemnly. ''We've got his

prints and we'll send them to FBI headquarters back East. If he's ever been in trouble with the law, we'll know his identity.''

"I'll bet he has," Mary Jo said coldly. "I'll bet he has! Did you see the way he looked? That cheap suit and that little mustache…''

"Honey, you can't tell a man's character by that," Dugin said indulgently. "Anyway, what would a sweet little lady like you know about such things?''

She straightened her billowing white skirt. "But of course I don't. I was just guessing. Would anyone care for a cold drink? I feel absolutely parched," she said, lightly touching her throat.

When the others declined her offer, Mary Jo wandered over to a bar set up on the wide patio. Jessica watched as she put some ice in a glass, then added a generous pour of liquor. No soda or water, Jessica noticed. The poor woman was obviously more upset than she'd let on. Well, she'd hardly be the first person to reach for a strong drink under stress. Who cold blame her? Jessica wondered if she should walk over and say a few words. Then she thought it best to let Mary Jo take a private moment to compose herself.

Mary Jo gave her drink a brief stir, then turned her back to the others and took a deep swallow. The straight bourbon delivered a familiar and satisfying burn. First genuine drink she'd allowed herself all day and it tasted mighty fine. If she had to be kissed, squeezed or oozed over by one more of these White-horn hicks she would scream. Playing the blushing bride had been more of a strain than she'd expected and she could barely wait for the show to be over. Even though that meant being left alone with her *darling* Dugin.

But Hensley and McCallum hadn't gotten tired yet of playing detective, she noticed. Her dead wedding guest had made their day. Mary Jo smiled to herself, struggling to control her expression. Poor old Floyd, he'd made quite a splash at her party, hadn't he? The man was clearly more interesting dead than alive. That was for sure. How had he ever tracked her down, now that was the mystery. Last she'd seen of Floyd, they were standing before a judge in Denver, and wearing matching brace-

lets; that lovely police model that comes with a key. But the charges didn't stick and once they'd been released, she and Floyd had a fairly bitter parting.

She'd lived nine lives at least since her days of running scams with Floyd Oakly. She'd always imagined he was either serving hard time, or dead. Floyd was just a two-bit operator; always was, always would be. Showing up here, for example. Bad move, Floyd. And on her wedding day, of all things. What could he have been thinking of? Didn't he remember how quickly she would pick up whatever he taught her, then show him one better? Thank goodness she'd been able to keep the blood off her dress. now that would have been a problem. She just didn't know how she managed to handle the stress.

Mary Jo sighed and finished off her drink. She placed the empty glass on the bar and took a deep breath. It looked like the last of her guests were about to go. Wearing a pleasant smile, she started across the patio to say her goodbyes, as a gracious hostess should.

As she joined the group, Jessica smiled and lightly touched her arm. "Feeling better?"

Mary Jo smiled and nodded. "Yes, thanks. I am."

"Don't let it spoil your day, Mary Jo," Jessica said kindly. "It was bad luck that it had to happen here, but you and Dugin have the rest of your lives to be happy together. I hope you both will be."

"Thank you, Jessica. You're so nice." Mary Jo hugged her warmly. "I'm glad you could come."

"So am I."

They left the bridal couple and went back to the car. Jessica looked at McCallum with open concern. He was very quiet, hardly communicative at all as they drove back to town.

"What's wrong?" she asked softly.

"That man," he said. "Why would someone murder him at a wedding? And what was he doing at the wedding in the first place, when not one of the guests knew him?"

"Someone probably did and was afraid to say so," she said.

"That's what I suspect." He sighed heavily. "Jessie, I'm

uneasy about the murder. This case has all the earmarks of a professional killer—not a gangland one, but an experienced one, just the same."

"Are you sure?" she asked.

"Oh, yes. I'm sure. The murderer knew exactly how to place that knife. It wasn't an amateur attempt."

"That means that someone at the wedding was a killer," she deduced. "Possibly a professional killer."

He nodded. "That's it."

She sighed heavily. "But this is a small Montana town," she protested. "We're old-fashioned, and people look out for one another...."

"We're part of the modern world, too," he said seriously. "And violence has become part of the American experience." He cradled her hand in his as he drove. "Don't worry. There may be a good motive, once we identify him, and it could even turn out to be self-defense."

"You don't think so."

He glanced at her with soft eyes. "Jessica, you already know me too well. God knows what our lives will be like in twenty years or so."

She smiled brightly. "We'll be just as happy as we are today," she assured him. "And little Jennifer will be in college, or getting married, too."

His fingers contracted around hers. "I hope we have that much time together, and more."

She returned the warm pressure. "So do I."

Their own wedding took place just a few weeks later, in July. They were married in the Whitehorn Methodist Church, with a small group of friends as witnesses. Jessica wore a simple white wedding dress. It had a lace bodice and a veil, even though it was street length, not long and elegant like Mary Jo Plumber's. But when, after their vows, Sterling lifted the brief veil to kiss her, she knew that the dress was completely incidental. The love they shared was the end of the rainbow for her. When his lips touched hers, she laid her hand against his hard, lean cheek

and felt tears sliding down her face. Tears of joy, of utter happiness.

Their reception was simplicity itself—the women at the office had baked cookies and a friend had made them a wedding cake. There was coffee and punch at the local community hall, and plenty of people showed up to wish them well.

Finally, the socializing was over. They drove to Jessica's house, where they would have complete privacy, to spend their wedding night. Later, they planned to live at McCallum's more modern place.

"Your knees are shaking," he teased when they were inside, with the door locked. It had become dark, and the house was quiet—even with Meriwether's vocal welcome—and cozy in its nest of forestland.

"I know," she confessed with a shy smile. "I have a few scars left, I guess, and even now it's all unfamiliar territory. You've been...very patient," she added, recalling his restraint while they were dating. Things had been very circumspect between them, considering the explosive passion they kindled in each other.

"I think we're going to find that this is very addictive," he explained as he drew her gently to him. "And I wanted us to be married before we did a lot of heavy experimenting. We've both suffered enough gossip for one lifetime."

"Indeed we have," she agreed. She reached up to loop her arms around his neck. Her eyes searched his. "And now it's all signed and sealed—all legal." She smiled a little nervously. "I can hardly wait!"

He chuckled softly as he bent his head. "I hope I can manage to live up to all those expectations. What if I can't?"

"Oh, I'll make allowances," she promised as his mouth settled on hers.

The teasing had made her fears recede. She relaxed as he drew her intimately close. When his tongue gently penetrated the line of her lips, she stiffened slightly, but he lifted his head and softly stroked her mouth, studying her in the intense silence.

"It's strange right now, isn't it, because we haven't done much of this sort of kissing. But you'll get used to it," he said in a tender tone. "Try not to think about anything except the way it feels."

He bent again, brushing his lips lazily against hers for a long time, until the pressure wasn't enough. When he heard her breathing change and felt her mouth start to follow his when he lifted it, he knew she was more than ready for something deeper.

It was like the first time they'd been intimate. She clung to him, loving his strength and the exquisite penetration of his tongue in her mouth. It made her think of what lay ahead, and her body reacted with pleasure and eagerness.

He coaxed her hands to his shirt while he worked on the buttons that held her lacy bodice together. Catches were undone. Fabric was shifted. Before she registered the fact mentally, his hair-roughened chest was rubbing gently across her bare breasts and she was encouraging him shamelessly.

He picked her up, still kissing her, and barely made it to the sofa before he fell onto it with her. The passion was already red-hot. She gave him back kiss for kiss, touch for touch, in a silence that magnified the harsh quickness of their breathing.

When he sat up, she moaned, but it didn't take long to get the rest of the irritating obstacles out of the way. When he came back to her, there was nothing to separate them.

Her body was so attuned to his, so hungry for him, that she took him at once, without pain or difficulty, and was shocked enough to cry out.

His body stilled immediately. His ragged breathing was audible as he lifted his head and looked into her eyes, stark need vying with concern.

"It didn't hurt," she assured him in a choked voice.

"Of course...it didn't hurt," he gasped, pushing down again. "You want me so badly that pain wouldn't register now... God!"

She felt the exquisite stab of pleasure just as he cried out,

and her mouth flattened against his shoulder as he began to move feverishly against her taut body.

"I love you," he groaned as the rhythm grew reckless and rough. "Jessie, I love you...!"

Her mouth opened in a soundless scream as she felt the most incredible sensation she'd ever experienced in her life. It was like a throbbing wave of searing heat that suddenly became unbearable, pleasure beyond pleasure. Her body shuddered convulsively and she arched, gasping. He stilled just a minute later, and his hoarse cry whispered endlessly against her ear.

He collapsed then, and she felt the full weight of him with satisfied indulgence. She was damp with sweat. So was he. She stroked his dark hair, and it was damp, too. Wonder wrapped her up like a blanket and she began to laugh softly.

He managed to lift his head, frowning as he met her dancing eyes.

"You passed," she whispered impishly.

He began to laugh, too, at the absurdity of the remark. "Lucky me."

"Oh, no," she murmured, lifting to him slightly but deliberately. "Lucky *me!*"

He groaned. "I can't yet!"

"I have plenty of time," she assured him, and kissed him softly on the chin. "I can wait. Don't let me rush you."

"Remind me to have a long talk with you about men."

She locked her arms around his neck with a deep sigh. "Later," she said. "Right now I just want to lie here and look at my husband. He's a dish."

"So is my wife." He nuzzled her nose with his, smiling tenderly. "Jessie, I hope we have a hundred more years together."

"I love you," she told him reverently. Her eyes closed and she began to drift to sleep. She wondered how anything so delicious could be so exhausting.

The next morning, she awoke to the smell of bacon. She was in her bedroom, in her gown, with the covers pulled up. The

pillow next to hers was dented in and the sheet had been disturbed. She smiled. He must have put her to bed. Now it smelled as if he was busy with breakfast.

She put on her jeans and T-shirt and went downstairs in her stocking feet to find him slaving over a hot stove.

"I haven't burned it," he said before she could ask. "And I have scrambled eggs and toast warming in the oven. Coffee's in the pot. Help yourself."

"You're going to be a very handy husband," she said enthusiastically. She moved closer to him, frowning. "But can you do laundry?"

He looked affronted. "Lady, I can iron. Haven't you noticed my uniform shirts?"

"Well, yes, I thought the dry cleaners—"

"Dry cleaners, hell," he scoffed. "As if I'd trust my uniforms to amateurs!"

She laughed and hugged him warmly. "Mr. McCallum, you're just unbelievable."

"So are you." He hugged her back. "Now get out of the way, will you? Burned bacon would be a terrible blot on my perfect record as a new husband."

"You fed Meriwether!" she gasped, glancing at her cat, who was busy with his own breakfast.

"He stopped hissing at me the second I picked up the can opener," Sterling said smugly. "Now he's putty in my hands. He even likes Mack!"

"Wonderful! It isn't enough that you've got me trained," she complained to the orange cat lying on the floor beside the big dog. Mack was already his friend, "now you're starting on other people!"

"Wait until Jenny is old enough to use the can opener," he said. "Then he'll start on her!"

Jessica looked at him with her heart in her eyes. She wanted the baby so much.

"What if the judge won't let us have her?" she asked with faint sadness.

He took up the bacon and turned off the burner, placing the platter on the table.

"The judge *will* let us have her," he corrected. He tilted up her chin. "You have to start realizing that good times follow bad. You've paid your dues, haven't you noticed? You've had one tragedy after another. But life has a way of balancing the books, honey. You're about due for a refund. And it's just beginning. Wait and see."

"How in the world did a cynic like you learn to look for a silver lining in storm clouds?" she asked with mock surprise.

He drew her close. "I started being pestered by this overly optimistic little social worker who got me by the heart and refused to let go. She taught me to look for miracles. Now I can't seem to stop."

"I hope you find them all the time now," she said. "And I hope we get Jennifer, too. That one little miracle would do me for the rest of my life. With Jennifer and you, I'd have the very world."

"We'll see how it goes. But you have to have faith," he reminded her.

"I have plenty of that," she agreed, looking at him with quiet, hungry eyes. "I've lived on it since the first time I looked at you. It must have worked. Here you are."

"Here I stay, too," he replied, bending his head to kiss her.

Fourteen

The petition was drawn up by their attorney. It was filed in the county clerk's office. A hearing was scheduled and placed on the docket. Then there was nothing else to do except wait.

Jessica went to work as usual, but she was a different person now that she was married. Her delight in her new husband spilled over into every aspect of her work. She felt whole, for the first time.

They both went out to the No Bull Ranch to see Maris Wyler and Keith Colson. The young man was settled in very nicely now, and was working hard. The homebound teacher who had been working with him since the summer recess was proud of the way he'd pulled up his grades. He was learning the trade of being a cowboy, too, and he'd gone crazy on the subject of wildlife conservation. He wanted to be a forest ranger, and Maris encouraged him. He was already talking about college.

"I couldn't be more delighted," Jessica told McCallum when they were driving back to town. "He's so different, isn't he? He isn't surly or uncooperative or scowling all the time. I hardly knew him."

"Unhappy people don't make good impressions. If you only knew how many children go to prison for lack of love and attention and even discipline.... Some people have no business raising kids."

"I think you and I would be good at it," she said.

He caught the note of sadness in her voice. "Cut that out," he told her. "You're the last person on earth I'd ever suspect of being a closet pessimist."

"I'm trying not to be discouraged. It's just that I want to adopt Jennifer so much," she said. "I'm afraid to want anything that badly."

"You wanted me that badly," he reminded her. "and look what happened."

She looked at him with her heart in her eyes and grinned. "Well, yes. You were unexpected."

"So were you. I'd resigned myself to living alone."

"I suppose we were both blessed."

"Yes. And the blessings are still coming. Wait and see."

She leaned back against the seat with a sigh, complacent but still unconvinced.

They went to court that fall. Kate Randall was the presiding judge. Jessica knew and liked her but couldn't control her nerves. Witness after witness gave positive character readings about both Jessica and McCallum. The juvenile authorities mentioned their fine record with helping young offenders, most recently Keith Colson. And through it all Jessica sat gripping McCallum's hand under the table and chewing the skin off her lower lip with fear and apprehension.

The judge was watching her surreptitiously. When the witnesses had all been called and the recommendations—good ones—given by the juvenile authorities, she spoke directly to Jessica.

"You're very nervous, Mrs. McCallum," Kate said with teasing kindness and a judicial formality. "Do I look like an ogre to you?"

She gasped. "Oh, no, your honor!" she cried, reddening.

"Well, judging by the painful look on your face, you must think I am one. Your joy in that child, and your own background, would make it difficult for even a hanging judge to deny you. And I'm hardly that." She smiled at Jessica. "The petition to adopt the abandoned baby Jennifer is hereby approved without reservation. Case dismissed." She banged the gavel and stood up.

Jessica burst into tears, and it took McCallum a long time to calm and comfort her.

"She said yes," he kept repeating, laughing with considerable joy of his own. "Stop crying! She may change her mind!"

"No, she won't," the judge assured them, standing patiently by their table.

Jessica wiped her eyes, got up and hugged the judge, too.

"There, there," she comforted. "I've seen a lot of kids go through this court, but I've seen few who ended up with better parents. In the end it doesn't matter that your child is adopted. You'll raise her and be Jennifer's parents. That's the real test of love, I think. It's the bringing up that matters."

She agreed wholeheartedly. "You can't imagine how I felt, how afraid I was," she blurted out.

Kate patted her shoulder. "Yes, I can. I've had a steady stream of people come through my office this past week, all pleading on your behalf. You might be shocked at who some of them were. Your own boss," she said to McCallum, shaking her head. "Who'd have thought it."

"Hensley?" McCallum asked in surprise.

"The very same. And even old Jeremiah Kincaid," she added with a chuckle. "I thought my eyes would fly right out of my head on that one." Kate checked her watch. "I've got another case coming up. You'd better go and see about your baby, Jessica." She dropped the formal address since the court had adjourned. "I expect you new parents will have plenty of things to do now."

"Oh, yes!" she exclaimed. "We'll need to buy formula and diapers and toys and a playpen—"

"We already have the crib," McCallum said smugly, laughing at Jessica's startled reaction. "Well, I was confident, even if you weren't. I ordered it from the furniture store."

"I love you!" She hugged him.

He held her close, shaking hands with the judge.

From the courthouse they went around town, making a number of purchases, and Jessica was in a frenzy of joy as they gathered up all the things they'd need to start life with a new baby.

But the most exciting thing was collecting Baby Jennifer from a delighted Mabel Darren, the woman who'd been keeping her, and taking her home.

Even Meriwether was a perfect gentleman, sniffing the in-fant, but keeping a respectful distance. Jessica and McCallum sat on the sofa with their precious treasure, and didn't turn on the television at all that night. Instead they watched the baby. She cooed and stared at them with her big blue eyes and never cried once.

Later, as Jessica and McCallum lay together in bed—with the baby's bed right next to theirs instead of in another room—they both lay watching Jennifer sleep in the soft glow of the night-light.

"I never realized just how it would feel to be a parent," McCallum said quietly. "She's ours. She's all ours."

She inched closer to him. "Sterling, what if her mother ever comes back?"

His arms contracted around her. "If her mother had wanted and been able to keep her, we wouldn't have her," he said. "You have to put that thought out of your mind. Sometimes there are things we never find out about in life—and then there are mysteries that are waiting to be solved just around the cor-ner. For instance, we're still working on the mystery murder at the wedding. We may solve it, we may not. The same is true of Jennifer's situation. But we've legally adopted her. She be longs to us, and we to her. That's all there is to it."

Jessica let out her breath in a long sigh. After a minute she nodded. "Okay. Then that's how it will be."

He turned her to face him and kissed her tenderly. "Happy?" he whispered.

"So happy that I could die of it," she whispered back. She pushed her way into his arms and was held tight and close. As her eyes closed, she thought ahead to first steps and birthday parties and school. She'd thought she'd never know those things, but life had been kind. She remembered what McCallum had said to her—that bad times were like dues paid for all the good times that followed. And perhaps they were. God knew, her good times had only just begun!

*   *   *   *   *

From the bestselling author
who launched the Montana Mavericks saga...

DIANA PALMER

In December 1999,
Mira Books presents

PAPER ROSE

Tate had come to her rescue in her teens, a bold and strong hero. Now Cecily was a woman on her way to a brilliant career, but Tate still thought of her as a girl who needed protecting. Her love for him was a paper rose, which longed for the magic to make it real.

Now a political scandal has an unknowing Tate caught in the middle, and it is Cecily who must come, secretly, to *his* rescue and protect him from a secret which could destroy his life. And in the process, her paper rose has a chance to become real....

Just turn the page for an exciting preview of PAPER ROSE.

Chapter One

In the crowded airport in Tulsa, Cecily Peterson juggled her carry-on bag with a duffel bag full of equipment, scanning the milling rush around her for Tate Winthrop. She was wearing her usual field gear: boots, a khaki suit with a safari jacket. Her natural platinum blond hair was in a neat braided bun atop her head, and through her glasses with large lenses, her pale-green eyes twinkled with anticipation. It wasn't often that Tate Winthrop asked her to help him on a case. It was an occasion.

Suddenly, there he was, towering over the people around him. He was Lakota Sioux, and looked it. He had high cheekbones and big black, deep-set eyes under a jutting brow. His mouth was wide and sexy, with a thin upper lip and a chiseled lower one, with perfect teeth. His hair was straight and jet-black. He was lean and striking, muscular without being obvious. And he'd once worked for a very secret government agency. Of course, Cecily wasn't supposed to know that—or that he was consulting with them on the sly right now in a hush-hush murder case in Oklahoma.

"Where's your luggage?" Tate asked in his deep, crisp voice.

She gave him a pert look, taking in the elegance of his vested suit. "Where's your field gear?" she countered with the ease of long acquaintance.

Tate had saved her from the unsavory advances of a drunken stepfather when she was just seventeen. He'd been her guardian angel through four years of college and the master's program she was beginning now—doing forensic archaeology. She was already earning respect for her work. She was an honors student all the way, not surprising since she had eyes for no man in the world except Tate.

"I'm security chief of the Hutton corporation," he reminded her. "This is a freelance favor I'm doing for a couple of old friends. So this *is* my working gear."

"You'll get all dusty."

He made a deep sound in his throat. "You can brush me off."

Her eyes lit up and she grinned wickedly. "Now that's what I call incentive!"

"Cut it out. We've got a serious and sensitive situation here."

"So you intimated on the phone. What do you want me to do out here?" she asked, sounding like the professional she was. "You mentioned something about skeletal remains."

He looked around her stealthily. "We had a tip that a murder could be solved if we looked in a certain place. About twenty years ago, a foreign double agent went missing near Tulsa. He was carrying a piece of microfilm that identified a mole in the CIA. It would be embarrassing for everybody if this is him and the microfilm surfaced now."

"I gather that your mole has moved up in the world?"

"Don't even ask," he told her. "All you have to do is tell me if this DB is the one we're looking for."

"Dead body," she translated, then frowned. "I thought you had an expert out here."

"You can't imagine what sort of expert these guys brought with them. Besides," he added with a quick glance, "you're a clam. I know from experience that you don't tell everything you know."

"What did your expert tell you about the body?"

"That it's very old," he said with exaggerated awe. "Probably thousands of years old!"

"Why do you think it isn't?"

"For one thing, there's a .32 caliber bullet in the skull."

"Well, that rather lets out a Paleo-Indian hunter," she agreed.

"Sure it does. But I need an expert to say so, or the case will be summarily dropped."

"You do realize that somebody could have been out to the site and used the skull for target practice?"

He nodded. "Can you date the remains?"

"I'll do the best I can."

"That's good enough for me. You're the only person I could think of to call."

"I'm flattered."

"You're good," he said. "That's not flattery."

"When do we leave for the site?" she asked.

"Right now."

After they retrieved her luggage from the baggage claim, he led the way to a big black sport utility vehicle. He put her bags in the back and opened the door for her. She wasn't beautiful, but she had a way about her. She was intelligent, lively, outrageous and she made him feel good inside. She could have become his world, if he'd allowed her to. But he was a full-blooded Lakota, and she was not. If he ever married, something his profession made unlikely, he didn't like the idea of mixed blood.

He got in beside her and impatiently reached for her seat belt, snapping it in place. "You always forget," he murmured, meeting her eyes.

Her breath came uneasily through her lips as she met the level stare and responded helplessly to it. He was handsome and sexy and she loved him more than her own life. She had for years. But it was a hopeless, unreturned adoration that left her unfulfilled. He'd never touched her, not even in the most innocent way. He only looked.

"I should close my door to you," she said huskily. "Refuse to speak to you, refuse to see you, and get on with my life. You're a constant torment."

Unexpectedly, he reached out and touched her soft cheek with just his fingertips. They smoothed down to her full, soft mouth and teased the lower lip away from the upper one. "I'm Lakota," he said quietly. "You're white."

"There is," she said unsteadily, "such a thing as birth control."

His face was very solemn and his eyes were narrow and intent on hers. "And sex is all you want from me, Cecily?" he said mockingly. "No kids, ever?"

She couldn't look away from his dark eyes. She wanted him. But she wanted children, too, eventually. Her expression told him so.

"Cecily, what you really want I can't give you. We have no future together. If I marry one day, it's important to me that I marry a woman with the same background as my own. I don't want to live with a young, and all too innocent, white woman."

"I wouldn't be innocent if you'd cooperate for an hour," she muttered outrageously.

He chuckled. "Under different circumstances, I would," he said, and there was suddenly something hot and dangerous in the way he looked at her as the smile faded from his lips, something that made her heart race even faster. "You tempt me too often. This teasing is more dangerous than you realize."

She didn't reply. She couldn't. She was throbbing, aroused, sick with desire. In all her life, there had been only this man who made her feel alive, who made her feel passion. Despite the traumatic experience of her teens, she had a fierce connection to Tate that she was incapable of feeling with anyone else....

THE WIDOW AND THE RODEO MAN

by Jackie Merritt

One

Maris Wyler disliked unexpected visitors. The black pickup truck that had pulled into her front yard was definitely unexpected and the man who got out was a stranger. She shielded her gaze from the strong afternoon sun to get a better look at him. He was tall and broad shouldered, a black Stetson shadowing his face as he headed toward the house. Maris had just come off the range, having tended her small herd of cattle on horseback for most of the day. She felt sweaty, gritty and in no mood for a caller. Nevertheless, she stepped off her front porch and walked out to greet him.

Something about the man seemed vaguely familiar, she thought as she drew closer. Though even face-to-face she couldn't quite place him.

"Can I help you?"

Her caller flashed a charming smile. "Hello, Maris. How are you?"

His familiar greeting put her a little off-balance. She tried, but her own smile faltered some. "Apparently we've met."

"Apparently you don't remember." His amused expression suggested that he'd rarely heard a woman say she'd forgotten meeting him. "Name's Luke Rivers. We met in Casper, Wyoming. A bunch of us from the rodeo had joined up in a little bar—"

Maris's hand jerked up. "I remember now." Her deceased husband's behavior that night wasn't a memory to elevate a widow's spirit. Ray had followed a flashy-trashy girl around like a panting puppy dog, embarrassing and angering Maris. Luke Rivers had broken the whole thing up by persuading Ray

it was late and time to leave. Maris never did know if Luke had gallantly come to her rescue to save her from further humiliation, or simply because it really was late and the woman Ray had been hitting on was Luke's date. Certainly they hadn't discussed it, and, in fact, had never seen each other again until this very moment.

"What are you doing in Montana? Is there a rodeo in the area?" Maris wasn't speaking with any great amount of friendliness. Ray's obsession with rodeo had been one of the poisons that had destroyed their marriage, long before his fatal accident. Luke Rivers—if she remembered correctly—was a rodeo man through and through, a substantial enough reason to keep a very wide chasm between them.

Luke leaned his hips against the front fender of his truck. Maris Wyler was nice to look at, even with that guarded expression on her face. She had long, sun-streaked, honey-brown hair, restrained at the back of her neck by something he couldn't see. Her skin was as tanned and smooth as honey, and he would bet anything she wasn't wearing any makeup. Her leanness and long legs were accentuated by her worn jeans and red T-shirt. She didn't look soft or at all helpless; rather, she impressed him as a tough, no-nonsense woman. That was okay; she was still nice to look at.

"I came to see Ray. Is he around?"

Maris stiffened. This was the second time an out-of-state pal of Ray's had dropped in, the second time she was going to have to explain why he wasn't "around."

"Ray's dead." The first old pal had gotten tears in his eyes, Maris recalled. Luke Rivers looked as though someone had just punched him in the belly.

"He can't be!" Luke heard his own ludicrous denial and shook his head to clear it. "I'm sorry. What happened?"

Maris recited without emotion. "He got drunk and ran his truck into a cement pier at an underpass out on Highway 191."

"Damn." Frowning, Luke moved away from the pickup and paced a small circle. He pulled off his hat and ran his hand

through his hair. "Damn," he repeated. "Now what am I gonna do?"

"What are *you* going to do?" Maris didn't care what Luke Rivers did about anything, but his remark was so quixotic that she repeated it with some sarcasm. "I can't see why Ray's death should have any effect on your life."

Maris watched him scowling and pacing. He was a tall, rangy, good-looking man, with thick black hair and vivid blue eyes. A lady's man, she'd bet, if the women who made themselves so blatantly available to rodeo men could be called ladies. They were in every town, hanging on the corral fences while the men took care of their horses, cracking jokes, laughing too loudly, trying to catch the men's notice.

Ray had noticed too many times to count, each occasion driving the spike in Maris's heart a little deeper. Luke Rivers would notice. She could tell just from his good looks that he was cut from the same cloth as Ray. Two peas from the same damned pod. Overly macho, strutting peacocks who thought the sun rose and set in their hind pocket just because they risked their stupid necks in the rodeo arena.

Luke stopped pacing and faced Maris with his hands on his hips. "Ray owes me three thousand bucks."

Maris's left eyebrow shot up. "Oh?" She almost laughed. Luke couldn't have known Ray all that well, or he would also have known that collecting that debt would be next to impossible. The only time Ray had ever repaid a loan was when the lender had harangued it out of him. Maris gave her head a brief, negative shake. "All I can tell you is that you're out the three thousand, Mr. Rivers."

"I have an IOU." Luke dug for his wallet and fished out a ragged piece of paper, which he handed to Maris.

She read it—IOU three thousand dollars. Ray Wyler—then handed it back.

"It's none of my affair," she said calmly.

Luke's face darkened. "I need that money."

Maris smirked. "I hope you're not thinking of collecting it from me. I'll tell you right now that I don't have three thousand

dollars, but even if I did I wouldn't use it to pay off one of Ray's gambling debts.''

''It wasn't a gambling debt. Ray came to me about two years ago and all but begged for that money. He said something about using ranch money…'' Luke stopped. What Ray had told him had been in confidence. *Luke, I took money out of the ranch account, and I've got to put it back before Maris gets the next bank statement. She'll brain me for sure if she finds out I gambled again.* It had been all but impossible for Luke to refuse. He had just earned a big purse in a bronc-riding contest, and only the day before Ray had saved him from being gored by an ornery old bull. He'd never been particularly fond of Ray Wyler, but the man had risked his own life to save Luke from certain injury.

''He used ranch money?'' Maris asked suspiciously. ''Two years ago, you said?'' There were so many incidents of Ray depleting the ranch bank account for some inane reason, to pay a gambling debt or to buy another piece of junk, to name two. There were acres of old cars, trucks and odd pieces of junk out behind the barn, and Ray had said the same thing every time he brought home another unnecessary and foolish purchase: ''I'm gonna fix it up and sell it for a big profit.''

He had never fixed anything. Ray Wyler had been a dreamer and a schemer, a gambler, a womanizer and, something that only Maris knew, an insurance-company swindler. But she wasn't thinking of her deceased husband's amoral character right now, she was thinking of that three thousand dollars. In the back of her mind was a bank statement with a mysterious withdrawal and deposit, each for three thousand dollars. Ray had sworn he knew nothing about it and had finally convinced Maris that the bank had made a mistake and merely corrected it. Since it hadn't affected the account's balance, Maris had let it go.

''Let me see that IOU again,'' she said to Luke. He handed it over and she studied the date and thought about that peculiar bank statement. It was easy to put together: Ray had withdrawn the three thousand, wasted it on something, probably gambling,

and borrowed the money from Luke to maintain the correct balance in their account to keep her from finding out that he'd lost so much money.

She wilted inside. Was she responsible for Ray's reprehensible schemes? For his conniving and manipulating Luke Rivers into giving him a loan? Obviously the IOU was genuine, and Luke had every right to expect repayment.

But she had to look after herself, and while she could probably scrape together the three thousand, she wasn't going to hand it over to Luke Rivers.

She passed the IOU back to him. "Sorry, I just don't have that kind of money."

There was a rising panic in Luke. A year ago he'd had a bad accident in the arena, resulting in a broken leg and collarbone. But worse than his own injuries was the death of Pancho, his horse. Pancho had broken his neck in that freak fall and had to be put to sleep, and everyone who had ever seen Pancho work knew he was one of the best cutting horses in the business. For Luke, losing Pancho had been like losing a piece of himself. His broken bones had healed, but would he ever find another Pancho? Especially when he didn't have the money even to start looking?

About two weeks ago he'd remembered that old IOU from Ray Wyler. Though it wasn't nearly enough to buy a horse of Pancho's talent and experience, three thousand would give him the means to get started again. He'd used all of his savings since the accident, and he was as close to being busted right now as he'd ever been. His current status was very little money, no horse and some aches and pains that would probably stay with him for the rest of his life.

But rodeo was all he knew, rodeo or getting a job on a ranch, which sure as hell didn't appeal to him. Anyway, he'd packed up and driven to Whitehorn, Montana, to find Ray Wyler and collect on that old debt.

Instead he was standing in the Wyler yard and being stared down by a woman whose stubborn expression suggested that he had a snowball's chance in hell of seeing that money again.

Whether she had the money or not really wasn't the issue, Luke realized. She wasn't going to pay Ray's IOU, and that was final.

Well, it might be final to Maris Wyler, Luke thought irately, but it wasn't final to him. He began looking around, taking in the house—a modest home—the barn and corrals, a number of other outbuildings and last, but certainly not least, a large pasture containing about a hundred horses. His gaze went further out to the snowcapped mountains he could see on the western horizon. The view was spectacular, in his opinion adding enormous value to this ranch. Grimly, he looked again at the horses. Money on the hoof, he thought. And plenty of it.

"I'll take some of those horses for payment," he said brusquely, turning around to look at Maris.

Her back became rigid. "You'll do no such thing. You will not touch one thing on this ranch, and if you try I'll call Sheriff Hensley, who happens to be a personal friend."

Anger was in the air now. Luke felt it, Maris felt it.

"You're not even going to try to make good on any part of that debt, are you?" he accused.

"Why did you wait two years to collect on it?" Maris spoke harshly. "Ray probably put it out of his mind five minutes after you gave him the money. Didn't you know him at all?"

Luke was staring at the horses. They were mostly quarterhorse stock, good-looking animals. "I thought Ray raised cattle. I don't remember him mentioning horses."

Maris wasn't going to get into that dismal story with Luke Rivers. "Like I just said, didn't you know him at all? Look, you might as well take your IOU and go on about your business. I'm not paying it, and—"

"The law might say otherwise."

Maris sighed wearily. "Take your best shot, cowboy. Frankly, I don't give a damn what you do about it. Your piddly little IOU is nothing compared to what else I'm facing." Maris turned to walk away.

Luke's eyes narrowed angrily. "It might be nothing to you, lady, but it's a hell of a lot to me. You don't have it so bad,

and your whining isn't impressing me in the least. You've got a damned nice little ranch here, a home, a—''

Maris whirled. "I was *not* whining! And your judgment of my situation doesn't impress *me* in the least. So why don't you just climb back into that fancy truck and take yourself off of my land?''

Fancy truck? Luke looked at his only asset, a six-year-old pickup that he'd kept in good repair and just happened to be clean and shiny from the recent wash and wax he'd given it. He was down to practically nothing, and Maris Wyler was taking slams at his one possession of any value?

Anger burned his gut. He wasn't giving up on that IOU, damn it, not when *her* assets were everywhere he looked. "I'd take payment on an installment basis, half now, half in a month or so,'' he said flatly.

Maris threw up her hands in exasperation. "Have you heard one word I've said?''

"Have you heard one word *I've* said?'' he shouted. "I'm flat broke, busted, and you're acting like I'm trying to steal something's that's mine in the first place. If you really don't have the cash, why not let me have a couple of those horses? At least I could sell them and eat until I figure out what to do next.''

"Sell them?'' Maris scoffed. "They're green, Luke, unbroken, wild as March hares. Who would buy them?''

"They're green?'' Frowning, Luke walked away, moving to the fence. The animals appeared docile, grazing on the lush grass in the pasture. "Mind if I take a closer look?'' he said over his shoulder.

"They'll run right over the top of you,'' Maris drawled with some sarcasm, at the same time thinking that might be a picture worth seeing. "Go ahead. Be my guest.''

Luke took off his hat to crawl between the strands of barbed wire, then settled it back on his head. Watching Luke closely, Maris heard footsteps behind her and then Keith's voice. "What's going on, Maris?''

Keith Colson was the one employee Maris was able to keep

on the ranch. Keith had been in trouble of one kind or another since childhood. An alcoholic, abusive father and no sensible adult supervision had left their marks on the sixteen-year-old, but since Maris had put him to work on the ranch, Keith hadn't been in even one small scrape with the law.

He was a handsome boy, dark and lanky, and he was willing to work hard at whatever chore Maris suggested. She had developed a genuine fondness for Keith, thinking on occasion that he could be her own son. Ray had been adamant about not wanting kids, and, in fact, had gone and had a vasectomy without Maris's knowledge. Months later, when he'd been drunk one night, he'd told her about it. She had wept for days, and then, as always, she had regathered her courage and carried on.

Keith was watching the man on the other side of the barbed wire. "What's he doing? Who is he?"

"His name is Luke Rivers, and I don't think he believed me when I told him those horses are green."

"Dang, Maris, he could get hurt."

"Yes, I expect he could," she agreed quietly. "But I think he's one of those men who do exactly as they want, when they want. In other words, no woman is going to tell Luke Rivers what to do."

Keith gave her a curious glance, but what was going on in the pasture was too interesting to miss and he quickly brought his gaze back to Luke Rivers.

Luke was walking very slowly. Any time he got within twenty feet of a horse, the animal kicked up its heels and ran off. Maris was right; these horses were completely wild, too spooky to let a human get near them. But some of them looked good, very good. As he'd already noticed, most were quarter horses, and they had marvelous symmetrical and muscular conformation. They were heavily muscled in their hindquarters, necessary for quality cutting horses. Generally, Luke knew, quarter horses had a gentle disposition, but these broncs had been completely ignored, maybe allowed to grow up on some isolated range without human contact. Then, obviously, someone had rounded them up and sold them to Ray Wyler.

Who was going to break them for Maris? Glancing back to where she waited, he saw a young fellow wearing a huge hat standing next to her. Maybe *he* was going to do the breaking.

Maris was watching Luke's every move and was impressed in spite of herself. He showed absolutely no fear, and though she wasn't normally afraid of horses, she gave the group in this pasture a wide berth.

Luke Rivers. The awful evening at that bar in Casper returned to Maris's mind. Ray had been drunk and disgusting, and she, with her very own eyes, had seen him take that girl out on the dance floor, his hands moving all over her and the rest of his body moving against her as if they were already checked-in at a cheap motel.

Maris had figured that she'd seen just about everything there was to see in life, but her own husband just about bedding a woman in a public place and obviously not caring that his wife was one of the witnesses, was a new low. Teary-eyed, she had scrambled to her feet, knocking down her chair in her haste.

Suddenly Luke had been there, righting her chair, getting Ray off the dance floor and that girl, talking and talking and talking to Ray, and finally escorting her and Ray out of that bar and to their motel, where he even offered, Maris remembered now, to help put Ray to bed.

She had thanked him but said no, that she could manage to pull off his boots and put him to bed on her own. She had sat up the rest of that night, Maris recalled with the pain of old bitterness, seeing again and again her husband standing there with that idiotic look of drunken ecstasy on his face. The next morning, after feeling just a little bit glad that Ray was sick as a dog with a hangover, she had brought their suitcases out to the car, helped Ray from the motel to the vehicle, gotten behind the wheel and started the long drive home. Not a word had ever been said about the night before, not during the drive or anytime after. As was her way, she had put the whole awful incident out of her mind, and to tell the honest-to-God's truth, she had never thought of Luke Rivers again.

But here he was, testing her word on the horses, and perhaps

doing a little more than that. Wasn't he studying them rather intently?

After Luke had seen all he wanted, he returned to the fence and crawled through it. "They're green, all right. Where'd they come from?"

"I have no idea," Maris replied. "Ray bought them and they were delivered by a trucking firm." She glanced at Keith. "Keith Colson, Luke Rivers."

Keith offered his hand. "Pleased to meetcha."

"Same here." Keith was a mere boy, Luke realized. If he knew how to break those horses it would be the surprise of the century. "Do you work here, Keith?"

"Yes, he does," Maris answered before Keith could. But she feared the boy might try to explain how he'd come by his job, and Maris didn't think Keith's sad and sorry background was any of Luke's business.

"Who else?" Luke questioned.

Maris gave him a well-aren't-you-the-nosy-one look, but decided to be truthful. "No one else right now. I had a few more hands, but I had to let them go."

Luke's gaze moved from woman to boy and back again. "And which one of you is going to break those horses?"

Keith's smooth, whiskerless cheeks got pink. "I could break 'em if someone showed me what to do."

"Don't let Mr. Rivers's question throw you, Keith," Maris said with a frosty glare at Luke. "He's only attempting to prove how superior he is to you and me."

"That's a mighty narrow-minded attitude," Luke stated gruffly. "Maybe I've got a good reason for asking about what help you've got on the place."

Her golden hazel eyes flashed. "I understand the reasoning behind any question you might ask," she said sharply. "But let me say it one more time. I do not have three thousand lying around gathering dust. I do not have three thousand gathering interest. *I do not have it!* Now, if there's any other way that you would like me to express my financial situation, name it and I'll be glad to comply."

Luke stared at her for several long moments, then turned on his heel and walked away. Startled, Maris watched him reach his pickup truck and get in.

Keith said, "He's madder 'n a wet hen, Maris. How come?"

She sighed. "Ray borrowed money from him two years ago and never paid it back. He came here today to collect, not knowing that Ray was gone."

"Jeez, that's tough," Keith murmured. "Seems like an all-right guy. He probably needs the money."

"Don't we all," Maris drawled. But as Luke Rivers's truck sped away and she was walking to the house, her own innate sense of fair play began to pinch. She could have handled the situation with a little more diplomacy, maybe explaining just how bad things really were for her right now.

Wearily she rubbed her forehead as she went into the house. How did a woman remain kind and considerate when her very foundation was crumbling a little more every day? There were payments on the ranch's mortgage to worry about, and utility bills, gas and oil for her car, groceries for her and Keith, Keith's small wage, and on and on. Right now the horses and few remaining cattle were faring just fine on natural feed, but come winter there would be hay and grain to buy, and what would she use for money?

Luke Rivers showing up and demanding payment for an old IOU she hadn't even known existed really was a final straw. Small wonder she hadn't been diplomatic, she thought on her way to the kitchen to scare up some supper. Keith, bless his heart, was a bottomless pit. He didn't care what she put on the table to eat as long as there was lots of it. Tonight it would be a dish she had grown up calling "goulash," a filling concoction of ground beef, macaroni and canned tomatoes. Bread and butter and milk would round out the meal, and for dessert there were still a few of those peanut-butter cookies she had baked the other day.

Luke drove away steaming. True, that IOU wasn't Maris Wyler's debt, but it sure as hell had been Ray's, and obviously

Maris had control of the family assets. Didn't one inherit liabilities right along with assets in an estate?

Luke shook his head. He knew beans about legal matters. He could take the IOU to a lawyer and get some answers, but the idea of getting into a legal hassle with Maris Wyler rubbed him wrong. There had to be another way to collect that money. He didn't think she doubted the authenticity of the IOU, and maybe she was as short of cash as she'd said. But she had other assets, such as those unbroken horses, and if he was willing to take the animals in lieu of cash, why was she so stubbornly opposed?

On the other hand, suppose she had agreed to giving him two or three of the horses? What then? They were all but valueless as they were, and he sure didn't have a place to take them for the breaking process. Turning untamed broncs into good cutting horses, which was what he would want to do with them, took time and patience. Well, he had the time and he had the patience, but that was all he had. In retrospect, he was lucky Maris had refused to give him the horses.

Reaching Whitehorn, he drove around and decided it was a pleasant little town. It had a courthouse, a police station, a library, a movie theater, two schools, two churches, a fire station, and various restaurants, food markets and a couple of saloons. He noticed the Hip Hop Café on Amity Lane, and the Amity Boarding House at the intersection of Amity Lane and Cascade Avenue.

But he bypassed the boarding house and drove around until he located a small motel on the highway leading to Interstate 90, where he rented a room for the night.

This wasn't over yet, he told himself as he stretched out on the bed with his hands locked behind his head, staring at the ceiling. Someway, somehow, he was going to collect that three thousand. Leaving Whitehorn, just driving away and forgetting that IOU, wasn't going to happen. He could be as stubborn as Maris Wyler, which she was going to find out.

Lying on that lumpy motel bed, Luke's expression became hard and determined. What he had to do now, tonight, was figure out his next step.

There had to be one. All he had to do was think it through.

Two

The following morning Maris woke up with a throbbing headache. Dragging herself out of bed, she went into her bathroom and took two over-the-counter pain pills. Then she eyed the bottle and wondered how many it would take to put her out of her misery for good.

Tears filled her eyes. Never in her life had she had such a horrible thought, and never in her life had she been a quitter. What was happening to her? There was a solution to every problem, and by all that was holy she was going to find the one that fit her situation. Returning the bottle of pills to the medicine chest, Maris turned on the shower full blast, dropped her nightgown and stepped into the stall. The water hadn't yet warmed up, but she felt she needed an icy shock this morning.

Fifteen minutes later, she was dressed and ready to face the day.

Maybe something good would turn up for a change, she thought hopefully on her way to the kitchen.

Luke went to the Hip Hop Café for breakfast, which, he discovered, wasn't at all what he'd expected before walking into the place. Nothing matched. There was a long chrome counter straight out of the fifties, and then a bunch of tables and chairs that had to have been picked up at garage sales, since none of them were the same. Some were constructed of old oak, some had red vinyl seats, some were painted in startlingly vivid colors. The café's walls were crammed with objects. He spotted an oval mirror with a seashell frame, baskets overflowing with ivy or straw flowers, posters by the score and hand-stitched fabrics in frames, one that read Home Sweet Home and another advising everyone to Have A Good Day.

The many objects, along with the many patrons occupying the place, gave Luke the impression of clutter. But the country music coming from the garish jukebox in a far corner and the buzz of conversation and laughter invited him in, and he walked to the counter and slid onto an empty stool.

The man on his left nodded. "'Morning."

"'Morning." Luke reached for the menu standing on edge between a sunshine-yellow plastic napkin holder and a container of sugar. "What's good in here?" he asked his neighbor.

"Everything's good at the Hip Hop. You must be new in town if you haven't eaten in here before."

The activity of the place was astounding. The waitresses not only delivered food from the kitchen with speed and efficiency, they chatted and joked with their customers. Luke's foul mood began lightening up, and he even smiled at some of the conversations he could hear going on around the room.

Then a young woman came through the swinging doors from the kitchen. Her dark, almost black hair was arranged in a French braid that hung down to the middle of her back. She had vibrant blue eyes and a trim figure, and was wearing a flowing skirt that nearly reached her ankles and a bright-pink blouse. Luke looked her over real good as she passed behind the counter, smiling and commenting to people as she went.

"That's Melissa Avery, the owner," Luke's friendly neighbor volunteered. "Real nice gal."

Melissa Avery not only looked like a "real nice gal," she was pretty enough to draw any man's attention. At any other time, Luke would have pursued the topic, such as asking the fellow next to him if Melissa was married. But this morning his mind was on more important matters than pretty women. Granted, Maris Wyler was damned attractive, but her looks weren't the reason he couldn't stop thinking about her. His stomach cramped every time he thought of hounding a woman for money, even though there was no other way to collect on that IOU.

He mentally counted the cash in his wallet—two twenties, a ten and three ones. Fifty-three bucks. In a secret compartment

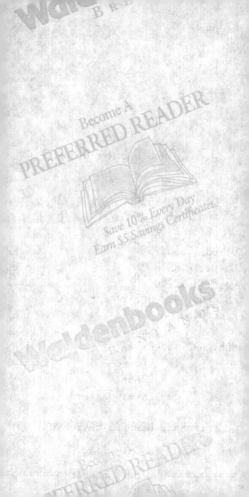

WALDENBOOKS

```
SALE        0579   102   2174   03-19-(
            REL    7.1   10   12:07:

01 0821766392                     6.99
02 0821758578                     6.50
03 0373652100                    12.95
PREF NO. 404800310  EXP 04/02
PREF DISC    26.44 10% OFF        2.64
             SUBTOTAL            23.80
MARYLAND  5.0% TAX                1.19
             TOTAL              24.99
             CASH               24.99
             PV# 0022174
```

PREFERRED READERS SAVE EVERY DAY

===========CUSTOMER RECEIPT===========

in the wallet was also an old, sharply creased hundred-dollar bill. That bill had been in that compartment for at least seven years, which was the last time Luke had been down to nothing. The first money he'd earned after being dead broke for nearly two weeks, he had folded that hundred and secreted it in that compartment, and ever since, knowing it was there had given him a modicum of security.

But that was all the money he had left, one hundred and fifty-three bucks, and the thought of using that hundred gave him a sinking sensation, as though he were going down for the count.

He *had* to collect that three thousand.

"Ready to order, mister?"

Startled, Luke looked up at the waitress. He'd been staring at the menu without absorbing anything written on it. "Uh...ham and eggs and some hash-brown potatoes. And coffee."

"Sure thing. How do you want your eggs?"

"Over easy."

"And what kind of toast? There's wheat, rye, white and sourdough."

"Sourdough."

The waitress stuck her pencil behind her ear and smiled. "I'll get your coffee. Your order will be up in a few minutes."

"Thanks."

"Bread's homemade," Luke's neighbor remarked. "Melissa turned this old place into a fine eating establishment."

A cup of coffee was set in front of Luke. "Thanks," he said to the waitress, then turned to his neighbor and offered his hand. "Luke Rivers."

"John Tully. I own the drugstore between here and the boarding house."

John Tully was around fifty, Luke figured, with a balding head and smelling of antiseptic. "Know of any jobs in the area?" Luke asked.

Mr. Tully frowned. "Well...can't think of anything right off. What kind of work are you looking for?"

Though he had initiated it, the topic depressed Luke. He didn't want a job, damn it, he wanted his three thousand dollars so he could get back on the rodeo circuit. "Ranch work," he said grimly.

"In that case you shouldn't have a problem. There are a lot of ranches around Whitehorn. Let's see now. You might try the Kincaid place first—it's the biggest. Then there's the Walker ranch, and Wyatt North's spread, and..." The man's eyes lit up. "Hey, I bet you could get a job at the Circle W." Then he started to chuckle.

Luke couldn't see that anything funny had been said, so he took a swallow of coffee—very good coffee, he realized—and gave Tully a chance to simmer down.

Then he stiffened. The Circle W was Ray Wyler's ranch! *Maris* Wyler's ranch, he reminded himself with an inward wince.

John Tully stopped laughing, though his round, chubby face still bore an amused grin. "You couldn't know, being new and all, but Mrs. Wyler changed the name of her ranch right after her husband died." For a moment Tully's grin vanished. "Fatal highway accident. Tragic business." His smile returned. "Anyhow, she took down the old Circle W sign and put up one that says No Bull Ranch. It's got everyone around here trying to figure out what she means by that name." Tully chuckled again. "No Bull Ranch. Could signify a lot of things, couldn't it?"

Luke wasn't laughing. "Could mean there's no bull on the place."

"Or no man?" Tully suggested with a masculine twinkle in his eye.

The waitress delivered Luke's breakfast. "Here you are, sir. Enjoy."

Luke picked up his fork, wondering why he hadn't seen that sign yesterday. He'd found the Wyler ranch by asking directions from a gas-station attendant in town, and he'd been anxious to see Ray. Then, too, maybe the sign wasn't in a prominent location. At any rate, he'd missed it completely, and

besides, he didn't think it was nearly as funny as John Tully did.

"Anyway," Tully continued, "Mrs. Wyler is undoubtedly in need of a good ranch hand. You might speak to her about a job."

"Yeah, I might. Thanks." Luke was glad to see John Tully picking up his check.

"Nice talking to you, Luke. Be seeing you again, I'm sure."

"Probably will," Luke muttered as the chatty druggist walked away. He dug into his food, which was hot and as tasty as any ham and eggs he'd ever eaten. Out of the corner of his eye he could see John Tully paying his check and talking to Melissa Avery, who was tending the cash register.

Depressed again, Luke concentrated on his food. He was just finishing up, when the café's door opened for another customer.

"Hi, Judd," Melissa called from the opposite end of the counter, where she had sat down for her own breakfast, a cup of coffee, a glass of orange juice and a plate of toast.

Luke paid no attention to the newcomer until someone else greeted him. "Hello, Sheriff." Then Luke slowly swiveled on his stool to get a look at the man Maris Wyler had used to threaten him with yesterday. So, he thought dryly, that tall, dark, muscular lawman was Maris's personal friend. That was what she had said. *The sheriff is a personal friend.*

For some reason Luke's lips thinned, probably because he didn't like the sheriff at first sight and it made no sense. Grabbing his check, he ambled past the sheriff, who was heading for an empty stool, and stopped at the cash register.

Melissa hurried over. "I hope you enjoyed your meal."

Laying down the check and his ten-spot, Luke looked directly into her stunning blue eyes. "It was the best breakfast I ever had."

Melissa smiled. "That's what we like to hear." She rang up the sale and gave Luke his change.

Remembering that he hadn't left a tip, Luke walked back to where he'd been sitting and dropped a dollar on the counter.

Then he sauntered out of the Hip Hop as though he hadn't a care in the world, just in case Melissa Avery was watching.

As he climbed into his pickup, however, his dark mood returned and Ms. Avery was completely forgotten. Sighing heavily, he started the engine and tried very hard to resign himself to making the rounds of the local ranches to inquire about work.

Right now life stunk. Big time.

Luke did a lot of driving. The Kincaid ranch was seventeen miles northwest of Whitehorn; the Walker ranch lay twenty-five miles west; and the North ranch was in the opposite direction entirely, thirty-five miles east. Then he crossed Interstate 90 and took a look at the Bain spread. When he turned around and reached the interstate again, he pulled his pickup to the side of the road. He'd found the major ranches in the area without too much trouble, but he hadn't stopped at even one and asked about a job.

All during the driving and the looking he'd been doing some heavy-duty thinking. John Tully was right; Maris Wyler *did* need a good ranch hand. He himself had realized yesterday that she needed someone with the know-how to break those broncs. If he had any genuine talent, Luke knew, it was in working with horses. He'd grown up on a ranch in Texas and there'd been plenty of green horses to train to the saddle. Of course, he'd loved rodeo a whole lot more than ranch work, and once he was old enough to take off on his own, he'd pretty much left the Rivers ranch to his parents.

Then his father died. He'd been notified and had made a mad dash for home. His mother was naturally devastated, but within a month she was pretty much her old self and noticing her son's increasing restlessness.

"I know you want to get on with your own life, Luke, so it probably won't bother you none that I'm selling the ranch and moving to town. Am I wrong in that assumption?"

He'd been so relieved that his knees had gotten weak. "That's a great idea, Ma. Just great."

Lila Rivers had smiled wryly. "That's what I thought."

Luke saw his mother about once a year. His visits always coincided with the rodeos scheduled in East Texas, but Lila never seemed to mind. Once in a while, though, she made subtle references to him getting married and settling down like the rest of the world. Luke's standard response was always a big laugh, a hug for his mother and a cocky "Heck, Ma, think of all the unhappy gals there'd be out there if I settled down with just one."

Though he was thirty-five years old, settling down wasn't in Luke's plans, certainly not in his immediate future. The thought of tying himself to a steady job actually pained him, but he was in a financial bind and had to do something. Still, he'd driven on past a half-dozen ranches today. He might have a job right now if he could get Maris Wyler, her unbroken horses and that three thousand dollars out of his mind.

Sitting alongside that vacant stretch of road, with the interstate on ramp no more than a hundred feet ahead, Luke pondered his options. His things were in the back of the pickup, and he could kiss goodbye that three thousand and leave Whitehorn and Maris Wyler in the dust right now. The interstate went west to Butte and east to Billings. He could find out where and when the next scheduled rodeo with any kind of decent purses would take place in either city.

So...why in hell didn't he do that? Why fight with a woman over money? Why worry about her being straddled with a hundred wild broncs and, apparently, no money to hire someone to break them?

He rubbed his mouth and then his jaw, scowling intently. He tugged on his left ear and glared at the interstate, at the traffic it bore, the eighteen-wheelers hauling freight, the motor homes, the pickups and cars.

After about ten minutes of deciding first one way and then another, he muttered a vicious curse, slapped the shifting lever into Drive and took off.

He drove under the interstate and headed back for Whitehorn.

* * *

Maris had been bending over and pulling weeds from her vegetable garden for at least two hours. Straightening her back with a muffled groan of relief, she wiped her sweaty forehead with the back of her forearm and eyed the neat rows of weed-free plants. A garden was always a must for Maris, but this year's crop was going to see her and Keith through the winter and seemed more important than usual. She would can and freeze everything that was possible to can and freeze, and come fall she would have Keith haul one of the steers to Grayson's Meat Packing Plant, which would supply them with beef to eat with the vegetables. They would make it through the winter— providing, of course, she managed to scare up enough cash to meet the mortgage payments on the ranch each month.

The movements of the horses in their pasture drew Maris's attention, and she chewed on her lip while considering their present value, certainly not for the first time. Unbroken, they might bring a hundred dollars apiece, and there were ninety-three horses. Finding buyers for ninety-three unbroken horses in the Whitehorn area was a fantasy, however, so anticipating ninety-three-hundred dollars was nothing more than a futile exercise.

Besides, they were fine animals, and with the proper training should be worth at least five times that amount. She had been delaying asking around about a good horse trainer, because anyone with experience and knowledge was bound to come high, and where would she get the money to pay his or her wage? It was a vicious circle, Maris decided bitterly for about the hundredth time in the past several weeks. No money, no trainer. No trainer, no money. Why in God's name had Ray thought selling the cattle to buy a herd of green horses made sense? That was what he'd done, with absolutely no warning—sold their best cattle and used the money to buy those horses. Maris hadn't understood Ray's motive for doing something so impractical at the time and she still couldn't figure it out.

"Maris, look what I found!"

It was Keith, and Maris turned around to see him coming

toward her with a scruffy, skinny black dog on his heels. "You *found* a dog?" she said dryly. "Where?"

Keith shrugged. "She just showed up out of nowhere. Maybe someone dropped her off on the road."

People did that, Maris knew, just stopped their cars and kicked a poor little kitten or dog out to fend for itself. A stray of that nature raised her hackles. Some pet owners behaved abominably.

She left the garden to inspect the pitiful dog. The animal cringed and trembled and then lay down with its head on its paws. "She's skinny as a rail," Maris said angrily. "Keith, go into the house and fix a bowl of bread and warm milk. This poor little dog might even be too weak to eat, but we'll give it a try."

Uncertain about touching the sad-eyed pooch until it knew her better, Maris sat down in the grass to await Keith's return. "Life dealt you a dirty blow, too, huh, girl?" The dog's tail weakly thumped the grass. "You'd like to be friends, wouldn't you? Well, maybe we will be." Maris shook her head in dismay. The last thing she needed right now was another mouth to feed, particularly one that couldn't possibly benefit the ranch.

But chasing off a poor hungry animal just wasn't in her. She pulled off her canvas garden gloves and examined her dirty, broken fingernails. "Might as well go without gloves," she mumbled dejectedly.

It was just that everything seemed to get her down these days, and she realized that she could easily shed tears over that sad little dog and her own work-worn hands.

Keith came striding up. "Here we go, girl." He set the bowl down in front of the dog, but the little pooch just lay there listlessly. "Come on, girl, you have to eat."

Keith, Maris saw, wasn't at all wary of the dog, as she'd been, and he scooped up a piece of milk-soaked bread from the bowl and held it to the dog's mouth. The animal's tongue flicked to wipe it away, and then she seemed to realize what it was. Struggling to her feet, she stuck her nose in the bowl and began eating.

"That's it, girl," Keith said soothingly. "Eat it all up."

"She probably needs water, too," Maris said while getting to her feet. After locating an old pan in the toolshed, she returned to fill it with water from the garden spigot and brought it to the dog.

"She didn't eat all the bread and milk," Keith said.

"She'll probably finish it later. Here, girl, have a drink of water."

The dog lapped up some water, then lay down again. "Do you think she's sick, Maris?" Keith asked worriedly.

"I think she's half-starved, Keith. But she ate a little, and now she needs to rest. She'll probably be fine in a day or two."

Keith was on his knees next to the dog, petting its matted back. "She's real pretty, don't you think?"

Maris almost smiled. This piteous, bony mutt certainly wasn't pretty. But Keith had had so little love in his young life, and if he felt some fondness for the stray it was fine with Maris. "She'll be a handsome dog, once she's fattened up," she said agreeably.

They both heard the vehicle approaching the compound. Keith saw it first. "Oh-oh, guess who's back."

Maris turned to see Luke Rivers's pickup pulling to a stop near her own truck. Her face turned stony. "Great. Another go-around with that man will certainly complete my day."

"Want me to talk to him?" Keith asked, willing, as always, to help Maris whenever he could.

"Thanks, but I think I'd better do it myself. Apparently he hasn't given up on that IOU Ray gave him." Maris had been sitting on the grass again, and she pushed herself up to her feet. "Do this for me, Keith. Stay within listening distance, and if Mr. Rivers gets too belligerent, call Judd and ask him to come out here, on the double."

Keith's youthful features turned hard right in front of Maris's eyes. "Do you think he'll try something funny, Maris? If he does, I'm gonna tear into him."

"No, Keith, no! Just do as I said about calling Judd. Luke Rivers is twice your size, and I don't want you getting hurt."

"Size ain't everything," Keith mumbled. "I ain't scared of him just 'cause he's bigger."

"I know you're not. If it makes you feel any better, I'm not scared of him, either. It's just that I'm not going to be harassed every day by Luke Rivers. If that's going to be the case, then Judd should be brought in to set him straight. Do you understand what I'm saying?"

"Guess so," Keith said rather sullenly. He wanted to protect Maris, and *would* protect Maris from any threat or danger. Calling the sheriff probably made good sense, but he wished Maris would realize that he wasn't a helpless little kid.

Drawing a deep breath, Maris detoured around the garden and walked toward the parking area of the ranch, where Luke was getting out of his truck.

"Before you start yelling," he said with the same scowl he'd worn all day, "give me a chance to say one thing, okay?"

"If that one thing is about Ray's IOU, the answer is no," Maris said flatly.

"It's not. Well, in a way it is, but mostly it's about something else."

Maris folded her arms. "Very well. Shoot."

Clearing his throat, Luke turned his gaze on the horse pasture. "You need someone to break those horses and I need a job. Here's my offer." His eyes connected with Maris's. "You give me room, board and a few bucks a week, and I'll put a smile on every one of those horses' faces. Some of them look to me like good cutting stock, which will take more work than the others. But when they're all broken to the saddle and acting as sweet as sugar, you'll get a good price for them. Then you pay me the three thousand, give me my pick of the lot for a bonus, and I'll get out of your hair for good."

Maris was slightly stunned. "Seems to me your offer is pretty heavily weighted in your favor. Why should you end up with the best horse in the herd, which I'm sure would be the case?"

"Because you won't have to pay me during the breaking process, except for a place to sleep, meals and, like I said, a

few bucks a week so I've got a little spending money. Look, you already owe me the three thousand, so you can't count that as pay. The horse would be my fee for doing the job.''

Maris stood with her arms folded across her chest, frowning at this overbearing man and his outrageous offer.

But was it really that outrageous? As he'd said, he was already owed the three thousand, although she really hadn't intended to pay that debt of Ray's. But fair was fair, and that aspect of Luke's offer wasn't out of line. There were other considerations, however.

''How do I know you can do the job?'' she asked.

''Because I'm telling you I can,'' Luke said gruffly. ''I grew up on a ranch. I understand horses and I'm damned good with them.''

Luke's macho confidence annoyed Maris. Ray had thought he'd been an expert in every possible field, when, in fact, his knowledge on any given subject had been extremely limited. Luke Rivers could be the same kind of person, all bluster and brag.

''How long would it take?'' Maris asked, unable to keep the suspicion and doubt in her system from influencing her tone of voice.

Luke heard the suspicion but ignored it. Again his gaze went across the fence to the grazing horses. ''There are about a hundred horses...''

''Ninety-three.''

''All right, ninety-three.'' Luke did some figuring in his head. Breaking a horse took time and patience, but a handler didn't pull only one animal out of a herd and work solely with it until it accepted humans and their commands. He would be working with seven, eight horses a day—one at a time, of course. Some would break easily and require only a few sessions; some would be stubborn, balky and mean and require dozens of repetitive sessions. But he knew how to spot the outlaws and would begin with the more docile animals. The whole thing shouldn't take more than ten weeks.

''I'll be out of here by the end of September,'' he told Maris.

Her eyes widened. "Less than three months?"

Luke nodded. "That's fact, not boast. By the end of September those horses will be ready to sell." The corner of his mouth turned up in a crooked half smile. "Maybe you can throw a big whoop-de-do and have an auction."

"An auction," she repeated slowly, though her blood was definitely flowing faster from Luke's promises and comments. An auction would be a dramatic way to sell her horses. She could advertise the event all over the area, using the newspaper and strategically placed signs.

But jumping into anything, however good it sounded, wasn't her nature. "Let me think about it overnight," she said.

Aw, hell, thought Luke. "Overnight" meant laying down another thirty bucks for a motel room.

"Come back in the morning and I'll give you an answer," Maris added.

Frustration made standing still impossible for Luke. He walked a small circle, rubbing the back of his neck, then took a breath and began again. "What's the problem? Do you think I can't do it?"

"I only have your word on that, don't I?"

"That's all you'll have in the morning, too. Maris, today was the pits. I drove about two hundred miles looking at the other ranches around Whitehorn, trying to work up the desire to ask one of them for a job. I *need* a job, but I don't want a job. Do you get my drift? This arrangement would benefit both of us. Your horses would be salable by the end of September, and I could get back to what I do best."

"Rodeo," Maris said, icicles dripping from every syllable.

Her tone stunned Luke. "Something wrong with rodeo?"

"Too many things to mention."

"But Ray—"

"Loved it, just as you seem to do. Forget it. Your preferences are none of my affair, nor are my attitudes of any interest to you. Getting back to your offer, I really do need tonight to think about it."

Luke's face hardened. "Fine. But would you mind if I bedded down in your barn while you're doing your thinking?"

"In my barn! You mean spend the night in there?"

"I have a bedroll."

Maris took a breath. Was he *that* broke? The boarding house in town didn't charge exorbitant rates, and she knew there was a little motel on the road to the interstate. But if he didn't even have enough money to pay for a room for the night...?

She groaned inwardly. Two strays in one afternoon. Keith was still sitting beside his half-starved friend, petting the dog's head and back, and now this, Luke Rivers asking to sleep in her barn because he couldn't afford the cost of a room.

"Fine," she said tiredly. "You can stay. But you don't have to use your bedroll. There's a room in the loft of the barn with a bed, and a small bathroom. I'll have Keith show you the way."

Shaking her head, Maris turned and walked away. Watching her go, Luke admitted total and complete perplexity about Maris Wyler. She was wearing cutoff jeans, an old T-shirt and sneakers, and the dirt on her clothing, hands and legs evidenced a day of hard work. For certain she wasn't the kind of woman Luke was usually drawn to. Melissa Avery, with her gorgeous blue eyes and long dark hair was much more his type. But it was Maris he felt in his loins, not Melissa. How in hell did a man figure that one out?

Well...at least he had a free bed for the night. And maybe by morning Maris would realize what a good deal he had offered her.

Like he'd said, it would benefit both of them.

Three

Maris did give Luke's offer a lot of thought that night, and there was one aspect of the arrangement that kept popping into her mind and turning her off on the deal: the fact that Luke Rivers, rodeo bum, would be living on the ranch. Forcing herself to remember the details of that night in the bar in Casper, she finally recalled the woman who had to have been Luke's date for the evening—a vivacious young blonde wearing tight, tight jeans and a low-cut blouse that displayed her ample cleavage. It was a disturbing image, indicating quite clearly the type of woman Luke Rivers preferred.

The problem, of course, was that she had no alternative solutions to choose over Luke's. If Luke wasn't just bragging and throwing his machismo around and he actually got those horses ready for sale by the end of September, her financial worries would vanish in the fall. Or most of them, at least.

Maris walked the floor half the night. There was so much to consider. Money for this, money for that. Putting the ranch up for sale had occurred to her, of course, but she loved the place, which had been in Ray's family for several generations. Ray had been the first Wyler in decades who hadn't been completely contented with his lot as a rancher. There'd been a restlessness in Ray, Maris had always known, some kind of inner force that made him seek excitement...such as the rodeo circuit...and gambling...and other women.

Despondent at the turn of her thoughts, Maris snapped off the light, crawled into bed and drew the covers up to her chin. A bright moon shone through the window, and she thought of Luke Rivers in that little loft bedroom. Did she want him in that room every night for weeks and weeks? Did she want him at the table with her and Keith, meal after meal? Then her

thoughts flipped. Was she judging Luke too harshly because he reminded her of Ray? Oh, not in looks, for pity's sake. The two men looked nothing alike. Ray had been a slight man, not much taller than her, with light hair and pale brown eyes, and Luke was...Luke was...

Well, he was just too darned good-looking, that's what he was. And he made her...uncomfortable. Yes, that was the word. Luke Rivers made her *very* uncomfortable. Now, why do you suppose that was? she thought with a perplexed frown. Certainly he wasn't apt to make a pass when he preferred leggy blondes with overdeveloped chests.

That entire subject was unnerving to Maris. Punching her pillow into a different shape, she grumpily told herself to put Luke Rivers out of her mind and get some sleep.

Luke didn't sleep well, either. His mind wouldn't shut down, and nearly everyone he'd ever known paraded through his brain. The specter that bothered him the most was the one of Ray Wyler. Why in heck had Ray bought so many unbroken horses? Luke was positive Ray hadn't been an experienced handler, and Ray's personality had been erratic and sometimes downright unstable. Luke would bet anything that Ray's idea of breaking horses had been to tie down the animal, throw a saddle on its back and ride it to exhaustion. He probably would have used the whip on the balky ones, too, beating them into submission. Luke hated cruelty to animals, and more than once had stepped between a man with a whip and a horse.

It was odd then the way his thoughts moved from Ray Wyler and horses to Ray Wyler and Maris. But Luke had seen for himself how Ray had treated Maris. The embarrassing episode in that Casper tavern could have been an isolated incident for the Wylers, but Luke really didn't think so.

Maris puzzled him. She conveyed determined independence and female vulnerability, both at the same time, and he'd be willing to bet that she'd huff up and do battle with anyone who dared to mention her vulnerability. Maybe she wasn't even aware of it herself.

Luke had one more point to ponder about Maris Wyler. He

had the impression that Ray's fatal accident hadn't happened that long ago, but she honestly didn't appear to be a grieving widow. True, she had a lot to deal with—the ranch, very little money and no help other than Keith. But she had told him about Ray's accident without a dram of emotion, and wouldn't a woman who had loved her husband be devastated for months after his death?

On the other hand, his own mother hadn't mourned openly for any great length of time after his father had died, and Luke was positive his parents had had a good and happy marriage. Maybe some women recovered more quickly than others. Or maybe they did their crying when they were alone.

He frowned at the possibility of Maris crying into her pillow after dark when no one could see her. The idea of her crying at all was surprisingly discomfiting.

"Aw, hell," he mumbled, and turned to his side to get more comfortable. Maris Wyler's emotions or lack thereof were none of his business. All he wanted from her was an agreement on the deal he'd offered. She wasn't all that great, anyway. Hadn't she let him drive to town for supper, rather than inviting him in to eat with her and Keith?

That was all he wanted from Maris Wyler, he thought again, getting drowsy, an agreement on his offer. Then he would break her horses, collect his three thousand dollars, pick himself a good cutting horse out of the herd and leave the Wyler ranch and Whitehorn, Montana, for good.

He'd be back on the rodeo circuit in October. It was a satisfying thought to fall asleep with.

Keith was preparing to leave the kitchen with a bowl of bread and milk for the stray dog, which had been bedded down on an old blanket in the toolshed.

Maris was stirring a pot of oatmeal on the stove. "Keith, please go by the barn and tell Luke that he's welcome to join us for breakfast."

"Okay." Keith stopped at the door. "Uh...are you gonna take his deal?"

Maris hesitated, then nodded. "I think so." She threw a hopefully brave smile at her young friend. "It's the only game in town right now, Keith."

"Yeah, guess it is."

From the kitchen window, Maris watched Keith go into the toolshed with the dog's breakfast. Before he came out again, she spotted Luke walking from the barn. "At least you're not a slugabed," she mumbled. It wasn't yet 6:00 a.m., and Luke's early appearance was a good sign.

Keith came out of the toolshed with the stray pooch on his heels. Luke veered directions to meet the boy halfway. "'Morning, Keith. Who's your friend?"

Bending over, Keith scratched the dog's ears. "I don't know her name. She's a stray. Someone probably dropped her off on the highway. She looks a lot better this morning than she did last night."

Luke grinned down at the scruffy animal. "Looks like she could use a bath."

Keith straightened. "Yeah, she does. I'm hoping Maris will let me keep her. I'd buy her food with my own money."

Luke could see that the boy was fond of the motley little mutt. "Can't think of any reason why Maris wouldn't let her stay."

Keith suddenly remembered what Maris had asked him to do. "You're invited to breakfast." Keith's cheeks got pink. "If you wanna eat with us, that is."

"Sure, thanks."

"Come on in, then. Breakfast was almost done when I came outside a few minutes ago."

Luke followed Keith into the house. The dog tried to follow, as well, but Keith stopped her at the door. "Stay, girl," he said, and the little dog sat down next to the steps.

"'Morning, Maris," Luke said. She was dressed in worn jeans and a white T-shirt, and she looked as fresh as the morning dew. He caught himself staring at her pretty, sun-streaked hair and abruptly turned his gaze.

"Good morning. Everything's ready. You two go ahead and sit down while I pour the coffee."

Luke waited until Keith sat at his place, then decided that the one nearest the stove would be Maris's spot at the table and sat in the third chair. In front of him was a large bowl of steaming oatmeal, a glass of orange juice and a cup awaiting coffee. The center of the table contained a pitcher of milk, a sugar bowl, a jar of peanut butter, a small bowl of jam—strawberry, it looked like—and a plate heaped with toast.

Maris came around the table and filled his cup with coffee, then went to her place and poured her own. Keith, Luke noted, had a glass for milk along with his glass of orange juice.

Maris took her seat. "Dig in," she said while looking at Luke. "It's not fancy but it's filling."

"It looks...great." Oatmeal was not his favorite breakfast food, but he would never say so. Maris got up to switch on the small radio on the counter. "For the weather report," she explained, resuming her place at the table.

They ate with very little conversation. Keith, Maris realized, was shy around Luke, and since she couldn't think of any small talk that made sense, they mostly listened to the morning news and finally the weather report. "Scattered clouds, with the temperature reaching ninety degrees. A great day, folks."

Keith devoured the last toast on the plate after slathering it with strawberry jam, then got up and carried his dishes to sink. "Want me to work on those fences again today, Maris?"

"Later, Keith." Maris stood up and began gathering her own dishes. "First I'd like you to drive to town and buy that skinny dog some regular dog food."

Keith's face broke out in a big grin. "Then she can stay?"

She smiled. "I think we need a dog on the place, don't you?"

"Yeah, I sure do."

"Remember, though, Keith, someone might come along and claim her. She could have merely strayed away from home on her own."

"I'll remember. I've been thinking up names for her, but I bet she's been called 'Blackie.' What do you think?"

"Seems appropriate," Maris said with a laugh. She dug out a ten-dollar bill from a pocket in her jeans and held it out to Keith.

"I'll buy her food, Maris," Keith said with a prideful lift of his chin. "I'd like to do it."

She studied the young boy. Keith's eyes contained a joyful light that touched her deeply. Nodding, she tucked the ten back into her pocket. "Drive carefully."

"I will. And thanks, Maris." Keith grabbed his big hat from the hook by the door and eagerly bounded out.

Luke started to get up and Maris reached for the coffeepot. "We need to talk. Would you like more coffee?"

He'd been wondering when she would get around to telling him her decision. Sinking back to his chair, Luke nodded. "Yes, thanks."

After their cups were refilled, Maris sat down and regarded Luke across the table. Impersonally, she hoped, since impersonal was the only way she wanted their relationship. "I'm going to accept your offer, if you accept my conditions."

His hopes ignited. "What are they?" he asked casually, pretending that his gut wasn't tied in a knot. This deal was maybe the most important of his life, the new start he desperately needed.

Looking directly at Luke's handsome face made Maris nervous, and she dropped her gaze to the table in front of her. "No drinking on the place. Not even beer. And should you overindulge somewhere else, don't come back here to sleep it off."

"Agreed," Luke said quietly. He wasn't much of a drinker—a few beers once in a while—so this condition was no hardship. "What else?"

"No women." Maris's face colored. "I mean, of course, no women on the ranch. What you do in your own time is of no concern to me. I just don't want you bringing a woman here. Keith is at an impressionable age, and—"

Luke broke in brusquely. "Don't worry about it. There won't be any women."

"Fine. Thank you," she said stiffly. "I won't expect you to work seven days a week, but I would like as much of your time spent working with the horses as you can manage."

"I don't need any days off. I probably will work seven days a week." He leaned forward slightly. "Maris, I want this job over and done with as soon as possible. Don't worry about me goofing off when I should be working."

"You want it over with so you can get back to rodeo," she said tonelessly.

"I know you don't like rodeo, but I'm not going to be embarrassed every time it comes up in conversation. It's what I do, Maris, what I've done since I was old enough to leave home."

Maris mustered up a shrug. "It's nothing to me." Her gaze sought Luke's across the table. "Well...do we have a deal then?"

"We do as far as I'm concerned." Relieved and elated that it had gone so easily, Luke shaped a tentative smile. "Should we shake hands on it?"

Maris got to her feet and began clearing the table. "I don't think that's necessary. We've struck a bargain and I'm sure we'll both abide by it."

Luke stood up. "If it's okay with you I'd like to look around the ranch. Snoop through the barn and the other buildings and take stock of what equipment you have."

"Do whatever you think necessary." At the sink Maris rinsed her hands and picked up a towel to dry them. "Wait a minute. There is one point we haven't discussed."

Luke was already on his way to the door. He stopped and turned. "What's that?"

"Your wage. You said something about a few dollars a week. I think we should agree on the amount, don't you?"

Luke tugged at his ear. "Well...yeah, guess we should. I was thinking about fifty a week. Is that all right with you?"

Maris's stomach sank and her face flushed to a dark crimson. "I...can't pay fifty a week."

This aspect of their discussion didn't set right with Luke. Pressuring a woman for money made him feel like a damned parasite. The only thing he really needed money for was gas for his pickup, and he probably had enough in his wallet to keep him going until the job was done.

"Let's forget that part of the deal," he said, wishing he hadn't mentioned a wage at all yesterday. He'd embarrassed her by suggesting fifty bucks a week, and he realized that he didn't like embarrassing her.

But Maris shook her head rather adamantly. "No, a deal's a deal. I can't pay fifty a week, but I can pay..." She hesitated, praying to God he wouldn't be insulted by such a paltry sum. "Twenty-five."

Luke saw the pride in her pretty golden eyes, the independence, whether natural or forced by circumstances, and he vowed on the spot to do the best job possible and pray that the sale of those horses would make things easier for her.

"Twenty-five is fine. Thanks."

Maris breathed a quiet sigh of relief. She was putting all of her eggs in one basket by relying on Luke Rivers, and only time would prove her right or wrong.

But even if he was all brag and bluster and she ended up with only half-broken horses, would she be much worse off than she was today?

Luke gave one sharp, definitive nod of his head. "Guess that's it then. I'll go to work now."

"Yes, go ahead," Maris said faintly as he again started for the door.

This time he stopped on his own. "I have a condition, too, Maris."

Startled, she looked at him. "What is it?"

"It's this. I know what I'm doing with horses, and I don't want you or anyone else interfering with my methods."

"Oh." *His* condition riled her. This was her ranch, after all, and her horses. A noticeable coolness crept into her voice. "I'm

sure no one will interfere. If I knew how to do the job I wouldn't need you at all, would I?''

''Good point. See you later.'' Luke left the kitchen and went outside. The first thing he did was suck in a huge gulp of fresh air. Making a business deal with a woman was an unnerving undertaking. Walking to the barn, he remembered that he'd never worked for a woman before, other than his mother.

But then, he hadn't worked for men very much, either. His entire life had been dedicated to rodeo, and there'd been five, six years back a ways that he was damned proud of. He'd won lots of money and earned a slew of trophies. Luke frowned. The money was gone, his mother had the trophies and thirty-five was an iffy age in the arena. He was paying the price of too many bad falls and this latest accident. Every morning he awoke with some new ache in his bones he'd fight to ignore. Some cowpokes seemed to go on forever, but most of the competitors were young, tough and full of vinegar. But what the hell else would he do if he didn't jump back into the rodeo circuit?

Grim-lipped, he decided that he couldn't worry about his age, or his aching bones. What the young guys lacked he had plenty of, and that crucial component was called experience. And he also had a reputation, a damned *good* reputation. Once he got hold of another great cutting horse, though there would probably never be another Pancho, he'd do all right. The steer-roping event had always been his specialty, and he'd rise to the top again with the right horse. He'd find the right horse in Maris's herd, and he'd train him to perfection exactly as he'd done with Pancho.

Feeling better about his future, Luke walked into the barn.

Maris did the dishes and tidied the kitchen, moving at a snail's pace. Ordinarily the job took no more than ten minutes; this morning she fiddled around for a good half-hour.

But the arrangement with Luke changed everything, and she kept thinking of the additional cooking, the extra food to buy and how strange it felt to have a man like Luke living on the

ranch. How would he and Keith get along? How would *she* and Luke get along? She felt disruptive undercurrents when she was with him, odd little sensations within herself that she couldn't pin down.

Maris stopped at the clean and shiny sink to stare out the window. What should be her chores for the day? What was Luke looking for down at the barn? Equipment, he'd said, but what sort of equipment? She should have asked, and maybe saved him some time and effort by explaining that she did or did not have what he needed.

Deciding that she could water her garden while lining out her day, she went outside to the garden area. She had just gotten started with the water hose, when she heard a vehicle approaching. It couldn't be Keith back so soon, she thought, and turned off the spigot to walk around the house to see who was coming.

Smiling at the sight of Judd's official black utility vehicle she continued walking to greet him as he got out. "'Morning, Judd."

"'Morning, Maris."

Judd was a tall, dark and mostly silent man. Since Ray's death he had stopped in quite a few times, and Maris appreciated his thoughtfulness. Twice he had asked her out for supper and they'd eaten at the Hip Hop Café. The evenings had been pleasant diversions, and Maris recognized and admired Judd's strong and honest outlook on life. He was everything Ray hadn't been—a complete opposite, to be perfectly accurate. A woman could do a lot worse than to take up with Judd Hensley.

"Everything all right on the Wyler ranch?" Judd asked.

Maris laughed with some wryness. "As right as can be expected."

But Judd, she saw, had become more interested in Luke's pickup than in her answer and was giving it a thorough once-over. "Got company?"

"A hired man, Judd. He's going to break the horses."

"Anyone I know?"

"I doubt it. He's not from Montana. Actually, he knew Ray and came here to—" Maris stopped short of blurting out the

whole story. That old IOU really wasn't anyone else's business. "See Ray." Maris's voice became quieter. "He didn't know Ray was gone."

"Too bad," Judd said. "Must be hard on you to tell old friends about it." Judd was still looking at Luke's pickup, which he was sure he'd seen in town yesterday. "What's this guy's name?"

"Luke Rivers. He knew Ray from the rodeo, Judd. That's what he does ordinarily." Maris could see Judd's wheels turning and decided to change the subject. Her financial situation really wasn't open for discussion, and as of this morning, Luke Rivers and her pitifully small bank account were oddly intermingled.

"Any news on that man who died at Mary Jo and Dugan's wedding?" she asked.

"He didn't just die, Maris. He was murdered."

"Murdered!" Maris's eyes got very big. "But I heard he was a stranger. Why would anyone murder a total stranger? And how come he was at the wedding in the first place? People don't usually crash weddings."

"All we've been able to discover so far is that his name was Floyd Oakley. Neither Mary Jo nor Dugan admit to inviting him to the wedding, so maybe he was just a transient looking for a free meal. We're working on it. That makes two strangers in our little town now, doesn't it? Floyd Oakley and Luke Rivers."

Appalled at Judd's implication, Maris rushed to defend Luke. "Oh, but Luke didn't arrive until after the wedding, Judd."

Judd cocked an eyebrow. "Maybe he didn't show his face out here right away. Maybe he'd been hanging around town for several weeks. Mind if I talk to him?"

Maris drew a nervous breath. "Well, no, of course not, but..." She couldn't believe that Luke could be a murderer. As hard-nosed as Luke could be, the idea struck her as utterly preposterous. But Judd Hensley wasn't a man to waltz around on a subject, either. She could see on his stern face that he was determined to talk to her new hired man. She wondered if Judd

really suspected Luke, or was simply feeling protective of her and maybe even rankled at the news that a stranger was going to be living on the ranch.

"He's in the barn, Judd. Let me run down there and get him."

"No...let's just walk down to the barn together," Judd said calmly.

"Uh...fine. That's fine." All sorts of things ran through Maris's mind during the short trek. Luke *had* come directly to the No Bull Ranch when he'd gotten to the area, hadn't he? But what if he hadn't? Would his presence in the area at the time of that murder automatically make him a suspect?

Uneasily she led Judd into the barn, calling "Luke? Are you in here?"

Luke stepped out of the tack room with a bridle in his hand. "Do you need me for something?" He saw the sheriff and involuntarily stiffened. "'Morning, Sheriff."

"Judd, this is Luke Rivers. Luke, Sheriff Judd Hensley."

They didn't shake hands. Maris sucked in an exasperated breath. It was all too obvious that Judd and Luke weren't going to be friends, though she wasn't vain enough to suppose their immediate animosity had anything to do with her. It was a male thing, she thought, an instantaneous clash of personalities.

"Didn't I see you in the Hip Hop yesterday morning?" Judd questioned evenly.

"I saw you," Luke replied. "So guess you could have seen me, too."

"How long you been in the area?"

"Three days. Why?" Luke looked at Maris for an explanation, but she was merely standing by and chewing on the inside of her bottom lip with a worried frown.

"You have proof of that, I suppose," Judd said.

"Proof? Why would I need proof? I drove into Whitehorn two days ago, asked directions to Ray Wyler's place at a gas station and came directly here. What's this all about, Sheriff?"

"We had a little trouble around here a few weeks back.

Where were you on..." Judd named the date in late June of Mary Jo and Dugan's wedding.

Luke's forehead creased in thought. Then his expression cleared. "I was in Denver, visiting friends." It was the truth. After his release from the hospital, most of his recovery time had been spent in Texas. Then, with that IOU in mind, he had started working his way north to Montana. Since he'd been out of commission for nearly a year he had made several stops during the trip to see old friends.

Judd decided to believe him...for the time being. Floyd Oakley, if that was his real name, thus far seemed to be a man without a past. His wallet had been empty except for a few dollars, a snapshot of a woman and an outdated Wisconsin driver's license. That license had provided Oakley's name, but Judd has his suspicions about its authenticity. Of course Judd knew he was a naturally suspicious person.

Regardless, Oakley had been murdered in his jurisdiction, either by one of the wedding guests or by someone who had slipped into the group unnoticed, done his dirty deed and then slipped away again, and he intended to identify the culprit, whatever it took.

He spoke to Luke again. "Are you planning to make Whitehorn your home?"

Luke's voice was cold and unfriendly. "This is my home, but only until Maris's horses are broken and salable. I'll be moving on then."

Maris could tell that Judd didn't like Luke calling the No Bull home. But the belligerent look on Luke's face said rather plainly that he didn't like Judd Hensley period. It struck her that they were squaring off right before her eyes, as stubbornly and determinedly as two bulls did in the presence of a juicy young heifer. The only elements missing were the lowered heads, snorts and the pawings of the ground.

But it was so dumb. She certainly wasn't a juicy young heifer, not by any stretch of the imagination, and her relationship with Judd so far was only friendship. As for Luke, he

couldn't even claim that. He was her employee and that was all he would ever be.

Maris cleared her throat, loudly, hoping these two macho men would get the picture that she wasn't very pleased with their attitudes. "Luke," she said deliberately, "are you finding the equipment you need to get started with the horses?"

Both men shifted their weight, breaking their staredown to look at her. Judd said, "Guess I'll be running along. You two have work to do."

"Yes, we do," Maris replied rather coolly.

But she walked Judd to his car. "Thanks for stopping by. You're welcome here anytime, Judd. I hope you know that."

Judd's dark eyes still contained suspicion. "How well do you know Rivers? You said he was Ray's friend, but did you know him, too, before he showed up?"

"I...knew him." It wasn't a total lie, Maris told herself. But she was not going to get into a long dissertation on when and how she and Luke had met. "Judd, I really don't think he's going to be any kind of problem."

Judd slid into his car. "Probably not, but just to be on the safe side, I'm going to check him out, see if he has a record. Anything's possible."

As the sheriff's car sped away, Maris heaved a sigh. Luke wasn't any fugitive from the law. Maris knew it instinctively. He was just a rodeo cowboy—one who was going to break her horses and help her get out from under a load of debt. She sure didn't need Judd chasing Luke out of town, at least not until his job was done.

Four

Luke entered the horse pasture with a coiled rope clasped in his right hand and held down around his thigh. He walked slowly, studying the horses, looking for one with a gentle disposition. Horses had personalities just as people did. Some were meaner than rat poison and never would gentle down enough for a novice rider. Others were easily trained, and that was what he wanted to start with, an animal that wouldn't throw a fit at every step of the process.

He spotted a gray mare with good lines and a well-shaped head. She lifted her head when she became aware of Luke, and he got a clear, unobstructed look at her eyes, which were constant and calm with no white showing. Quick, darting eyes that displayed a large amount of white on a horse usually indicated a spooky, erratic animal.

Cautiously and slowly he moved closer to the mare, uncoiling the rope as he went. When she didn't bolt and run, as the other horses had been doing if he got too close, he began talking in a quiet, soothing voice. "There's a nice girl. Stay steady, girl. No one's going to harm you." The chant continued, soft and singsong, until Luke was within roping distance. He didn't move quickly until he threw the loop, and it landed precisely where he'd aimed it, squarely over the mare's head.

She squealed and reared in an attempt to get rid of the noose around her neck, but Luke dug in his heels, wound his end of the rope around his leather-gloved hands and hung on.

Maris was watching from outside the fence, utterly fascinated. Ray had practiced roping quite a lot, but he had never attained the expertise she had just witnessed. Luke began walking up the rope, getting closer to the mare. He was too far away for Maris to hear what he was saying, but she could tell he was

talking to the horse. Gradually the mare calmed; gradually Luke got closer. When there was about six feet of rope between him and the animal, he started urging her to follow him. The mare took a step and stopped. Luke tugged lightly on the rope. "Come on, girl," he crooned. The mare took a few more steps, and then Maris shook her head in amazement: Luke was leading the mare toward the gate in the fence!

Quickly she ran over and opened the gate. Luke and the mare passed through it and she closed it again. Luke had left the corral gate open, and he led the mare into the corral as easily as anything Maris had ever seen. Though Luke had issued no instructions, other than for her to bring out a sack of apples, Maris closed and latched the corral gate.

"Toss me one of those apples," Luke said softly. Maris dug one out of the sack and threw it to Luke, who caught it deftly in his left hand. Using the apple as a bribe—the mare ate it directly out of his hand—he loosened the loop around the mare's neck and released her.

Recoiling the rope, Luke walked over to Maris. "This one's going to be easy. Give me a couple more of those apples." He stuck the apples in his shirt pockets, giving him the appearance of breasts and causing Maris to laugh.

Then he walked over to the section of corral rail where he'd earlier placed an old feed sack and slowly walked back to the mare. First he offered her another apple, which she willingly took from his hand, then he began tentatively and gently rubbing the sack over her neck. She turned her head, looked at him and snorted, but she stood still and let him rub her with the sack. Patiently he rubbed the sack over her hind quarters, her belly, her neck and finally her head.

"Why is she letting you do that?" Maris asked, keeping her voice down so she wouldn't startle the mare.

"Probably because it feels good," Luke said quietly. "Rubbing and touching is the first step to familiarity."

Maris equated his comment to humans and flushed hotly. She hadn't had any rubbing and touching for a long, long time. Ray had been gone so much, and during the year just prior to his

death, he had seldom come near her. When he had, it had been quick and emotionless sex and she had received no pleasure from it. That mare was receiving more loving, tender, patient caresses right now than Maris Wyler had gotten in longer than she cared to remember.

And the man doing the caressing, the rubbing and the touching was truly a sight for any lonely woman's eyes. His wide shoulders stretched the seams of a blue chambray work shirt, and then his torso tapered to a flat, firm belly. Everything below his belt was equally magnificent—his tight behind, his long, muscular thighs. Oh, God, Maris thought frantically. Am I having a sexual fantasy in broad daylight? And about Luke Rivers?

Suddenly she felt as though she couldn't get enough air, and she hopped down from the corral fence where she had perched herself and walked away. As intriguing as watching Luke work was, it had set off something ridiculously sensual in her system, and the last thing she wanted was another rodeo man muddling up her life.

Keith drove into the yard at about the same time Maris reached the house. She veered directions to see Blackie jumping out of the pickup right behind Keith. "Everything go okay?" she called, glad of any diversion to get her mind off Luke.

From the back of the pickup Keith picked up a huge sack of dry dog food. "Everything went fine. How's it going here?"

"Luke's in the corral, working with the first horse, and Judd stopped by for a few minutes."

Keith swung his gaze to the corral and saw what was happening. "Luke's a fast worker."

"Could be," Maris agreed dryly, recalling her hot flash a few minutes ago. "Anyway, looks like you've got Blackie all set."

Keith hoisted the bag of dog food to his shoulder. "These large sacks were marked down. Thought I may as well take advantage of the sale."

"Put it in the toolshed," Maris called as Keith walked off with his twenty-pound burden.

"Okay," he called back. Blackie was no more than six

inches behind her newly adopted master's bootheels. In watching the boy and dog, Maris nodded with fond approval. Keith had needed something of his very own, and maybe Blackie, stray, straggly little pooch that she was, was it.

Maris didn't immediately proceed into the house. Instead she stood with her hand splayed at the base of her throat and endured a peculiar throbbing in the pit of her stomach. Automatically her gaze slipped back to the corral and its occupants. Never would Luke throb over her, and her doing so over him was the height of foolishness, especially when she really wanted nothing but hard work from him. Actually, his deadline was rather ludicrous. How could any one person tame ninety-three wild horses in less than three months?

But that gray mare was responding incredibly well, she had to admit. Was Luke's touch special? He was still rubbing the animal, and talking to it. What was he saying? What magic was he breathing into that pretty mare's ears?

Sighing, slightly disgusted with her own lurid imagination, Maris turned her back on the corral, Luke Rivers and the mare. She had her own work to do...if she could only think of what it was.

By supper, Luke had moved the gray mare and three other horses into another pasture. Seated at the table with Keith and Luke, Maris said, "Please explain why you're moving the horses." She paused then added, "And don't take my curiosity as interference."

Luke looked at her sharply, then nodded. "Right. I'm picking out the calmest horses from the herd, one by one. Today's sessions with the four I moved to that other pasture went well, and I don't want them relearning bad habits from their pals. By the way, do either of you ride?"

"I do," Maris volunteered. "We used to have several good horses, and I enjoyed riding each of them. There's only one on the ranch now, though."

"What happened to the others?" Luke asked.

"Ray traded them for a car. It's behind the barn with the rest

of the—'' she stopped short of the word *junk* ''—things he purchased over the years.''

Keith's eyes lit up. ''It's a Corvette, Luke, a Sting Ray Coupe. Sure wish I knew how to get it running. It's really cool.''

''A Corvette, eh? Out behind the barn? Maybe I'll take a look after supper.'' He glanced at Maris. ''If you don't mind, of course.''

She shrugged. ''Why would I mind?''

Luke returned to his original question. ''Do you ride, Keith?''

The boy's cheeks got pink. ''I've only been on a horse a couple of times, Luke, but I really liked it.''

''Why, Luke?'' Maris questioned.

''Well, in a few days some of those horses are going to be ready for a rider. I'll ride them first to make sure they'll obey commands and won't try to throw the person off their back, but then they're going to need a lot of riding.''

''Heck, I'll do it,'' Keith exclaimed excitedly.

Maris frowned. She didn't want Keith getting hurt riding half-broken horses. ''Will it be dangerous?''

Luke glanced over at her and thought she'd never looked prettier than she did this evening in that red blouse she was wearing. ''I wouldn't put anyone on a dangerous horse, Maris. There are some in that pasture that will never be calm enough for either of you to ride. Here's my plan. Mother—that's the gray mare—will be the first horse I'll be riding. When she's ready for some real action I'm going to use her to move the three stallions from the main pasture to another. Probably the one with the cows. That big red bozo is the head honcho of the herd, and getting him and the younger stallions away from the other horses will calm them all down. It's going to have to be done from horseback, and Mother's going to be my mount.''

''Interesting,'' Maris commented. She was smiling. ''Are you going to name every horse?''

''Probably,'' Luke admitted with a grin. ''That tan gelding I

worked with after Mother has a curly tail, so his name is 'Curly.'"

"Naturally," Maris said with a laugh. "And the other two?"

"Zelda and Mickey."

Both Maris and Keith were laughing now. "So, we have Mother, Curly, Zelda and Mickey so far," Maris said.

"And Bozo," Luke reminded.

"Oh, yes, the big red stallion."

"You can sure count on me to ride 'em when they're ready," Keith said with unabashed enthusiasm.

"I'll do it, too," Maris said, though she cast a concerned glance at Keith. "Just be certain it's safe, Luke."

Taking a swallow of coffee, Luke saw and recognized Maris's affection for Keith. Was he a relative? The son of a friend who'd needed a summer job? He was a nice kid, Luke felt, and eager to get involved. Keith could be a big help with the horses, but from the protectiveness he detected in Maris's attitude toward the boy, he had better discuss it with her before mentioning it to Keith.

"It'll be safe, Maris," he told her. "You have my word on it."

His word. Maris fell silent. How good was Luke Rivers's word? Ray's "word" had been wasted breath, his promises forgotten the second they came out of his mouth. She had learned not to count on anything Ray said, but what about Luke? Regardless of the two men's common obsession with rodeo, she probably shouldn't be too hasty in judging them as being alike.

"I'll hold you to that," she told Luke with a steady look across the table. Luke returned the look, and their gazes suddenly locked in a brand-new and disturbing way. Maris felt that unnerving throbbing again; Luke admired her red blouse and the startling color of her hair and eyes. Keith was eating and noticed nothing, but both Luke and Maris were all too aware of the attraction between them. Both dropped their eyes and awkwardly began eating.

An unfamiliar nervousness sprang to life in Luke's gut. Maris

Wyler was off-limits. He sent her a quick, furtive glance. She *was* off-limits, wasn't she?

Maris's appetite was gone. She'd eaten about half the food on her plate, but it suddenly looked as tasteless as sawdust. She sat there, however, and pretended to eat by pushing the food around on her plate and occasionally bringing a teensy bite to her mouth.

Finally Luke and Keith were finished. "There's pudding for dessert," Maris announced tonelessly, wishing they would say they were too full for dessert. That look exchanged with Luke had put her on edge, because now she wasn't sure that he *wouldn't* throb for her.

At long last—it seemed an eternity to Maris—the meal was over. Luke pushed back his chair and got up to take his dishes to the sink. Keith and Maris did the same, and then the two men left the kitchen to go outside and Maris was alone.

Weakly she leaned against the sink counter. That "throbbing" business could be getting out of hand. How could she stop it? There must be a way to put an end to it.

Outside, Keith said, "Want to take a look at that Corvette, Luke?"

"Yeah, I'd like to see it." They began walking—with Blackie right behind them—toward the barn. "I didn't know there was a car parked back there."

Keith let out a whooping laugh. "There's a lot more than a car back there, Luke. Wait till you see."

Luke had figured that he'd explored the ranch pretty well, but obviously he'd missed the acreage behind the barn. His eyes widened with outright shock when he and Keith rounded the back corner of the barn and he saw what was out there: cars, trucks, tractors, a row of old refrigerators, electric motors rusting on the ground, a riding lawn mower, and much more, too many items to take in at one time. Knee-high weeds had grown up so thickly as to obscure some of the smaller objects.

"Good God," Luke muttered.

"The Corvette's over there," Keith said excitedly, starting to plow through the weeds and debris to a particular location.

Luke followed the boy to a red car propped up on blocks, its tires missing. There were rust spots in the red paint, but the body wasn't banged up. "I tried to start it one day," Keith confessed. "But nothing happened. The engine looks okay to me, but I'm not much of a mechanic. Do you know anything about engines, Luke?"

"Very little." He opened the Corvette's door and peered inside. "It has a four-speed manual transmission." The interior of the car was black leather and in pretty good condition. An idea was taking shape in his mind. He wasn't interested in old cars, but he knew someone who was. Maris just might pick up a sizable piece of cash for this baby.

"I'm going in to talk to Maris, Keith. There's a good chance that a fellow I know might be interested in buying this car."

"Really? Hey, that'd be great."

Blackie was sniffing around, and Keith began throwing a stick for Blackie to chase and bring back. "She's a real smart dog, Luke. Knows lots of tricks."

Grinning, Luke walked off. "See ya later." He hurried around the barn and to the house, where he walked in without any warning.

Maris jumped a foot. "Good Lord, you scared the stuffing out of me. I thought you were down by the barn with Keith."

"I was." She was just finishing up at the sink, Luke saw, wiping down the counters. "Maris, that Corvette has some value. Maybe some of that other stuff does, too, but I know a guy who collects old Corvettes and he just might be interested in yours. What do you say I give him a call?"

Holding the dishcloth, Maris turned. "You mean someone might actually pay good money for that junk?"

"That Corvette isn't junk, Maris. If my hunch is right, it's worth a good sum of money."

"And you know someone who might be interested? Well, yes, by all means, give him a call." It had never occurred to Maris that some of Ray's old junk might have any value. None of the vehicles ran, she knew, and everything was dirty and rusted and half-hidden by weeds. The place was an eyesore,

and one of her plans for the future, should she manage to save the ranch, was to hire a truck to haul off all that junk. To think that someone might buy even one item as it was, broken, rusted and not very pretty, was a thrill she could never have anticipated.

Luke sat down at the kitchen table to use the wall phone next to it. He dialed a long-distance number and spoke to Maris. "Hope Jim's at home." While Jim's phone rang in his ear, he watched Maris puttering, apparently too antsy to stand still.

Then the phone was picked up. "Hello?"

"Jim? This is Luke Rivers. How are you?"

"Luke! Well, I'll be a son of a gun. Thought you dropped off the face of the earth. Where you been, boy?"

"It's a long story, Jim, and I'm using someone else's phone. What I called about is an old Corvette I ran across. Are you still collecting them?"

"Sure am. What'd you find, Luke?"

"It's a Sting Ray Coupe. Original paint with some rust in spots, four-speed transmission and black leather interior, also original. It needs work, but it's nothing you couldn't handle."

"Do you know what engine it's got?"

Luke could hear the excitement in Jim's voice. "No, I don't. Frankly I didn't even look at the engine, though I know it's got one. But I wouldn't know what I was looking at if I stared at it for three days. Anyway, I was wondering if you'd like to come to Whitehorn, Montana, and take a look at it?"

"Whitehorn, Montana, eh? Well, sure, why not? You might have stumbled across a real find, Luke. Who owns it?"

"The lady I'm breaking a herd of horses for. It's the No Bull Ranch, Jim, about thirty miles northeast of Whitehorn."

Maris's stomach was churning with excitement. From Luke's end of the conversation, his friend Jim was indeed interested in the Corvette.

But now they were chuckling over the name of her ranch. Maris shot Luke an exasperated look, wanting to say, "Get to the point. Pin him down about when he can come and see the

Corvette.'' She said nothing, just stewed to herself and wiped the counters again, though they were already gleaming.

Luke put down the phone with a satisfied expression. "He'll be here within the week."

Maris's excitement totally eluded her control. "Oh, Luke, that's great! What if he buys it? How much do you think it's worth? To think it was sitting out there all this time and I never dreamed someone might buy it. Honestly, I feel so silly."

Luke got to his feet. "He hasn't bought it yet, Maris."

"But you think he might."

"I think there's a good chance, yes." He came around the table. "But I have no idea of the car's value, Maris. I have heard that some classic older cars bring high prices, but I don't think you should hang your hat on a large sum."

"Any sum looks good right now, Luke."

Luke was enjoying the spark of hope in her eyes and realizing an odd fact: it made him feel good to make Maris happy. His next thought wasn't nearly as high-minded, however. Recognizing desire streaking through his body, he drew a slow, uneven breath.

Maris blinked, suddenly aware that they were alone and that the kitchen was getting very dim, as she hadn't yet turned on any lights in the house. "Uh...maybe I'll go out and take a look at that Corvette myself." She started for the door, only to be stopped by a big hand on her arm. Her eyes lifted to Luke's, and what she saw caused that throbbing to begin again. "Please...don't," she whispered, wondering why in God's name her voice was deserting her at a time like this.

"Maris..." Luke took her by the shoulders and slowly brought her forward. She smelled wonderful, of soap and lotion and other feminine scents.

She couldn't move. In her mind's eye was a picture of Luke and Mother, the mare. Her own system was resisting common sense. His hands, his marvelous hands, were gently kneading her shoulders, and she knew he was going to kiss her.

He brought his face down to hers and very tenderly touched her lips with his. It felt so good and she didn't back away, so

he did it again. Her hands rose to clasp his forearms, and when he looked at her, he saw the glaze of pleasure in her eyes.

That was all he needed to see. Almost roughly, he swept her into a full embrace and kissed her the way a man *should* kiss a woman, with passion and possession and a message of raw hunger. Maris's knees got as limp as last year's carrots. When had she last been kissed like this? When had she *ever* been kissed like this? Luke's lips molded hers to fit his, then urged hers open to take his tongue. It was hot and slick and bold as brass, delving into every nook and cranny of her mouth. A red haze was developing behind her closed eyelids, and the throbbing in her stomach was intensified further by the sensation of his strong arms around her, the length of his body pressing into hers, by his male scent and heat.

It was a lover's kiss, and it scared her. Her own response scared her. Breathing hard, she twisted her head to free her mouth. "Stop," she moaned.

"Maris, honey..." He didn't want to stop. Where that explosive passion had come from, he would never know, but Maris had suddenly become the most desirable woman he'd ever known.

"Please." Extricating herself from his arms, she took a backward step and then had to hang on to the back of a chair to remain upright and steady. "This isn't me, Luke. I don't do this sort of thing." Her voice was shaky and thin.

He looked at her strangely. "What do I say to that? You kissed me back, Maris."

"I know, but you took me by surprise."

Luke took a forward step. "What's wrong with you and me sharing a kiss?"

It was not a subject to debate with him, not when she still felt his kiss on her mouth and her legs would barely hold her up. "Intimacy is not a part of our arrangement," she croaked, trying to sound calm and in control and failing abysmally.

Luke looked at her for the longest time. "But what if intimacy is what we want?"

Her eyes jerked upward to see his. "Do you always get what you want?"

"No, but I always try. Don't you, Maris? Don't you at least try to get what you want? What you need?"

"That's enough." Her legs felt a little stronger, and she left the chair and began moving toward the door. "Don't make any more passes, Luke. I want and need those horses broken, a whole lot more than I want what you just offered."

"There's no reason why you can't have both," he said softly.

She paused at the door to look at him. "You're wrong. There is a reason, and it's very important to me. I never did and never will have an affair." She opened the door. "Especially with a man whom I know in advance is only going to be around for a few months." Showing him her back, she stepped outside, and an enormous surge of relief hit her, because Keith and Blackie were coming toward her and the house. Keith's presence would deter Luke's determination to persuade her into thinking his way.

"Where's Luke?" Keith called.

"Right here," Luke said in a voice that caused Maris's back to stiffen. Without even addressing her, he had let her know that he didn't agree with her attitude against kisses and affairs.

Luke walked past both her and Keith. "I'm going to bed. Good night."

Keith looked at Maris with a perplexed expression. "What's wrong with Luke?"

Maris took a breath and lied through her teeth. "I couldn't begin to guess. Call it a mood." She formed a smile for Keith. "I think I'll go to bed, too. Good night, Keith."

"Well, heck," Keith mumbled. "It's still light out and everyone's going to bed."

"If you turn on the TV, please keep the volume down. 'Night, Keith." Maris went back into the house and directly to her bedroom.

She wasn't over the shakes yet, but she was beginning to wonder if anything would ever be normal again until after Luke Rivers left the No Bull.

Five

Luke waded through the weeds behind the barn, going from vehicle to vehicle to look them over, then inspected numerous electric and gasoline motors all but concealed by huge clumps of dandelions and overgrown wild grasses. He paused at the riding lawn mower and finally stopped his wandering near the row of old refrigerators, shaking his head in amazement, wondering why a man would collect and save so much junk. Maris had been right to ask if he'd known Ray at all; obviously he hadn't.

All morning while working with the horses, the junk strewn behind the barn had kept popping into his mind. What was junk to one person was pure gold to another. Take that Corvette, for example. Rusting away behind the barn it was worthless. But to Jim Humphrey the car was a collector's find. And if Jim found the car to his liking and bought it, it would no longer be worthless to Maris but cash in her pocket.

What if some of these other things could also be turned into cash? That was the question hounding Luke this morning, although the cold shoulder Maris had given him at breakfast was hardly an incentive to approaching her with any new ideas. He shouldn't have kissed her. Now she acted as though he was just lying in wait for another opportunity to grab her, which simply wasn't true. He understood the word *no* as well as Maris did and would abide by her wishes, even though he knew damned well that she had kissed him back and enjoyed it every bit as much as he had.

But...that was behind him. Behind *them*. Maris would soon realize it wasn't going to be repeated, and then she would relax around him again. In the meantime, he would act as though nothing had occurred in her kitchen last night, and he would

begin by going up to the house right now and talking to her about the veritable gold mine in back of the barn. Starting on his way, Luke had to chuckle. ''Gold mine'' was a terrible exaggeration, when the truth was that she might pick up a few bucks by selling some of that junk. But his impression of her financial straits was that even a few bucks would be welcome.

Maris had told Keith to finish repairing the section of fence he'd been working on for several days now, so Luke hadn't seen the boy since breakfast. He hadn't seen Maris, either, but then, he'd been so engrossed in whatever horse he'd been working with in the corral, he hadn't been watching for her. She hadn't, however, come near the corral.

He strode across the compound from barn to house and rapped on the screen door, as the inner door was wide open. ''Maris?''

Maris was in the kitchen, making sandwiches for lunch. She'd been out helping Keith with the fence repairs, and had returned to the house only a few minutes ago. Wiping her hands on a section of paper towel, she went to the screen door. ''Lunch will be ready in a few minutes.''

''Great, but that's not why I'm here. I need to talk to you about something.''

''Oh. Well, come on in.'' Maris backed away from the door and returned to the counter, with its array of bread, cold meat and condiments. She had vowed to remain aloof of Luke's personal charms, but she had to allow communication on anything concerning the horses. ''What is it?''

Luke was standing near the refrigerator, as that location provided a side view of what she was doing. ''I just took another look at the stuff behind the barn and I think some of it could be sold.''

Maris sliced a sandwich in half. ''Other than the Corvette, that stuff is pure junk. Why would anyone want it?''

''Some of it could be fixed up, Maris. Cleaned up, at least. That riding mower is missing its battery and its tires are flat, but maybe those are the only things wrong with it. If we could get it in shape and slap a coat of paint on it...''

Maris turned. "Do you have the time to do it?" It wasn't said kindly. If they were still counting on that September 30 deadline, which she was wholeheartedly doing, then every minute of Luke's time was already scheduled.

Luke's face hardened. "I'll find the time. Keith could help and so could you."

"Me!" Maris emitted a sardonic laugh. "I'm hardly a mechanic. Besides, with tending the herd and keeping this place from falling apart, I've got enough to do."

"Well, you can damned well find the time to wield a paintbrush and use a little soap and water!"

"Don't you dare get angry with me because I didn't jump for joy at your suggestion!" Maris drew a calming breath. She didn't want to argue with Luke; they were skating on thin ice as it was. "I'm sorry. Let's not fight about something so silly. I appreciate your calling your friend about the Corvette but—"

Luke folded his arms and interrupted. "Maybe you're not as broke as you let on. Appears to me that a person who's as short of money as you've led me to believe would jump at the chance to make a few bucks."

Maris's eyes widened. "I have not misled you, and I'm not a liar. But trying to sell that junk would be a waste of time."

"Come out there with me."

"Why?"

"Maris, don't be so damned obstinate. I'm trying to help you out here."

Her mind was cluttered with problems, and Luke was one of them. Why, even now when he was angering her by pushing her into doing something she thought utterly senseless, was she so aware of his good looks? And remembering how she'd felt in his arms?

With her jaw clenched, she draped a clean towel over the food on the counter. "Fine," she snapped. "I'll go with you."

They made the trek in silence, but Maris's temper had cooled considerably by the time they had rounded the barn and reached the junkyard. Luke began talking. "There are—I counted them—fifteen motors of various sizes and types lying in these

weeds. There are tools, electric saws, a lathe, woodworking equipment and on and on. You can see the old cars, trucks and tractors for yourself, and I have no intention of trying to put any of them in running order. Other than the riding lawn mower, which I think needs only minor repairs.''

"There is also a room filled with junk," Maris said wearily, far from convinced that anything out here—other than the Corvette—was worth two cents.

"A room? Where?"

"Through that door."

It was just another door to get into the barn, Luke had figured. "Is it locked?"

"Is anything on the ranch locked?"

Shooting her an irate look—she sure wasn't being very cooperative—Luke made his way through the weeds to the door and pulled it open. He stepped in and then stared in utter amazement. Picture frames, paintings, old clocks, tables, chairs, bedsteads, boxes and boxes of hand tools, stacks of galvanized pails, golf clubs, skis, tennis rackets—he had never seen so much stuff crammed into one small room before. Everything was coated with a thick layer of dust, but it had been protected from the weather and he could see that the wood tables and chairs, for instance, weren't warped and misshapen.

"Maris," he said slowly. "You could hold a yard sale to end all yard sales."

Ray's obsession with junk had annoyed and irked Maris so intensely for so long that she found it difficult now to alter her attitude. "Who would want it?" she scoffed, looking directly at an ugly lamp without a shade. "Would you want that thing in your house?"

Luke followed the direction of her gaze and had to laugh. "No, I wouldn't want that thing in my house. But someone else might fall in love with it."

"Yeah, right," she drawled. But one of the old clocks had drawn her attention. It was a grimy, dull-black color, but it had an ivory face and had the configuration of an ancient Greek building. Winding her way through the litter, she reached the

clock and touched it. Then she tried to pick it up, and found that she could hardly budge it. "This thing weighs a ton!" she exclaimed.

Luke came over to peer at it. "Looks like it's made out of marble."

Maris turned to survey the hundreds of objects crowded into the room. "Do you really think people would buy some of this junk? Wait! I know the person to ask, Winona Cobb. You had to pass her place on your way here, the Stop 'n' Swap? You must have seen it. Her front yard is littered with old sinks and hubcaps, and there are animals running everywhere. Winona is as eccentric as they come, but if anyone's an expert on junk around here, it's her."

"I don't think you need advice from anyone about holding a yard sale, Maris. Haven't you ever stopped at a garage or yard sale and seen the kind of stuff people are selling?" Luke gestured at the clutter. "You've got great junk, Maris."

The remark tickled Maris's funny bone. "Great junk?" she choked out as she started laughing.

Luke smiled broadly, enjoying the sight and sound of Maris laughing. When she had calmed down, he said, "Let's do it, Maris. Let's throw a yard sale that'll set Whitehorn back on its heels. You'll make a small fortune, I guarantee it."

Maris was beginning to warm to the idea. "It would take a lot of work. Everything in here needs a good cleaning."

"Keith and I could haul it outside and you could use the hose on most of it."

"We'd have to set it up in the front yard." Maris laughed wryly. "The No Bull would look like Winona's place."

"Only for a few days. Anything that doesn't sell we can haul to the dump."

It was really beginning to sink in. What didn't sell would be hauled to the dump. She would be *rid* of it, once and for all.

"The big pieces out back couldn't be moved to the front yard, though," Luke told her. "But Keith and I could chop down the weeds and clean up the area so people could check out the items for sale."

This time Maris was the one who folded her arms. "And who's going to be working with the horses while you're chopping weeds and hauling around furniture?"

"The horses come first," Luke said firmly. "Damn, Maris, I can do more than one thing at a time. Can't you? Can't anyone who really sets his mind to it?"

Maris's wheels were turning. A good two-thirds of the things in this room were light enough for her to carry outside for cleaning all by herself. Keith could chop down the weeds out back, and then she could put him to work helping her with the yard sale. Luke wouldn't have to do all that much on it and the horses wouldn't be neglected, which, of course, was a much more important undertaking than getting rid of this junk.

But the thought of the ranch being junk-free, finally, was elating. Someday she wanted white painted fencing around the close-in pastures instead of barbed wire, and someday she wanted every single building painted the same color. She'd been thinking—for a long time—of a soft blue-gray color with white trim.

"Someday" was still a long way off, but getting rid of this junk was an extremely satisfying first step to attaining her dream.

A smile lit her face. "You're absolutely right. I'll do it!"

"*We'll* do it."

Maris started out of the musty room. "Keith and I will do most of it. I want you to..."

Luke grabbed her arm, halting her flight. "Are you telling me to stay out of it?"

Surprised, she lifted her eyes to his. "It was your idea and I appreciate it, but you said yourself that the horses come first."

"And they will. But I can also help clean up this stuff."

Why was he so insistent on doing more than he'd bargained for? He was still holding her arm, they were still looking into each other's eyes, and it suddenly occurred to Maris to wonder if he wasn't doubling his work load because of her.

She flushed. What had happened in her kitchen last night was in Luke's eyes, and Lord help her, she wanted to move

closer to him, to walk into his arms and have him hold her, and kiss her, and touch her.

Luke knew exactly what she was thinking. "There's something happening with us, Maris. We can pretend it isn't, we can act as though we're nothing more than boss and employee, but we both know that's not true."

She dampened her suddenly dry lips. "I...told you how I feel about an..." She avoided the word *affair.* "Don't push me into something that can only hurt me after you're gone. This has never happened to me before. I knew only one man, I've slept with only one man, and he was my husband. Do you think I could sleep with you and then forget it after you drive away?"

Her words, so candid, so frank, startled Luke. "Ray was the only man? Ever?"

Oh, dear God. How could she have said such a thing to him? Profoundly embarrassed, Maris glanced away.

Luke looked at her turned face with its high color for a moment, then released her arm. "I told myself I wasn't going to try anything else with you. I'm sorry. It won't happen again." It was a monumental effort to speak so calmly, when what he wanted to do was dust down one of those old tables and lay her on it. He could almost see himself peeling down her jeans and opening his own, almost *feel* himself inside of her, loving her, kissing her sensual mouth and beautiful throat. The intensity of his desire for Maris was overwhelming and impossible to comprehend.

They walked out of the room not looking at each other, both shaken, both trying very hard to appear nonchalant and undisturbed.

"Well," Maris said with false brightness, "I'd better get back to the house and finish up lunch. It'll be ready in about ten minutes. Keith is probably on his way in."

"Go ahead. I'll be up in a few minutes." As Maris disappeared around the corner of the barn, he mumbled, "Run away, little girl, and keep on running, 'cause the big bad wolf is right on your heels." Then his own words disgusted him, and he

parked his hips against one of the old tractor wheels to berate himself.

But he was so hard he ached, and no amount of self-reproach was going to cool him off. Damn! Cursing under his breath, he hurried around to the front of the barn, went inside, took the stairs to the loft two at a time, threw off his clothes, gave his stubborn, erect member a poisonous look, turned the shower on to Cold and stepped under the icy spray.

Maris was becoming enthused about the yard sale idea. It would take at least two weeks to get everything ready, she figured. Along with cleaning each item, there were signs to make and distribute. Advertising the event in the newspaper was crucial to the success of the venture, but the ad shouldn't come out until the week just prior to the weekend of the sale. First things first, Maris thought determinedly, and the first chores, of course, were the sorting and cleaning.

That very afternoon she began by carrying out the stack of galvanized pails—three and four at a time—washed the dust out of them with the garden hose and turned them upside down to dry. During lunch she had told Keith of her plans, and he had immediately and eagerly offered to get involved. "Go back and finish the fence repairs," she had told him. "That job is nearly done and we have to keep our priorities in order. What Luke is doing comes before anything else. When he wants either of us to start riding those horses, that's what we'll do."

Luke had been rather grim lipped and silent throughout the meal. Not because of the horses and not because of the yard sale. But his own damned system was in some sort of rebellious mode and it was all because of Maris. He wasn't blaming her. It was himself, his own suddenly overactive libido that had him symbolically climbing the walls. He told himself to stop being such a damn fool. Women were a dime a dozen. He could walk into almost any tavern and find several of them sitting on bar stools or at tables with that expectant, inviting expression in their eyes. Of course, not every woman who went to a tavern

without an escort was looking for a man. In his experience, however, the percentages were definitely in his favor.

But it wasn't a woman he hadn't even met yet that had his blood racing; it was Maris. Maris Wyler, rancher and the widow of his old pal Ray. Maris, with her sun-streaked hair and lean, sensual body. And Maris wasn't cooperating. She wanted to cooperate, he knew, or thought he knew. But Maris had high morals and strict standards, and she was right about him leaving the minute those horses were sold, so he couldn't blame her for saying no. Understanding Maris's attitude didn't alter his own, however.

After lunch, Luke had gone into the pasture and roped a nervous piebald gelding. He alternated further sessions with Mother and the other horses already in the training process with new trainees. The piebald wasn't being taken in by Luke's gift of apples, nor did he let Luke get close enough to rub him down with the feed sack.

The sun was high in the sky and hot. The piebald danced around the corral like a puppet on a string, and Luke patiently kept after him until his shirt was wet with sweat. Maris was hauling out straight-backed wooden chairs from the storage room, and she just happened to be setting one down on the grass, when she looked over to the corral and saw Luke tossing his shirt.

She stood up straighter and stared, drawing in a slow, uneven breath. With the leather gloves on his hands, his faded jeans, his boots and no shirt, he was the most gorgeous specimen of mankind she had ever seen. Intent on the piebald, Luke wasn't aware of Maris watching. He deftly roped the horse's back leg with one loop, then the animal's opposite front leg with another. The ropes were pulled taut and tied to posts in the corral fencing. Blowing and snorting, the piebald tossed his head in fury, but he was unable to rear or run, and Luke walked over to the water spigot at the trough and got himself a drink. That was when he spotted Maris.

In one smooth, fluid movement, he hopped over the corral

fence and walked over to her. "That one's got a temper. He'll cool down after a while."

"You tied him down."

"Have to with some of them." Luke eyed the chairs. "Aren't these too heavy for you to be hauling around?"

Maris was trying not to look at his naked chest, but it wasn't possible to look at Luke at all without seeing it, especially when it was such a large chest. The impressive muscles of his shoulders, arms and chest rippled when he moved, and his skin was tan and looked as smooth as satin.

"They're not too heavy," Maris murmured, slightly breathlessly. "You're very good with a rope."

The left corner of Luke's lips turned up in an acknowledging half smile. "I've had a lot of experience. I wish you'd let me or Keith carry the heavy stuff."

"These chairs aren't too heavy for me. I'll let you know when something is. How long do you think it will take for that horse to calm down?"

Luke shrugged. "Not long. I'm going to put a saddle on Mother while I'm waiting."

"She's ready for riding?"

"No, but she's ready for a saddle. I'll leave it on her for two or three hours. She has to get used to the weight of a saddle on her back and the stirrups bumping her during movement."

Maris was beginning to understand that Luke had a pattern in his training of the horses. She smiled over it. "You work like an assembly line."

That little half grin flashed again. "Guess you could say that. I'm pretty satisfied with the way things are going. 'Course, I've saved the worst of the lot for last. When Mother's ready for riding it'll go a little easier. As I told you before, I intend to move Bozo and the other stallions out of the herd. They'll all be much calmer then."

"The stallions disrupt the others?" In spite of her determination to avoid looking directly at Luke's chest, she spotted a two-inch scar near his left nipple.

"The stallions are constantly aroused and keeping the herd, especially the mares, stirred up."

"Like when a bull is turned into the cows' pasture," Maris murmured absently, her thoughts on that scar.

"Did you used to have a bull?"

Putting Luke's manly chest with its two-inch scar out of her mind, Maris sighed. "He was sold with most of our other cattle. That's when Ray bought these horses."

Luke frowned. "Was he going to hire someone to do the breaking for him?"

She merely shook her head. "I don't know," she said, sounding a little broken herself. The subject was defeating, one of the trials she had lived through with Ray without ever understanding why he did what he did.

Bending over for the garden hose, she turned the spray on the chair. "Some of these things are going to need scrubbing with soap and water," she remarked. "Anything wood will have to have a coat of furniture polish, as well."

Luke was almost sorry he'd suggested the yard sale. Already he could tell that Maris was going to make too much of it. Everything for sale didn't have to look as though it had just come off of a showroom floor.

He watched her for a moment, then began walking off, heading for the barn for a rope and a saddle to take out to Mother's pasture. "See you later."

"Yeah, see you later," Maris said under her breath. But she looked up to get another glimpse of Luke's remarkable torso. A small groan rose in her throat. No man should look the way he did without a shirt.

Maris was busily scrubbing a filthy table with a sponge and a bucket of warm, soapy water, when a car drove into the compound. A strange car. "Maybe that's your friend coming to see the Corvette," she called to Luke.

The roan in the corral was behaving much better than the piebald, and Luke had been rubbing the animal down with the blanket. He turned to see the car and then grinned when Jim

Humphrey got out. "That's him," he called to Maris. "Come and meet him."

Maris dropped the sponge into the bucket and dried her hands on one of the old towels she'd brought out from the house, along with a basket of cleaning supplies.

The three of them met about midway between Jim's car and the corral. "Hey, Rivers, you look half-broken yourself," Jim exclaimed with a big grin. He glanced at Maris. "Hello, ma'am. Are you the reason this big galoot seems to be finally settling down?"

Maris's face turned beet-red. Luke quickly came to the rescue. "This lady is Maris Wyler, Jim, the owner of this place. I'm working for her."

Jim grabbed Maris's hand and energetically shook it. "Glad to meetcha, Maris. Then you must be the proud owner of that Corvette Luke called me about."

Despite Jim's hasty and certainly uncalled-for assessment of the situation, Maris couldn't dislike him. He was a jolly-looking man with a cherubic face and a constant smile. She couldn't help noticing the enormous diamond on his pinky ring, or his casual but unmistakably expensive clothing. Obviously, if Jim Humphrey liked the Corvette, he could afford to buy it.

"It's out behind the barn, Mr. Humphrey. Would you like to see it right away, or perhaps you'd rather come into the house and have something cold to drink first?"

"Corvette first, cold drink later," Jim boomed with a hearty laugh. "And for Pete's sake, call me 'Jim.'"

Maris smiled. "If you wish. Luke, would you show Jim the car? There's something I need to do in the house." It wasn't true. There was nothing she needed to do in the house, but she was suddenly nervous about the car, and Luke could probably handle it much better than she could.

The two men walked off, talking and laughing. Apparently they were old friends and glad to see each other. Maris did go into the house, first so she wouldn't look like a liar, and second because she was too flustered to return to her sponge and bucket of soapy water. Jittery, she moved from one window in the

house to the next. What if Jim liked the car and actually bought it? How much would he pay for it? Would he make an immediate decision or ask for time to consider it?

Oh, damn, maybe she *should* have gone with them. At least then she would know what they were saying about the car.

To do something besides worry and fret, Maris made a pitcher of lemonade, using fresh lemons. It was almost an hour before she saw Luke and Jim coming around the barn, and by then she was totally frazzled. Springing to life, she fixed a tray with the pitcher of lemonade and three glasses containing ice cubes. Before the two men had reached the tiny patio at the back of the house, Maris had the tray sitting on the round table and she was smiling, as any sane and sensible person would be doing.

"Is that lemonade I see in that pitcher?" Jim asked jovially.

"It certainly is," Maris replied. She filled the three glasses and passed them around. They drank and looked at one another and smiled at one another and everything seemed just peachy. "Well," said Maris. "Would you like to sit down?"

"For a minute," Jim replied.

They all sat around the table. "Wonderful lemonade. It's not from a mix, I'll bet," Jim said.

"No, I used fresh lemons."

"I can always tell the difference," Jim said with unmistakable pride in his apparently trustworthy palate. "Well, young woman, I can tell you right now that I want that car. All we have to do now is settle on a price."

Relief washed through Maris, immediately followed by panic. "Uh...price, yes. Well..." She looked to Luke for help, but he was sipping his lemonade and ignoring her silent plea. To his way of thinking, it was Maris's car and she should do the dickering. Of course, if old Jim should offer too little for the 'Vette, he might step in and help Maris out.

"I'll tell you about your car, Maris," Jim said matter-of-factly. "The body can be repaired without too much expense, but Corvette wheels are costly and it has no tires. The standard engine in that model was a 300-bhp V8, but your 'Vette has

the engine I'd hoped to see in it. It has the L-71 Tri-carb, which makes it a 435-bhp. Plus, it has the four-speed manual transmission. Put it all together, and we're talking power, young woman, power and speed.''

Maris smiled weakly, grasping none of it. ''I'm sure it would be a very pretty car...if repaired, of course.''

''Pretty!'' Jim guffawed so loudly, Maris jumped. ''A Corvette is an object of rare beauty, Maris.'' He talked on and on, using phrases like ''independent suspension'' and ''cubic inches'' and then talking about wheelbase measurements and front/rear weight distribution.

Finally Jim ran down and stopped lauding the merits of his favorite automobile. His expression became serious. ''The thing we don't know is how much work the engine needs, Maris. How long have you owned it?''

''Um...about two years.''

''And it was running then?''

''Oh, no,'' Maris replied. ''It never ran while we owned it. My husband traded—''

Luke hastily interrupted. ''That's all beside the point, Jim. Maris never drove the car and I really don't think she knows very much about it. Isn't that true, Maris?''

''Very true.'' Thank God Luke had finally spoken. Why on earth had he been sitting there all this time without saying something?

''Well...'' Jim looked off into the distance, apparently pondering the matter. ''I'm prepared to pay three thousand for the car.''

Maris's mouth dropped open. She had never even come near a figure that high. One thousand had been a hope, but certainly not three.

''It's worth more than that, Jim,'' Luke said with a male-to-male laugh. ''You know it, I know it.''

''Thirty-five hundred,'' Jim said, adding, ''there could be damage to the undercarriage, Luke. Without putting it on a lift, there's no way of knowing.''

''Five thousand,'' Luke said calmly.

"Five!" Jim laughed. "You're dreaming, Luke."

Luke sat there as cool as could be. "When that car is refurbished, it'll be worth twenty-five thousand, maybe more. That's something else we both know." It was a bluff. Luke knew that classic automobiles carried a high value, but he'd pulled that figure of twenty-five thousand out of the air.

"Yeah, but how much will it take to refurbish it? I'll go four thousand, and that's being damned generous, Luke."

"Forty-five hundred and we've got a deal," Luke returned.

Maris's startled gaze was going back and forth between the two men. They were actually thrilled to be sitting here dealing on the price of her car! She would have accepted the three thousand and been glad to take it. But she could see that Jim had *expected* some debate on the price and would probably have been disappointed not to get it.

Silently sighing, she sat back in her chair. Men and women were completely different creatures. Was it any wonder they didn't get along? Or that they rarely understood one another?

Jim stood up and offered his hand. "Deal!"

Luke nudged Maris. "He's talking to you, Maris."

"Oh!" Hastily she got to her feet and shook hands with Jim Humphrey. "Thank you." Forty-five hundred dollars for what she'd considered to be just another piece of junk behind the barn. She could hardly believe it.

Six

That night before going to bed, Maris looked again at the five-hundred-dollar check Jim Humphrey had given her. "You'll get the balance when I pick up the car, Maris. Probably in a week or two."

So she still didn't have a large sum of money in her possession, but things were definitely looking up. If the yard sale was a success and then the horse auction, she could start running the ranch the way it used to function. From old accounting records and photograph albums, Maris had proof that the Circle W had once been a thriving, profitable operation. Her dreams went further than those old records and photos, though. It wasn't that she yearned for wealth, but she did want financial security. Living in beautiful surroundings would be wonderful, too. When she was married to Ray, she'd never known one minute to the next what to expect. She'd make plans for the ranch, only to have him pull the rug out from under her. Now that she was on her own and getting out of debt things would be different.

Maris put away the check, opened a window for fresh air, turned off the light and crawled into bed. Her body was tired. Other than sitting down for meals and to talk to Jim Humphrey, she had been on her feet and working at one job or another all day. She lay there thinking of all that was going on—the preparations for the yard sale, Luke's work with the horses, the unexpected windfall of Jim Humphrey buying that old Corvette.

A frown creased her forehead as a startling thought struck her: everything happening on the ranch was Luke's doing! Because of that IOU, Luke had come up with the idea of him breaking her horses and holding a big whoop-de-do—his word—auction; Luke was the one who'd recognized the value

of the Corvette and then just happened to have a friend who collected older-model 'Vettes; and last, it was Luke who had suggested the yard sale.

Rather than feeling grateful that Luke had such a versatile imagination, Maris felt slightly wounded that every good idea to make money for the ranch had come from him. Where had *her* imagination been hiding? Why hadn't she seen the potential of Ray's junk?

Agitated and suddenly not tired at all, Maris threw back the blankets and got out of bed. Finding her robe and slippers without a light, she put them on and walked through the dark house to the kitchen, where she stood at the window and stared out at the compound to ponder Luke's involvement not only with the ranch but with her. The man had nothing of his own other than a pickup truck, and no one could ever accuse Luke Rivers of being dense or dull-witted. He recognized opportunity and didn't hesitate to act upon it, and wasn't a widow with a nice little ranch that could be a whole lot nicer a perfect opportunity for an unscrupulous man to better his lot in life?

A dull ache began in Maris's chest. Was that why he'd kissed her? Did he think her so lonely and vulnerable, so in need of a man, that she would be easy to woo into submission and ultimately some kind of partnership that would give him control of her ranch?

But he was looking forward to leaving at the end of September, a voice in Maris's head reminded. Anxious to return to rodeo.

Another voice argued, *That could all be an act to put you off guard.*

Was it an act? Was Luke unscrupulous? Was she a fool?

Her business arrangement with Luke regarding the horses didn't make her a fool, Maris decided. Neither did grasping his idea for the yard sale. And certainly she appreciated his assistance in selling the Corvette.

But most definitely there was some of the fool lurking within her when she admired, with weak knees and a palpitating heart,

his physique without a shirt, or responded with soft, pliant lips to his kisses.

As she stared out into the darkness, her gaze lingered on the ground area lighted by the lamp at the top of a tall pole near the barn. Her chin lifted in a show of defiance, though there was no one to see it. There would be no more kisses between her and Luke, no more girlishly breathless glances at him while he worked with the horses. She would not be taken in by an unscrupulous man, however much he turned on the charm.

Maris narrowed her eyes. Someone—it had to be Luke, as Keith had gone to bed several hours ago—was down by the barn. She squinted to see what he was carrying and couldn't quite make it out. Why on earth was he still up, and what was he doing?

Without further speculation, Maris sped from the kitchen and through the door into the night. Her slippers fell softly on the grass of the backyard lawn and then on the hard-packed dirt between the lawn and barn. Luke had gone inside and turned on a light. She found him in the tack room.

Thinking that Maris had retired because of the dark house, he looked at her with surprise. "Anything wrong?"

Her gaze darted, as though searching for something out of place, or missing. "What are you doing out here so late?"

"Putting away the saddles I used on Mother and Zelda this afternoon. Why?"

His dedication annoyed her, probably because of her doubts about his scruples a few minutes ago. "You don't have to work all night, you know," she said tartly.

Luke held up a hand. "Wait a minute. You couldn't possibly be angry because I'm doing my job, so why don't you just come right out and say what's got your tail in a knot?"

Maris's head lifted until she was looking down her nose at him. "I don't think you need to use that tone of voice with me."

"You can use any uppity tone you please but I can't speak my mind? Forget that notion, Maris." He brushed past her. "It's late and I'm beat. Good night."

She stared, openmouthed because he would be so rude, as he headed for the tack room door, and felt fury solidifying in her belly. "Sometimes I think you forget which one of us *owns* this ranch and which one merely works on it." She hurled the words at his retreating back.

Luke came to an abrupt halt and then slowly turned around. "What's that supposed to mean? Why don't you cut the crap and tell me why you're out here at eleven o'clock at night trying to pick a fight?" He took a step toward her. "Is that what you want, Maris, a no-holds-barred fight? Maybe I've been doing something that's been rubbing you wrong. Or maybe I *haven't* been doing something you want done real bad."

She was suddenly wishing she hadn't come out here at all, let alone yelled at him. "I didn't mean to pick a fight," she said as haughtily as she could manage. "I saw you carrying something, and I merely wondered what you were doing out here so late."

"Yeah, right. When I told you what I was doing, what did you do?"

"I..." She tried hard to remember. "I didn't do anything!"

Luke took another forward step. "You told me in a smart-assed way that I didn't have to work all night. You were ticked when you walked in here, and since you were nice as pie during dinner, something happened to change your mood. What was it?"

The dark glower in Luke's eyes was intimidating. His un-buttoned shirt and beltless jeans were intimidating. Maris's eyes widened. "You were in bed and then remembered that you'd left the saddles on the horses!"

"So?"

"So, nothing. I'm sorry I bothered you." This time Maris brushed past him. He was only half-dressed, the same as her, even though her robe was ankle-length and tightly closed by a sash. Maybe she did want to pick a fight with him, but this was neither the time nor the place to do it.

Luke neatly hooked a finger into the sash at the back of her

waist and yanked her backward. His arms closed around her. Maris gasped. "Just stop it! I didn't come out here for this!"

He was breathing into her hair, causing her scalp to tingle. "*I* think this is exactly what you came out here for. *I* think you were lying in your bed all alone and picturing me out here alone in my bed. It's a terrible waste, isn't it, you in one bed, me in another?" His voice had grown husky. "Damn, Maris, we could make some mighty sweet music together."

Her traitorous mind painted the image he'd suggested. Sweet music. Her eyes closed as the throbbing between her legs began again. Her aching breasts reminded her of the many unhappy, lonely nights she'd spent as a woman tied to a man who hadn't considered her pleasure since the first year of their marriage. The first few months, to be more accurate.

But what made Luke any different? Hadn't she and Lori, her best friend, talked endlessly about that very subject? And wasn't Lori's attitude virtually the same as her own—that a happy, romantic marriage was just a fruitless fantasy?

Besides, Luke wasn't offering marriage. He was offering her his bed and a night of sweet music.

She went limp and spoke listlessly. "Let go of me."

Her abrupt change of mood startled Luke into obeying. But he was breathing erratically and his body was uncomfortably geared up for that "sweet music."

"Go on. Get out of here," he said wearily. He couldn't resist a parting shot, however. As Maris hurried through the door, he yelled, "The next time you come looking for a fight—or something—in the middle of the night, count on getting it!"

Maris ran from the barn and kept on running all the way to the house.

"Keith, would you mind doing the grocery shopping for me this week? I don't want to stop working on the things for the yard sale." The telephone rang. Maris went to pick it up and said, "Hello, would you hold for a moment, please?" Then she held her hand over the phone's mouthpiece to finish up with

Keith. "The grocery list and money are on the counter. Your paycheck is there, too."

Grinning, Keith walked over to the counter and gathered up the money, the grocery list and his paycheck. Earning his own money was the greatest feeling he'd ever had. "Thanks, Maris. See ya later." He went out the door whistling through his teeth.

Maris returned to her caller. "Sorry to keep you waiting."

"It's just me, Maris."

"Lori! Hi, how are you?" Maris sat down. "It's been ages since we talked."

"I'm fine...busy, as usual. How are you?"

Lori Parker Bains was a nurse and a midwife. She was an absolute doll with her gorgeous blond hair and big blue eyes, but her looks had never gone to her head and she had been Maris's best friend since childhood. Lori had married her high school sweetheart, Travis Bains, but it hadn't lasted, so, in a way, she and Maris were in almost the same boat as far as their manless lives went.

Maris took a breath. "I've been busy, too. There's a lot going on right now."

"You needn't say another word. I've heard all about the hunk you've got working out there. The word around town is that he looks like Mel Gibson."

"The movie star? Good Lord, where did you hear that?"

"From the gals at the Hip Hop. Incidentally, John Tully is taking all the credit for sending him out to your place to ask for a job. Seems very proud of himself for having been so helpful."

Maris groaned. "Oh, God. Do you mean to tell me the whole town is talking about Luke working out here?"

"Afraid so, kiddo. Is it true? Does he look like Mel Gibson?"

"Of course he doesn't look like Mel Gibson. I've never heard of anything so ridiculous. He's nice-looking, but he's certainly not movie-star material." If she were Pinocchio, her nose would be four inches longer, Maris thought disgustedly.

Luke might not look precisely like Mel Gibson, but he was every bit as handsome.

"Methinks the lady doth protest a little too much," Lori quipped in her ear with a laugh.

"Come and meet him for yourself," Maris retorted.

"At the very first opportunity, my friend."

They talked for about fifteen minutes, about other topics than Luke Rivers, then signed off with promises to see each other very soon.

Maris sat there more than a little disgruntled. Damned gossips. Why was everyone else's business so interesting to some people? Didn't they have enough to do keeping their own lives on course? Or were they so bored with their own routines and ruts that they became titillated over a widow hiring a man to break her horses? Of course, Luke really *was* unusually good-looking....

Slapping her palms on the table, Maris pushed herself to her feet. She was tired of the topic, and if one person—other than Lori, of course—dared to mention Luke Rivers to her with a smug twinkle in his or her eye, she would let him have it with both barrels.

Luke was riding Mother. Maris stood with the soapy sponge in her hand and surprise on her face. He was in the secondary pasture, putting the mare through a variety of paces—a walk, a gallop, a trot. Mother tossed her head every so often, but obeyed Luke's commands. Dropping the sponge into the bucket of water, Maris deserted the old sideboard she'd been scrubbing down and hurried over to the fence to watch.

The grace and ease of Luke's performance awed Maris. He was a wonderful rider, using both the reins and his legs to guide the mare. Around and around the pasture they went, then, without warning, Luke would head the mare for the fence, draw back on the reins and call "Whoa!" The mare stopped, of course, not wanting to tangle with barbed wire. But Maris could see that the animal was learning what the word *whoa* meant.

Maris stayed at the fence for some time, but when she real-

ized that Luke wasn't merely taking a short ride, she returned to the sideboard. Before reaching into the bucket for the sponge, she brushed back a stray lock of hair on her forehead with the back of her hand. At the same time she spotted an approaching vehicle. Smiling, she started walking to the parking area to greet Jessica Larson McCallum. Only last week Jessica had married Sterling McCallum, and if two people were ever more mismatched, Maris hadn't met them.

But the newly wed Jessica had a glow these days that was pure magic, which couldn't help denting Maris's theory that men and women simply were not compatible.

"Hello, Jessica," she called ahead.

"Maris, how are you?" Jessica called back while getting out of her pickup truck.

"It's nice seeing you. Come inside and we'll have a glass of iced tea."

"Thank you. I could use a cool drink."

Jessica was tall and slender and quite pretty. In sending her a sidelong glance on their way to the house, Maris decided that Jessica was *very* pretty. Had falling in love added depth to her looks?

They entered the house through the kitchen door. "How is Sterling?" Maris asked.

"Wonderful, beautiful, loving, lovable..." Jessica stopped to laugh. "I could go on and on and bore you to tears."

"You're happy."

"Ecstatic, Maris. And baby Jennifer...well, words escape me when it comes to Jenny. But—" smiling teasingly, she pulled out her wallet "—I just happen to have a few pictures of her."

The baby had been left on the Kincaids' doorstep in April. No one could understand why they had been chosen, though everyone seemed to agree that boring, Milquetoast Dugin Kincaid was hardly the type of man to be roaming around the countryside, fathering children. Certainly Jeremiah Kincaid, Dugin's father, although still a vigorous man with an eye for pretty women, had been too old for those kinds of shenanigans. Of course, Maris thought, looks can be deceiving. It was more

likely though that whoever left the baby chose the Kincaids simply because they were the wealthiest folks in town.

After the baby had gone into the social-services system Sterling McCallum had tried to find her mother, or anyone related for that matter, without success. Jessica, who was the head of social services, had gotten so involved with the child she'd arranged to become Jennifer's foster mother after marrying Sterling. Now, if everything worked out, Jessica, Sterling and Jennifer were going to be a happy family.

Looking at the photos, Maris's eyes filled with tears. She would never have such a beautiful little family, but maybe she could adopt a child on her own. Adoption was probably the *only* way she would ever have a baby of her own. ''Oh, Jessica, she's the most beautiful baby I've ever seen,'' Maris said, all but bawling with emotion.

Jessica was blinking back a few tears of her own. ''Sterling and I think so.''

Maris handed back the wallet and went to the refrigerator for the pitcher of iced tea.

''How's Keith doing, Maris?''

Jessica was the social worker who had brought Keith to the Wyler ranch. Jessica had called soon after Ray had died and explained his situation, and Maris's heart had immediately gone out to the troubled, abused boy. She'd needed no time at all to consider helping Keith Colson; instead she'd told Jessica to bring him at once.

Maris brought the tea and two tumblers containing ice cubes to the table. ''Keith is doing great, Jessica, and that's—'' she grinned ''—no bull.'' The two women laughed over Maris's little pun. ''Seriously,'' Maris continued, seating herself at the table with Jessica, ''he's a great kid.'' Her gaze met Jessica's. ''I wish he were my son.''

Jessica sighed softly. Maris had a good heart. Most people who suffered a sudden loss, as she had with Ray, wouldn't have been able to take a boy like Keith into their home and treat him so kindly.

''I know you're grieving, Maris, but time heals all sorrows.

Most of us have lost someone important. It just takes time to get over it. Not that you'll ever forget Ray, but in time your pain will diminish.''

"Grieving?" A moment of embarrassment pinkened Maris's cheeks. She liked Jessica, but didn't know her very well, certainly not the way she knew Lori, so there were some subjects she couldn't talk about with ease. And maybe she should be grieving. Maybe she should be wallowing in self-pity because her husband had died. "Uh...yes," she said lamely.

"Is Keith working somewhere on the ranch right now?" Jessica inquired. "I'd like to say hello."

Keith was a much more comfortable topic. "He went to town today." Maris smiled. "Armed with my grocery list for the week."

"And the cash to purchase the food?"

"I would trust Keith with anything on the ranch, Jessica." Maris leaned forward. "I would swear on a Bible that he will never get into trouble again."

"If that's true, it's your doing." Jessica reached out and touched Maris's hand. "Thank you. I just knew that all Keith needed was a chance, Maris. You've given it to him, and I truly believe that what goes around comes around. For your own kindness, you'll be rewarded in some way. You'll see." Jessica began gathering up her purse. "I'll be running along. Tell Keith hello for me. I'll drop in again when I'm out this way."

"Anytime, Jessica."

It wasn't until Maris was back outside and scrubbing the sideboard that she realized Jessica hadn't mentioned Luke. Apparently there were some people in the area who didn't listen to gossip, thank goodness.

While Keith carried in the groceries, Maris began putting them away. When everything was unloaded, Keith laid some money on the counter. "That's your change."

"Thanks, Keith." Placing canned goods on a shelf, Maris said, "Jessica stopped by to say hello." Instantly a wary glint appeared in Keith's eyes. "I told her you were doing great, so

please don't worry about your future. You're welcome to stay here for as long as you want.''

Keith looked down at his boots. ''Uh...even after school starts?''

Maris went to the boy and took his hand. ''Keith, I told you before that you can finish your schooling from here. Jessica told you the same thing. This is your home now.'' She smiled. ''What on earth would I do without you? You're the only family I have.''

Keith rarely mentioned his own family, especially his abusive father, and Maris never pushed him into talking about his past. But sometimes, like now, Keith's youthful dark eyes contained more pain than she cared to see in anyone's eyes.

''Enough of that,'' she said lightly, giving Keith's hand a playful shake. ''I've got a new job for you. Luke has been riding Mother and Curly today. What I want you to do is to ignore everything else and help Luke with the horses.''

''No kidding?'' Keith's lapse into sadness completely vanished. ''Can I start right now?'' he asked eagerly.

Maris started putting food away again. ''Go out and talk to Luke about it. I really haven't had the chance, what with one thing and another all day. But you heard him say those horses were going to need a lot of riding once he got them to a certain stage.''

''Uh...Maris, I bought you a little gift.''

Maris had noticed the bulge in his shirt pocket, but really hadn't given it any thought. Now Keith reached into the pocket and brought out a small object wrapped in pink tissue paper. ''It ain't much,'' he mumbled sheepishly, holding out the tiny package. ''But it sort of reminded me of you...when I saw it.''

With her heart melting, Maris accepted the package. So she wouldn't cry, she forced a little laugh. ''They always say the best presents come in small packages.'' Gently she removed the tissue wrapping and saw a delicate, heart-shaped porcelain trinket. ''Oh, it's beautiful, Keith.''

''It's a little box,'' he explained. ''The top comes off.''

The ''top'' was decorated with miniature red roses and green

leaves. Never had a gift touched Maris more. But why would this fragile, lovely little object remind Keith of her?

"The woman at the store told me that ladies keep things in little boxes like this." He frowned. "But it sure wouldn't hold anything very big, would it?"

It was already holding something for Maris that was more valuable than diamonds—Keith's affection. "I'll find something to put in it, never fear, and I intend keeping it on the top of my dresser so I can see it every day. Thank you." She gave him a quick kiss on the cheek and then saw the pleased surprise on his face. "I'll treasure it always. Run along now and talk to Luke."

The boy bounded from the house and let the screen door bang behind him. Maris smiled wistfully and looked at the tiny box in her hand. "It really is beautiful," she whispered. No one had ever given her anything quite like it before. She was not a porcelain-and-miniature-roses sort of woman.

At least she had never thought of herself that way.

Luke noticed Keith hanging on the corral fence. The horse he was working with at the present was a handsome animal. It had the configuration of a quarter horse with the distinct black-and-white spotted markings on its rump and loins of the Appaloosa. This was the first horse of Maris's herd that really excited Luke. He'd already named him Rocky, and he liked the way the animal moved, even though Rocky wasn't exactly receptive to Luke's advances.

Giving both Rocky and himself a breather, Luke walked over to the spigot, turned it on and splashed water over his head, arms and bare chest. "Hot today," he called to Keith.

"Yeah, real hot," Keith agreed.

After shaking the water out of his eyes, Luke ambled over to the fence. "So, how's it going in town?"

Keith shrugged. "Same as always."

"Do your friends live in town?"

"Uh…yeah, most of them." It was a tough question to answer, because his previous friends weren't going to be his

friends when school started and he had to start mingling with his peers again. That was okay with him. He liked living like normal folks, and he wasn't going to screw up and do something to ruin what he had on the No Bull. Which meant finding new friends, kids who didn't get their kicks from stealing and vandalizing other people's property.

"Maris said I should talk to you about helping with the horses. She said you were riding Mother and Curly today. Are they ready for riding now, Luke?"

"Mother is. You can start riding her in the morning. I'll ride Curly a little more before turning him over to you." Luke grinned. "Glad to have you on the team, Keith, but I can almost guarantee you're going to get tired of riding before we're through with the herd."

"I won't, Luke. I know I won't." Keith gazed admiringly at the horse in the corral. "He's kind of special-looking, ain't he? How come he's got those spots on his rump?"

"Those spots are called a blanket, Keith. He's an Appaloosa, and someone bred him to get that exact effect in his coloring. Breeding Appaloosas isn't a simple matter. Mating an Appaloosa stud with an Appaloosa mare doesn't guarantee an Appaloosa foal."

"No kidding? That's kind of odd, ain't it?"

Luke ran his fingers through his wet hair, smoothing it back from his forehead. "It's just a trick of nature, I guess."

"Did you grow up on a ranch?"

Luke nodded. "In Texas."

Keith looked at the handsome animal standing on the other side of the corral. "You sure were lucky, Luke. I really like living on a ranch."

Luke was studying the boy. "Then you lived in town before this summer?"

"I've been here since May—just after Ray died."

"I see." There was a story behind Keith's connection to Maris and the ranch, Luke decided. For one thing, no one ever mentioned his family, or if he even had one. In fact, Maris had been very closemouthed about Keith right from the first.

"Are you related to Maris?" Luke quietly asked.

"No, but I wish I was. Hey, he's pawing the ground. Is he getting mad, Luke?"

Luke looked back at the Appaloosa and grinned. "He'd rather be out in the pasture. Well, I'd better get back to work. Me and Rocky are going to be friends, though he doesn't know it yet."

"You named him Rocky? Cool," Keith commented with an approving grin. "Is it okay if I stay out here and watch you work?"

"Yeah, it's fine. Just don't yell or make any sudden movements, okay? And keep Blackie on your side of the fence."

"Okay."

At supper that evening Keith talked on and on about Luke and Rocky. "You should've seen how Luke calmed him down, Maris. He rubbed him all over with an old sack, then with a blanket. Rocky loved it."

"I've seen the process," Maris said with a glance at Luke, who instantly sent her a grin that she saw as masculine smugness. Obviously he was basking in Keith's enthusiastic admiration and the whole situation worried her. Luke Rivers, after all, was not the best role model for a boy like Keith.

That was something she should have considered before this, she realized uneasily. Keith was all but bursting with elation because he was going to be helping Luke with the horses, and she couldn't very well reverse herself on that decision now.

She made another decision. After dinner was over she would talk to Luke and ask him to avoid telling Keith stories about his wild-and-woolly good times on the rodeo circuit. Maris actually shuddered at the thought of that sort of camaraderie developing between the two of them. She would be crushed if Keith followed in Ray's and Luke's footsteps, particularly since it would be her fault for exposing the boy to a man of Luke's feckless nature.

Immediately after dinner, she firmly resolved that whatever it took, she was going to talk to Luke alone. This was not going to be a conversation for Keith to overhear.

Seven

"Luke, would you teach me how to use a rope the way you do?"

Still seated at the dinner table, though everyone had finished eating, Maris let her gaze drift from boy to man. Keith was no longer shy with Luke and was, in fact, developing a bad case of hero-worship. Maris opened her mouth to intervene, but Luke answered before she could suggest that learning to use a rope really wasn't a very high-priority item.

"Be glad to, Keith. How about a lesson right now?"

Keith's excitement had him up and heading for the door at once, and Maris's heart sank. Luke, grinning at the boy's enthusiasm, stood up to follow.

"Luke," Maris said in a low voice. "I need to talk to you."

Luke's entire expression changed, his face taking on a predatory cast. "Anytime, babe. Just say the word."

Maris's eyes flashed angrily. "I *said* talk!"

"Luke? Are you coming?" Keith called from just outside the door, obviously anxious to get started with his roping lesson.

"I'm coming." Almost lazily Luke moved around the table, stopping very close to Maris's chair to lean over and whisper, "What's it going to be this time, honey, another fight or something with a little spice to it?"

She lifted her eyes to send him a venomous look. "It's happens to be something very important, and I do not appreciate your crude jokes."

Laughing deep in his throat, Luke went through the back door to join Keith. Maris continued to sit at the table, while anger wreaked havoc on her nervous system. How dared he call her "babe" and "honey"? If only she didn't need his profi-

ciency with the horses so badly. For a few seconds she indulged in a gratifying mental image of herself telling him what a careless, negligent, pleasure-seeking jerk he was, and then to get his gear together and get the hell off of her ranch.

Reality began overriding her anger. Luke wasn't careless or negligent when it came to the horses, and their training was moving along at a rapid pace. With Mother and Sugar and Zelda and all the other animals he'd been working with, he showed endless patience and an unquestionable expertise. She couldn't do something so stupid as to lose her temper and destroy the best thing she had going for the ranch, regardless of his insolent reminders that he would gladly take her to bed.

Besides, there'd been a teasing note in his whispery voice when he'd leaned over her. She probably presented a comical challenge to a man like him, which wasn't a particularly flattering idea to Maris. Yet what other amusement was there for Luke on the No Bull but to bait her and then watch her feathers ruffle? And dumb her, she bristled on cue. No wonder he'd walked out laughing.

The table full of dirty dishes suddenly seeped into her senses. Sighing dramatically, she got up to do the dishes.

But come hell or high water, embarrassment or even another argument, she was going to have that talk with Luke before she went to bed tonight. Keith had made remarkable headway since coming to the ranch, and Luke Rivers was not going to undermine that progress by painting outlandish scenes of romance and adventure on the rodeo circuit for the impressionable teenager.

Maris was just finishing up with the dishes, when the telephone rang. Wiping her hands on a dish towel, she picked up the phone. "No Bull Ranch. This is Maris."

"You're not really serious about changing the name of your ranch, are you, Maris?"

"It's already been done, Judd. Hi, how are you?"

"But I thought you were just kidding around with that new sign."

"The Circle W was the Wylers' ranch, Judd. The No Bull is mine."

"Now that doesn't make any sense at all, Maris, not when it's the same darned ranch."

"It's not 'the same darned ranch,' Judd, but it'll be a while before it's obvious to anyone but myself."

"Maris, are you all right?" She could hear concern in Judd's somber voice. "You're talking kind of funny. Is everything all right out there?"

Worrying Judd Hensley was the last thing she wanted to do. She was fond of him and appreciated his attention. "Judd, I'm fine and so is everything else."

"Well...the reason I called was to ask you out for supper on Friday night. Melissa's advertising an all-you-can-eat fish fry at the Hip Hop, and I thought you might enjoy it."

"I would, but..." Maris bit down on her bottom lip. With all that was going on right now, did she want to leave the ranch for an evening? "Judd...would you mind terribly if I begged off? I'm working very hard to get a yard sale organized, and frankly, I'm completely exhausted at the end of the day."

"A yard sale, you say? What're you planning to sell?"

"Every piece of junk on the place."

"Those things that Ray had stored out behind the barn?"

"Yes." Recently she'd been thinking of certain articles in the house that she'd be glad to see the last of, as well. Ray's gun collection for one. She hated guns, and there were eight rifles and almost as many handguns in a locked gun cabinet in her living room. Cabinet and all were going to be added to her growing list of sale items.

"Well...I'm disappointed about Friday night, but we'll do it another time. By the way, how's your hired man working out?"

"Luke is a wizard with horses, Judd. He's working out very well." Maris had been wondering if Judd would get around to mentioning Luke.

"Uh, Maris, I've been hearing some rumors about—"

"Don't say it, Judd," she interjected sharply. "I despise gossip, especially when it's totally groundless."

Judd was silent a moment. "Sorry I brought it up. I'll call again, or drop by, Maris."

"Do that, Judd."

After goodbyes, Maris put down the phone. So, even Judd had heard the gossip about Luke doing more than just working for her. Someone was mighty busy spreading lies, or perhaps no more than amused hints and sly innuendo. Maris had never been the subject of this sort of gossip before, and she didn't much care for the feeling it gave her.

But what could she do about it? It would die down after Luke left. Until then she would just have to grin and bear it.

Maris was becoming impatient. The sun had slipped down below the mountains, it was nearly dark and Luke and Keith were still tossing loops at fence posts. They were getting along famously, she saw from a window, talking and laughing together, whooping when Keith actually succeeded in roping a post. She didn't want to go out there with some heavy-handed comment about needing to speak to Luke in private, but it was getting late and she was not going to go to bed without having that crucial conversation with Luke.

From the window it appeared to Maris that Keith was having the time of his life, which raised some extremely disturbing ambiguities within her. She wanted Keith to have fun—he'd had little enough of that before coming to the ranch—but she didn't want him having fun with a man of Luke Rivers's ilk. Though she could tell they were talking at intervals, she couldn't make out their words, and what if Luke was boasting about wine, women and song on the rodeo circuit? Wouldn't tales of that sort influence a young man, maybe start him thinking that rodeo would be a great way to go?

With intense relief, she finally saw Keith handing his coiled rope to Luke and starting for the house. The yard light, which was on a sensor responsive to darkness, flashed on and provided enough light for Maris to see Luke going into the barn.

Keith came in through the kitchen door. "Hi." He went directly to the refrigerator and took out a gallon of milk. "Roping

sure is fun, Maris. You should've come down and watched. Luke said I did real well for a beginner.'' After pouring himself a tall glass of milk, Keith grabbed a handful of cookies and sat at the table to eat his snack.

Maris leaned her hips against the sink counter. ''You like Luke, don't you?''

''Yeah, he's an all-right guy.''

''Does he talk very much about himself?''

Keith looked up. ''Why would he do that? Don't you like him, Maris?''

She drew a slow and uneasy breath. ''I like him just fine. I was just curious about…well, about what the two of you might have discussed.''

Keith grinned. ''We talked about roping. He's an expert, Maris. He can do all kinds of tricks with ropes.''

''I'm sure he can.''

Gulping the last of his milk, Keith got up and rinsed his glass at the sink, the way Maris had requested he do when he'd first come to the ranch. ''I'm hitting the sack, Maris. Luke said I could start riding Mother first thing in the morning.''

''Good night, Keith. See you in the morning.'' Maris wanted to kick herself. There was no way she could tell Keith that she'd changed her mind about him working with Luke and the horses, not when Keith's excitement was almost tangible.

Maris pushed away from the counter. That talk with Luke was imminent.

Luke had just stepped out of the shower, when he heard someone knocking on the door of his loft quarters. ''Just a minute,'' he yelled from the tiny bathroom. Wrapping a towel around his hips, he crossed the living room and pulled open the door.

His near nudity shocked Maris into momentary speechless-ness. Then she stammered, ''Uh…put some clothes on. I'll wait out here.'' Shivering with an internal chill, she folded her arms around herself in the barren loft and tried not to listen to the sounds in Luke's room. His bare feet made a soft slapping noise on the wood floor. A door opened—the closet?—and then she

heard the rustle of clothing. Her heart seemed to be beating unusually fast. Her mouth felt dry. She would have to ask him for a glass of water.

The look on Maris's face when he'd opened that door, wearing a towel, made Luke chuckle while he yanked on a pair of clean jeans. But he returned to her with a straight face. "Come on in. *Mi casa es su casa.*"

"Indeed it is." Maris swept past him into the room. Damn him! All he'd put on was jeans, and he hadn't even closed the button at his waist. She suspected that he already considered her a prude, so she wouldn't mention more clothing if her life depended on it.

"Have a seat," Luke drawled.

There were two places to sit in there, one straight-backed chair and the bed. Maris chose the chair. Luke sat on the edge of the bed, leaning forward with his forearms resting on his thighs. "Must be something mighty important eating at you to bring you into my lair," he said with deliberate and mocking somberness.

"I'm not here to bandy words with you, Luke, so please cut the macho lines, okay?"

He changed positions, leaning back on his elbows, half sitting, half reclining. His spread thighs seemed to be pointing directly at her, a flagrant display of manly assets that could only have been more clearly defined without the jeans.

Maris got up, moved the chair to another location—one without such an arresting view—and sat down again. "I want to talk to you about Keith."

"About Keith?" Luke's teasing came to an abrupt halt and he sat up. "What about Keith?"

Her mouth was dryer still. Telling, or even asking, Luke how to behave on any level wasn't a pleasant prospect. "Could I have a glass of water?"

He looked at her peculiarly, then pushed to his feet. "Yeah, sure." Disappearing into the bathroom for a moment, he returned with a paper cup of water.

"Thank you." Maris drank it down, every drop.

"What about Keith, Maris?" Luke repeated.

It couldn't be put off any longer. She lifted her chin. "I don't want you filling his head with romantic nonsense about rodeo life. It's *not* romantic, and it's not even very civilized, and..."

"Hold on a minute." Luke's expression had become as hard as granite. "In the first damned place, you don't know what you're talking about. How many rodeos did *you* compete in? How many did you even attend? But that's not the point. You have your opinion of rodeo and I have mine. What *is* the point is why you would think I would discuss it with Keith, and second, if it did happen to come up in conversation when we're together, what makes you think I would romanticize the subject? Rodeo is hard work and tough competition. Most of the men and women competing for the prize money love the sport and work damn hard to prove themselves. Where do you get the nerve to call it uncivilized, when you don't even understand it?"

Maris smirked. "I understand it perfectly."

"No, babe, you don't," Luke said sardonically. "You're against rodeo because Ray loved it, and that's the long and the short of it."

Maris leapt to her feet. "You smug bastard. Just a regular Mr. Know-it-all, aren't you? Well, let me tell you something. If Ray had stayed home and taken care of this ranch instead of traipsing all over the country to chase prize money—which he never won—and women—which I'm sure he found by the droves—this ranch wouldn't be nearly bankrupt. And you have the gall to stand there and tell me not to blame rodeo?"

"He wasn't gone all the time, Maris. What did he do when he was home? Even with rodeo a big part of his life, this ranch shouldn't be bankrupt."

It was the God's truth, the *stunning* truth, and Maris's fury wilted right before Luke's eyes.

"He drank," she said listlessly. "I ran the ranch, or tried to, and with him spending every cent coming in, I couldn't keep it afloat." Her eyes flashed with renewed anger at the pity she saw in Luke's. "None of that is any of your business. I will

always despise rodeo and nothing you can say or do will ever change my mind. I meant what I said about Keith. He's a good kid and he's going to make something of himself. I don't want him influenced by a bunch of fairy tales about how wonderful bumming around the country to break his neck in some rodeo arena is.''

Arguing with Maris over the pros and cons of rodeo life was a no-win proposition. Luke sucked in a long, slow breath. ''Who is he, Maris? How come he's living here with you? Where's his own family?''

Maris hesitated. ''If I tell you about his background, will you keep it to yourself? What I mean is, unless Keith himself mentions it, will you act as though you know nothing about it?''

''He's been in trouble with the law, hasn't he?'' Luke said quietly.

''Do you promise?''

''Yes, I promise. I'll never mention it to Keith. What happened?''

Maris walked to a window and looked out at the black night. This side of the barn was opposite to the yard light, and there really was nothing to see, other than her own reflection in the windowpane.

''He lived with his father and grandmother. Terrance, his father, is an alcoholic. He beat not only Keith, but his own elderly mother. No one knew it. Keith started getting into trouble at school, then he got caught shoplifting. Sterling McCallum and Jessica got involved in the case. They suspected something terribly wrong in the Colson home, but Keith would never admit to anything. Finally, I guess he just couldn't take any more abuse. He got hold of an unloaded gun and tried to hold up Bill Murray's car lot. It was a cry for help. Every time he got in trouble, he eventually got sent back to his father. The poor kid decided that going to jail would be better than living with Terrance. It was Sterling and Jessica who saved him from juvenile detention. Sterling, actually. He called me and told me the story. I needed some help on the place—'' Maris turned around to face Luke ''—but that wasn't the reason I agreed to

Keith's coming here. I can't bear the thought of youngsters being abused, and I wanted him to have a chance at a decent life. It's been working, Luke. You must be able to see for yourself what a great kid Keith is.''

Forgetting everything but her vehement concern for Keith, Maris went to Luke and laid her hand on his arm. "I don't want him to become enchanted with some unstable vocation like rodeo. I want him to get an education and to do something with his life. He's so young—young enough to be my own son—and I've become very attached to him.''

"He's what, sixteen? To be your son, you would have had to have him when you were a kid.''

"I'm thirty-two, Luke." She was looking into his eyes. "That's not important. Keith's future is. Will you downplay your obsession with rodeo if he should ask about it? He likes you. He admires you. But I don't want him to be like you,'' she said, finishing in a tortured whisper.

Never had anyone said something that hurt Luke more than what Maris had just said: *I don't want him to be like you.*

He tried to put it out of his mind. "So where's Terrance Colson now?''

Suddenly realizing that she'd been hanging on to Luke's arm, Maris backed away from him. "He's in jail. Keith's grandmother moved away. I don't think there's any other family. Luke, will you cooperate with me on this?''

Without a dram of expression on his face, he nodded. "You have my word.''

This time she didn't question the value of his word but believed him wholeheartedly. Something she'd said had reached him, thank God. "Many, many thanks,'' she said with all the gratitude she felt inside, making her voice slightly unsteady. "I won't forget this, Luke.''

Luke ran all ten of his fingers through his damp hair. "I have a feeling that neither will I, Maris.'' *I don't want him to be like you.* "Would you like me to walk you to the house? It's awfully dark out tonight.''

Maris shook her head. "Thanks, but I'm not afraid of the

dark, and the yard's pretty well lit once I get beyond the barn. Good night, Luke.''

She slipped out, closing the door behind her. He sank to the bed and sat there staring down at his own two bare feet. He was thirty-five years old and owned nothing but a six-year-old pickup truck and an IOU for three thousand bucks. A cynical smile tipped one corner of his lips. Maybe Maris wasn't wrong about rodeo, after all.

There was a bustle on the ranch in the ensuing days, which elated Maris. Keith and Luke worked nonstop with the horses, and often she heard their laughter ringing throughout the compound. She rode out every morning to tend the cattle, then spent the rest of the day on the yard sale. There were only a few more items left to clean and make ready.

During lunch one day she mentioned the weeds behind the barn. ''They have to be chopped down,'' she said, looking at both Keith and Luke.

''We'll do it right after lunch,'' Luke assured her.

''Great. Thanks. I made up a bunch of posters announcing the sale, and I'm going to bring them into town this afternoon to display in store windows. I've also put an ad in the newspaper. I can hardly believe the sale is going to be this weekend.'' She bit down on her lip, worried suddenly. ''What if no one comes to it? What if no one cares that I'm having a yard sale?''

''They'll come,'' Luke said.

''They will, Maris,'' Keith earnestly agreed.

Of course people will come, Maris told herself repeatedly during the drive to town. She smiled grimly. Maybe some would come just to get a look at her hired man.

With her stack of posters, Maris started making the rounds of Whitehorn's commercial establishments. No one refused her request to exhibit her signs in their windows, and she got to talk to a lot of old friends, many of whom promised to come and see what she had for sale this weekend.

John Tully, the drugstore owner, beamed from ear to ear when she showed him the poster. ''A yard sale, eh? Well, I

could use a new yard. Maybe I'll buy yours." He laughed as though he'd just invented wit, and Maris, out of friendship, laughed with him at the tired old joke.

John put the poster in a prominent spot in his best window. "How's that?"

"That's great, John. Thanks. Well, I have a few more of these to distribute, so I'd better be running along."

John followed her to the door. "How's that fellow Rivers working out?"

"Just fine, John." Maris put her hand on the door to open it.

"I sent him out to your place, you know. We met in the Hip Hop one morning and he asked if I knew of any available jobs in the area. Naturally, the minute he said he wanted ranch work, I thought of you trying to run your place with just a boy for help."

"That was kind of you, John."

John kept smiling. "Guess it turned out better than I thought."

"Better how, John?"

"Well, with the two of you becoming…um…friends…"

Maris heaved a discouraged sigh. "Don't believe everything you hear, John. Incidentally, do you happen to recall who told you that Luke and I were becoming…um…friends?"

"Well, let me see, Maris." The druggist scratched his balding head. "Uh…seems like it was Lily Wheeler."

"Now, why doesn't that surprise me?" Maris drawled sarcastically. Before John Tully could come up with a reply, Maris was going out the door. "Bye, John. Thanks for the use of your window."

Lily Mae Wheeler. Maris fumed all the way back to the ranch. That woman would try the patience of a saint. She knew everything about everybody in town and within a fifty-mile radius thereafter, and if you happened to run into her on the street, you couldn't shut her up no matter what you did. Lily could talk faster than anyone Maris had ever known, and ob-

viously the woman didn't need much oxygen, because she rarely ever slowed down for a breath of air.

But how on earth Lily Wheeler had gotten wind of Luke working on the No Bull, Maris would never know. But then, how did Lily get most of her information? The woman just naturally attracted news, even plain, everyday and rather dull news such as a stranger in town landing a job on a ranch thirty miles from town.

Judd should hire Lily to unearth the murderer of Floyd Oakley, Maris thought wryly. She must have plenty to say on *that* subject.

Eight

Maris had advertised the yard sale to begin at nine in the morning and end at four in the afternoon. At ten minutes after eight on Saturday morning a car arrived. Maris was walking among her sale items, removing sheets that she'd been using to protect some of the better pieces from nighttime dampness, and she looked at the car with surprise.

Winona Cobb got out and called a cheery, "Hello, Maris."

Winona was at least seventy, but seemed to have more energy than people half her age. She was short and stout, a round little butterball of a woman with iron gray hair and a chipper smile. Today she was wearing a purple tunic and her usual jewelry—a large amethyst crystal pendant and assorted bracelets. Maris had always considered Winona to be a true eccentric. Along with the junk she collected, which she sold, swapped or merely stacked in untidy piles inside her small shop or in her front yard, she kept animals—dogs, cats, chickens and goats. And bees, lots of bees. She sold the honey they produced, and it was very good honey. Winona had a way with the insects and they never stung her—even though she never wore protective clothing. People called her a "bee charmer." But Maris wasn't especially fond of bees buzzing around her head and she never stopped at Winona's place anymore. Ray used to stop often. Ray had not only stopped, he had swapped and even bought. Winona was apt to recognize some of her own junk in today's sale, Maris thought with droll amusement.

Oh, yes, there was one more side to Winona Cobb, Maris recalled as she resigned herself to the woman jumping the gun on the opening of the sale and walked out to greet her: reputedly, Winona had psychic powers. Sometimes she had visions that came upon her like sort of a fit, or spell. Winona also told

fortunes; if you asked nicely and she was in the mood, although Maris had never availed herself of Winona's services.

"Hello, Winona." She was already looking around, quite avidly, Maris noted.

"Where'd you get all this stuff?" Winona asked.

"From a room in the barn," Maris replied evenly.

Winona gave her a sharp-eyed, almost suspicious look. "How'd it get in the barn?"

Maris had to physically choke back laughter. "Ray put it there."

Winona grunted. "Never knew he had so much goods. How come you're selling it?" Her gaze landed on the old marble clock, which Luke had carried outside for Maris to clean, then carried it again when she asked him to place it on the sideboard. "What's that?"

"An antique clock. It's genuine black onyx, Winona, and the face is real gold and ivory." Those were facts, not fancy. The clock, once cleaned and quite beautiful, had raised Maris's curiosity enough that she had made a trip to Whitehorn's library to research old clocks. She had found a photograph in a book that depicted a clock very similar to hers. *Circa, late 1800s. Value, $400-$500.* The book was a year old, so it was quite likely that the value of her clock was even higher than quoted.

But this was only a yard sale, after all, and she had put a price of two hundred dollars on it.

Winona looked at the tag and sniffed. "No one's gonna give you two hundred for an old clock, Maris."

Maris smiled. "Then I'll keep it. I rather like it."

By eight-thirty, Winona had checked each and every item in Maris's yard, even the old trucks and cars behind the barn. "What about that Corvette?" she asked.

"It's sold, Winona. See the Sold sign on it?"

"Oh, yeah, I see it now." She turned to Maris. "Where's that hired hand I've heard so much about?"

Inwardly Maris stiffened; outwardly she smiled coolly. "He's here somewhere. Both he and Keith will be helping with the sale." Actually, what they were doing before the sale began

was attempting to separate the stallions from the other horses still remaining in the main pasture.

Keith was riding Mother and Luke was riding Rocky. Both animals were reasonably well behaved now, and Luke had successfully roped the two younger stallions and led them to the cattle pasture, which was the most distant fenced field from the buildings.

Bozo, the big red stallion was a whole different ball game, however. Over and over again he cleverly dodged the rope and ran off kicking up his hind legs and snorting. "He's a sly devil," Luke called to Keith, though the comment was accompanied by a rather pleased smile. The stallion's spirit reminded him of Pancho's. No one but Luke had ever ridden Pancho, and Luke suspected that Bozo, too, would be a one-rider horse. Before he could even begin the training process, however, he had to catch him.

Winona's keen eyes caught sight of the two men on horseback, though the pasture was some distance from the barn. "What're they doing?" she asked Maris. "That smaller fellow is Keith Colson, isn't he?"

Before Maris could say more than "Yes," Winona was on her way to the pasture. Maris breathed an exasperated sigh. Obviously the woman was determined to get a closer look at Luke.

But what did it matter? Maris thought. She had nothing to hide. Luke was a hired hand and the twenty-five dollars she handed him at the end of each week was proof of their platonic relationship. He always looked at the money with sardonic amusement and she always pretended to not notice. But the cash he'd received thus far must all be in his wallet, as he hadn't left the ranch even once since he'd begun working with the horses.

Winona stopped at the fence; Maris did the same. "Keith looks well," the older woman commented. Her piercing gaze moved to Maris. "You like him, don't you?"

"Yes. Very much."

Winona looked off across the pasture again. "Terry Colson

was born mean, you know. It wasn't just his drinking that caused him to beat his son and mother."

"You knew him?"

"I lived here all my life, Maris. I know everyone."

"Yes, I expect you do," Maris said with a smile.

"Except for that lanky fellow on the Appaloosa."

Maris was watching Luke, admitting to herself the splendid way he rode and looked, admiring even the hat on his head and the boots on his feet. Feeling Winona's eyes boring into her, a flush crept into her cheeks.

"You like him, too, don't you?" Winona said.

Maris's face got redder. "I...he..."

"Oh, for pity's sake, don't be embarrassed about it. Do you think anyone expects a young woman like yourself to live alone for the rest of her life?" Winona began walking off. "I've seen enough. Thanks for letting me look around."

Maris hurried to catch up. "Did you see anything you wanted to buy?"

"Nope. Just wanted to find out what it was you were selling." Winona climbed into her car. "Drop by and say hello sometime."

Maris nodded. "I will." She meant it. It wouldn't hurt her one darned bit to dodge the bees and the goats to say hello to a neighbor. "Bye, Winona."

In the pasture Luke admitted defeat with Bozo...for the time being. Coiling up his rope he spoke to Keith. "We'd better unsaddle now. It's almost nine."

They rode toward the gate. "Do you really think people will come to the sale?" Keith questioned.

"They'll come," Luke said confidently. He grinned at his younger companion. "We'll be ready for them, right?"

"Right," Keith agreed. He'd been assigned to handle the cash box, and was mighty proud about Maris's putting so much trust in him. He looked at Luke and couldn't imagine anything better than the two people he liked most becoming more than just friends. "Maris is real pretty, don't you think?"

Luke laughed. "Yeah, she is. What're trying to do, boy, match us up?"

Keith's face got red, but he grinned. "Seems like a good idea to me." Whooping then, he nudged Mother into a gallop.

As Luke kept Rocky at a walk, his laughter faded. Keith might think it was a good idea, and it set all right with him, too. But Maris was another story. Her opinion of rodeo riders sure wasn't one to encourage a man.

The number of people, who seemed to arrive in droves, stunned Maris. For hours she went from one group to another, discussing the various merchandise, and selling it!

Melissa Avery fell in love with the sideboard. "I have the perfect spot for it in the Hip Hop." She also bought most of the mismatched chairs and tables. "I'm planning on expanding the café," she told Maris.

John Tully bought the clock, after arguing Maris down to one hundred fifty dollars. A young couple purchased the bedstead and two dressers. A rancher bought the entire stack of galvanized pails and the riding lawn mower.

And so it went throughout the day. One man, who owned a gas station and dealt in used vehicles on the side, bought all the old, broken-down cars and trucks—other than the Corvette, of course—from behind the barn. After that transaction was made, Luke toted the miscellaneous motors around to the front of the building, as there was no longer a reason for him to hang around the larger equipment.

The hand tools went, the coat tree with the brass fittings, much of the glassware and, finally, one by one, Ray's gun collection.

By four Maris was exhausted. There were still some things unsold, and most of the larger items that were sold hadn't yet been picked up. But the cash box was overflowing, and when the last car drove off, Keith brought it to Maris with a totally amazed expression.

"There must be thousands of dollars in here, Maris."

Maris's weary spirit suddenly revived. "Let's count it." She

and Keith started for the house. Maris stopped and turned. "You, too, Luke. Come on."

"No, you two go ahead. I'm going to take a shower."

Concealing her disappointment that he didn't want to be included in the most exciting part of the day, she nodded and proceeded to the house. She and Keith sat at the kitchen table.

"I don't believe this," she said while sorting the cash from the checks, then stacking the cash by denomination. "Keith, look. There are six one-hundred-dollar bills." They counted the cash and added up the checks, and Maris sat back, weak with incredulity. "Three thousand five hundred and sixty three dollars. And that's not counting the change." There was a small mountain of coins. "I'm looking at it with my own eyes and I still don't believe it."

Keith chuckled gleefully. "Hundreds of people came, Maris."

"Everyone from the whole area, I think."

"There's not much left out there for tomorrow."

"I know, but my signs said Saturday *and* Sunday, so we'll have to be here. Keith, this calls for a celebration." She picked up two of the twenties. "Would you do me a huge favor and go to town? I want three of the biggest, best steaks you can find. We'll cook them on the charcoal grill. How does that sound?"

Keith's eyes lit up. "Terrific! Sure, I'll go." He took the money from Maris's hand.

"And stop at the bakery and pick out something really special for dessert."

"A pie?"

"Or a cake or…whatever looks good to you. Okay?"

"Gotcha. I won't be long."

"Drive carefully," Maris called as Keith dashed out. She sat back again, sighing and shaking her head at the stacks of cash on the table. The sale was a lifesaver. She could catch up on the mortgage payments and certainly all the small bills that had been coming in the mail with Past Due stickers could be paid in full. Plus, she reminded herself, she would be receiving the

balance due from Jim Humphrey on the sale of the Corvette. Oh, what a wonderful feeling it was to have the money to get herself back in the black.

Then she thought of Luke and that IOU. The means to pay him the full amount was sitting right in front of her. Her heart skipped a beat. If she paid him off, would he leave the ranch and her stranded with a herd of partially broken horses?

Oh, he wouldn't, she mentally argued. Surely he wouldn't.

But dared she take that risk? He had agreed to receiving payment from the sale of horses, and that was the arrangement she must hold him to.

Not nearly as excited as she'd been, Maris gathered up the money and brought it to her bedroom, where she put it in a shoe box in her closet. The coins remained on the table, and she returned to the kitchen to scoop them into a plastic bowl. Later, when she had the time, she would sort and count them. For now, she stuck the bowl in a cupboard.

Then she went outside to organize what items were left for tomorrow's sale. She was busily moving things around, when Luke walked up.

"Need some help?"

"Sure, thanks. I thought it would be best to close the gaps."

She was placing everything that wasn't already sold in one small area of the yard. Luke pitched in and the job was completed in about ten minutes. Maris stopped and looked thoughtfully at the goods. "There sure isn't much left."

"It was a success, all right." Luke had showered, shaved and put on clean jeans and shirt. The sale had been a success because they had worked their fannies off today. In fact, on this ranch they all worked their fannies off *every* day. He had never worked harder or put in longer hours in his life, and the funny thing, he realized while studying Maris studying the remnants of today's sale, was that he wasn't resentful, annoyed or unhappy about it. For some unimaginable reason he was unusually content, and Lord knows he'd never been content with ordinary labor. So...what was going on with him, pray tell?

"Well," Maris declared briskly, placing her hands on her

hips to look at Luke. "You're all cleaned up and I'm a mess. I've got to do something about that. Listen, I sent Keith to town to buy some steaks. I think a little celebration is in order after today's big success, don't you?"

"Uh..." He'd been planning on going to town himself. For weeks now he hadn't even started his pickup, let alone gone anywhere. It was Saturday night and he'd been thinking of a few beers and maybe looking for a place with a live band. While showering, he'd toyed with the idea of asking Maris to go along, but had decided she would only say no. Now here she was, talking about a celebration dinner, and it wasn't as easy for him to say no as it was for her. "Sure, sounds great," he told her, thinking that he could go to town *after* dinner.

"Good. I'm going in now." Maris started away. "Oh. If you wouldn't mind digging out the barbecue grill—it's in the tool-shed."

"Wouldn't mind at all. I'll get it."

"Thanks." He hadn't asked how much money she had taken in today, Maris thought gratefully as she went into the house and directly to her bedroom and bath to clean up. She paused at her closet to look over her modest wardrobe. Regardless of her fervent hope that Luke wouldn't suggest she pay him now instead of after the horse auction, she felt rather festive and didn't want merely to pull on a pair of clean jeans for the evening. Something pretty, she thought, while moving hangers around to check the garments. Something feminine. It had been ages since she'd bought any new clothes, but anything other than jeans would look new to Luke.

Frowning, she stopped to chide herself. She wasn't dressing up for Luke, was she? Did she want him to see her feminine side? Lord knows there'd been nothing feminine about her since he'd shown up.

Still, he'd kissed her. Maris's heart beat faster at the memory. He was a handsome, exciting, sexy man, whatever he did for a living or how short a time he'd be in the vicinity, and she was almost constantly aware of him. Common sense to the contrary,

she was attracted to Luke and couldn't help believing that he was attracted to her.

But where could it go? Dismissing the whole discomfiting topic with a toss of her head, Maris pulled out a faded denim skirt and a yellow blouse. The outfit would satisfy her desire for something other than jeans, but it couldn't possibly give Luke any ideas about her "dressing up" for him.

They ate outside at Maris's small patio table. The food was great, the heat of the day had passed and the evening air was soft and silky. But all was not right. During the meal Maris had noticed that Keith seemed distracted and nervous, which wasn't like him. Upon returning from town with the steaks and a delicious-looking chocolate-and-raspberry torte, he had disappeared to shower and clean up. He'd returned to the kitchen wearing his best jeans and shirt and Maris had smiled teasingly. "My, you look handsome."

A slow flush had colored his cheeks, but he'd grinned and gone outside to sit with Luke, who was watching the steaks on the grill so Maris could finish the green salad she'd started earlier. Blackie, who was never very far away from Keith, lay nearby, her head on her front paws.

The food was wonderful, and they ate it with gusto and enjoyment. But Keith's unusual mood worried Maris. Since coming to the ranch, the boy had had his silent moments, which she'd considered only normal, given his background. But this was different. She wanted to ask if anything was wrong, but hesitated to do so in front of Luke, as it might embarrass Keith.

They were just finishing up with dessert, when Keith suddenly blurted, "Maris, could I use the truck tonight?"

Maris slowly put down her fork. This was a first, and obviously what had been on Keith's mind throughout the meal. She wanted to handle it sensibly. "To do what, Keith?"

His face was crimson and he was staring down at his plate. "I...asked a girl to see a movie with me tonight." He lifted his eyes. "She's a real nice girl, Maris. I...sort of liked her in school last year, but we never really spoke...very much. She was at the store when I was picking out the steaks. Any-

way…we got to talking and I asked her to go to the movie with me, and she said yes.''

An enormous relief flooded Maris's system. She'd been worried about dark, terrible things concerning Keith, not about something as innocent and natural as this. She glanced at Luke, who she could see was maintaining a completely impassive expression, though there was a spark of masculine amusement in his eyes. Maris looked at Keith again. Anxiety was written all over his handsome boy-man face. He'd gone way out on a limb, making a date with a girl, when he didn't know if he would have transportation. No wonder he'd been nervous.

"Yes,'' Maris said quietly. "You may use the truck, Keith.''

He jumped to his feet, no boy-man now but all boy, excited and eager to be off. "Thanks, Maris. Thanks a lot. I have to go right now or I'll be late.'' He started away, then stopped. "I won't be home late. Um…no later than midnight, okay?''

Maris smiled. "Okay.'' Her gaze followed Keith to the truck, which was immediately started and then gone. Blackie whimpered. "It's all right, Blackie,'' Maris said soothingly. "Keith will be back.''

"You're a nice woman, Maris,'' Luke said softly.

The comment startled her. "But who likes nice women, right?'' she quipped as she took the steak bone from her plate and brought it to Blackie. The little dog instantly settled down with her treat.

"Nice men?'' Luke drawled.

They were alone. With Keith gone, she and Luke were completely alone and the sun was going down. This, too, was a first. She could get very flustered right now, Maris realized. She could clear the table, and flutter from patio to kitchen and look very silly dashing about, simply because she was alone with a man who had kissed her and the sun was going down.

She took her chair again, calmly, coolly. "I'm not sure I've ever known any nice men.''

"Present company excluded, of course.''

That smooth-as-honey tone didn't fool Maris. Beneath it, he was laughing at her. But he was not going to rattle her, she

vowed. "Our criteria for what constitutes 'nice' probably differs, don't you think?"

He shrugged, casually, adorably. Damn him, thought Maris, and damn myself, too. Why was she noticing every tiny detail of his appearance? The minute crinkles at the corners of his eyes, for instance. And the way his shoulders filled his white shirt.

"It appears to me that our criteria for anything differs," he replied. "'Course, that could be because you're female and I'm male. Men and women don't think alike."

"That should be my line," Maris said dryly.

He grinned. "Why's that?"

"Because it's something women know and men don't. Usually," she added. "How come you know it?"

"My mother told me," he said solemnly.

Maris stared, then laughed. "You're pulling my leg, right?"

"I never joke about my mother."

Was he yanking her chain, or what? "Is your mother living?"

"Alive and thriving in Texas."

"And your father?"

"He died ten years ago. Ma sold the ranch and moved to town. I see her about once a year." Behind the conversation Luke was thinking of his plans for the evening—heading for Whitehorn and a few beers. But this was an opportunity if he'd ever stumbled across one. Just once he'd like to see Maris Wyler relaxed and enjoying herself. Maybe tonight was the night. "What about your folks?" he questioned.

Maris sighed softly. "Gone, both of them. And I was an only child. Do you have any brothers or sisters?"

Luke hooked his arm over the back corner of his chair. "Nope. It's just me and Ma."

"If you see her only once a year, I hope you call her often," Maris said, then wished she hadn't. "Sorry. I'm sure you're not looking for advice from me."

"It's okay. I know I don't call her enough."

"Feel free to use my phone, Luke. Anytime."

He nodded. "I'll take you up on that. Maybe tomorrow. Maris, would you like to go somewhere?"

Her eyes widened. "Go where?"

"I don't know. For a ride, maybe?"

"Um…" Oh, Lord, what should she say? A ride in Luke's truck was hardly a romantic outing, and yet, why had he suggested it?

"Hey, I've got a really great idea," Luke exclaimed. "You haven't ridden any of the horses yet. How about us taking a ride right now?"

"But it's getting dark." Despite her common-sense objection, the idea was appealing. "Which horse would I be riding?"

"Mother. I'll take Rocky."

He was fond of Rocky, Maris knew. Maybe the Appaloosa would be the horse he picked to take with him when he left at the end of September. Disturbed by that image, she became very still.

"Come on, say you'll go," Luke said.

"I…have to clear the table and…and do the dishes."

Luke got up and began stacking plates. "Clearing away will take three minutes. I'll help you with the dishes when we get back."

Uneasily Maris pushed herself to her feet. "That wouldn't be necessary, but Luke…I don't know. It's almost dark."

"A great time of day for a ride." He headed for the house with most of the dirty dishes.

Maris gathered up the rest and followed. He was insisting and she really would like to do it. But was a moonlit ride on a velvety night a wise move for her to make with Luke?

Then she thought of the consequences of a firm refusal. Luke would either take that ride alone or go to his quarters in the loft of the barn. It was such a beautiful evening, and she would spend it in her kitchen, washing dishes, and then go to bed. With Keith gone, the house would be empty and lonely. Very, very lonely.

"All right," she said as she placed her load of dirty dishes

in the sink on top of those that Luke had carried in. "Let's go."

Luke's pleased grin was a yard wide. "Great! Let's do it to it!"

Together they walked back outside, laughing at his silly remark. Maris closed the door behind them.

The moment Maris mounted the mare Luke realized she might have ridden quite a lot before, but she wasn't completely comfortable on a strange horse.

Maris's mind was elsewhere. "I should have changed into jeans," she said, arranging her skirt around her legs.

"You look great in a dress," Luke said quietly. He was standing next to Maris and the mare, making sure Maris was well seated, worrying some about her riding a strange, newly broken horse in the dark. He put the reins in her hands. "Hold them evenly, a little loosely. Mother responds well to a light touch."

"All right." Maris recognized the giddiness in her system. The moon was coming up, full and huge. Doing something like this, impulsive and unplanned, was completely alien to her present life-style. She had become rather staid, she knew, but there'd been a time when she had laughed easily and blossomed under a handsome man's attention. That was what she was feeling tonight, a blooming, an unusual radiance, and more than a little daring. Maybe her rare mood was because her financial worries were easing, or because the moon was full and bright.

Then again, it could be because of being alone with Luke.

"Are you set?" he asked. "Do you feel comfortable in the saddle?"

"I'm fine." She laughed for no reason, merely because it felt good to laugh. "Come on. Get on Rocky and let's go."

Frowning slightly, Luke left her side to mount the Appaloosa. "Maybe we should just ride around the pasture."

"No way," Maris exclaimed. She was ready for adventure and picturing the miles of open land beyond the fences. "The

night is heavenly. Let's ride and ride and ride,'' she said with a dreamy sigh.

Luke's pulse rate took a noticeable jump in speed. Maris was beautiful in the moonlight, and her mood was one he'd never witnessed before. The husky tone of her voice and her carefree gestures told him that anything could happen tonight.

Anything.

Nine

The landscape was beautifully eerie in the moonlight. Trees and bushes, sparse in number, cast long, dark shadows upon grass and ground that appeared silvery and spectral. The air was still and unusually warm for a Montana night.

Luke tended the gates and they left the fences behind and headed into open country. Blackie was following, staying about ten feet behind. Maris looked back at the dog. "With Keith gone, Blackie has apparently attached herself to us," she remarked to Luke.

Luke glanced back. "Seems so." His gaze lingered on Maris. "How're you doing?"

"Luke Rivers, are you worried about Mother or me?" she asked teasingly.

"Mother can take care of herself."

"And I can't?"

"You're not used to riding a strange horse."

"Well, I like riding and I'm doing just fine. And I rode plenty of strange horses before Ray traded them for that Corvette." Maris wished she hadn't mentioned Ray. She didn't want to talk about Ray tonight, but with Luke's next words, she knew they were going to.

"Did Ray ever ride with you?"

"Occasionally. But Ray was usually busy with one thing or another."

There was a trace of bitterness in Maris's voice, which piqued Luke's curiosity. "Where'd you two meet? I know Ray grew up right here, but what about you? Have you always lived in the Whitehorn area?"

Maris took a breath, not completely comfortable with Luke's

questions. "I came here as…a bride. I grew up in another small town, Demming, Montana. Have you heard of it?"

"Can't say that I have. So you met Ray in Demming?"

"No, in Bozeman. I was in college…" She sensed Luke's sudden, sharp look. "In my final year. I was planning to teach at the elementary level." She had met Ray Wyler through friends, and had fallen s͞o hard her teaching plans had almost immediately taken second place.

Luke was frowning, all but scowling, recalling his own lack of education. He'd been so enthralled with rodeo that he'd barely made it through high school. His folks had wanted him to attend Texas A&M and had offered to pay for everything—tuition, housing, books, even spending money—and he'd refused and gone off to join the rodeo circuit, leaving behind his high school diploma and the ashes of his parents' hopes.

For the first time ever he doubted his wisdom in that decision, wondering, in fact, if there'd been any wisdom involved. He could have gotten an education, *then* roamed the globe, chasing rodeo, if that was what he still wanted. But today, tonight, riding along with Maris Wyler, he would be able to say, "My school was Texas A&M." It would surprise and maybe please her. Instead he had nothing to say on the subject of education.

His voice became a little gruffer. "You met Ray in Bozeman, married him and moved to the ranch. Did all of that take place in rapid succession?"

Maris was looking straight ahead. "We got married the day after I received my diploma."

Luke uneasily shifted his weight in the saddle. "You must've loved him."

"It was a long time ago, Luke. Let's talk about something else." She had loved Ray madly, and had come to the ranch brimming with starry-eyed dreams for their future. Remembering their first happy weeks together, their first months, was painful, and she didn't want to dwell on that or what had come after.

"But you did love him," Luke persisted, not ready to drop the subject.

Maris drew in and then released a long breath, finally allowing a terse "Yes."

"What happened?"

"What makes you think something happened?"

"Maris, I was with the two of you in Casper, remember?" There was no love between them that night in Casper, Luke would swear. A man who loved his wife—and he'd been around plenty of guys who did—didn't play around with other women right in front of her. Ray had been a total jerk that night, a drunken, loudmouth fool who hadn't seemed to care one damned bit that Maris was sitting at a table and seeing everything he did.

"I really don't want to remember that night. It's no kindness to remind me of it, Luke."

"It proved that something happened to kill the feelings the two of you had for each other when you got married," Luke said stubbornly.

Maris shot him a fierce look. "Which really isn't any of your business, is it?"

"Technically, no. But I have this great big lump of curiosity in my gut, Maris." He nudged Rocky a little closer to Maris's horse. "Tell me about it. Please."

Maris gave a short, bitter laugh. "Tell you about my marriage just to satisfy your curiosity? Really, Luke—"

He broke in, brusquely. "You have to know why I'm curious." Just then Blackie darted in front of Mother's front hooves. The mare spooked and reared. Maris let out a yelp of confusion. Luke could see her losing the reins and falling backward. He leaned far to the right, snaked out an arm and caught her by the waist. "Hang on to me," he yelled. Maris clutched at his shirt with one hand and the other went up around his neck. It happened so fast. One second she was peacefully riding Mother, the next she was draped across Luke's lap and the mare was hightailing it for parts unknown.

Luke pulled Rocky to an abrupt halt. "Are you all right?"

"Just shaken up," Maris said hoarsely. "What happened?"

"Blackie ran under Mother's hooves. Scared her."

Maris shivered. "Not as much as she scared me." Luke was holding the reins with one hand and Maris with the other. His solid body and arms felt like sanctuary, and asking to be put down on the ground never entered her mind. "Thanks," she whispered raggedly. "You're very quick."

"Quick in some things, slow in others," he said with his lips sunk into her hair, which had the most arousing scent he'd ever encountered. His reply was a reference to his dull-witted refusal to go to college when he'd had the chance, though it was also a hint of how he would like to make love to her. "You're not comfortable," he said huskily. "Put your left leg over the saddle horn. We'll head back."

"Maybe I should ride behind you." It was a sensible suggestion, arising from the recognition of the intimacy of their embrace. It *was* an embrace, make no mistake. His body cradled hers, and with her legs separated by the saddle horn she felt extremely vulnerable.

"Are you afraid of me, Maris?"

"No, of course not, but..."

Luke's lips thinned slightly. "Maybe you should be. We're getting closer to making love every hour that we spend together, and you have to know it as well as I do." He clucked his tongue and got Rocky moving. "Say something, Maris."

Her heart was beating like a jackhammer. "I...I'm not sure what to say. Do you really believe that?"

"Wholeheartedly," Luke said, grim lipped.

"Have I said or done anything to give you that idea?"

"Yeah, you have. You've smelled sweet and looked beautiful. You've smiled and worked hard and treated Keith kindly. You've cooked my meals and washed my clothes. You've worried in front of me and worried even harder when you thought no one was looking. You don't have the remotest understanding of how pretty you are, and you'll turn sometimes, unexpectedly, and dazzle me with the beauty of your face and smile. And

when I kissed you, you kissed me back. Yeah, you've said and done a lot to give me that idea.''

Maris gulped and whispered, ''Not intentionally, Luke.''

''You've watched me working with the horses, Maris.''

''Only because I was interested in your methods.''

''You do most of your watching when I'm working without a shirt.'' He transferred the reins from his right hand to his left, which was the arm supporting her back. Then he stopped Rocky and tipped Maris's chin with his fingertips to look into her eyes. ''I want you, lady, and you want me.''

She couldn't move, merely sat there in his arms, on his lap, absorbing his maleness and declaration of intent. ''I don't know how to deal with you, Luke,'' she whispered.

''Yes, you do.'' His mouth brushed hers once, gently, then settled into a serious kiss. She felt hunger in that kiss, from him and within herself. Her own happiness, for which she had once held such high hopes, was only an old memory and seemed so far away as to have involved a woman other than herself. This was real and happening now. A man's strong arms around her. His mouth moving on hers, molding it, urging it to open for his tongue. His scent, the feel of him.

Luke lifted his head. ''See? You know exactly how to deal with me.'' Before she could even think of a reply, let alone say it, he kissed her again. Somewhere within the maelstrom of wildly beating hearts, which she could hear, and labored breathing, another unique and sensual sound, and kisses, another and another, she was vaguely aware of Rocky moving, heading for home.

Regardless of the solidity and strength of the man holding her, Maris was becoming too dizzy to put much trust in her perch. She clutched at Luke's arm and turned her head to break their kiss. ''Please...let me get down. I have to get down, Luke.''

He readily grasped why she had made the request. Making love on the back of a moving horse was utterly ludicrous. Especially when the horse had been completely green no more than two weeks ago and still wasn't all that certain about people

climbing all over his back. Rocky was skittish and prancing sideways instead of honing in on a straight line for the ranch.

"Whoa," Luke commanded the horse while pulling on the reins. "We'll both get down and walk back. It's not that far. I'm going to dismount first so I can help you down. Hang on to the saddle horn for a second." Swinging his left leg over the horse's rump, Luke slid to the ground. Because he wasn't completely positive of Rocky's reaction to all of this unfamiliar maneuvering, Luke tied the reins around a small tree before assisting Maris.

He returned to Rocky's right side, reached up and laid his hands on Maris's waist. "Put your hands on my shoulders," he instructed.

She obeyed and he lifted her down from the saddle. Only he didn't immediately set her feet on the ground. Instead, he brought her up against himself and let her slide down very slowly. A small gasp escaped Maris. The friction of clothing against clothing and body against body created a rippling thrill that took her breath.

The "Don't, Luke" she whispered came from her sane and sensible side; something else inside of her prevented her from physically moving away from him. The reactions of her own body to Luke Rivers were startling, and yet she understood them. She had lived without a man's love and affection for so long that her system was bound to respond to so much male chemistry, wise or not.

"Maris," he whispered, drawing her closer still, seeking her lips. His kiss was hot and heavy, and she found herself leaning into him and kissing him in the same hungrily demanding way. His hands moved on her back, from shoulders to hips and up again. Her breasts were chafed, almost harshly, by the pressure of his chest, and there was no ignoring the power of his arousal moving suggestively against her abdomen.

She knew she should break this up and didn't seem to have the strength to do it. Maybe the full moon was making her a little crazy, she thought. Certainly kissing a rootless man and reveling in the delectable sensations dancing and darting within

her own body was an extreme departure from her usual behavior.

But it felt so good and she felt so alive, so *glad* to be alive, and she raised on tiptoes to nestle against him. Luke's response was a deep-throated growl of pleasure. He pulled the bottom of her blouse from the waistband of her skirt and growled again when his hands glided over the smooth, hot skin of her back. A deft flicking of his fingers unhooked her bra, then he stepped away from her only enough to permit his hand to squeeze between them.

His hand on her bare breast brought a gasp from Maris, but the small sound neither intruded upon nor hindered their feverish kisses. It had never been like this for Maris before, where everything within her burned with sensation and yearning. Even during the early months of her marriage, when she had doted on Ray and responded to him in bed, she had never felt so overwhelmed by desire.

But it wasn't right. She shouldn't be standing in the middle of a dark field under a full moon and making love with Luke Rivers. Yet even knowing with every certainty that she was inviting future heartache, she couldn't leave his arms. Couldn't resist one more kiss. Couldn't stop his exploration of her body.

Instead she moaned while he caressed her breasts and aroused her nipples into hard peaks, and then let him unbutton her blouse so he could bend his head and lavish kisses to each sensitized crest. He gently tugged one into his mouth and sucked. Her fingers curled into his hair while her mind spun dizzily. "Luke...oh, Luke," she whispered raggedly.

Straightening his back, he brought her close again and mated their mouths for a long kiss that had her clinging to his shirt for support. Lost in sexual turmoil, Maris only vaguely registered her skirt being drawn up. He caught the elastic top of her panties and slid them down her thighs, and then his hand was seeking her most private spot. She jumped when he found it.

"Relax, honey," Luke whispered thickly, though he suspected neither of them would relax again until they had finished what they'd started tonight. No, that was wrong. The excite-

ment between them had begun long before tonight. Their first kiss might have been the beginning, or maybe it went clear back to the day he'd come to the Wyler ranch looking for Ray to collect on that IOU.

When it began was immaterial. They were together now, single-minded and focused on the grand finale. Kissing her sensual mouth, his hand lingered between her legs. Her every reaction raised his own blood pressure another notch. Then he whispered, "Now, Maris, right now, right here." He unzipped his jeans.

Her body was in flames and caught in a whirlpool of intense longing. But the sound of his zipper created a chink in her dazed mind. "Wait...Luke...wait," she stammered huskily.

He lifted his head and looked at her. "Wait for what, honey?"

"I...please...this isn't right."

He snorted out a brief, disbelieving laugh. "What isn't right?"

"You...and me. Like this." Her whole body felt damp and prickly. Her clothing was half on, half off. His hand was still between her legs, and some erotic portion of herself that she hadn't even known existed was in control of her physical side. Her brain, however, was objecting, albeit dimly and rather ineffectively, to such audacious behavior.

Luke brought his hands up to cup her face. He gazed into her eyes. "We're adults and unattached, both of us, and we're doing nothing wrong."

She was embarrassed by the turn of her thoughts, but couldn't stop herself from expressing them. "But...you only want me for tonight."

Luke went very still. "Meaning?"

"You have to know that I don't... What I mean is..."

"Do you want me for more than tonight? And please don't deny the wanting. I can feel it, Maris. I can see it on your face."

"In other words," she said in an agonized whisper, "you would consent to an affair with me while you're here."

"Consent?" Luke emitted a short, clipped laugh. "Hell, yes, I'd consent. Why wouldn't I?" His eyes narrowed on her face again. "Why wouldn't you?"

"Is it really that simple for you?"

"It's not simple at all." As if to prove it, he took possession of her mouth in a kiss that wasn't even slightly simple. Within it emotions flowed back and forth between them, sizzling emotions, complex emotions. Maris's entire life didn't exactly shoot through her mind, but she was suddenly bombarded with a hundred fleeting glimpses of herself before meeting Ray and after meeting Ray. Influencing every image was her present loneliness, which was probably the only reason she was in Luke's arms this very minute. At least he wasn't devising lies about being in love with her, or making false promises not to leave her in September.

She wasn't in love with him, either, she remembered, and maybe it was time to stop being so rigid and straitlaced. Accept him as he is, a voice said in her head. He's handsome and sexy and just possibly the kind of man you need right now. You certainly aren't looking for another husband, are you?

Indeed she was not. The mere thought of legally tying herself to another man put a bad taste in her mouth. Being independent had many more pluses than minuses. Sure she had her moments of loneliness, but Luke was more than willing to remedy that particular affliction, and so what if it was only a temporary cure?

She wrapped her arms around his waist and snuggled against his hard body. Breathlessly she whispered, "Forget everything I just said, Luke. I don't want to talk at all, not about anything."

Holding her, Luke frowned in surprise and then smiled, just a little; he didn't want to talk, either. Maris's cheek was against his chest and she could hear the hard, fast beat of his heart. "We won't talk," she whispered. Talking would change everything. As a logical thinker, she looked for logic in moods, attitudes and actions. There was no logic in tonight's activities and talking would only confuse her.

She tipped her head back and Luke promptly kissed her up-turned lips. In seconds she felt as though there had been no interruption, no doubts at all. She wanted Luke simply because he was a powerfully attractive, sexy man, and because she desperately needed closeness and intimacy with another human being. It had never happened to her before, but she was no longer questioning its logic.

"Luke," she whispered, and started unbuttoning his shirt. The shadowy planes of his muscular chest were finally hers to explore, and she ran her hands over his smooth, taut skin and into the triangular patch of hair between his nipples. "You're a dangerously handsome man." Her voice was low and not very steady.

Luke laughed softly, deep in his throat. "Are you calling me dangerous because I make you feel like a woman? That's not danger, Maris. This is the way it should be between a man and a woman, exciting, thrilling, erotic." He covered her hands with his own and pressed her palms to his chest. "I like you touching me." He paused, then added, "I like everything about you."

Her eyes lifted to lock with his. "You do?"

Without warning, Luke moved away from her. "I do." Taking off his shirt he spread it out on the grass. On his knees, he looked at her. "Give me your skirt and blouse."

He was making them a bed, Maris realized. Mesmerized by him, the beautiful night and her own aching body, she stepped out of her skirt and handed it to him. Her fingers undid the few remaining buttons of her blouse he hadn't already opened, and she slid the garment from her shoulders and dropped it near the makeshift bed. Luke stopped to look at her in the moonlight. "Damn, you're beautiful," he said hoarsely. "Come here."

Maris sank to her knees on her own skirt. Luke finished removing her bra, and she felt the burn of his hot gaze on her bare breasts. Then he yanked off his boots and socks, and slithered out of his jeans and undershorts. She stared and stared, entranced by the utter beauty of his maleness.

But he was doing the same with her, drinking in the sight of

her body without clothes. They sat there looking at each other—then, quite suddenly, it wasn't enough to merely look.

Luke pulled her down, placing her on her back. His kisses started out tender and gentle, but quickly became rough and hungry. He took a breath of air deep into his lungs and told himself to take it easy. At this rate, things would be over almost before they'd begun, and that wouldn't be fair to Maris. There were all kinds of women in the world, he'd discovered through the years. Some deserved teeth-gritting patience from a man, some didn't. Maris was in the first category. In fact, Maris Wyler was in a class all her own. He had never—never—felt this way about any other woman.

Frowning slightly, he lifted his head to see her face. Her eyes, even though dusky with shadows, held a dreamy cast. She touched his cheek. "What is it, Luke?"

He had no glib reply, no immediate answer of any sort. Recognizing special feelings for a woman was foreign to his experience. "Um…nothing important," he mumbled, deliberately blocking out everything but the woman beneath him. She was beautiful in the moonlight, beautiful and sensual and eager to make love. Why in hell was he wasting time?

His kisses began at her forehead and moved slowly down to her nose, her lips, her throat. Her hands moved over him, lingering on the muscles of his back, then sliding down to his hips. "Touch me all over," he whispered. "I want to feel your hands on me."

The images behind Maris's closed eyes were of Luke working in the corral without a shirt, his sweaty skin glistening in the sun, the leather gloves on his hands, the snug fit of his jeans. Those mental pictures were as arousing as having Luke naked in her arms. In one tiny corner of her mind lurked the knowledge that she would regret this tomorrow. But tomorrow seemed so far away. For once in her life she was going to live for the moment.

Luke's mouth glided down to her breasts, where he gave each perfect mound equal attention. "Sweet…so sweet," he whispered.

"It...it's torment," Maris moaned as he gently sucked on her nipple.

"Do you want me to stop?"

"No...no. I couldn't bear it if you stopped now."

"Then it's good torment."

"Yes, oh, yes."

Luke's hand slid down to the soft hair at the base of her belly, and then farther, deep into the secrets of her body. "Is this good torment, too?"

Maris groaned. "You know it is." She couldn't lie still. Her hips arched upward. "Luke...please..."

He knew what she was asking for in that husky, ragged tone, but he also knew that once he entered her he wouldn't last very long. "Easy, honey," he whispered, and lay down beside her. Nimbly he adjusted her position, placing her head in the crook of his left arm so he could kiss her mouth while he made sure she reached the pinnacle with his right hand.

Writhing beneath the incredible stroking of his fingers, Maris felt a gathering in her lower abdomen, the beginning of the end, a radiating pleasure. "Luke...oh, Luke."

"Go with it, honey," he whispered. "Don't fight it."

She could do nothing *but* go with it. The spiraling thrills were consuming her, so strong and overpowering she could barely breathe and had to tear her mouth from Luke's to gasp for air. Then, moaning, she buried her face in the curve of his neck and shoulder and savored the delicious sensations rippling throughout her body.

Luke held her for a few minutes, giving her time to come down from that awesome peak. But he knew that too much time would completely deplete her desire, so at a huge release of breath from Maris, he moved on top of her. Watching her face, he slowly slid into her. Her lips parted. There was a look of bewitchment in her eyes. Luke couldn't know it, Maris realized, but never had she felt so wanton before, so completely submerged in lovemaking.

Her hips lifted to meet his first thrust. Taking his face be-

tween her hands, she brought his head down for a breathy, passionate kiss. "You are an amazing lover," she whispered.

Her words sent Luke's spirit soaring. An amazing lover. Yeah, by damn, he was.

But so was she. "Maris...Maris..."

They were kissing again, their bodies moving together in perfect harmony. He slid his hands under her hips. "Put your legs around me," he whispered thickly.

She did it, and then things got really wild. A red haze of pure lust burned behind Luke's eyes. He couldn't slow himself down any longer, and his thrusts into her velvety heat became faster, harder, deeper.

"Making love to you is like riding the tail of a comet," he whispered hoarsely.

"For me, too, Luke," she gasped. Without intent, her fingernails dug into his back. "Don't stop. Please don't stop."

"No way, baby. I couldn't stop now even if I wanted to. Even if *you* wanted me to."

Maris's moans turned to whimpers, and her whimpers became cries. "Luke...Luke...*Luke!*"

He went over the edge himself. "Maris..." He wanted to say more, but he was suddenly too weak to do more than collapse upon her.

It seemed an eternity before either was able to move. Maris lay under him with her eyes closed and listened to her own heart returning to its normal beat. Her skin was damp with perspiration—so was Luke's—and suddenly the night air didn't feel as warm as it had.

As she opened her eyes and felt the weight of Luke's limp body clamping her to the ground, her system went into shock. Had she lost her mind tonight? She stared at the full moon and blamed it for her aberration. It was a common belief that people behaved peculiarly when the moon was full, but making love on the ground with a man who would never commit himself to anything or anyone—other than rodeo—was insane, not peculiar. Especially when they had used no protection.

"Oh, God," she moaned.

Alarmed at the agony in her voice, Luke raised up. "What?"

"Let me up."

"Honey, what's wrong?"

"You need to ask? Luke, we didn't use any protection." She pushed on him. "Let me up."

"Well...sure...but..." Luke moved to the ground, but he caught her hand before she could leap up and dash away. "Tell me you're not sorry about this."

Maris jerked her hand out of his. "If I did it would be a lie." She grabbed a corner of her skirt and yanked. "Please get off my clothes."

He got to his feet. "Maris..."

"I can't talk now." Hastily gathering her clothing, she looked around the dark landscape and spotted a large bush. While Luke watched, confused and a little queasy over her attitude, Maris disappeared behind the bush.

With a distinct lack of enthusiasm, he found his own clothes and began dressing.

He was standing next to Rocky when Maris reappeared. "The last thing I expected was immediate regret," he said gloomily. "Why do you feel that way, Maris?"

She stopped. "Something happened to me tonight, Luke. I don't know what it was—"

"How about needing a man?" he interjected cruelly.

She flinched, but forced herself to stand there. "I'm not blaming you."

"You're not. Well, for some damned reason that doesn't make me feel a whole lot better. If you're not blaming me, then you're blaming yourself, and that's just plain idiotic. Needing sex is as natural as needing food and water. Are you ashamed of being human?"

"Having sex is not the same thing as sitting down to a meal, so that argument leaves me cold. I'm walking back to the ranch. Alone. You ride Rocky home. I need to think."

The ice in her voice unnerved and angered Luke. "Lady, you are one mixed-up human being. Ten minutes ago you couldn't get enough of me and now you hate my guts."

Maris's jaw dropped. "I don't hate you! Why would you say such a thing? I...I'm confused. Can't you understand that? I've never done anything like...like what I did tonight in all my life."

"Why didn't you think about that *before* we made love?" Luke put the question harshly. Maris's attitude hurt. Maybe she was confused, but so was he. He didn't want her talking this way, acting this way. While making love he'd had visions of...visions of... Well, they weren't clear, but for a fact they had included Maris.

Maris looked at him for a long moment. Then she lifted her chin. "I should have. Good night. I'm going home." Turning, she started walking.

"Maris!" She kept going. "You can ride behind me." She kept going. "Damn you," he shouted, and then wondered in the echo of his own anger if he wasn't damning himself.

Ten

Maris had a hard time falling asleep that night. Again and again she got up to prowl around the house and question her behavior with Luke. Taking momentary pleasure while ignoring the aftermath was so unlike her that the episode was deeply unsettling.

The only time she made sure she was in her room was when Keith came home. With her lights off she listened to the boy's stealthy movements in the house, obviously an attempt not to wake her. It was a few minutes before midnight, exactly as he had promised. Her heart melted just a little for Keith. He was a dear and she loved him as a woman must love her own son.

Then she remembered how careless she and Luke had been tonight and that she could be pregnant this very minute.

A sudden abandoned joy leapt through her body. A baby. Maris had been sitting on the edge of the bed and she got up to pace, curling her arms around herself. What if it was true? What if Luke had made her pregnant tonight?

She stopped pacing to calculate dates, then frowned at the result. Her most fertile time wouldn't be for another day or two. This was something she understood very well. Before learning of Ray's vasectomy she had faithfully kept track of her monthly cycle, steadfast in her hope of becoming pregnant. The habit had stayed with her, albeit absentmindedly and without cause, but she was always able to pinpoint which stage her body was undergoing.

Disappointment created a furrow between her eyes. It was highly unlikely she had conceived tonight. If she and Luke had made love—by mere coincidence, of course—when her cycle was at its peak, she could have had the child she'd always yearned for.

Her mouth was suddenly cotton dry as a shocking idea struck her: seducing Luke at the right time to conceive. Luke would never know, she told herself. He was leaving right after the horse auction, and she couldn't imagine a reason why he would ever return to Whitehorn. Ray's death hadn't been that long ago. She could tell everyone the baby was Ray's. She had heard of ten-and eleven-month babies, and often, she had also heard, a first baby came late.

Oh, my God, she thought frantically. Could she actually do something so deceitful?

But Luke was probably her one and only opportunity to have a child with no one being the wiser. And it wasn't as if he would care, even if by some improbable chance he should figure out her scheme. He was a drifter, a man who by his own admission visited his mother only once a year. He had no ties and obviously wanted none. He would undoubtedly be surprised if she instigated further lovemaking, but why would he question her motives? He would believe, as he had tonight, that she merely needed a man.

Trembling, Maris crawled into bed and pulled the covers up to her chin. Her eyes were wide and staring. *Could she do it?* Could she deliberately trick Luke into thinking she wanted his body once or twice more merely because she was lonely? This was Saturday night, or rather, a very early Sunday morning. Monday or Tuesday would be her fertile period. But how would she accomplish it? With Keith on the place, how could she spend time alone with Luke?

Her morals battled with her intense desire to have a baby. Again she relived that awful moment when Ray had told her about his vasectomy. He had cheated her out of something that was only every woman's right—the right to bear children. *Life* had cheated her, Maris decided bitterly. If Luke was the kind of man who needed a family she wouldn't even consider doing something so underhanded. But he was a loner, a man who actually worked at remaining rootless and unencumbered. Aside from that one personality flaw he was a perfect candidate to

father a child, physically strong and healthy, reasonably intelligent and ambitious in his own way.

By morning Maris had decided that yes, she could do it, and then no, she couldn't, so many times, she got up bleary eyed and depressed. She made pancakes for breakfast, then took a cup of coffee to her bedroom while Luke and Keith ate. The thought of food made her stomach roll, though the coffee tasted good. The truth was that she didn't want to look Luke in the eye this morning. She didn't want to see what had happened between them on his face, and she was sure there would be some sort of reminder in his expression.

Groaning because there was no way to avoid him once the yard sale began, Maris got ready for the day. Her skin was pale, she saw in the bathroom mirror, and she applied some blusher to her cheeks and lipstick to her lips.

When she finally braved the kitchen again, Luke and Keith were gone. A glance out the window told her where they were: working with a horse in the corral. Maris sighed. Luke was the most constant, the hardest-working man she'd ever known. Compared to Ray's lackadaisical interest in any aspect of the ranch, Luke was a saint.

Standing at the window and squinting to watch the two men and the horse within the corral, Maris knew that she couldn't delude and manipulate Luke into giving her a baby. How could she have even thought of something so dishonest and conniving? Some of the tension drained from her system. Feeling better at having ultimately made a sane and sensible decision, she tackled the breakfast dishes. When the kitchen was tidy, she went outside to await any visitors to her yard sale, though she really didn't expect a repeat of yesterday's onslaught.

The first car that arrived was familiar. Smiling, Maris walked out to greet Lori Parker Bains. "Lori, hi." She gave her friend a hug. "Gosh, it's good to see you."

Lori was carrying a small box. "I made a batch of fudge last night. I brought you some."

"Homemade fudge? I haven't made fudge in years. Thanks."

Lori frowned. "Maris, are you feeling well? You look a little peaked."

And that was when the first lie came out of Maris's mouth, without warning, without intent. "I...I've been a little queasy in the morning for the past few weeks." Maris could hardly believe she'd said that, and to her best friend, to boot. She felt embarrassed, and her face burned.

"Every morning?" Lori asked with a serious edge to her voice. "Maris, queasiness in the morning is a symptom of pregnancy. Do you suppose...?"

Maris felt about two inches high. Lori was the one person in Whitehorn who knew how much Maris had always wanted a child. However, Lori was a nurse and a midwife, and if anyone had the training and talent to see through Maris's lie, it was her.

"I doubt it very much," Maris said firmly, wishing to God she hadn't told that abominable lie. *Why* had she lied? Hadn't she decided not more than a half hour ago in the kitchen that she wasn't going to trick Luke into anything?

"Beside a queasy stomach, how else have you been feeling? Are your breasts tender?"

Maris's breasts were very tender this morning, but only because of the extremely ardent attention Luke had given them last night. "Uh, sort of," she mumbled.

Lori was beaming. "And what about getting up in the night? Are you using the commode a little more than usual?"

"No." She absolutely could not tell one more lie to her best friend. "It's nothing, Lori, really. Just forget I said anything, okay?"

"Forget it? Maris, if you are pregnant it's very important to begin prenatal care as early as possible. Your baby will benefit by it and so will you."

Maris felt as though her stomach had dropped somewhere down by her knees. Never had she rued an impulse more than she did this one. "It's nothing, Lori. I swear it." She forced a bright smile. "Did you come to look over my sale items? There

isn't much left. It was a little crazy here yesterday and most of the good stuff was sold.''

Lori was not distracted by Maris's change of subject. ''Promise me one thing, at least. If you don't want to see a doctor right away, buy one of those home pregnancy tests.'' She named a brand. ''It's really quite reliable, Maris.''

Buy a home pregnancy test in Whitehorn's one drugstore? Maris's heart sank. John Tully would have a field day spreading that news around town.

''I'll think about it.''

''Maris, you have to do more than think about it,'' Lori said in her most professional voice. ''Look, I know what you're thinking. There's only one place in Whitehorn that carries that product, and you would just as soon keep your condition private until you know for sure. How about if I buy the test and bring it by sometime tomorrow?''

''That...would be nice,'' Maris said weakly. Out of the corner of her eye she spotted Luke walking across the yard, which presented a golden opportunity to desert the topic of pregnancy. ''There's Luke Rivers. Would you like to meet him?''

Lori turned to see Maris's hired man. ''Wow,'' she whispered. ''Maris, he's gorgeous. I would love to meet him.''

''Luke,'' Maris called. When he looked her way, she beckoned him with her hand.

He began ambling toward the two women. Earlier this morning Maris hadn't even looked at him, and he had to question why she was friendly again.

''Hi,'' he said when he'd reached Maris and her companion. ''Lori Bains, Luke Rivers.''

Smiling, Lori offered her hand. ''Nice meeting you, Luke. I've been hearing your name quite a lot around town.''

''Is that right?'' Luke shook Lori's hand and grinned. ''Why would anyone be mentioning my name?''

Lori shrugged prettily and Maris felt an uncharacteristic pang of envy. She could never look the way Lori did, not if she spent the rest of her life trying every cosmetic on the market and even resorting to plastic surgery. Lori's blond hair challenged

the sun's bright light, and Lori's smile could grace a toothpaste ad.

"Well, you're new to the area, for one thing," Lori replied. "And you're single and good-looking." She smiled teasingly. "People just like to talk, Luke, especially in a small town."

"Guess that's true." Luke thought that Lori was one of the prettiest women he'd ever seen. She was also very friendly and, he suspected, a warm and compassionate person.

But it was Maris who was making his skin tingle, not Lori Bains. He gave Maris a melting look. "How are you this morning?"

Maris turned three shades of red. "Fine...just fine." As she had feared, every detail of last night's misadventure was in his eyes. "Uh, Lori wanted to meet you."

His gaze returned to Ms. Bains. "Well, it was good meeting you, Lori. I'm sure we'll see each other again before I leave."

"Oh? How long will you be here?"

"Until the end of September." Luke looked at Maris. "That's still our agreement, isn't it?"

"Yes," Maris said quietly, wondering why he would ask her that. Nothing they had said last night or at any other time could possibly be construed as a deviation of their agreement.

"Well, I'd better get back to work." Nodding at Lori, he walked away.

Both women watched him for a few moments. Lori spoke first. "Luke is in love with you, Maris."

Maris's eyes widened in shock. "Don't be silly! Luke can hardly wait to get out of here."

"Do you mean to tell me that you don't feel something from him?" Lori looked exceedingly doubtful. "Hasn't he said or done anything to let you know he's interested? He is, Maris, believe me. I saw the way he looked at you."

"Your imagination is running wild, Lori. He didn't look at me any differently than he looked at you."

"Hogwash. Well, I can't make you like him, but I do. Not for any romantic reason," Lori added. "But he seems like a darned nice guy to me."

Maris was more depressed than ever. Not only had she told that abysmal lie to her best friend about feeling queasy every morning—apparently to pave the way, she thought disgustedly, just in case she changed her mind again about using Luke—she'd felt the heat of Luke's gaze and knew that he was thinking of further intimacy between them.

But as for him being in love with her, that was utterly ridiculous. She was glad to see another car arriving. "Look around if you want, Lori. I'll go say hello to the Jensons."

Sheriff Judd Hensley drove in around two that afternoon. He was out of uniform and in his own car, obviously enjoying a day off. There were so few things left to sell that Luke and Keith had gone back to work with the horses and Maris was tending the sale by herself.

Judd walked up. "Hello, Maris."

"Hello, Judd."

Judd was looking around. "Appears that I should have come by yesterday. I heard that people were buying your stuff like crazy. Seems to be the truth."

"The sale was a huge success," Maris agreed. "I never dreamed so many people would show up. As you can see, there are only a few odds and ends left."

Judd's steady gaze rested on her. "How are you doing?"

"Just fine, Judd. Please don't worry about me."

Judd jerked his head toward the corral. "I see you've still got Luke Rivers working for you."

"And doing a very good job," Maris replied evenly. She drummed up a smile. "The next event for the No Bull Ranch is going to be a horse auction at the end of September. I'll be putting out signs and notices in the newspaper to advertise the sale in a few weeks."

"An auction, eh? Sounds like a good idea, Maris." Judd paused briefly. "What happens after that?"

Maris drew a breath. "Then Luke will be leaving and I'll be back in the cattle business."

"He'll be leaving?"

"He's only here to break my horses, Judd. I told you that."

"Yeah, guess you did." Judd paused. "How about having supper out with me tonight?"

Supper out with anyone was the last thing Maris wanted for tonight, but maybe spending time with another man besides Luke would put her back on course. "Sure, why not?"

Judd shaped one of his rare smiles. "I'll pick you up around six, all right?"

"I'll be ready."

After Judd left, Maris went to the patio and sat down. She'd hardly had a chance to catch her breath yesterday, but people had merely dribbled in today. Judd could very well be her last customer, she decided, and then turned her thoughts to what she could prepare for Keith's and Luke's supper.

She bit down on her lip, suspecting that Luke wasn't going to like her going out with Judd tonight. But last night's foolishness didn't give Luke any say in what she did or did not do. Last night had been a mistake. What in God's name had caused her to behave so brazenly? Loneliness was no excuse for completely losing herself in a man's arms.

Then, sitting there in the quiet, she thought again of a baby, and of the names she had chosen shortly after her wedding day. Her first son would have been named Robert Ray Wyler, after his father. Her first daughter would have been named Samantha Ray Wyler, also after her father. It would be wise, of course, to keep the "Ray" in either name, should she become pregnant.

Maris shuddered. Why was she still thinking that way? She wasn't going to do it, so why couldn't she eradicate the idea from her mind?

Blackie wandered over and lay down beside Maris's chair. "Blackie, my friend," she said quietly. "A dog's life is very simple compared to a human's. Be glad you're a scruffy little mutt, okay?" Patting Blackie's head, Maris got to her feet and started for the house.

Luke saw Maris going in. "Just keep him moving in a circle like you're doing, Keith." The bay gelding was on a long lead, and Luke had shown Keith how to swing a rope with one hand

while hanging on to the lead with the other. It was another step in the training process, teaching the horse to obey a human's commands and not to fear a rope. "I'm going up to the house to talk to Maris about something. I won't be long." Taking hold of a corral post Luke vaulted over the fence.

"Sure thing," Keith agreed. "I'll keep him moving."

Luke jogged to the house and walked in. "Maris?"

She was in the kitchen, putting together a casserole of rice, vegetables and chicken, which would be baking in a slow oven until suppertime. Luke's coming in without Keith put her on guard. "What is it?"

"I think we should talk about last night."

Maris turned her back on him, giving the casserole her full attention. "There's nothing to talk about."

"Nothing?" Luke went to stand beside her at the counter and crooked his head around to see her face. "You're calling what happened last night nothing?"

"No, it's just that I don't see any good reason to talk about it."

"You don't. Well, supposing I do?"

"Don't pressure me, Luke."

"Stop puttering and look at me."

"I'm not puttering. I'm making dinner. Yours and Keith's. I won't be here."

Luke narrowed his eyes on her. "Where will you be?"

"I'm having dinner with Judd."

The bottom fell out of Luke's stomach. "You're going out with Judd? Why?"

Maris sent him a quick, nervous glance. "Because he asked me. He's a good friend, Luke."

"How good a friend, Maris?" Luke's voice was lethally quiet.

"Not the way you're thinking. He's a *friend*. Do you understand the definition of the word?"

"Don't patronize me, Maris. I might not have gone to college like you did, but I'm not stupid."

She realized that she had hurt him, and she turned to face

him. "I never meant to imply you were. But last night shouldn't have happened." Oh, Lord, he was handsome. Just looking at him made her spine tingle. He was sweaty and smelled musky and male. His heavy dark hair was damp and drooping down his forehead. There was a fierce, defensive pride in his eyes. "I'm sorry," she whispered, deeply shaken by what she was feeling for him. "It just...shouldn't have happened."

Luke kept looking at her. His past relationships had been sweet but brief and he'd never wanted them any other way. Maris was different. He was different because of her. He didn't want her going out with Judd Hensley or any other man.

But nothing came out of his mouth.

"Luke? Do you understand?"

He nodded. "Yeah, I understand." Whirling, he strode from the kitchen, gave the screen door an unnecessarily hefty shove, causing it to bang loudly behind him, and headed for the corral.

Clenching her hand into a fist, Maris brought it up to press against her lips. Which one of them was hurting more, she wondered with tears dribbling down her cheeks, her or Luke?

A second later she wiped them away with a kitchen towel. Another car was arriving. Pasting a smile on her face, she went outside. Her smile became genuine when she saw Jessica. "Hi."

"Hi, Maris." Jessica got out and opened the back door of her car. "I have Jennifer with me." Jessica began unbuckling the safety straps of the baby's car seat as she thought to herself. She missed her truck, but having the car was much more practical with Jennifer.

Maris felt a burst of joy at sight of the baby. "Oh, Jessica, she's so beautiful."

"Yes, isn't she?" Jessica said proudly. Lifting the sleeping child from the car seat, Jessica held her daughter so Maris could look at her. "She's so special to Sterling and me, Maris."

"That's how it should be with a baby," Maris said softly, her gaze riveted on the child's adorable little face.

Jessica spotted Luke and Keith in the corral. "I need to speak

to Keith, Maris.'' She smiled. ''Would you like to hold Jennifer while I do it?''

''I'd love to hold her.'' Jessica passed the baby to Maris's arms. ''Oh, she's wonderful,'' she whispered emotionally. ''I'll sit on the patio with her.''

''I shouldn't be very long with Keith,'' Jessica said, then started walking toward the corral.

Maris resumed her chair on the patio and stared in awe at the sleeping child on her lap. She touched Jennifer's tiny fingers and then undid the lower portion of her lightweight cotton blanket to look at her little feet. The baby's warmth and powdery scent penetrated Maris's clothing and skin to wind around her soul.

She wanted a baby of her own. Every cell of her body ached from the wanting, and it wasn't wrong, she told herself. Wanting a child was natural and right. She wasn't warped or crazy to yearn for motherhood. Nature intended for the female of every species to procreate.

Luke looked up to see a woman standing at the corral fence. ''Hi,'' he called.

''Hello.''

Keith turned. ''Mrs. McCallum!''

''Hello, Keith. Could you leave your work for a few minutes to talk to me?''

Keith's face was red, but he remembered his manners. ''Mrs. McCallum, this is Luke Rivers.''

Luke nodded a greeting. ''Nice meeting you, ma'am. Keith, you go on and talk to Mrs. McCallum.''

Keith considered vaulting the corral fence the way Luke did, but he figured he'd better try it for the first time when no one was around, and he went through the gate. ''Anything wrong, Mrs. McCallum?''

Jessica began walking, leading him away from the corral. ''I'm not here to deliver bad news, Keith,'' she said calmly. ''At least, I don't consider my message bad news. You'll have to make up your own mind on that score.'' They stopped under a large elm tree. She looked Keith in the eye. ''Keith, your

father would like you to visit him.'' There was a sudden sharp withdrawal in the boy's eyes. ''You don't have to do it. You never have to see him again if you don't want to. But you should know what's been happening with him in prison. He has joined Alcoholics Anonymous and has voluntarily requested emotional therapy. The prison psychologist sent me a report that indicates definite progress in Terrance's attitude and out-look.''

Jessica touched Keith's arm. ''I'm not advising you one way or the other on this, Keith. I'm merely passing on Terrance's request.'' The boy was silent for so long, looking off into the distance, that Jessica spoke again. ''You don't have to make up your mind this minute, Keith. Maybe you'd like to think about it for a while.''

''Why does he want to see me?''

Jessica looked at the boy. ''I don't know. Perhaps he's think-ing about making amends. You're his only child and he's get-ting old, Keith. Without alcohol pickling his brain, maybe he's sorry for what he did to you.''

''He'll start drinking again when he gets out of jail,'' Keith mumbled.

''That's possible. It's also possible that he will never touch liquor again.'' Again Jessica touched Keith's arm. ''It's your decision, Keith. No one can make it for you, nor should they. I'm going now. Call me after you've given it some thought.''

Jessica began walking toward the patio. ''Mrs. McCallum?'' Keith called.

''Yes?'' Jessica stopped and turned.

''Uh...I'll go and see him. Can I go tomorrow?''

''If I can arrange for your transportation that soon, I don't see why not. I'll call you as soon as I know, all right?''

Keith nodded. ''Thanks.''

Jessica smiled. ''You're quite welcome. Incidentally, you seem to enjoy working with horses.''

''Luke's teaching me a lot.''

''I'm pleased to hear it. Goodbye for now, Keith.''

''Bye.''

Jessica continued on to Maris's patio. "Well, are you tired of holding Jennifer?"

Maris lifted her eyes to baby Jennifer's mother. "I could never get tired of holding a baby, Jessica. I'm not completely certain—I haven't seen a doctor yet—but I think...I think I might be pregnant." Maris licked her suddenly dry lips. "Please don't mention it to anyone. I don't want it to get around until I know for sure."

Jessica's eyes misted over. "Oh, Maris, how wonderful for you. Don't worry, I won't say a word to anyone."

Maris remained on the patio after Jessica had driven away, though she had turned her chair to face the corral and Luke. Her arms still felt the imprint of baby Jennifer's firm little body and there was a lingering scent of baby powder on her clothes. Her face bore a look of determination, even though her stomach roiled with guilt. She was going to get pregnant, and that man out there in the corral was going to be the baby's father.

That decision was final.

Eleven

Maris tried very hard to be an attentive dinner companion to Judd that evening, but her mind was at the ranch with Luke and not on the busy Hip Hop Café or the excellent stir-fry dish she had ordered.

"Something's bothering you, Maris," Judd said after he'd had to repeat himself several times to get a response from her. "Would you like to talk about it?"

"I'm sorry, Judd." Reaching across the table, Maris patted his hand. "I don't know where my mind is these days."

"You're not over Ray's death yet," Judd said with a somber expression. He was also thinking of himself, of the death of his son and of his divorce. It had been seven years and he still wasn't over those two tragic events. Maris was a courageous woman, but Ray's death had to have hit her hard. "How could you be?" Judd stated logically. "It's only been a few months."

Two and a half months to be exact, Maris thought. Who would be stupid enough to believe she'd been pregnant when Ray died?

But who, Maris decided next, would be rude enough to mention dates to her face? There would be talk, of course, and more than likely Luke's name would come up. *He lived on the ranch with Maris for several months, you know. If you ask me, Luke Rivers is the father of that baby.*

It wouldn't matter, Maris thought with sudden fierce resolve. She would have her baby, and the gossips could speculate from then until doomsday and they would never know for sure.

"I'm pretty much over Ray's death," she told Judd, speaking calmly and certainly honestly. There'd been a time when losing Ray would have nearly killed her, but those days were long gone and she didn't like thinking about them.

It was getting dark when they left the Hip Hop. "How about a drive somewhere?" Judd asked. "You don't have to hurry home, do you?"

"No, I suppose not." Maris hoped her reluctance didn't show. After they were in Judd's car and driving along, she thought about Judd's invitation that afternoon and why she'd felt so obliged to accept. He'd been kind and considerate since the night he had come to the ranch to tell her about Ray's death. She recalled every word:

"Judd!" Maris had answered the doorbell, and was surprised to see the sheriff on her front porch. It was late, or early, depending on one's point of view: 2:30 a.m.

"May I come in?"

"Well…yes, of course." Nervous suddenly, Maris pinched the lapels of her robe together. The sheriff didn't make calls in the middle of the night without cause and Ray wasn't home yet. Silently she led Judd to her living room.

"Sit down, Maris," he said gently.

She sank to the sofa. "Something happened to Ray, didn't it? Is he all right?"

Judd sat next to her, compassion in his dark eyes. "Ray's dead, Maris."

Shock bolted through her system, all but immobilizing her. "Dead?"

Judd reached for her hand. "It was a highway accident. He drove into a cement pier at an underpass."

Maris swallowed because her throat felt so tight and sticky. "Was anyone else hurt?"

"No one. He was alone and no other vehicles were involved."

Maris leveled a demanding look on the sheriff. "Tell me the truth. Was he drunk?"

"I don't have the coroner's report yet, but I was there and my own opinion is that yes, he was very drunk."

"Dead drunk," Maris said with intense bitterness. It was a macabre pun and not funny. Tugging her hand out of Judd's, she raised it and her other to cover her face. Her eyes burned,

but there were no tears. Her heart ached for Ray's wasted life, but there was no real sorrow. It was as though she had known for a long time that something like this was going to happen.

She felt Judd's hand on her shoulder. "Maris, is there anyone you would like me to call to come out here and be with you?"

She dropped her hands and spoke dully. "I'll be all right, Judd."

Ever since, Judd had checked on her regularly. He wasn't really courting her, she felt, nor did she think that he was falling in love with her. She turned her head to look at him. It was too bad they *weren't* falling in love. Judd was steady as a rock, and wasn't that the very quality she would hope for in a man, should she ever marry again? Instead, she was getting much too involved with Luke, who was a lot more like Ray than Judd could ever be.

Judd realized he was being stared at and sent her a glance. "What?"

Maris smiled. "I was just thinking. You're a nice man, Judd."

He chuckled cynically. "Not everyone would agree with you on that point."

"Maybe not, but it's still the truth." Judd took his duties as sheriff very seriously, and there were people in the area—especially those of Terrance Colson's ilk—who had nothing good to say about Judd.

But Maris saw beneath his reticent, stern exterior. He was a proud, solitary man and she suspected that he viewed her as bearing the same traits. Judd's own marriage had ended in divorce after he and his wife had lost their eight-year-old son in a tragic accident. Judd was no stranger to loss or loneliness. Maris *was* lonely, too, but her loneliness hadn't begun with Ray's demise. Only one person, Lori Bains, knew that Maris's unhappiness had started within the first six months of her marriage.

Maris sighed. Everyone had to live with his or her own past, but the water under her bridge was murky and dark with shat-

tered dreams and ideals. It was up to her to bring some sunshine into her life; she was the only one who could do it.

Judd drove out to the Laughing Horse Indian Reservation, turned around and took some side roads back to town. They talked about impersonal topics, the library's current fund drive to increase its reference material, the new houses being constructed on the outskirts of Whitehorn and local politics. Maris had held up her end of the conversation, but she was glad to see the lights of Whitehorn. It surprised her when Judd drove past the turn onto Highway 17, which led to her ranch.

He sent her a small smile. "Let's have some dessert before calling it a night."

What could she do but agree? "All right."   .

Judd stopped at a fast-food restaurant that featured ice-cream specialties. "A banana split sounds about right to me," he commented as they got out of the car.

Maris ordered a chocolate soda and Judd ordered a banana split with extra caramel sauce. The rich desserts were delivered to their table. Judd picked up his spoon and began eating. After a few bites he said, rather casually, "Maris, I hope you know I would never deliberately say anything to you that would hurt your feelings."

She gave him a questioning look. "Yes, I know. What's on your mind, Judd?"

Judd spooned another bite of ice cream and banana into his mouth, chewed briefly and swallowed before answering. "There's talk around town about you and Luke Rivers."

Maris sat back. "That's not news, Judd. I would have been a lot more surprised to hear you say that no one ever mentions it."

"Well, for my part, I'll be glad to see the last of Rivers."

"Why is that?"

"Just a feeling that he could be trouble, Maris."

Instantly defensive, Maris leaned forward. "Let me tell you about Luke Rivers, Judd. He's up before dawn every morning and only stops working for meals. He hasn't taken any time off since the day he started working for me. If Ray had possessed

even one-tenth of Luke's drive, our ranch would have prospered. Luke is kind to Keith and..."

"Kind to you?" Judd said softly.

Maris drew a breath. "We get along, but there's nothing..." The lie got stuck in her throat. "I despise gossip, and I'm surprised you're listening to it."

"If there's no truth to it, it shouldn't bother you."

"You must believe it or you wouldn't have mentioned it."

"That's not true, Maris. I only wanted you to know about it."

"So I could do what, Judd? Get all fired up and kick Luke off the ranch?" Disgustedly Maris pushed aside her unfinished soda. "I'm not going to tell him to leave. I need him to break those horses and he's doing a darned good job of it. If the lily-white citizens of Whitehorn weren't talking about me, they'd be talking about someone else. Maybe I'm doing someone I don't even know a big favor."

"Don't be bitter, Maris."

She laughed and it was indeed a bitter sound. "May we go now? I'm tired and would like to go home."

Judd tried to make amends during the drive from town to Maris's ranch. She replied to everything he said, but her tone of voice remained unrelentingly cool. Finally Judd came right out and apologized. "I'm sorry I even brought it up, Maris."

"So am I, Judd," she said wearily. No one could possibly grasp her situation. If she explained everything from her current financial picture to the sham her marriage really had been, they would understand, but even when things had been unbearable with Ray she'd kept her private life private. Occasionally she had unloaded on Lori, but even Lori didn't know it all.

Other than one small light illuminating the kitchen window, the ranch was dark when they arrived. Obviously Keith and Luke had gone to bed, which she'd expected, as it was after ten. Judd walked her to the back door. "We're still friends, aren't we, Maris?"

"Yes, we're still friends, Judd. I hope we always will be. Thank you for dinner. Good night."

"Good night. I'll drop by in a few days."

"Do that."

Judd walked off. Instead of going in, Maris stood with her hand on the doorknob and listened to his car driving away. She glanced behind her to the dark barn and thought of Luke in bed, undoubtedly sound asleep. There were faint noises in the night—the movements of the horses, the chirps of crickets in the grass, the rustling of leaves in a nearby tree.

She didn't want to go in to her lonely bed. Her heart began fluttering wildly, because what she wanted to do was brazen and brash. But, standing there in the dark, she knew she was going to do it.

Feeling breathless and keyed up, she went to her car for the flashlight she kept under the seat. Getting to the barn in the dark wouldn't be a problem, but once inside the pitch-black structure she would need a light. She left her purse in the car, then sped across the compound to the barn. Quietly opening one of its smaller doors, she stepped inside. The inky blackness was as she'd anticipated and she switched on the flashlight.

For a moment her courage deserted her, and she shook in her shoes while pondering how much she had changed since meeting Luke. Until Luke, Ray had been her one and only lover. Her high school and college boyfriends had never moved her enough to get past her strict morality. Ray had sweet-talked her into bed on their third date, but only because she had been so in love with him. She had been a stupid, gullible, naive girl to fall for Ray's line of patter, although even now, in retrospect, she believed that he had loved her for a while. Their problems had begun when she'd happily settled into marriage and he couldn't. Settling into anything for any length of time just wasn't in his nature, she had ultimately learned.

A creaking noise in the old barn startled Maris back into the present. Nervously she shone the flashlight on the ladder to the loft. She wasn't here only because she wanted a baby, she realized. Luke had brought an excitement into her life she couldn't

have imagined before experiencing it. His leaving in September was going to create a void that would take a lot of time to accept, but until then he was here and why should she deny herself the pleasure of being in his arms?

Quietly she crept up the ladder, then tiptoed across the wood floor to the door of the loft bedroom with her heart beating like a tom-tom. Maris slowly turned the knob and pushed the door open. Even without the flashlight she could make out Luke's form in bed. He was on his left side, facing the window, which put his back to the door and her. His even, shallow breathing told her he was deep in sleep, and she wondered if she should just walk around the bed and awaken him, or if there was a better way.

That "better way" took shape in her mind. Before she could lose her nerve she laid the flashlight on a chair and started undressing. She did it quickly, piling her things on top of the flashlight and leaving her shoes on the floor. Naked and barefoot, she moved silently to the bed, cautiously lifted the blankets and then very slowly sat down. Her weight jiggled the bed slightly, but Luke never moved. Taking a very deep but very quiet breath, Maris stretched out and drew the blankets over herself.

Then she lay there with her heart pounding. It was a large bed and Luke was several feet away. She could probably stay here all night without his knowing it until he woke up in the morning.

But she hadn't taken this daring, brazen step just to sleep on one side of the bed while Luke slept on the other. She began inching over, thinking that it was a wonder the hammering of her heart didn't awaken Luke, as loud as it was in her own ears. The closer she got to him the more she felt his radiating warmth. It was what she needed, his heat, his passion.

She took the final slide and lay against his back, realizing with mounting excitement that he slept in the nude. Swallowing the choking sensation in her throat, she turned to her side and slid her arm across his waist, nestling her body against his. Her insides began the meltdown she had known would happen, and

she started pressing kisses to his back and shoulders while the hand that was over him began caressing his chest and belly. He made an odd little sound, but Maris could tell he hadn't yet awakened.

Her hand went lower, and when she was holding his manhood and it was getting hard and full in her grasp, she could no longer breathe silently. His hips began moving, thrusting himself against her hand, and his breathing wasn't even and shallow as it had been before.

He came awake suddenly, startling Maris, raising up and turning over to pin her to the bed. He said nothing, but he found her lips in the dark and kissed her roughly, almost savagely. There were no other preliminaries before he kneed her legs apart and thrust into her, hard and fiercely. It was wild and crazy and the most erotic experience of Maris's life. She writhed beneath him, moaning and whimpering, urging him on, arching to meet his tempestuous lunges.

Then the feverish pleasure began for Maris, the delicious spasms in her lower belly. She cried out. "Luke...Luke..." He finished only seconds later and collapsed upon her, weak and drained.

She lay with her eyes closed. It had happened so fast. Never could she have visualized her body performing with such haste.

Luke lifted his head and uttered one harsh word: "Why?"

Nervous suddenly, Maris swallowed. "Dare I be flip and ask why not?"

"You refused to talk about us today, then you come crawling into my bed tonight. Tell me why, Maris."

He wasn't speaking kindly. There was anger in his voice, and resentment. "You liked it, didn't you?" she said.

"Hell, yes, I liked it. Any man would like it, but I still want to know why." Luke was trying to make out her features in the dark. "What happened? Did your boyfriend get you all worked up and then leave you hanging?"

Maris gasped. "I told you Judd and I were only friends. Why won't you believe that?"

"Because it sounds like a damned fairy tale," Luke mut-

tered, moving to the side of the bed to sit up. He grabbed a handful of tissues from the box on the nightstand and tossed them to Maris. "You're a sexy woman, and maybe I can't see old Judd keeping his pants zipped for a whole evening with you."

"For your information, Judd has never even tried to kiss me!"

"Then maybe he doesn't like women." Moving quickly, Luke lay on top of her again, surprising Maris to a startled gasp.

"That is a reprehensible remark and this is a ridiculous conversation. Get off of me so I can get up."

Luke studied her shadowed face. "No, I don't think so. You started this, baby, but I'm going to finish it."

"You already finished it!"

He chuckled softly, deep in his throat. "That was only round one, Maris. Round two is just coming up."

She could feel what was "coming up," quite distinctly. "Luke, it's getting very late. I...I could come back tomorrow night." And the night after that, as well, she thought. Three nights in a row during her fertile time would almost guarantee pregnancy.

And then an awful thought struck her. Luke was very careless about using protection. Maybe he, too, had had a vasectomy! Her body went limp. That was it, she thought morosely, the reason he made love without protection.

"Wonderful idea," he whispered, bringing his mouth down to hers. "Tomorrow night and every night after that."

Until you leave, Maris thought dully. Damn! She'd been naïve again, gullible, dreaming her own silly little dreams, just as she'd done with Ray.

But then Luke's kisses began seeping into her senses. He had the most incredible mouth, with lips that were both soft and firm, and a unique way of angling his head for a perfect union. The taste of him had her head spinning. His weight merely snuggled the configuration of his body into hers, and in mere

seconds she was kissing him back and straining against his feverish skin with her hands locked together behind his head.

They kissed and cuddled and touched each other. Luke's hands were everywhere, caressing her breasts, her thighs, her belly. She ran her fingertips over his muscular build, absorbing and reveling in his maleness. A disturbing thought crept through the pink haze of desire clouding her mind: she cared for him, maybe even loved him. No, no, a voice in her head cried. That wasn't supposed to happen. She wasn't ready to fall in love, and certainly not with a man of Luke's transitory nature. Yet, spellbound by their intimacy, she couldn't force herself to break away from his arms, his kisses, his hard, sexy body.

A second shock followed on the heels of that one. Luke abruptly raised his head and huskily whispered, "I've been really lax about protection, Maris. We don't want you getting pregnant, do we? We won't take any more chances. Don't move, honey. Let me get something out of my wallet. I'll only be a second."

The bed was so large that he had to break all contact with her to reach his wallet on the nightstand. Sudden shock had Maris stiff and chilled. He *hadn't* had a vasectomy. He was perfectly capable of making her pregnant, but now he was going to eliminate that possibility by using a condom. And fool that she was, she was falling in love with him, while to him she was merely a convenient and very easy lover!

Seared with humiliation, she scooted to the edge of the bed and got off of it. Luke turned. "What are you doing?"

Maris stumbled to where she'd left her clothes and began feeling around for her underwear. "I…I have to go."

Frowning, Luke snapped on the bedside lamp, nearly blinding Maris for a minute. Blinking against the sudden infusion of light, she turned her back, quickly drew on her panties and reached for her bra. She could feel Luke's stare and sensed his perplexity.

"Maris…" There was a note of confusion in his voice. "I don't get it. What happened?"

"Nothing happened, except I realized just how late it really is," she lied. This whole affair—the most appropriate name for their relationship—needed rethinking. She wasn't going to get pregnant if he used protection, but what bothered her more was recognizing how emotionally involved she was becoming with Luke. He was going to leave at the end of September, and if she continued sleeping with him, making love with him, she was going to be in for some heavy-duty heartache.

Luke got up and yanked on a pair of jeans. "If this doesn't take the damned cake, nothing does," he muttered angrily.

Maris was hurrying into her dress, her blue-and-white checked shirtwaist that she'd worn for her dinner date with Judd. "You have no right to be angry with me," she told Luke. "Nor any reason."

"Lady, I didn't come sneaking into your bed. You came to me!" He rounded the foot of the bed and stopped right in front of Maris. "Just what the hell is going on with you? You want me, you don't want me. How do you think that makes me feel?"

"Blame it on hormones," Maris mumbled, making sure her dress was buttoned and tidy.

"Extremely changeable hormones, apparently," Luke said dryly. "Where do we go from here, Maris?"

She looked at him with a raised eyebrow. "Where do we go? Where do you want us to go, Luke?"

"Well, I sure didn't want everything to just stop cold like it did."

"An evasive answer, if I ever heard one." Buckling her belt around her waist was her final step in dressing, other than slipping into her shoes.

"Maris, you're a hell of a lot more evasive than I could ever be," Luke said darkly.

She couldn't rebut such a blatant truth. Luke had promised her nothing and she was fully cognizant of his obsession with rodeo and his plans to return to the circuit as soon as possible. As for her role in this fiasco, she had been plotting and praying for pregnancy, using him and his body to accomplish her goal.

The whole damned plot was backfiring, which was probably no more than she deserved. Regàrdless, falling in love seemed to be an awfully high price to pay for a few days of fantasy.

Well, that was over. Any more fooling around with Luke would cause her nothing but future misery. Already just thinking of the day that he would drive away created an ache she damn well didn't need.

Seeing that she was ready to go, Luke moved closer and put his hands on her shoulders to probe the depths of her eyes. "Be honest with me, Maris. Please. Tell me what you're thinking, what you're feeling."

She certainly couldn't tell him that she was falling in love with him, nor could she confess her foolish hopes of becoming pregnant.

Her gaze remained steady, though her knees were shaking. "You're good in bed. I like making love with you."

A bleakness entered Luke's eyes. "And that's it, all of it."

"What else could there be?" That peculiar, slightly hurt look in his eyes made Maris's blood run faster. "Is there more for you?"

He took a breath, releasing it slowly. He would never beg a woman, not for anything. "No."

Maris's spurt of hope died. "That's what I thought." She picked up the flashlight. "Good night."

"Want me to walk you to the house?"

"Please don't. If Keith should happen to wake up when I go in, I'd rather he not see us together."

"Maris, he's not a child. Don't you think he knows what goes on between men and women?"

"That's beside the point. I want Keith's respect."

"You have Keith's respect. Why would him adding up two and two about us change that?"

Maris went to the door. "I won't take that risk. Good night, Luke."

Luke followed her down the ladder, then stood at the door of the barn and watched her winding her way to the house. She

was the confusingest woman he'd ever known, the most stubborn, the most irritating.

The most exciting. "Damn," he muttered with his lips in a thin, grim line. If she liked him in bed so much, why had she suddenly turned off on him?

Maris stole into the house on tiptoes. She almost turned off the kitchen light without looking around, but fortunately she saw the piece of paper taped to the refrigerator just as she reached for the light switch.

Walking over to it, she pulled it loose. It was a note from Keith:

Maris,
I'm going to see my dad tomorrow. Mrs. McCallum arranged for someone to pick me up at five in the morning. I'll probably be gone all day. See you when I get back, unless you're up in the morning before I leave.

Keith

Maris had mixed feelings about Keith visiting his father, but it wasn't her place to judge.

Sighing heavily, she turned off the light and made her way to her bedroom in the dark. Nothing was ever easy or simple, not one blasted thing.

Twelve

Maris made sure she was up, dressed and ready to say a few words to Keith before he left the next morning. "How did this happen, Keith?" she asked gently.

Keith explained Jessica's message, adding, "Mrs. McCallum said I didn't have to go, but..." The boy looked down at the floor for a moment, then lifted his gaze to Maris's. There was maturity in his eyes and a strength that Maris hadn't seen before. "It's something I have to do, Maris."

She couldn't doubt his sincerity, or the gravity of his decision. "I understand, and I'd like to say how very proud I am of you." Unable to resist the impulse, Maris put her arms around Keith and hugged him. To her surprise, he returned the hug without embarrassment. It was a lovely moment for Maris, and she had to blink back tears.

A car horn honked outside. Immediately she put on a bright smile. "That must be your ride. Take care, Keith."

"I will. See you tonight. Tell Luke...tell 'im I'm sorry about not being here today to help with the horses."

"He'll understand."

After Keith had gone Maris put on a pot of coffee. She didn't expect Luke to walk in quite this early, but he was suddenly filling her kitchen. "Good morning," she said calmly, though her pulse did a great deal of fluttering.

"'Morning. Where'd Keith go so early?"

"To visit his father." Maris related the facts behind Keith's departure. "He said to tell you he was sorry about not being here to help you today."

"He's a nice kid." Luke looked at the gurgling coffeepot. "Not quite ready yet?"

"In a few minutes. I'll make breakfast while it's brewing."

Luke took his place at the table, not to rush Maris with breakfast but because he wanted to watch her, and the chairs around the table were the only things to sit on. After several silent minutes he said, "Guess we're going to be alone on the place today."

Maris concentrated on her pancake batter rather than look at him. "I can deal with that."

"But maybe I can't."

Maris's heart skipped a beat. "You have work to do and so do I. Keith being away should make no difference to our day."

"Is he going to be gone all day?"

"I...don't know," she said.

"And you talk about me being evasive," Luke said with a snort of derision.

Maris turned to face him. "Last night you asked me for honesty, so here it is. I'm getting in too deep with you, and if we don't stop...uh, sleeping together, it's going to hurt like hell when you leave."

His gaze remained steady. "And you didn't think about that before coming to my room last night?"

A flush heated Maris's cheeks. Her confession could only go so far. Mentioning her hope of getting pregnant would shock him and humiliate herself. "Obviously not," she replied, turning back to the counter.

She was right, Luke was thinking with a frown of personal discomfort. This thing with Maris wasn't one of those brief and expendable affairs that dotted his past. Its differences weren't readily grasped or understood, but they bothered Luke all the same. Maris bothered him. This ranch bothered him. Everything going on these days bothered him. He watched broodingly while she poured pancake batter onto the hot griddle. It would be best for both of them if he left now, before, as she'd said, they got in too deep.

"Maris, would you rather I left right away?" he asked.

Her back was to him and she bit down hard on her bottom lip. Instead of suggesting he *never* left, he had immediately come up with leaving sooner than planned. Hurt over his in-

sensitivity, she said rather caustically, "You're thinking I have the money to pay that IOU, aren't you?"

"No, that is not what I was thinking. But I guess it's true, isn't it?"

Maris scooped up some pancakes with a spatula and dropped them on a plate, which she brought to the table and set down in front of him. She spoke without friendliness or warmth. "We have a business agreement, Luke. If you left now, I'd be stuck with a herd of half-broken horses."

"I think Keith could finish the job. They wouldn't be ready for sale by the end of September, but he knows what to do now. I'm only mentioning it for your benefit. If you don't want me around anymore, you have the means to send me packing. And don't forget that Jim Humphrey will be showing up with the balance due on the Corvette."

"He seems to be taking his own sweet time about it."

"Jim's rarely in a hurry. He'll be around one of these days."

The thought of Luke loading his pickup with his gear and driving away today made Maris feel a little sick. She wasn't ready for that yet. Beside, maybe Keith could finish breaking the horses and maybe he couldn't. Certainly the process would take him much longer than it would Luke, especially after school started and Keith was busy with his studies.

Maris brought two cups of coffee to the table, gave one to Luke and sat down with the other. "I don't want you leaving until after the horse auction," she said with a granitelike look over the rim of her cup. "That doesn't mean we have to… to…"

"Just say it, for hell's sake," Luke said with a flash of anger. "We made love, and don't get all surprised and shook if we do it again." He hadn't even started eating, and he leaned forward, ignoring the plate of food between his elbows. "Do *you* know what makes one woman special to a man? I sure as hell don't, but I do know this—I want you all the time and that's never happened to me before. Last night makes me think you're going through some of the same damned misery. Tell me I'm wrong."

She took a breath. "You're wrong."

Luke's expression could have curdled milk. "I guess that's clear enough." He got to his feet. "I'm going to work."

"What about breakfast? You didn't eat anything."

"I'm not hungry." He strode from the kitchen and out the door, every line of his body exuding fury and frustration. Maris sat looking down at the table, undergoing some of that "damned misery" Luke had mentioned. Maybe it was masculine logic for him to say he wanted her and almost at the same time suggest leaving today instead of after the horses were broken, but it was pure gibberish to her. Maybe because she was falling for the big jerk. Falling too hard, too fast. This was the last possible scenario she could have dreamed up while making that deal with Luke.

It occurred to Maris while she was taking care of chores around the ranch and avoiding the corral that morning that she hated worrying about what Luke really thought of her. In the first place she already knew how he felt. She'd been available and willing, and he was male. End of subject.

But deep within her the subject was far from exhausted. She had crossed a line with Luke that had always been inviolate, and why had she been so responsive to him when other men— Judd, for one—simply hadn't interested her beyond friendship? Even before Ray's death and she had been alone so much there had been opportunities for sexual adventures with other men, and she had always repelled any and all advances. It was as though she had lost some sense of herself where Luke was concerned, which was a mystifying deviation from personal standards and ethics that she didn't find particularly comforting.

Then there was that foolishness about hoping to get pregnant and passing the child off as Ray's. Maris knew she had behaved stupidly with Ray many times. In retrospect, what good had come out of her turning a blind eye to his faithlessness, his lack of respect for her and his own roots, his dishonesty, and his out and out laziness? Rather than fight with him about a problem—he'd been extremely adroit at sidestepping an ordinary

discussion hinting at any flaw or fault in his behavior—Maris had simply buried her pain and kept her mouth shut.

But thinking she could use Luke to get pregnant with no one catching on really was the most absurd idea of her life, far surpassing any mistakes she had made with Ray. Obviously the day that Luke finally left the No Bull, Maris Wyler would be much better off.

The stickler in that conclusion was Maris's own emotions. Never before had she felt what she did in Luke's arms. Just looking at him across the compound sent feverish tingles through her body. Wishing he were a different kind of man, one who was looking for solidity and stability, was wasted energy. He was addicted to rodeo, and to living a transient, disorderly life. No woman would change him, she was certain, especially a plain countrywoman like herself.

When Luke didn't come in for lunch, Maris brought some sandwiches and a thermos of lemonade out to the corral. "I know you're angry with me, but you have to eat." He was shirtless again, and his bronzed skin gleamed with perspiration. Maris tried not to notice.

He took the food from her hands. "Thanks. And I'm not angry, Maris—I'm confused. I guess I don't understand you. Maybe what's really got me confused is that I don't usually try to understand women." He held her gaze. "Does that make any sense to you?"

"Uh...no. I mean, should it?"

Releasing a long breath of resignation, Luke looked off into the distance. "Probably not. It's just that..." His voice trailed off. "Forget it. Do you want one of these sandwiches?"

"I already ate, thanks." Maris looked beyond Luke into the corral and saw the snow-white mare he'd been working with. "She's a pretty horse, isn't she?"

"I've been calling her Snowflake."

"It suits her. I like it. Is she taking to the training?"

"Pretty well. She definitely has spirit."

"You know," Maris said speculatively, "I'd kind of like to keep one or two of the horses for myself."

"Snowflake might be a good candidate. We'll see how she turns out. Maris..." Luke had just swallowed a big bite of sandwich and was washing it down with a drink of lemonade. He wiped his mouth. "I've been wondering again where Ray might have bought these horses. They're not just common broncs. Oh, a few of them are, but most have great conformation, indicating good bloodlines. Do you realize that if you could prove ancestry on some of these animals that their value could easily double or triple?"

Maris's eyes widened. "How would I prove ancestry?"

"By finding out who owned the horses before Ray bought them. You said a trucking firm handled their delivery. You must have been given something, a receipt, a manifest, bills of sale, something, from the truckers."

A frown creased Maris's forehead. "Ray took delivery. As a matter of fact, I wasn't here that day. I had gone to Dillings for something—a dental appointment, I think."

"But there must be some paperwork somewhere, Maris. I think you should take a look around the house and try to find it."

Slowly Maris nodded. "And then what?"

"If you can find out who owned these horses before Ray bought them, we'll go and talk to the person and ask him or her about the animals' history. Might get some real good information."

Maris frowned slightly. "I should have thought of doing that before this."

"You've had a lot on your mind," Luke reminded her.

"Yes, but..." Breathing a sigh, Maris questioned her ability to run the ranch, which she'd never done before. Raising animals had been brand-new to her when she'd married Ray and come here, but when it became apparent—very quickly—that Ray had very little interest in operating the place as it should be operated, she had gradually assumed his duties and responsibilities, until she had ended up running the whole show. Obviously she still didn't see every opportunity and grasp every subtlety of profitable ranching. Surprising to realize was that

Luke did. He'd immediately seen dollar signs in Ray's old junk and had suggested the yard sale. It was Luke's doing that had sold the Corvette, and now he'd come up with this, an idea that just might increase the value of the horses.

Her voice was rather disapproving when she spoke. "You'd make a good rancher."

Luke looked at her with a restrained, unreadable expression, though without question he'd grasped Maris's reproachful tone. "It must be in the genes."

Resenting his overly casual, cavalier reply, Maris couldn't stop herself from expressing her opinion. "You're wasting your life in rodeo. You're talented with animals and have a natural instinct for business. There isn't anything you couldn't do if you put your mind to it. Certainly you're the hardest-working man I've ever met, and—"

"That's enough, Maris," Luke broke in. He'd been having some of the same thoughts that Maris had just put into words, but his mind wasn't made up yet, not about anything, and whatever decision he arrived at concerning his future, he was the one who had to make it. He handed her the empty thermos. "Thanks for lunch. I'm going back to work."

Walking to the house, Maris alternated between anger over Luke's wasting his talents and regret that she'd been so quick to tell him so. She didn't even speak to Keith in that censuring tone, believing that everyone should have the freedom and space to choose his own path in life. But Keith was sixteen years old and had plenty of time to make those choices, where Luke was old enough that he should already have done so.

He has done so, a voice in Maris's head said loud and clear. Indeed he'd chosen his path years ago, and why would he veer from it now?

Sighing despondently, Maris went into the house. Like it or not, sensible or not, she had feelings for Luke Rivers that she wished she could eliminate with a toss of her head, or something equally as mundane. In the depths of her soul, she knew it wasn't going to happen.

* * *

One of the bedrooms in Maris's house never had contained a bed from the time she'd moved in. Ray had used it as a combination storage room and office, haphazard as his record keeping had been, and though Maris had gone through some of the boxes and thrown out things she considered useless—even while Ray was alive—the room still couldn't be considered well organized. It was, in fact, the only room in the house that Maris didn't keep neat and clean at all times. It was where her Christmas decorations were stored, for one thing, and numerous other cartons containing seldom-used items.

There was also a desk—a huge old thing with a dozen drawers—and two file cabinets. Maris was digging through the drawers, looking for some scrap of paper from that trucking company, when she suddenly sat back, impatient and unsettled with herself and everything else going on at the present. In fact, what she really was, she thought unhappily, was depressed—depressed because she'd gone to Luke's bed last night, and because he was outside and she couldn't stop thinking of him. Her future was so miserably uncertain, which added to her depression, and the thought of going through all of the boxes and files in this room made her want to bawl, another indication of the depression gripping her.

Knowing that if she sat there much longer she'd fall apart completely, she got up and left the room, closing the door behind her. She'd look for those papers, but not today. What she needed right now, desperately, was to go somewhere, to get away from the ranch and Luke and responsibility, if only for an afternoon.

After changing from her jeans and T-shirt to a pair of white slacks and a green blouse, she quickly applied a little makeup and ran a brush through her hair. Grabbing her purse, she dashed from the house and out to her pickup.

Luke saw her leaving and stood in the corral with a scowl on his face. In his mind's eye he saw her meeting Judd Hensley again.

But last night she'd come from Hensley to him, which had to mean something. Maris wasn't the kind of woman to keep

two men on the string, so it was doubtful that she'd be meeting the sheriff again today. Luke had no prior experience with jealousy, yet he recognized the condition in his body and didn't like it.

Sighing heavily, once again admitting utter confusion, he returned to work.

The simple act of driving away from the ranch gave Maris's spirit a decided lift. She loved this wide open country, she loved its distant mountains and enormous sky. The air was so clean and clear it seemed to sparkle.

Maris switched on the radio and drove with the window open, enjoying the music and the warm breezes tossing her hair around. Though she'd left without a destination in mind, she automatically headed for Whitehorn. Everyone that she might want to see was at work, which was probably best, she thought, as she really wasn't fit company in her present mood, though unquestionably she felt much better than she had a half-hour ago.

Still, she didn't feel like talking, answering questions, or pretending that everything was wonderful, which would certainly be the case should she run into any of her friends. Other than Lori, that is. With Lori she could be honest and herself.

Except, Maris remembered with a pang of genuine remorse, she had deliberately lied to Lori about the possibility of her being pregnant. It was Luke's fault, she thought with an angry twist to her lips. Everything happening lately was Luke's fault. Damn Ray for borrowing money from Luke and not paying it back! Without that IOU, Luke never would have come to the ranch. She would never have made love with him, or never gotten that stupid idea about having his baby, or...

Cynically Maris shook her head. Everything wasn't Luke's fault—it was Ray's! God, she was going off the deep end, looking for someone, anyone, to blame for her own sins. What she should be doing is giving thanks that Luke *had* come along. Without his help, she'd have been in such terrible financial condition by now that she might have already lost the ranch.

Reaching the outskirts of Whitehorn, Maris slowed the pickup to the speed limit and slowly cruised Center Avenue. On impulse she made a right turn on Kinsey Way and pulled into the movie theater's parking lot, which was all but vacant, as the theater didn't have matinees during the week.

Leaving the truck, Maris began walking. Again she had no destination in mind, but it was pleasant strolling along and peering at the courthouse, the mayor's office and into the windows of Whitehorn's few shops that sold clothing. It was long past the lunch hour, so as Maris approached the Hip Hop Café, she figured the odds were in her favor for not running into anyone she knew.

She went in and was glad to see only a few patrons, none of whom she recognized.

"Hi," a waitress called. "Sit wherever you'd like, ma'am. As you can see, this isn't exactly the rush hour."

"Thanks," Maris called back, and chose a table in the far corner. She ordered a piece of apple pie and a cup of coffee from the friendly waitress. The pie was delicious, and Maris was thoroughly enjoying it, when the café's door opened and a woman came in. Maris had met Mary Jo Kincaid one time, but she doubted that Mary Jo even remembered the introduction, so it was quite a shock to see the woman suddenly spotting her and then walking over to her table showing a warm and friendly smile.

"Maris, how are you?" Mary Jo asked in her sweet way.

"Just fine, Mary Jo. How are you?"

"It just wouldn't be possible for me to be any better, Maris. I'm so very, very happy married to Dugan. You were at our wedding, weren't you?"

Maris's heart sank with undeserved embarrassment. Didn't the woman know whom she'd invited to her own wedding? "No," she said simply, hoping Mary Jo would realize her own faux pas and drop the subject.

"Oh, that's too bad. It was quite an affair," Mary Jo said in a way that implied that Maris had deliberately missed Whitehorn's event of the year. Maris frowned slightly but her own

good nature prevented her from correcting Mary Jo's mistaken impression.

The woman was hovering, obviously hoping for an invitation to join her, Maris realized uneasily. "Uh...would you like to sit down?"

"I would indeed. Thank you." Mary Jo pulled out a chair and gracefully sank onto it, laying her expensive-looking handbag on a corner of the table. "My, this is nice. I was hoping someone would be here that I know." She looked up at the waitress, who had just appeared. "Oh, there you are. I'll have a small bowl of sugar-free gelatin and a pot of herbal tea, please."

Maris searched her brain for something to talk about, recalling the little she knew about Mary Jo. Apparently she had suddenly turned up one day in Whitehorn and established herself by landing a job in the children's library. It wasn't long before she began dating Dugin Kincaid and then, rather quickly, they had gotten married. It was two months before their wedding that baby Jennifer had been left at the Kincaid ranch. And yes, Maris remembered now, someone had been murdered at the ranch on their wedding. Judd had told her about it, a man by the name of Floyd Oakley.

As if guessing Maris's thoughts, Mary Jo said, "Well, even if you didn't attend the wedding, I'm sure you heard about the unfortunate...incident. You know, that fellow that was found murdered on our property? Fred something-or-other I think was his name...."

"Floyd Oakley, you mean?" Maris corrected her.

"Yes, that was it. Poor Mr. Oakley. Never even got his share of all that free champagne, I imagine," Mary Jo said, looking a bit embarrassed to be smiling at her own joke.

"Well, it must have been awful for you, having to deal with such a horrible situation on your wedding day."

Mary Jo lowered her gaze to examine her manicured nails and thick, diamond-studded wedding band. "Oh, you know what they say, the show must go on." She gave a brave little laugh. "I tried my best to keep a smile on my face, for Dugin

and his daddy's sake. Even though I was quite shaken up,'' she admitted in a low, serious tone.

"I can imagine," Maris replied, though she guessed that it took quite a bit—maybe even more than a murder on her wedding day?—to shake up this lady.

"Dugin was wonderful. He's just my tower of strength," Mary Jo added sweetly.

"Dugin is a very…kind man," Maris said, searching for a reply that would be both tactful and still basically truthful.

Having known Dugin for years, she sincerely found it hard to imagine him *anybody's* tower of strength. He was known to be spoiled, weak-willed and totally dominated by his father, Jeremiah. Dugin's older brother, Wade, had been Jeremiah's favorite. But Wade had died years ago, in Vietnam. It was said that Jeremiah would have much preferred mourning Dugin, if the tough old cowboy had been offered the choice. But maybe that bit of gossip wasn't entirely fair to Jeremiah. Maris had always known him to be a fair man, if a bit hard at times.

Mary Jo certainly didn't share the popular opinion of Dugin, though. It was newly wed enthusiasm that had clouded her vision, Maris thought and on those grounds she could be exempt from having a rational perspective. After all, it had taken her quite a long time to see Ray clearly, and even then it had taken her longer to fall out of love with him. She wondered if Mary Jo was indeed in love with Dugin, or just in love with his money.

"I certainly admire you, Maris," Mary Jo said suddenly.

"You do?"

"You, a widow, running a ranch all on your own." Mary Jo shook her head. "In my book, *that* takes courage and a tremendous amount of strength. Both physical and emotional, I mean."

Maris took a sip of her coffee. "It's just my life. I really don't think of it as being superwoman or anything like that," she said with a smile.

The waitress arrived with Mary Jo's order and Maris thought it a good moment to excuse herself. "Speaking of the ranch,

I'd better be heading back. Nice talking with you, Mary Jo,'' Maris said, getting up from the table.

"Nice visiting with you, Maris. Let me know the next time you're coming into town. Maybe we can have lunch.''

"Well, my visits are usually in sort of a rush. Just running in for supplies or some other emergency. But maybe we'll bump into each other again sometime,'' Maris replied. She picked up her purse and left a dollar and some change near her plate for a tip. "So long, Mary Jo.''

"Bye, Maris.'' Mary Jo looked up at her with a warm smile.

Maris left the table feeling a little sorry for Mary Jo and a little guilty at brushing off her offer to get better acquainted. It wasn't easy to be new in a town like Whitehorn, where most people knew each other for years. She had once been in the same position herself. But Maris didn't have much time for socializing, and Mary Jo just wasn't her type. In fact, there was something about the woman that made her downright uncomfortable, Maris decided.

Mary Jo watched as Maris paid her check at the cash register and left the café. Then her eyes fell on the money next to the empty coffee cup. Her fingers virtually tingled, instinctively about to reach for it. She made a little fist instead, then took a spoonful of her diet gelatin.

Mary Jo laughed to herself. It was hard sometimes to re- member that she was now the wife of the richest man in town and hardly in need of stealing a tip from a poor little waitress. But grabbing for that loose cash came just as automatically to her poor old body as breathing. And she always did have a light hand. Light as a feather, Floyd used to say. But old Floyd had always taken too much credit for her success. Sure, he'd taught her some of the finer points. But she'd been basically a self-taught operator when they'd met. Plying her trade as a truck-stop hooker, she'd quickly learned how to double her prof- its by cleaning out a john's wallet right under the poor guy's nose—or some other unsuspecting part of his anatomy.

The trick was not to get caught. If you got caught, you had

to pay. Painfully, too. It hadn't taken her long to learn that rule either. And she'd never forget it.

But no telling how far you could go if you *didn't* get caught, Mary Jo reminded herself as she sipped the last of her tea. Her diamond wedding band sparkled in the late afternoon light, catching her gaze. She held out her hand, admiring it. How far she had come. Floyd had been impressed. And to think this was only the start. Just the first step in her plan.

The waitress came by just then, interrupting her thoughts. "Anything else today, ma'am?"

"Just the check, please," Mary Jo said.

The waitress totaled the order and tore it off her pad. "Would you like me to take that up to the cashier for you?"

Mary Jo glanced at the amount and nodded. The check came to a little under three dollars. She took out her wallet; the smallest bill she had was a ten. She pulled it out and handed it to the girl with her check.

"Here you go. And you keep the change, honey," she said generously.

The waitress stared down at the money a moment, then back at Mary Jo. "Gee, thanks. Thanks a lot."

"That's all right." Mary Jo closed her purse with a loud snap and got up from the table. "It's my pleasure, honestly," she added with a charming smile.

Luke was still working, Maris saw when she drove into the ranch compound and parked the truck. She sat there a moment, thinking about her next move with Luke. After last night was it any wonder he'd expected more from her this morning than the cool reserve she'd shown him? Then there was that lecture she'd laid on him, which had been rude and presumptuous. Her next move with Luke should be an apology.

Getting out of the pickup, Maris headed for the corral. Luke saw her coming and went over to the spigot to splash water over his sweaty face and chest. He was drying off with a towel when Maris walked up to the fence.

She got right to the point. "I owe you an apology. We both

know how we each feel about rodeo versus ranching, so there's no point in my constantly haranguing you about the choices you've made in your life. I'm sorry.''

''Well, now, I sure didn't expect to hear that from you,'' Luke said calmly. ''But I appreciate it. Thanks.''

''You're welcome.'' She looked at the horse he'd been working with, a black gelding with a white blaze on its forehead. One by one he was making his way through the herd, but he had to be getting tired of the same routine, over and over. ''You must have the patience of Job,'' she told him. ''Doing virtually the same thing every day. Isn't it starting to wear thin?''

He looped the towel he was holding around his neck and walked over to the fence where Maris was standing. ''I guess I do have patience, Maris. And it doesn't stop with the horses, either.''

''Meaning?'' Her heart was suddenly beating harder. Looking into his shimmering blue eyes was definitely raising her blood pressure.

He suddenly became bold and brash and gave her an impudent grin. ''How about the two of us taking a shower together? You can wash my back and I'll wash yours.''

Maris gulped. ''You never give up, do you?''

''Not when a woman crawls into bed with me all of her own volition. Maris, we're good together.'' His eyes narrowed slightly. ''I wonder if you realize just *how* good. If I asked about your previous sex life, would you give me a straight answer?''

''If I asked about yours, would you give *me* a straight answer?'' she retorted.

He thought a moment. ''Yes. Do you want to hear about it?''

''Every detail?''

''If that's what you want, yes.''

Maris scoffed. ''I don't believe you.''

''Try me.''

She took a breath. ''No, I don't think so.'' Turning, she walked away, heading for the house.

"Someday we'll talk about it, Maris," Luke called. "You'll see."

"Maybe when hell freezes over," she called back over her shoulder.

Thirteen

Keith got back late that night. Maris awakened when he came in, but though she was curious—and a little worried—about his day, she remained in bed. Keith would tell her what he wanted her to know in the morning, she decided, and if he told her nothing at all, she wouldn't push him. Seeing his father in jail had to have been a traumatic experience, but it wasn't her place either to sympathize or offer guidance. That was for Jessica McCallum to do.

Once awake, however, Maris didn't immediately fall back asleep. Keith went directly to his room, and in a very few minutes the house was silent again. As Maris stared into the dark, the day flicked through her mind.

Sighing, Maris turned on her side to face the window. Was she falling in love with Luke? Was she really so stupid as to fall for another man who couldn't stay in one place for more than a few weeks without getting antsy? Hadn't she vowed several years back that if she ever found herself single again for whatever reason, she would never get married again?

Maris's lip curled wryly. Luke had hardly proposed marriage, so that line of thought was a little ridiculous. But a relationship went either forward or backward, and "forward" to Maris meant marriage. What it might mean to Luke was a complete mystery, other than lots of hot sex and then a cheery "So long, babe. See you one of these days."

"God," Maris moaned aloud. Her agony was all her own fault. She should have set Luke straight the night they took that horseback ride. Instead she'd gotten all female and giddy and responded to him as though he were her only hope for life itself. Then there was that business of her going to his room and getting into his bed. How could she have done something so

moronic? Small wonder that Luke had seen today as another opportunity. If she had agreed, he probably would have kept her in bed all day.

That thought brought Maris's body temperature to a fever pitch. She moaned again. Wanting Luke was becoming a painful, miserably uncomfortable habit, particularly when her sane and sensible side refused to comply.

Would September ever arrive? Nothing would be normal again until Luke Rivers left for good, she thought for perhaps the hundredth time in the past few weeks.

Keith was unusually subdued during breakfast the following morning. Maris smiled across the table at him and he managed a thin smile in return. But he wasn't offering information about yesterday and she couldn't bring herself to ask. He ate quickly and, grabbing his hat from the wall hook near the back door, started out. "I'll be at the corral, Luke."

Luke nodded. "I'll be there in a few minutes, Keith." When Keith was gone, Luke looked at Maris. "Do you think he's all right?"

"I think that yesterday was difficult for him."

"Everyone has problems." Luke took a swallow of coffee. "Keith, you, me, everyone."

"What problems do you have?" Maris sounded skeptical.

"You don't think I have any?"

Maris was silent a moment. "Yes, I think you have problems, though I doubt very much that our opinions would coincide on what they are."

Luke surprised Maris by grinning. "You tell me yours and I'll tell you mine."

"You're teasing," she said shortly, getting up to begin clearing the table.

"I'll be serious if you will," Luke responded quietly, all signs of levity gone from his voice.

Maris turned, one eyebrow cocked. "Fine. How about if you go first?"

"Me first? Well...I think I'd rather have you go first."

"That's just about what I figured you'd say." She hadn't believed for a second that he would really talk about himself. Not about anything truly private, such as feelings, at any rate.

Luke finished off his coffee and got to his feet. Maris was heading for the sink with a stack of dishes and didn't see him walk around the table and come up behind her. But no sooner had she deposited the dishes in the sink than his hands were on her upper arms, drawing her back against his chest. "You look mighty pretty this morning," he said huskily, breathing into her hair.

"Luke, don't. Please don't." Her voice had instantly and foolishly become hoarse. "Keith is right outside."

"Keith is down by the corral. In fact..." Luke peered around her and out the window. "I can see him from here. He's sitting on the top rail of the corral fence with his hind side to the house." Forgetting the window, Luke lifted the back of Maris' hair and pressed his lips to her neck.

The thrills began compounding in Maris's body. "You're making me angry," she whispered.

"Yeah, I can tell," he murmured, nuzzling her neck and the side of her face. His hand crept around her waist to the front of her jeans, which he deftly unsnapped and unzipped. Then that wily hand slid down into her clothing, under her jeans, under her panties, and stopped right where he wanted it to be.

"Luke, no!" Maris grabbed at his hand.

"Tell me it doesn't feel good," he whispered. Her gripping his hand through her jeans and panties was no deterrent to the movement of his fingers. She could feel him rubbing his aroused manhood against her behind, and the whole thing was so erotic she couldn't find her voice to speak.

Instead she moaned, softly and deep in her throat. His fingers were pure magic, opening her, stroking her most sensitive spot. "You're hot and wet," he whispered. "I'm burning up. Let's go to your room for a few minutes. That's all it would take, honey, just a few beautiful minutes."

A wildness swept through her. Not only was she on fire with

sexual need, there was a very good chance that Luke was too worked up to remember protection.

"Do it here," she said thickly.

"What?"

Ignoring his surprise, Maris turned quickly and opened the buckle on his belt. Excitement whipped through Luke with the impact of a tornado. He yanked down her jeans and his own. Then he lifted her to sit on the counter and buried himself inside of her hot, velvety depths. She was utterly swamped with overwhelming desire. Her fingers ran through Luke's hair and gripped his broad shoulders.

As Luke had predicted, it took only a few beautiful minutes. Dazed and dizzy, clinging to her lover, Maris moaned as the rapturous spasms began. Luke's cry of release was seconds behind her own.

Panting and disheveled, Luke brought her head to his chest. "Maris...damn. You're really something."

She jerked her head away to look outside and make sure Keith hadn't suddenly decided to come to the house. And then, without warning, she burst into tears.

"Hey, hey, what's this?" Luke put his arms around her.

To her complete humiliation, she couldn't stop crying and instead sobbed uncontrollably into his shirt.

"Maris...honey... what's wrong? Why are you crying?"

"It's perfectly obvious, isn't it? I...I'm totally disgusting!"

"You're what?" Luke pushed her away to see her tear-streaked face. "Listen, *I* might be a little disgusting, and sure as grass is green a whole lot of other folks are definitely in that category. But not you, Maris, not you. Why would you say such a thing? Why would you even think it?"

"After what I just did, you have to ask?" She could hardly force herself to look at him.

"Making love makes you disgusting?" It was written all over Luke's face what he thought of that sentiment. "Are you deliberately looking for a guilt trip, or does it just come natural to you?" He gave her shoulders a gentle shake. "Maris, you're

only human, the same as everyone else. Why are you so hard on yourself?"

Being assigned the same slot as "everyone else" didn't elevate Maris's flagging spirit, not when Luke's life revolved around men like Ray and easy women. Maris's shoulders slumped. That's what she had become, easy pickings. All Luke had to do was put his hands on her and she melted into a chunk of mindless desire. Emotionally she was a mess, and the urge to cry about it was again filling her eyes with salty tears.

"I'm not being hard on myself," she said, her voice cracking. "But there is such a thing as common decency, you know." Pushing on Luke's chest, she forced him to step back. "You've got work to do. Keith is waiting."

"Now you're mad at me," Luke observed grimly.

She had slid off the counter and was scrambling to straighten her clothes. "At you, at myself, at the whole damned world!"

"That's silly, Maris."

"So I'm silly. Sue me!" Maris started from the kitchen. "Go to work, Luke."

He walked out of the house, scowling and shaking his head. Why in hell did he keep going back for more of Maris's illogical, inconsistent, irrational behavior? What made her so appealing he couldn't keep his hands off her? She was pretty, sure, but so were a million other women.

Enough was enough. The next time he got that itch around Maris, he would ignore it if it killed him. And that was a promise.

Luke put Keith to riding the horses in the secondary pasture, those that had already gone through the training process. Recalling how Blackie had spooked Mother the night Maris had been riding the mare, Luke cautioned Keith to keep a sharp eye out for anything that might alarm his mount. "Ride each one for about an hour," Luke instructed. "Make sure they're responding to your commands."

Luke's own plan for the day was another go at Bozo, the big red stallion. Riding Rocky, he roped the stallion and led the

balky animal into the corral. Once he was freed within the enclosure Bozo's eyes contained a feral gleam, and anytime Luke tried to approach him, Bozo would swivel around and kick at him with his hind feet. After a good hour of trying to coax the stallion into calming down, Luke admitted defeat. There was only one way to break Bozo, and that was to ride the buck out of him. After this morning Luke was in the proper frame of mind to take on a bucking bronc. Determinedly he set about doing so.

First he called Keith from the pasture. "I need your help with this brute." Luke roped Bozo from two directions, tying the ends of the taut ropes to opposite sections of corral fencing, virtually immobilizing the large animal. With murder in his eye, Bozo squealed, tossed his head, swished his tail and kicked out his hooves, but that was all he could do.

Taking up a saddle, watchful of those flying hooves, Luke threw it over the stallion's back.

Keith's eyes were as big as saucers. "What're you doing, Luke?"

"I'm gonna ride the ornery out of this stallion," Luke replied grimly. Bozo was prancing and doing his best to get rid of the burden on his back, but Luke managed to connect and tighten the cinch belt. It took some time, but he finally forced the bit into Bozo's mouth. "Here's where you come in, Keith. Once I'm in the saddle and give you the word, cut those ropes loose."

"Cut 'em, as in using a knife?"

"Right."

Keith grinned with sudden excitement. This was going to be some show. "I'll wait for your word."

Luke smoothed the leather gloves on his hands, then moved quickly, leaping onto the saddle without using the stirrup. Bozo went crazy. Luke twisted the reins around his left hand. "Cut 'im loose!" he yelled to Keith.

Unfettered and enraged, the stallion threw himself around and around in a tight circle. Luke hung on. Bozo arched his back and went straight up in the air, coming down hard on all

four feet, jarring Luke so hard his teeth hurt. Bozo fishtailed, bucked, squealed and reared, but Luke held on.

"Holy smoke," Keith mumbled in awe.

Alerted and alarmed by the noise coming from the corral, Maris came running up. "What's going on?"

"Luke's riding the ornery out of Bozo," Keith explained. "I've never seen anything like it, Maris."

Maris was staring at Luke and Bozo. *She'd* seen similar displays before, at various rodeos. Only rodeo broncs were usually goaded into anger and Bozo was crazed with genuine fury. "My God," she whispered. One mistake and Luke would be mashed potatoes. "You damned fool," she mumbled. Her heart was in her throat, beating hard and fast.

Keith was practically turning inside out with excitement. "Look at Luke go," he cried.

Maris was looking and the sight within the corral made her knees weak from fear. Bozo threw himself into the fence; Luke drew up his leg just in time to avoid it being crushed by a post. The stallion went airborne again, a mighty leap that put space in between Luke's seat and the saddle. Coming down was another jarring blow. Gritting his teeth, he pulled the reins tighter, sawing the bit against Bozo's tender mouth.

The battle between horse and man went on and on. Maris found herself holding her breath one minute and gasping for oxygen the next.

"Bozo's getting winded," Keith exclaimed.

"So is Luke," Maris retorted. "This really ticks me off."

Keith sent her a look. "How come?"

"I'm not paying Luke enough money to get himself killed," she snapped.

"Heck, he isn't gonna get killed, Maris," Keith said with every confidence. "He's the best rider there ever was. Yee-hah!" Keith yelled as Luke survived another bout of fishtailing from Bozo. "Ride 'im, Luke! Show 'im how it's done!"

Then, suddenly, it was over. His massive chest heaving from exhaustion, Bozo stopped dead in his tracks. Luke took a long breath, then leaned forward and stroked the stallion's neck.

"Atta boy, Bozo. Good boy." He nudged the horse with his knees. "Take a few steps, boy." The stallion obeyed. Luke walked him around the corral, then called "Whoa" and pulled gently on the reins. Bozo stopped.

Luke looked over to grin at Keith and saw Maris. She wasn't smiling. "Uh...were you watching?" Without answering, she whirled and walked off. Luke's gaze met Keith's. "She didn't like it, huh?"

"She said she wasn't paying you enough money to get yourself killed," Keith confided.

Luke turned his head to watch Maris stomping off across the compound. Something within him sighed. "She was already mad at me, so I guess one more reason doesn't matter."

Keith looked curious. "How come she's mad at you?"

"Uh...it was something that happened this morning." But while Luke was walking Bozo around the corral, he knew that wasn't the whole truth. Maris was either hot for his body or hot under the collar *because* of him. How could a mere man figure out that one?

Maris was determined to find that bill of lading, or whatever document Ray had been given when the horses were delivered. There had to be something, she knew, but where had Ray put it? Surely he wouldn't have thrown it away, not when he'd never thrown anything out in his entire life.

It was late that afternoon when she finally found a sheaf of papers at the very bottom of a cardboard box without any sort of label. Other than those important documents, the box contained an assortment of magazines and pamphlets related to the breeding and raising of quarter horses. Quickly Maris thumbed through the papers and nodded with satisfaction. The name of the trucking firm was there, as well as bills of sale for the ninety-three horses, all signed by a Katherine Willoughby with a rural Wyoming address.

"Great," Maris declared aloud. Now she could contact Ms. Willoughby and find out if there were any existing records of ancestry on the horses she'd sold Ray.

* * *

Bending over the corral spigot, Luke splashed water on his face and naked chest. He straightened and gave his head a shake to get the wet hair out of his eyes. Keith had shed his shirt, too, and when Luke moved aside, he wet himself down the same way Luke had.

"It's gonna rain, Luke." Keith looked up at the sky. "Not too many clouds yet, but the humidity is really climbing."

"Feels like it," Luke agreed. The summer heat had become oppressive this afternoon. He'd sweated more today than any-time since starting this job. So had Keith. Luke grinned at the boy. "Water's dripping off the end of your nose, kid."

"Yours, too," Keith retorted. "Hey, Luke, I've never seen anything like that ride you took on Bozo today. Do you think I'll ever be as good as you are with horses?"

Maris's cutting words on that subject were suddenly in Luke's mind: *I don't want Keith giving up everything else for rodeo, Luke. I don't want him to be like you.*

Luke walked over to pick up the feed sacks and blankets he used on the horses, which had been dropped on the ground in a heap. He began draping them over the corral fence. "Well, that depends," he said calmly. "First, I suppose, you have to decide if that's what you want to do with your life. Got any plans?"

"Plans? Like what kind of work I want to do after high school, you mean?"

"Yeah, plans like that. Only don't rule out college without some really serious thought. I did, and the older I get the sorrier I am that I stopped my education with a high school diploma."

Keith smirked openly. "How in heck would I ever go to college? That takes money, Luke."

Luke swung another blanket over the corral fence. "It sure does, but I've heard there are scholarships available to good students. Have you ever looked into it?"

"I've heard some talk about scholarships and loans, but my grades were never that good."

"You're a bright kid. Shouldn't be too tough to change that

pattern,'' Luke commented. He stopped with his hands on his hips. "I'm not preaching, Keith. I'm not even advising. I just don't like the idea of you or any other kid in high school selling himself short. You can do or be anything you want. If breaking horses for a living suits you, then fine. Be the best damned handler you can be. But if in the back of your mind are some dreams that you're afraid wouldn't stand a snowball's chance in hell of coming true because you don't have the bucks, then don't settle for common labor. Go after that education, like I wish I'd done.''

Rubbing the back of his neck, Luke gave a wry little laugh. ''Guess I *am* preaching. Sorry. I'm the last guy who should be dishing out sermons.'' He walked across the corral to where he'd hung his shirt on a post.

Keith followed, his youthful forehead furrowed by a frown. ''Luke, do you have a dad?''

''My dad's dead, Keith. My mother's living, though. Down in Texas.''

''I'm just the opposite. My mom ran off when I was just a little kid, and I think she's dead, but my dad is...alive.''

Luke guessed what was coming and decided to play dumb about Keith's background. ''Is that so? Then this is just a summer job you have here with Maris, I guess.''

''Uh...not exactly. Didn't she tell you about me?''

''Maris doesn't tell me much of anything about anyone, Keith.''

''Oh. I thought you two were getting along pretty good. Guess not. I forgot you said she was mad at you.''

Luke hung his shirt around his neck. ''She'll get over it.'' He paused and looked toward the house. ''Or maybe she won't,'' he said softly, more to himself than to Keith. ''Anyway, what would she be telling me about you, if she were so inclined?'' Keith's troubled expression hit Luke hard. The boy was hurting. ''What is it, Keith?'' he asked gently.

''My...my dad's in jail,'' the boy blurted out. ''That's where I went yesterday, to see him. He...he wants me to live with him again when he gets out in a few months. Luke, can people

change? I mean, can they do terrible things and then change and be different? He said he's changed. He said he stopped drinking and that he'd never hit me again. He made a bunch of promises and he...he cried. I never saw him cry before." Keith stared down at the ground. "I didn't know what to tell him."

Luke's suddenly livid brain lined up a whole slew of curses. Whether or not it was his place to give advice to Keith, he was going to do it on this subject. "Tell him to prove his promises, Keith. Tell him you're staying here until he does. Give him a year. If he doesn't drink for a year after he gets out of jail, then you might think about living with him again. That's what I'd do, and I wouldn't feel guilty about it, either."

Keith stood there staring into Luke's hard blue eyes for the longest time. Then the boy nodded. "Thanks, Luke. I think that's what I needed to hear."

"Feel free to come to me anytime you need to talk, Keith. I don't have the smarts to answer every question you might think up, but I'll try to be honest with my answers, okay?"

Keith smiled shyly. "Okay."

"Let's get back to work. I want you to take Snowflake for a ride around the pasture."

"Snowflake it is!" Keith exclaimed, heading for the saddle he would use on the white mare. Lifting the saddle, he stopped for a parting shot. "Whatever else I might do to earn a living, Luke, I'd still like to be a good enough rider someday to stay on a bronc the way you did with Bozo today."

Luke laughed. "Sure, kid, anything you say. Now, go catch Snowflake and give her a good workout."

Supper was a quiet affair that night. Maris had decided to locate Katherine Willoughby without Luke's help, maybe just to prove that she didn't need him making *every* decision concerning the ranch, so she ate with very few comments. Keith seemed engrossed in his own thoughts, mulling over Luke's advice, which seemed sounder the more he thought about it. And Luke was silent because he wasn't feeling particularly

friendly toward Maris and didn't give a damn if she knew it. She was the only woman he'd ever known who could turn him inside out with a word, a look, a gesture, and he wasn't overly pleased about it.

About three-quarters of the way through the meal Maris caught on to Luke's sour mood. Her chin lifted as she sent him a defiant look. He sent one right back to her, even more defiant than hers had been. They glared at each other until Maris began feeling foolish and broke the staredown by looking at Keith. "More potatoes, Keith?"

"No, thanks. I'm getting stuffed."

"More potatoes, Luke?" she asked sweetly.

"No, thanks." Luke got up and took his plate to the sink. "Good night." He walked out.

Maris felt awful. She had pushed him too far this morning and he wasn't going to let her forget it. Uneasily she picked at the food on her plate until Keith was through eating. He, too, took his plate to the sink and said good-night, and all within the space of five minutes she found herself alone at the table, alone in the kitchen.

She was still sitting there fifteen minutes later, pondering and ruing her many mistakes with Luke, when she heard his pickup start up and drive away. She jumped to her feet and ran to a front window, to see the truck disappearing in a cloud of dust, heading for the highway. Her stomach suddenly tied itself into a painful knot. Where was he going? And to do what?

Those questions and a few others were still with her when she went to bed at ten o'clock and Luke hadn't yet returned. What's more, she had called information for Katherine Willoughby's telephone number and learned that there was no phone, either listed or unlisted, in that name at the Wyoming address written on those bills of sale. "Is there a phone at that address in someone else's name?" she had questioned the operator.

"I'm sorry, but I do not have that information, ma'am."

"Is there anyone in your company who does?"

"You might try calling the business office in the morning, ma'am."

"Thank you, I will." Utterly depressed, Maris put down the phone. That Wyoming address was hundreds of miles away, but if there was no way to reach Katherine Willoughby by telephone, how else could she talk to her but to make that long drive?

Fourteen

After leaving the No Bull, Luke merely drove around for a while, taking roads he hadn't been on before to see where they might lead. His curiosity about the unexplored country of the area was weak, however, and it soon petered out to indifference. When that low hit him, he drove on into Whitehorn and parked his truck on the street in front of the Sundowner Saloon. The exterior of the building was old brick, unplaned weathered boards and darkly tinted windows. The place appeared to Luke's eyes to be a neighborhood bar, which seemed appropriate for his state of mind, as he wasn't looking for excitement, loud music or crowds. Opening the heavy wood door, he stepped inside and looked around.

Three men sat at the bar, two together, one at the far end by himself. A table was occupied by a group of three, one man and two women. Along the wall opposite of the bar was a row of booths, and the one way back in the corner was occupied by a man and a woman. Country music, notably muted, came from the jukebox and a big-screen TV over the bar was tuned—with the sound all but turned off—to a baseball game that no one seemed to be watching. The place was quiet, dimly lit, and everyone appeared to be minding their own business. Luke went on in and slid onto a bar stool, putting space between himself and the other men at the bar.

A short, chubby, male barkeep slapped down a paper napkin in front of Luke. "What'll it be, friend?"

"A glass of beer."

The drink was placed on the napkin. Luke laid down one of the twenties in his wallet and the barkeep rang up the sale and delivered Luke's change, placing it next to the napkin.

"Raining out there yet?" the man asked.

"Not yet." Picking up his glass of beer, Luke took a swallow, then deliberately turned his head to avoid eye contact with the barkeep. He wasn't here for conversation and wanted the man to know it. The bartender moved down the bar to the lone patron at the far end.

Staring into his glass of beer, Luke broodingly watched the tiny bubbles rising to the top of the amber liquid. Nothing felt right. His life was out of sync. Loose ends were developing by leaps and bounds and he didn't like the feeling. He thought of Keith and the advice he'd given the boy, which he probably shouldn't have done. On the other hand, he'd only told Keith how he felt, and that shouldn't be a crime. At least he had tried to encourage the teenager toward further education, which should please Maris if she ever heard about it.

He sipped his beer and scowled over Maris's image in his mind. She was not the type of woman he was normally drawn to. Maris was one of those strong-willed women who would have outfitted her own wagon in the old days and made the trek west, fighting off bachelors and would-be Lotharios every step of the way. Still, she took life much too seriously one minute and then became all woman in his arms the next. Her mood swings were impossible to understand for a simple country boy like himself, which raised some mighty disturbing questions. Why did he care? Why did he care that she made love with him willingly, eagerly, then turned on him as though he had held her down and ripped off her clothes by force? Why couldn't he simply enjoy her friendly moods and ignore the others? After all, it wasn't as though he were attempting to forge some sort of permanent bond between them.

In the background of Luke's troubled thoughts he could hear the conversations of the other patrons. The two guys sitting together on his right were talking about fishing. At the table with the man and two women mixed topics were being discussed, though right at the moment the young women were discussing childbirth, while the man sat there beaming, obviously thrilled with the subject. Those three were a convivial group.

It was the couple sitting in the corner booth who began sounding a warning bell in Luke's system. Although they weren't screaming at each other or even speaking overly loud, they were fighting. Arguing intensely and trying to keep it quiet. He glanced over his shoulder at the duo and saw a woman of about forty, with bleached hair and layers of makeup, and a man maybe a little younger, wearing a cowboy hat and a fierce expression. With the music and the other talk in the room, Luke could make out only bits and pieces of their animosity.

"You did it. Why don't you stop denying it?" the woman hissed.

The man's head was turned toward her, and Luke couldn't make out his reply, though from the set of his jaw he was angry through and through.

The saloon door opened and two men walked in. "Hey, Pete," one called to the bartender. "Bring us a beer." They sat in a booth.

Pete delivered the drinks and stood by the booth to chat about the impending rain. "Been a long dry spell" was Pete's opinion. The two men agreed that the area needed a good drenching.

Luke took another swallow from his glass and tried to relax, though the tension in his body felt like a fixed condition. He was normally a pretty loose guy, so it wasn't at all difficult to blame Maris for feeling as though his backbone had turned to granite. He wouldn't have to put up with her on-again off-again attitudes for much longer, he reminded himself. September first was just around the corner. In a few more weeks he'd have his money, a new horse and be gone.

For some reason that thought was no longer satisfying. Monotonous long drives between rodeo sites and strange motel rooms had lost their appeal. Not that those aspects of his chosen vocation ever had been all that appealing, but neither had they really bothered him before. Picturing himself wandering from rodeo to rodeo until he was too old to compete created what felt like a lead weight in his gut. Did he have Maris to thank for that aberration, too?

Thin-lipped with annoyance, he picked up his glass for another sip of beer. Pete was behind the bar again, delivering drinks to the two fishermen. A sharp crack rang out, followed immediately by a wail from the woman in the corner booth. Startled, Luke swiveled on his stool to see the man from the booth getting up and heading for the door. The woman was crying, holding her face. Luke's eyes narrowed. That bastard had hit her!

He got off the stool, strode toward the man and tapped him on the shoulder just as he reached the door.

The guy turned, snarling. "Whadya want?"

Luke's expression was as cold and forbidding as a glacier. "I don't know the circumstances and I ain't asking, but hitting a woman for *any* reason makes a man lower than pond scum, mister."

"Are you calling me pond scum?"

Luke could hear the woman sobbing in the corner booth. The two women from the table had gone over to her. "I think I said *lower* than pond scum," Luke replied in a lethal tone. He sort of expected what happened next: the guy threw a punch.

A feeling of elation rushed through Luke as he sidestepped the blow. "I'd be a little careful if I were you," he warned. "Beating up women is more your style than fighting with a man, isn't it?"

"You son of a bitch!" the man screamed, and jerked out his arm again, clipping Luke on the jaw. Luke backed up a step, then rushed the guy with a flurry of punches that targeted his face and gut.

The men in the place jumped to their feet. Pete reached for the phone and dialed the sheriff's office. The guy came at Luke again. More punches were thrown. Luke's lip was cut and bleeding. The guy's nose was gushing blood. People were shouting. A couple of the men tried to break up the fight, but one was in the wrong place at the wrong time and received a blow from Luke that had been aimed at his adversary.

"Hey, just watch it," the newcomer yelled angrily.

Tables and chairs were knocked askew as the fight continued.

Other than the three women in the corner booth, the saloon's patrons gathered around, though staying back far enough to elude the melee.

The guy was as big as Luke and just as strong, he realized. But he was quicker on his feet and getting in a lot more punches. The exhilaration of adrenaline kept him fast and cool-headed. He connected a hard fist with the guy's face, and the man sank to his knees.

Luke stood there rubbing his knuckles, which were bruised and hurting like hell. Moving to the bar, he picked up a cocktail napkin and dabbed at his bleeding lip. Just then the door burst open and two deputies walked in. In seconds they sized up the scene. One chair was broken, two tables were overturned and there were some shattered glasses on the floor.

"He started it," Pete said with an accusing finger pointed at Luke.

"Benteen threw the first punch," one of the fishermen volunteered, which was the first time Luke had heard the name of the man he'd fought and beaten to his knees.

"Doesn't matter who started it," a deputy said calmly. "Pete, are you pressing charges?"

"Damned right. Look what they did to my place. This is a decent place, and I ain't putting up with drunken brawls."

The door opened and Judd Hensley walked in. "What's going on in here, Pete?"

Pete was only too glad to relate the story. "Jim Benteen was on his way out, almost to the door, when this guy here jumped him."

Judd's stern gaze went to Luke. "Luke Rivers. Now, why doesn't this surprise me?"

"Maybe because you surprise easily," Luke retorted grimly.

Lori Bains did a double take at Luke's name. Sitting beside Melva in the booth, holding a napkin she'd filled with ice cubes from the drinks on the table to Melva's bruised eye, she mumbled, "Oh-oh." She had met here with Louise and Larry Hawkins, friends who just today had learned they were going to have a baby. Her celebration drink had been a glass of white

wine. Larry's had been beer and Louise had ordered sparkling water. But they'd been talking so excitedly about the baby, Lori simply hadn't noticed Luke come in. Then, once the brouhaha had gotten started, she had rushed to soothe Melva rather than watch the fight, which she wouldn't have watched anyway, as men pounding on each other sickened and disgusted her.

But Maris wasn't going to like her hired man brawling in a public place and getting himself arrested. She sighed.

Jim Benteen staggered to his feet, saw Luke and charged into him again.

"Jesus!" Luke yelped, taking the man's weight in the gut. The deputies rushed to pull Benteen back with warnings to cool down.

"Put the cuffs on him," Judd commanded. He looked at Luke. "Cuff him, too. Charge them both with drunk and disorderly, and public brawling."

"I'm not drunk," Luke said angrily as his arms were yanked behind his back and the cuffs slapped on his wrists.

"No? Well, we'll find that out at the station. Pete, we'll make sure someone pays for the damage in here tonight."

"Lock 'em both up," Pete said disgustedly.

The deputies escorted Luke and Benteen through the door and to a police car. Judd ambled over to the booth with the women. "Melva, let me see your face." Lori lowered the ice-filled napkin so Judd could check the damage for himself. His mouth tightened; Melva's right eye was bruised and swollen. "Melva, are you going to file charges this time?"

The woman's uninjured eye dripped tears. "I know I should," she said bitterly.

"We all know that, but are you going to do it?"

"I...don't know. I need to think about it. Lori, let me out. I wanta go home."

"Would you like me to drive you?" Lori asked gently.

"No, I can get there myself. But thanks."

Lori got up and Melva quickly slid from the booth, gathered her purse and made a hasty exit. Larry had come over to the booth. "Are you okay, honey?" he asked his wife.

Louise slid from her side of the booth. "I'm fine. Lori, we're going to leave. I'll call you, okay?"

"Yes, do that."

Judd's stern eyes rested on Lori. "Sit down and talk to me for a few minutes."

"Sure, Judd."

They sat on opposite sides of the booth. "I'd like to hear from you what happened in here tonight," Judd said.

"I'll tell you what I can, Judd. It all happened very fast. One second everything was quiet and peaceful, and the next..." She took a breath. "I guess Luke came in when I wasn't looking. At any rate, I wasn't aware of him sitting at the bar. I could tell Melva and Jim were arguing, but I really wasn't paying them any mind. Anyway, he hauled off and hit her. There was no mistaking the sound of the blow. Melva started crying. Jim got up and started for the door. By then me and everyone else were stunned and watching. I still didn't recognize Luke, as his back was to the room, but he tapped Jim on the shoulder and said something to him. Jim threw a punch and the fight was on. That's really all I know, Judd. Melva won't file charges, will she?"

"I doubt it. She never does." Judd got to his feet. "Thanks, Lori."

Lori was frowning. "Judd, are you going to call Maris?"

"I don't know. Probably not. It's late, and a night in jail won't hurt Rivers none. Maybe he'll call her. See ya, Lori."

After Judd walked over to the bar to talk to Pete, Lori left the booth, got her purse from the table where she'd been sitting before the fracas and quietly left the Sundowner. Outside she drew in a breath of fresh air and walked to her car. Behind the wheel she sat there chewing on her bottom lip. Maris should be told. Maybe Luke would call her and maybe he wouldn't. Should she, Lori, keep her nose out of it? She'd suspected the day Maris had introduced Luke that there were feelings between the two of them, though Maris had been quick to deny any such thing.

Feeling uneasy, Lori pondered the problem. She and Maris

were close, but Maris always held some portion of herself in reserve. During her and Ray's marriage there'd been times when Maris had needed to talk, times when she'd sounded off, but even when she'd been angry and hurt and at her most communicative, Lori had always sensed something held back. The truth was that Maris might resent anyone's assuming she would care that Luke had been arrested for public brawling, even Lori.

She was still sitting there, when Judd came out of the Sundowner. To reach his car he had to pass hers. He came around to the driver's side. Lori rolled down the window.

"I've been thinking, Lori. Maris should be told. Are you planning to call her?"

"That's what I've been sitting here debating," Lori admitted. "Judd, maybe she should hear it from you."

Judd nodded. "All right. If Rivers doesn't call her, I will. Good night, Lori."

Maris awoke to rain on the roof. It sounded nice and she lay there for a few minutes just listening. Then, for some reason, she turned her head and glanced at the clock on the bedstand, which read 11:25. Almost eleven-thirty. Maris frowned. What had awakened her? Maybe Luke's truck returning?

Climbing out of bed, she walked through the dark house to the kitchen window. Though the hard rain obscured the compound, she could see that Luke's truck was still absent. Her nerves tautened as well as her mouth. How many nights had she worried and lost sleep because Ray wasn't home?

Whirling, Maris returned to her bedroom and crawled under the covers. Damned if she was going to lose sleep over Luke!

Luke had been locked in a tiny cell with bars on three sides. He could see Jim Benteen in another cell some distance away. One of the deputies had dabbed Luke's cut lip with antiseptic and given Benteen an ice pack for his bleeding nose. Luke had again stated, rather fiercely, that he wasn't drunk and demanded a test to prove it.

The test proved negative, so he couldn't be charged with drunk and disorderly, only disorderly and brawling in public.

In his present frame of mind he didn't give a damn *what* they charged him with. Sitting on the cot in his cell, he glared at the drab cement floor. If he ever saw a man hit a woman again he'd do the same damned thing, arrest or no arrest.

The sheriff came into the cell block, the heavy metal door clanging loudly behind him. He stopped at Benteen's cell. "Anyone you want to call, Jim?"

"I already did," Benteen said sullenly. "He'll be down to bail me out."

"I'm surprised you didn't call Melva," Judd said dryly.

"I'm through with that bitch," Benteen mumbled.

"I think I've heard you say that before. This time I hope you mean it. You'd be doing Melva a big favor." Judd strode the corridor down to Luke's cell. "You're entitled to a telephone call, Rivers." Luke slanted him a glance but said nothing. "Did you understand what I said?"

Luke smirked. "You're speaking English and there's nothing wrong with my hearing. Yes, I understood what you said. So what?"

"So, is there anyone you want to call?"

"No."

Judd studied the man in the cell for a long moment. "What about Maris?"

"What about her?" Luke's voice was flat.

"Well, you're working for her, damn it. Don't you think she might wonder where you are?"

"In the middle of the night? We don't sleep in the same bed, Sheriff," Luke drawled sarcastically.

Judd's skin reddened. "I never thought you did. Wait, let me rephrase that. I never thought of *Maris* that way."

Luke turned his face toward the one solid wall of the cubicle until Judd realized he wasn't going to prolong that line of conversation.

The metal door opened and a deputy entered the area. He unlocked Jim Benteen's cell. "You're outta here, Benteen."

Luke watched the man stagger to his feet. "Bet he didn't test negative," Luke muttered.

Judd merely shook his head and followed the deputy and Banteen from the cell block.

Stretching out on the cot, Luke crooked an arm over his eyes to block out the bright lights. He swore he'd stay in this god-awful place for the rest of his life before he'd ever call Maris and ask for her help.

Maris was still awake, listening to the rain and pondering the misery of life in general, when her phone rang. Frowning, she sat up, switched on the bedstand lamp and picked up the phone. "Hello?"

"Maris, this is Judd."

A chill went up Maris's spine. Judd didn't phone at midnight just to chat. "What's wrong?"

"Has anyone else called you tonight?"

"No one. Judd, what's going on?" A note of panic had entered Maris's voice.

"It's just something I figured you'd want to know. Luke Rivers has been arrested. I've got him here in jail."

"In jail! What on earth for? What happened?"

"He was brawling in the Sundowner Saloon. Pete's filing charges."

Maris's shoulders slumped. Brawling and drinking, no doubt. God, she hated drinking. Alcohol turned some people into fools or, worse, bullies. Sober, Ray had been reasonably amiable; drunk, he'd been belligerent, quarrelsome and mean. What if Luke was the same?

Still, the thought of leaving him in jail was abhorrent. "Judd…uh…how drunk is he?"

"He isn't drunk, Maris."

A dizzying relief rocketed through her. "In that case I'll be down to bail him out."

"Figured you'd say that," Judd said on a sigh. "But I won't be here, Maris. I'm beat and heading for the barn. Deputy Rawlins will be on duty. He'll take care of the paperwork."

"Thanks, Judd. Talk to you soon."

"You're acting like you'd rather I hadn't gotten you out of

jail," Maris said, taking her eyes from the road to send Luke's stony profile a resentful glance. "Did you enjoy being locked up?"

"Of course I didn't enjoy it, but Hensley shouldn't have called you."

"Why not?"

Luke jerked his head around and glared at her. "Because what goes on between you and me is no one else's business, especially his."

"Well, your being in jail could hardly be *my* business unless someone told me about it, now could it?"

"I didn't want you involved. My truck's parked in front of the Sundowner. Take a right."

"I know where the Sundowner is," Maris snapped. "Why didn't *you* call me?"

"I just told you. I didn't want you involved."

"I don't believe you. You didn't call because you're angry with me. You left the house angry and you drove away angry. You were angry all day—don't deny it—which is probably the reason you risked your damned neck riding Bozo."

"I rode Bozo to break him, not for any other reason," Luke retorted sharply. "Damn, women are something."

"Meaning?" Maris sent him a glowering look.

"Meaning you've got me going in circles," Luke muttered darkly. "Why in hell wouldn't I be angry? Besides, if you'd care to remember, when we talked about my breaking the horses you laid down some pretty stiff rules."

"What I said was no drinking or women on the ranch. Obviously you went elsewhere to do your drinking."

"I had one lousy glass of beer, for your information."

"But you got into a fight. Looks to me like your anger got a little out of control."

"You have no idea what happened, so don't go making any snap judgments, Maris."

"Fine, I won't. In the meantime, why don't you fill me in?"

Luke was staring straight ahead. The wipers were slapping

away the heavy rain on the windshield. "I don't want to talk about it. There's my truck. Pull over."

His ungrateful attitude infuriated Maris. She had gotten out of a warm bed to drive through a dark and rainy night to help him out, and he hadn't even said thanks. She stopped her car next to Luke's truck. "Thank you, Maris," she mimicked. "Why, you're very welcome, Luke."

Luke had his door partially open, and was ready to hop out. He stopped to look at her. "You're right. Sorry. Thanks for coming to the rescue. See you at the ranch."

Maris's anger suddenly drained away. "Luke, I know you don't understand me, but I really don't mean to make you angry. You said that I've got you going in circles. You should know that I'm feeling pretty much the same about you."

Without warning, he slid across the seat, clasped the back of her head and pressed his mouth to hers. It was a hard, rough kiss that set Maris's heart to pounding. Her body responded immediately, and she attempted to gentle the kiss by parting her lips and seeking his tongue.

He broke away and narrowed his eyes on hers. "Why did you kiss me back?"

She swallowed. "Why did you kiss me at all?"

He muttered a curse. "You're driving me crazy." With that quixotic message, he slid back across the seat and got out in the rain, giving the door a hard slam behind him.

Perplexed, Maris sat there until he had gotten into his truck and started the engine. Then she slowly pulled away and headed for home.

Obviously they were driving each other "crazy," because her heart still hadn't settled down from that wild kiss and now she was wondering if it ever would again. God help her, she thought dismally. She had to be falling in love with Luke, and if that wasn't asking for trouble nothing ever would be.

Luke drove about a hundred feet behind Maris's car during the rainy miles to the ranch, his shoulders hunched forward, his features grim. He had given a part of himself to Maris Wyler that he'd never given to any other woman, and he didn't know

how to get it back. Call it heart, call it soul, he thought resentfully, angrily, but when he left the No Bull after the horse auction, he'd be leaving without it.

It was the strangest sensation he'd ever experienced, but he couldn't think of one single way to alleviate its sting. That damned IOU had brought him more pain than any one man deserved, physical as well as emotional. Right now his split lip hurt like hell—a sane man wouldn't have kissed a woman so hard with a split lip—and the bones in his body that he'd broken in his fall last year were aching and throbbing, probably from both the fight and the damp weather. He felt like a bag of weary, hurting old bones, and he could hardly wait to reach the ranch and crawl into bed.

They finally got there. Maris parked the truck, got out in the rain, ran over to Luke's pickup and yanked open the door before he could. "Are you okay? I was thinking on the way home that you might need some aspirin or something."

Nimbly Luke crawled out of the truck, keeping his numerous aches and pains to himself. "I don't need anything, thanks." He started for the barn.

Frowning, Maris watched him for a minute, then shivered from the cold rain penetrating her clothing and ran for the house. But instead of going directly to her room, she stood at the kitchen window and tried to see the barn through the downpour. Eventually a light came on in the loft, appearing as a ghostly beam in the dreary night.

Sighing unhappily, she left the window and went to bed.

Fifteen

It was still raining in the morning. Luke and Keith put on waterproof ponchos and went out to work with the horses, while Maris sat down and began making calls to the business offices of Wyoming's telephone company. She got nowhere. "Sorry, ma'am, but that information is not available," she was told repeatedly. All she wanted was to know if there was a telephone under another name at Katherine Willoughby's old address, but apparently the telephone company considered that privileged information.

Finally, frustrated and irate, she dialed the sheriff's office and asked for Judd. He came on the line.

"Sheriff Hensley."

"Judd, this is Maris. Listen, I need a tremendous favor. Can you go through legal channels or contacts or however you do these things and find out if a certain address in Wyoming has a telephone? I've been on the phone for hours trying to get the information, but no one will give me an answer."

"I can try, Maris. What's the address?" She recited the data. "Might take a while. I'll call you back when I know anything. Incidentally, Rivers has to appear before Judge Mathews on Thursday at 9:00 a.m. Did he tell you?"

"Your deputy told us both last night. Luke will be there. Judd, if Luke paid for the damage to Pete's place and he dropped the charges, wouldn't that be the end of it?"

"Pete's pretty upset, Maris. I doubt if he'd drop the charges for any reason."

"Hmm." Maris was thinking hard. "Well, thanks, Judd. I hope you have better luck getting that information than I did."

"What do you need it for, Maris?"

"You know the horses Ray bought? Well, I located the bills

of sale and they were signed by a Katherine Willoughby with that address. I want to speak to her about the horses' ancestry. Luke thinks there's some good blood in the herd, and if we could prove it my horses would bring a much better price at the auction. But there's no phone in her name and I thought it might be listed under someone else's name.''

''I'll do what I can, Maris. Talk to you later.''

Maris got up from her chair with a determined expression. While Judd was throwing his legal weight around on that address and telephone number, she was going to take a little drive into town.

Walking into the Sundowner Saloon took courage for Maris. She wasn't accustomed to visiting taverns by herself, and seldom had even done so in the company of others. At least there were very few patrons on this rainy day, she thought gratefully while going to the bar.

A pudgy middle-aged man behind the bar came over to her. ''Hello,'' Maris said with a smile. ''I'm looking for Pete Riddick.''

''You found him, ma'am. What can I do for you?''

Maris extended her hand over the bar. ''I'm Maris Wyler.''

''Wyler? Uh…would you be Ray's widow?'' Pete shook her hand.

''Yes. Mr. Riddick, there was a fight in here last night, and one of the men involved, Luke Rivers, works for me.''

Pete's face lost most of its friendliness. ''Mrs. Wyler, I try to keep a nice, peaceable place here, the kind of place a man can bring his wife for a drink and feel comfortable.''

''I understand.'' Maris glanced around. ''It's very… pleasant.'' She looked for damage and couldn't spot any. There was a row of booths along the far wall and tables and chairs separating the booths from the bar. Her gaze returned to Pete Riddick behind the bar. ''Let me get right to the point, Mr. Riddick. If I paid you right now for whatever damages were incurred by that fight, would you consider dropping the charges against Luke?''

Pete cleared his throat. "You'd pay right now?"

Maris withdrew a handful of cash from her purse. "Yes, right now."

"I have a list of the damage," Pete said, as though issuing a warning.

"May I see it?"

"Just a second. I'll get it." Pete walked to the back bar and picked up a piece of paper. Returning, he handed it to Maris.

She read it quickly: *Two tables...$250. Three chairs...$150. Glasses...$30.*

"I'm gonna ask the judge for an extra two hundred for the trouble of having to order new things," Pete said.

"So we're talking about six hundred and thirty dollars," Maris said with a wince she couldn't completely conceal. She'd brought the last of the cash from the yard sale with her, never dreaming the cost of the damage would require nearly all of it.

But her bills were current and the bail money she had handed over to the deputy last night—two hundred and fifty dollars—would be returned if the charges were dropped. The values that Pete Riddick had placed on his things were much too high, considering that every stick of furniture in the place showed evidence of longtime usage.

She wasn't going to argue values, however. Not when there was a chance Judge Mathews would make an example of Luke and sentence him to some jail time. The summer was waning. Labor Day was only a week away, and Maris wanted desperately to stick to her plan of a horse auction at the end of September. Luke had to be free to finish his work with the horses, and besides, she really couldn't bear the thought of him sitting in jail and coming out with a record that would follow him ad infinitum.

To whet Mr. Riddick's appetite for immediate payment, Maris counted out the correct sum and laid it on the bar. "The truth is, Mr. Riddick, I need Mr. Rivers at the ranch, and Judge Mathews might not be in a benevolent mood on Thursday."

Pete rubbed his mouth, his gaze on the neat stack of cash.

"Well, I don't like causing a widow lady undue stress, Mrs. Wyler. Ray used to drop in now and again, you know."

"Yes, I know." Ray had "dropped in" at every saloon and tavern in the Whitehorn area on a regular basis. The Sundowner could have been the place in which he'd done his drinking the night of his fatal accident. Maris had never attempted to find out which establishment had allowed him to walk out too drunk to drive, because, in truth, she never had blamed anyone else for anything Ray had ever done. Her philosophy had always been that adult human beings were responsible for their own actions. Which she'd sort of been forgetting, she thought with an inward wince, recalling how she'd been looking for someone to blame for her own recent behavior.

"Well, what do you say, Mr. Riddick? Do we have a deal?"

Pete eyed the money again. "Would you tell Rivers that he's not welcome in here again?"

"If that's what you want, yes. Mr. Riddick, what really happened last night?"

"Rivers started the fight, Mrs. Wyler."

"Do you know why?"

"All I know is that Jim Benteen was on his way out and Rivers stopped him with some remark about pond scum." Pete shook his head in disgust. "They weren't even sitting anywhere near each other, Mrs. Wyler. Jim was in that corner booth and Rivers was sitting at the bar, just about where you're standing now."

Maris tried to visualize the scene. Why on earth would Luke leave his seat and start a fight with a man he didn't know? There wasn't any sense to be made out of something so irrational, but then she remembered that Luke had been in a foul mood when he'd left the ranch and maybe that was all the incentive he'd needed to pick a fight.

She sighed. There was an awful lot she didn't know about Luke, though in God's truth she never would have thought him the type of man to engage in barroom brawls. She especially wouldn't have thought him capable of *instigating* that kind of trouble.

"There were women in the place, too," Pete said, as though the presence of the fairer sex increased Luke's crime a hundredfold.

Maris felt as though the wind had just been knocked out of her. A woman. Of course. She should have figured that out for herself. Jealousy clawing at her insides startled her, and she suddenly wanted this over and done with. Pushing the money forward, she asked again, "Do we have a deal, Mr. Riddick?"

Pete hesitated, then reached for the cash. "Yeah, we do. I'll call the sheriff and tell him to drop the charges." He folded and tucked the money into his pants pocket. "Just be sure and tell Rivers to stay away from here."

"Gladly," Maris said coolly. "May I have a receipt?"

Driving into the ranch compound, Maris saw that the corral was vacant. The rain, coming down in sheets, had apparently driven Luke and Keith inside. She went into the house, calling, "Keith?" When she got no response, she figured Keith was with Luke.

The phone rang, and she picked up the kitchen extension. "No Bull Ranch. This is Maris."

"This is Judd. Pete Riddick called and dropped the charges against Rivers."

"He said he would."

"How'd you talk him into it?"

"I didn't do much talking, actually. But I did lay cash on the bar to pay for the damages."

"Rivers didn't gain any respect from me by sending you to do his dirty work," Judd growled.

"Luke doesn't even know about it."

"He doesn't. Well, now, seems like you're taking mighty good care of your hired hand, Maris."

"Judd, please. I need Luke out here, and..."

"Yeah, I think maybe you do. About that information you asked me to dig up—there's no longer a telephone at that address you gave me, but there's a Katherine Willoughby living in Sheridan. Got a pencil handy?"

"Right here." A little sick at heart over Judd's comment about her "needing" Luke—it certainly hadn't been said in a flattering tone of voice—Maris wrote down the address and telephone number Judd recited in her ear. "Thank you, Judd. I really appreciate this."

"You're welcome. I've gotta go, Maris. Another call." The phone went dead.

After hanging up, Maris sat there feeling rather numb. Obviously Luke and Jim Benteen had fought over a woman. Judd believed she and Luke were carrying on an affair, which they were. Sort of. And now she had to tell Luke what she'd done about getting his charges dropped, and she suddenly wasn't so sure that she should have done anything without discussing it with him first.

Well, there really wasn't any reason to rush out into the rain to impart the news. Grim lipped, Maris dialed Katherine Willoughby's Sheridan number. It was answered on the third ring.

"Hello?"

"Is this Katherine Willoughby?"

"Yes, it is." The woman's voice was melodious and pleasant.

"My name is Maris Wyler, Ms. Willoughby. About four months ago you sold ninety-three horses to my husband, Ray Wyler. Do you recall the transaction?"

"Certainly. And please call me 'Katherine.'"

"Thank you. Um...those horses were very green, Katherine, and I have a man breaking them. He's quite familiar with horses and mentioned that some of them appear to have excellent conformation and might be from a good bloodline. That's why I'm calling. Do you have any information on the herd's ancestry?"

"Not at my fingertips, Maris. Your husband, Ray, was apprised of the situation at the time of the transaction."

Maris took a breath. "Ray died shortly after buying the horses, Katherine. I'm sorry to have to bother you with this, but he told me nothing about the herd and I really do need any information you might have access to."

"Oh, you poor dear. Please accept my condolences. Losing

a loved one is most difficult and very trying to the spirit. Well, let me begin at the beginning. Those horses belonged to my father, who became very ill about three years ago. I moved out to the ranch to care for him, and with him being gravely ill for so long, the horses were certainly my last concern and totally ignored. That is the reason they were so completely untrained. They grew up on the range without any human contact whatsoever. Your hired man is correct in his assumption that most of the herd has good blood, and I know Dad kept excellent records regarding their lineage. However, after Dad died I sold the ranch, lock, stock and barrel, and I can't think what I might have done with those records, or even if I kept them.''

"Ray didn't inquire about the herd's lineage?''

There was a lengthy silence in Maris's ear. Finally Katherine said, ''I honestly can't remember, Maris. But it seems only sensible to assume he didn't, or I would have given him the data. Are you certain you don't have it?''

"Very certain, Katherine. I've gone through everything in the house and really only found the bills of sale a short time ago.''

"Well, I'm glad you have those, at least. Maris, give me a few days to gather my wits and think about those records. I was quite shaken over my father's death, even though I knew it was coming. At any rate, there are blanks in my memory connected to those unhappy days and the ensuing weeks when I was selling Dad's property. Give me your telephone number. I'll call you one way or the other.''

Maris recited her phone number. ''I can't tell you how much I appreciate your cooperation in this, Katherine.''

"I think I understand, Maris. Besides, it's information you should have…if I can just think what I might have done with those records. Goodbye.''

"Goodbye, Katherine, and thank you again.''

"You're quite welcome, my dear. I'll be calling.''

Maris put down the phone with excitement pumping through her system. Luke was right; her horses weren't just run-of-the-mill range animals. If Katherine found those records and they

could be presented at the auction with each horse, the value of the animals would increase greatly.

This was very good news, and Maris became anxious to tell Luke about it. Besides, he might even look upon her talking Riddick into dropping those charges as good news. Sometimes she was such a pessimist, she chided herself. Why on earth *wouldn't* he be relieved over not having to appear in court?

Going to the kitchen door to brave the rain in a run for the barn, Maris stopped to frown at the wall hooks and what they contained. Keith's poncho was hanging there, and why would he have brought it to the house, then returned to the barn without it?

She gave her head a small shake to clear it. These days everything seemed like a problem of one sort or another. But Keith running around in the rain without his poncho was hardly a major crisis.

Yanking up the hood of her own rain jacket, Maris left the house and jogged to the barn. Inside she lowered the hood and called, "Luke? Keith? Anybody here?" Luke's pickup was parked in its usual spot, so the question was merely to let them know she was in the building.

Luke appeared at the top of the ladder. "I'm up here."

"Figured you were." Maris started up. "It's really pouring out there."

"We had to quit working."

Maris reached the second floor. "So what're you two doing to pass the time, playing cards or something?"

"Keith's not here."

"He's not? He's not at the house, either. Where is he?"

"Don't get panicky. Jessica McCallum came along and took him for a ride."

Maris heaved a sigh of relief. "Oh, thank goodness. I couldn't imagine where he might have gone on foot in this downpour."

The loft was chilly and damp. "Come on into my room. I've got the electric heater going," Luke said.

Maris followed him into his room. Luke closed the door. "You know who Jessica is, don't you?" Maris said.

"I figured it out the first time she came around."

"Yes, well, she must want to talk to Keith about something." Maris loosened her jacket. "She comes out to see him every so often."

"Have a seat," Luke offered.

"I'm too excited to sit. Luke, I finally made contact with Katherine Willoughby." Maris related what Katherine had told her about her father, his ranch and his horses. "So if she can locate those records, we'll have proof of their lineage to present at the auction. Isn't that great?"

"It'll only be great if she *finds* the records, Maris."

"Yes, but I have a very strong feeling that she's going to find them."

Luke grinned slightly. "Woman's intuition?"

Maris grinned back, until she remembered what else she had to tell Luke. "Um...I went to see Pete Riddick at the Sundowner, Luke."

His grin disappeared. "To do what?"

Deciding to present this news as though he couldn't possibly be offended, Maris put on a big smile. "I paid him for the damages to his place and he dropped the charges against you. Isn't that wonderful?"

"You paid him? How much?"

"Luke, the amount doesn't matter. But now you don't have to appear in court. The whole thing's over. Aren't you thrilled?" He didn't look thrilled, she saw with a sinking sensation. "Don't tell me you're upset because I just possibly might have saved you from spending some time in jail, for pity's sake!"

"I wouldn't have gone to jail," Luke said stonily.

"How can you be so certain?"

"Because of the circumstances."

Maris's lips thinned. "Oh, is two men fighting over a woman acceptable behavior these days? If it is, I certainly haven't heard about it."

Luke's eyes narrowed on her in a hard look. "Who told you that?"

"No one had to tell me. Pete said there were women in the place when the fight broke out, and I can put two and two together as well as anyone else."

Folding his arms across his chest, Luke leaned his hips against the bureau. "So you've got it all figured out, have you? You know something, Maris? I'm beginning to understand why Ray drank."

Her eyes widened in shock. "How...how dare you say such a thing to me?" she said hoarsely, on the verge of tears. There was no way she could defend herself against such an unfair accusation, but as quickly as her throat had filled with tears, just as quickly the urge to cry vanished and was replaced by cold fury. "You bastard," she said, her eyes shooting daggers. "There are a lot of things I will never put up with from a man again, and mental cruelty is one of them."

Luke wasn't exactly calm, either. "What the hell do you think your assumption that I fought with Benteen over a woman was, if not mental cruelty? Clean up your own act before you start judging mine, Maris."

"Are you saying a woman was not the cause of your fight last night?" Her words dripped skepticism.

"Actually a woman *was* involved, but not in the way you're thinking." Luke pointed an angry finger at her. "I didn't have to go to court to get tried and convicted, Maris. You did that all by your lonesome. And you're far from perfect, lady, damned far, *too* far to be acting so superior. You know what your biggest problem is? You're afraid of being human."

"And just what is that supposed to mean?"

"You know what it means, as well as I do."

"You're referring to our...our..."

Luke raked his hair into a mess. "For crying out loud, say it like it is. We didn't commit murder, Maris. We made love. Making love doesn't make you a criminal. You've got nothing to be ashamed of. You're a good and decent woman."

"Decent women do not go to bed with the hired help," she snapped.

Luke's lips thinned. "Sometimes you talk like a damned fool."

"And you're a jerk!" Maris started for the door, then stopped. "Since you asked, I paid Riddick six hundred and thirty dollars, *which* I'll be only too happy to deduct from that three thousand I never owed you in the first damned place!"

She stormed out. For a second Luke was dumbfounded by the staggering sum she had paid Pete Riddick. But then he bounded from the room and caught Maris by the arm before she could start down the ladder. "Do you know what was broken in his place last night? One damned chair. A few tables got knocked over, but I would swear on a Bible they weren't damaged. Oh, yes, a few glasses got shattered. Does one chair and a few glasses add up to six hundred and thirty bucks to you? They sure don't to me, sweetheart, and besides, Benteen should have paid half the damages, *which* he would have been forced to do if you hadn't stuck in your nose and stopped us from going to court!"

Maris jerked her arm out of his hand. "Don't you ever touch me again, and don't worry about me doing you any more favors, you...you ingrate!" Her bravado was all on the outside, however. Internally she was cringing because Luke was right. Benteen *should* have paid half the damages. She *should* have kept her nose out of it.

But she had pictured Luke as guilty and drawing a jail sentence from a coldhearted judge, and she needed him to finish breaking the horses. It was all too much, and she suddenly felt her legs giving out. Moving to one of the heavy beams that supported the roof of the barn, she leaned against it, all her fighting spirit gone.

"Oh, damn," she moaned, turning to hide her face from Luke.

He looked at her forlorn figure and felt his own anger losing impetus. "Maris, it's done. Just forget it," he said wearily. "Deduct the sum you paid Riddick from the three thousand. I

just don't give a damn about it anymore. I'll finish breaking your horses and get the hell out of Montana the minute they're sold." He hesitated, then added, "And I'm sorry I made that crack about why Ray drank. I don't know where it came from, because it's not how I feel about you at all."

His apology didn't alleviate the pain his remark had caused Maris, but she stopped hiding her face and turned around. He looked utterly miserable, she saw, which, perversely, made her feel even worse than she had. "I...I'm sorry, too. I thought I was helping by going to see Pete Riddick. And I'm sorry I called you names. I seem so on edge lately." She ran her fingers through her damp hair, pushing it back from her face. "I'd like us to get along for the remainder of your stay here. Do you think we can manage to do that?"

"We can try," Luke said quietly. Even though she was damp, a little disheveled and unquestionably upset, Maris made him think of sex. He'd rather kiss her than fight with her any day of the week. He took a long breath for caution, because in the back of his mind was a question that wouldn't go away. If he made a pass right now, would she melt as she'd done before? Or would a sexual advance from him at this point finish destroying their already deteriorating relationship?

Maris was again thinking of the mystery woman who had caused the fight, though "not in the way she'd been thinking." What had Luke meant by that? However badly she wanted to know, she couldn't bring herself to ask.

"I'm going to the house," she said, sounding tired and defeated.

"Put your hood up. The rain is still coming down hard."

She looked Luke in the eye. "Maybe I will and maybe I won't. Don't give me advice, Luke. I don't like it any more than you do. And maybe I do talk like a damned fool sometimes, but so do you."

"Aw, hell." Luke groaned. Turning on his heel, he returned to his quarters and slammed the door behind him. If that was Maris's idea of getting along, she must have slipped a cog.

He frowned at that notion. She hadn't been that edgy when

he'd first gotten to the ranch. In fact, she hadn't been that edgy until today. Maybe his getting arrested had upset her a lot more than she'd indicated last night when she'd bailed him out. But that conclusion didn't seem completely accurate, either, not when she had gone out of her way today to make sure he didn't spend some time in jail.

Standing at the window and watching Maris running through the rain—with her hood up—to the house, Luke shook his head and admitted that he knew only two things for sure with this peculiar lady. One, he never stopped wanting her, and two, as he'd told her last night, she was indeed driving him crazy. Sad to realize, there couldn't possibly be a cure for what ailed him as far as Maris went. Not when he couldn't even give the disease a name.

Glancing at the clock every few minutes, Maris made supper. Jessica keeping Keith this long—a good three hours—had never happened before and didn't feel quite right to Maris. Worrying that something was wrong, she browned a chicken, then put it in the oven to bake, along with three large potatoes.

Her thoughts weren't only on Keith, however. What woman had been involved in Luke and Jim Benteen's brawl last night? And *how* was she involved? Why hadn't Luke come right out and explained? Did he think it was none of her business and never planned to tell her about it? What was strange was that Pete Riddick's explanation of the fracas hadn't pinpointed a woman. He'd merely said that he didn't like that sort of thing occurring in his place with women present.

At five-thirty, the normal dinner hour, Luke rapped on the kitchen door and walked in. "Isn't Keith back yet?"

"No, and I'm getting very worried. Did Jessica say anything about keeping him so long?"

"All she said was that she needed to talk to him and would he please take a ride with her."

"I see." Maris thought a moment. It was possible that Jessica was seeing to Keith's supper, though it really wasn't at all like her to be inconsiderate of Maris's routines. Regardless,

Keith wasn't the only mouth to feed on this ranch and Luke was probably hungry. "Everything is ready, Luke. We may as well go ahead and eat. I can warm the meal for Keith if he hasn't already eaten when he gets home."

Sixteen

They weren't at the table more than five minutes, when a motor noise announced an arriving vehicle. "It's them," Maris said with obvious relief. Rising, she went to the window. Though true nightfall was still some hours away, the rain and heavy cloud cover darkened the area. Still, Maris could identify Jessica's car. "It's them," she repeated with a glance back at Luke.

Luke had started eating, but he laid down his fork. "Don't wait," Maris said. "Keith will be right in." She resumed her place at the table, anticipating Keith bounding in at any moment and plopping into his chair.

But minutes passed and then more minutes, and still Keith didn't appear. They could hear the idling engine of Jessica's car and Maris began worrying again. "Something's wrong," she murmured, more to herself than to Luke. Maris wondered if she should go outside and speak to Jessica, then argued herself out of it. If Jessica wanted to talk to her, she wouldn't be sitting in her car.

Finally the door opened and Keith walked in. Maris stood up and smiled, although Keith's down-in-the-mouth expression really didn't invite smiles. "I'm glad you're home," she said to the boy. She saw him swallow and noted the paleness of his face. "Is anything wrong, Keith?" she asked gently.

"Jessica wanted to come in with me, but I told her I could do this. My dad died."

"Oh, Keith. What happened?"

"He died in his sleep last night. The doctor said he had a heart attack." Keith held out a folded piece of paper. "Jessica wrote this just now so I could bring it in to you."

Jessica's writing her a message was the reason Keith hadn't

immediately come in, Maris thought, accepting the paper. "Shall I read it now?" she asked Keith. "Dinner's on the table. Are you hungry?"

"I'm not, Maris, thanks. I think I'll go to my room, if you don't care."

"Of course I don't care." She went to Keith and put her arms around him. "If or when you feel like talking, I'll be here."

Luke had gotten to his feet. "So will I, Keith."

"Thanks, Luke." The boy shuffled from the kitchen with his head down.

Maris slowly sank to her chair. Luke returned to his. They looked at each other across the table, empathy and sympathy mingling on the path of their gazes. "I had better read this," Maris said quietly, indicating the note from Jessica:

Maris,
I tried calling you several times today, but you were apparently out. Now Keith prefers going in and telling you about Terrance by himself and I feel as though I should honor his request. He hasn't cried, Maris, which maybe is only to be expected, given his sad and abnormal relationship with his father. He has also said very little today. We went to the prison, then to a funeral home to make arrangements for Terrance's interment. I'm sure it was all quite traumatic for Keith, though he showed very little emotion throughout.

At any rate, I will be calling tomorrow. Keith is going to have to wade through this on his own, Maris, though it will be enormously therapeutic for him to know that we all care about his pain and that he has friends who will remain constant.

Jessica

Maris lifted her eyes to Luke's. "Would you like to read it?"

He nodded. "If you don't mind."

She handed the paper across the table. It was while Luke was

intent on Jessica's handwriting that Maris felt the first gush of tears. Sniffling, she got up for a tissue and blew her nose. But once flowing, the tears wouldn't stop. Standing with her hips against the sink counter, she wept silently and wiped away tears.

Luke started to say something as he raised his eyes from the paper, but stopped short when he saw Maris crying. "Did you know Terrance Colson?"

"No. I recognized him on the street, of course, but I never knew him personally."

"Then you're crying for Keith."

"I...I guess so." With a fresh tissue, she wiped away another spate of tears. "I didn't cry for Ray," she said, and covered her face with her hands.

The unhappy, embittered tone of her voice startled Luke almost as much as what she'd said. He got up, rounded the table and gently pulled her into his arms. She wept into his shirt and accepted the comfort he was offering. What she'd said was the God's truth. Instead of sorrow over Ray's untimely death, she had felt resentment that he would die so unnecessarily. Before his death she had cried too many times to count, but after the accident and even at the funeral her eyes had contained deeply rooted anger instead of tears.

Luke's natural warmth lessened the chill in her soul. It felt good to be held and soothed and treated as someone special. Her thoughts turned from sorrows the world over to the immediate present, to how she felt in Luke's arms. It wasn't shocking anymore to think about falling in love with him, though remembering that his time here was running out created an almost unbearable ache in the vicinity of her heart.

Jessica's comment in her note about Keith's having to wade through this by himself rang true for Maris, as well. She, too, had something to wade through. Foolishly she had become emotionally involved with a wandering man, and she would pay for it, possibly for the rest of her life.

She stepped back, though Luke's hands remained on her

shoulders. His eyes contained concern and caring, which touched her deeply. "Are you all right now?" he asked softly.

"Yes, I'm fine." It was a lie, but if she said, "No, I might never be all right again," he would force her to talk about old events and hurts that she didn't even want to think about, let alone discuss. "Finish your dinner, Luke. Wait, let me put your plate in the microwave for a minute." Darting away from him, she whisked his plate of food from the table and into the microwave to reheat.

They sat at the table, though neither had much appetite. Maris was despondent and showed it. "Is it best to leave Keith be, or should one of us go to his room and talk to him?"

"I think we should give him some space for a while, Maris. When he's ready to talk he'll come to us." ·

"He's so young to be all alone in the world." Maris's eyes filled again.

"He's not alone. He has you and he has me, too, if he wants me."

"But you're not going to be around much longer." Maris bit down on her lip. Keith would miss Luke, too. He had started out shy and reticent around Luke, but she'd known for some time now that the boy enjoyed working with Luke and being in his company. Then Maris remembered Mrs. Colson, Terrance's mother. "Keith has a grandmother somewhere. I'm sure Jessica must have notified her."

Luke acknowledged the information about Keith's grandmother with a nod, though his mind was strangely stuck on Maris's remark about his impending departure. The thought of driving away and putting Maris, Keith and the No Bull out of his life was intensely disturbing. But what could he say? *Maris, I've been thinking about staying.* How would she receive such a remark? Their arrangement ended in September. Once the horses were sold she and Keith could easily care for the few beeves on the ranch. She'd mentioned turning the No Bull back into a cattle ranch, but that would take time, and resources she didn't have. Unless the horse auction was a rousing success,

that is, which was a distinct possibility should Katherine Willoughby locate her father's breeding records.

They finally stopped pretending to eat and pushed their plates back. Tonight Maris was in no hurry to clear the table and get the dishes washed. By the same token, she noted, Luke didn't appear in any hurry to leave, probably because of the weather. Before it started raining he'd been going out to the corral or one of the pastures after dinner to work with the horses till dark, and tonight's heavy rainfall pretty much eliminated any outside activity.

Absently she toyed with the salt shaker, turning it around and around on the table with the tips of her fingers. "Where will you go from here?" she asked in a very low and quiet voice.

Luke blinked, as though suddenly coming awake. "I don't know."

"Where's the next big rodeo in October?"

"I don't know that, either."

"Haven't you done any checking into it?"

"No, I haven't." Luke leaned forward. The ceiling light was reflecting in Maris's hair, appearing as shiny golden and reddish highlights. "Maris...I said some things to you today..."

"And I said just as bad to you, Luke. Let's not start apologizing again. Not tonight."

He could see the unnatural glistening of her eyes, the pallor of her skin. Old Terrance's death had affected her very strongly. Oddly, it had also brought Ray's death closer and somehow made it more grievous for Maris.

"All right," he agreed, getting to his feet. "I'll say goodnight." He glanced at the dirty dishes on the table. "Unless you'd like some help with the dishes. In fact, why don't you let me clean the kitchen and you go and lie down?"

As though jerked to her feet by an invisible hand, Maris stood and began stacking dishes. She wasn't an invalid, for heaven's sake, just shaken up. "Thanks for the offer, but I'd rather keep busy."

Without another word Luke left. He and Maris had no real

relationship and why did he keep thinking they did? There was an ache in his gut, a sadness, that he didn't know how to combat. It was for everyone on the No Bull, for Keith and what he must be going through, for Maris and her strength and her weaknesses, so at odds with each other, and for himself, a man who had mindlessly drifted for nearly twenty years and now realized that he would never again be content with that careless, freewheeling life-style.

After the kitchen was back in order, Maris sat in the living room. She kept listening for some sound from Keith's room, some indication of his presence. There was nothing, and she couldn't stop thinking of him in there alone. The mantel clock ticked off the minutes, then the hours. Finally she got to her feet. Unnerved or not, she couldn't sit up all night.

Passing the door to Keith's room on the way to her own, Maris stopped to listen again. Unable to bear the silence any longer, she slowly turned the knob and pushed the door open only enough to see into the room. Keith was fully dressed, wide-awake and lying on top of the bed covers, with the nightstand light burning.

"Keith? Are you all right?"

His head turned on the pillow to look at her, then, abruptly, he swung his feet to the floor and sat up. "I don't know, Maris. How does a person know if he's all right?"

This was not a child speaking to her, Maris realized as she entered the room and sat down on its one chair. She had thought of Keith as a boy since Jessica had first brought him to the ranch, but he had lost the last remnants of childhood today and looked and sounded like a man.

"Good question," Maris said quietly. "I'm sure it's one that most people ask themselves at one time or another. There's so much stress involved with losing a family member that days of confusion aren't at all out of the ordinary. It happened to me when my parents died."

Keith lifted his eyes to look at her. "And when Ray was killed?"

Maris took a breath. ''There was stress at that time, yes, but it was different than when my parents died.''

''Different how?''

Maris thought for a moment. Keith needed honesty right now, but how much honesty was she strong enough to give him? His eyes looked old and weary, she saw. He was obviously struggling with his own private memories of his father, and quite possibly feeling guilty because he hadn't loved Terrance. It was that guilt Maris wanted to eliminate.

''I didn't love Ray, Keith. I was sorry he died, but the sorrow was for his wasted life, not for me. I believe that when someone dies whom you love very much, then the grief you feel is for yourself. You know how much you're going to miss this person, and you actually torture yourself by remembering the good times you'd had together. That's the way it was with my parents. With Ray...'' Maris paused, realizing that this was the first time she had said these things aloud. ''With Ray I almost felt a sense of relief. He had caused me a great deal of heartache and unhappiness, and I felt... I thought...'' Her voice faltered. There were so many aspects of her marriage she couldn't tell this young man about. She shaped a shaky little smile. ''I think I've said enough for you to understand.''

''Dad never loved me,'' Keith said in a voice so low Maris could only just hear him. ''He probably never loved anyone. He was never nice, Maris, not to anyone, not the way you and Luke are.''

Maris stood up to pull her chair closer to the bed. Seated again, she reached for Keith's hand and looked directly into his eyes. ''I want you to know with all your heart and soul that this is your home. I'd like you to consider me as family, Keith. Is that possible?''

He nodded. ''I'd like that, Maris. When I went to see my dad that day, he said he wanted me to live with him when he got out of prison. I didn't want to. I didn't believe he had changed. Luke said for me to tell him to stay sober for a year and then maybe I would live with him again.''

''Luke said that? Then you discussed it with him.''

Keith nodded again. "Luke's great, Maris." Keith's eyes dropped and his old shyness suddenly reappeared. "I wish *he* were my dad."

Sitting back, Maris took a long breath. Reminding Keith of Luke's approaching departure at this emotional moment would be cruel. Luke might be nice in Keith's eyes, but he had his faults, make no mistake. Barroom brawling was one that Maris could hardly overlook. For a second the faceless woman involved in that brawl flashed through Maris's mind, and her lips thinned slightly. Luke might not be a Ray Wyler or a Terrance Colson, but he was far from perfect.

But disenchanting Keith by saying so would only hurt the boy and he already had enough pain to deal with. Besides, Keith may as well remember Luke as being only "nice" after Luke was gone.

Sighing, Maris patted Keith's hand. "Feeling any better?"

"I guess so."

"It will take some time, Keith."

"Will...will you go to the funeral with me? It's set for the day after tomorrow."

"Absolutely. I'll be right by your side every minute." Maris saw the mist forming in Keith's eyes. He was trying hard not to cry, but she could see that the dam was finally breaking. It was what he needed to do, to just let go of his tightly contained emotions and bawl.

But her witnessing his breakdown would only embarrass him. Briskly Maris got to her feet. "I'm going to bed. If you need me in the night for anything, knock on my door."

"Thanks, Maris." Keith's voice was thick with tears.

"Good night, honey," she whispered, and bent over to kiss his cheek. "I love you like the son I never had. Remember that. Always."

She hurried across the room to the door, then stood in the corridor and felt her own influx of tears and sorrow.

The sun was bright the next morning. Maris prepared breakfast and was pleased when Keith made an appearance. Luke

came in and they sat at the table.

"How're you doing, buddy?" Luke asked the boy.

"All right, Luke. I want to work today."

"Good. I really need your help. There's only a handful of unbroken horses left in the big pasture, and I'm planning on starting the training process with each one of them today."

Maris's heart skipped a beat. "Then we're going to meet the deadline?"

"No question about it," Luke replied. "I'd get some advertising out about the auction, if I were you."

"I'll work on it," Maris murmured.

Two hours later she was painting signs announcing the auction, when the phone rang. "Maris, this is Katherine Willoughby. I located Dad's breeding records. I'm shipping them to you today—it's quite a bulky package—so watch for it, dear."

Maris's knees went weak and she had to sit down. "I can't thank you enough, Katherine. I'll reimburse you for the shipping cost if you'll let me know the amount."

"I'll put a little note in the parcel. I hope the records will be of some help to you, Maris."

"I'm sure they will. Thank you again, Katherine."

Elated, Maris put down the phone and let out a yell. "Yahoo!" She started for the door, anxious to tell Luke the good news, but the phone rang again and she returned to answer it.

"Is this Maris?"

"Yes, it is."

"Jim Humphrey here." He chuckled in her ear. "Bet you thought I was never going to pick up that Corvette. I got tied up with other things, but I'll be there this coming weekend. Just wanted to let you know."

"That's wonderful, Jim." Another burst of elation had Maris grinning. This was a good day, a *great* day.

Again she started for the door and again the phone rang. Maris looked back at it with a disbelieving expression. What next?

"Maris, this is Jessica. How is Keith doing?"

"Surprisingly well, Jessica. He's out working with Luke today. Would you like me to call him in so you can speak to him?"

"No, that's not necessary. You can pass on my message. Maris, the county will pay for new clothes for Keith to attend his father's funeral. I'd like to pick him up and take him shopping this afternoon."

"The county?" Keith was not a charity case, damn it! Not to her, he wasn't. "Jessica, I will buy Keith whatever he needs for the funeral."

"That cost is not your responsibility, Maris."

Maris thought of that two-hundred-fifty-dollars bail money sitting at the sheriff's office, which she hadn't yet picked up. It would be more than enough to buy a suit of clothes for Keith, which was something she should have thought of before this.

"I want to do it, Jessica. Keith has become very important to me."

"He really is an exceptional young man, isn't he? I have very high hopes for his future, Maris."

"So do I, Jessica."

"Well, I can see he's in very good hands." Maris could hear the pleased smile in Jessica's voice. "Until he turns eighteen I will have to keep an eye on him, but I have a very good feeling about Keith now. And it's all your doing, Maris. Thank you."

"It's I who should be thanking you, Jessica. You brought him into my life, and I couldn't be happier about it. One thing has come to mind, though, Jessica. Has anyone contacted Keith's grandmother?"

"I called and spoke to her sister, Maris. Mrs. Colson is very old and unwell. Her sister said she barely recognizes anyone anymore, and she couldn't possibly make the trip to attend the funeral. I told Keith about it yesterday."

"I see. I just wanted to be sure she'd been notified."

After a few more words, they hung up. This time when Maris started for the door to go outside, the phone remained silent.

She had a marvelous idea, and she could hardly wait to pass it on to Keith.

He was in the corral with Luke and another Appaloosa. Maris leaned on the fence and called, "Hey, you two, I've got a whole slew of things to tell you. Can you take a break for a few minutes?" They were both working without shirts, but it wasn't Keith's youthful torso that had Maris mesmerized. Luke's skin was as dark as a hazelnut and glistening with perspiration in the bright sunlight. The core of her felt every rippling muscle of his beautiful body as surely as if he were touching her, and the sensation literally took her breath.

At that very instant, while Luke was removing his gloves and Keith had already started toward her, a thought struck Maris nearly dumb: she had missed her period. It had never happened before. She'd rarely ever been even a day late, and now she had completely missed a period and she'd been too preoccupied with other things to notice something she had never failed to keep very close track of.

She began trembling and had to hang on to the fence to at least appear steady and in control of her senses. But this could be the real thing. She could be pregnant. Oh, Luke, she thought with a remorseful look in his direction. Tricking a man as she'd done with Luke was unforgivable.

But it hadn't seemed so terrible before falling in love with him, she realized with panic eating a hole in her stomach. If it was true, would she tell him now?

Oh, God…oh, God…

"What's up?" Luke asked, strolling over to the fence, which Keith had already reached.

"Uh…uh…" Maris's mind was so full of unconnected topics, she couldn't settle on one.

"You said you had something to tell us," Luke reminded her.

"I did. I do." Gratefully her dizzy brain remembered Katherine's call. "Katherine Willoughby found her father's breeding records and is shipping them to me."

Luke's face lit up. "Hey, that's great."

"Yes…yes, it is. Oh, Jim Humphrey called and he'll be here this weekend to pick up the Corvette."

Luke was grinning. "You're just full of good news. Anything else?"

"Something for Keith." She was beginning to calm down, thank God. "Keith, I'd like you to have some new clothes for the…for tomorrow."

"You would? I was just gonna wear my jeans."

"Would you rather just wear jeans? I was thinking of a suit."

The boy smiled shyly. "I've never had a suit."

"A suit and tie would be very appropriate," Maris said.

Keith looked at Luke. "What'll you be wearing, Luke?"

With a glance at Maris, Luke cleared his throat. "A suit and tie." He hadn't given the subject one second's thought, but if Maris wanted Keith in a suit and tie, then he'd go along with it, though it probably surprised the heck out of Maris that he even owned a suit and tie.

"Okay," Keith said. "How much will it cost? I've got about fifty bucks…"

"I'm paying for it, Keith. Now, here's the big question. Do you want to go shopping by yourself or would you like someone to go with you?"

Keith's boyish smile flashed. "I'd like someone to go with me." Maris smiled broadly, thrilled that he would want her company and advice. "I'll go call Susie right now and see if she can go," Keith said, hopping the fence and heading for the house at full speed.

Maris's mouth dropped open. "I thought he meant me."

"Susie's his girlfriend," Luke said calmly.

"The girl he took to the movies that night? But they only had that one date, didn't they?"

Luke shrugged. "Apparently it was enough."

Maris sucked in a slow breath. "Well, this is a surprise."

"Don't let it get you down, honey," Luke said gently. Reaching across the fence, he laid his hand on her shoulder.

Maris brought her gaze around to him and it hit her again.

She could be pregnant with his baby and he was leaving in less than a month.

Luke's hand slid up under her hair to the back of her neck. "You look beautiful today," he said huskily.

The words came out of her mouth before she could stop them. "So do you."

He laughed, softly, sensuously. "Maybe after Keith leaves we can...talk."

"Keith!" Maris began backing away. "There's something I have to tell him."

"Well, hell," Luke muttered, watching her hurrying to the house. For a minute there her mood had been the one he liked. Liked, hell! It was the one he *loved*. The one in which she got all dewy-eyed and excited and game for anything.

But then he relaxed. Keith would be leaving and maybe, just maybe, he could coax her back into that sweet, female mood.

Maris went into the house calling, "Keith?"

He came out of his room wearing clean jeans and shirt. "She can go, Maris. I'm going to pick her up in half an hour."

"That's wonderful, but there's something I need you to do before you pick up Susie. It won't take but a minute. Stop at the sheriff's office and they'll give you two hundred and fifty dollars in cash."

"How come?" Keith looked completely mystified.

"Uh...it's money they owe me. Use what you need of it for a nice suit and accessories. I would suggest a white shirt and a tie in subdued colors. Get some shoes, too, some *real* shoes."

Keith grinned. "No boots or sneakers, huh? Okay, I'll stop and pick up the money." He started out, then did an about-face. "Thanks, Maris. You think of everything."

Maris collapsed onto the nearest chair. She came up with everything, all right, she thought disgustedly, even devising that awful plot to get pregnant without Luke's knowledge.

But then the thought of a baby refired her earlier elation, and she sat there and fantasized about having a child in the house and in her own arms, until she remembered that she had to call Judd and tell him to release that bail money to Keith.

Jumping up, she dashed to the phone.

Seventeen

When Keith drove away in Maris's pickup, Luke washed up at the corral faucet, dried himself with his shirt, draped the shirt over a post fence, strode to the house and walked in. Maris was just hanging up the phone, and he went to her, took her by the hands and brought her to her feet.

Her eyes became very wide and startled. "No, Luke."

"Look me in the eye and tell me you don't want me," he said gruffly.

"I..." Her blood was suddenly racing. "It would be a lie."

"That's what I thought." Bending, he placed his hand behind her knees and scooped her off the floor and against his chest. "Which way to your bedroom?"

She buried her face in his neck. "Down the hall. Last door on the right." It was no use, she thought. She'd tried keeping Luke from doing something like this and had obviously failed. Maybe, without realizing it, she'd even been inviting one more repeat of their tempestuous lovemaking before he went away.

Today he seemed in a hurry. He set her on her feet next to her own bed and began undressing her. "Go slower," she whispered. Their eyes met, and the grim expression in his evolved into warmth and desire.

"Sorry." Gently he tugged her forward and pressed his lips to hers. Maris felt his kiss all the way down to her toes. A strange mixture of joy and misery made her feel reckless, and she snuggled closer and thrust her tongue into his mouth. After he was gone she would remember each time they had made love, and maybe he deserved the same cruel fate. She would make today as memorable as she could. He would not drive away without memories, not after today.

His naked chest seemed to beg for attention, and Maris ran her fingertips, her nails, over his smooth, dark skin.

"Baby," he whispered raggedly. "Why do I want you so much?"

She'd been asking herself the same question, only in her case the answer was becoming acutely evident. Apparently Luke wasn't thinking beyond the pounding beat of his own blood, which was sort of sad. And yet, if he said right now that he was in love with her she would be aghast. Heaven knows she had long stopped comparing him to Ray, but there were still worrisome similarities, such as fighting in a bar and, for that matter, going there in the first place. What else did a person go to a tavern for but to drink? Then there was the biggest similarity of all, rodeo. Luke's obsession for rodeo actually surpassed Ray's.

No, she didn't want to hear that Luke loved her, or that he would drop in and see her if and when he ever returned to this part of Montana. His departure after the horse auction had to be final and the end of their relationship.

Even with those thoughts deeply entrenched in her mind, Maris sighed seductively and responded to his desire with every cell in her body. She kissed him as demandingly, as passionately, as he kissed her, and her caresses were as bold and intimate as his.

Suddenly it was she who seemed in a hurry. Groping for the buckle on his belt, she opened it and then the zipper of his fly. He unbuttoned her blouse and pushed it from her shoulders. Their kisses had become hungry and greedy, landing willy-nilly on noses and chins and lips. She pushed down his jeans and undershorts while he did the same with her jeans and panties.

But their clothing got hung up on Luke's boots and her shoes, and they separated to hastily rid themselves of the obstructions. Naked then, Maris drew back the spread and blankets. They tumbled to the bed, legs entwined, to kiss and touch and explore each other's bodies.

"You're so beautiful," Luke whispered. His mouth opened on her breast. His tongue teased her nipple until it had formed

a rigid peak, causing an unbearable ache between her legs. He seemed to know, because he slid down in the bed and began kissing her inner thighs, gradually going higher. Moaning softly, eyes closed, Maris curled her fingers into his hair, all she could reach of him. His tongue was like hot satin on her most sensitive spot, and in minutes a starburst of pleasure began in her lower abdomen.

"Luke...Luke..." she whimpered, needing his arms around her at this unique and special moment.

He heard and understood her cry. Moving up in the bed, he gathered her into his arms and kissed her lips. He held her against his chest until her trembling had ceased.

Then he tipped her chin and looked into her eyes. The mist of tears and the softness he saw touched his soul. Tenderly he kissed her. "Maris...we need to talk," he said hoarsely.

"Not now. Please...not now." If he talked about love she would fall apart and confess how much she cared for him. She would tell him that nothing mattered but loving him, and it wasn't true. Or it wouldn't be true once this incredibly sensual interlude was over. But in her present mood she would say foolish things, things such as his need for the excitement of rodeo being no detriment to their relationship, and that she didn't care if he hung out in bars and got into fistfights and was arrested. She did care. Those things caused her great pain, and she didn't want to tell romantic lies because of his sexual power and then regret them later.

For a moment Luke nearly forced the issue. They *did* need to talk. He wanted to understand why she'd become so important to him, and why she made love with him if he wasn't equally as important to her.

But he was unmercifully aroused and talking could come later. Maris surprised him by sitting up. But she wasn't eluding his embrace, he realized, not when she smiled mysteriously and then straddled his hips. He sucked in a huge breath of air as his excitement increased to the bursting stage.

Leaning forward, she feathered kisses across his lips. Her long hair caressed his shoulders and the sides of his face. The

crests of her breasts softly touched his chest, and she deliberately moved them back and forth in exquisite torture.

His eyes were partially closed, his breathing deep and labored. "What're you doing to me?" he said thickly.

"Do you want me to stop?" she whispered with a seductive smile.

"No way."

Laughing softly, she took his sexy bottom lip between her teeth and gently nibbled. Luke's hands rose up to cup her bottom. "Incredible," he murmured.

"What's incredible?"

"Your...uh, hips." Her nibbling at his mouth was driving him crazy. "If you raise up just a little..."

"Yes? If I raise up just a little you'll do what?"

"Do it and find out," he growled.

Maris appeared to be thinking very hard. "Could it be this?" Lifting her bottom, she reached down to his manhood and held it upright, positioning them both for a perfect union. Very slowly she took him inside herself, until she was sitting precisely on the juncture of his thighs.

"That's it," Luke said with his eyes closed and supreme pleasure all over his face.

He was fully inside of her, lying flat on his back, and the sensation was unbelievably exciting for Maris. "I kind of like this," she said playfully, albeit in an unusually husky voice.

"I kind of like it, too."

"It makes me feel quite powerful."

Luke's eyes opened. "Like you're the boss?"

"Like I'm in control."

His eyes were dark and smoldering. "You are. What are you going to do now, boss?"

"Hmm. Maybe this." With her hands on his chest she slowly raised her hips and then slid down again. "How was that?"

"That was good. That was *very* good. Do it again."

"Again? Once wasn't enough?"

Her teasing tone delighted Luke. Never had she teased him about anything. Nearly every day Maris let him see another

side of her. A lot of the time the side she exposed wasn't altogether pleasant, but he was beginning to realize she was a many faceted woman. A complex woman.

But he could tease, too. "Well...maybe once *was* enough. I'll let you decide. You are in control, you know."

Her teasing expression vanished. "So I am. Maybe I'll keep you in this position for hours."

He laughed, a trifle grimly. "I wouldn't last for hours, baby, but give it your best shot."

She fell forward and whispered into his ear. "I know what you want, you devil." Then she straightened and began moving her hips up and down, using her knees on the bed to propel herself.

He clutched at her thighs. "That's it. That's fantastic. Don't stop. Don't even slow down." His right hand crept over his own belly to locate and then stroke the core of her pleasure.

"Luke...oh, Luke," she gasped, stunned that she would be this needful so soon after the heights she had just reached no more than ten minutes ago. It was almost laughable that she had decided to give him a memory about today that he would never forget. *She* was the one who would never forget this day, and didn't she already have enough incidents to suffer over after he was gone?

But there was no stopping now. Nor, as Luke had pleaded, even a chance of slowing down. She was caught by the rhythms of their intense lovemaking, soaring and feeling more alive than ever in her life. She loved this man, adored him, and she just might die when the day came for him to drive away in his fancy pickup.

Her eyes flooded with tears, and when the powerful and beautiful spasms of release began, she fell forward, too dazed even to wonder if Luke had come to the same dizzying fulfillment.

He had, and he held her in an embrace so tight he marveled that she didn't complain. "Straighten out your legs, honey," he whispered. Mindlessly she obeyed. Luke turned them to their sides. "Do you want to get up?" Damn, he thought. He hadn't

used protection again. What in hell was wrong with his brain? When he was hot for Maris and she cooperated, everything sensible simply disappeared.

She was starting to come out of that magical haze, starting to think again. "Uh...yes, I'd better." Still dazed, she slipped from his arms and got off the bed. Somehow she made it to the bathroom without tripping over anything, though how she'd accomplished it she would never know.

Automatically she refreshed herself, then, standing before the bathroom mirror, she studied her reflection and saw the dejection in her eyes. Her heart was already broken and Luke was still here. How would she bear it when he wasn't?

Wrapping a large bath towel around herself, she returned to the bedroom. Luke had stacked the pillows and was lying against them with his eyes closed, and wearing an expression of utter satisfaction. Hearing her come in, he lifted his lids and smiled at her.

"Hi, baby." Maris didn't smile back and his spirit deflated. Every damn time they made love she got depressed right after. "Don't do this, Maris."

"Don't do what?" Listlessly she began picking up her clothes.

Luke sat up. "I think you know." He watched her gather clothes for a moment. "Maris, come over here. Please."

She heaved a despondent sigh. "Luke, I don't like myself very much right now. Just get up and go, please."

Leaping off the bed, Luke grabbed her by her upper arms. "We're going to talk. Come and sit down."

"Talk about what?"

"About us, damn it! What else would I want to talk about?"

"Don't shout at me," she said sharply.

"Then talk to me. Right now, right here." He began pushing her toward the bed. "Sit down."

She shook off his hands. "Don't give me orders." She wasn't yelling. In fact, her voice had become steely, steady and lethally quiet.

Luke took a breath. "I'm sorry. Maris, would you please sit down and talk to me?"

Apparently this "talk" was inevitable and it may as well be now as later, she thought. "Yes," she said, and marched to the closet for a bathrobe, which she put on with her back to him. Then she went over to the room's one chair and sat down. "Go ahead."

Luke scrambled for his jeans and yanked them on without bothering with his underwear. He turned to look at Maris. "The first thing I wish you'd tell me is why you get angry and depressed every time we make love."

A snotty retort nearly made it to her lips, but she decided against it. It was time for the truth with Luke. "I like you more than I should. I don't want to like you. I don't *want* to sleep with you. I don't want anything between us but our original deal. Second, I have never casually slept around. I turn into someone else with you, the kind of woman that I have never respected or even wanted to know. I believe that only people deeply in love with each other should be making love. I believe that it's up to the woman to say no to a man, because men can and do sleep around and it means nothing to them. Nor does the woman mean anything to them. I..."

"Whoa," Luke said, sounding as breathless as if he'd been the one making that long speech. "Let's start with why you don't want to like me."

Maris's left eyebrow went up. "I think that's perfectly obvious. You're leaving in a few weeks, aren't you?"

Luke hesitated. "That's been my plan all along, yes. But let me ask you this. Don't you ever let yourself like anyone who isn't living on the ranch?"

"We're not talking about ordinary liking, and you know it," Maris said with cutting asperity.

"Ah, that's good." Luke nodded enthusiastically, surprising her. "Now we're getting somewhere. You don't just *like* me. It's possible that you even—" he cleared his throat "—love me."

Maris's face drained of color. "Don't presume too much,

Luke. However I feel about you, it's going to come to a screeching halt very soon now. I'd just as soon not get in any deeper than I already am, and if you had any feelings at all for me you wouldn't even be mentioning the word *love*."

"Because you and I couldn't possibly have a future together, right?" He practically stopped breathing, almost praying for some word, some sign from Maris that would indicate otherwise. She disappointed him.

"That's *exactly* right. Let me tell you something, Luke. I will never again make any sort of commitment to a man who has not only completely settled down in one place, but who wouldn't have it any other way."

"A man like Judd Hensley." Just saying the sheriff's name caused Luke's spine to stiffen.

Maris scoffed. "Don't bring Judd into this. I don't have to explain my friendship with Judd to you, nor do I intend to try."

"Don't expect me to believe Hensley hasn't made a pass, Maris," Luke said with some sarcasm.

"Judd has *never* made a pass," she said with icy distinction. "You're exactly like Ray was. You simply cannot visualize a nonsexual relationship between a man and a woman."

Luke's face shut down. "I'm *nothing* like Ray was."

"Nothing! Good grief, do you take me for an idiot? He couldn't enter enough competitions to satisfy his obsession with trying to kill himself in a rodeo arena, and he was forever fighting in bars. Usually over a woman, I might add."

Luke's lips tightened into a thin line. He looked at her for a long time, then said brusquely, "So you feel that my career choice and one fight in a bar make me like Ray. Maris, what's your friend Lori's telephone number?"

Maris blinked. "What?" Walking over to the telephone on the bedstand, Luke repeated the question. "Why do you want Lori's number?" Maris asked incredulously.

"Because she was at the Sundowner that night and I'd like you to hear from her what really happened."

"Lori was there? I don't believe you. She would have called me...or something."

"She was there, Maris. Believe it." Luke picked up the phone and pointed it at Maris. "Call her."

Perplexed, Maris stared at the phone in Luke's hand. Lori had been there? She'd seen the fight and what had caused it? If that was true, why hadn't Lori called and told her about it?

Maris lifted her chin. Lori was a very busy woman and many times weeks passed without either of them calling the other. It could also be that Lori simply didn't want to carry tales. "Why don't you leave Lori out of this and tell me what happened yourself?"

"Because I don't think you'd believe me. I don't think you believe *anything* I say. For some crazy reason you've got me mixed up with Ray. It's like Ray went away and I showed up and nothing had changed."

"That's the most ridiculous thing I've ever heard." But the sneer in Maris's voice wasn't nearly as definite as she'd meant to convey. Without question she had lumped Luke and Ray in the same untrustworthy category many times. By the same token, she had also recognized their differences. Ray had been as lazy as they came and no one could ever accuse Luke of shirking responsibility. As far as his work with the horses went, anyway.

She had only discussed Ray with Luke in general terms, and maybe it was time to get specific. Maris stood and went to the window. "You're not like Ray. I'm sorry I said you were. Oh, there are similarities, make no mistake, but you're not mean or lazy or unkind, and he…" Her voice cracked. She was getting painfully close to the very memories she had diligently avoided since Ray's death.

"He what, Maris? Tell me, please."

Maris sighed. She had opened this can of worms all on her own, whetting Luke's curiosity, and maybe he *should* hear the facts of his friend's true nature.

She turned to face Luke. "You and Ray were good friends, weren't you?"

"Uh…let's just say we ran into each other quite a lot."

"At various rodeos."

Luke nodded. "Yes, but that didn't make us good friends, Maris. What were you going to say a minute ago?"

"Are you sure you want to hear this?"

"I'm positive. Maris…" Luke moved close enough to touch her and very gently brushed a strand of hair from her cheek. "Tell me your secrets, honey, and I'll tell you mine."

"You have secrets?"

"There's one that's been eating a hole in my gut for weeks now."

Instinctively she knew his "secret" was about her. He was going to talk about love, and she was just stupid enough to listen and then confess her feelings for him. He was right. Ray had died, Luke had shown up and nothing had changed.

But that wasn't completely true, either. *She* had changed, and she'd meant what she'd said about never again committing herself to an unstable man. Yes, she would tell him her secrets, and if that didn't get her point across to Luke, nothing ever would.

"Very well." Needing some space between them, Maris went to the other side of the room. "When Ray and I were married, I was very deeply in love with him." She noticed Luke's flinch but let it pass without a reaction from her. "He brought me here and I immediately found a second love, the ranch. He showed me around the place and I was so starry-eyed I only barely noticed the evidences of neglect. It was around the middle of September and we had a beautiful fall that year. Every day was sunny and warm, and Ray was full of smiles. We drove somewhere to eat out almost every night. We slept late in the morning. He always had something fun lined up for the day and I rarely had any free time to even do any housecleaning. 'We're on our honeymoon,' he'd say if I mentioned that the carpets needed vacuuming or the laundry was piling up. And he never did any real work outside. Once in a while he'd go down to the barn and putter around for an hour or so, but that was about it.

"The weather changed. There was no snow, but it got very cold very fast. One morning I awoke and heard the cattle bawl-

ing. You know how far the pastures are from the house, so it was a muffled sound, but incessant and disturbing. I couldn't figure out what was causing it, so I slipped out of bed, put on some warm clothes and went out to investigate. It was bitterly cold. The thermometer read five below zero. I hurried to the fields and found the animals milling around the water ponds, which had completely frozen over.

"It seemed like a simple enough problem to me, and I rushed back to the house to wake Ray and tell him about it, assuming, of course, that he would take the news as I had. Obviously holes had to be chopped through the ice so the animals could drink."

Maris drew a breath. "He became enraged when I shook him awake and explained the situation. Cursing and throwing things around, he got dressed and stormed out of the house. I was so stunned I didn't know where to put myself. Would he want my help outside? Would my presence anger him further?

"I made a pot of coffee and worried myself sick. Had I done something to anger him? To that point I hadn't seen him angry and it scared me. Would he calm down outside and come back in sweet as sugar? I realized that awful morning that I really didn't know my husband.

"Well, he didn't come in at all. About three hours later, from the kitchen window, I saw him getting into his pickup and driving off. He got home around midnight that night, so drunk he could barely walk. I helped him into bed, then I sat up the rest of the night, crying and accusing myself of doing something to make him angry enough to drink himself into a stupor."

Maris went to the chair and sat down. "That was the beginning. Ray was never the same after that. He told me he hated the ranch and he was no longer very fond of me. He started going off by himself, to one rodeo or another. I chopped through the ice when the ponds froze over. I delivered hay to the fields when there was too much snow for the cattle to paw through to reach the grass.

"I knew what my options were—leave Ray or stay and take

whatever he dished out. I hated fighting and did everything I could to avoid dissension. But he got mean when he drank, and he—'' She stopped to swallow. This was something she had never told anyone. "He started hitting me.''

"Hitting you!'' Luke looked as though someone had just hit *him*. "And you still stayed?''

Maris didn't answer. Instead she said, "I had wanted a baby from the day we were married. One night he told me that he'd had a vasectomy *after* we were married. He laughed about it. He had let me hope and pray for a child. He had watched me taking my temperature to check for my fertile times, and all along he'd known he couldn't become a father.''

"Mental cruelty,'' Luke mumbled. Clearly he was dumbfounded by Maris's history. "He must have loved you to marry you, so what changed him?''

"I disappointed him, Luke. He wanted a playmate, which was exactly what I'd been during his courtship. But you see, I took marriage seriously and Ray did not. He didn't want to run the ranch the way it needed to be run. He didn't want to be tied down by a wife who thought animals should be properly cared for. I honestly don't know how the ranch survived after Ray's father died and Ray lived here alone. He must have worked sometimes, however erratically or begrudgingly, probably doing only what absolutely had to be done to keep the place together. When I finally faced reality and took a really good look at everything, the signs of neglect were everywhere. Fencing was falling down. Every building needed repairs and paint.''

Maris threw up her hands and got to her feet. "There's so much more I could go on for the rest of the day. But I'm sure I've said enough for you to understand why I get depressed, as you pointed out, every time we make love. No, you don't seem to be like Ray in temperament. But you do have some of his traits, and that scares me, Luke. I admit to being weak with you. I admit that I'm enormously attracted to you, but you have to do a little admitting, too. One, you're always going to be a traveling rodeo rider. Two—''

"Stop." Luke spoke quietly, but the intensity of the expression on his face was enough to stop Maris from enlarging her list. "It's time you heard my secrets."

"I...I'm not sure I want to," Maris said falteringly.

"Fair is fair. I listened to yours—now you listen to mine." Luke walked a small circle in the middle of the room, taking in a long breath at the same time. Maris watched with her heart in her throat. He finally stopped and looked at her. "Here goes," he said in a tone of voice that sounded as though he were preparing to dive into an erupting volcano. "I'm thirty-five years old, I've traveled thousands of miles, I've met hundreds of women, and until coming here I thought everything was great. Oh, sure, I was broke, but I figured I'd collect that three thousand from Ray and make a new start."

He narrowed his eyes on Maris, who was standing stock-still and staring at him rather nervously. "Did I ever tell you *why* I was broke?"

"No," Maris said cautiously.

"I took a bad fall about a year ago and broke several bones. My horse broke his neck and had to be put to sleep. He was the best cutting horse..." Luke looked away for a moment, embarrassed to find himself on the brink of tears. "Anyway, I used up my savings in getting well. You know, if I hadn't had that accident I might never have remembered Ray's IOU."

"This happened while you were competing in a rodeo, right?" There was sudden frost in Maris's eyes. "I'm sorry about your mishap and your losing your horse, but a man risking his neck in rodeo just doesn't make any sense to me."

"It's no damned different than any other sport! Do you hate football players, too?"

Maris's jaw dropped. "I never thought of it that way."

"Well, try, okay? Maris, the only reason you hate rodeo is that Ray used it to get away from the ranch. After what you just told me, he might even have used it to get away from you." At her hurt expression, he took the sharp edges off his voice. "Honey, I'm trying to tell you something. I feel...different now. I've been trying to figure it out for weeks. It's you. It's

Keith. It's working with the horses. It's watching you do your gardening, and the way you worked your tail off on that yard sale. It's the way you run the ranch and take care of the cattle. It's how you treat Keith and how much he likes and respects you. It's…''

He chewed on his bottom lip. He shoved his hands into the pockets of his jeans and yanked them free again. He raked his hair and darted nervous glances at her. And finally, when she was starting to think of dashing out of the room and probably the house altogether to avoid what was coming, he blurted, ''I'm different because I love you.''

Maris wilted. ''I don't want to hear this.''

''You already did, but I'm going to say it again. I love you and I'm pretty sure you love me, too.''

Sinking weakly to the edge of the bed, Maris hid her face behind her hands. ''I knew you were going to do this to me— I just knew it. Luke, go away. I mean, pack your things and *go away!*''

''Not on your life, sweetheart.'' He knelt beside her. ''It took every ounce of courage I could find to tell you my secret, and now that it's been said I'm sure as hell not going to disappear.''

Dropping her hands, Maris jerked her head up. ''Not until you get the itch to wander again. And it will happen, Luke. Maybe I've gone overboard with my dislike of rodeo, but don't expect me to believe that you've suddenly lost a lifelong yen to compete.''

''That's exactly what I expect you to believe,'' he said softly. ''You know what my big problem is now? I don't have anything to offer you.''

''Offer me?'' Her voice was as unsteady as she felt inside, all quavery and woozy.

''Maris, I'd like to stay here and help you run the ranch. But I don't have anything to contribute. Why would a woman want to marry a man who has only two assets—a six-year-old pickup and an uncollectable IOU?''

''Marry?'' She was going to faint, she could feel it starting in her midsection and working its way up to her brain. She

strove for clarity. "Uh...you're going to collect on that IOU after the horse auction."

"Let's talk about that after we decide on the marrying part of this conversation."

She tried to swallow the massive lump in her throat. "Luke, I can't...I can't marry you. And it's not because of your assets. I explained about Ray..."

"I'm not Ray. I won't yell at you because the ponds freeze over. I won't leave you alone to chase after either a rodeo or another woman, and I will never, never lay a hand on you. Except to make love." He managed a hopeful, lopsided grin. He'd laid his heart on the line with Maris, something he'd never done with any other woman. "Those are promises, Maris, vows. You're the only woman I've ever talked to like this, the only woman I've ever been in love with."

Maris's chest was so tight she could just barely breathe. Didn't Luke understand anything she had told him? Ray had made promises, too. Ray had...

No! Ray hadn't promised anything. Ray had led her into love and marriage with no more than a sexy grin, a persuasive personality and a dishonest glibness. She probably knew Luke ten times better right now than she'd known Ray on their wedding day.

It scared her that she was weakening, leaning toward Luke's unusual marriage proposal, forgetting about him fighting in the Sundowner, forgetting that he'd lived a restless, roaming life and, probably most important, that very few people possessed the strength of will to change lifelong habits and routines.

She looked into his eyes, then raised her right hand and laid it on his cheek. He had told her—begged her, actually—to call Lori and hear from her best friend what had really happened at the Sundowner. She had to call Lori anyway, to ask her to pick up one of those home pregnancy tests at Tully's Drugstore for her. She would also ask Lori about the fight.

"Luke," she said quietly. "I'm not saying no, all right? But I need some time to think about it."

He closed his eyes for a blissful moment, then buried his

face in her lap. "You'll say yes," he whispered. "I know you will." Maris heard, but said nothing. She merely stroked his hair, very gently, very tenderly. Whatever decision she finally came to, she was in love with Luke.

That love could be either a blessing or a curse. Only time would tell.

Eighteen

Keith, with Susie's help, bought a handsome dark-gray suit and the correct accessories. Maris was impressed by their choices and said so, though she hadn't yet met Keith's young friend. The next day Luke, Keith and Maris dressed up for Terrance Colson's funeral, and they drove to the somber event in a hushed mood, using Maris's truck.

The saddest part of it for Maris was that other than the three of them, the only person at the service was Jessica McCallum. If Terrance had had any friends, they weren't announcing it by attending his funeral. Maris mentioned Susie to Keith and he said, "I asked her not to come. I didn't want her here, Maris."

He seemed so grown-up, Maris thought. The suit and tie added years to his appearance, but it wasn't only his clothes that made him look older. Maturity was in his eyes, in the set of his mouth and shoulders. Giving him a small smile of understanding, Maris curled her hand around his arm.

Later, after the brief service was over, Jessica spoke to them all, though her message was unquestionably for Keith. "If you need anything, please let me know."

The drive back to the ranch was almost as silent as the drive out. Maris felt Luke's emotional tension much more than she felt Keith's, and she was relieved when the trip was over. Keith had every right to introspective sobriety today; Luke was tense because of their conversation yesterday. Every time he looked at her, which was often, she felt his head in her lap again, her hand in his hair. Each time she remembered what he'd said. *You'll say yes. I know you will.*

Possibly she would. Possibly she wouldn't. Weighing Luke's hopes and her ambivalence from every angle didn't seem crass to Maris. She had vowed never to marry again. While that oath

might be a bit overboard, vowing to avoid another unstable man was not, and certainly she had done that, too.

No one discussed plans for the balance of the day, but Maris immediately went to her room to change clothes. When she walked into the kitchen a short time later, Keith was on his way outside. He stopped for a few words.

"Thanks for being there, Maris."

"I wouldn't have had it any other way." Her gaze flicked over his jeans and boots. "Are you going to work?"

"Luke needs my help."

Maris glanced out the window and saw Luke down by the corral, also wearing jeans and boots. The men on the No Bull were both hard workers and even on a day like today would not evade responsibility. Was there a chance the three of them could actually become a family?

Maybe she should be thinking in terms of the *four* of them, Maris thought uneasily. She would call Lori the minute Keith was out of earshot.

He grabbed an apple from the bowl of fruit on the table and left through the kitchen door. Maris sat down and eyed the telephone. Love wasn't enough to guarantee harmony between a couple, she reminded herself, thinking of Luke and Ray and everything in between. But was she judging Luke too harshly because of her years of unhappiness with Ray?

Slowly, reflectively, Maris picked up the phone and dialed Lori's work number. The receptionist asked her to hold for a few minutes, as Lori was busy with a patient. With the silent telephone at her ear, Maris doodled on a pad and thought about Luke and his many promises. His concern about having nothing of a material nature to contribute to their relationship was touching, though anyone's net worth had never been of great significance to Maris. Still, she could see why he might have doubts about that aspect of his proposal.

She heaved a long-suffering sigh. Nothing was ever easy. If she said yes to Luke she might regret it within months, as she had with Ray. If she said no, she might regret it for the rest of her life.

"Maris?"

"Lori, hi. Have you got a minute to talk?"

"I have *fifteen* minutes to talk. I'm on a break. How've you been? I've been meaning to call for weeks, but the baby business is booming these days and I've been working practically nonstop."

"I've been meaning to call you, too. So much for good intentions, right? Lori, do you recall our conversation about that home pregnancy test?"

"Sure do. Are you ready to try one? Maris, if you're certain of your condition now, you really should make an appointment with your doctor."

"I'm not certain, and I think I'd rather try the test first. Could I impose on your busy schedule and ask you to pick one up for me?"

"I'll do it today. Are you hoping to get a positive reaction? I know you've always wanted a child, but you're alone now and single parenting can be very trying."

"Trying or not, I'm hoping very much that the test will turn out positive, Lori."

"Then I hope it does, too. So...what else is happening on the No Bull? How's Keith?"

"His father died. Did you hear?"

"No, I didn't." Lori paused. "I suppose I should be sorry, but I really can't muster up any sorrow for a man who did what he did to his family. How did Keith take it?"

"Quietly. I don't think he can muster up much sorrow, either."

"Understandable. Well...how's Luke? He's still working for you, isn't he?"

"He's still here. Lori, about Luke...he said you were in the Sundowner the night he got into that fight with Jim Benteen."

"I was there with Louise and Larry Hawkins, Maris. Judd called you that night, didn't he? I was going to call, but when he said that he planned to, I decided to stay out of it."

"He called, Lori, but... Well, no one's told me what really happened."

"Luke didn't?"

"When I questioned him about it, he said to call you."

Lori laughed. "He did, huh? Well, I suppose he's not proud of being arrested, but after it was over and I grasped what had happened, I was very proud of him. He's quite a guy, Maris."

"Tell me about it, Lori."

"Sure, glad to. I was sitting with my back to the bar, yakking with Louise and Larry, and I honestly didn't see Luke come in and sit at the bar. You know the layout of the Sundowner, don't you? Well, Melva Waterman and Jim Benteen were sitting in that back corner booth. Those two have lived together off and on for a good ten years, Maris, and when they're in an off mood, they fight. That's what they were doing that night, hissing at each other like two spitting cats, and drinking heavily, to boot.

"All of a sudden this loud cracking noise came from the booth. Melva let out a wail and everyone in the place knew that Jim had struck her. He got up to leave and was nearly to the door, when Luke stopped him. Something was said between them. I didn't hear what it was, because Louise and I went over to Melva to see if she was all right.

"The next thing I knew, Luke and Jim were fighting, knocking over chairs, trying to kill each other it looked like. Pete called the sheriff. I'd made a makeshift ice pack out of napkins and ice from the drinks on the table, and was holding it to Melva's eye.

"The deputies arrived, though the fight was pretty much over by then. Benteen was on his knees and Luke was leaning against the bar, blowing on his bruised knuckles. Sometime along in there Judd walked in and I realized who Luke was. It all happened pretty fast, but I would give Luke a pat on the back any day of the week for what he did, Maris. There were other men in the place and none of them did one blasted thing about Jim hitting Melva.

"That's the story, Maris. Apparently Luke doesn't like men beating up women."

Recalling Luke's shocked reaction when she'd told him that

Ray had hit her, Maris bit down on her lower lip. "Apparently not," she said after a moment, her voice husky and emotional.

"I wonder why Luke didn't tell you about it himself," Lori mused.

"He said it was because I wouldn't believe him. He added that I doubted everything he says," Maris said quietly.

"Do you?"

Maris took a rather shaky breath. "Maybe it seems that way to him. I haven't always been...kind to Luke." *Not only that, I tricked him into making me pregnant.* Maris felt about two inches high. "Lori, thanks for the story. I'll let you get back to work now."

"I'll drop off that test sometime today, probably this evening."

"Thanks, Lori. See you then." Maris nearly hung up, then said, "Lori? Are you still there?"

"You darned near lost me," Lori said with a laugh.

"I'll pick up that test myself."

"Really? What about John Tully catching on and spreading it around town?"

"To hell with what John Tully or anyone else might think," Maris said emphatically.

"Good girl. See you when I see you, okay?"

"Bye, Lori."

Maris put down the phone. Ray had fought in bars just for the hell of it; Luke had fought to protest Benteen's treatment of Melva. There was a world of difference between Ray's temperament and Luke's. And Judd himself had told her Luke hadn't been drunk. She'd been too quick to judge, and who was she to judge anyone's ethics or behavior, anyway? It took a pretty sneaky woman to make love with a man just so she could get pregnant, and in the process make plans never to let him know about his own child should her deceitful plot be successful.

But she hadn't only made love with Luke to get pregnant. She must have fallen in love with him very early in their relationship to have made love with him that first time. Hadn't

she stood around outside, trying to look busy, just so she could watch him working without his shirt? He had affected her right from the first and she had fought and denied the feelings developing within her as hard as she could, simply because he was a rodeo rider.

Getting to her feet, Maris went to the window over the sink. Luke was in the corral with a reddish brown horse; Keith was nowhere to be seen, probably putting the already trained horses through their paces in one of the pastures.

Maris's pulse began a faster beat. Her own nerve astounded her. Going to the back door, she stepped outside and shouted, "Luke?"

He turned his head toward her. "What?" he yelled back.

"Could you come to the house?"

"Yeah. Be right there."

She went inside to quiver and tremble and pray she was doing the right thing.

Luke loped from the corral to the house and went inside. "What is it?"

Maris's legs felt about as steady as a bowl of gelatin. "I...I love you."

His eyes widened, but surprise didn't prevent him from closing the gap between them in two long strides and pulling her into his arms. "I love you, too, baby."

Her face was against his bare chest, and she could smell the musky maleness of his sun-heated skin. "There's something I have to tell you," she whispered tremulously.

"Tell me anything."

"You're not going to like it."

"Try me."

"Yes...I have to." Maris pushed herself free of his embrace. "I..." She couldn't look at him. "I think I'm pregnant."

He was stunned for a moment, but then a slow grin broke out on Luke's face. "Maris, that's great! Why would you think I wouldn't like it?"

She swallowed nervously. "Because I...I planned to lure you

into making me pregnant, knowing you were going to leave in September. You never would have known about the baby.''

He sat down. Rather, he plopped into the nearest chair as though every ounce of strength in his body had suddenly deserted him. ''I don't believe you'd do something like that,'' he mumbled.

''It's true, Luke,'' she whispered with her eyes cast downward.

''Why are you telling me about it now?''

''Because I'm ashamed. And sorry. I always had so much to say about your...uh, faults, or what I considered faults, and then I did something worse than you've probably ever done.''

''But you really are pregnant?'' Luke asked, as though needing to hear it again.

''I'm not a hundred percent sure yet, but I think so.'' He still looked shell-shocked, she saw with a sinking sensation. Maybe he didn't want children. Oh, God, why hadn't she considered that before calling him in to confess her sin?

But no, he'd declared her pregnancy great. What had stunned him was her deceit. He probably hated deceit and anyone capable of it.

The strangest sense of calm suddenly descended upon Maris. She wasn't any more perfect than the next person. She was willing to overlook Luke's flaws and only he could decide if he was able to accept hers.

''If you don't love me now, I won't be angry, Luke,'' she said quietly.

He jerked his eyes toward her. ''Don't love you? Do you think my feelings for you are that shallow? There are only a few things that could destroy my love for you, lady. One of them is infidelity and the others... Well, I can't think of them right now, but it would take something pretty damned serious to turn me off on you.''

Thrilled at his attitude, Maris opened her mouth to say that she felt the same about him, but the front doorbell rang before she could express herself. She nearly jumped out of her skin. ''Who on earth could that be?''

Luke got up. "Why don't we go and find out?"

It was a deliveryman with a large cardboard carton. "I have a delivery for Mrs. Maris Wyler," he said cheerfully.

"I'm Mrs. Wyler."

"Sign here, please." The man held out a clipboard containing a receipt.

Maris glanced excitedly at Luke. "It's the package from Katherine Willoughby." Quickly she signed the receipt and the deliveryman tore off a copy and handed it to her. Luke picked up the carton. "Thank you," Maris told the man.

"You're welcome. Have a good day, Mrs. Wyler." Whistling, he walked off to his truck.

Luke carried in the carton. Maris quickly closed the door and followed him to the kitchen. "Set it on the table. Do you have a knife?"

"Right here." Luke pulled a jackknife out of his pocket. The box was opened in no time, and they could both see that it was crammed full of file folders.

Maris took out the top folder and read its label. "'Satin Dolly.' Oh, my goodness, Luke, it just occurred to me. How will we decide which horse belongs to which file?"

"We'll figure it out." Luke picked up a folder and began thumbing through the papers in it. He smiled. "Everything's here, sire, dam, grandsire, grandam, and even farther back than that. Physical descriptions, time of birth..." He looked at Maris. "Do you realize what you have here?"

"Uh...records?"

"Damned good records. I wonder why Ray neglected to ask for these files when he bought the horses."

"I think the key word in that statement is 'neglected,' Luke."

Their gazes meshed for a long moment. "If you hadn't taken care of this ranch, there wouldn't be a No Bull, would there?" Luke said.

"I'm sure the ranch would still be here, but I wouldn't own it." Maris smiled a trifle grimly. "Me and the bank, that is."

"You said you planned to go back into the cattle business, once the horses were sold."

"That's true."

Thoughtfully Luke looked at the carton of breeding records. "How about raising horses instead?"

"Luke, I understand the cattle business. Raising horses is a whole other ball game."

His gaze pinned her with its intensity. "*I* understand horses."

Maris's heart skipped a beat. "We're talking about you and me now, aren't we?"

"We're talking about a lot of things, Maris, mainly our future. Are you going to marry me? I said I didn't have much in the way of assets to offer you, but there's one I didn't think of until now. There's very little I don't know about horses." He laid his hand on the carton of records. "With these we could breed and raise the best cutting horses in the country. There's always a demand for good cutting stock, Maris. Ranchers use them as well as rodeo riders. I paid ten thousand dollars for Pancho and he was worth every cent. That's the kind of price you could get for properly trained cutting stock."

"Ten thousand!" Maris drew a startled breath. "Do you mean to say that my horses are worth…" She multiplied ninety-three times ten thousand and gasped. "Nearly a million dollars?"

Luke chuckled. "No, I don't mean that at all, though it would be great, wouldn't it? I'd say that about half your herd has the traits needed for good cutting stock. What I would do is keep the best and sell the rest, which would result in enough animals to get started in the horse breeding business *and* the cash to keep the ranch going through the winter. By spring I'd have some of those horses so well trained, ranchers and rodeo riders would be begging to buy them."

"We would still hold the auction," Maris said, a little breathless over Luke's ambitious and exciting ideas.

"Definitely. With these records of ancestry, any of your horses will bring a good price. But some of them will never be

more than what they are right now. A good cutting horse needs to possess three qualities, Maris—the ability and desire to learn, a lot of endurance and a natural freedom of movement. I could go on and on about that subject, and I will if you think my idea is worth pursuing. But our first decision isn't about the horses, is it?''

She knew what he meant. "No, I guess it isn't," she said quietly, though her heart had started beating double time.

"It seems relatively simple to me," Luke said almost casually. "I love you and you love me. Maris, I'm asking you to be my wife." His nonchalance vanished. "I'm also asking you to believe in me, aren't I?"

"Yes," she whispered. "But that coin has two sides. Can *you* believe in *me* after what I did?"

"You really weren't going to tell me about the baby?"

"No," she said meekly.

"Last night you said you needed time to think about my proposal. What changed your mind?"

"I called Lori and she told me why you fought with Jim Benteen. Lori's proud to even know you, and Luke...so am I." Tears were beginning to blur Maris's vision. "I love you. I fought it so damned hard. I kept telling myself you were like Ray, but you're not. You're not like anyone else I've ever known."

A corner of his mouth turned up in a wry little half smile. "I can say the same about you, believe me."

She couldn't help laughing, though it came out rather shaky. "I guess that's a compliment."

Luke moved to pull her into his arms. "Here's a much better one. You're a beautiful, sensual, intelligent woman, and I want to spend the rest of my life with you. If you want to sell every horse on the place and raise cattle, that's what we'll do. If you want a dozen babies, that's what we'll have. Marry me, Maris. Make me the happiest man on earth." He grinned then, surprising Maris. "Make my mother the happiest woman on earth. She's always wanted me to settle down. 'Like normal folk' is

the way she puts it. Think what a favor you'd be doing her by marrying her son.''

''And giving her grandbabies?'' Maris threw her arms around Luke's neck. ''Oh, Luke,'' she said on a sob.

He squeezed her tightly to himself. ''Was that a yes, honey?''

''Yes...yes...*yes!*''

Epilogue

Luke asked Keith to be his best man at the wedding and Lori acted as Maris's matron of honor. It was a quiet affair, with just a handful of Maris's closest friends in attendance. The bride was indeed pregnant, having seen a doctor for verification of what she already knew. Keith was bursting with pride over his role in the affair, and actually strutted during the small reception held at the ranch after the ceremony, Maris saw with great affection. Of course Susie was there, and Keith's machismo was directed at her. She was a pretty little thing, but what Maris really liked about her were her plans for her future.

"Oh, yes, I'm definitely going to college," she told Maris while they chatted over a cup of fruit punch. "Keith has been talking about Montana State U, in Bozeman, so I'm also considering that school. He told me that Luke really gave him a pep talk about going to college."

Maris sent first Keith then Luke a pleased glance across the room. "Is that a fact? Montana State U, hmm? That's my school."

After the wedding there was a lot of work to do to get ready for the horse auction. School had started for Keith, but as long as he kept up with his homework, Maris and Luke thought it was fine for him to continue working with the horses.

Maris worked hard on the piles of records that Katherine Willoughby had sent. Finally, she and Luke managed to figure out which records belonged to each horse in their herd. As they had planned, Luke picked out the best of the lot for breeding. He was pleased with their bloodlines and temperament, and assured Maris that they had the start of a fine stock.

As she worked with Luke through the last weeks of Septem-

ber, Maris was thrilled not only by the thought of the growing life inside her, but by the wonderful new future she and Luke were building together with each passing day. Luke felt badly that he wasn't able to give his bride what he called a "proper honeymoon," but she felt those first days—and nights—of their marriage couldn't have been happier, or more satisfying.

The auction was a great success, with buyers coming from miles around and the bids flying fast and furiously. Next to her wedding to Luke, Maris thought it had to be the most exciting day of her life. Luke himself ran the auction with impressive professionalism and flare. Maris was thrilled as the high-figured sales totaled up, and feeling quite proud that day to be Luke's wife.

With the proceeds from the auction and the money received from Jim Humphrey for the Corvette, Maris set about making some much needed repairs on the ranch. And there was still enough extra money for Luke and Maris to fly to Texas. The trip was not only their honeymoon, but Maris wanted very much to meet Luke's mother. Lila Rivers actually wept when Luke introduced his bride, then she wiped her eyes and served them a sumptuous home-cooked meal.

They didn't sleep at Lila's house, however. There was a very nice motel in that small Texas town and they rented a room for the five nights of their stay, the time they had allotted themselves to be away from the ranch, as there was so much to do before the cold weather set in. Their honeymoon days would be spent with Lila, but they wanted to be alone at night, which Lila Rivers understood and graciously accepted as only natural for a newlywed couple.

Maris had splurged on some lovely new nightgowns, and she picked what she thought was the most appealing to wear on their first night in the motel. She came out of the bathroom all perfumed and pretty for her husband, and saw Luke already in bed. One small light was on, casting the room in soft shadows.

His gaze washed over her, ardent and loving. "Stand there for a second and just let me look at you," he said huskily. Maris got warm all over from the heated head-to-foot inspection

she received. "Damn, you're beautiful," he whispered. "Come here." He held up the sheet in invitation.

Maris slid into bed and was immediately brought into a feverish embrace. "I love you, baby," Luke said hoarsely.

"And I love you." She wrapped her arms around him and held on tightly, almost fiercely. "I love you so much it scares me."

He nuzzled his mouth in her hair. "It scares you because you loved Ray and it didn't last. We're going to last, Maris. Count on it. I don't want you scared or worried about anything. I'm always going to be there, honey, always. You can talk to me about anything. Let's make a pact right now. I saw this in a movie a long time ago and even then it made good sense to me. Let's never go to bed angry. If either of us does something to annoy or anger the other during the day, let's talk about it and make up before we go to bed."

Maris smiled tremulously. "That's a wonderful idea, Luke. I swear I'll do my part."

"And I'll do mine. We'd be fools to let anything undermine what we have, Maris." He tipped her chin to look into her eyes. "And we're not fools, either of us. We're going to have the best marriage ever, honey." His mouth covered hers in a passionate, loving kiss, and in seconds neither was thinking of anything beyond the ecstasy and joy of being together.

Before they left Texas they told Lila about the baby. Again she shed tears. Maris took her mother-in-law's hands in her own. "Will you come to the ranch when the baby is born?"

"May I?"

"Lila, you may come anytime you wish, but I would be particularly pleased if you were there when the baby is born." Maris smiled. "And as I said before when I was telling you about Keith, you have to meet him. Luke and I both think of him as our son, which sort of makes him your grandson."

During the flight home, Maris put her head back and thought of her incredible happiness. She felt Luke take her hand, and she turned her head to smile at him. "I love you," she whis-

pered. Then she realized that he was pressing something *into* her hand, a small piece of paper. "What is it?"

"Take a guess."

Instead of guessing, she unfolded the little square of paper and looked at it. It was Ray's IOU, and across the face of it Luke had printed in bold letters PAID IN FULL.

Her lips twitched with a smile, then she gave a little laugh. But when Luke laughed, too, she began giggling. They lost it then, both of them laughing so hard that other passengers started smiling at them.

They finally calmed down. Maris looked at the IOU again. "I'm going to frame this and hang it in our bedroom."

"You're kidding."

She leaned over and kissed his lips. "Without this little piece of paper, you never would have come to the ranch. It's a keepsake, my love. I might not hang it on the wall, but I'm definitely going to keep it." Her eyes took on a teasing twinkle. "And when the No Bull Ranch is famous for its marvelous cutting horses, bred and trained by that also famous handler, Luke Rivers, no less, and we've been rich for so long we can't even recall when we weren't, then I'm going to take out this ancient IOU and remember that it brought us together."

Luke grinned. "Incidentally, there was so much going on before we left the ranch, I don't think anyone told you that Blackie is going to have pups."

Maris's jaw dropped. "How did she get pregnant?"

"The usual way, I suppose," Luke said dryly.

"But she's the only dog for miles!"

"Apparently not."

Maris settled back with a contented smile. "Do you realize that you changed my entire life?"

"Do you realize that you changed *my* entire life?"

They looked at each other for the longest time. "It was fate, wasn't it?" Maris said softly. "We were destined to be together."

"I think that's as good an explanation as any," Luke mur-

mured, leaning forward to kiss her sweet, sexy lips. "I wish we were alone right now."

"Patience, my love," she whispered throatily. "We have the rest of our lives."

And indeed they did.

*   *   *   *   *

SLEEPING WITH
THE ENEMY
by Myrna Temte

This book is dedicated to Kathie Hays,
who keeps my head on straight (most of the time),
my plots on track and my morale up.
Thanks, Kemo sabe!

Prologue

Glaring at the man seated on the other side of his desk, Congressman William C. Baldwin of Montana silently cursed the day he'd let his fear of losing an election run away with his good sense. At first meeting, Jeremiah Kincaid came across as just another big, friendly rancher, a real salt-of-the-earth kind of a guy, who wore cowboy boots and a Stetson whether he was in Montana or in the nation's capital. Surprisingly handsome for a man pushing seventy, he also had a well-earned reputation for being quite a charmer with the ladies.

But underneath that affable good-old-country-boy exterior, lurked a greedy, bullying, unscrupulous son of a bitch who had the disposition of a rattler with a sore tooth. Baldwin loathed and feared Kincaid, but he was doing his damnedest not to let it show. What a lousy way to start the New Year.

"Come on now, be reasonable, Jeremiah."

Kincaid sat back in the maroon leather wing chair and let out a derisive snort of laughter. "Reasonable? I don't have to be reasonable, Billy boy. That's why the Whitehorn Ranchers' Association decided to buy a congressman."

"You and your associates made some contributions to my campaign, but you don't own me," Baldwin said.

"The hell we don't! I could be wrong, but I don't think all of those contributions were exactly legal."

"And might I remind you, Mr. Kincaid," Baldwin retorted, "that it was just as illegal for you to give them to me as it was for me to accept them."

Jeremiah laughed. "Yeah, but we'll never get more than a slap on the wrist." He gazed around Baldwin's office, as if he were taking in the plush furnishings for the first time. Then he chuckled and shook his head. "This setup ain't bad for a poor

miner's kid. Be a shame if you lost it all and had to go back to a half-assed law practice in Butte. Mighty slim pickin's in Butte these days, from what I hear.''

"It won't do any good to threaten me," Baldwin said. "I'd help you if I could, but what you're asking is impossible."

Kincaid raised an eyebrow at him. "Nothing is impossible in Washington."

Exasperated, Baldwin picked up the letter Jeremiah had tossed in front of him half an hour ago and shook it. "This *is*. The Northern Cheyennes *own* that land. They have every legal right to refuse to renew your grazing leases.''

Kincaid propped his elbows on the arms of his chair and laced his fingers together. "I don't give a damn about their legal rights. My friends and I have held those leases for over forty years. We've put up fences and built irrigation systems and made all kinds of other improvements, and we're *not* gonna hand it all over to a bunch of lazy, good-for-nothin' Indian drunks. Hell, we should've exterminated all of 'em when we had the chance.''

Some people might agree with those sentiments, Baldwin thought grimly. But only a man as rich and powerful as Jeremiah Kincaid would have the gall to say them out loud, in such a calm, implacable tone of voice.

"Times have changed," Baldwin said. "Every president since Nixon has endorsed the self-determination policy for Indian tribes. If the Bureau of Indian Affairs doesn't even have the power to renew those leases, why do you expect me to have it?''

"You're on that subcommittee on Native American affairs, and on the appropriations committee. One of them oughta give you an opportunity to clear up this mess, if you really want to.'' Kincaid tipped his head to one side and studied Baldwin for a moment, a speculative gleam entering his cold gray eyes. "But then, maybe you don't really want to.''

"Of course I do, Jeremiah. Why the hell wouldn't I?''

"I met a real pretty little Indian gal while I was out there waitin' for you to let me in. Told me she works for you. Maybe

you've got somethin' extra goin' on the side with her, and you don't wanna tick her off.''

"You mean Maggie Schaeffer?" It was Baldwin's turn to laugh and shake his head. He wouldn't have minded doing exactly what Kincaid was implying, but this time, at least, he was innocent. "Don't be ridiculous. I'm old enough to be her father.''

Kincaid let out another one of his derisive snorts. "So? I'm old enough to be her grandpa, but if I wanted her, Billy boy, I'd *have* her.''

Just the thought of a nice young gal like Maggie Schaeffer with this randy old coot turned Baldwin's stomach. "Maggie's one of my best research aides, Jeremiah. Our relationship is strictly professional.''

"I don't care whether it is or not," Kincaid said. "Pretty as she is, it wouldn't take much to start a few rumors flyin' around. I don't think your new little wife would like that. Ya know, I really like Georgina, but she doesn't strike me as the kind of gal who'd stand by her man if he was involved in a dirty ol' sex scandal. Do you read me?''

"Yeah. I read you, Jeremiah." Baldwin stood then, forcing an end to the conversation. He didn't offer to shake Kincaid's hand. "I'll do what I can.''

Kincaid got up and set his black Stetson on his head. "A smart fella like you shouldn't have any problem gettin' a bunch of Indians under control, especially that sorry bunch up at Laughing Horse. It's just February now, so you've got four months before the June deadline, Congressman. We'll be expecting some results.''

The second the door snapped shut behind Kincaid, Baldwin collapsed into his chair, leaned back and closed his eyes. Damn that old man to hell and back, he knew exactly which buttons to push, which fears to exploit.

Bill Baldwin had put in twenty years of honest government service—honest by Washington standards, anyway. He'd golfed with presidents. He'd been a hero in Vietnam. And now he'd made one lousy decision in a moment of panic, and Jeremiah

Kincaid would destroy him without turning a hair if he didn't deliver the goods.

For a moment, Baldwin considered going public with the truth about his campaign finances. That would take some of the wind out of that old blowhard's sails, now wouldn't it? He wished he still had that much nerve.

Baldwin picked up the letter and glanced at the signature again. Well, Jackson Hawk, Tribal Attorney, whoever the hell he was, must have plenty of nerve. Jeremiah Kincaid controlled the Whitehorn Ranchers' Association, the town of Whitehorn, and the county, too. To take the old coot on like this, Mr. Hawk had to be crazy. Either that, or he had balls like a Hereford bull.

Unfortunately, Baldwin knew his own balls weren't that big anymore. He was almost fifty years old, and he'd grown accustomed to the perks and privileges of his office. He liked having money and a glamorous young wife who made other men drool. And the only way he ever wanted to go back to Butte on a permanent basis was in a coffin.

Damn it, he'd worked too hard for too long to give everything up for the sake of a few Indians who never voted. Hell, they probably wouldn't know what to do with that land if they ever *did* manage to get it back from Jeremiah and the Whitehorn Ranchers' Association. Possession *was* nine-tenths of the law. Of course, it wouldn't do his image much good if the press found out he was hassling an Indian tribe.

There had to be a way to get Jeremiah off his back without bringing the wrath of every bleeding-heart liberal in the whole damned country down on his head. If he could find an Indian to do most of the dirty work for him…maybe somebody from the Bureau of Indian Affairs who needed money. No, that wouldn't work. The folks at the BIA had gotten way too concerned about their own image lately. What about the Bureau of Land Management? No, they wouldn't have jurisdiction.

When the solution finally hit him, he smacked his forehead with the heel of his palm and laughed at his own stupidity. He'd send Maggie out to Laughing Horse on a fact-finding

mission, and use her research to close down that miserable place for good. The Northern Cheyenne didn't need two reservations. Since most of them were on welfare, it wouldn't hurt a thing if the Western Band got moved over to Lame Deer to live with the others.

Hell, he should have thought of this before. He'd have to take his time and plan it carefully, of course. Maggie wouldn't like it one bit when she found out what he was really doing with her work. But hey, this was politics. Rule number one in this game was, you did whatever you had to do to cover your ass. If he played his cards just right, Maggie Schaeffer would cover his nicely.

One

"Yes, Aunt Sally, I'm still listening," Jackson Hawk said into the telephone receiver, rolling his eyes in fond exasperation. "Of course I'll be polite. I'm always polite. Tell Uncle Frank he can stop nagging me any time now."

While Aunt Sally rattled on with a seemingly endless stream of advice, all of which he didn't need, Jackson propped his feet on the corner of his desk and rubbed the back of his neck with his free hand.

"Whoa! *Ne-xohose neheseha!* Say it again in English, Aunt Sally. Yes, I've been studying Cheyenne again, but I can't follow you when you talk so fast. Uh-huh. Uh-huh. Oh, yeah? Tell him I said he's been lying around like an old woman for too long. If he doesn't like the way I'm doing his job, he'd better hurry up and get well so he can do it himself."

Aunt Sally dutifully relayed the message. Jackson chuckled when he heard his uncle's outraged howl in the background. "Yeah, I thought that'd get a rise out of him."

A knocking sound drew Jackson's gaze to the doorway. A pretty young woman he'd never seen before stood there, clutching a black leather briefcase. The color of her hair, skin and eyes told him she had a substantial amount of Indian blood, but the gray wool coat draped over her arm, her conservative navy blue business suit, her sensible pumps and her short, chic hairstyle made her look out of place. And there was an obvious air of tension about her that made him wonder if she'd ever set foot on a reservation before. He held up one finger to indicate that he'd just be a moment.

"Aunt Sally, I have a visitor," he said when his garrulous aunt paused to take a breath. "I don't know. I don't know that,

either. I'll call if anything important comes up. All right. Take good care of yourself, too.''

Jackson hung up the phone, swung his feet to the floor and swiveled his chair to face the desk again. The woman still stood in the doorway, looking as if she'd rather be someplace—no, make that *any*place—else. Must be from the government. He'd guess she was a Fed, although she certainly had better-looking legs than the last one he'd had to deal with. The rest of her wasn't too shabby, either. But a Fed was still a Fed, and it never hurt to be cautious.

"May I help you?" he asked.

She gave him a tentative smile. "I'm sorry I interrupted your phone call." When Jackson merely shrugged at her apology, she continued. "I'm looking for Mr. Frank Many Horses. I believe he's the tribal chairman?"

"He's on a medical leave," Jackson said. "I'm filling in for him at the moment. And you are?"

He'd never seen a Fed blush before, but this one did. Quite prettily, too. Then she uttered a soft, husky laugh that charmed him right down to the scuffed toes of his cowboy boots. He decided she was more cute than pretty. But on her, cute looked damn good.

"Excuse me," she said, stepping into the room. "I guess I've spent so much time alone in the Library of Congress lately, I've forgotten my manners. I'm Maggie Schaeffer. From Congressman Baldwin's office in Washington."

Baldwin? Jackson thought, barely managing to keep a grimace of disgust off his face. What was that snake up to now? He'd never met the man personally, but he'd heard enough about him from Uncle Frank to be suspicious.

"What can I do for you, Ms. Schaeffer?"

"Oh, dear." She walked closer to the desk. "You weren't expecting me, were you, Mr., uh... I'm sorry, I didn't catch your name."

Jackson stood and briefly shook the hand she offered. It was small and soft and delicate, and he felt oddly reluctant to let

go of it. "Hawk. Jackson Hawk. I'm the tribal attorney here at Laughing Horse. And, no, I wasn't expecting you."

She shot him a startled glance, as if she couldn't believe he was really an attorney. Of course, she probably hadn't met many male lawyers who wore their hair in braids. His jeans and faded blue sweatshirt weren't exactly standard office attire, either. Well, tough. He didn't live or dress by the white man's rules anymore.

A worried little wrinkle appeared between her eyebrows. Then she squared her shoulders and gave him a rueful, lopsided grin. Damn, but she really *was* cute. And young. Probably only in her mid-twenties, which made her at least ten years younger than he was. Maybe that was why she worked for an S.O.B. like Baldwin—she was too young to know any better.

"Well, I apologize again, Mr. Hawk," she said. "Someone from the congressman's office in Whitehorn was supposed to call and set up an appointment for me for the first of March. Obviously, there's been a mix-up. I can come back tomorrow, if this isn't a convenient time."

Jackson gestured toward the straight-backed wooden chair on the other side of his desk. "It's as convenient as it's ever going to get. Have a seat." When they were both settled, he asked, "What brings you to Laughing Horse, Ms. Schaeffer?"

"I'm sure you're aware Congressman Baldwin serves on the House Subcommittee on Native American Affairs."

When he nodded, she smiled at him like a teacher rewarding a student for a correct answer. Then she went on in a brisk, businesslike tone that reminded Jackson of the years he'd spent working for a Wall Street law firm, pretending he wasn't an Indian. Her cuteness faded; when the gist of her mission became clear, it vanished completely.

"At the last meeting of the subcommittee, it came to the congressman's attention that conditions here at the Laughing Horse Reservation have not improved as much as they have on Montana's other reservations," she said. "He's quite concerned that we find a way to rectify the situation."

"Yeah, I'll bet," Jackson muttered.

"Excuse me?" She looked him straight in the eye, without the slightest hesitation.

It was a small thing, really, just one of those funny little differences between the Indian and white cultures that had caused tons of misunderstanding. It had taken him years to learn to look whites directly in the eye when he talked to them. That she did it so well told him a lot about how thoroughly she'd been assimilated into white society. He wondered if she even knew that most traditional Indians would consider such an action rude. Well, it wasn't his job to teach her.

"It's nothing. Go on, Ms. Schaeffer."

She shot him a doubtful look, but continued in that same irritating, businesslike tone after a moment. "My assignment is to interview some of the people here, make a list of the specific problems you're facing and formulate recommendations for legislation. If you could call a special meeting of the tribal council—"

"No."

Both of her eyebrows shot up beneath her wispy bangs. "I'm afraid I don't understand."

"That's obvious, Ms. Schaeffer. You don't have a clue about what life is like on this or any other reservation, and neither does your boss."

Jackson saw sparks of anger flash in her eyes, and she opened her mouth, as if she were going to say something. But then she inhaled a deep breath and pursed her lips, obviously struggling to rein in her emotions and come up with an appropriate response. He could hardly wait to hear it.

She spoke slowly and distinctly, as if she were choosing each word with great care. "You're absolutely right, Mr. Hawk. Which is precisely why Congressman Baldwin has sent me here to collect data. I'll do everything possible to avoid taking too much of your time. One or two meetings should be enough."

"No."

He saw more sparks, and heard a huffy little note of indignation in her voice when she replied. "May I ask why not?"

Jackson leaned back in his battered swivel chair and smoth-

ered a grin as best he could. He probably should be ashamed of himself, but he wasn't. If he was honest, he'd have to admit he was enjoying this immensely.

Since taking over for Uncle Frank two months ago, he'd been forced to deal with representatives from the federal, state and county governments on a daily basis. All of them wanted something from him or his tribe, but they didn't want to give anything in return. And they didn't care whether or not they understood the people they were supposed to be serving.

Well, he'd finally had enough of trying to accommodate these idiots. He felt stupid for ever having thought this one was cute. Hell, she was just another insensitive bureaucrat. The fact that she was Indian herself only made it all the more inexcusable, as far as he was concerned. Damn it, she should know better, and by the time he was done with her, she *would,*

Lacing his fingers together over his belt buckle, Jackson stared at her until the tension nearly crackled between them. "Why not? Because we're sick and tired of being studied like bugs under a microscope. And because I don't think you really want to understand our problems, Ms. Schaeffer."

"I beg your pardon?" She drew herself up as tall as she could and still remain seated. It didn't help a whole lot, because she was only about five foot four when she was standing. "I didn't come all the way to Montana from Washington for the fun of it, Mr. Hawk."

"I'm sure you didn't," Jackson said. "You came here looking for easy answers, so you can write your little report and make points with Baldwin. Well, here's a news flash, Ms. Schaeffer. There aren't any easy answers. If you really want to understand the problems of this reservation, you come out here and live with us for a year."

"Don't be ridiculous. I couldn't possibly stay for a year."

"Then don't waste the taxpayers' money writing another useless report about Indians."

"Why are you being so obnoxious about this with *me?*" she demanded, poking the center of her chest with her index finger.

"I certainly don't have any prejudice against Indians. I was chosen for this assignment because I *am* one."

Jackson had to chuckle at that. "You may have the blood, honey, but you don't have the soul."

Red patches bloomed over her cheekbones. She jumped out of her chair as if the seat had suddenly caught fire and propped her fists on her hips. "If you're implying—"

"I'm not *implying* anything," Jackson said, rising from his own chair. Bracing both hands on the top of his desk, he leaned forward until his nose nearly brushed hers. "I'll call you an apple right to your face, if you want. You know what that means, don't you? Red on the outside, white on the inside?"

"I've heard the term."

"I'm sure you have. You're trading on a heritage you know nothing about to further your career, and I'll be damned if you'll do it at my tribe's expense. Go on back to Washington and find somebody else to write about."

Her chin rose another notch. She slowly lowered her fists to her sides, her movements stiff and jerky enough to make Jackson suspect she was having a hard time fighting off an urge to punch him in the face. "I'm afraid I can't do that, Mr. Hawk. And might I remind you that I'm a *federal* employee?"

"So was Custer, lady. He didn't belong here, either."

She gave him a glare that should have singed his eyelashes off. Then she put on her coat, picked up her briefcase and rested the bottom of it on the seat of the chair. "You really think you know everything about me, don't you?"

"I know enough."

"Perhaps. But then again, perhaps not."

He didn't like the grim smile that slowly curved the corners of her mouth. He straightened to his full height. "What's that supposed to mean?"

"It's not important. But get one thing straight. With or without your help, I *will* write my report. Congressman Baldwin will be using it to draft legislation that will directly affect the people on this reservation. Since you have refused an oppor-

tunity to offer input, you'll have only yourself to blame if you don't like the results. Have a nice day, Mr. Hawk.''

Jackson remained standing behind his desk, listening to the angry clicks her heels made on the tile floor as she marched down the hallway. When he heard the exit door open and close, he swore under his breath, plunked his butt into the chair and reached for the phone.

Not only was the woman an apple, he'd bet his law degree she was an apple with some kind of an ax to grind. One of his old friends from Georgetown University's law school worked on Capitol Hill. Bennie Gonzales had a network of contacts among congressional staffers that a gossip columnist would kill for. If there was anything worth knowing about Maggie Schaeffer, Bennie already knew it, or he could get it within an hour. The call went through, and when he'd chitchatted enough to be polite, Jackson made his request.

"Maggie Schaeffer," Bennie said. "That name's familiar. Let me think a second. Maggie Schaeffer, Maggie Schaeffer... Yeah, I've got her now. Research aide for Baldwin. Native American. Kinda short. Cute. Hair like Katie Couric's?''

"That's the one," Jackson said, grinning to himself as he imagined Bennie sitting behind a desk piled high with papers, tapping his forehead, as if that would help him spit out pertinent facts faster. "What do you know about her?"

"I've met her once. She's got a good rep. Supposed to be one of the best researchers on the Hill. Has a master's in public administration from Harvard."

"Do you know if she's ever worked with Native American issues?" Jackson asked.

"Not that I remember. She's done a lot of work on labor and transportation issues, though. Did a report on the timber industry a few months ago that was really excellent."

"That's all you know about her?"

"Professionally," Bennie said. "I heard a rumor about her last week, but I doubt there's any truth in it."

"What?"

"You know Washington gossip. Everybody's always sup-

posed to be sleeping with their boss. I can't imagine Maggie with ol' horse-faced Baldwin, though.''

Jackson couldn't imagine that, either, and it was surprising how distasteful he found the idea. ''Are you sure this rumor was about the same Maggie?''

''Oh, yeah. The word was, Baldwin was shipping her out of town because his wife was jealous. The source really wasn't all that reliable, Jackson. I wouldn't jump to any conclusions.''

''All right, Bennie. Thanks. I owe you one.''

Jackson hung up the phone, then leaned back and propped his heels on the desk again. Should he call his uncle about Maggie Schaeffer or not? Kane Hunter, the doctor who served the reservation, had said they weren't supposed to upset Uncle Frank, but it had been two months since his heart attack. At this point, Jackson figured discovering he'd been kept in the dark about a potential problem with a congressman would upset his uncle more than hearing about it now.

Bracing for a scolding he probably deserved, Jackson grabbed the phone again and punched in his uncle's number. Sure enough, when he finished describing his encounter with Baldwin's aide, Uncle Frank cut loose with a list of insults, spoken in rapid-fire Cheyenne. Jackson caught one that sounded like ''turnip brain'' and considered himself lucky he couldn't understand the rest.

''All right, I get the message,'' he said, when his uncle started to slow down. ''I don't know how you stand dealing with these people all the time, Uncle Frank. They drive me nuts. It made me feel better to finally tell one of them off.''

''The job isn't about making *you* feel better, Jackson,'' Frank said, his voice deeper and gruffer than usual. ''It's about doing what is best for the *tribe*. And what is best for the tribe is to stay on polite terms with our congressional delegation.''

''I know, I know. But why should we waste our time like that? I'm telling you, this lady knows nothing. What good will it do for her to write a stupid report about us?''

''There's probably a warehouse in Washington as big as the Pentagon that's full of stupid reports about Indians,'' Frank

countered with a chuckle. "One more won't hurt anything, nephew. Besides, what right have you to judge anyone for being an apple?"

Jackson winced as his uncle's pointed question struck home. What right, indeed? Maggie Schaeffer wasn't doing a blessed thing he hadn't done himself—for almost half his life. He'd been back on the res for four years now, but he still didn't like to be reminded of the man he'd once been. Maybe that was why he'd reacted so strongly to Ms. Schaeffer—he couldn't look at her or listen to her without remembering his own folly.

"You know what you have to do, Jackson," Frank said, after a moment's silence.

"Yeah. Don't worry, I'll take care of it." Jackson swung his feet to the floor. "Answer one more question, Uncle Frank. How do you always manage to say the one thing that will make me squirm the most?"

Frank let out one of his deep, rumbling laughs. Jackson treasured that sound, especially since he'd come so close to never hearing it again. "Haven't you figured that out yet, kid? I'm a wise old Indian. Just like in the movies."

Breathing deeply in an attempt to bring her chaotic emotions under control, Maggie Schaeffer tossed her briefcase onto the passenger seat of her rental car and slammed the door. It didn't help much. She marched around the front end, unlocked the driver's door, climbed in behind the wheel and slammed that door, too. She poked the key at the ignition, but her hand was trembling too much for her to fit it into the narrow slot.

She dropped the keys into her lap and pounded the steering wheel with the side of her fist. "Damn that arrogant jerk!"

There were better words to describe Jackson Hawk, but she refused to lower herself that far. Her chest was so full of rage it ached, and she blinked back the tears of frustration stinging the backs of her eyes. She would *not* let him get to her. He wasn't worth it. It wasn't the first time she'd been called an apple, and she doubted it would be the last.

"So why does it still hurt?"

Maggie sniffed, then sighed and shook her head. She'd grown up surrounded by white people. Her mother had been the only other Indian she knew until she left home. Beverly Schaeffer hadn't seemed very different from the other kids' mothers, though, and since Maggie had worn the same kind of clothes, played with the same toys and taken the same lessons after school as the other kids, she hadn't felt all that different, either.

Oh, once in a while somebody would make a remark about her being an Indian, but she hadn't thought much about it then. Her mother and father had kept her too busy being an adored only child for her to worry about being inferior to anyone. She'd certainly never felt that way about herself.

Still, she'd always known she wasn't exactly like the other kids. She wasn't white, and she never would be. Her mother's refusal to talk about her own childhood, her relatives and Maggie's biological father had raised more than a few questions in Maggie's mind about her Indian heritage. One of her secret goals when she went off to college had been to meet other Indian students and find out if she would feel more at home with them than she did with her white friends.

"Hah!" she muttered, rolling her eyes in disgust at the painful memories flitting through her mind. She'd been rejected by white people over the years, but they had usually been so obviously ignorant, she was able to ignore them. It had hurt a thousand times more when her fellow Indian students took one look at her and despised her on sight.

It wasn't *her* fault she hadn't been raised on a reservation. It wasn't *her* fault she'd been raised with plenty of money, or that she'd received a better education in an upper-class white suburb of Denver. It wasn't *her* fault she had a white stepfather, or that he'd been allowed to adopt her. And yet she'd been rejected by her fellow Indian students for all of those reasons.

Sighing again, Maggie gazed through the windshield, silently reading the black letters painted on the door of the huge complex that housed the tribal offices, a restaurant, and heaven only

knew what else. "Welcome to the Laughing Horse Tribal Center. Home of the Northern Cheyenne, Western Band."

Well, if this was really the home of the Northern Cheyenne, then Maggie Schaeffer had as much right to be here as Mr. High-and-Mighty Hawk did. Her mother had been born and raised here. Maggie herself had been born here.

If she had received a warmer welcome, she might have found the nerve to look up a few of her relatives. She wouldn't dream of doing that now, though. Any relatives she had living here might well be as mean and nasty as Jackson Hawk.

Just thinking the wretched man's name was enough to raise gooseflesh on her arms. The meeting had started out so well. And then, in the space of a heartbeat, his attitude had changed from cautiously welcoming to downright hostile. What on earth had she done wrong?

It was hard to believe she'd thought he was so handsome at first—the handsomest man she'd ever seen. In a primitive sort of way. She closed her eyes for a moment, imagining his face.

He had smooth, coppery skin stretched over a bold blade of a nose, sharply defined cheekbones, and a firm jaw and chin. His long black braids did nothing to detract from his masculinity; he was so tall, his shoulders were so broad, his voice was so deep and rough, she doubted anything would be able to do that.

But it was his eyes she remembered best. Black, black eyes, shining with intelligence, glittering with anger, eyes that had looked into the darkest corners of her soul. And found her wanting.

A shiver zipped up her spine, and she felt a hollow, aching sensation in the center of her chest. Sighing, she opened her eyes and shook her head. It didn't matter whether or not he liked her. There was no point in feeling sorry for herself. She had a job to do. Perhaps someone at the BIA office would help.

She looked up at the sprawling building again, searching for a sign to tell her which way to go. Her stomach fluttered, her heart contracted, and a strangled gasp escaped her lips. There, at the top of the steps, stood a man wearing jeans, a denim

jacket, and a black Stetson with a white feather sticking out of the hatband. It was Jackson Hawk. Though he also wore a pair of aviator sunglasses, she just knew he was staring straight at her.

TWO

Jackson stepped outside, slid on his sunglasses to soften the sun's reflection off the snow and felt a sharp tug at his heart-strings that was part guilt, part relief. So, she hadn't left yet. Though her powder-blue rental car was only a compact, Ms. Schaeffer looked awfully small and fragile behind the wheel. And why was she just sitting there with her head back and her eyes shut? Maybe he'd given her a headache.

That was only fair, he thought with a wry grin. She'd sure as hell given him one. Then she sat up and looked right at him. His stomach lurched as if he were in an elevator that had suddenly plunged twenty stories. Her shoulders went rigid. Her chin came up. Even from this distance, her eyes looked as huge as a doe's during hunting season.

Damn. He hadn't thought he'd been mean enough to send her into a fight-or-flight response. She climbed out and stood behind the car door, facing him, her expression clearly indicating she'd give him one hell of a fight long before she would ever run from him. Well, good. He would have really felt bad if he'd scared all the spunk out of her.

Shoving his hands into his jeans pockets, he ambled down the steps and crossed the sidewalk. She braced one arm across the top of the car door and propped her other hand on her hip. Her face betrayed no emotion now, but he could see her chest rising and falling with rapid, choppy little breaths.

When she spoke, her voice was so carefully controlled it was a challenge, whether or not she intended it to be one. "Is there a problem, Mr. Hawk?"

Yeah, there was a problem. He'd never been any good at making apologies. He hoped he could figure out a way to do this without having to swallow a whole crow, feathers and all.

"Not exactly."

The top of her head barely reached his shoulders. She looked up at him expectantly, and for an insane instant, he wanted to touch the graceful curve of her neck. He cleared his throat, shoved his hands deeper into his pockets and inclined his head toward the vehicle.

"Havin' trouble with your car?"

"No."

"Good. The road between here and Whitehorn's not the best."

Her eyebrows shot up beneath her bangs again, and the corners of her mouth tightened. "Is that supposed to be a subtle way of telling me to leave?"

Feeling like an idiot, Jackson shook his head. "That's not what I meant."

"What exactly *did* you mean?"

No one could ever accuse her of having less-than-perfect diction.

"Nothing, really. I was just, uh, tryin' to make a little conversation."

Her eyes widened slightly at that. Jackson felt even more foolish when he saw the light of understanding turn on in her big, dark eyes and heard a trace of amusement slide into her voice. "Why?"

"It's no big deal," he said, raising one shoulder in a half shrug. "I just realized I may have been a little...abrupt when you were in my office."

Oh, damn. She was on to him, all right. He hadn't given her any reason to make this easy for him, but she was enjoying his discomfort entirely too much. Her voice took on a sweetness that made him grind his back teeth together.

"Abrupt? Don't be so modest, Mr. Hawk. I would have called your behavior insulting, at the very least."

"You don't have to be sarcastic," he grumbled.

She tipped her head to one side and gave him a wide-eyed look. "I don't? You certainly were."

"Yeah, I know. And I'm sorry, all right?"

Straightening away from the car door, she crossed her arms over her breasts. "Funny. You don't sound very sorry to me."

"Well, I am."

She grinned openly at that. What he wouldn't give to kiss that sassy little smile right off her face. She'd probably deck him, but he figured the pain just might be worth it.

"Be honest, Mr. Hawk," she said. "You're not the least bit sorry about the way you treated me. You're just afraid I'll make trouble for you with Mr. Baldwin."

Jackson stiffened. Man, she could really be a snot when she put her mind to it. "I'm not afraid of you, or of Baldwin."

"Not personally, maybe," she agreed. "But I think you're afraid of anything that might threaten your tribe. If I were in your position, I know I would be."

Jackson shrugged again. She was right, of course. But he'd be damned if he'd admit it out loud. "Are you gonna accept my apology or not?"

She rolled her eyes in disgust, then leaned inside the car and grabbed her briefcase. "Don't worry, Mr. Hawk," she said, straightening to face him again. "I'm not in the habit of blaming a whole group of innocent people for the actions of one rude jerk. Now, if you'll excuse me, I'm going to find the BIA office."

Punching the lock button, she stepped out from behind the door, shut it, and would have brushed right past him if he hadn't reached out and grabbed her arm. She stiffened, but didn't try to pull away. Oh, no, she had too much dignity for that. She simply glanced down at his hand, then looked up at him again, her expression one of bored patience.

Jackson couldn't hold back a chuckle of admiration. She was small, all right, but every inch of her was packed with feisty determination. Releasing her, he held both hands up beside his head in a classic gesture of surrender.

"All right, all right. I really am sorry, Ms. Schaeffer. My behavior was inexcusable. Please accept my apology."

"Why should I?"

"Because Frank Many Horses is my uncle, and he's gonna

kick my butt up between my ears if you don't," Jackson admitted with a sheepish grin. Encouraged by her startled laugh, he rushed on. "And because, honest to God, that's the best apology I know how to make. Besides, the BIA can't help you as much as I can."

She smiled back at him, naturally this time, as if she finally believed in his sincerity. Damned if she wasn't cute after all. "And just how do you intend to help me?"

"We could start with a tour of our social agencies. That'll give you an idea of what we're trying to accomplish."

"Thank you, Mr. Hawk," she said. "I would appreciate that very much."

He eyed her pumps doubtfully. "Do you have any boots with you? We'll have to walk, and it's pretty muddy in places."

She shook her head. "Don't worry, I'll manage."

Jackson held out his hand in an after-you gesture. She rewarded him with a gracious nod and set off in the direction he'd indicated. Oh, brother, he thought, falling in step with her businesslike stride. This was gonna be a *long* afternoon.

To his surprise, however, it didn't turn out that way. Though she didn't loosen up much with him, Maggie radiated a genuine warmth toward everyone else she met that excused her occasional lapses in Indian manners. She did more listening than talking, and she asked intelligent, probing questions that made people eager to tell her more. Even crusty old Earnest Running Bull at the alcohol rehabilitation center invited her to come back when she had more time.

They arrived at the day-care center fifteen minutes before the start of the story hour. To Jackson's surprise, after checking out the facility, Maggie sat right down on the floor with the kids and listened to Annie Little Deer's rendition of the Cheyenne creation story as raptly as any of the three- and four-year-olds. When little Emma Weasel Tail crawled onto her lap without an invitation, Maggie smiled and cuddled her close, as if she honestly enjoyed holding the child in her arms.

At that point, even Jackson, with his well-developed cynicism toward government employees in general and Feds in par-

ticular, couldn't deny he might have been a tad hasty in judging her. In fact, he could almost believe he'd finally met a Fed with a heart. Unbelievable as it seemed, he was actually starting to like Maggie Schaeffer.

The thought made him nervous. It was okay to give her a grudging sort of respect. It was even okay to think she was cute and lust after her curvy little body. But it wasn't okay to feel well...drawn to her. And it definitely wasn't okay to want her to smile at him the way she'd smiled at Earnest Running Bull— not as much as he wanted her to, anyway.

Something about her assignment smelled fishy. For one thing, Jackson just couldn't buy the story about the House Subcommittee on Native American Affairs suddenly noticing the problems at Laughing Horse. For another, Congressman Baldwin had never been interested in helping the Northern Cheyennes, or any of the other tribes in Montana. Why was he interested now?

Though he was intrigued by and attracted to Maggie Schaeffer, Jackson couldn't afford to forget she worked for Baldwin. Hell, according to Bennie, she might even be sleeping with the bastard. Whether or not that was true, Jackson sincerely doubted she would ever choose the tribe's interests over those of her boss. She seemed too ambitious for that.

He also couldn't afford to like her enough to let down his guard just because she'd let a little girl climb into her lap. Well, he'd finish giving her this damn tour, and then he'd go back to work and mind his own business. He didn't have time for Feds. Not even cute ones.

Entranced with the story and the child who had unabashedly climbed into her lap, Maggie gently brushed her cheek against the little girl's glossy black hair. Her mother must have heard this story when she lived here. Why had she never shared such a beautiful tale with her own daughter?

The children were as bright, sweet and eager to learn as any of the kids Maggie had baby-sat when she was in high school. But after brief conversations with the people at the employment

office, the welfare office, the Indian Health Service clinic and the drug and alcohol rehab center, she knew the chances for long, happy lives were slim at best for too many of them.

Hearing about the poverty and despair so many of the adults on this reservation lived with had been disturbing enough. Realizing these adorable little ones were destined to face the same problems made her fighting mad. If there was any way she could help these people, she intended to find it.

She felt a tingly, almost itchy sensation at the back of her neck. Great. Jackson Hawk was staring at her again. What *was* the man's problem? Was he this suspicious of everyone who visited the reservation? Or the res, as most of the people called it, she reminded herself.

But back to Mr. Hawk. What did he think she was going to do to these people, anyway? What did he think she *could* do? Maybe the real question was, what did he have to hide? Everyone she'd met had greeted him with friendliness and respect, but had there been a subtle attitude of reserve toward him? Or had she simply imagined that?

Well, if there was some kind of skulduggery going on, she would find out what it was, and she'd best be getting on with the process. Releasing the little girl, Maggie climbed to her feet and tiptoed across the room, so as not to distract the children's attention. Then she thanked the center's director for the tour and followed Jackson outside.

There was still quite a bit of snow on the ground, but surely, with all this sunshine, spring couldn't be too far off. Hundreds of questions formed in her mind as she walked beside Jackson, but she kept them to herself. He definitely was not the chatty type.

The last stop on the tour turned out to be what Jackson called the "Indian school," which was housed in a barnlike prefabricated structure northeast of the tribal center.

"It's pretty quiet around here right now," he said, flipping on the lights in the entryway. "But it'll really be busy when the school buses from Whitehorn show up at four o'clock. This program's my favorite."

Maggie followed him down a hallway, occasionally pausing beside him and peeking into the rooms. "Why is that, Mr. Hawk?"

"This is where our children learn how to be Indians. It meets a lot of other needs in the community, too. The kids have a place to go after school and get help with homework their parents may not be able to provide. We try to have at least two volunteer tutors available every day."

They moved on to the next room, and he continued. "This is the crafts room. The older women come in a couple of times a week and teach the girls how to sew and do beading. There's also a room where the boys can learn to make bows and arrows and drums, and we have a peer counseling center for the teenagers."

There was also a dining hall, and, finally, a gymnasium. Jackson raised one hand and gestured toward the vast open space. "The elders teach our traditional dances in here. We also hold community meetings here, and when it's not in use for some other purpose, the boys play basketball."

He led her back to the entrance then, extinguished the lights and turned to her when he'd locked the door. "If you want to meet a good cross section of folks from the res, this is the place to come. You'd probably learn more here than you would from a tribal council meeting."

Maggie looked up at him and wished he'd take off those sunglasses. Darn it, he really *was* a handsome man, one she would like to know better. While he hadn't exactly gone out of his way to charm her this afternoon, he had at least been civil, and she sensed that he cared deeply about his community.

"Is there some reason you don't want me to attend a tribal council meeting?" she asked.

He raised one shoulder in a half shrug, a characteristic gesture she had noticed from the beginning. "Not really. You'll have to attend one if you want to learn about our economic development plans. I just wanted you to know there are real people here, not just a bunch of statistics."

Maggie chuckled, and felt rewarded when he flashed her a

broad grin. "I do realize that, Mr. Hawk. Thank you for giving me a wonderful tour."

They set off for the tribal center again. "How long will you be in the area?" Jackson asked.

"I had only planned on a week, but I'm beginning to see what you meant about needing a year to understand the problems."

Her remark earned her another grin, which prompted her to consider the possibility of extending her visit. She really couldn't stay for an entire year but if there were other things she could accomplish in the congressman's Whitehorn office, in addition to her research at Laughing Horse, a few months might not be out of the question. She glanced at her watch and figured out the time difference between Montana and Washington. If she called in the next fifteen minutes, she could probably catch the congressman at his office.

"Tell me, Mr. Hawk," she said, halting at the foot of the steps leading up to the tribal office, "is there a pay phone nearby I could use? I need to make a long-distance call."

"If you've got a credit card, you can use the phone in my office."

Jackson escorted her inside and left her alone to make her call in private, with a gruff "Help yourself." Perplexed by his sudden mood shift, Maggie stared at the closed door through which he had disappeared for a moment. Then she shook her head and reached for the phone. First things first. If she had any luck with the congressman, she would have time later to figure out what made Jackson Hawk tick.

The temptation to eavesdrop on Maggie's conversation was great, but Jackson forced himself to move away from the door and start a pot of coffee. Since he'd spent the afternoon playing tour guide, he'd have to stay late to finish the paperwork he'd neglected. He didn't regret the loss of his work time, however.

As his uncle had said, staying on polite terms with Montana's congressional delegation was important to the tribe. Jackson figured an afternoon was a small price to pay to repair the lousy

impression he'd made earlier. Maggie had obviously enjoyed herself and, he hoped, learned something about the Laughing Horse Reservation.

Now she would spend a few days visiting with people, and then she would go back to Washington. Her report would be filed and forgotten, and he could forget he'd ever met her. At least he hoped he'd be able to forget her.

Shoving his hands into his pockets, he ambled over to the window and gazed out at the parking area in front of the building. The sight of Maggie's rental car brought up a vivid mental picture of her holding little Emma Weasel Tail in her lap. Jackson shook his head in disgust at the warm, fuzzy feeling the vision produced in his chest.

"You've just been alone too long," he muttered, turning back to the coffeemaker.

That was true enough. His marriage had ended four years ago, and he hadn't been seriously interested in a woman since. What he couldn't understand was why Maggie Schaeffer, of all people, was the one who had made him realize how much he'd missed spending time with a woman.

Oh, sure, she was cute. Even sexy, in an understated sort of way. It didn't hurt that she was well educated and intelligent, either. But she wasn't any more right for him than his wife, Nancy, had been.

If he really wanted to have a woman in his life, he should pursue Sara Lewis, the curator of the Native American Museum in Whitehorn. Sara was every bit as educated and intelligent as Maggie, but she understood and embraced traditional Indian values, and she was as committed to the tribe as he was. Unfortunately, though he liked and respected Sara, he was no more attracted to her than he was to his sisters.

Well, if *Maheo,* the Creator, intended for him to marry again, Jackson figured, a suitable woman would eventually come along. Meeting Maggie Schaeffer had only served as a reminder that he still had a libido. Maybe he should start paying more attention to Aunt Sally's attempts to find him a "nice Indi'n gal."

Hearing the office door open behind him, Jackson turned and felt his heart slide clear down to the toes of his boots. Wearing an infectious grin almost as wide as her face, her dark eyes sparkling with excitement, Maggie stood in the doorway. How was he supposed to resist her when she wrinkled her impish little nose at him? Didn't she know bureaucrats weren't supposed to do things like that?

"Well, I've done it," she announced, holding her hands out like an actor preparing to take a bow.

"Done what, Ms. Schaeffer?" Jackson asked.

She wrinkled her nose at him again, hurried across the room and stopped in front of him. He caught a whiff of the light floral fragrance she wore. He'd noticed it a time or two during their tour. It reminded him of wildflowers. Oh, jeez, *wildflowers?* What the hell was the matter with him?

Her eyes taking on an earnest, hopeful expression, she laid one hand on his forearm. "We didn't get off to a very promising start, but I thought we'd made some progress this afternoon. Would you mind very much if we called each other by our first names...Jackson?"

A shiver of pleasure rippled down his spine when she said his name, her voice soft and a little husky. Somehow, at the moment, it didn't seem to matter that she was all wrong for him. He liked feeling her touch him. Though he knew she only intended it to be a conciliatory gesture, he liked it too damned much.

He pulled back enough to dislodge her fingers from his arm, then, irrationally, wished he hadn't done that. Man, he was gonna be in big trouble if she didn't go back to Washington soon. "Well, yeah. I guess we could. If you want, uh... Maggie."

There went her nose again. "It didn't hurt *that* much, did it?" Her eyes glinted with a gentle, teasing light that made it impossible to do anything but smile at her. "Anyway, I'm sure it will make working together more pleasant for both of us."

"Working together?" Jackson shook his head in confusion. "Have I missed something?"

"Well, we won't exactly be working together, but I'm sure I'll be seeing you fairly often during the next two months."

"Two *months?*"

"Oh, didn't I tell you? No, I guess I didn't." She laughed and dodged around him when the coffeemaker started to spit and hiss, a sure sign that the brew was ready. "Ah, plasma..." she said, reaching for the pot. Then she stopped, as if she'd suddenly remembered she was a visitor. "Sorry. I'm such a coffee hound. Do you mind if I have a cup?"

"Help yourself," Jackson said, feeling more confused with each passing second. She poured him a cup first and handed it to him before filling one for herself. "What didn't you tell me?"

"I took your advice, Jackson."

She sipped, then closed her eyes and sighed with obvious pleasure. If a little swallow of coffee made her sigh like that, what did she do in bed when she— Refusing to allow himself to finish the thought, Jackson shook his head again.

"What advice?" he asked.

"Your advice about living here for a year so I can understand the people's problems. I knew Congressman Baldwin would never agree to a year, but I did talk him into two months. Actually, I can stay until the middle of May, if I need to."

"You can?"

"Uh-huh. It was surprisingly easy to convince him. I'll have to work in the Whitehorn office once in a while, but for the most part, I'll be right here on the res. Isn't that great?"

Jackson gulped, then stared at her, wondering where this bubbly little elf had come from. This couldn't be the same woman he'd disliked so intensely a few short hours ago. He'd found her to be more likable as the afternoon wore on, but he never would have dreamed she could be so...vivacious. Yeah. That was the right word—*vivacious*. And she was smiling at him. Really giving him her killer-diller smile, and damned if it didn't make his heart beat a little faster.

"I said, isn't that great, Jackson?"

With a start, he realized he hadn't answered her question. "Uh, yeah. It's, uh, great, Maggie."

She shot him a puzzled look. "Is something wrong? I know it's not a whole year, but I thought you'd be pleased I'd be working on this for more than a week."

"I am, Maggie. Pleased, I mean. It's more than anyone else from the government has ever done."

"I really want to do a fair and honest study, Jackson. I know it won't solve all of your problems, but it could be the start of some good things for everyone here."

"I hope it will be."

"Me too." She gazed deep into his eyes for a moment, then glanced away, as if she'd somehow embarrassed herself. "Well, I guess I'd better go back to town and develop an action plan."

Jackson took the cup she held out to him, set it on the counter by the coffeemaker and waited for Maggie to retrieve her briefcase from his office. She returned carrying it, and she suddenly looked like a bureaucrat again. Before he could stop to consider the wisdom of offering her advice, the words popped out of his mouth.

"We're not usually too formal around here, Maggie. If you really want people to talk to you, you should ditch the briefcase and the suits."

She glanced down at her clothes, then looked up and grinned. "I'm so used to these things, I never would have thought of that. I'll stop at the trading post and see what I can find. Thanks, Jackson. Thanks for everything. I'll see you tomorrow."

A moment later, she was gone. Jackson poured himself another cup of coffee and walked into his office. Though it didn't have much in the way of comforts, compared to the cushy office he'd had in New York, he'd never minded working here. But now the whole building seemed too quiet. Too empty. Too lonely.

The phone rang then. Jackson wasn't surprised to hear his uncle's voice on the other end of the line. The moccasin telegraph had always been active on the Laughing Horse Res.

"Everything's fine, Uncle Frank. Oh, you talked to Earnest

Running Bull, did you? Annie Little Deer, too? That's quite a network of spies you've got.''

While his uncle fired one question after another, Jackson propped his feet up on the desk and rubbed the back of his neck.

''Yeah, she turned out to be okay. Was she cute?'' Jackson rolled his eyes, crossed his fingers and lied. His irrational attraction to Maggie was the last thing he wanted to have blabbed all over the res. It didn't mean anything, anyway. Just a few hormones acting up.

''Hell, I didn't notice. She's gonna stay for two months, Uncle Frank. No, I didn't charm her. I didn't have to. She figured out she didn't know anything all by herself. I still don't trust her, though.''

Now the advice started. ''Yes, Uncle Frank. I know. I know. Hey, have a little faith in me, will ya? I'll keep an eye on her. Yes, I promise.''

Hanging up the phone, Jackson assured himself he'd keep an eye on Maggie Schaeffer, all right. But, for his own peace of mind, he'd do it from a distance. Uncle Frank wasn't the only one on the res who had a network of spies.

Three

For the next two weeks, Maggie immersed herself in becoming more acquainted with the people who ran the social agencies at Laughing Horse, and with their clients. Following Jackson's advice, she bought jeans, sneakers, and beautifully decorated shirts and sweaters made by a co-op of Northern Cheyenne women at the trading post. Her new clothes were comfortable and practical, and she believed they did help her to blend in with the reservation residents.

She also exchanged her briefcase for a large purse, in which she carried a small notebook. She didn't take many notes, however. Before long, she found herself so involved with whatever was going on at the day-care center or the clinic or the employment office or the Indian school, she simply didn't have time. She didn't need notes to remember the conversations she had during the day, anyway.

These people were absolutely fascinating, and one of the things she liked best about being around them was their humor. They teased and harassed each other without mercy, but there was usually an underlying tone of affection that went along with it. Given the problems they often dealt with—unemployment, alcohol and drug abuse, domestic violence and so on—Maggie realized they probably needed a strong sense of humor to survive.

Though people treated her with courtesy and respect, Maggie also realized she was only seeing the surface of their lives. It would take time, probably a lot more time, for them to learn to trust her enough to really open up with their concerns. While it was frustrating, she tried to understand, and told herself she would know she'd finally been accepted when they started to tease her as they did each other.

She visited with the tribal police, the elderly people who told stories at the day-care center, the waitresses at the tribal center's restaurant. She interviewed the postmistress, the salesclerks at the trading post and the members of the women's sewing society. She talked to the Catholic and Protestant clergy who served the reservation, and the tribal priests and medicine men.

Every night she returned to her motel room in Whitehorn, feeling physically and emotionally drained, but eager to write up her impressions and insights on her laptop computer. Every morning she went back for more, always asking, "Why do you think that happens?" and "What should be done to change things?"

At first she regularly dropped by the tribal offices and tried to talk with Jackson Hawk, hoping to verify her perceptions of the things she was learning. Unfortunately, he rarely had time to see her, and when he did, his manner was cool and distant. She was puzzled, disappointed and a little hurt by his attitude, but she finally decided to leave the man alone and get on with her business.

If she occasionally felt lonely and depressed from observing the grinding poverty of the res, Maggie reminded herself there were more bright spots in her days than dark ones. One of the brightest was Sara Lewis, the curator of the Native American Museum, who was one of the volunteer tutors at the Indian school. Sara had welcomed Maggie and befriended her from the moment they met. Maggie admired her tremendously.

Tall and statuesque, Sara was cheerful, organized and dedicated. Her thick, shiny black hair fell to her waist when she wore it down, and her beautiful dark eyes carried a serenity that seldom wavered. Proud of her Northern Cheyenne heritage, Sara knew who she was and where she belonged, in a way Maggie envied.

Eager to spend time with her new friend, Maggie signed up to help tutor the junior and senior high students in the after-school program. The kids were as cautious about accepting her as their parents and grandparents, but on March 15, Maggie

still caught a disturbing glimpse of what life was like for them at the public schools in Whitehorn.

A group of high school girls came into the study room and spread their books and papers out on a big round table. Their mood was unusually glum, and Maggie was just about to go ask Sara for advice on how to handle them when a girl named Wanda Weasel Tail broke the silence.

"You went to college, didn't you, Ms. Schaeffer?"

Another girl—Nina, if Maggie remembered her name correctly—rolled her eyes in disgust and slammed her chemistry book shut. Maggie nodded at Wanda. "Yes."

"Did you like it?" Wanda asked.

Maggie nodded again. "It was a lot of hard work, but I enjoyed most of it."

"Was it worth it?" the girl persisted. "I mean, all that hard work, you know? Did it make white people treat you better?"

"I'm not sure I can answer that," Maggie said slowly, choosing her words with care. "I guess in some ways it did, but I didn't grow up in an Indian community. I've always been so used to white people; I've never had many problems in dealing with them."

"But college helped you get a good job, didn't it?"

"Of course it did. I wouldn't be working for a congressman if I hadn't gone to college."

"Aw, Wanda, give it a rest," Nina muttered. "You're not gonna go to any college. None of us are."

"Why do you say that, Nina?" Maggie asked. "You're all doing very well in your classes, and there are scholarships available for Indian students."

"It's not the money." Nina's eyes flashed with anger for a moment, then suddenly took on a dull, defeated expression that wrenched Maggie's heart. "We're not even gonna graduate from high school, because we're all flunking English."

"Now, I know that's not necessary," Maggie said firmly. "I can help you with almost anything that's giving you trouble. And if I can't, I'm sure Miss Lewis can. That's why we're here."

"It's not that we don't know how to do the assignment," Wanda said. "We just can't do it."

Maggie pulled out a chair and sat down with the kids. "I'm afraid I still don't understand. What's the assignment?"

"It's our senior research paper," Nina said. "You know, one of those ones with footnotes and all that garbage?"

"Why can't you do it?"

"Because they have to be typed, and we don't have any typewriters or word processors," one of the other girls said.

"And because we don't have time to do the research at school, and the librarians won't let us check out any books," Wanda added. "They say they never get 'em back when Indian kids check 'em out, so they won't let us take 'em home."

"But that's ridiculous!" Maggie squawked.

Nina shrugged. "That's the rules, Ms. Schaeffer."

"Rules can be changed," Maggie said.

"Not these rules," Wanda said. "You don't know those librarians."

So furious she could hardly see straight, Maggie shoved back her chair and stood. "Well, those librarians don't know me, either. I want a list of your research topics, girls. And I promise you, one way or another, you're going to write your papers."

"Oh, yeah?" Nina scoffed. "So what're you gonna do, Ms. Schaeffer? Beat up the librarians?"

Maggie gave her a grim smile. "If I have to. But I don't think it'll come to that."

"What about the typing?" Wanda asked. "None of us have taken it, because we can't do the homework. 'Cause we don't have equipment, you know? The papers are due next month."

Fearing she would explode with some inappropriate remarks if she didn't get out of this room fast, Maggie collected the papers with the girls' research topics. "You just do the writing, and let me worry about the rest. Get busy on your other homework for now. I have to go talk to someone."

Unable to concentrate on his work, Jackson tossed his pen onto the desk, swiveled his chair around and gazed out the

window at the Indian school. He told himself he really wasn't hoping for a glimpse of Maggie Schaeffer, but he didn't believe it for a second. Though he hadn't seen her for three days, she was seldom far from his thoughts.

How could she be, when everyone he ran into asked him what he knew about her? Hell, he hadn't needed a spy network to keep up with her movements; she was the talk of the entire reservation. She'd even earned herself a nickname. She was now known as Maggie the Little Fed Who Actually Listens, which was high praise indeed for an outsider who'd been here such a short time.

Sighing, Jackson started to turn back to his work, then caught a flash of movement that drew him to the window again. Uh-oh. The Little Fed was headed this way, in one heck of a hurry, and she looked mad enough to spit nails. Jackson whipped around and picked up one of the court documents he'd been reading, so that he'd look busy if she was coming to see him.

Sure enough, she stormed into his office a moment later, bristling with righteous indignation. Without so much as a greeting, she waved a fistful of crumpled papers at him. "Do you have any idea what's going on at Whitehorn High School?"

"Lots of things are going on at the high school," Jackson said, hiding a grin. Man, the lady was *steamed.* "Could you be more specific?"

"The discrimination, Jackson! Outright, blatant, illegal discrimination. Why are you letting them get away with it?"

Jackson climbed to his feet and stepped out from behind his desk, approaching her with one hand held up like a traffic cop. "Whoa! Calm down, and tell me what this is all about."

She took a deep breath and blew it out, ruffling her bangs with the breeze she created. "You're right. I'm sorry I barged in here like this. But it just makes me so furious, I want to hit somebody!"

"I can see that." Jackson gestured toward the straight-backed chair. "Sit down. I'll get you a cup of coffee, and we'll talk about it, okay?"

She obediently sat for a moment, then bounced out of the chair, as if she couldn't contain all the energy generated by her fury. She followed him to the coffeemaker, yapping at him like an enraged pup while he filled two cups.

"I'm telling you, Jackson, this situation is absolutely intolerable. No one deserves the kind of treatment the kids are getting. Those librarians should be drawn and quartered, tarred and feathered, ridden out of town on a rail."

Jackson handed her one of the mugs. Grasping her shoulder with his free hand, he gently herded her back into his office and pushed her into the chair again, then parked his butt on the edge of his desk. The aroma of the coffee finally got to her, and when she stopped to take a sip, he asked, "What's this about librarians?"

Maggie shot him an impatient look, but proceeded to explain the high school students' dilemma. By the time she finished, he felt ready to spit a few nails himself.

"We've got to do *some*thing, Jackson," she said. "For heaven's sake, the dropout rate for Indian kids is high enough, without those idiots making it impossible for them to succeed. You should take the librarians and the principal and the whole lousy school district to court and sue them for damages."

"I wish I could, Maggie," he said, shaking his head in disgust. "But I can't do it right now."

"Why not?" she demanded. "Those kids don't have a minute to lose. You're the tribal attorney—"

"Yes, I'm the tribal attorney, and at the moment, this tribe has more important legal matters to contend with."

"Such as? What on earth could be more important than helping those kids graduate from high school?"

"The tribe's economic survival. We're in a fight for our lives, and I can't take on any more than I already have."

That shut her up for an instant. But only for an instant. When she spoke again, however, her voice had softened. "What's going on, Jackson?"

Taking a moment to consider the wisdom of telling her, Jackson studied her face. She cared deeply about the kids, he was

certain of that. But could he trust her with information as sensitive as this? Well, shoot, he'd already spilled half of it, and if she kept poking around on her own, she'd probably hear the rest, anyway.

"Have you ever heard of Jeremiah Kincaid?" he asked.

She nodded. "I've met him, once. In the office in Washington. As I recall, he's the president of the Whitehorn Ranchers' Association."

"That's right. He's pretty much run the whole county for the last thirty years. His father ran it before that."

"What's he got to do with the tribe?" Maggie asked.

"I'll get to that in a minute. But first, I want you to tell me something."

"I will if I can."

"You've been talking to all kinds of people here for two weeks now," he said. "What's the most common problem you've heard about?"

She didn't even pause to think about it. "Unemployment. Some decent jobs would probably solve a lot of the other problems I've heard about, too."

"Exactly. And why do you think we have so much unemployment?"

"A lack of education is one reason."

"Yeah, it sure is," Jackson agreed. "And racial discrimination's another. But a lot of other tribes have even less education per capita than we do, and their unemployment figures are about half of what ours are. How do you suppose they manage that?"

She tossed her head impatiently. "I don't know. Why don't you just *tell* me?"

"All right," Jackson said, smiling at her impatience. "They have a better land base, Maggie. And they've managed to keep the whites out and employ their people themselves. We haven't been able to do that."

"Now you've *really* lost me," she complained. "Are you saying Jeremiah Kincaid and the Whitehorn Ranchers' Association are trying to steal your land?"

"In a way. See, until the Indian Self-determination Act was passed in 1975, the government treated Indian tribes as wards, with the Bureau of Indian Affairs acting as a legal guardian. Anything the tribal governments wanted to do had to be cleared through the BIA, and the BIA had the power to lease out lands that weren't being used. Mr. Kincaid and his pals got in pretty thick with our local BIA superintendent, and were granted long-term leases at rock-bottom prices on almost half our land."

"Can't the leases be revoked?" Maggie asked.

"They don't need to be. They're due to expire on the first of June. When I informed Mr. Kincaid the tribe would not be renewing those leases, the ranchers' association filed a lawsuit against us."

"On what grounds?"

"Guys like Kincaid don't need solid grounds, Maggie. They buy judges and congressmen, and even U.S. senators."

Her eyebrows swooped into a scowling *V*. "Now, wait a minute—are you implying my boss takes bribes?"

She was quick, all right, Jackson thought with a grin. And so damned earnest. "I don't know. Does he?"

"I hardly think so, Jackson."

"What was Jeremiah Kincaid doing in his office?"

"I don't know, and I wouldn't tell you if I did. I have *some* integrity, you know." She shot him a huffy glare that dared him to challenge her last statement. "But constituents visit him every day. That doesn't mean he takes bribes."

Jackson shrugged. "You're right. But I have to tell you, it makes me damn nervous to find out Kincaid's been to see him. I'll bet he's one of Baldwin's biggest campaign contributors."

"So what if he is?" Maggie demanded. "Congressman Baldwin doesn't have any control over the courts."

"No, but he has a certain amount of control over legislation concerning Indians. And when it comes to Indians, Congress has the power to do any damn thing they want. Frankly, I'm worried about Baldwin's sudden interest in us. It was clever of him to send you out here."

"You think he's using me somehow? To harm the tribe?"

"It's a possibility."

She gaped at him for a second, then firmly shook her head. "No. He wouldn't do that. I *know* he wouldn't."

"For God's sake, Maggie, how naive *are* you?" Jackson stood and paced the length of the room and back. "If you really believe that, you need to go to the library and read the history of federal policy toward Indian tribes. Look up the Allotment Act, the relocation program and the termination policy."

"Oh, come on, Jackson. That's all in the past."

"Are you willing to stake the tribe's survival on it? I'm not. Any time whites have wanted our land, ninety-nine times out of a hundred, we've lost it. Kincaid wants our land, and believe me, he's got plenty of powerful friends to back him up."

"But he can't possibly win in court. Can he?"

"Haven't you ever heard that possession is nine-tenths of the law? The leases were supposed to expire in January, but he's already managed to get a six-month extension. And damn it, we *need* those acres. If we can ever get them back, we've got plans that will put one hell of a dent in our unemployment problem."

"But I still don't see how anyone could use me or my work to help Kincaid. Mr. Baldwin asked me to report the truth about conditions here. That should help you, not hurt you."

Jackson shrugged. "Maybe it doesn't have anything to do with your report. For all I know, he might already be drafting legislation to force us to renew the leases or sell the land, and he wanted you out of the office so you wouldn't be around to protest if you found out about it."

"That's a pretty paranoid—"

"I'd rather be paranoid than stupid."

"Well, gee, thanks a lot." Maggie got up and walked stiffly to the doorway.

"Wait a minute." Jackson hurried after her. She turned to face him, hurt showing in her eyes. "I didn't mean that the way it sounded. I'm just afraid you're too trusting."

"Well, it's obvious you don't trust me, either," she said,

thumping her chest with one finger. "After all, I *do* work for the evil congressman."

She was so damn cute when she was furious, Jackson had to grin. "Actually, I kind of admire your loyalty to your boss. I only wish I knew how much loyalty you feel toward the people here. You don't have any real connection to us."

She raised her chin to a proud, almost haughty angle. "I'm as Northern Cheyenne as you are, Jackson Hawk. And I happen to have a very direct connection to the Laughing Horse Reservation."

"What are you talking about?"

"Take a look at your tribal rolls. I'm listed as Margaret Speaks Softly. My mother was listed as Beverly Speaks Softly."

Jackson frowned. He'd heard that name before—recently, in fact. When the memory surfaced, he had even less reason to trust Maggie. "I've heard of her. She left over twenty years ago and never came back. Married some big-shot white man, didn't she? The guy who owns all those motels?"

"That's right. My father's name is Calvin Schaeffer."

"Then you're half white? You don't look—"

"No. My biological father was Northern Cheyenne, too. He abandoned Mama before I was born. When he died, Cal adopted me. He's been a wonderful father, Jackson. I love him very much."

Well, that explained a lot of things about Maggie Schaeffer, Jackson thought. "You never even said you were Cheyenne. Why the hell didn't you tell me this before?"

"You were so busy judging me and telling me I didn't belong here, I didn't think it was any of your business. I'd appreciate it if you wouldn't spread this around. It's no one else's business, either."

"You have family here, Maggie."

"I know, but I'm not too sure I want to meet them. My mother must have had her reasons for staying away. Until I find out what they were, I'd rather not have any contact."

It was too late for that, Jackson thought, grimly shaking his

head. She'd already met her grandmother, Annie Little Deer. Annie's husband of fifty years had died a month ago, and Jackson remembered her mentioning her long-lost daughter. He believed Annie would love to know Maggie was her granddaughter. But it was Maggie's decision to make.

"All right," he said. "I won't tell anyone."

"Thank you. Since you're not going to be able to help the kids, do you mind if I take a shot at it?"

"What are you going to do?"

"You *still* don't trust me...." she said, shaking her head as if in amazement.

"Should I?"

"Yes, damn it. What have I done to make you believe I would ever willingly hurt anyone?"

"Nothing," he said. "But I told you, I can't afford to deal with any other legal hassles right now."

"I won't create any. All I plan to do is visit the superintendent of schools tomorrow morning. There's got to be Federal funding for Indian children in this school district. I think I can rattle his cage enough to make him take some action."

Jackson smiled at the thought of her doing that. She'd go after the guy like a mama grizzly protecting her cubs. It would serve the son of a bitch right.

"All right," he said. "The superintendent's name is Edward Reese. We've got BIA records of all the funding allocated for our kids during the past five years. Would you like to see them?"

Her mouth curved into a wicked grin. "Would I ever!"

He led her into Frank's office and dug the appropriate file out of the cabinet. She scanned the contents and tucked the folder under her arm. Promising to let him know how the meeting went, she left with a cheery wave. Jackson shook his head in bemusement.

Maggie Schaeffer had a healthy temper, and she wasn't afraid to show it. But when an argument ended, she didn't seem to hold a grudge. He liked that about her. That, and a lot of other things.

In fact, the only thing he didn't like about her was her boss. Damn it, an Indian woman as intelligent and educated as Maggie had no business working for a jerk like Baldwin. She should be working for her people in some capacity. So why the hell wasn't she? They could use her talents right here at Laughing Horse.

"Forget it," Jackson muttered. "Calvin Schaeffer's daughter would never live on a reservation. Not in a billion years."

Eager to study the file Jackson had given her, Maggie drove to Whitehorn, stopped at a fast-food restaurant for dinner and hurried back to her motel room. Two hours later, she set the folder aside, confident she was prepared to tackle Mr. Reese. If the man proved difficult, Jackson had given her plenty of ammunition to handle him with.

She got up and wandered over to the window, telling herself she shouldn't be thinking about Jackson. He was suspicious and irascible, and sometimes he could be an absolute stinker. He was also intelligent; though he invariably infuriated her, she had to admit she enjoyed the challenge of arguing with him.

And she still thought he was the most attractive man she'd ever seen. Lord, those eyes of his made her feel all shivery and jittery inside. However, unless he was yelling at her, Jackson masked his emotions so well she usually found it difficult to guess what he was feeling or thinking.

It had seemed as if they'd reached some level of understanding this afternoon. His giving her the file had been a demonstration of trust. Hadn't it? Surely he didn't think she would betray her own people, even if she hadn't ever lived with them.

"You probably don't want to know what he really thinks of you, Schaeffer," Maggie muttered to herself.

Sighing, she turned away from the window, crossed the room and flopped down on the bed. Linking her hands behind her head, she stared up at the water-spotted ceiling. Every time she talked with Jackson Hawk, she ended up feeling confused about something. Her attraction to him, her background, her career— after today, especially her career.

Darn him, anyway, she'd worked long and hard to get a job on Capitol Hill. Congressman Baldwin was a good boss and a kind, decent human being. He had an impeccable record; she'd checked it out before accepting a position with him. He couldn't be involved in the sleazy kinds of things Jackson had implied. He just couldn't.

She wasn't nearly as naive as Jackson obviously thought she was, either; if Mr. Baldwin was involved in corruption, she would have seen or heard something about it by now. So why was she suddenly doubting him? And her own judgment?

The phone on the bedside table rang before she could find a suitable answer. She picked up the receiver and smiled when she heard her father's voice.

"I haven't heard from you in ages, Maggie," he scolded. "How are you?"

"I'm fine, Dad. I've just been awfully busy."

"Busy doing what?"

Touched by his interest, she launched into a description of her activities during the past two weeks, finishing with the story about the kids. She wasn't ready to talk about Jackson yet. As always, her father listened intently. And, as always, he picked up on her turbulent emotions without her having to tell him directly.

"You sound like you could use a hug," he said. "I wish I could be there to give you one."

Imagining her big, burly father, with his unruly red hair and his hazel eyes that usually sparkled with laughter, Maggie felt a lump form in her throat. He gave the world's best hugs, and she suddenly missed him desperately. "Me too, Daddy."

"Oh, it's *Daddy*, huh?" he said with a soft chuckle. "That sounds pretty serious. What's wrong, honey?"

Maggie shrugged, then remembered he couldn't see her. "It's nothing, really. I mean, nothing's happened that I can't handle. I'm just feeling a little..."

"Confused and overwhelmed?" he asked.

"Yeah. That about covers it. The reservation is exactly what I expected in some ways, but not in others."

"What did you expect?"

"I knew I'd see a lot of problems, of course. And I've certainly seen them. I just didn't realize I'd feel so personally affected. When those girls told me what was happening to them, I felt like it was happening to *me*."

"Aw, Maggs, it's natural for you to identify with those people. They're Indians, and so are you."

"Am I?" Shaking her head, she choked out a bitter little laugh. "I look like them on the outside, but I don't have all that anger and despair on the inside. I guess I really am an apple."

"You're not an apple. You're just Maggie. And Maggie's one heck of a special lady."

"You've always made me feel that way," Maggie said. "But here, I feel so ignorant. I don't know anything about being a Northern Cheyenne. I don't know their stories or their customs or their history. Why didn't Mama ever teach me those things?"

Her father was silent for a long time. Fearing she'd upset him, Maggie tried to smooth things over. "I'm sorry, Dad. I shouldn't have said that."

"It's okay. I'm just not sure how to answer your questions, that's all," he said. "But go ahead and ask them."

"Are you sure you don't mind?"

"Of course, not. Honey, you know I loved your mother, but she wasn't a saint. I always thought you should know about your Indian heritage, but she'd get so angry when I'd try to talk about it, I finally stopped bringing it up."

"Was she ashamed of being an Indian?"

"No, I really don't believe she was. I think she faced an awful lot of discrimination, though, and she would have done anything to protect you from it."

"Even give up her own family?"

"That's what she did, all right. She never would tell me why, either. She didn't seem to be angry with them, but...well, who knows what really goes on in someone else's family? All I can

say for sure is, I never understood her attitude. Have you met any of her relatives?"

"I don't think so. There's one older lady who tells stories at the day-care center who gives me funny looks sometimes, but she's never said anything."

"I know your mother had at least one sister and a brother. And I'm pretty sure her parents were still alive when she left. Maybe you should look them up."

"I don't know, Daddy. Mama would be furious if she knew what I was doing. I feel like I'm betraying her memory, just being here."

"You couldn't do that if you tried." Her father sighed. "Maggie, your mother chose the way she wanted to live. But she's gone now, and you need to make your own choices."

"I know, but—"

"But nothing. Her family is your family, too. When I'm gone, you won't have anyone from my side. And besides that, I hate to think of you living the rest of your life with so many unanswered questions. It's not fair to you."

"I'll, uh…" Her voice cracked, and her eyes suddenly filled with tears. "I'll have to think about it."

"You do that. And trust your instincts, honey. They've always been pretty darn good ones."

"I will. Thanks, Daddy. I love you."

"I love you, too—and remember, I'm so damn proud of you I can hardly stand it."

Maggie hung up the phone and wiped her streaming eyes with the back of one hand. Then she crawled off the bed and went into the bathroom to splash cold water on her face. Honestly, she rarely cried, and she didn't know why she'd started to now.

"It's just stress," she muttered, turning away from the mirror. "You've been under too much stress."

She suspected the reasons were a lot more complicated than stress, however. Her father was right in at least one respect. She *did* have a lot of unanswered questions about her mother. Maybe it was time she found some answers. But first, she was going to help those kids—or die trying.

Four

Deciding the occasion called for a professional appearance, Maggie dressed in her gray pinstripe suit the next morning. Then she slid the file Jackson had given her into her briefcase and drove to the school-district administration building. She introduced herself at the front desk, asked to see Mr. Reese and followed his secretary down a carpeted hallway to an office at the end. The secretary, Mrs. Adams, knocked on the door and opened it.

Before she could say anything, Maggie brushed past her into the large office. Flashing what she hoped was a brilliant smile, she crossed the room to the massive teak desk and extended a business card to the scowling man sitting behind it.

Edward Reese appeared to be in his mid-to-late fifties. He wore his gray hair in a bristly crew cut. A pair of black horn-rimmed glasses perched precariously in the middle of his sharp nose. His navy wool suit, white shirt and subdued tie fairly shrieked, "Conservative."

He accepted the card without speaking, glanced at it and did a double take—when he caught Congressman Baldwin's name, no doubt, Maggie thought cynically. Suddenly all smiles and cordiality, he heaved his considerable bulk out of his high-backed leather chair and shook the hand Maggie offered him.

"This is quite a surprise, Miss Schaeffer," he said. "Welcome to Whitehorn."

"Thank you, Mr. Reese." She glanced apologetically at his pristine desktop, then smiled at him again. "I'm sorry to interrupt your busy schedule."

"I'm never too busy for a member of Bill's staff." Reese waved toward a chair to Maggie's right. "Have a seat."

So it was *Bill*, was it? Maggie thought, mentally raising an

eyebrow. Mr. Reese had obviously had years of practice at power games. Well, he would soon learn she was no amateur. She settled herself in the chair he had indicated and smoothed the hem of her skirt over her knees. Then she opened her briefcase and took out a legal pad and a pen.

"This shouldn't take long," she assured him, closing her briefcase and setting it on the floor. "I'm here on a fact-finding trip for the congressman. I need to ask you a few questions about the students from the Laughing Horse Reservation who attend your schools."

His eyes narrowing slightly, Reese leaned back in his chair. "Ask whatever you want."

"Thank you. How many Native American children are you presently serving, Mr. Reese?"

"That varies from week to week," he said. "The Indian families are frequently unstable. I'm afraid their children's attendance records tend to be rather hit-and-miss."

Ignoring the condescension in his smile, Maggie continued. "Could you give me an average number?"

"It's usually somewhere between four and five hundred."

"I see." Maggie dutifully wrote down the man's answer. "What percentage of your budget comes from federal funds for these children?"

"Approximately twenty percent."

Though Maggie knew the figure was closer to forty percent, she noted the answer without commenting. "Would you say the funds you receive for Native American children are adequate?"

Reese pushed his glasses up against his face and studied her for a moment. Maintaining a neutral expression, Maggie calmly returned his scrutiny.

"Frankly, Miss Schaeffer, they're not," he said. "Students who come from a deprived background, such as most of our Indian students have, need extra help and attention. We could do much more if our funding were increased, of course, but we do the best we can under the circumstances."

"I'm sure you do, Mr. Reese." Maggie made a show of

consulting her legal pad. That should be about enough rope to let this pompous ass hang himself, she thought, giving him a disarming smile. "I just have a few more questions. Could you tell me what percentage of the Indian high school students actually graduate?"

Reese sighed and sadly shook his head. "I'm afraid only about twenty percent of them graduate."

"Eighty percent of them drop out?" Maggie widened her eyes in feigned astonishment. "My goodness, isn't that an awfully high rate? Even for a minority group?"

He raised his hands in a what-can-you-do? gesture. "As I said, we do our best for all of our students, but the Indian kids simply don't have the discipline they need to succeed academically. They start drinking and taking drugs. Some of them commit suicide. Many of the girls get pregnant. You, of all people, must know what it's like on a reservation, Miss Schaeffer."

"I'm learning, Mr. Reese," Maggie said, struggling to maintain a calm, professional tone after his obvious dig regarding her background. Perhaps she should inform this twit of her master's degree from Harvard. "In fact, I've spent quite a bit of time tutoring some of your high school students lately."

"Oh, really?"

"Yes, they have a marvelous after-school program out at Laughing Horse. The students have mentioned some of the problems they've been having in school." She leaned back and crossed her legs, settling more comfortably in order to enjoy wiping that smug smile off Reese's chubby face. "I'd be happy to share them, if you're interested."

Leaning forward, he rested his forearms on the desk. "Of course. We're always looking for ways to improve communication with our Indian students."

"Well, the first one is something I'm afraid I just don't understand." Opening her briefcase, Maggie pulled out the file Jackson had given her and studied the top sheet inside. "The kids told me they couldn't take typing because they didn't have access to equipment to do their homework. According to my figures, however, during the past five years, federal funds were

allocated for fifty computers for Whitehorn High School. Is there some reason—''

"Excuse me," Reese said sharply, interrupting her. "Where did you get those figures?''

"From the Bureau of Indian Affairs," Maggie replied, trying for an innocent expression. "They keep very complete records, Mr. Reese. Would you like to compare them with yours?''

He pursed his lips and studied her, giving her the impression he was trying to calculate the wisdom of disputing the figures. She seriously doubted he wanted to open his own records for her inspection. Sure enough, he gave his head one decisive shake. "That won't be necessary.''

"Well, as I was about to say, I don't understand why the Indian students aren't aware those computers are available for their use. Don't you have a computer lab at Whitehorn High?''

"Of course we do. The Indian kids just don't use it.''

Maggie shot him a doubtful look. "The students I spoke with are all very concerned about getting their senior English research papers typed. As I understand it, that's a graduation requirement?''

Reese nodded.

"Well, I'm sure you understand that, because of their *deprived* backgrounds, none of those kids have computers at home," Maggie said. "Frankly, Mr. Reese, I would think that if you really wanted to increase the number of Indian graduates, your staff would make sure those students have plenty of opportunity and encouragement to use the equipment the taxpayers have provided for them.''

Her thinly veiled sarcasm was not wasted on the superintendent. A dull red flush climbed up his face and disappeared into his crew cut. "Are you implying we *don't* want our Indian students to graduate?''

Maggie smiled. "Heavens, no, Mr. Reese. I'm sure a dedicated educator like yourself must be terribly embarrassed by this school district's abysmal performance in serving your Indian students.''

"Now, see here," Reese said, thumping his index finger on

the desk. "It's not the school district's fault. Those kids are lazy. They don't show up half the time, and when they do, they're not prepared for class."

Dropping all pretense of pleasantness, Maggie glared right back at him and brought out her second round of ammunition. "Perhaps they would *be* prepared for class, if they were allowed to check out library books, like the white students."

Beads of sweat popped out on Reese's forehead. "They never bring the books back—"

"*Never?* I doubt that's true. Tell me, do your white students *always* return library books?"

"Of course they don't." He shifted around in his chair, as if the plush seat had suddenly become uncomfortable. "However, we have a reasonable chance of collecting fines to pay for the books the white students don't return. That's not the case with our Indian students. Surely you can understand that we can't afford to give books away."

"Certainly. And I believe you've just given me an idea for solving these problems." Maggie pulled her briefcase back onto her lap and put away her things. Then she stood. "Thank you, Mr. Reese. You've been very helpful. I won't take up any more of your time."

He heaved himself to his feet again and braced his knuckles on the desk. "Wait a minute. What are you planning to do?"

"The federal government gives this school district twenty thousand dollars a year for new library books, specifically intended for Native American students," Maggie said, drawing herself up to her full height. "I'm going to recommend to the agencies involved that those funds go directly to the Northern Cheyenne tribal council. The same will be true of the equipment funds, and any other funds I find are being misappropriated."

"Misappropriated!"

"If you were a Native American parent, what would you call it?" Maggie demanded. "The children need books and computers. If you can't allow them access, we'll have to find another way to get it for them. The after-school program at the

reservation has plenty of room for library and a computer center.''

''You can't do this!''

''Oh, but I *can,* and what I'm proposing is only the beginning,'' she said, digging the knife in a little deeper. ''It's obvious your schools are not capable of meeting the Indian students' needs. There *are* other communities within busing distance. If this discrimination continues, the tribal council may well decide to make new arrangements for the children's education. Have a nice day, Mr. Reese.''

With that, Maggie strolled out of the room, mentally dusting her hands every time she heard another outraged sputter coming from the superintendent's office. She nodded politely at the secretary, then continued unhurriedly out to her rental car.

The first fit of giggles erupted when she was safely inside the vehicle. Another followed, and then another and another, until she gave up trying to control them and whooped with laughter. Finally regaining enough composure to start the car and back out of the parking space, she headed for the res.

''Hey, Jackson, wait until you hear about this!''

Jackson looked up at the sound of Maggie's voice in the hallway outside his office, as did his Uncle Frank. She charged into the room a moment later, wearing one of her power suits and an exuberant smile that was bright enough to compete with the spring sunshine streaming through the window. Dropping her briefcase on the floor, she raised one fist in triumph and wrinkled her nose at him.

''Jackson, you should have been there!'' she crowed. ''It was great! The look on his face was absolutely priceless!''

Jackson exchanged an amused glance with his uncle. Maggie followed the direction of his gaze and blushed when she saw the older man.

''Oh, I'm sorry. I didn't realize you had company.''

Frank Many Horses chuckled and muttered to Jackson, ''You didn't notice she was cute, huh? You need glasses, nephew.''

Ignoring the remark, Jackson introduced Maggie to his uncle.

"I've been wanting to meet you, Mr. Many Horses," she said, offering her hand, along with a sincere smile. "I've heard so many nice things about you."

While Frank shook her hand, Jackson cleared a stack of folders off another chair and pulled it over for Maggie. She shook her head when she saw it.

"I didn't mean to interrupt you. I'll come back later."

"It's all right, Maggie," Jackson said. "I told my uncle about your visit with Reese this morning. He's as interested in hearing what happened as I am."

Giving him a delightfully wicked grin, Maggie waggled her eyebrows at him. Then she was off, enthusiastically acting out her part and Reese's part until Jackson and Frank were laughing so hard they had to wipe tears from their eyes. She ended with a flourish, cheerfully bowing in response to their applause.

Jackson studied her glowing face and shining eyes and thought she was absolutely beautiful. That she had achieved such beauty by accomplishing something good for the tribe enhanced his attraction to her. He wished he could pull her into his arms and kiss her sensible pumps right off her feet.

"Can you really do all that?" Frank asked a moment later.

A sober expression came over Maggie's face, and Jackson appreciated her reluctance to promise something she might not be able to deliver.

"I'd need some authorization from the tribal council, but I'd be happy to try, Mr. Many Horses."

Chuckling, Frank slapped his knee and grinned at Jackson. "There will not be a problem with the council."

Jackson nodded in agreement. "I don't think we should rush into anything, though. Maggie's performance this morning is bound to shake things up. Why don't we wait and see what happens?"

"That won't help the seniors, if they don't finish their papers on time," Maggie said quietly. "And some of those kids have real college potential, Jackson."

She was right, of course. Which meant they needed a quick

solution. Before he could come up with one, however, the telephone rang.

He answered it, listened for a moment, then covered the mouthpiece with one hand. "It's Congressman Baldwin, Maggie. You can take it in Frank's office, if you want."

"Thanks. I'll do that."

Frank shot him a worried look when she left. "What would you bet ol' Reese has already been on the phone to Washington?"

Jackson nodded grimly. The possibility of Maggie getting into trouble with her boss over this had occurred to him. He knew it also must have occurred to her, and he'd admired her willingness to get involved anyway. Still, he had to admit he was curious to see how she would handle it. He eyed the phone with longing, then sighed and hung it up.

Uncle Frank had fewer scruples about eavesdropping than he did, however. Jackson watched in amazement as his big, barrel-chested uncle tiptoed to the open door and stood to the left, his head cocked to one side. Since Jackson couldn't see his face, he had no idea what, if anything, his uncle could hear. The temptation to join him was too strong to resist. Taking a position on the right side of the doorway, he listened intently.

"*I* didn't create the problem, Congressman. Mr. Reese and his staff did. They're systematically discriminating against those students—and misappropriating federal funds."

Jackson grinned. Maggie's voice sounded cool and professional, but he'd tangled with her enough to recognize the note of steel that meant she was prepared to dig in her heels but good.

"I disagree, sir," she said. "As a federal employee, I believe it was my duty to intervene. I couldn't possibly have ignored the situation."

She was silent for a long moment. Jackson held his breath in anticipation of her next response.

"I know you have to stand for reelection next fall. Yes, I'm aware I'll be unemployed if you lose. But under the circum-

stances, I did the only ethical thing I could do." There was another pause. Then she said, "Do you want my resignation?"

Frank shot Jackson an appalled look. Jackson shrugged and shook his head. Maggie had gone into this willingly, and there was nothing they could do to help her.

"No, I don't want to resign, but I will *not* apologize to Mr. Reese. And I *will* resign if we don't take appropriate action here. The Northern Cheyenne are also your constituents, Congressman. They're only asking for justice."

The next pause was even longer. "All right. I appreciate your understanding. Thank you, sir. Yes, I'll be in touch. Goodbye, sir."

Racing back to their chairs like a couple of naughty schoolboys in danger of being caught, Jackson and Frank barely got themselves settled before Maggie walked back into the room. Her expression was thoughtful, but not tearful, Jackson decided after studying her face for a moment. Damn, but he was proud of her. The look in his uncle's eyes indicated he felt the same way.

Uncle Frank cleared his throat. "Is everything all right, Ms. Schaeffer?"

Smiling slightly at him, she nodded. "Everything's just fine, Mr. Many Horses."

"My friends call me Frank," he said gravely. "I would like it very much if you would also call me that."

Her smile brightened. "Thank you. Please call me Maggie." She picked up her briefcase. "Well, I'd better get back to work and leave you gentlemen to your meeting."

"We appreciate what you did for the kids this morning, Maggie," Jackson said.

She gave him another one of those wicked grins. "Believe me, it was *my* pleasure. And one way or another, I'm going to get the kids what they need."

Frank and Jackson eyed each other until they heard the outer door shut. Then Frank leaned back, laced his fingers together behind his head and stretched his long legs out in front of him.

"The Little Fed has a big heart, nephew," he said.

Jackson nodded. "So it would seem."

"Courage, too." Frank added. "And strong convictions."

"Yeah," Jackson said. "She sure didn't take any bull from Baldwin, did she?"

Frank chuckled. "Didn't sound like it. Why do you suppose he backed down?"

"From what Bennie Gonzales told me, I'd guess Baldwin knows she could get another job on Capitol Hill without breaking a sweat. Or maybe he was afraid she'd expose him if she quit."

Or maybe, Jackson silently reminded himself, Maggie and Baldwin were lovers. He didn't want to believe it, especially not now. But this whole assignment of hers still had a funny smell to it.

"Could be," Frank agreed. "She say anything about what she's gonna put in her report?"

"I haven't talked to her that much," Jackson said.

Frank shot him a knowing grin. "Yeah, I heard you've been hidin' out in the office a lot lately. You haven't been avoidin' that little gal, have ya?"

"I've been *busy,* Uncle."

"Uh-huh. Maybe *too* busy. I think she's got you runnin' scared."

"You're way off base," Jackson insisted, though he didn't expect his uncle to believe him. Hell, he wasn't too sure he believed himself. When it came to Maggie Schaeffer, he wasn't too sure about anything. "I'm not interested in her that way."

A touch of impatience entered Frank's voice. "It's time you took an interest in women again. Maggie looks like a pretty good one to start with, if you ask me."

"I didn't ask you, uncle."

"That's a fact. But women like her don't come along every day. She had lunch with the good doctor the other day. Kane looked plenty interested."

"Well, good for Kane," Jackson muttered, suddenly wanting to track down his old friend at the clinic and punch his face in. Aw, damn, he was really losing it.

Frank's eyes danced with amusement. "She didn't look all that interested in him, though. Not like she looked at you."

"Uncle, I know you mean well—"

Frank cut him off with an impatient snort. "That's right, I do. I want what's best for you and what's best for the tribe. A woman like Maggie could be one hell of an asset for us."

"I'd do a lot of things for the sake of the tribe," Jackson said. "But I wouldn't marry that woman just to—"

Frank interrupted him again. "Who said anything about marriage?"

"You did. You implied it, anyway."

"No, I didn't." Frank laughed and pointed a finger at Jackson. "You thought up that word all by yourself. And you were thinkin' it about Maggie, too."

Jackson pinched the bridge of his nose with his thumb and forefinger. "You're giving me a headache, uncle. Knock it off, will ya?"

Frank climbed to his feet and smiled down at Jackson. "All I meant was, it would be a good idea if you got to know her better. For the sake of the tribe, of course."

"I don't have time," Jackson grumbled. "I'm still doing your job, too, remember?"

"What if I came back to work?"

"Did Kane say you could?"

"Oh, sure. The doc told me that a week ago."

Delighted with the news, Jackson grinned. "You sly old wolf, why didn't you tell me?"

"Because you're getting good experience," Frank said, his tone completely serious. "And I'd like to know the tribe is in experienced hands if I drop over dead someday."

"You're not gonna do that, uncle."

"How do you know? How do any of us know when that time will come? I want you to be ready just in case."

"What makes you think the people would elect me to chair the tribal council? Most of them despised me for years."

"You've changed since you came back, Jackson. Their opin-

ions have changed with you. The council would never have let you fill in for me if you hadn't won their respect.''

"I don't know if I really want your job," Jackson said. "It's a real pain in the butt sometimes.''

"That's for sure. But it makes you feel good to do things for the tribe, doesn't it?''

"Yeah," Jackson admitted. "It does.''

"The Little Fed felt the same way this morning. I could see it in her eyes. We need somebody with her knowledge and enthusiasm.''

"All right, uncle. When you come back to work, I'll spend more time with her. Just don't expect any big romance, okay?''

"Whatever you say, nephew.'' Chuckling, Frank headed for the doorway. "Whatever you say. I'll be in tomorrow.''

Jackson tried to get back to work when his uncle left, but the effort was futile. After ten minutes of zero concentration, he threw down his pen in disgust, leaned back and propped his feet on the corner of the desk. It was time to do some serious thinking.

He was interested in Maggie Schaeffer, all right. And it was a hell of a lot more than a professional interest. The Little Fed just plain turned him on. With her smiles and her laughter. With her temper and stubbornness. With her intelligence and courage and convictions.

Realizing he hadn't even gotten around to thinking about her body yet made his chest feel tight. He took a deep breath to calm himself, but a sick sensation invaded his stomach. Damn it, he shouldn't *like* her so much.

His relationship with Nancy had started out the same way. The liking had grown into love, of course, but not even love had been enough to hold their marriage together. He'd been so hurt and humiliated when she left him, he'd wanted to crawl into a hole and never come back out. Only his anger at learning she'd never really loved him at all had kept him going. Not the real him, anyway. The Indian him.

The sick feeling in his gut came from realizing that Maggie fascinated him more than any woman he'd ever met, including

his ex-wife. He might be able to fall in love with her, but she would never be able to love the real him, any more than Nancy had. Damn it, he wouldn't go through that again. He couldn't.

At the same time, he knew himself well enough to know that his attraction to her was not going to go away on its own. Avoiding her hadn't helped a bit. So, maybe Uncle Frank had the right idea. If he spent more time with Maggie, he might discover things about her that would turn him off.

If that didn't happen, well, he still didn't have to get romantically involved with her. He was thirty-six, not sixteen. He could control his libido, and he'd outgrown having affairs years ago. Since an affair was all he'd ever be able to have with Maggie, sex wouldn't be an issue between them. Hell, for all he knew, she wasn't even attracted to him.

Liar! a voice inside his head shouted at him. Jackson shrugged in dismissal. He'd caught her looking at him with more than professional interest a few times. He'd noticed that her eyes lit up whenever she saw him, and she smiled at him in a way that always made him aware of his masculinity. So what?

Maggie didn't strike him as a woman who gave herself lightly. She knew she'd be leaving in a few weeks. He doubted she was any more interested in starting an affair than he was. She'd probably deck him if he tried to kiss her.

That thought wasn't nearly as comforting as it should have been, but Jackson figured that was just his ego talking. He'd already promised his uncle he would get to know Maggie better, and he would. He might even allow himself to develop a friendship with her. But he wouldn't go one step farther than that. He just couldn't afford to do otherwise.

So why did he still have this awful, sinking feeling in his gut that the decision might not be his alone to make?

Five

After leaving Jackson's office, Maggie grabbed a set of casual clothes she'd stashed in the car and changed in the women's rest room at the tribal center restaurant. The aromas of french fries and hamburgers sizzling on the grill made her stomach rumble. She glanced at her watch, noting with surprise that it was almost noon. Heavens, where had the morning gone?

She hurried back out to her car, dumped her suit and pumps into the back seat, then returned to the restaurant. Three people nodded and smiled at her as she seated herself in a booth by the window, and with a jolt she realized she was beginning to feel as if she belonged here. That was silly, of course. She would be going back to Washington in a few weeks to resume her career and her "real" life.

And yet, when she considered it for another moment, the idea of belonging at Laughing Horse didn't seem quite so ridiculous. These people didn't see someone "different" when they looked at her; they simply saw a woman who looked like themselves. She was one of them. It was a liberating concept, in a place few people would have associated with freedom.

Maggie glanced around, met with more nods and smiles, and felt a warm glow ignite deep in her chest. These people were *her* people. She'd known that intellectually from the beginning, but this was the first time she'd actually *felt* it.

That was why she'd taken up the teenagers' cause. Why she'd felt such a strong sense of accomplishment when she told Jackson and Frank about her morning's work. Why she'd risked her job when her boss reprimanded her.

Though she rarely held a grudge, the memory of that phone call still rankled. She hadn't thought Congressman Baldwin could ever be so insensitive to any of his constituents' needs,

not to mention their civil rights. But after what he'd said to her, she had to wonder if perhaps Jackson was right to be suspicious of Baldwin's sudden interest in the tribe's welfare.

A waitress came and took her order. While she waited for her cheeseburger and fries, Maggie tried to sort out her troubled thoughts. She had always considered herself a loyal employee. She'd thoroughly enjoyed researching the political issues the congressman dealt with, and she'd seldom questioned how he would use that information or how his actions would affect peoples' lives. Now, for the first time in her career, she had to question both of those things.

Just where did her own responsibilities for what happened in the political process begin and end? And where did her loyalties lie in this instance? With Congressman Baldwin and the U.S. Government? Or with the Northern Cheyenne? If they were really *her* people…

"Hey, the food's not *that* bad here," an amused male voice said from somewhere above her head.

Startled, Maggie looked up and found herself gazing into Jackson Hawk's dark, dark eyes. Her stomach did a little flip that had nothing to do with hunger. Sweet, merciful heaven, when he smiled, he was one handsome hunk of man.

"Mind if I join you?" he asked.

Maggie gestured toward the opposite bench seat in invitation. "By all means."

Suddenly nervous, she cleared her throat, then sipped from the glass of ice water the waitress had brought her. Jackson's long legs bumped against her knees as he settled himself in the booth. The resulting jolt of sexual awareness raised her temperature five degrees. She took another sip. Oh, this was absurd. She saw handsome men every day on Capitol Hill without getting hot and bothered.

Propping his forearms on the table, he leaned closer. She caught a whiff of a clean, outdoorsy scent. His braids hung down in front of his shoulders, and she had a sudden urge to reach out, tug off the leather strings tied to the ends and see what his hair looked like unbound. Judging from the plump,

shiny coils of his braids, she suspected it would be thick and smooth. It would probably glide through her fingers like warm—

"You were on top of the world this morning," he said. "What put that frown on your face?"

She shook her head, trying to dispel the pleasurable, caressing effect his deep, quiet voice had on her ears. Lord, it made her think of darkened bedrooms and murmured intimacies between lovers. *Get a grip,* she told herself, praying he hadn't already noticed her reaction to him.

Jackson had been friendlier than usual since yesterday, but she couldn't forget he'd already called her stupid, naive, and an apple. She doubted he even thought of her as a woman. It would be absolutely humiliating if he knew she was sitting here lusting after his bod.

"Nothing important," she said. "I was just thinking about something."

He looked as if he wanted to question her further, but the arrival of her lunch provided a distraction. Jackson ordered an identical meal, then sat back and watched while Maggie piled condiments on her cheeseburger. His intent regard made her feel jittery inside and turned her fingers into uncoordinated sticks at the ends of her hands.

"I liked your uncle," she said, hoping to distract him again. "Is he your mother's brother, or your father's?"

"My mother's. He liked you, too."

"Good. I want to interview him, when he's well enough."

"He's well enough now," Jackson said. "In fact, he's coming back to work tomorrow. That's why I tracked you down. I've got a proposition for you."

"Oh, really?" she asked, raising an eyebrow at his word choice. "Would you care to explain that?"

Jackson grinned and pointed at her plate. "Go ahead and eat while it's hot, Maggie. Mine'll be coming in a minute. I'll talk while you chew."

She dunked a french fry in a puddle of ketchup and popped it into her mouth, then looked at him expectantly.

"Since Uncle Frank's coming back, I'll have some free time," he said. "You haven't seen much of the res beyond the tribal center. I'd be happy to drive you around, so you can see the rest of it and meet more of the people. Are you interested?"

An hour ago, she would have eagerly accepted his offer. Given the way her attraction to him appeared to be getting out of hand, however, she wasn't at all sure she wanted to be cooped up in a vehicle with him for hours at a time. On the other hand, she needed to explore the outer reaches of the reservation. She'd probably spend half her time being lost if she tried to travel those lonely back roads alone.

For heaven's sake, she chided herself, dithering about this was ridiculous. She was an adult, and a professional. She could handle this...infatuation or hormonal surge or whatever the heck was wrong with her. The way they tended to fight with each other, she'd be over it in no time.

"Yes, I'm interested," she said. "Thank you."

"You're welcome. We'll start tomorrow afternoon."

The waitress arrived with Jackson's order. He put his cheeseburger together and bit into it enthusiastically. A drop of mustard squirted out the side and clung to the corner of his mouth. Maggie stared at that little yellow dot and gulped.

She'd never thought there was anything even slightly erotic about watching someone eat, but at this moment, she wanted to lick that drop of mustard away and then kiss him. Long and hard. Until he gasped for air. No doubt about it, she was losing her mind.

And then, bold as any hooker in downtown D.C., Jackson looked up, winked at her, and went back to munching his burger. He knew! Oh, God, the wretched man knew exactly what she'd been thinking all along! She didn't know whether to laugh or cry or howl with mortification.

A fourth option—hitting him over the head with the ketchup bottle—held enormous appeal. Unfortunately, Al Black Bird, one of the tribal policemen she had interviewed, was sitting at a nearby table. She didn't particularly want to tangle with all six foot six and two hundred and fifty pounds of him.

Jackson continued to eat as if nothing unusual had passed between them. Promising herself she'd get even one of these days, Maggie picked up her own burger and forced her concentration onto her meal. When they were finishing, a short, wiry-looking white man wearing a dark gray uniform entered the restaurant. The room suddenly fell silent as everyone turned to stare at him. His face flushed beneath his curly blond hair, but he murmured something to the cashier, then walked quickly to Maggie's booth.

"Excuse me, ma'am," he said, "are you Maggie Schaeffer?"

"Yes, I am."

"My name's Harvey." He pointed to the white letters embroidered on his shirt.

Hoping to ease his obvious tension, Maggie smiled. "It's nice to meet you, Harvey. May I help you?"

He pulled an envelope out of his hip pocket and handed it to her. "I have a delivery for you, ma'am. If you'll sign that top form, and tell me where you want the stuff, I'll unload it for you and be on my way."

Mystified, Maggie opened the envelope and found a bill of lading from Conway Electronics in Billings. She gasped at the listed inventory, then quickly flipped the top sheet over and read the note her father must have faxed from Denver to the store. Barely suppressing a delighted whoop, she stuffed the papers back in the envelope and grinned at Jackson, who was staring at her with a perplexed frown.

Then she stood, stuck one hand out and wiggled her fingers at him. Lowering her voice, because everyone else was staring at her, too, and listening with avid interest, she said, "Your keys, Jackson. I need to get into the Indian school."

"What for?"

"I don't want to explain it here," she said. "It's sort of a surprise for the kids."

"Do you mind if I tag along?"

"You'll get put to work if you do," she warned him.

He slid out of the booth and plunked his Stetson on his head. "I'll take my chances."

Harvey headed for the exit as if he couldn't get out of there fast enough. Maggie followed him, leaving Jackson to bring up the rear.

"Hey, Maggie, what about your check?" the cashier called as she hurried past.

Maggie looked over her shoulder and grinned at the woman. "Give it to Jackson, Gretchen." It wasn't much of a payback for that outrageous wink, but for now it would have to do.

Jackson paid both checks, then left the restaurant, chuckling to himself. He knew exactly why she'd stiffed him with her bill, and he figured he deserved it.

He really shouldn't have winked at her like that, but he hadn't been able to resist. How anyone with a face as expressive as hers had ever survived in Washington was beyond him. Her reaction to their knees' bumping under the table had confirmed his suspicion that she was attracted to him and stroked his ego at the same time. The fun part had been watching her try to hide what she was feeling. And fail miserably.

If he had any smarts at all, he wouldn't have found it so amusing. Or so endearing. But, hey, it was no big deal. Just a little harmless teasing between friends, right?

Ignoring the jeering inner voice that shouted *Liar!* at him again, Jackson shoved his sunglasses on his face and left the restaurant. Maggie and the delivery man stood beside a long white van parked at the curb, talking about the great spring weather. When Jackson joined them, they all piled into the front seat of the vehicle, with Maggie in the middle. She gave the driver directions, then shot Jackson an excited grin.

"You want to tell me what this is all about?" he asked.

"Computers." She handed him the envelope she'd received from Harvey. "Take a look."

Holy smokes, Jackson thought as he studied the bill of lading. There must be thousands of dollars' worth of equipment

in the back of this rig. Tens of thousands. Then he flipped over the top sheet and found a note that explained the situation.

Dear Maggie,

Kids who work as hard in school as the ones you described to me last night deserve a helping hand. The goodies are for the after-school program. Let me know if they need anything else. Take care of yourself, honey, and God bless.

Dad

Playing for time, Jackson carefully folded the papers, poked them back into the envelope and handed it to Maggie. She smiled at him expectantly. Damn. She obviously thought he'd be as delighted as she was to get this equipment for the kids. He wished he could be, if only to keep that smile on her face.

The driver pulled over in front of the Indian school. Jackson leaned across Maggie and said, "Sit tight for a minute, Harvey. We need to talk about something."

He climbed down and offered Maggie his hand. Shooting him a wary look, she scrambled out of the van without his assistance. Her refusal to touch him was irritating, but he clamped down on his annoyance and walked toward the building, turning to face her when he was sure they wouldn't be overheard.

Her chin raised to a challenging angle, she propped her fists on her hips. "All right, what's the matter?"

Oh, brother, Jackson thought grimly, here we go again. Aloud, he said, "I'm not sure the tribal council will want to accept this stuff."

She gave him a perplexed frown. "Why on earth wouldn't they? It's just a gift. And a pretty darned nice one."

Jackson shrugged one shoulder. "Sometimes gifts come with strings attached. We've learned that the hard way."

Her frown deepened. "When my father gives a gift, that's exactly what it is, Jackson. A *gift*. He doesn't expect anything in return. What could he want from the tribe, anyway?"

"He's into motels, isn't he? Other tribes have them. Maybe he wants to build one here."

"Would it be so awful if he did? Laughing Horse could certainly use one, and it would bring in jobs and tourist money."

"Yeah, it probably would," Jackson said. "But that isn't the kind of decision we make lightly, Maggie. We have to consider the negative effects it might have, too."

"Such as?"

"More garbage and sewer problems. Strangers coming onto the res, bringing in drugs, and who knows what else?"

She rolled her eyes at him. "Oh, come on, Jackson, don't you think you're reaching a little bit? Why are you really worried about this? Because my dad's white?"

Jackson shrugged again. "That's part of it. Rich white guys usually try to take something for nothing, not give it. We've learned that the hard way, too."

"My father is a kind, generous man. He would never try to force a business deal on anyone."

"How can you be so sure of that?"

"I grew up with the man!" She glared at him for a second, then gave her head an impatient shake. "All right, think about it logically. Dad doesn't need any more motels. Certainly not enough to try to bribe an Indian tribe with a few computers."

"A *few?*" Jackson jerked his thumb toward the van. "I saw the list, Maggie. There must be twenty computers out there."

"And printers, software, modems and CD-ROM players," she agreed with a fond smile—for her father, no doubt. "If I know Dad, there's probably a case of computer paper and extra printer ribbons out there, too. Believe me, he can afford it."

"But why would he give all that stuff away?"

"That's just the way he is. He was always donating things to the schools I attended."

"Why would he do this for *us,* Maggie? He's never been here. He doesn't know anyone on this reservation but you. Why would he care that much about a bunch of Indian kids he's never met?"

"Has it ever occurred to you that you might have a problem with bigotry, Jackson?" She exhaled an angry huff, then shook her head again and continued before he could defend himself.

"Dad's always tried to help people take charge of their own lives. Half of his executive staff didn't have high school diplomas when they started working for him. I couldn't begin to tell you how many employees he's sent to college over the years. He never cared what color they were, either."

"Look, I didn't mean to offend you, or accuse your father of anything," Jackson said slowly. "It's just pretty damned unusual for anyone to be so generous."

"Well, he's a pretty damned unusual man. Perhaps you should meet him before you judge him the way you judged me."

Jackson winced inwardly when that remark struck home, but he refused to let her sidetrack him. "It's not that simple."

"Why not? You've accepted corporate donations before, haven't you?"

"Yeah, and sometimes that's hurt us more than it's helped us. We've depended on the white man's charity for too long. At some point we've got to start depending on ourselves and solve our own problems."

"And you think *this* is that point?" she demanded.

"It's as good as any," Jackson shot back. "I don't want these kids to think all they have to do to get what they want is whine to some rich white guy about how poor they are. I want them to understand they've got to work for it."

"That's a noble sentiment, but how are they going to work if they don't have the skills to get jobs that will pay them a living wage?" Jabbing her finger toward the van, she said, "There are *jobs* in those boxes. And not just for the kids. Some of the unemployed adults could learn to use those computers while the kids are in school."

"It's still charity, damn it. We'll never regain our pride as a people until we learn to provide for our own needs. There's a principle involved here."

"If you want to use a principle, try the one that says if you

give a man a fish, you feed him for one day. If you teach a
man to fish, you feed him for a lifetime. That's all my dad's
trying to do here. And I don't think it's the people's pride
you're worried about, Jackson. It's your *own*.''

"That's not true.'' He shoved his hands into his pockets to
stop himself from shaking her senseless. Why the hell did she
always have to make such a big deal out of everything? "It's
a question of values. *Indian* values, which you obviously can't
understand.''

"Because I'm an apple?'' She snorted in disgust. "Please
try to explain it to me, and I'll do my best to follow along.''

"It's looking for a quick fix. Taking the easy way out. Whatever you call it, it does nothing to build character.''

"You think poverty *does?*''

Jackson closed his eyes for a moment and sucked in a deep
breath. Beating down this woman's arguments was like swat-
ting mosquitoes in a swamp. Every time you squashed one,
three more appeared to suck your blood.

"The point I'm trying to make,'' he said, opening his eyes
and glaring at her, "is that *real* Indians, *real* Northern Cheyenne, are more concerned with values and character and the
long-term survival of our tribe than we are with chasing the
almighty dollar. That's why we haven't built a casino here.
Another good example is the way our cousins over at the Lame
Deer reservation handled the coal companies a few years ago.''

Maggie crossed her arms over her chest and leaned one
shoulder against the building. "What did they do?''

"They weren't much better off economically than we are
now, but they're sitting on one of the world's biggest coal de-
posits,'' Jackson explained. "Nobody paid any attention to it
until the energy crisis hit back in the seventies. Then, all of a
sudden, the coal companies and power companies started offering them millions of dollars for the privilege of strip-mining
on the reservation. Can you imagine how tempting it was for
them to grab that money and let Mother Earth take care of
herself?''

Maggie nodded "But they didn't?''

Jackson shook his head. "Nope. There was a big legal hassle, because the tribal council had already signed leases, on the advice of the BIA. But when they saw what was happening to the environment a few miles north of the reservation, at Colstrip, the tribe raised hell until they got those leases canceled. If they ever do develop their energy resources, it'll be on their own terms, and in a way that won't destroy their land."

"That's fascinating," Maggie said. "But I still don't see why you're being so pigheaded about the computers. They're not going to harm the environment or anything else."

"It's the *principle,* Maggie. Accepting this huge gift will not help us learn to manage our own resources, any more than taking the coal companies' money would have helped our cousins learn to manage theirs. If our kids need computers, then the tribe should find a way to provide them."

She studied him for so long, he began to hope he'd finally gotten through to her. Then she dashed his hopes with a firm shake of her head.

"You couldn't find time to confront Ed Reese for the kids. How long will they have to wait for the tribe to help them? Until it's too late to graduate with the rest of their class?"

"Probably. But it won't be the end of the world. They can get their GED certificates and still go to college."

"Oh, yeah? And how will they feel about it, Jackson? Don't you think they'll feel cheated? Damn it, it's not fair."

"Grow up, will you?" Jackson snapped. "Life is rarely fair for anyone, much less Indians."

"But this time it could be," she insisted. "Those kids have *earned* their diplomas. Denying them the chance to walk across that stage with their classmates is only going to teach them that their hard work *won't* be rewarded. The only thing it will motivate them to do is give up. Can't you see that?"

Jackson didn't want to, but when she put it that way, he had to admit she might have a point. Graduation night was always one of the worst nights of the year for underage drinking on the res. Last year, five Laughing Horse kids had been killed in an alcohol-related car accident. Grudgingly giving in to the in-

evitable, he fished his keys out of his pocket and beckoned to Harvey to start unloading.

"All right," he said as he unlocked the door. "You win this time, but don't solicit any other donations unless you clear it with the tribal council first."

"No problem. I didn't solicit *this* one. But if I ever get the urge, I'll leave it up to the *real* Indians. God knows I wouldn't want to taint anyone with my inferior white values."

Surprised at the pain he detected behind her sarcasm, Jackson shot her a quick look. Oh, man, her chin was trembling, and her long eyelashes were moving at top speed, undoubtedly blinking back tears. She always fought him so fiercely, he tended to forget the possibility of hurting her feelings.

She turned her back to him, yanked the door open wide and flipped down the doorstop for Harvey. Then she stepped inside, switched on the lights and marched down the hall to the tutoring center. Cursing under his breath, Jackson hurried after her.

When he entered the room, she was systematically pulling chairs away from the study tables. He cleared his throat. If she heard him, she ignored him.

"Look," he said, approaching her with a tentative smile. "I didn't mean anything personal."

She shoved a chair into his path, but didn't speak. He set the chair aside and, stepping closer, put his hand on her shoulder. She jerked away as if he'd stabbed her with a needle.

"Hey," he protested. "I'm trying to apologize for whatever I said that hurt your feelings."

Refusing even to look at him, she yanked another chair out of the way. "Forget it. Thanks for unlocking the door. I'll handle things from here."

"You said you were going to put me to work."

"I changed my mind."

"It's not like you to hold a grudge, Maggie."

"How would you know?"

"We've fought before, and you never did. It's one of the things I like about you."

She shot him a disbelieving glare. "Yeah, right. Why don't you be honest, Mr. Hawk, and admit you don't like me at all?"

"Because it's not true." He walked around the end of the table, smiling to himself when she straightened to her full height and faced him, like a boxer bracing for the next round. Well, fine. He'd rather have her come out swinging at him than see her in tears. "You want to tell me what I said that upset you so much?"

"No. Go away. I've got work to do."

As if to prove her point, Harvey entered the room, pushing a dolly loaded with boxes. "Where do you folks want these?"

Maggie pointed to the nearest wall. "Just stack them over there, Harvey."

Jackson waited for the other man to leave, then approached her again. "Come on, out with it. It won't be much fun touring the res together if you're mad at me."

"I've changed my mind about that, too. Thanks for the offer, but I'd prefer to drive myself."

"Don't even think about it," he said, feeling his temper starting to heat up again. "This is rough, desolate country. You've got no business being out there alone."

She opened her mouth as if she would argue the point. Fortunately, Al Black Bird walked into the room, cutting her off before she could get out a syllable.

"What's goin' on in here?" the big tribal policeman asked.

Maggie gave him a brief explanation, then went back to banging chairs around.

"Did you need something, Al?" Jackson asked.

Al tipped his baseball cap back and stuck his hands in his jeans pockets. "Yeah. Somethin's happened I think you'd better be in on, Jackson."

"What is it?"

Al glanced at Maggie, then raised an eyebrow at Jackson, as if asking whether or not he should talk in front of her. Jackson nodded.

"George Sweetwater was huntin' rabbits in the brush about

ten miles past your place this mornin',", Al said. "He found some bones out there, and he thinks they're human."

Staring at his friend, Jackson said, "Human bones?"

"Yeah. An arm and a hand." Al shrugged his beefy shoulders. "George said they look like they've been there for years. There's an old burial ground out that way, but I couldn't tell from his description whether the bones came from there. If they didn't, we could be lookin' at a homicide."

"Any idea who it would be?"

"Nope. We don't have any outstanding missing-persons reports on file. But I think you should come check it out with me. It never hurts to have a credible witness, you know?"

"Go ahead, Jackson," Maggie said quietly. "I can handle the rest of this."

He didn't doubt she could handle damn near anything, but it didn't feel right to leave her with this dispute unresolved.

"Really," she insisted. "I'll just set up a couple of the computers, and let Sara and the kids help with the rest."

Al lumbered to the doorway. "Let's go, Hawk. I want to get out there before the Feds do. I don't want them touchin' anything until we can figure out if those bones belong to an ancestor. I want to call in your old pal, Tracy Roper, 'cause I know she'll shoot straight with us."

"I'll be right there," Jackson answered. Turning to Maggie, he said, "Let's meet at my office at one tomorrow. We can finish sorting this out then, okay?"

He walked to the doorway and turned for one last look at Maggie. She stood there, staring at him with those big dark eyes of hers. There was a wounded sort of vulnerability about her that reached down into his chest and gave his heartstrings a hard yank. He gulped, searching for something to say that would make things all right between them again.

He finally settled for an unsatisfying but practical warning. "Don't turn on more than three computers at one time until we can get an electrician in here to check out the wiring."

Her only response was a nod. Biting back a frustrated curse,

Jackson left. Al waited for him at the front door, grinning like he'd just won a medal for marksmanship.

"Whoo-whee," he said. "That was some tension between you and the Little Fed in there."

Jackson brushed past the policeman. "Shut up, Al."

Al caught up with him in two strides. "Oooh, touchy, are we? You got the hots for her, or what?"

Jackson scowled at him over the top of the four-wheel-drive wagon that served as a cruiser. "Mind your own damn business."

Al slid into the driver's seat and fired the engine while Jackson climbed in on the other side. "Can't say as I blame you," he said, as if Jackson hadn't spoken. "That Maggie's somethin' else. I really like the way she smiles, you know? Kinda lights up the whole room. She sure wasn't smilin' at you, though, buddy. Whatcha do to her?"

"Damned if I know," Jackson muttered. Then he put on his sunglasses, dragged the brim of his hat down over his face, crossed his arms over his chest and slid down until his head rested on the back of the seat.

"Hey, if you don't wanna talk, all you have to do is say so." Chuckling, Al grabbed the microphone, radioed his position to the office and drove away from the curb.

Jackson tuned him out, his thoughts immediately returning to Maggie. Damn it, he knew better than to let a woman manipulate him with tears. So why did the memory of Maggie struggling not to shed them make him feel so stinkin' guilty? Especially when she was too immature to just come out and tell him what he'd done? Talk about manipulative!

But the hurt in her eyes and in her voice had gone deeper than that. Just picturing the way she'd looked before he left made him feel like he'd kicked a defenseless puppy. Which was about the most ridiculous notion he could imagine.

Maggie was hardly defenseless. She'd taken on both Reese and Baldwin this morning, and she'd still had plenty of steam left to rake him over the proverbial coals. That woman could take on a tank and win, for God's sake.

The funny thing was, in the everyday scheme of things, she didn't come across as a combative sort of person. Too many people on the res liked her for that to be true. In fact, other than their first meeting, when he'd deliberately provoked her, the only times he'd seen her temper flare had been connected with her efforts to help the teenagers.

He could hardly blame her for that; in fact, he admired her protectiveness toward those kids tremendously. Because of it, he'd actually started to look forward to showing her the rest of the res, in spite of his ambivalent feelings toward her.

Maybe his ambivalence was the key to this whole mess. He'd been trying so hard not to like her more than he should, he'd convinced her he didn't like her at all. Aw, hell, now that he thought about it, it wasn't hard to see how she'd come to that conclusion.

He'd treated her like she was nothing but trouble on the hoof from the beginning. Even when it had become perfectly clear that she was only trying to help, he'd questioned everything she did, not to mention the integrity of her boss and her father. And he'd been damn suspicious and condescending, because...well, because he was scared spitless to trust his reactions to her.

It hadn't *really* been necessary to make such a big stink about those computers. While he believed wholeheartedly in the principle of self-reliance, he could bend a principle when circumstances warranted it; building self-esteem in the tribe's young people warranted almost any amount of bending.

He could have just said thank-you on behalf of the tribe and accepted Maggie's father's generous gift. But had he? No, he'd thrown it back in her face, and made all kinds of nasty remarks about a man she obviously loved a lot.

It was time to stop acting like a jackass. As Uncle Frank had said, women like Maggie didn't come along every day. He'd fought his attraction to her for as long as he could, but he might as well admit it was no use.

Maggie challenged him, intrigued him, infuriated him and confused the hell out of him. If he allowed himself to get close

to her, she might well break his heart. But damn it all, whenever he was with her, he felt more alive than he had in years. And somehow, some way, he just had to find out what made her tick.

Six

When the hollow sound of Jackson's bootheels hitting the tile floor had faded away, Maggie swallowed at the lump in her throat. Then she gritted her teeth, squared her shoulders and went back to work. She would *not* cry over that man. And she was *not* going to tour the res with him, either. She'd rather get lost out in the boondocks and never be heard from again than accept the tiniest scrap of help from that arrogant jerk.

By tomorrow she would have her emotions back under control, and she'd tell him what he could do with his proposition and where he could put his *real* Indian values. With anger fueling her energy, she rearranged the room, set up three of the systems and loaded the software onto the computers' hard drives, finishing as the school buses arrived from Whitehorn.

A moment later, the building's main doors crashed open and an excited babble of voices filled the hallway. Wanda Weasel Tail burst into the room, followed by a herd of other teenagers.

"Miss Schaeffer! Miss Schaeffer!" Wanda called, gleefully racing over to Maggie. "You'll never guess what happened today. We got library books!"

"I don't know what you did to those librarians," Nina Walks Tall said, "but I wish I'd a been there to see it."

Janie Brown Bear dumped her backpack on the big round study table, headed after the other girls, then stopped and did a double take when she spotted one of the computers. Her mouth fell open, and an awed expression came over her face as she looked around the room. "Hey, where did all this stuff come from?"

The other girls stopped chattering for a second, shooting irritated glances at Janie. She pointed at a gleaming monitor. Wanda and Nina followed the direction of her finger. Then, as

if they'd communicated some signal only teenagers could hear, all three girls started jumping up and down and shrieking in delight.

More kids rushed in to see what was going on. Their surprised and happy shouts brought people running from all over the building. Luckily, Sara Lewis was among the newcomers. After assuring the crowd that everyone would eventually have a chance to use the machines, she shooed out the folks who were supposed to be somewhere else with the skill of a born organizer.

Then she organized those who remained into a work detail to set up the remaining systems. When Maggie relayed Jackson's warning about the wiring, Sara called the employment office at the tribal headquarters. Two unemployed electricians arrived in short order.

For the next two hours, Maggie hurried from group to group, checking connections, demonstrating how to load software and marveling at how well the kids cooperated with each other. They were so appreciative and eager to learn, she wanted to hug them all. Their excitement over the new equipment provided a sorely needed balm to the emotional wounds Jackson had inflicted.

By the time the last reluctant straggler left for home at dusk, however, she felt wrung out. She wanted a hot shower and solitude. Hours and hours of solitude, and at least twenty-four hours of sleep. She nearly groaned out loud when Sara suggested a celebration as they walked out of the building together.

"I'm really whipped, Sara," Maggie said. "Would you be offended if I asked for a rain check?"

"After what you've accomplished today, you couldn't offend me if you tried," Sara replied with a sympathetic grin. "As long as you promise to tell me what you did to Reese. I want to hear every gory detail."

Maintaining a deadpan expression, Maggie shrugged. "Oh, it was nothing. I just walked into his office, shoved a gun in his face, and he caved right in."

Sara laughed. "Yeah, right. Do you realize all the teachers

in Whitehorn are wondering why they suddenly got orders to take their Indian kids to the library today? Some of my friends called me to talk about it. And I'll bet we can get the school district to set up evening or weekend keyboarding classes out here for the kids and the adults. This is really going to open up some opportunities, Maggie. It's just wonderful.''

"I'm glad I could help, but it wasn't that big of a deal.''

"It was a very big deal to the kids,'' Sara said. "Now, tell me, where did all of that stuff come from?''

Fearing Sara would react as Jackson had if she knew the source of the new equipment, Maggie said, "It was a corporate donation, Sara. I just happened to mention the kids to a C.E.O. friend of mine, and he sent the computers right out.''

"We should all have such friends,'' Sara said with a grin. "You'd better watch your step, though. You've made a big impression on the kids. I wouldn't be surprised to see every one of those girls walk in with short hair tomorrow.''

Recalling her conversation with Jackson, Maggie winced. "Lord, I hope not. I'm not exactly great role model material for Indian kids.''

"How can you say that?'' Sara demanded, scowling at her. "You gave them hope, and showed them one person can make a difference. Sounds like pretty good role model material for any kind of kids to me.''

Wishing she'd kept her mouth shut, Maggie shook her head dismissively and forced a smile. Sara was not about to be put off so easily, however. Pausing beside her car, she studied Maggie through narrowed eyes.

"You should be higher than a kite. The library books were a major victory by themselves, but to get the computers, too, is a miracle.''

"Look, I've really got to go,'' Maggie said. "The road to Whitehorn's bad enough in the daytime. I'd rather not tackle it when it's any darker than it already is.''

Sara grasped Maggie's arm when she would have turned away. "Wait a minute. What's wrong, Maggie?''

"It's nothing. Really. I've just had a long day.''

Though she raised a doubtful eyebrow, Sara released Maggie's arm. "Okay. I can understand that, I guess. But if you ever want to talk or anything, you know where to find me."

"Yeah. Thanks, Sara. I'll see you later."

Maggie headed on toward the tribal center. The last rays of the sunset had faded to a deep navy blue, and the stars were coming out. Maggie slowed to look at them, suddenly feeling terribly small and alone. Seeing her little rental car sitting all by itself where she'd parked it in front of the tribal offices this morning reinforced the feeling.

Sara honked and waved when she drove away from the school, dispelling Maggie's blue mood for a moment. She waved back, then nearly had a coronary when she turned around and saw a man step out of a doorway on the other side of the street. She was always ultracareful about being out alone at night in Washington, but Laughing Horse had such a small-town ambience, she hadn't thought much about her personal security.

She stopped walking, hoping he would go the other way. The man didn't. He looked big and dark, and his face was obscured by the deep shadows cast by the brim of his Stetson. And he was walking straight toward her, as if he meant business. Adrenaline surging, she backed up a step, then another, struggling to stay calm and remember what she'd learned in the self-defense class she took last year.

"Relax, Maggie, it's me," Jackson said.

She halted her retreat, pressing one hand over her heart, as if that would still its frantic pounding. He stopped less than a foot in front of her, tipped back his hat and looked down at her, his forehead creased with concern. "Are you all right?"

"Fine. You just scared the devil out of me," she said with a shaky laugh. She took two steps back to put a more comfortable distance between them. "What are you doing here so late?"

"Waiting for you."

"Why?"

He spread his feet farther apart and stuck the tips of his fingers into his back pockets. "I wanted to talk to you."

"Oh, please," she said. "Couldn't it wait? I don't have enough energy to fight with you again today."

"I said talk, not fight."

"We don't seem to be able to do one without doing the other." She sidestepped around him and made a beeline for her car.

He followed her, easily catching up with his longer stride. "Yeah, I know. I wanted to apologize for that."

Maggie shot him a skeptical look, then stuck her key in the door lock. "Don't bother. I know you don't like me, and that's your privilege, Jackson. Believe me, I can handle it."

"It didn't look that way to me," he said. "When I left, you were damn near ready to cry."

Nuts. She'd hoped he hadn't noticed. "I got over it."

"Well, I didn't." Raising one hand, he brushed the backs of his knuckles across her cheek. "I felt guilty all afternoon."

She pushed his hand away, not because his touch felt bad, but because it felt too good. "I cry sometimes when I'm really angry. It's embarrassing, but it's no big problem."

"You weren't just angry. You were hurt."

"Even apples have feelings, Mr. Hawk."

He smiled at that. "So do bigots, Ms. Schaeffer. You know, when we start arguing, neither one of us knows when to shut up. Were you ever on a debating team?"

His question pulled a reluctant grin from her. "How did you know?"

"Just a wild guess." He chuckled, then gazed at her for a long moment, his expression turning sober. "But you've got one thing wrong, Maggie. I don't dislike you."

She rolled her eyes at him. "Give me a break. I don't feel like getting into that again now, so—"

He laid one finger across her lips. "This is one of those times you should shut up. I tried to tell you this before I left, but you weren't ready to listen. The truth is, I like you a lot. I'm even...attracted to you."

Maggie raised her eyebrows in disbelief. Chuckling again, Jackson traced her upper lip with his forefinger. Soft as dandelion fluff, his touch left a trail of tingling nerve endings behind it.

"You don't believe me?" He stepped closer, crowding her against the side of the car, framing her face between his big hands when she tried to lean away from him. "Well, I guess I'll have to prove it to you."

Staring in stupefaction, she watched his head slowly descend, the brim of his hat blocking out what little light there was on the deserted street. Though she'd literally seen it coming, she started when his mouth brushed against hers.

"Easy, I won't bite..." he murmured. He slid his right hand into her hair, above her ear, and curved his long fingers around the back of her head. "Close your eyes, Maggie."

His voice was so low, so gentle, she obeyed automatically. And then his mouth closed over hers with a passion that stole the oxygen from her lungs and demanded a response.

"God, you're sweet." He tilted his head in the opposite direction, then took her mouth again, as if he had all the time in the world.

Kissing Jackson was better than anything she'd imagined, and she'd fantasized enough about him to have imagined plenty. She'd thought it would be hot and exciting, maybe a little dangerous and overpowering. It was all of those things, and more. It was like her first dive off the high board, like taking on raging white water in a flimsy rubber raft, like the great shrieking rush you get just before you hit the end of a bungee cord.

She opened her mouth, eager for the taste and feel of his tongue stroking hers. He accepted her invitation with a muffled groan. She raised her hands to his chest. Her fingertips pressed into his hard muscles, and she felt his heart hammering beneath her palms. She heard his harsh, choppy breaths—or maybe they were hers. She didn't know or care. The only thing she knew for certain at the moment was, she wanted to get closer. Much, much closer.

As if he'd read her mind, he dropped his left arm to her hips and pulled her flush against him. Her mouth went dry and her knees went weak when the rigid length of his arousal pressed into her belly. It felt…intimate. Too intimate. Too fast. Too out of control.

Wrenching her mouth from his, she said, "Jackson, no. Stop. Please, stop."

His arm around her hips loosened, but he didn't let her go completely until she found the strength to push against his chest. He shook his head, as if to clear it, then dropped his arms to his sides and turned away from her. Well, damn, she thought, shivering from the sudden lack of warmth. Knowing Jackson, he'd probably add being a tease to her long list of faults.

To her surprise, however, he looked over his shoulder and gave her a rueful grin. "Now do you believe me?"

"About what?"

"That I'm attracted to you."

"Oh, uh, well…sure," she stammered, fighting to suppress the fit of hysterical laughter bubbling up inside her. God, how had she gotten herself into this situation, with Jackson Hawk, of all people? "I, uh, I guess so…"

"You only *guess* so?" Turning back around, he waggled his eyebrows at her. His rueful grin became wicked. "You want more proof? I'll be happy to give you another demonstration."

"No, Jackson." She wrapped her arms around herself and backed away from him. "Thank you, but once was, uh, sufficient."

He held up both hands in a classic gesture of innocence. "I know things got a little carried away there for a minute, but you don't have to be afraid of me."

"I'm not, really. I'm just a little, uh…stunned."

"You didn't hate it, did you?"

"No." Her voice came out in a hoarse croak. She cleared her throat and tried again. "No, I didn't hate it."

"Does that mean you liked it?"

"Do you really expect me to answer that?"

He gave her another one of those wicked grins. "If you don't, I may have to try it again. Just to make sure I didn't get the wrong signals, or anything."

She couldn't help laughing at such a blatant attempt at manipulation. She couldn't resist taking a poke at his ego, either. "It was okay. On a scale of one to ten, I'd give it about a... four."

"Only a four, huh?" He hung his head, then looked up at her and winked. "I guess I'll have to practice."

"Why this sudden change of heart, Jackson?"

"It's not really sudden." He rested his hip against the side of her car and crossed his arms over his chest. "You were right about some of the things you said today."

"What things?"

"Bigotry, for one. I don't like it in other people, and I sure don't like it in myself. But it's there, all right." Sighing, he shook his head. "You've been catching the brunt of some things that happened a long time before I met you. I'm sorry, Maggie. You didn't deserve it."

There was no doubting his sincerity this time. Maggie gazed into his dark eyes and saw stark memories of pain. Feeling privileged that he had trusted her enough to let her see it, she stepped closer. "Do you want to talk about it?"

"Not right now." He reached out and caressed her cheek with the tips of his fingers. "I know you're tired. We'll have lots of time to talk when we're driving all over the res."

She pulled back, scowling at him. "Is that why you kissed me? Because I said I'd changed my mind?"

Jackson straightened away from the car, dropped a quick, hard kiss on her lips, and opened the door for her. "No. I kissed you because I damn well wanted to. In fact, if you don't get out of here in the next thirty seconds, I'll probably do it again, because I still want to."

Maggie slid into the driver's seat, then rolled down the window when Jackson shut the door for her. "I'm not comfortable with this. I don't mix business relationships with personal ones. If you're expecting—"

"I'm not expecting anything," Jackson said, interrupting her. "Why don't we pretend we just met, and try to be friends, for starters?"

"Do you really think that's possible? Just being friends?"

His wicked grin returned. Bracing one hand on the window opening, he leaned down until they were eye-to-eye. "I like my women willing. You won't have any problem resisting me, if my kisses only rate a four, Maggie."

Oh, you wretch, she thought, smiling in spite of her better judgment. "That sounds like a challenge."

"You started it. But, hey, if you don't think you can handle it..." Allowing his voice to trail off, he shrugged as if it didn't matter to him whether or not she accepted it.

Though she wasn't at all certain she *could* handle his challenge, Maggie wouldn't have admitted it to him under torture. "All right. I'll see you tomorrow at one."

She started the car and backed out of the parking slot as Jackson raised one hand to wave her off. Tapping the brake, she stuck her head out of the window and called to him, "Hey, Jackson? That kiss was closer to a six."

Then she drove away, with the sound of his laughter echoing in her wake. She smiled all the way to the junction with highway 191, the road back to Whitehorn. In truth, that kiss had been more like a fifteen, but she didn't want him to get any more conceited than he already was. Besides, it would be fun to see how hard he was willing to work to improve his score.

As she turned south and the miles passed, however, doubts about the wisdom of getting more personally involved with Jackson crept into her mind. Whether or not either of them wanted to admit it, they were heading in that direction. He was the most complicated, fascinating man she'd ever met, and by far the best kisser. Knowing he was as physically attracted to her as she was to him had given her ego a nice boost.

What worried her was that if Jackson continued to be as charming as he'd been tonight, it might not be all that difficult for her to fall in love with him. She couldn't afford to do it. There was the promise to her mother, for one thing. For an-

other, much as she was enjoying her time at Laughing Horse, she didn't want to live there permanently. It was impossible to imagine Jackson living anywhere else.

Her mother had consistently advised her to stand on her own two feet and never depend on a man to support her. Maggie had taken the advice to heart, and she had no regrets for having done so. While she was starting to have some uneasy feelings about Congressman Baldwin, she loved her work a great deal. She wanted to get married and have children someday, but not at the expense of her career.

"Wait a minute, Schaeffer," she muttered. "You're getting way ahead of yourself. Jackson didn't say anything about love or marriage. He just wants to take you to bed."

It was a disheartening thought, but one she couldn't ignore. She hadn't been living in a convent, after all. She'd dated enough to know what men wanted from women, and it usually wasn't a commitment. Her unwillingness to engage in sex without one had ended more than a few promising relationships.

She hadn't mourned over her lost relationships, though. Not for long, anyway. Her life was busy and fulfilling, and only one of those men had ever turned her on enough to tempt her into bed with him in the first place. Of course, if any of the others had ever kissed her the way Jackson had, she might not be feeling quite so virtuous.

Lord, just thinking about it was enough to make her toes curl and her heart pound with anticipation of the next one. And there would, undoubtedly, be a next one. Oh, drat the man. He certainly had a gift for keeping her in a constant state of confusion about *some*thing. How did he manage to do that?

Reducing her speed as she entered the Whitehorn city limits, Maggie heaved a weary sigh. Well, it was too late to back out now. When she arrived at the motel, she would go straight to bed and get a good night's sleep. She had a feeling she would need every bit of strength she could muster in order to deal with Jackson Hawk tomorrow.

Jackson spent the next morning helping his uncle catch up on tribal business. The hours passed in a flurry of paperwork

and arguments over how he'd handled this problem or that one, but Maggie was never far from his thoughts. After a long night of too little sleep and too much reflection, he had come to the brilliant conclusion that he never should have kissed her.

He honestly hadn't intended to. He'd only meant to make sure she was okay and try to reestablish a decent working relationship. But then he'd watched her come out of the school with Sara and heard almost every word the two women had said.

Knowing Maggie *had* been higher than a kite when she came back from her confrontation with Reese, that she'd been high again when the computers arrived, and that he'd smashed her pleasure in both events, had made him feel like a mean bastard all over again.

His guilt had grown when she left Sara and crossed the street, looking so discouraged. Then he'd unwittingly scared the hell out of her; he didn't even want to imagine what a woman from a crime-ridden city like Washington must have felt when he came at her out of the darkness the way he had. And when she'd stood there in the street, fiercely rejecting his apology...well, damn, he'd have done almost anything to earn her forgiveness.

Like an idiot, he'd gone too far, of course. But then, he seemed to overreact to just about everything when he was with Maggie. He knew he'd overreacted to the power of that kiss, too. He would have rated it higher than a four or a six, but it hadn't really been all *that* spectacular. Had it?

The only way to be absolutely sure, of course, was to kiss her again. He wanted to. Oh, yeah, he wanted to do it so bad, his lips itched. But what if it *had* been as spectacular as he remembered? He could get addicted to that kind of pleasure. And then he'd want more and more and more. Oh, hell, who was he trying to kid? He'd already made love to her in his fantasies at least fifty times.

No matter where he was or what he was trying to do, Maggie nagged at the edges of his mind, like a pesky fly that wouldn't

go away, but wouldn't land anywhere so he could swat it. Like a TV with the sound turned low enough he couldn't quite hear it, but loud enough that he couldn't quite ignore it, either. Like a song whose melody haunted him, but whose lyrics he could only half remember.

She was just always *there*. He didn't know if he really wanted to resist her. Or if he even *could* resist her if he really wanted to. Now, if that wasn't a confusing mess for a supposedly rational lawyer to find himself in, he'd like to know what was.

"I don't know where your brain is, nephew, but it sure as hell ain't here," Frank said, scowling at Jackson. "What's goin' on with you?"

"Nothing."

Frank threw down his pen, shoved back his chair and stood. "Well, I'm starvin' to death. Let's get some lunch."

"I can't, uncle. I'm taking Maggie for a tour of the res this afternoon."

A knowing smile spread across Frank's face. "Well, I guess that explains it."

"Explains what?"

"The nothing that's goin' on with you." Chuckling, Frank walked out the door, calling, *"Ne-sta-va-voomatse,"* as he left.

"Right, I'll see you later, uncle," Jackson replied.

He glanced at his watch and felt a sharp surge of anticipation in the center of his chest. Since it was almost one o'clock, and Maggie operated on white man's time, she should be here any minute. Would she be nervous about seeing him again? he wondered. As nervous as he was about seeing her?

Disgusted with himself for that admission, he gathered up the papers he'd been working on, muttering, "For God's sake, it was just a kiss."

His heart lurched when he heard the outer door open, followed by muffled footsteps. And then Maggie appeared in the doorway of his office, wearing jeans, sneakers, and a bright purple shirt with intricate beading on the collar under her jacket. Her shy smile warmed him, driving every rational, self-

preserving thought from his head. Damn, but he was glad to see her.

"Hello, Jackson," she said.

"Hello, Maggie."

She paused just inside the doorway, as if she weren't sure what to expect from him. "Are you ready to go?"

Smiling at her, Jackson pushed himself to his feet. Before he could say anything, however, the outer door opened again.

"Hello?" a feminine voice he didn't recognize called from the end of the hallway. "Is someone there?"

Maggie looked at Jackson, her eyebrows raised in a silent query. When he shrugged to let her know he wasn't expecting anybody, she stepped back into the hallway and said, "Down here, ma'am. May I help you?"

"Well, actually, I was hoping I could help you," the woman said, her words accompanied by the staccato clicking of high heels striking the tile floor.

Maggie shot Jackson an amused glance. A second later, he understood why. The woman who walked into his office was a delicate, fortyish blonde who looked as if she ought to be heading for a ladies' luncheon at a country club.

She wore a pastel-pink suit with a short, straight skirt, a white scoop-necked blouse, and pearls at her ears and throat. She carried a small handbag the same color as her shoes, three-inch spikes that had, no doubt, been dyed to match her outfit. Her makeup was subtle and flattering, every strand of her shoulder-length hair was combed into place, and her perfectly manicured fingernails told him any work she did with her hands was rarely more strenuous than arranging flowers.

The woman stood in the middle of the room for a moment, glancing from Jackson to Maggie and back to Jackson, obviously trying to figure out which one of them was in charge. Impatient to learn her business and get on with his afternoon with Maggie, Jackson said, "What can we do for you, miss?"

"Oh, it's Mrs.," she said, raising her left hand to her necklace, flashing a ring with a diamond the size of an acorn in it. Then she gave him a sweet smile and offered her dainty right

hand to him. "Mrs. Dugin Kincaid. But please, call me Mary Jo. Everyone does."

"Jackson Hawk," he said, reluctantly shaking her hand. Oh, great, he thought grimly, *Maheo* knew he'd always wanted to be on a first-name basis with Jeremiah Kincaid's daughter-in-law. Maggie came forward and offered the woman a chair.

"It's a pleasure to meet you, Mary Jo," she said, shooting Jackson a warning scowl. "I'm Maggie Schaeffer. I'm working with the tribe on a temporary assignment for Congressman Baldwin."

The woman settled herself on the straight-backed wooden chair, responding graciously to Maggie's efforts to make polite small talk. After five minutes, Jackson had heard all the get-acquainted chitchat he could stand. He cleared his throat to gain the women's attention.

"What brings you to Laughing Horse, Mrs. Kincaid?" he asked.

"Well, I know this may sound a bit strange, but if you'll bear with me, I'll do my best to explain," she said. "You see, Duggie and I were having dinner at the club last night, and I heard this rumor about you folks out here, and I just *had* to find out if it was true. I mean, I didn't really know if I'd be welcome, or anything, but then I thought, why not? It never hurts to ask, does it?"

Jackson broke in when she finally paused to take a breath. "Excuse me, Mrs. Kincaid. Would you mind telling us what the rumor was?"

"Oh, silly me, didn't I tell you?" She let out a giggle that was annoyingly girlish for a woman her age, tipped her head to one side and batted her eyelashes at him. The effect was less than charming, as far as Jackson was concerned, but he answered as patiently as he could.

"No, I don't believe you did."

"Well, what I heard was that you folks will be starting a children's library out here soon, and I just happen to be a children's librarian. You see, I used to work at the library in town, but I had to quit when I married Duggie, because he's on the

library board and he didn't really think it was proper for his wife to work for money. We have a certain…position to maintain in the community, you know.''

Her light, breathless chatter grated on Jackson's nerves almost as much as the ultrafeminine little gestures she made with her hands did. Honest to God, watching her talk was like watching hummingbirds zipping from flower to flower in his mother's garden. He caught another warning scowl from Maggie, however, and decided to keep his mouth shut for the moment.

''Anyway,'' Mary Jo rattled on, ''I just love children, and since it's all right if I volunteer to work for a worthy cause, I hoped you might be willing to allow me to organize your new children's library. I really am a very good librarian.''

''We've discussed the idea of starting a children's library, but I'm afraid we're still at the thinking stage,'' Jackson said. ''We don't have any definite plans.''

''Oh,'' Mary Jo said, her shoulders slumping, as if she were terribly disappointed. ''I see. Then it was just a rumor.''

''That was an awfully kind offer,'' Maggie said. ''Organizing a library must be a huge undertaking.''

Mary Jo gave her a sad smile. ''Well, yes, it is, but I would have loved doing it. I'm just not used to being idle, and I miss being around children so much.''

''There's an after-school tutoring program you might enjoy,'' Maggie suggested. ''We can always use volunteers to help the children with their homework.''

Mary Jo perked right up, beaming at Maggie as if she'd offered her a winning lottery ticket. ''Really? That sounds wonderful. Could I work with the little ones?''

''You'll have to talk to Sara Lewis about that,'' Jackson said, sending Maggie a warning scowl of his own. It was bad enough this woman was a Kincaid, but her personality alone would drive him to drink, if he had to be around her much. ''She's in charge of the program.''

Mary Jo flashed him a brilliant smile. ''I'll do it today. Oh, this will be such fun. You know, I've always been fascinated with Indians, and they talk about you folks in town all the time.

Why, this morning one of our neighbors told me you found a body out here yesterday. Is that just another rumor?''

''No, it's partly true, Mrs. Kincaid,'' Jackson said, hoping to scare her off for good. ''We've only found a skeletonized arm and hand so far, but Dr. Hunter has assured the tribal police they were human remains.''

Mary Jo shuddered delicately. ''How gruesome. Do you think there was...murder involved?''

Encouraged by her shudder, Jackson decided to lay it on good and thick. ''We won't know for certain until we find the rest of the skeleton, but I wouldn't be surprised if it was. We've had such a bad history of violence at Laughing Horse, the FBI is sending in a forensic specialist to study the case.''

''Really? Do you think they'll be able to solve it?''

Jackson studied Mary Jo for a moment. Nuts. The woman seemed to be more interested in learning the gory details of a crime than scared. This was one weird lady. She made all the right noises, but somehow, they just didn't ring true.

''I guess we'll see,'' he said. ''You should be extremely careful when you come out here, Mrs. Kincaid. If there was foul play attached to those bones, the murderer is probably still running loose, right here on the reservation.''

''Oh, my goodness,'' Mary Jo murmured. She shuddered again, then stood and said, ''Well, I must go now, but I'll be back to work with the children. And I will be careful, I promise. Thanks again. I'll see you later.''

With a cheery wave, she left the room, trailing a cloud of expensive perfume. Jackson waited until he heard the outer door bang shut before looking at Maggie. Arms folded across her chest, she was studying him as intently as he'd studied Mary Jo Kincaid. Uh-oh. It didn't take a psychic to tell him he was in for it again.

Seven

Maggie met and held Jackson's challenging gaze for the space of a heartbeat, then lowered her hands to her sides. She had spent the morning in her motel room, organizing her notes and thinking about him. After analyzing their stormy relationship to date, she had decided to take Jackson at his word and accept his suggestion that they start over and try to be friends.

In the spirit of that decision, she was determined to reserve comment on his behavior toward Mary Jo Kincaid until he asked for her opinion. And maybe, with luck and patience, they could learn to have calm, rational discussions, instead of fierce, energy-draining debates.

"I'm ready to leave, if you are," she said with a smile. "Do you want to take your car or mine?"

His eyebrows rose halfway up his forehead, and he stared at her for a moment. Then his face and shoulders relaxed, and the corners of his mouth curved into a grin. He grabbed his hat from the top of the bookshelf behind his desk, plunked it on his head and motioned for her to precede him through the doorway.

"We'll take my truck. I want to show you the grazing leases first, and the roads are rough out there."

Neither of them spoke again as they headed out of Laughing Horse in his battered red pickup, traveling southwest on a gravel road. Maggie settled back in the seat and gazed out the side window. The homesteads gradually came fewer and farther between, bearing little resemblance to the well-kept farms and ranches she'd seen on the outskirts of Whitehorn.

There were no stately red barns, no satellite dishes, no elaborate sprinkler systems. Many of the houses were unpretentious clapboards with faded and peeling paint and the Spartan,

cookie-cutter sameness of government construction. Others were little more than log cabins or tar-paper shacks surrounded by sagging fences and the rusting carcasses of junked vehicles, farm machinery and appliances. Some had a few chickens scratching at the dirt in the front yard, a privy and a sagging clothesline out back. Occasionally she saw a horse or a mangy-looking dog, but if there were people around, they remained out of sight.

Maggie had seen plenty of urban poverty before, but she found this rural variety wrenched her heart with equal, if not greater, force. Americans frequently heard about the problems of the poor in their cities on the nightly news. These grim, isolated pockets of dreariness were much easier for the media to ignore; the people who struggled to survive out here were all-too-often forgotten.

In stark contrast to the homesteads, the landscape provided a backdrop of breathtaking scenery. To the west, the jagged, snowcapped peaks of the Crazy Mountains soared into the clear blue sky like a prayer reaching for heaven. The grass covering the foothills was turning green. A large bird, probably an eagle or a hawk, floated on the air currents high overhead.

Such poverty in the midst of so much rich natural beauty struck Maggie as some kind of a cruel joke. Did her mother's family live in a ramshackle place like that one? Did Jackson? He finally broke the silence, startling her out of her reverie.

"Well?" he asked.

Maggie looked at him, raising one eyebrow at the gruff demand in his voice. "Well, what?"

"Aren't you going to tell me what a paranoid bigot I am again?"

"Do you really want me to?"

"Not particularly, but I know that's what you're thinking. You might as well go ahead and say it."

Chuckling at his disgruntled tone, she shifted around on the seat until she was partially facing him. "I think you're hearing the voice of your own guilty conscience, because you fibbed to Mrs. Kincaid."

A grin tugged at the corners of Jackson's mouth. "No, I didn't. Nothing I said was really a lie."

"Oh, huh! The story I heard, was that the elders were pretty darn positive those bones came from the old burial ground, which was why they've locked them up until the FBI's forensic specialist can get here. And you deliberately led that poor woman to believe there's a vicious killer on the loose."

He shrugged. "She can believe whatever she wants. But tell me, what did you really think of her?"

"I'm not sure," she said. "She was nice enough, I guess, but maybe a little...strange."

"Only a little?" he shot her a disbelieving look, then turned his attention to the road again and shook his head.

"Well, actually, I thought she was pretty ditzy," Maggie admitted with a laugh, "but I thought she seemed sincere about wanting to help."

"She wants something, all right, but I doubt it has anything to do with the library, or the kids."

"Why, Jackson?"

"For starters, good ol' Duggie and his father despise Indians. I can't believe either one of them would approve of her volunteering to work out here, no matter how worthy the cause. It just doesn't fit, unless there's some other motive involved."

Maggie opened her eyes wide and lowered her voice to a spooky whisper. "Maybe she's on a mission to infiltrate the tribe and spy for Jeremiah. Maybe she's a pervert who gets off on kiddie library books. Maybe she's a commie pinko rat!"

Jackson snorted with laughter. "Stop makin' fun of me, Schaeffer. There's something weird about that woman, and you know it."

"Agreed, but can you really imagine that ditzy little woman being involved in Jeremiah's business affairs? And if he wanted to send in a spy, wouldn't you expect him to be more subtle than to use his own daughter-in-law?"

"Who knows what to expect from that guy?"

"What if Mary Jo's last name was Smith or Jones, instead of Kincaid? Would you still be suspicious of her?"

"Probably. Does that make me a bigot?"

"I didn't call you a bigot," Maggie said, struggling to hold on to her patience. "I said you might have a problem with bigotry. For whatever it's worth, I think we all have a touch of it somewhere in our souls."

"Okay. So why do you think I have such a problem with it?"

"Because you seem to suspect the motives of every white person who offers to do anything good for the tribe. Why don't you trust any of them?"

"Why do you trust all of them?"

Maggie shook her head in exasperation. "I don't. But I at least try to give people the benefit of the doubt until they prove me wrong, Jackson."

"That's fine on a personal basis. But when you're responsible for the well-being of two thousand people, you can't afford to make mistakes."

"Somebody must have really hurt you to make you feel that way," Maggie said quietly.

Jackson laughed again, but there was no humor in it this time. "Don't try to psychoanalyze me. I'm not one bit more suspicious of whites than anyone else who grew up on the res."

"Yes, you are, and it's really a personal thing with you. Come on, Jackson, talk to me. If we're going to be friends, I need to understand."

He pulled over to the side of the road, switched off the ignition and turned to face her. "Look, Maggie, I'm not saying this to be insulting, but I don't think anyone with your background really *can* understand."

Maggie opened her mouth to protest, but he held up one hand like a traffic cop. "Give me a minute, and then you can yell at me all you want. The truth is, you've had a rich white daddy smoothing the way for you with his money and influence. My guess is, all the stuff he donated to your schools probably bought you a lot of acceptance from the teachers and the other kids."

"You mean, they didn't all love me for my charm, intelli-

gence and good looks?'' Maggie asked, her tongue firmly planted in her cheek.

He shot her a quelling glance. ''Your intelligence and good looks, maybe. I wouldn't bet on the other one. Anyway, what I was trying to say is, the rest of us weren't that lucky. We couldn't even go to school in Whitehorn back then.''

''Where did you go?''

''To a BIA boarding school in Oklahoma.''

''What was it like?''

''I guess it was better than my parents had it, but I thought it was worse than being sent to prison.'' Jackson's eyes took on a faraway cast. ''My father was a traditional medicine man. He was determined we would know our own culture, and we spoke very little English at home. The teachers at the school were equally determined to turn us into little white people. We weren't allowed to speak anything *but* English there. Since I was more afraid of the teachers than I was of my dad, I focused on English. My Cheyenne vocabulary is still at a six-year-old's level.''

''It must have been hard for your parents to let you go so far from home, when you were still so little.''

''They didn't have a choice. If they wanted to receive any of the government benefits they needed to survive, all of their children had to be enrolled. It was blackmail, really, and it broke my father's heart to see his children being systematically stripped of everything he'd tried to teach us.''

''How often did you get to go home, Jackson?''

''Once a year. For about six weeks in the summer. All year long, I'd live for those few days at home, but then I'd get here and everything would feel so strange, I couldn't relax. My father would try to undo all the damage he thought my teachers had done to me, and we didn't get along very well. It became a classic Catch-22.''

''In what way?'' Maggie asked.

''At school I was too Indian. At home I had too many white ideas. Wherever I was, there was always somebody ready and willing to tell me there was something wrong with me.''

Jackson gave Maggie a lopsided grin that made her want to weep for the sad little boy he must have been.

"How did you ever cope with that?" she asked.

He studied her face for a moment, then scowled at her. "Don't feel sorry for me. I was one of the lucky ones. At least I was tough enough to survive."

"Some of them didn't?"

Jackson grimly shook his head. "There were always kids who couldn't stand the homesickness and the regimentation. Some of them decided suicide was the only way out. Others ran away and died of exposure before anyone found them, or they just plain vanished. Who knows what happened to them?"

"God, that's awful. You didn't ever think about..."

"Killing myself? Sure I did. I was just too damned mean to give anybody the satisfaction of getting rid of me."

"Oh, Jackson, that's a terrible thing to say."

"That's how it felt sometimes, Maggie. Especially after they shook up the whole system and I had to come back and go to high school in Whitehorn. Believe me, I was one screwed-up kid. I don't know how my parents tolerated me at all."

"Most teenagers rebel at one time or another," Maggie said.

"Yeah, well, I did more than my share. Most of the other kids got into alcohol or drugs, but I chose the one way guaranteed to hurt my father the most."

"What was that?"

"I turned my back on the tribe. I let everybody know I couldn't wait to leave the res, and that I never intended to come back. If I had to choose between the white world and the Indian one, by God, I was gonna go with the winners."

"Is that why you went to law school?"

He nodded. "I thought if I could study hard enough, assimilate enough and make enough money, it wouldn't matter who I was or where I'd come from. People would have to accept me, whether they wanted to or not."

"So, I'm not the only apple around here," she said.

"Not hardly. It takes one to know one." Uttering a bitter laugh, he shook his head again. "That's why you bugged me

so much the first time we met. You reminded me too much of myself. I guess I owe you another apology for that.''

She nodded in acceptance, then asked, ''Why did you come back here, Jackson?''

''I finally realized I'd been fooling myself and selling my soul at the same time. Whites will accept you to the degree you can assimilate, but sooner or later, you'll slip up and remind them you're an Indian. When you get right down to it, equality's just a myth.''

''You really believe that, don't you?''

He shrugged one shoulder, as if to say it didn't matter what he really believed. ''That's what I experienced. When I figured that out, I decided to come home and learn how to be the man *Maheo* created me to be. I am Northern Cheyenne, and I will always *be* Northern Cheyenne, and if I have anything to say about it, this tribe will never be at the mercy of whites again. When it comes to Indians, they don't have any mercy to spare.''

''They're not *all* like that, Jackson,'' Maggie said, quietly chiding him.

''Oh, I'm sure there's a few good guys out there. But I haven't had much luck in separating the good ones from the bad ones. I'm not willing to risk being wrong anymore.''

''So you hate the whole bunch. Don't trust anyone. Is that the way you want to live your whole life?''

''I didn't choose it, Maggie. But I've learned the hard way that if you stick your neck out with whites, the chances are too damn high you're gonna get your head chopped off. Maybe you're just too young to understand betrayal.''

''I'm not too young or too naive to understand anything,'' she said. ''I've been betrayed by whites and other Indians, and I know how much it hurts. But if you go into every new relationship expecting betrayal, you're setting yourself up for a self-fulfilling prophecy. That's a defeatist attitude.''

He gazed at her for a long moment, his expression completely unreadable. ''I prefer to think of it as realistic. And one of these days, you're gonna find out I'm right.''

When she made no reply, he started the engine and drove

back onto the road. Releasing a resigned sigh, Maggie turned to her window. So much for ending their fierce debates, she thought with a wry grin. But, while their discussion had become more heated than she would have liked, Maggie believed she and Jackson were making progress toward understanding each other.

She was beginning to understand him, anyway, she thought, sneaking a sidelong glance at him. He'd put his aviator glasses on, and she wondered whether it was for protection from the sun or to shield his eyes from her view because he felt he'd revealed too much. Well, he'd better get used to it. By telling her about his childhood, he'd only whetted her appetite to learn more about him.

Somewhere inside that big, strong, sexy man, there was a hurt, confused, lonely little boy who had never really felt accepted. Her childhood had undoubtedly been easier than his, and maybe she couldn't relate to everything that had happened to him. But she knew more than he thought she did about feeling lost and left out. And wondering if she would ever really belong anywhere. Perhaps they could find some answers together.

The road deteriorated into a rutted path, forcing Jackson to concentrate more on his driving and less on Maggie, but she still occupied a large part of his mind. She'd drifted into a thoughtful silence about five miles back, and he'd give a small fortune to know what was going on in that head of hers. Nuts.

He shouldn't have told her all that stuff about boarding school. It wasn't relevant to anything going on with the tribe now, and he'd probably sounded like a big baby, whining over a scratch that should have healed and been forgotten a long time ago. She was such a good listener, he'd have to watch himself, or he'd wind up boring her to tears with the story of his whole damn sad life. The idea made his skin crawl.

Spotting the turnoff he'd been looking for, he shifted into a lower gear, warned Maggie to hang on and gunned the engine. The pickup jolted and bounced violently over rocks and pot-

holes, but ultimately conquered the track, which ran straight up the side of a steep hill. Knowing the top of it ended in a cliff, he slammed on the brakes as soon as the truck leveled out.

Maggie shot him a wild-eyed, indignant look as the dust settled. He grinned at her, then climbed out of the cab and hurried around to open the door for her. She jumped to the ground and stalked away from him, hands curled into fists at her sides. She came to an abrupt halt a moment later and gazed off into the distance as if entranced.

He walked over and stood beside her, his face turned toward the sun, allowing Maggie a modicum of privacy while she absorbed the view he had seen so many times before. Though he had few of the spiritual powers of his father, Jackson knew this ground was sacred. He silently offered prayers to *Maheo* and each of the four directions, then glanced at Maggie.

Her eyes shone with the awed wonder of a child. When she spoke, her voice held a hushed reverence. "Oh, Jackson, this is so…beautiful."

For once, they were in complete accord. As if Mother Earth had chosen this particular spot to display her most impressive gifts to their best advantage, a lush valley stretched for miles before them, reaching all the way to the point at which the mountains blocked the horizon. Sunlight sparkled on a blue ribbon of water cutting a lazy, serpentine path through the center of the valley. Clumps of aspen and cottonwood trees along the river would soon provide shade for sleek Hereford cows and their recently born calves.

"What is this place?" Maggie murmured.

"It's ours," he said. "The land we're trying to get back from the Whitehorn Ranchers' Association."

"No wonder they want it. It looks like Eden."

"It's a paradise for cattle, all right. It's got all the best grass and water. Kincaid and his friends have gotten rich off this valley."

"What will you do with it?" she asked.

"The same thing they're doing. Raise cattle. So many of our

people have worked for the white ranchers, we've got plenty of expertise to draw from.''

''Won't it take an awful lot of money to get started?''

Jackson nodded. ''We're already working on grant proposals.''

''Let me know when you're ready to submit them. Perhaps I can speed up the process.''

''I'll keep that in mind,'' he said, smiling at her. ''I may need your help first to settle a disagreement among the tribal council members.''

''Me? How could I do that?''

''Sweet talk your buddy Earnest Running Bull into giving up the idea we should raise buffalo instead of Herefords.''

''Buffalo?''

''Sure. This whole area was a bison feeding ground long before the white men showed up. Our people used to hunt here every summer. We're standing on a buffalo jump right now.''

Maggie looked up at him, her eyes wide with surprise. ''You're kidding.''

''Nope. The men would climb up into those hills back there,'' Jackson said, pointing over his right shoulder with his thumb. ''They'd bunch up as many buffalo as they could, and drive them off this cliff. The animals would break their necks when they fell, and the women would be waiting down below to finish them off and start the butchering.''

Leaning out, Maggie peeked over the edge of the cliff. A huge chunk of dirt in front of her toes broke loose and smashed on the boulders below. Arms flapping wildly for balance, she teetered for an instant, and would have pitched forward to disaster if Jackson hadn't grabbed the back of her Windbreaker and yanked her back to safety.

''That,'' she said, uttering a shaky laugh, ''was close.''

Jackson couldn't have agreed more, but since his heart was still stuck in his throat, he didn't try to talk. Instead, he wrapped his arm around her shoulders, urged her farther back from the ledge and held her against his side, while he waited for his

lungs to start working again. She threw both arms around him and buried her face in the front of his shirt.

A fierce sense of gladness washed over him. Gladness she hadn't fallen. And gladness that, despite their previous disagreement, she had felt she could turn to him for comfort. Vivid pictures of what would have happened if he hadn't grabbed her in time flashed through his mind, and suddenly none of the things they'd argued about seemed important.

"It's all right, Maggie," he said, stroking her glossy hair with a hand that was none too steady. "It's all right."

She felt good in his arms. It had been so long since he'd held a woman like this, he'd almost forgotten what pleasure a simple human touch could bring. She turned her face to the side. With her ear still pressed against his chest, she gazed up at him from under her long lashes.

"Your heart's pounding like crazy," she said.

"That's because you scared the hell out of me."

"You saved my life, Jackson."

"Next time you're mad enough to strangle me, remember that."

"I'd probably kiss your whole face right now, if you weren't so darn tall."

"Is that a fact?"

"You betcha, kemo sabe."

Tickled by her ridiculous reference to the Lone Ranger's faithful Indian friend, Tonto, and the way she wrinkled her impish little nose at him, Jackson put his hands on Maggie's waist, picked her up and carried her back to the pickup. Then he plunked her tush down on the hood, braced his hands on either side of her and looked her right in the eye.

"I'm not too tall now, am I?"

Returning his challenging grin with one of her own, she lifted his Stetson off his head and set it behind her. She took his sunglasses next, carefully laying them on his hat brim. Finally she linked her fingers at the back of his head and pulled him closer.

His heart started racing again as she kissed his eyes shut.

Her breath struck his face in sweet little puffs as she moved on to his nose, his cheekbones, his forehead. His lips tingled, wanting their turn, but she playfully denied them in favor of his temples, jaw and chin.

"You missed a spot, Schaeffer," he grumbled, opening one eye to glare at her.

She kissed it shut again. "Don't be so impatient," she said, punctuating each word with another soft kiss, retracing her previous route. "I'll get there eventually."

It was the gentlest form of torture, but torture nonetheless, especially when she started stroking her thumbs behind his ears, while her fingers massaged the back of his neck. He didn't know why he tolerated it, except that it was...fun. Like Maggie. He'd bet his truck she'd been one of those adorable little girls who loved to flirt and tease and giggle.

And suddenly she "got there," reminding him in no uncertain terms that she was all woman, not a little girl. Her lips brushed tentatively over his, then zeroed in for a kiss that sent blood rushing to his groin in one hell of a hurry. She clasped the sides of his head, as if she feared he might try to escape, and slid her tongue into his mouth.

Damn. It was even better than the last time. All of his senses were on overload, but he couldn't taste enough, feel enough, breathe in enough of her essence. A primitive part of him wanted to seize control—just grab her and lay her back on the pickup's hood, strip off her jeans and bury himself to the hilt in her softness. But another part of him was enjoying her gentle seduction too much to risk frightening her into ending it. Or, worse yet, never doing it again.

Her hands were on his chest now, stroking and petting, and the sweet, hungry little sounds she was making were driving him out of his mind. She took the kiss hotter, wetter, deeper. He *had* to touch her with his hands. *Had* to pull her closer and feel her breasts rub against his chest. *Had* to nuzzle the side of her neck.

It was like racing down a mountain on a runaway train—too fast and powerful to stop, both exhilarating and terrifying while

the ride lasted. And all along you knew it would have to stop sooner or later, and the end wouldn't be pretty. Already it was starting to happen.

She was calling his name, trying to get his attention, slamming on the brakes. Damn it, she wanted him. He felt it in the way her body clung to his, even as her hands halfheartedly pushed at his shoulders. He could silence her protests with another kiss, overwhelm her silly female restraint with passion.

It wouldn't be rape. Not even close. But it wouldn't be right, either. Eventually she would regret her loss of control, and come to hate him. And then he would hate himself.

Forcing himself to release her, he stepped back. His chest heaved like a bellows as he sucked in head-clearing oxygen. When his thundering pulse finally subsided, he looked at Maggie and felt his heart contract.

Still sitting on the pickup's hood, she had her hands clasped in her lap, her shoulders hunched and her eyes focused on the ground. Then, with agonizing slowness, she raised her gaze to meet his. The wariness he saw in her eyes made him feel like crawling under a flat rock.

"I'm sorry," she said. "I never intended for it to get so..."

"Hot?" Jackson suggested. "Wild? Crazy? Passionate?"

Her cheeks flushed. "All of the above."

"I didn't either, Maggie." Shrugging one shoulder, he crammed his hands into his pockets and tried to give her a grin. "Some chemistry, huh?"

"Yeah." Her answering grin was crooked to start out with. A second later, it vanished, leaving her with a somber expression. "But it can't happen again."

"Because you don't mix business and personal relationships?"

"Yes. I'll only be here a few more weeks, so there's no future in pursuing this for either of us."

"You have to have a future with every guy you kiss?"

"Not if I'm sure it'll stop with kissing. That's not true with you, Jackson."

"Are you afraid of me?" he asked. "Is that what this is all about?"

"No." She slid off the hood and, with her feet planted firmly on the ground, faced him squarely. "I'm more afraid of myself. I don't usually get so, um...carried away."

"You think I *do?*" he demanded.

"That's beside the point. We were supposed to be starting over as friends, and I can't afford to be anything more than that with you." She walked around to the passenger door, opened it and put one foot on the running board. "This game with the kisses is too risky for me. It has to end now."

"What do you want to do?" Jackson asked, propping his hands on his hips. "Pretend it never happened?"

"That's right. Otherwise, I'll have to drive myself."

The look in her eyes told him more clearly than words that she meant exactly what she'd said. Which didn't leave him much choice. The crazy, stubborn damn woman was liable to get herself killed if she went off alone, and his uncle would skin him alive if he let her do it. Of course, he'd never forget that kiss, and neither would she, but if this was how she wanted to play it, he'd go along with her. For now.

"Okay, Maggie," he said. "We'll do it your way."

She climbed into the cab, shut the door and fastened her seat belt. Jackson followed suit and carefully turned the pickup around so that he wouldn't have to back down the hill. Neither of them spoke, even after they'd bounced and jolted their way to the bottom. He turned right, heading farther out, to show her the actual boundary to the leased land.

Maggie asked an occasional question, appearing to be completely at ease with him. Now that she'd settled the issue of their sexual attraction to her satisfaction, why shouldn't she be at ease with him? Jackson smiled to himself and kept on driving. As far as he was concerned, they had settled nothing. In fact, that second dynamite kiss had changed everything.

He had no clear vision of where he wanted their relationship to go. He sure as hell wasn't ready to declare that he loved her, or propose marriage. But for the first time in a long, long time,

he felt there were possibilities to be explored, and he damn well intended to explore them all.

   Granted, on the surface, he and Maggie didn't have much in common. He could have named a whole handful of barriers to having a meaningful relationship with her. None of them had stopped this powerful attraction, however, probably because there was a hell of a lot more to it than just sex. Not that he had any objection to sex for its own sake, but he'd found he liked it better if he had an emotional attachment to his partner. He suspected the same was true for Maggie.

   He also suspected there was more to her reluctance to get involved with him than a simple desire to keep her business and personal relationships separate. She might not be afraid of him, but she was afraid of something, all right. One way or another, he intended to find out what it was.

Eight

"Come on, you've done enough for one day."

"Give me ten more minutes." Maggie tossed a quick smile over her shoulder at Jackson, then turned to the computer monitor again. "I've only got one more page to go, and Wanda needs to start editing tomorrow."

"I need to work in the office for a couple of hours before we take off tomorrow," Jackson said. "You can finish it then."

Out of the corner of her eye, she saw his hand sneak toward the keyboard, his index finger aimed at the save button. "Stop that," she said, rapping his hand with her knuckles. "I want to see how she wraps this up."

Sara Lewis chuckled. Pushing her chair away from the computer next to Maggie's, she stood and rubbed the small of her back. "You might as well give it up, Jackson. When the Little Fed's on a mission, she won't quit till she's good and ready."

"Tell me about it," he said in a dry tone. "She runs my butt all over the res all day, and then drags me in here to type research papers until my fingers bleed at night. She's wearin' me down to a nub."

"So, go on home to bed," Maggie suggested without taking her eyes from the screen.

"No way," he said. "Shut up and keep typing."

Maggie lifted both hands from the keyboard and looked over at Sara. "Has he always been this bossy?"

Sara chuckled again. "He can't help it, Maggie. It runs in his family."

"Well, tell him he doesn't have to escort me all the way in to Whitehorn every night. I'm a big girl now, with a driver's license and everything. I can get back to the motel all by myself."

"Oh, no." Sara held up crossed forefingers in front of her

face, as if warding off a vampire. "I'm not getting in the middle of one of your spats. Leave me out of this."

"Wise move, Sara," Jackson told her. "I wouldn't listen, anyway. She thinks just because she's not in D.C., there aren't any dangers for a woman traveling alone at night."

Maggie rolled her eyes in exasperation and went back to typing. Honestly, ever since she'd almost fallen from the buffalo jump two weeks ago, Jackson had been driving her batty. Not that he'd given her a single legitimate reason to complain.

There had been no unnecessary touches, no teasing innuendos, no more kisses. While she still suffered the pangs of the strongest sexual attraction of her life every time she got within six feet of him, being around her didn't seem to faze him a bit. He was invariably helpful and solicitous of her comfort, but for all the notice he took of her as a woman, she could have been his sister or an elderly aunt.

Of course, that irritated Maggie to the roots of her hair, but after the way she'd told him to back off, what could she possibly say? *Hey, Jackson, I've changed my mind. Why don't you start hitting on me again?* Not in this or any other lifetime.

As if the physical attraction weren't enough to contend with, the wretched man kept revealing new, utterly appealing sides to his personality. Last week, for instance, they'd called on a young woman who had four-month-old twins. While the mother was pouring her heart out to Maggie about the problems her husband was having in finding a steady job, both babies had started fussing.

Jackson had scooped the kids into his arms and left the kitchen. When her conversation ended half an hour later, Maggie had followed her hostess into the living room, where they'd found him sitting in an old wooden rocking chair, with a sleeping baby draped over each shoulder and a smug grin on his face.

And take yesterday. They had visited an elderly man who was crippled with arthritis and lived in a trailer with a dilapidated porch attached to the front. While Maggie conducted her interview, Jackson had poked around in the old fellow's garage, found a hammer and nails and repaired the wobbly steps leading up to the porch.

Today he'd merely chopped wood for over an hour and milked a cow for a harassed grandmother who was baby-sitting four grandchildren and tending to her husband, who was dying of lung cancer. Who did he think he was? The Mother Teresa of the res?

Maggie found it extremely difficult to remain emotionally aloof from a man who did things like that and then acted embarrassed when simple gratitude was offered in return. She couldn't even indulge in the cynical suspicion he was only doing those things to impress her. She'd heard too many stories about Jackson's previous kindnesses, from too many people, to believe that of him.

"Earth to Maggie. Yo, woman, wake up!"

Startled out of her reverie by the sound of his voice right next to her ear, she looked up into Jackson's dark, amused eyes, and discovered she couldn't look away. Lord, she must be more tired than she'd realized. Because at that moment, she wanted nothing more than to wrap his long braids around her hands and pull him down for a bone-melting kiss.

As if he'd read her thoughts, his gaze dropped to her lips and lingered there. Her throat constricted in an involuntary swallow. Then he grasped the back of her chair and unceremoniously dragged her away from the keyboard. Before she could gather a coherent protest, he'd hit the save key, backed out of the word-processing program and turned off the computer.

"That's it, Schaeffer. We're outa here. You're gonna be too sleepy to drive if you wait any longer."

Unable to argue, she climbed to her feet, stretched out the kinks in her shoulders and exchanged a weary grin with Sara. "The kids are going to make it, aren't they?"

"You'd better believe it. They've done excellent work in the short time they've had to pull these papers together," Sara said. "They're getting so excited about graduation."

"That's great," Maggie said. "We should be thinking about a party for them. Maybe we could hire a disc jockey, or—"

Jackson barged between the two women, grabbed each of them by an arm and hustled them down the hallway to the exit, scolding them as they skipped to keep up with his long strides.

"Think we're on Indian time around here? Get a move on, ladies. It'll keep till tomorrow."

He practically shoved them outdoors, then went back to turn off the lights and lock up the building. Maggie shot him a dirty look, which sent Sara into gales of laughter.

"Listen," Sara said when she'd regained her composure, "there's no reason the two of you have to go through this every night."

"I know," Maggie retorted. "But that big dope in there must have flunked listening in kindergarten. I just can't get him to understand I can take care of myself."

"That's not what I meant," Sara said. "I've got a spare bedroom you can use, if you're interested."

"You mean tonight?"

"Tonight, and any other night you want. You're spending so much time out here, you might as well move in with me. It's nothing fancy, but I'd be glad to have you."

"That's a great offer, Sara, but I couldn't impose on you."

"If I thought you'd impose, I wouldn't have offered," Sara replied.

"Are you sure you wouldn't mind?" Maggie asked. It really would be a godsend to skip the awful drive back and forth to Whitehorn every day.

Sara shrugged. "I grew up in a house smaller than mine is, with my grandmother, mother, older brother and father—at least until he ran off. One skinny little Fed isn't gonna get in my way." As if that settled the issue, she dug around in her purse and pulled out a key.

Maggie tucked it into her jeans pocket and gave Sara a quick hug. "Thanks, pal. I'll move in in the morning."

Sara got into her car and rolled down the window. "It's the little blue house right behind the jail. Your room's the one off the living room."

"See you tomorrow night." Maggie waved as her friend drove off, then turned when the door to the building opened behind her.

No matter how much she tried to convince herself otherwise, she always felt her heart lift at the sight of Jackson coming her way. Just this once, she allowed herself to enjoy the sensation.

She liked the way his broad shoulders moved with his loose-limbed cowboy walk. She liked the scruffy clothes he wore that allowed him to do nice things for people without worrying about getting himself dirty. She even liked that tired, scowling expression on his handsome face.

If circumstances had been different, she would have opened her arms to him, hugged him for being the big-hearted man he was beneath that gruff, cranky exterior he often hid behind, and soothed away his weariness with kisses. She'd learned so much about him in the past few weeks, but there was much, much more she wanted to know. More than she could ever learn in the time she had left at Laughing Horse. Maybe more than she could learn in a lifetime.

Fearing her thoughts and emotions would show on her face, she turned away and climbed into her car. When Jackson had done likewise, she backed out of her parking space and headed for Whitehorn. She tried to put him out of her mind, but with his headlights shining a constant reminder in her rearview mirror, it was impossible to forget he was right behind her.

And with each passing mile, the conviction grew that, with or without his headlights in her mirror, no matter how much time or distance she put between them, she would never be able to forget Jackson Hawk.

Gripping a mug of coffee in his left hand, Jackson steered the pickup with his right on his way into Laughing Horse the next morning. As usual, his thoughts were on Maggie. Also as usual, they were confused and frustrated.

Keeping his hands off her the past two weeks hadn't been easy, but he'd done it. The question uppermost in his mind at the moment was whether or not it was time to change tactics. There'd been a second last night, just after he caught her zoning off at the computer, when he could have sworn she wanted him to kiss her. If Sara hadn't been there, he would have done it, consequences be damned.

In the clear light of a new morning, however, those conse-quences seemed a hell of a lot more important. The more he'd worked with Maggie, the more he'd come to appreciate just how special she really was. They'd visited some people and

seen some situations that had made *him* want to throw up his hands in defeat—battered wives; children abandoned to grandparents who were too old to keep up with them; angry, bewildered young men and women who couldn't find anything better to do with their lives than to try to drown their despair in alcohol or drugs.

Considering the privileged background she'd grown up with, Maggie's capacity for empathizing with these people was nothing short of astonishing to Jackson. No matter how poor the household, she treated each person with dignity and respect, and graciously accepted whatever hospitality was offered. Time and time again, he'd watched sullen, bitter people fall victim to the magic of her smiles.

She had a unique gift for focusing her attention on the person in front of her and responding without defensiveness or judgment. The pattern that followed had become as predictable to Jackson as the sun rising in the east. Before long, the interviewees would be sitting up straighter, dropping their flip or sarcastic answers to her questions, speaking with more assurance and conviction as they finally began to believe that whatever they said honest-to-God mattered to her.

What they didn't know was how much all that warmth and understanding cost Maggie in emotional terms. Oh, she didn't let on about it. She didn't rant and rave, the way he often wanted to, or cry, which seemed more appropriate for a softhearted woman like her. But day after day he'd seen it—a slow, steady drain on her energy, leaving behind a quiet, tense little ghost in place of the bubbly little elf he'd come to love.

Love? a voice inside his head inquired. *Did you say love?*

Jackson's response was both automatic and emphatic. No. It couldn't be love. He felt a lot of emotions toward Maggie—admiration, gratitude for her efforts on behalf of the tribe, lust, and even a certain amount of affection. But he was only exploring the possibilities of a deeper relationship with her at this point. He didn't love her as in "falling in love with." Uh-uh. No way.

Why the hell not? the voice demanded.

"I don't know her well enough yet," Jackson muttered.

Bull. She's perfect for you, and you know it.

His gut clenched, and every muscle in his back and shoulders tightened. "She doesn't love me."

How do you know? Have you asked her?

"Of course not. I just know, all right?" A clammy sweat had broken out on his forehead and the back of his neck. "Even if she did, it wouldn't work out."

Oh, you're psychic now, huh? You can read her mind? See into the future?

"I didn't say that."

Then why are you being so negative? Don't you think you're man enough for her?

"I didn't say that, either."

But you're too damned chicken to find out, aren't you?

"Now, look," Jackson said, forcing the words out through gritted teeth. "She's got a career and a life of her own in Washington. She even said there's no future for us—"

And you're just gonna take her word for it? Sheesh! Women change their minds all the time. If you had the balls to go after her, you could help Maggie change hers.

The clammy sweat was moving down to his palms. Jackson tightened his grip on the steering wheel. "She wouldn't stay here."

You don't know that. Cluck, cluck, cluck.

"She'll leave me like Nancy did."

She's not Nancy. Cluck, cluck, cluck.

"There's not enough time," Jackson insisted.

And you're wasting what little you've got left, pretending to be her buddy. You've gotta do something, you big jackass. And you'd better do it damn fast.

"Do what? Seduce her? Kidnap her? Hold her hostage?"

How the hell should I know? But you'd better think of something, or she'll leave for sure, and you'll end up alone and clucking for the rest of your life.

With that thought reverberating in his mind, Jackson pulled up in front of the tribal offices, put the pickup in Park and set his empty mug on the dash. Drumming his fingers on the steering wheel, he considered the situation from every possible angle.

Maggie was scheduled to return to D.C. in a month—six

weeks, if he was lucky. While that really didn't give him much time, he couldn't rush her, either. They'd made a good start on building a friendship, but if he pushed her too hard to deepen it, she was liable to finish her assignment and get the hell out of here. Okay, so he had to be careful.

On the plus side, he was certain she'd begun to identify with the people of Laughing Horse. On the minus side, her father and her career represented powerful ties to the white world.

Could he find a way to break those ties? Not likely. The best he could probably hope for would be to neutralize them with equally strong ties to him and to the tribe. Was it possible to do that in a month?

Jackson didn't know the answer, but he'd fail for sure if he didn't try. Maggie had spent all of her time here documenting the reservation's most desperate problems. Maybe if she saw some of the better parts of life on the res, she'd find the idea of staying more attractive. And maybe it was time for him to be more open about himself.

If he'd learned anything from his divorce, it was that it wouldn't do any good to pretty things up for her. If she ever did fall in love with him, it had to be with the "real" him. With the Indian him. He couldn't deny who and what he was for anyone, ever again. Not even Maggie.

The thought made him nervous as hell, but he was not without weapons in this fight for her affections. What he had to do now was put them to good use. The question was, where should he start?

After a busy morning spent checking out of the motel, moving into Sara's house and typing the rest of Wanda's research paper, Maggie climbed into the passenger seat of Jackson's pickup. She sat back and took a moment to catch her breath while he drove west out of Laughing Horse, on the same road he'd taken to go to the buffalo jump.

He took the north fork this time, however. Ten miles beyond it, he made a left turn onto a dirt lane cut into a stand of towering ponderosa pines. Since Jackson appeared to be in one of his quiet moods, Maggie contented herself with watching the

scenery. The lane twisted and turned back into the trees, growing narrower and more weed-choked the farther they went.

"Whose place is this?" she asked after fifteen minutes of bouncing from one pothole to the next.

"Mine."

"Did you forget something this morning?" she asked.

"Nope."

"Then why are we stopping here?"

"Because I think it's about time you interviewed me," he said, giving her a smile that was far too bland to be completely innocent. What the heck was he up to, anyway?

"Do you really think that's necessary?" she asked. "We've spent a lot of time together."

"And we've spent all of it talking about other people. Don't you want to hear about my ideas for the tribe's future?"

"Don't I already know most of them?"

"Maybe. But I want to be officially on the record."

Jackson slowed down. Maggie glanced away from him, then felt her mouth drop open when she caught sight of the clearing ahead of them. He braked to a complete stop, as if he knew she needed a moment to absorb the entire scene.

Sheltered on two sides by the pines, the two-story log home perched at the top of a small rise, facing east. Front picture windows looked out over a broad field of native grasses. Solar panels covered the roof, and a rock chimney protruded at the north end of the building. A detached two-car garage sat fifteen feet to the south. A pair of pinto horses grazed in a fenced pasture beyond the garage.

"It's lovely, Jackson," she murmured, giving him a bemused smile.

He muttered a soft "Thanks" and drove on up to the garage. He climbed out of the cab, hurried around the front of the pickup and opened her door for her. When she stepped down beside him, he took her hand and led her inside.

Most of the main floor had been left in one large, open space, with room divisions suggested by the placement of furniture rather than interior walls. A sofa and two easy chairs were grouped around an oval braided rug in front of the fireplace. A

trestle table and matching chairs created a dining area, which was separated from the kitchen by a freestanding work island.

Sunlight poured in through the large windows in each exterior log wall, accenting the warm golden tones in the wood used just about everywhere—the built-in bookcases, the kitchen cabinets, the banister flanking the stairway to the second floor. Thriving green plants, fat pillows covered in calico prints and an overflowing box of toys in the living room added vivid colors to the cozy atmosphere.

Jackson hung his Stetson on a peg mounted by the door, then led the way to the kitchen. "Come on. Let's see what we can find for lunch."

Maggie followed at a slower pace, pausing in the dining area to study a small but intricately carved wooden statue of a hawk, its wings spread as if it were poised for flight.

"My father made that for me when I was six," Jackson said. "He told me it was a little piece of home I could take to boarding school with me."

"It's beautiful. He's very talented."

Leaving the statue, Maggie walked slowly to the work island.

"He was," Jackson said. He took a can of chili out of a cupboard and set an aluminum pot on the stove. "He died four and a half years ago."

"I'm sorry. I know how much it hurts to lose a parent."

With swift, economical movements, he dumped the chili into the pot and switched on the burner, then went to the refrigerator for a block of cheese and an onion. "The hurt, I can handle. I have a harder time coping with the guilt."

"Why do you feel guilty?"

"Because I helped to kill him."

Jackson turned away from her undoubtedly shocked expression and rummaged in drawers and cupboards, coming up with a knife, a cutting board and a grater. He left again and came back with a couple of bowls, shoving one of them, the cheese and the grater across the countertop to Maggie. She eyed him with exasperation for a moment, then picked up the cheese and went to work while he attacked the onion.

"I don't believe that, Jackson."

He gave her a long, steady look. "I didn't do it with a knife or a gun, but I helped kill him, all right."

"What happened?"

Jackson cleared his throat and went back to chopping the onion. "When I told you I turned my back on the tribe, I wasn't kidding. After I started college, I never came home if I could avoid it. And I was damn good at avoiding it."

"Because you didn't get along with your father?"

"That was part of it," he agreed. "But it was more because of the pressure I always felt from everyone to come back to the res. Have you ever watched the boys play basketball after school?"

Though she felt confused by the abrupt change of subject, Maggie nodded. "I'm no expert, but some of them look awfully good out there."

"They *are* good. Good enough for full-ride basketball scholarships, but the recruiters don't offer them to Indian kids anymore."

"Why not?"

"Because they won't stay in school. They get stuck in some big dorm with a bunch of white strangers. They're scared and lonesome and their classes are harder than they expected. They come home for a weekend and go out drinkin' with their buddies, and all they hear is how they're never gonna make it, and how they think they're better than everybody else. It's like the friends who got left behind can't stand to see them succeed."

"That's a shame," Maggie said.

"It's a damn waste. Every high school basketball star I saw leave this place for college before I did ended up right back here before the first year was over. I decided that wasn't gonna happen to me. I'm the only guy from this reservation who actually got a degree out of sports, and I never could have done it if I hadn't stayed away."

"Was that hard for you?"

He stirred the bubbling chili, then brought two more bowls to the work island and poured the contents of the pot into them.

"The first year was the worst, because my family kept begging me to come home. After that, they kinda gave up. It got

to be a real pride issue. I wasn't like those drunks on the res. I was this tough guy who could make it on his own.''

''That's a perfectly understandable reaction,'' Maggie said. ''Don't be so hard on yourself.''

''Thanks for the sympathy,'' he said with a wry smile. He carried the bowls to the table, and pulled out a chair for her. ''But that's not why I'm tellin' you all of this.''

''Okay, I'll bite,'' Maggie said, bringing the cheese and chopped onion to the table. When they were both seated, she asked, ''Why are you telling me this?''

''Because I want you to understand why the tribe's welfare is so important to me. It's more than a convenient career choice.''

''I figured that out a long time ago,'' she said. ''But go ahead and finish your story.''

''There's not much left. I went to law school at Georgetown, married a white woman, and went to work for a big Wall Street firm.''

''Whoa, back up one,'' Maggie said, hoping her eyes weren't bugging out as far as she thought they were. She'd heard he was divorced, but nobody had ever mentioned that little tidbit of information about him before. ''You married a *white* woman?''

''I told you I was an apple, didn't I?'' he said, raising one shoulder in a half shrug.

Maggie glanced toward the living room. ''Whose toys are those, Jackson?''

He laughed. ''Relax, I don't have any kids. I keep the toys around for my nieces and nephews. I've got a bunch of 'em.''

''Oh. Go on, then. What happened next?''

''We were a nice yuppie couple. Nancy was a stock trader. We raked in all kinds of bucks, and had one hell of a good time. Then, one day, my youngest sister tracked me down and told me our father had suffered a coronary. He was in intensive care in Billings, and he was asking for me.''

''Did you get home in time to say goodbye?''

Jackson nodded. ''Yeah. He was stabilized by the time I got there, and everyone seemed to think he'd be all right. But then he demanded to see me alone. He begged me to take care of

my mother if he didn't make it. I promised I would. Hell, I'd have done anything to ease his mind. But he had another heart attack right then, and they couldn't bring him back. He'd never even met my wife.''

Her eyes stinging with unshed tears, Maggie reached across the table and laid her hand over his clenched fist. ''Sometimes those things just happen. It wasn't your fault.''

''Yes, it was. If I'd come home once in a while, or at least stayed in touch, I would have known he was having health problems and refusing to go to the white man's doctor. Hell, I could have paid his doctor bills with the money I blew on tickets for Broadway shows and numbered prints. He was the tribal council chairman, and I could have used my law degree to help him the way I'm helping Uncle Frank now.''

''It's always easy to see those things in hindsight, Jackson, but you can't change anything. What good does it do to beat yourself up like this?''

He pulled his hand out from under hers. ''It helps me to remember what my pride and selfishness caused, and appreciate the beauty of the tribal system. When my father died, I found out I wasn't one bit different from those drunks on the res. I'd be one of them, if Uncle Frank hadn't straightened me out in time.''

''So, you're working for the tribe as a way to atone for your father's death?''

''There's no way I could ever do that. But when I cut myself off from the tribe, I hurt myself as much as I hurt anyone else, including my father. At this point, I'm still tryin' to get my own identity back.''

''I'm not sure I understand what you mean.''

''It goes back to the issue of values, Maggie. To a Cheyenne, preserving the tribe is a sacred responsibility. We're taught from an early age it's more important to share and get along with the group than it is to seek personal glory and achievement. Competing successfully in the white society meant I had to deny almost every lesson my parents had taught me. It took my father's death to make me realize my values were so screwed up, I didn't know who I was anymore.''

''Is that when you moved back here?''

"About six months later. My wife hung in there as long as she could, but my sudden search for my native roots seemed pretty bizarre to her. When she filed for divorce, I came home."

Maggie winced. "First your father, then your wife. That must have hurt."

"It did at the time. But in the long run, I think it was for the best that my marriage ended when it did. At least there weren't any children involved, and now I'm where I belong."

Jackson pushed back his chair and cleared away the empty bowls. Sensing he needed a moment's privacy, Maggie stayed at the table. A lump grew in her throat as she let her gaze roam from one end of the room to the other. This was by far the nicest house she'd visited on the res, but it was obviously meant for a family.

Did Jackson ever feel lonely here? she wondered. As lonely as she sometimes felt in her Washington apartment? Or did the tribe offer all the companionship he wanted? He was so self-contained, she couldn't be sure, but she had the impression he hadn't made as complete a transition back to his native roots as he had led her to believe. Perhaps he'd found a measure of contentment, but he didn't really seem…happy.

He returned to the dining area. "You look too serious, Schaeffer. Why don't we take a break and go for a walk?"

"That sounds great." Standing, she rubbed her fanny and gave him a rueful grin. "We've been sitting too much lately."

Chuckling, Jackson went back to the refrigerator, pulled out a couple of carrots and pointed them toward the rear of the kitchen. "We'll go out that way and visit the horses first."

Glad to see his mood lightening, Maggie followed him outdoors. "Oh, wow…" she said, pausing at the bottom of the steps to study his backyard.

There were crooked hopscotch boxes drawn in colored chalk all over the small cement patio. A sandbox filled with toy trucks and plastic pails sat off to the right. A wooden jungle gym filled the space between a couple of spindly-looking trees she couldn't identify, and beyond that was a vegetable garden that had been tilled, but not yet planted. A huge cottonwood tree grew behind the garden.

"This is quite a spread ya got here, Mr. Hawk," she drawled,

hustling to catch up with him. "Looks like your nieces and nephews visit a lot."

"Yeah, they do," he said. "The rest of my family lives about five miles up the road. I try to make it fun for the kids to come visit Uncle Jackson."

"Why don't you live with the rest of your family?" Maggie asked. "Everyone else around here seems to do that."

"When I first came back, I wasn't welcome. It's taken time to heal the wounds I caused, and earn my family's respect again." He grinned suddenly and looked back at the house. "They all thought I was nuts when I started building this place."

"You built it yourself?"

"Most of it. Uncle Frank helped me clear the trees and put up the walls. I think he figured if I stayed busy enough out here, I wouldn't be tearin' up the bars in Whitehorn."

"It's a beautiful house, Jackson, but why did you make it so big?"

"I intended to give it to my mother, but she was too attached to the house my dad built for her. She let me help her fix that one up, though. And, you know, I guess there's still enough apple left in me, I kinda like havin' my privacy."

"Have all the wounds with your family been healed, then?"

"You'll see for yourself next week. I've been given strict orders to bring you over for supper when we're done typing the kids' papers. Would you mind?"

"Why would I mind?"

He turned to her with a broad smile. "Because they've all been tryin' to marry me off for the last couple of years. You'll be a prime candidate as far as they're concerned."

"How big of a group are we talking here?" Maggie asked, silently ordering her heart to stop its sudden thumping. He hadn't said *he* thought she'd be a prime candidate, only that his family would. Since she had no intention of staying here, what did it matter, anyway?

"I have two younger sisters and two brothers. They're all married and have at least three kids apiece. Then there's Uncle Frank and Aunt Sally and their four kids and their families. My

mother also has two younger sisters, who'll probably bring their whole families along, and on my father's side—''

· "Enough, enough!" Maggie said with a laugh. "I get the picture."

"I doubt it. They're about as subtle as a bunch of terrorists with machine guns when it comes to matchmaking.''

"Would you rather I declined the invitation?''

"Nope. Just givin' you fair warning, so you won't feel embarrassed.''

If he only knew how many of the elderly members of the tribe had already extolled his virtues to her when he'd been out chopping wood and the like, he wouldn't worry about that, Maggie thought with a grin. They arrived at the fenced pasture. Jackson called the horses over and gave Maggie a carrot. She fed it to one of the mares, while he fed the other one.

"They're beautiful," she said, stroking the animal's smooth neck. "Do you ride them much?''

He shook his head. "They're not broke yet. I got 'em about a week before you came, as payment for some legal work. I'm really gonna have to watch the kids this summer. Some of the boys are gettin' to the age where they'll try to ride anything with four legs.''

The horses lost interest when the carrots ran out. Jackson and Maggie strolled along the fence line toward the trees. At the end of the pasture, they came to a small creek. Maggie spotted a ring of stones with a pile of ashes in the middle. Next to it was a waist-high dome-shaped frame built with saplings and fishing line.

"Is this going to be a tent for the kids?'' she asked, walking closer to inspect it.

Jackson laughed. "Aw, come on, Maggie. Haven't you ever seen a sweat lodge before?''

"Uh, no. We didn't have too many of those in Denver. Is it like a sauna?''

"Yeah. We use it to purify ourselves and to pray. It's part of our religion.''

"Are you really into this religion thing?''

"I'm learning about it. Uncle Frank helped me with a vision

quest when I'd been home for a year. I pierced for the first time at the Sun Dance last summer.''

Sweat lodge, vision quest, Sun Dance? Maggie shook her head in amazement. Every time she thought she was starting to see him clearly, he tossed out some new thing that blurred her image of him all over again.

"What?" he asked, sitting on a log near the campfire ring. "You look confused."

She ambled over to join him, collecting her thoughts as she walked. "All of this sounds kind of...mystical," she said, for lack of a better word.

The corners of his eyes crinkled with amusement. Clutching one hand to his chest as if he'd been mortally wounded, he said, "You don't see me as a great Indian mystic?"

"No."

"Why not?"

Chuckling, she rolled her eyes at him. "You're too hard-headed for that. Too much of a lawyer. Too modern."

He accepted her description of him with one of his half shrugs. "It's not easy to shed all those years of living in the white world, Maggie."

"They're a part of who you are, Jackson," she said. "Why would you want to shed them?"

"They're what makes it so hard for me to grasp all the mystical stuff that came so naturally to my father. He wasn't stupid, by any means, but he was a very simple man in a lot of ways. I mean, he didn't have to stop and think about right and wrong in any situation. He just always seemed to know what was best for the family and for the tribe."

"He lived in simpler times. He probably didn't have to make as many choices as you do," Maggie said.

Giving her a sad smile, Jackson nodded in agreement. "You're right. He didn't have many choices to make, because Indians had very little control over their lives back then. But he had such...vision. He was a true spiritual leader. I wish I'd listened to him more."

The regret in his voice tore at Maggie's heart. It sounded to her as if Jackson had set up his father as some kind of a saint whose standards he could never meet.

"Jackson," she said softly, continuing only when his gaze rose to meet hers. "Different times call for different skills and styles of leadership. The tribe desperately needs your particular skills right now, and you were only able to develop them because of the years you spent in the white world. Don't deny those years. And don't discount the contribution you're making because it's not what your father's might have been."

"Thanks," he said, his voice equally soft, equally sincere. "I hadn't thought of it that way before."

She turned toward him, lifting one knee to balance more comfortably on the log. "So tell me about *your* vision. What do you want to see happen for the tribe in the next ten years?"

His mouth curved into a thoughtful smile, and he gazed into the distance. "I want to see economic security and independence, our own businesses and entertainment facilities. I want us to have a real hospital, staffed with our own doctors, nurses and medicine men. I want us to have our own schools, where our kids can learn to be proud of who they are before they have to deal with whites. I want our young people to have job opportunities right here on the res. They shouldn't have to choose cultural annihilation or welfare to survive."

"What else?" Maggie asked, when he paused for a moment.

"I want to see more tribal unity. People taking more pride in themselves and more responsibility for themselves. We've got to find some answers to the drug and alcohol problems before they damage another whole generation. And I want us to stop seeing ourselves as a conquered people. As powerless victims."

"How would you accomplish that?"

"I like what I've seen happening since you've been here, Maggie. Especially with the kids. But I think we need to focus more attention on the old ways, too. Our religion has a lot to teach about living a meaningful life."

"And you think you don't have vision?" Maggie asked, raising both eyebrows at him. "That's a pretty tall order for only ten years, Jackson."

He shot her a self-conscious grin. "You think it's too much?"

"My dad always told me you might as well shoot for the

stars. It seems to me, though, that what you're really wanting is for the tribe to withdraw from the white world even more than it already has.''

''Absolutely,'' Jackson said. ''We need to rebuild our strength from within. In order to do that, we've got to limit the amount of white interference in our affairs. The grazing leases are one example. The Whitehorn schools are another.''

''I can see that,'' Maggie said, searching for words to suggest an alternative view that wouldn't raise his hackles.

''I can already hear the 'but' in your next sentence,'' he said, heaving an exaggerated sigh that made her smile.

''But,'' she said, ''I think you'll need to maintain a careful balance there, Jackson. The tribe can't employ everyone, and the white world is not going to go away while you're rebuilding from within. You'll need people who can cope effectively in both worlds.''

''I agree.'' He leaned closer, gazing so deeply into her eyes, she felt as if he could see down into her soul. ''We'll need people like you, Maggie. Why don't you quit working for Baldwin and come to work for the tribe? You could coordinate our social programs and help us develop new ones. Write grant proposals. Help us plan economic development.''

Unable to believe she'd heard him correctly, Maggie stared at Jackson in stupefaction. He calmly returned her regard, as if he expected her to be pleased with his suggestion. And the really astonishing thing was, she was almost tempted to consider it. But, of course, she couldn't. Not without breaking her promise to her mother, which she would never, ever do.

''That's impossible,'' she said, forcing a flat note of finality into her voice.

''Why?'' he asked. ''Uncle Frank's crazy about you. A word from him to the tribal council, and—''

She stood, cutting him off with a vehement shake of her head. ''No. Don't even think about it, Jackson. And don't you dare bring it up with your uncle.''

''Maggie—''

''No.''

He rose to his feet and held out his hands, as if in a plea for a reasonable discussion. ''Just think about it for a second.''

She backed up, shaking her head even more vehemently. "Which part don't you understand, Jackson? The *n* or the *o?* I already have a career."

"So, you'll have another one. You wouldn't make as much money, but—"

"Money is not the issue."

"Then what *is* the issue?"

"I don't belong here. You've said it yourself often enough."

"That was weeks ago. And I was dead wrong, Maggie. You could belong here just fine, if you wanted to."

"I *don't* want to," she said, knowing, even as she said them, that those words were not entirely the truth.

"Okay," Jackson said, shoving his hands into his jeans pockets. "It was just an idea."

Eyes narrowed with suspicion, she studied him for a moment. "Why are you giving up so easily?"

"Isn't that what you wanted?"

"Yes." She stepped closer, frowning at him in confusion. There was something seriously out of whack with this conversation, but she couldn't quite grasp what it was. It was almost as if she were talking to a slightly different Jackson from the one she was used to. "But it's not like you to be so agreeable."

"Excuse me?" he said, giving her a wounded-puppy look. "Are you saying I'm a disagreeable kind of a guy?"

"Usually."

Laughing, he casually slung his arm around her shoulders and turned her toward the house. "Okay, be that way, Schaeffer. Come on. Let's go back to work."

She walked along beside him, telling herself there was no need to feel so threatened. If Jackson had been more willing to be open about himself today, it was simply the logical result of their growing friendship. He wouldn't suddenly challenge the boundaries she'd demanded, after he'd accepted them for weeks.

And yet she couldn't deny a nagging suspicion that something important had changed. Call it a premonition, an intuition, or plain old instinct, she knew darn well he was up to something. Something he knew she wasn't going to approve of when she figured it out. It really wasn't like him to be so agreeable.

Nine

A week later, Maggie sat at Sara's kitchen table, working at her laptop computer. Sara had gone to bed hours ago. Maggie knew she should have done likewise, but there didn't seem to be much point. She would only thrash around all night, as she had every other night since her visit to Jackson's house.

There was simply no ignoring the growing urgency she felt about finishing her report and getting back to her own life— her *real* life—now, while she still could.

She paused to rub her burning eyes and stretch her stiff shoulders, muttering, "Oh, damn the man."

Her insomnia was all Jackson's fault, of course. If he hadn't suggested she go to work for the tribe, she'd be sleeping at this very moment, instead of sitting here in the dead of night, racing to finish her rough draft. Trying not to think about him or his insane job offer.

And it *was* insane. Why couldn't she remember that? Why did the notion of staying here tantalize her imagination to the point of making her question her goals, her life-style, even her own conscience? Was it the job itself she found so attractive— the thought of helping Jackson to achieve his goals for the tribe? Or was it really the possibility of staying close to him?

"Damn the man," she muttered again, burying her face in her hands.

A vision of his face appeared in her mind's eye, and she didn't know whether to burst into hysterical laughter or weep with frustration. He was up to something, all right, and the word for it was *temptation*. If she hadn't experienced it herself, she never would have believed he could be so diabolically cunning. The sneaky wretch had her right where he wanted her.

And what, exactly, had he done? Nothing! That was the worst part—feeling the subtle, relentless pressure to do what he

wanted, but not being able to call him on it, because he never did anything overtly out of line.

He hadn't tried to kiss her again, or made any suggestive remarks. But a woman would have to be blind to miss the masculine admiration in his eyes whenever he looked at her now. She'd have to be deaf not to hear the new warmth in his voice when he spoke to her. She'd have to be unconscious or dead to be unaware of the sexual vibrations he'd been putting out all week.

He hadn't mentioned the job offer again, either. Instead, he had taken a more active role in the interviews she conducted, painting seductive word pictures of what Laughing Horse could be like as he elaborated on his dreams for the tribe's future. And he always managed to make her feel as if those dreams would never come true without her help.

It was blatant manipulation, but she had precious few defenses against it. When she was with him, she felt sexy, intelligent and wanted—hardly the kind of emotions to put any woman in a mood to resist. But did he want her as a mate for himself, or as an employee for the tribe? And could he ever really accept her for who and what she was, including her white background and father?

Ah, yes, now those were excellent questions, weren't they? They were also the only things that had kept her from tumbling head over heels in love with Jackson. If she wasn't extremely careful, he would turn her entire life upside down. Shaking her head in disgust at her own confusion, she went back to work.

A moment later, she heard a noise at the doorway and jerked her head up in time to see her hostess enter the room. Wrapped in a green terry bathrobe, Sara scuffed the toes of her slippers across the floor, filled the teakettle with water and lit a burner. Then she turned around, crossed her arms over her breasts and leaned back against the counter.

"All right, Schaeffer, what's going on with you?"

"I'm just getting in a little extra work," Maggie said, resisting the urge to squirm beneath Sara's probing teacher's gaze. "I'm sorry if I woke you."

"I haven't been to sleep yet. Too many weird vibes coming out of this kitchen. Are you and Jackson feuding again?"

Maggie wished the problem was that simple. "No, we've been getting along fine."

"I thought you had three more weeks to finish your report."

"I do," Maggie admitted.

"Then what's the big rush?" Sara demanded.

The teakettle shrieked. Sara moved it to a cold burner, spooned decaffeinated instant coffee into two mugs and filled them with hot water. Then she carried them to the table and sat down across from Maggie.

"Do you want me to move out?" Maggie asked.

"Of course not. I just want to know what's bothering you. Maybe I can help."

While she was tempted to unburden herself, Maggie was all too aware that Sara had to get up early for work the next morning. "I'm okay."

"Uh-huh. That's why you're typing at 2:00 a.m.? Because you're okay?"

"It's not a big deal," Maggie insisted. "And it would take too long to explain."

"I'm not goin' anywhere," Sara said dryly. "Certainly not to sleep, while you're out here actin' like a speed freak. You might as well spill your guts."

Sighing with resignation, Maggie told Sara about Jackson's invitation to work for the tribe.

"I think it's a great idea," Sara said. "Why does it upset you so much?"

"It's ridiculous, Sara. I can't just quit my job and move clear across the country."

"Why can't you? Is there a man you don't want to leave?"

"No."

"Is it the people here? I know some of them can be cantankerous, but—"

"No. They've been wonderful, and I'd really like to help them."

"Is it Jackson?"

"What about him?"

"You *know* what about him," Sara told her in a chiding tone. "You're falling in love with him, aren't you?"

Maggie opened her mouth to utter a third denial, but found

she couldn't force the short syllable past her lips. Too agitated to sit another second, she shoved back her chair and paced across the room. Sara silently watched her make three round-trips to the doorway and back, then started to chuckle.

"It's not funny." Maggie wrapped her arms around herself in an effort to ward off the chill sinking into her bones. "I feel like I'm getting into something way over my head."

"You're really good for him, you know," Sara said in a mild tone. "Everyone's noticed it."

"Noticed what?"

"He smiles and laughs more when you're around. He's more relaxed. He's even putting up with that weird white lady you recruited for the tutoring program."

"Mary Jo's not weird," Maggie protested.

Sara simply stared at her with a deadpan expression. "She keeps asking about those bones George Sweetwater found. Don't you think that's a little weird?"

"Well, maybe a little. But she shows up regularly, and the kids like her, don't they?"

"I'm not sure they do. It's more like they're trying to figure her out. She's not always very patient with them."

"Do you want me to talk with her about that?"

Sara shook her head. "I can handle her. Now, stop trying to change the subject. What I want you to talk about, is Jackson. Are you falling in love with him or not?"

"I'm getting there, I guess," Maggie grumbled. "That's why I have to finish this report and get the heck out of here."

"That doesn't make any sense."

"I'm not sure how he feels about me, Sara. Even if he was in love with me, we could never make a relationship work. It's just...futile."

"I can't believe I'm hearing this garbage from you, of all people," Sara said. "We all thought it was futile to try to get our kids fair treatment in the Whitehorn schools. You marched in there for one measly hour and showed us we were wrong."

"That was different."

"Hah! If you can get Reese to toe the line, Jackson'll be a cinch. I'll admit I was a little surprised when I first noticed there was something going on between you two, but trust me,

the sparks are flying in both directions. It wouldn't surprise me if he took you home to meet his family any day now.''

Feeling the blood draining out of her head, Maggie returned to her chair and collapsed into it. ''I'm having dinner at his mother's house tomorrow night. The whole family is supposed to be there.''

Sara slapped the table and hooted with delight. ''See? What'd I tell ya? No man in his right mind takes a woman to something like that unless he's serious about her.''

Maggie groaned and shook her head.

''Aw, c'mon, Maggie. We're talkin' about love here, not a funeral. You're lookin' at this all wrong.''

''Am I? What about my career, Sara? It happens to be very important to me, it's not portable, and I'm not going to give it up just because some man crooks his finger at me.''

''If it was just any old man, I might agree with you,'' Sara said. ''But it's not. It's Jackson. If you really love him—''

''Damn it, Sara, you don't understand. I *can't* love him. I *can't* live on a reservation. I shouldn't even be here now.''

Sara straightened up and studied her as if she'd finally heard at least a hint of the desperation Maggie was feeling. ''Okay,'' she said softly. ''Then why don't you explain it to me?''

''It has to do with my mother.'' Maggie paused to swallow the lump that had suddenly formed in her throat, then recounted what little she knew of her mother's background.

''Speaks Softly,'' Sara murmured, when Maggie had finished. ''I've heard that name before, but I can't remember where.'' She shrugged after a moment. ''Well, I'll think of it someday. So what does this have to do with Jackson?''

''My mother died from cancer five years ago. The last time I saw her when she was still lucid, she made me promise I would never go back to the blanket.''

Sara jerked back as if she'd been slapped. Her nostrils flared, and her eyes took on a frosty expression. ''Go back to the *blanket?* Did she actually *say* it that way?''

Maggie nodded. Before she could speak in her mother's defense, however, Sara stood, grabbed her empty mug and carried it to the sink. She banged it onto the drain board with such

force, Maggie was surprised it didn't shatter. Then she returned to the table, sat down and crossed her arms over her breasts.

"Sara, I didn't mean to offend you."

"I know you didn't, but it makes me angry, and very, very sad, to hear that phrase. And coming from one of our own people, well, it reeks of self-hatred and shame and denial of who we are. *We* were here first. This was *our* land, but we were willing to share it with the whites. *We* didn't violate the treaties we made with them. Was it our fault we ended up with only blankets?"

Not knowing what else to say, Maggie whispered, "I'm sorry."

Sara shook her head. "It's not your fault, Maggie. I feel sorry for you, though. What your mother did to you wasn't fair."

"What do you mean?"

"She denied you your heritage while you were growing up. And then she made you promise to give it up permanently, when you had no idea what you were surrendering."

"I don't think you really understand, Sara."

"No, Maggie. *You* are the one who doesn't understand. If you honor your mother's last request, you'll never know who you really are. You will have given up the right to be a real Indian. A real Northern Cheyenne."

Maggie felt her temper starting to flare, and made no effort to control it. "You know, Jackson has said things like that to me, too, and I find them extremely offensive. What is this *real* Indian stuff, anyway? Do I have to earn a merit badge to get into the club? Buy a membership card? What do I have to do to prove myself to you people? Huh?"

"You don't have to prove anything to anyone but yourself," Sara said quietly. "If you're happy with yourself and the way you live, it's nobody's business but yours. But I've been watching you ever since you came here, and I don't think you're all that happy."

"Why not?"

"Why did you come here in the first place?"

"It was my job, Sara."

Sara leaned forward, pinning Maggie with an unblinking stare. "It was an excuse. An excuse to break your promise, just

a little bit, so you could learn about your own people. If you're honest with yourself, you'll admit you *like* being with us, and you *want* to belong here. You *want* to be a part of this tribe. You're just afraid to make the commitment."

"I didn't know you had a degree in psychiatry."

"Can the sarcasm," Sara said. "It's not me you're really mad at."

Maggie glared at her for a moment, then sighed and shook her head. "You're right. I'm just all...confused."

"Welcome to the human race. It seems to me, though, that you're trying to figure out two issues at once. Maybe if you separated them, it wouldn't be so hard to figure out."

"You mean the, uh, Indian thing and Jackson?"

"Yeah. There's really no point in worrying about a relationship with Jackson until you decide whether or not you're willing to go back on your promise and become a part of the tribe. He's here to stay, Maggie. He's committed to his eyeballs, and I think you know that."

Maggie nodded. "It's one of the things I admire most about him. And you're right about something else. I *do* like being here. I can see so many things I could do for the tribe, and I *like* being a part of things. But I feel guilty about it."

"Because of your mother."

"Yes. I always knew she loved me, Sara. Whatever she did, she only did it to protect me. She wasn't a bad person."

"I never thought she was," Sara said. "I think she was misguided, but she had to have been a pretty special lady to raise a daughter like you."

"Thanks. But where does that leave me now?" Maggie asked. "If you were in my place, what would you do?"

"I'd find her family and see if anyone could tell me why she left and why she never came back."

"What difference would that make?"

"I'm not sure," Sara admitted. "I'll tell you one thing, though. Jackson Hawk is no saint, but he's one of the finest men I've ever known. If I was in love with him the way I think you are, I wouldn't give him up without a damn good reason."

"That assumes, of course, that he's in love with me, too," Maggie said. "Big assumption, Sara."

Sara grinned. "Aw, he'll get around to telling you one of these days. Are you okay now?"

"Yeah. I'm better, anyway. Go get some sleep."

"Right. See you tomorrow, Maggie."

Maggie waited until she heard Sara's bedroom door shut, then exhaled a ragged sigh. It was time to make a decision. Countless times, she had considered asking Jackson to introduce her to her relatives. She'd always chickened out, because it had felt like an invasion of her mother's privacy, at best. At worst, outright disrespect.

But so many of the things Sara had said were on target. What if she was right about Jackson's feelings for her, too? Her heart skipped half a beat, then lurched into high gear as the truth finally hit her.

Oh, God. She had to meet her relatives as soon as possible. Had to resolve her guilt over her promise to her mother. She wasn't just falling in love with Jackson Hawk. That was already a done deal.

Fighting the worst case of nerves he'd suffered in years, Jackson parked in front of Sara's house the next evening and willed himself to calm down. It was only a dinner, he told himself. His family would like Maggie, and she would like them. No need to get himself all worked up.

If he knew what had been troubling her all day, he'd have an easier time believing his own assurances, but he hadn't been able to coax anything out of her. Damn, he hated trying to guess what was going on in a woman's mind. One of the things he liked most about Maggie was that she usually told him exactly what she thought, with little or no encouragement. But not today.

He'd never seen her so distracted. While he knew it was probably a sign his recent tactics had shaken her up, he couldn't tell if he'd made any real progress toward his goal. Had he been putting too much pressure on her? Not enough? The wrong kind?

Well, he'd had enough of the indirect approach. As soon as this damn dinner was over, he'd have a talk with her and get

the whole thing out in the open. Then they'd both feel better. At least he hoped they would.

Muttering under his breath, Jackson climbed out of the pickup, hurried up the walk and knocked on the door. Maggie opened it a moment later and smiled at him, and his heart rolled over like a well-trained pup. She'd traded in her jeans for a pair of slim-fitting black slacks. With them, she wore a red long-sleeved silk blouse, cinched in at the waist by a black leather belt. Dainty silver earrings complemented her short hair, and a matching pendant winked at him from the V neckline of her blouse.

She looked casual and classy, sweet and sexy, all at the same time. And if he didn't get to kiss her again soon, he was gonna go totally out of his mind. Knowing he couldn't trust himself to keep his hands off her if they spent much time alone, he declined her invitation to come inside. Once he got her settled in the passenger seat, he made a U-turn and headed straight for his mother's place.

As he'd expected, the simple family dinner had escalated into a full-fledged party. Luckily, the weather had been unseasonably warm during the past two weeks, making a picnic possible tonight. The air was fragrant with the scent of the pine trees and smoke from the barbecue pit. Vehicles of every kind and vintage lined both sides of the long driveway. The big yard surrounding the house teemed with people.

The teenagers had taken over the front porch. One group of women hustled back and forth between the kitchen and the rows of picnic tables, setting out food and fussing over the arrangement of salads, baked beans and frybread. Another group cooed over the babies and gossiped between frantic dashes to keep the more adventurous toddlers away from the irrigation ditch that formed the southern boundary of the yard.

The men played their traditional role of helping the women by staying the hell out of their way. Translated into action, that meant occasionally tending the barbecue pit or gathering around a metal horse trough filled with ice, beer and soft drinks, smoking cigarettes and swapping lies and jokes. The kids charged around in packs of five and six, laughing, yelling and generally adding to the commotion.

Meeting a clan as large and diverse as his would have been daunting for anyone. The one time his ex-wife had been here, she'd acted like she was afraid of catching a disease if she touched anyone or anything. Maggie couldn't have been more gracious. The longer Jackson watched her chatting and laughing with his relatives, the more convinced he became that she belonged here. With him. He could hardly stand to wait until dinner was over to start trying to convince her.

When the time finally came, he casually offered to take her for a walk, and guided her away from the party. They strolled past the barn in silence. Once they were out of sight and earshot of the others, he led her over to the corral fence.

Maggie rested both hands on the top rail. ''What's up, Jackson?''

''I thought you might like a break from the horde. Are they driving you crazy yet?''

She laughed. ''No, your family's wonderful.''

Turning toward her, he braced his elbow on the rail, buying a little time to search for the right words. ''I'm glad you feel that way. It makes it a little easier to confess something.''

''Oh? What have you done now?''

''It's more what I haven't done,'' he said, returning her teasing grin with a rueful one of his own. ''For the past week, I haven't been very honest with you.''

Her grin faded. ''In what way?''

''I really haven't given up on the idea of your coming to work for the tribe. I've been trying to put you in situations where you'd see how much we need your skills.''

''Is that all?'' she asked with a chuckle. ''I hate to tell you this, Jackson, but you're about as subtle as your family.''

He gave her an unrepentant wink. ''Well? Did it work? Have you thought about it at all?''

''Yes.''

He prompted when she didn't go on. ''And?''

''And, I'm...intrigued with the idea.''

''How intrigued?''

She looked away from him, pausing, as if she were wrestling with some inner decision. Impatience clawed at Jackson's gut, but he forced himself to remain silent. Then she looked at him

again. Though her eyes held an anxiety he'd never seen before, her voice was filled with conviction.

"There's something I need to do before I can seriously consider any kind of a future relationship with the tribe."

"What is it, Maggie?"

"I need to understand what happened to my mother. I need to meet her relatives."

Jackson released the breath he'd been holding, in a silent sigh of relief. This he could help her with. "I'll set up a meeting tomorrow, if you want."

She grimaced. "That soon?"

"Frankly, I've been wondering why you haven't wanted to meet them before this."

"It's not that I haven't wanted to." Biting her lower lip, she hesitated, then glanced away again. In a hoarse whisper, she finally admitted, "But I'm scared."

Needing to touch her, he cupped the side of her face with his palm and forced her to look at him. "Why, Maggie?"

"What if they don't want to meet me? I mean, what if they hated my mother, for some reason? Don't you think they might hate me, too?"

"Hate you?" Stroking her cheek with the backs of his knuckles, he laughed softly at the absurdity of any such notion. "Honey, believe me, that won't happen."

"How can you be so sure? Do you know why my mother left and never came back?"

"No. But you've already met your grandmother, and she likes you just fine."

"I have a grandmother?"

He nodded. "Yup. You also have three aunts, two uncles and a slew of cousins on your mother's side of the family."

"Oh, my," she murmured, her voice sounding so wistful it wrenched Jackson's heart.

"Don't you want to know who they are?"

She shook her head. "I don't think so. If I ran into one of them before the meeting, I'd probably freak out or something. Do you, uh, know anything about my biological father's family?"

"Yeah. I was curious about why he wasn't listed on the tribal

rolls with you and your mother, so I did a little discreet checking.''

''What did you find out?''

''He was from Lame Deer. You've got a bunch of relatives over there, too. I'll be glad to go with you, if you want to make contact.''

''Thank you. That's awfully sweet of you.''

''Yeah, that's me, all right. I'm always a real sweet guy.''

Her low, husky chuckle wrapped around him like a warm blanket on a frigid night. Her eyes caressed his face with shared humor, and her teasing grin was as blatant an invitation to a kiss as he'd ever seen. Then she wrinkled her sassy little nose at him.

Uttering a half laugh, half groan, he said, ''Aw, Maggie,'' and gathered her into his arms.

She didn't seem to mind. When he lowered his head to capture her mouth, she went up on tiptoe and met him halfway. Her arms slid around his neck. Her lips parted. She welcomed his tongue with eager little moans.

The magic was still there, sweeter and more intense than the last time he'd kissed her. God, how had he lived without doing this for so long? He held her tighter, reveling in the sensations created by her body pressing against his from chest to thighs.

Her name pounded in his head in rhythm with the thundering of his heartbeat. Maggie, Maggie, Maggie... Determined to stay more in control this time, he shifted his mouth to the right and contented himself with peppering quick, light kisses across her cheeks, her eyelids, her temples and, finally, the tip of her sassy little nose. Then he rested his forehead against hers.

''Hey, Maggie, ya know what?''

''What, Jackson?''

''Pretending we're just friends doesn't work for me.''

She sighed, but didn't open her eyes. ''It doesn't work for me, either, but I don't know what else to do. Maybe we should stay away from each other.''

''Is that what you really want?''

Slowly shaking her head, she looked up at him. ''I like being with you, Jackson.''

"I like being with you, too. I like it a lot. I like kissing you even more."

"Yeah, me too." She dropped her gaze. "Whenever it happens, though, I, uh, seem to forget that it's not nice to be a tease. I'll understand if you'd rather keep your distance."

"That's the last thing I want," he said. "I'd like to see you stay here for the tribe's sake, but that's not the only reason I've been pressuring you, Maggie. You know that, don't you?"

"I thought there might be more to it, but I wasn't sure."

"Well, now you are. I want you so bad, I ache with it."

She gulped, then looked up at him again. "I don't think I can handle an affair with you, Jackson."

"Did it ever occur to you I might want more than an affair?"

"What are you saying? Is this a...proposal?"

"What if I said yes?"

She pulled out of his loose embrace. "I don't know."

"Relax," he said. "It's not a proposal, but my intentions aren't completely dishonorable. For now, I'd just like to give our relationship a chance to grow and see what happens. Know what I mean?"

Her eyes narrowing with suspicion, she backed up a step. "I'm not sure I do."

"C'mon, Maggie, lighten up a little, will ya? All I'm askin' is for us to admit we're more than pals and do some of the things other couples do. Like hold hands, or hug or kiss once in a while. It might even be fun to go out on a date and talk about something besides work. Now does that sound so damn bad?"

Feeling foolish for practically yelling at her when he'd been trying to woo her, Jackson scowled while he waited for an answer. Honest to God, he thought he'd behaved pretty well when she called a halt to their kissing before. Considering how much he wanted her and how fiercely she'd responded to him, he'd damn near been a saint.

The corners of her mouth twitched, then slowly curved up in a smile that was worth every bit of aggravation she'd caused him. "No, Jackson, it doesn't sound bad at all. As long as you understand that's as far as I can go until I find out about my mother."

He held out his hand. She slid hers into it. And without another word, they set off for his mother's house again. It was a far cry from where he hoped to end up with her, but at least it was a start.

Ten

The next afternoon, Maggie climbed into the passenger seat of Jackson's pickup, fastened her seat belt and clamped her hands between her knees to stop them from shaking. Jackson slid behind the wheel and drove north on a gravel road they'd never taken before. She wished she had a pair of aviator sunglasses like his to hide behind.

"Nervous?" Jackson asked.

"Yes. You know, it's weird, but I wasn't half as nervous when I went to see Mr. Reese."

Jackson shot her a teasing smile. "Hell, he's lots meaner and uglier than your grandmmother."

"My head knows that." Maggie wiped her damp palms on her jeans. "But the rest of me hasn't gotten the message yet."

Steering with his left hand, he reached across the bench seat with his right, grabbed her left hand and laced their fingers together. "You're only gonna meet your grandmother and one of your aunts today. I promise, it'll be okay. Annie was tickled to death when I called her this morning."

"Annie?"

"Yeah. Annie Little Deer is your grandmother. And Rose Weasel Tail is your aunt."

"Then Wanda's..."

"Your first cousin," Jackson finished for her. "You couldn't have asked for nicer relatives, so stop worrying."

Maggie digested that information for a moment, then blew out a quiet sigh. "You weren't supposed to tell me, Jackson."

"You were gettin' so tense over there, I was afraid you were either gonna pass out or barf all over my pickup. Besides, if I didn't tell you now, there wouldn't be any time for you to settle down. We're almost there."

Her stomach lurched. She yanked her hand away from Jack-

son's and held it over her eyes. "Lord, I won't know what to say to them. Turn around. I can't do this."

He pulled to the side of the road and turned off the engine. Then he unfastened his seat belt, slid over next to Maggie and hauled her onto his lap. "It's okay," he murmured. "I'll be right there with you. They're probably just as scared as you are, Maggie."

"I'm being ridiculous, aren't I?"

"A little. But I won't tell a soul."

Smiling at her own foolishness, she rubbed her cheek against the front of his shirt, taking comfort from his warmth and the strong, steady beating of his heart beneath her ear. She wished she could stay here all day. But, of course, she couldn't. Her grandmother and aunt were waiting.

She gave him a quick, hard kiss for luck, then scooted off his lap and ordered him to drive on before she lost her nerve again. In what seemed like only a few seconds, he turned into a rutted driveway. Gnarled old cottonwood trees flanked both sides of the lane. When the house came into view, Maggie's heart sank.

Small and shabby, it had the peeling paint and junk-filled yard of almost every other house on the reservation. But it wasn't just any other house. Her mother had been born, taken her first steps and said her first words there. It was difficult to believe anyone, much less her own mother, could have started out in this decrepit little cottage and ended up in a gorgeous home in one of Denver's most exclusive subdivisions.

"Are you ready?" Jackson asked as he shut off the engine.

No. She would never be ready for this, but it was too late for retreat. The front door opened. Two women stepped out onto the sagging porch and stood there, silently watching and waiting. Though they didn't touch, an aura of unity surrounded them, as if they had stood on that porch many times, lending each other strength while they watched and waited for a loved one to return.

Maggie inhaled a deep breath, clutched her purse and the carton of cigarettes she'd brought as a traditional gift of tobacco for her grandmother to her chest and said, "Let's go."

She popped the door latch, climbed down and slowly crossed

the yard, unable to take her gaze off the women whose blood she shared. Annie was an inch shorter than Rose, her face heavily lined by at least seventy years of sun and struggle. Her hair had a liberal sprinkling of gray among the darker strands, and she wore it pulled back in one long braid. She was thin to the point of gauntness, but she held her back straight and proud, and a keen intelligence shone from her black eyes.

Rose was a rounder, younger-looking version of Annie. She wore her hair in a similar style, but it was a thick, lustrous black that reflected the bright sunshine. She had the same proud bearing as her mother, and she studied Maggie with the same intense interest.

Maggie stopped at the foot of the steps, raising one hand to shade her eyes. Her mouth was as dry as the parched ground. Her heart was thumping so hard, everyone must be able to hear it. Then she felt a hard, reassuring arm wrap around her waist, steadying her.

She looked up at Jackson, found empathy and support in his wink, and abruptly felt her anxiety fade to a manageable level. It was the strangest sensation, as if by his mere presence he'd replenished her depleted supply of courage. She gave him a grateful smile, then turned back to her grandmother and aunt.

Finally able to see past her own fear, she suddenly noticed her grandmother's. Annie's chin was quivering. Her lips were clamped together. Her fingers were clasped in a tight knot in front of her abdomen. All those small clues formed a picture of a woman fighting to control a powerful emotion. And there was a desperate eagerness in Annie's misty eyes that told Maggie the emotion was not rejection.

Clearing her throat, she climbed the first step. "Hello, Grandmother."

As if those two quiet words had unlocked a set of floodgates, tears spilled from Annie's eyes, leaving glistening tracks down her lined cheeks. Her hands jerked apart. She opened her arms in a silent invitation. Maggie ran up the last two steps and squeezed her eyes shut as her grandmother's bony little arms closed around her in a fierce hug.

A moment later, Annie pulled back and raised her hands to

Maggie's face, tracing her features with trembling fingertips, smiling through her tears.

"Welcome, little one," she whispered. "I never thought I would be blessed to see you again. You look like my Bevy."

"Thank you," Maggie murmured, blinking back tears of her own. "She was a beautiful lady."

"Quit hoggin' her, Mama," Rose said. "I want a hug, too."

Laughing, Maggie turned to her aunt and received another warm welcome. Then Rose took over, drawing Annie, Maggie and Jackson inside, leading the way to a cozy kitchen at the back of the house, talking constantly, as if she intended to make up for all the lost years in one afternoon.

Jackson elbowed Maggie in the ribs, gestured toward Rose with his thumb and whispered, "That's where you got your gabbiness."

"Oh, hush," Maggie whispered back, but the thought pleased her immensely.

She'd noted many times before that no matter how poor a Cheyenne home might look on the outside, the inside was invariably neat and clean, and whatever food the people had was generously shared with visitors. Annie Little Deer's home was no exception. Feeling too excited to eat, Maggie almost groaned when she saw the kitchen table.

Big dishes of vegetables and salads fought for space with heaping platters of beef, chicken and frybread. Four freshly baked pies sat on the counter beside the stove. Her grandmother and aunt must have been cooking nonstop since Jackson phoned this morning. The gesture touched Maggie deeply, and she did her best to do the meal justice.

Jackson and Rose carried most of the conversation while they were eating. When Rose stood to clear away the dirty dessert plates, however, Annie got up and brought a fat, dog-eared photo album to the table. Maggie and Jackson scooted their chairs closer for a better view of the book. Picture by picture, memory by memory, Annie revealed a part of Beverly's life Maggie had never known.

There were photographs of Beverly as a young child, with Rose and their other sisters, Carol and Susan, playing with dolls, lined up on a horse's back, having a water fight with their

brothers, William and Henry. As the pages turned, the children grew into gangly adolescents and then into good-looking young men and women. Toward the end of the book, a heartbreakingly handsome young man began to appear in the photos with Beverly.

"Your father," Annie said, "Daniel Speaks Softly."

"What was he like?" Maggie asked.

"He was a good boy," Annie said. "Polite, smart, ambitious. He could fix any kind of a machine. He loved your mother very much."

"Then why did he leave her?"

"He got into an argument with his boss and lost his job. Couldn't find another one, because the boss spread lies about him all over Whitehorn. Then he felt ashamed and started drinkin'." Annie sighed and shook her head. "My Bevy, she tried real hard to make him stop, but it wasn't no use. He just up and left one day. Didn't even know you were on the way."

Jackson pointed to a photo of Beverly, smiling down at a squalling infant in her arms. "Is that Maggie?"

Rose peered over Jackson's shoulder and laughed when she saw the picture. "Oh, yeah. We were all crazy about that kid, but she had a set of lungs on her you could hear for miles."

Maggie smiled over her shoulder at Rose, who reached out and affectionately ruffled her hair.

"And from what Wanda tells me, she still makes a lot of noise in certain places," Rose said, with a wicked grin. "Like school district offices. We owe you big-time for that one, sweetie. Thanks."

"You're welcome," Maggie said.

Annie closed the album, then got up and pulled open a drawer. Returning to the table, she set a small, intricately beaded pouch shaped like a turtle in front of Maggie. "I made this for you when you were born. I want you to have it."

Maggie picked it up and studied both sides, feeling something hard, like a little stick, between the layers. "This is beautiful. What is it?"

"A charm to make you grow up healthy and protect you from evil. This is an old Cheyenne custom. When you have babies, I will make charms for them."

"What's inside it, Grandmother?"

"A piece of your navel cord. That's what makes the medicine work." Annie shot a sly grin at Jackson, then looked back at Maggie. "This Hawk kid, here—I think he might give you pretty babies. You like him?"

Maggie felt her face grow hot. She heard Jackson let out a deep, rough chuckle, but didn't dare look at him. "Yes, I like him, Grandmother, but we haven't known each other very long."

"Pah!" Annie said, waving aside Maggie's cautious words. "What's to know? He's a big, handsome fella. Got steady work, a nice house and a decent family. You could do a lot worse."

"Thank you, Annie," Jackson said.

She shook a bony finger at him. "Don't get all conceited, Jackson Hawk. She could do a lot *better* than you, too. You get this girl of ours, I'll expect you to take good care of her."

"Yes, ma'am," Jackson said.

"I don't need anyone to take care of me." Maggie shot him a warning look. "I can take care of myself."

"Yeah, sure," Annie agreed. "Most of us can. But it don't hurt to have a good-lookin' man around to give you them pretty babies."

"Don't give him any more ideas, Grandmother," Maggie complained. "He's got enough of his own."

"He's a randy one, eh?" Raising her eyebrows, Annie turned her scrutiny on Jackson again. "You behave yourself around our girl, Jackson Hawk. Show her respect, or her uncles will pay you a visit. You understand me?"

His eyes glinting with unholy glee, Jackson nodded solemnly. "Yes, ma'am. I understand."

Annie nodded back at him, then leaned forward, bracing her forearms on the table. "Tell me about your mother, Maggie. This Mr. Schaeffer she married—was he good to her?"

"Oh, yes," Maggie said. "He's a wonderful man. Would you like to see a picture of them together?"

"Please."

Maggie dug her wallet out of her purse and pulled a photo-

graph from it's plastic sleeve. "This was taken at Lake Louise, up in Canada, about a year before she got sick."

Annie accepted the picture, holding it carefully by the edges. Rose came over and stood behind her, laying one hand on Annie's shoulder, as if in a gesture of comfort. Annie's face contorted with grief.

After a moment of silent struggle, her expression cleared, and she said softly, "My Bevy looks happy. Like when she was a little girl."

"Yeah, she does," Rose said. "See what pretty clothes she's wearing?"

Annie started to hand back the picture, but Maggie refused to take it. "I still have the negative. You keep that one, Grandmother."

"Thank you." Annie looked up at Maggie, then down at the photograph again. "You said she got sick?"

"She had breast cancer. The doctors did everything they could, but she never liked going to the doctor much, and they found it too late to help her."

Annie's voice softened to a hoarse whisper. "Did she... suffer?"

"It got bad toward the end," Maggie said, "but she had the best care Dad and I could give her. We still miss her a lot."

Gently laying the picture on the table, Annie said, "We also miss her, Maggie. I'm happy you finally came to see me. It's like having a little piece of my Bevy back."

"Did you know who I was that first day, when we met at the day-care center?" Maggie asked.

Annie nodded. "I was pretty sure."

"Why didn't you say something, Grandmother?"

"I didn't know how much you knew, and I didn't want to force a relationship on you, if you didn't want to know us."

"I didn't know if you would want to see me," Maggie said. "I only knew Mama came from this reservation, and that she never wanted me to come here. Can you tell me why she felt that way? Was there a family fight, or something like that?"

Annie stiffened, then turned her gaze away from Maggie. "It had nothing to do with the family. We loved Bevy and she

loved us. She wanted you to have a better life. That is all I have to say.''

''But—''

''We will not speak of this again.'' Annie pushed back her chair and stood, suddenly looking old and exhausted. ''Thank you for coming to see me. You'll come back for Wanda's graduation dinner. You can meet the others then.''

In other words, here's your hat, what's your hurry? Maggie thought grimly. She looked to Jackson for guidance as to whether or not she should push for more information. He shook his head and got to his feet. Maggie exchanged a stilted good-bye with her grandmother and walked back to the front door.

She had almost reached the pickup when the door of the house opened behind her and Rose came out, softly calling her name.

''Wait, Maggie. Please.''

Maggie turned around in time to see her aunt reach the bottom step and jog across the short distance between them.

''I don't want you to leave like this,'' Rose said. ''Mama didn't mean to hurt your feelings.''

''I know she didn't, Aunt Rose. Don't worry about it.''

Rose took Maggie's right hand between both of hers and held on as if she feared her niece would run away. Anxiously searching Maggie's face, she said, ''Mama's got real old-fashioned ideas about some things. You're probably imagining something worse than what really happened to your mom.''

''Will you tell me?'' Maggie asked.

''Sure, honey.'' Rose looked over at Jackson. ''This is kinda private, so we're gonna go for a little walk, okay?''

''No problem,'' he replied. ''Take your time.''

Maggie gave him a grateful smile, then walked around the side of the house with her aunt.

Jackson stood beside his pickup until Maggie and Rose were out of sight. Then he climbed in behind the wheel, rolled down the windows and stretched his legs across the seat. Rose had said Maggie was probably imagining something worse than what had actually happened to Beverly, but the admission that something *had* indeed happened to Maggie's mother worried

him. Her remark about Annie's being old-fashioned about some things made him suspect sex had been involved.

Women everywhere were vulnerable to male predators, but Indian women had always been especially helpless when it came to dealing with white men. Having grown up on a reservation, Rose was bound to have developed a stoic attitude toward the indignities Cheyenne women had often been forced to endure. But Maggie had grown up in an environment where women didn't learn to accept such indignities. Would Rose understand that, if she was planning to tell Maggie her mother had been raped?

The longer they were gone, the more anxious he felt. After ten minutes, he climbed out of the pickup and rearranged the jumble of tools he always carried around in the back. After twenty minutes, he started to pace back and forth between the pickup and the gravel road. After thirty, he decided to go looking for them.

As he rounded the corner of the house, the women came out of a stand of willows fifty yards away. Rose had her arm around Maggie's shoulders, but from this distance he couldn't see much more than that. Wanting to give them the privacy they needed to finish their conversation, he backtracked before they spotted him and got into the pickup again.

Five minutes later Maggie climbed in beside him, her face pale and set. Reminding himself she would tell him what she'd learned if and when she felt like it, he turned the vehicle around and drove away. She sat utterly still, looking straight ahead with the unblinking stare of a shock victim.

Gritting his teeth against the rage he felt at seeing her so upset, Jackson stomped on the accelerator. She still hadn't spoken by the time they arrived at his house, and she made no objection when he took her inside. Her hand was so icy in his, he was surprised she wasn't shivering.

He led her to the sofa. She obediently sat at one end, pulled her knees up to her chest and hugged them to her with both arms. Swearing under his breath, Jackson raced upstairs for a blanket, raced back to the living room and wrapped her up. Then he hurried out to the kitchen and made her a mug of strong, sweetened tea.

When he offered it to her, she looked up at him with a blank, shattered expression for a heartbeat, then slowly shook her head. Jackson set the cup on the coffee table, sat beside her and took both of her hands between his.

Briskly rubbing them, he said, "Maggie, honey, talk to me. What did Rose tell you?"

Maggie shook her head again, but then her face crumpled and a harsh, racking sob shuddered through her body. He pulled her into his arms and held her, wishing he could take away her pain and knowing he couldn't. The tears came next, soaking his shirt while she gasped for air each time another sob shook her. And finally she raised her fists and pounded on his chest, crying, "No, no, no! Oh, Mama, no!"

Her energy spent, she sagged against him. Resting his cheek on the top of her head, Jackson held her, rocked her, murmured comforting words to her until even the silent weeping stopped. At last she pulled away, wiping her eyes with the backs of her hands.

"I'm sorry," she said, her voice still raw with emotion.

"You have nothing to be sorry for." He handed her the mug. When she'd taken a swallow, he asked, "Can you tell me what this is all about now?"

She took another swallow, then set the mug down and nodded.

"My, uh...my mother..." She choked, gulped, shook her head, as if in frustration.

"It's all right," Jackson said. "Take your time."

"When I was born, my m-mother had to go into W-White-horn to the hospital." She paused to inhale a deep breath. "She had to have a C-section because I was in the b-breach posi-tion."

A sick feeling invaded the pit of Jackson's stomach as he sensed what was coming, but he silently waited while she paused to take another breath.

"When, uh...when her periods still hadn't started again about eight months later, she went back to the doctor who had performed the operation. He laughed at her, Jackson. And he t-told her to f-forget about it."

"Why?"

Maggie's eyes suddenly glittered with fury. Her voice dripped venom onto every word. "Because that lousy son of a bitch had given her a hysterectomy while she was still under the anesthetic. Nobody had bothered to tell her about it."

Jackson uttered a vicious curse. Maggie nodded in agreement. Then she continued.

"He, uh…he said he had every right to do it to any dirty squaw who came to him expecting free emergency service. He'd made it his personal mission to save the taxpayers from having to support any more lazy damned Indians. Aunt Rose told me she knows of at least ten other women he sterilized involuntarily."

"Nobody ever took him to court?"

Maggie shook her head. "The women were all too ashamed to talk about it, and none of them thought they'd get any justice from the white courts if they did."

"He's not still practicing, is he?"

"No. If he was, I'd probably kill the bastard. Unfortunately, he's already dead. He murdered her, Jackson. It was because of him she wouldn't go to the doctor when she found the lump in her breast. I know it was."

"Damn, Maggie, I'm sorry that happened to your mother."

"Me, too. God, she must have felt so violated, and to him, it was like spaying a dog or a cat." Maggie turned to him, her eyes stark with pain. "I can't even imagine hating anyone that much. Can you?"

"No. But that kind of hatred's been out there for a long time," Jackson said. "After what she went through, I don't understand why your mother willingly spent the rest of her life with whites."

"I didn't, either. Aunt Rose said Mama blamed everything on her own ignorance of white people. I guess she thought she could save me from being that ignorant by raising me off the res. It was just pure luck she met Dad."

"How did that happen?"

"He hired her to clean the rooms in his first motel. She could have made more money as a waitress, but she took the motel job because he allowed her to bring me to work with her."

"He sounds like a nice guy."

"He is. Oh, God, I should call him. I don't think he knows any of this."

"Do it tomorrow," Jackson suggested. "You've had enough for one day."

"You're right." Leaning her head back against the sofa cushion, she closed her eyes. "You know what makes me feel the worst about this?"

"What?"

"When I was little, I used to beg my mother for a brother or a sister. Can you imagine how much that must have hurt her?"

"You were just a kid. You didn't know."

Tears trickled out from beneath her lashes. "I know, but she loved babies so much. After she was diagnosed, she used to go up to the hospital when she wasn't sick from the chemotherapy. And she'd rock and cuddle the babies who were born addicted to drugs. She said it comforted her as much as it did them. And that miserable excuse for a doctor took away her right to have any more babies of her own."

Jackson pulled her into his arms again. She clung to him for a moment, then pushed herself away. Refusing to look at him, she whispered, "I'm sorry. Knowing what he did to her makes me feel like I'm dirty inside."

"You're not the dirty one, Maggie. That damned doctor was."

"I know, but somehow I feel too...violated myself to touch anyone. I need to be alone for a little while."

Though he hated the thought of leaving her when she looked so forlorn, Jackson nodded and got up. "All right. I'll check on the horses and mess around in the garage or something. Call me if you need anything."

As he reached the back door, she called to him. "Hey, Jackson? Thanks."

"That's what friends are for," he said.

Then he walked into the mudroom, where he spied the stack of tarps and blankets he used for the sweat lodge. He hesitated for a moment, wondering if the idea forming in his mind would help Maggie put this painful episode into perspective.

Well, why not? he asked himself. Her spirit needed healing.

While his idea might not be too kosher, she wasn't a traditional Indian. Hell, she wouldn't even know the difference. Grabbing the pile of blankets, he hurried out the back door.

Exhausted and numb, Maggie curled up in the blanket again. Jackson had been so sweet, she hoped she hadn't hurt his feelings by asking him to leave her alone. But it couldn't be helped. She'd learned so many things today, she needed some time to digest them all and regain her composure.

Gradually, the daylight faded. Her clamorous thoughts subsided, and the peace and quiet of the house sank into her bones. She lost all sense of the passage of time. Her eyelids grew heavy.

"Maggie," a deep, familiar voice said close to her ear. "Maggie, wake up."

She forced her eyes open and sat up. What she saw made her wonder if she was having a weird dream. Closing her eyes, she shook her head to clear it. When she opened them again, Jackson was still standing in front of her, wearing nothing but a pair of black gym shorts and sneakers. He held out what looked like a purple T-shirt. In a voice that sounded as if it were coming from the bottom of a well, he asked if she needed some help.

"Help with what?" she asked.

He waved the T-shirt under her nose. "You need to take off everything but your underwear and put this on."

"Why?"

"We're gonna do a sweat. It'll make you feel better."

At the moment, she seriously doubted anything could accomplish that. But Jackson had a determined look on his face, and she still felt too groggy and disoriented to argue with him.

"Okay, okay..." she grumbled, holding out her hand. "I'll put it on."

"Do you need some help?" he asked again.

"No. Just give me a second to wake up."

"All right, but don't take too long. Everything's ready, and I can't leave the fire unattended. I can see it from the backyard, so I'll wait for you there." He handed her the shirt and walked

to the door, then added, "Wear your shoes, too, or you'll get stickers in your feet."

Moving slowly, she stood up. When she heard the door shut, she stripped down to her bra and panties and pulled the T-shirt over her head. The soft fabric covered her from her neck to her knees. It held a fresh scent, as if it had been dried on a clothesline. Then she obediently put on her shoes, made a pit stop in the bathroom and went out to join Jackson.

A cool evening breeze washed away the last vestiges of drowsiness. Jackson smiled at her as she crossed the patio, holding out a hand in welcome. It felt natural to slide her hand into his and walk beside him under a sky filled with stars.

Looking up at them, she said, "How long did I sleep?"

"Five hours," he said.

"Tell me about this sweat thing. Why is it going to make me feel better?"

"It's a purification ritual. It'll help you find your center of balance again, and connect you with Mother Earth. We usually have more people than this, but we'll do our best with just the two of us."

The sweat lodge came into view. A patchwork of blankets covered the sapling frame. The fire ring beside it held a pyramid of rocks surrounded by glowing embers. A pitchfork leaned against a nearby tree.

Jackson released her hand, then grasped her shoulders and turned her to face him. "It'll be pitch-black when we get inside the lodge and close the flap. I'll bring in the rocks four times, and it'll feel like you're being roasted alive."

"Gee, it sounds like fun," she muttered.

Ignoring her smart remark, he went on. "If you can't breathe, put your face close to the ground or lie down. It'll be cooler down there. You can leave anytime you need to, but try to stay with me through all four rotations. Okay?"

Following his directions, she ducked through the low canvas doorway and crawled to the far end of the lodge. She sat cross-legged and inhaled slow, deep breaths, reminding herself she was not claustrophobic. The only furnishings were a bucket of water with a metal dipper and a portable cassette player. Weird,

she thought. Using a modern machine in an ancient ceremony was definitely weird.

A moment later, Jackson carried in a load of glowing rocks, balancing them on the tines of the pitchfork. He dropped them in a hole dug in the center of the floor.

Then he quickly shut the flap and crawled to a spot beside her, dragging the bucket of water behind him. The temperature rose immediately. When the glow of the rocks died down, Maggie couldn't see a blessed thing. She heard a soft click, and the sound of Indian drums touched her ears. Well, that explained the cassette player. The rocks flared again when Jackson sprinkled something over them. Wisps of smoke rose from the pit. A wonderful aroma filled the air.

"This is cedar, for purification," Jackson said, his voice low and reverent, blending with the drums. "Breathe it in. Take it with your hands and rub it over yourself."

Determined to give this a chance, she followed his instructions. He poured a dipper of water over the rocks next, creating a hissing cloud of steam. Suddenly it was hotter. Hotter than anything she'd ever felt before. Hotter than even hell could be.

Sweat gushed from her skin. The air was too thick to breathe. Panic seized her. She had to get out. Get out. Get out!

Jackson's voice reached out to her, calming and soothing her, even though she couldn't understand the words he was chanting. They must be in Cheyenne. She bent down as Jackson had instructed, finally succeeding in dragging the searing air into her lungs. The drumbeats echoed through her head in a steady, relentless rhythm.

Her mind whirled with half-formed thoughts and fleeting images. Her heart picked up the cadence of the drums. She clung to Jackson's voice as if it were her only link to sanity, while the heat continued to come at her in overwhelming waves. Just when it was about to become bearable, she heard Jackson moving toward the doorway.

Cool air rushed in, shocking her skin, raising goose bumps as high as the Rockies. He brought in another load of rocks and flipped the canvas flap shut, and the cycle of heat and steam started all over again, opening her pores to another cleansing bath of sweat.

Slowly, slowly, her mind cleared. Her anxiety merged with the steam and floated into the night. She felt the earth, hard and cool beneath her. Heard the drums and Jackson's voice as if they were somewhere inside her. Sensed a deep and expanding unity of spirit with him that was like nothing she had ever known.

The lodge became a womb, the steam a protective cushion of fluid, the drums her mother's heartbeat. She was safe here. Safe from guilt and grief and humiliation. Safe from rage and hurt and confusion. She was one with the darkness, one with Jackson, one with all of the people who had ever experienced this ceremony. Here, finally, was a place where she felt, to the bottom of her soul, that she belonged.

When the fourth cycle ended, she didn't want to leave. The world outside was too exposed and frightening and lonely. But when Jackson held out his hand to her from the doorway, she went to him.

He helped her to her feet, then enfolded her in his arms. And suddenly, as if by magic, she felt safe again.

Eleven

"Thank you," Maggie whispered. She hugged Jackson with all her strength, then leaned back and gazed up at him. "That was absolutely incredible."

He tucked a strand of her hair behind her ear. "I thought you were pretty incredible. Your first sweat can be intimidating, but you handled it like a champ."

"Hearing your voice helped." She shivered from the memory of the intimate connection she had felt with him.

Jackson released her, untied one of the blankets on the sweat lodge and wrapped it around her. "Can't let you get chilled. Why don't you go to the house and take a shower? I'll clean up here."

"No, I want to help. You went to a lot of trouble to do this for me."

"It was my pleasure."

He leaned down and dropped a playful kiss on her mouth. That brief contact wasn't enough. She wanted much, much more. When he started to straighten up, she raised one hand to the back of his neck and held him there. His muscles tensed. His gaze locked with hers, and in the black depths of his eyes she saw a fierce hunger that matched her own. Oh, God. The intimate connection was still there, and she wanted—no, needed—to feel it with her body, as well as with her heart and mind.

She lifted her other hand to his neck and pressed her lips to his. The blanket slid off her shoulders, hitting the ground with a muffled plop. His arms surrounded her, pulling her flush against him.

Conscious thought ceased. Ancient instincts took over. He was all hot, naked skin, hard bones and muscles, strong, seeking hands. Her senses feasted on him. The slickness of his tongue

stroking hers. The salty taste of his neck. The aroma of wood smoke mixing with his own musky scent. His hoarse groans of need and want. The rough calluses on his hands when he slid them beneath her shirt and caressed her back and sides.

She strained closer. Cupping his hands under her bottom, he hiked her up. She wrapped her legs around his hips, clutched at his back with her hands, rubbed her breasts against his chest, reveling in the strength of his erection pressing into her most private parts. God, she loved being wanted like this. Needed to be needed like this. Never, ever, wanted these exciting sensations to end.

But suddenly he was pushing her hips away, untangling her arms from around his neck, denying her his mouth. Her feet touched the ground. He held her by the waist until her wobbly legs would support her. Then he let her go, curling his fingers into fists at his sides, as if to prevent himself reaching for her again. They stared at each other, chests heaving with ragged breaths that rent the night's stillness.

"We can't do this, Maggie," he said. "Not now."

"I want you, Jackson. And you want me. Don't deny it."

"I don't want to deny it." He glanced down at his groin, then gave her one of his half shrugs and a rueful smile. "I couldn't if I wanted to. But you've had one hell of an emotional day, and I don't want to take advantage of you when you're so vulnerable. I didn't bring you out here to seduce you."

"Fine." Grinning wickedly, she stepped toward him, her palms itching to touch him again. "I'll seduce you."

He grabbed her hands and held them together in front of her. "No, Maggie. Stop and think about this, before I run out of nobility. Believe me, I don't have much left."

"Jackson, I know what I'm doing."

He inhaled a deep breath, then released it with a shuddering sigh. "Humor me. I don't want you to have any regrets. Go up to the house and wait for me. If you still want to make love with me when I get there, we will. If you don't, there won't be any problem. Deal?"

Maggie knew she wouldn't change her mind. She had never felt so close to anyone, and nothing in her life had ever felt this right. Unfortunately, she could see that he had his heart set

on protecting her, and she could hardly fault him for forcing her to make a clear and conscious decision. In fact, she loved him for it, more than she'd ever dreamed she could love anyone.

"Okay, deal," she said. "But don't take forever."

Releasing her hands, he stepped back. She turned and walked away, plotting wonderfully wicked things she would do to him the next time she saw him. Unbraiding his hair topped the list. After that, she'd think of something.

She entered the kitchen, turned on the lights and dutifully sat down at the table to wait. She even tried to think of reasons not to make love with him. But there weren't any.

Until now, she had spent her whole life looking toward the future, studying to achieve the goals her mother had set for her and working to become the kind of woman who would make her mother proud.

The sweat lodge had forced her to live in the moment. It had taught her the joy of feeling all her feelings, no matter how intense they might be. It had shown her how empty her heart had been before she met Jackson.

When she finished her report, she would have to choose between going back to Washington and staying here with her people. It would not be an easy choice to make. But she wasn't going to worry about that now.

No, tonight she was not Beverly's daughter. She wasn't the congressman's aide or the Little Fed. She was simply a woman who deeply loved a man. She didn't need or want promises, commitments or obligations. The future would take care of itself. At this moment, the only thing she really wanted was to spend one night in Jackson's arms. Whatever she had promised her mother, she deserved that much happiness.

The back door opened and closed. Standing, she turned to face the doorway. Her heart soared when Jackson appeared. Catching sight of her, he halted in his tracks and rocked back on his heels as if he'd run into an invisible barrier. His gaze locked with hers, and in his eyes she saw everything she could have wished for—longing, hope and hunger, all mixed up with a resigned acceptance of the possibility that she'd changed her mind.

Unable to speak past the lump in her throat, she held out her arms to him. He crossed the room with long, deliberate strides, dumped the cassette player he carried on the table and studied her face intently, as if he were searching for the slightest sign of doubt. She looked back at him just as intently, holding her breath, praying he would see the feelings she couldn't express with words.

Finally, a slow, sensuous smile moved over his face, and then she was in his arms, hugging, kissing, laughing with the sheer joy of holding him. He lowered one hand to the backs of her knees and lifted her high against his chest. Chuckling at her startled yelp, he carried her up the stairs and into the bathroom.

He kissed her as if she were a tasty morsel he intended to savor to the fullest. Then he set her on her feet, turned away to start the water in the shower, and came back to her as the room began to fill with a steamy mist.

Beneath his tender ministrations, her clothing fell away. She sighed with delight when he kicked his gym shorts into the corner, revealing himself completely for the first time. He was a proud, virile warrior, created with long limbs and sleek, hard muscles, perfect for hunting and fighting off enemies and pleasing the eyes of his woman.

The admiration in his eyes when he looked at her said he found her equally pleasing, allowing her to shed all modesty and inhibition. Boldly she stepped forward and tugged off the leather strings at the ends of his braids. His hair immediately began to unwind. She helped it along, sliding her fingers through the thick ebony sections, spreading it out on his broad shoulders.

"I've wanted to do that for a long time," she said.

He held the shower curtain open with one hand and offered her the other. "Come."

She stepped into the bathtub, lifting her face to the water while he climbed in behind her and enclosed them both in a warm, intimate world. A world not unlike the sweat lodge. Surrounding her with his arms, he urged her to lean back against his chest.

Then he rubbed a bar of soap over her breasts and belly with his right hand and followed it with his left, working up a frothy

lather on her skin. He scrubbed her arms, her legs, even her feet, then turned her around and scrubbed her back and buttocks with the same gentle thoroughness. Each slick, circular stroke of his hands sensitized a new swath of nerve endings until she burned with wanting him:

She held out her hand in a silent demand for the soap, returning his wicked smile when he slapped it into her palm. Oh, she would make him burn the way she burned, need the way she needed, want the way she wanted. But while the act of scrubbing him elicited groans of pleasure from deep in his throat, it also intensified her own arousal until she could barely contain it.

At last he took the soap away and handed her a bottle of shampoo. When she poured a generous dollop into her palm, he went down on one knee, nuzzling her breasts and belly, stroking her back and buttocks with his hands, while she rubbed the shampoo into his scalp. Exploding shampoo bubbles released a scent of citrus into the air. His hair flowed between her fingers like ropes of wet silk.

He lapped at the drops of water that collected in the grooves of her collarbones, followed some that drizzled into the valley between her breasts with his tongue, flicked at others that clung to her nipples. His hands grew bolder, sliding up and down the backs of her thighs, then the fronts, coming dangerously close to the one place she most wanted to feel his touch, but never quite reaching it.

Her knees quivered. She clutched his head against her abdomen, fearing she would collapse if she didn't hold on to something. In one smooth motion, he rose to his feet, anchoring her with a strong arm around her waist. Murmuring soothing nonsense phrases, he massaged shampoo into her hair, then ducked them both under the spray for a final rinse before shutting off the water.

After a few swipes of a towel over his hair and torso, he lifted her from the tub and made short work of drying her off. Then he scooped her up against his chest again. She wrapped her arms around his neck and felt his heart thudding against her side. Her own heart picked up the rhythm, pounding with anticipation as he carried her to his bedroom.

She would not have been surprised if he'd dumped her in the middle of the bed and taken her immediately. Nor would she have objected; she couldn't imagine feeling any more aroused than she already did.

Jackson had other ideas, however, wonderful, inventive, erotic ideas that he proceeded to demonstrate one by one. Using his hands and lips, his teeth and his tongue, he explored her body with maddening patience. He knew when to linger and when to move on, when to tantalize and when to stimulate, when to soothe and when to incite.

As it had in the sweat lodge, time stretched out until it lost all meaning. Her world narrowed to the circle of light cast by the lamp on the nightstand, to the man in her arms and the incredible sensations created by his touch. By the time he retrieved a foil packet from somewhere in the headboard, she was filled with such a fierce need for release, she wasn't about to wait for Chief Slow Hand to take care of the precautions.

Grabbing the packet out of his hand, she ripped it open with her teeth, tossed the foil aside and rolled the condom onto his engorged shaft with a minimum of fuss. Then she kissed her way up his torso, giving him a taste of his own sweet medicine before she captured his mouth with an urgent demand for satisfaction. And then he was beside her, sliding his right arm under her shoulders, hoisting her left leg over his hip, entering her with a powerful thrust that nearly made her weep with relief.

But there was no time for tears. The man with infinite patience had vanished. In his place, she found a man determined to drive her out of control in the shortest time possible.

Murmuring dark, delicious words that would have shocked her under any other circumstances, he thrust into her relentlessly, like the echoes of the drums she could still hear pounding in her memory. He nipped at the juncture of her neck and shoulder, soothed it with his tongue, caressed her breasts with his free hand. And the drums beat on, harder and faster. Her hips found the rhythm, meeting each thrust with equal power.

Again she found herself clinging to his voice as she reached and strained for something elusive. Elusive, but desperately important. A oneness. A connection of spirits that could be found

only in sweat-drenched flesh and the drumbeats and the steamy friction where their bodies came together again and again in a pleasurable sort of violence.

And still he urged her on, praising her, commanding her, invading every part of her consciousness, until there was only heat and light and the drumbeats. Always the drumbeats. Driving her up and up in an endless quest. Suddenly they were there, reaching that mystical, elusive peak together in a chorus of ecstatic shouts. And for one utterly sweet moment, their souls embraced.

The drums gradually faded into the strong, steady thud of Jackson's heart beneath her ear. Ragged breathing softened to contented sighs. She curled into his warmth, felt him brush a gentle kiss on the top of her head, then slid into a deep, exhausted sleep.

Jackson awoke to the first golden rays of dawn with an arm and shoulder that had gone numb and a warm, naked body plastered against his side under the covers. He lifted the sheet and felt a wave of tenderness threaten to swamp his heart. Maggie's head lay in the crook of his shoulder, her hair standing up every which way in adorable little spikes. She had one arm and a leg draped over him in a boneless sprawl, and her mouth was curved in a soft smile that suggested happy dreams.

Man, she was something else, he thought, grinning as he tucked the covers around her neck and shoulders. He'd expected her to be an enthusiastic lover, but he hadn't expected her to take him on like such a tigress. Just remembering the fire in her eyes when she'd snatched the condom out of his hand brought on an erection he could have used for a tent pole.

And to think he'd given her a chance to back out. He might have lived the rest of his days without ever knowing what real passion felt like. After all that had happened between them last night, surely she must love him.

There was no use trying to deny it. He was deeply and irrevocably in love with Maggie, and he wanted her to stay with him forever—as his wife, and the mother of his children. He hadn't realized how much he wanted kids until yesterday, when

Annie had told Maggie he could give her pretty babies. God, yes, he could. And he would, if only she would let him.

But what if she didn't feel the same way about him? The only predictable thing about Maggie was that she always found a way to do the unpredictable. Last night there had been no promises, no commitments, no words of love spoken.

What if she'd only wanted one night with him? She'd said she didn't want an affair, but when he'd hinted at a proposal, she sure hadn't turned any cartwheels, either. He squeezed his eyes shut, hoping he could also squeeze out these nagging doubts. Damn.

He wanted to shake her awake and demand a commitment. Or, better yet, make love to her again, and seduce one out of her. But as stubborn and independent as Maggie was, he figured trying to manipulate her or crowd her in any way would be the worst mistake he could make.

Much as he hated to admit it, this was probably one of those times when a wise man would back off and allow his woman the time and space she needed to make her own decision. That didn't mean he couldn't do his damnedest to help her make the right one. But ultimately, she would only stay with him if that was where she honestly wanted to be.

Unable to lie still any longer, Jackson slowly eased his shoulder from under Maggie's head, replacing it with a pillow. A million tiny needles attacked his arm as the blood flowed back into it. Biting back a hiss at the discomfort, he gently removed her arm and leg and slid out of the bed.

A pouty little frown crossed her face, but she shifted around, wrapped her arms around the pillow and settled back to sleep. He stood there, filling his eyes with her, imprinting this moment on his memory until the temptation to crawl back in there and make love to her again became almost irresistible.

Promising himself there would be time for that later, he gathered up a clean set of clothes and left the room. He took a quick shower, dressed and braided his hair, then hurried downstairs to the kitchen. Since neither of them had eaten last night, breakfast in bed seemed like as good a place as any to start convincing Maggie she couldn't live without him.

Hot coffee and orange juice, buttermilk pancakes with his

mother's homemade huckleberry syrup, bacon and scrambled eggs—what more could a woman want? He tossed a dish towel over his shoulder, loaded everything onto a cookie sheet and carefully hauled it up the stairs. Maggie hadn't moved a centimeter since he'd left, nor did she when he entered the room.

Setting the tray on his dresser, he poured a mug of coffee and carried it to the bed. He held it under her nose, letting the fragrant steam act as an alarm clock. Her nose twitched. She yawned and stretched. Finally, one eye popped open, studying the cup with considerable confusion.

"Morning, gorgeous," he said. "Think you could eat some breakfast?"

Her other eye popped open, and for a second she stared at him as if she'd never laid eyes on him before. Then she shook her head, started to sit up, and made a desperate grab for the sheet when she realized she was naked. Tucking it under her arms, she frowned at him, while a rosy blush raced up her neck and into her cheeks.

He set the cup on the nightstand and sat on the bed, facing her. Bracing one hand on the far side of her hips, he raised his other hand to stroke her flushed cheek.

"There was no shame between us last night. There's no need for any now."

Her eyes opened wide, and he could actually see the memories of what they had shared return to her. The blush intensified, but her frown slowly reversed itself into a sweet, sexy smile.

"Don't look at me like that if you're hungry for food," he warned her, stealing a quick kiss from her lips.

As if on cue, her stomach rumbled. She pulled away with an embarrassed laugh. "Could I please borrow a shirt? I need to visit the bathroom, and I'm not really, um, used to morning-afters. You know?"

Yeah, he knew what she meant, and in a way, her modesty pleased him, though it also amused him. Her curvy little body held no secrets from him, but if she wasn't comfortable strutting around naked in front of him just yet, that was okay. He went to the dresser and found her a bright red T-shirt.

She accepted it with a grateful smile, tugged it on over her

head and climbed out of bed. The shirt should have looked silly on her. The shoulder seams hung halfway down her arms, and the hem almost reached her knees, but it draped her curves in a way that made his mouth go dry and his hands tremble with a fierce need to scoop her up, put her back in that bed and keep her there for at least a week.

His thoughts must have shown on his face. Maggie shot him a wary smile, then turned and scurried down the hallway to the bathroom. He let out a deep, shuddering sigh and told himself to get a grip. She was bound to have a lot of things on her mind today. The last thing she needed was sexual pressure from him.

But, damn it, he'd finally found a woman who had given him a taste of heaven. Why couldn't they just fall in love, get married and live happily ever after like anyone else? It didn't seem fair that this situation had to be so blasted complicated.

"So, who ever promised you life would be fair?" he muttered, turning away to straighten up the bed.

The sheets were still warm from her body, and the pillow she'd been sleeping on carried her unique scent. His chest tightened. His throat closed up. An icy sweat broke out on his forehead. He couldn't lose her now. He just couldn't. And he couldn't play it cool and pretend to give her time and space. Jeez, that sounded like something his ex-wife would have said. Yuppie ideas, if he'd ever heard any.

Those asinine notions had no place in an open, honest relationship, which was the only kind he wanted. Either Maggie loved him or she didn't. Either she wanted to be with him or she didn't. She wanted to live with her people or with whites.

She had to make a choice. It was as simple as that. But would she make the one he wanted? And how hard did he dare push her to make it?

Maggie breezed into the room then, her face glowing from a scrubbing. Her hair still stood up every which way, but she'd combed out the spikes. And that damn red T-shirt still made him feel randy as hell.

Clearing his throat, he fluffed up the pillows, then held the covers open in an invitation for her to climb in. She did so, with a smile that seemed both polite and nervous. Biting back

an impatient snort, he grabbed the tray from the dresser, settled it on her lap, then sat down facing her again.

He stripped off the tinfoil he'd wrapped around the plates to keep the food warm. She oohed and aahed and thanked him for going to so much trouble, but her bright chatter couldn't hide the shadows in her eyes. Not from him, anyway. Just as he couldn't hide his tension from her, which had, no doubt, put those shadows in her eyes in the first place.

Damn it, this was supposed to be fun! He'd wanted to pamper her and care for her, but she looked like a kid trying to choke down liver and onions and brussels sprouts. Heedless of the pitcher of syrup or the juice glasses or the coffee cups, he dropped his fork onto his plate with a clatter, leaned across the tray and gave her a long, hard kiss.

When he pulled back, he clasped his hands on either side of her head and looked into her eyes. "Are you regretting what we did last night?"

"No," she said softly, meeting his gaze without hesitation. "I could never regret that, Jackson."

Thank God, he thought, feeling one knot of tension in the pit of his stomach relax. Lowering his hands to his lap, he mustered a half smile. "Then what's wrong? Now that you've had your way with me, don't you respect me anymore?"

She laughed, and another knot in his stomach relaxed. "Of course I do, you silly man." Then her expression grew sober. "I'm just not sure where we're supposed to go from here. I told you, I'm not used to this."

"You weren't a virgin last night," Jackson said, frowning when he realized he might not have known it if she had been. After all, he hadn't made a practice of deflowering virgins, and Nancy certainly hadn't been one when he met her. "Were you?"

"Not quite," she admitted. "There was one guy back in college, but that relationship didn't work out. To tell you the truth, I wasn't impressed enough with sex to try it again. Until last night."

"How do you feel about it now?" he asked, his voice sounding strained and hoarse to his own ears. "Were you, uh, impressed?"

Her lips slowly curved into a knowing smile, and her voice took on a husky note. "Oh, yeah. Incredibly impressed."

Though another knot relaxed in his stomach, the tension didn't dissipate this time. It simply moved lower. Straight to his groin, in fact.

"I'm glad," he said. "I was impressed, too, Maggie. In case you're wondering, I don't feel casual about it. I mean, it...well, it really meant something to me."

"I know, Jackson. It meant something to me, too. I'm just not sure what to do about it."

She couldn't offer him an opening like that and not expect him to take advantage of it. Still, there was an air of skittishness about her that told him it wouldn't hurt to be cautious. The trick would be to find a way to give her a gentle nudge in his direction, instead of a shove. Tipping his head to one side, he forced himself to choose his words as carefully as he would if he was defending a client charged with murder.

"Listen, Maggie, I know you have a lot to think about, in terms of your mother and your relatives and your career. And I don't want to add any pressure to what you're already feeling. But if you're ever interested in negotiating that proposal we joked about at my mother's place, all you have to do is say so."

Not bad, he told himself as he watched another smile spread over her face. You've let her know you're serious about her, without backing her into a corner. But it wasn't enough, damn it. It was just more of that stupid yuppie thinking. Had he become such an emotional coward he would settle for less than a baby step, when what he really wanted was a giant leap? Not hardly.

Picking up her hand, he turned it over and placed a kiss in the center of her palm. Then he looked into her eyes and said, "Move in with me. My intentions are absolutely honorable, and I want every spare moment you've got to show you how good we can be together."

"Isn't that a little risky? It will offend some of the more traditional people, Jackson. Like your family."

"That's their problem. I'm falling in love with you, Maggie. I want to be with you."

There. He'd said it, and it hadn't even hurt much. At least it wouldn't if she didn't reject him out of hand.

"Oh, Jackson, I don't know." Biting her lower lip, she studied him with big, sad eyes. "I'm confused about so many things right now."

"But I'm not one of them. You love me, honey. You proved it last night." He leaned closer, until their lips lightly brushed. "Want me to help you prove it again?"

A strangled sound, somewhere between a laugh and a groan, came out of her mouth. She raised her hands to his chest, but didn't push him away. "I can't think straight when you get so close."

"Good." He licked her bottom lip. "Don't think. Just feel."

"The food, Jackson—"

He shoved the tray off the bed, chuckling at the way she flinched when it crashed to the floor. "To hell with the food and the mess and what anyone else thinks." Grasping her by the shoulders, he lay back, pulling her on top of him. "You belong with me, Maggie. Let me convince you."

She rested her forehead against his, giggling when he snuck one hand under the hem of her shirt and squeezed her bottom. "Oh, you fight dirty, Mr. Hawk."

"And you love it, don't you, Ms. Schaeffer?"

"I guess that will depend."

"On what?"

"Whether or not you can convince me."

He rolled her onto her back and gazed into her laughing eyes. Then he straddled her hips and nuzzled the side of her neck while he pushed the T-shirt up to her armpits. What followed was a joyous romp that left the bedclothes hopelessly tangled and both of them weak and satiated.

Raising himself up on one elbow, he tucked a finger under her chin, coaxing her to look at him. When she did, he said, "Move in with me, Maggie."

She studied him for a long moment, then nodded gravely. "All right, Jackson. But I don't want you to hover over me, or talk about my mother, or the future. Okay?"

"No. I don't understand."

She laid a finger across his lips. "I need time to think, Jack-

son. I want to finish my report and present it to the tribal council. When it's all done, then we'll see where we are. That's my best offer. Take it or leave it."

He didn't like her offer much, but he could see by the stubborn set to her chin that she meant every word. He might be setting himself up for another broken heart, but it was too late to back out now.

"I'll take it."

Twelve

Maggie moved in with Jackson later that afternoon, phoned her father to tell him about Beverly, and for the next two weeks enjoyed the sort of idyllic existence most people long for, but rarely achieve. When Jackson left for the office in the morning, she settled in at the kitchen table with her notes and her laptop computer. What had started as a monumental jumble of comments, complaints and vague impressions slowly began to take on a coherent shape.

She took a break at noon every day, driving into Laughing Horse to have lunch with Jackson and Frank if she needed to clarify something for her report. Other days, she visited her grandmother and Aunt Rose to learn more about her mother and the rest of her relatives. Then she went back to work, until Jackson came home and coaxed her away from the computer with a kiss and a hug, which usually led to more passionate pursuits.

They cooked together, took long, rambling walks together, worked in his yard and planned his garden together. If occasional doubts and worries about the future crept into her mind, it was easy enough to banish them in the haven of Jackson's arms. And while she knew similar doubts assailed him at times, he kept his promise and never mentioned them.

Instead, he taught her more about her people—their history, their religious traditions and beliefs, what he remembered of their language. He opened his heart and his mind and his life to her in a way no one had ever done before. Each day and each night, she fell a little more deeply in love with him.

The words of love and commitment she knew he desperately wanted to hear trembled on the tip of her tongue every time he made love to her. But something, some invisible force, or perhaps an unrecognized fear, continually held the words back.

She couldn't understand or explain it. It seemed that all she could do was wait for some kind of a mystical sign that would tell her what she must do.

And so, she loved him and worked and waited.

Finally, on the twenty-third of April, the afternoon arrived that would tell her whether or not she had accurately captured the tribe's needs and aspirations on paper. Frank Many Horses reserved the gymnasium at the Indian school for a special meeting of the tribal council. Any other interested members of the tribe were invited to attend and participate, as well.

Maggie surveyed the crowd during Frank's introduction. Realizing practically the entire population of the res had come to hear what she had written, she felt her palms grow damp. She looked at Jackson, who was sitting beside her, and found him looking back at her with such love and support in his eyes, her throat tightened with emotion.

Of course, that was the precise moment Frank chose to end his introduction. Taking a deep breath for courage, Maggie rose to her feet and approached the microphone. Her voice trembled a little at first, but gradually the rows and rows of faces became elders she had interviewed, teenagers she had tutored, friends and relatives. They listened with rapt attention, encouraging her with solemn nods and sporadic applause.

When she finished, a thoughtful hush filled the big room. When she asked for questions or suggestions for revision, fifty hands shot into the air. Jackson brought her a glass of water. Frank came to the podium to help her call on people by name.

For hours, the people debated point after point, amazing Maggie with their recall of the details in the report and their determination to be heard. She wished the members of the U.S. Congress could see this living example of participatory democracy in action. Though individual concerns were passionately expressed, the discussion remained doggedly focused on what was best for the tribe as a whole.

By the time the meeting adjourned, Maggie felt as if the people had made her report their own and accepted her into their hearts. She walked across the street to the tribal offices with Jackson and Frank, alternating between exhaustion and exhilaration. While Frank went into his office to check the an-

swering machine, Jackson pulled her into his arms and kissed her as if he were starving for the taste of her.

Then he moved on to nibble at her earlobe, murmuring, "You were wonderful today."

"Yes, I was," she agreed, taking giddy delight in sharing her triumph with him. "They all seemed really excited."

Pulling back, he smiled. "Of course they were. You acknowledged their problems, and then you made them look beyond the problems to the possibilities. You have a rare gift for bringing people together and helping them find a consensus, Maggie."

"More, more, tell me more." Chuckling, she wrinkled her nose at him. "My ego loves it."

"I'd rather kiss you again."

"Mmm... That sounds nice too."

Before she could collect her kiss, however, Frank loudly cleared his throat and came back out to the reception area. "Sorry to interrupt, but there was a message for Maggie from Baldwin's office in Whitehorn. The lady said it was urgent."

Sighing with resignation, Maggie settled for a quick smooch, then took the pink message slip from Frank and went into his office to make the phone call. Her eyes met Jackson's when she turned to close the door, and something in his gaze made her hesitate. It wasn't anger, exactly. No, it was either frustration or impatience—perhaps a combination of the two.

Whatever it was, it clearly said her time for thinking was running out. Very soon now, he would demand an answer to his proposal. Unfortunately, she didn't have one to give him. Not yet, anyway.

As Jackson watched, Maggie's eyes opened wide for a moment before she quickly closed Frank's office door. Well, good, he thought. And he didn't feel a damn bit guilty because of that look of reproach she'd managed to squeeze in the instant before the door had shut completely.

He'd been as patient as any man could hope to be for the past two weeks. In some respects, they'd been the best two weeks of his life. Living with Maggie, making love with her, sleeping and waking up with her in his arms, had been about

as close to heaven as he figured mortals were ever allowed to get.

Oh, he knew they'd been on some sort of a pseudo-honeymoon since she'd moved in with him. If they continued to live together, sooner or later they'd get on each other's nerves and have a spat now and then, like any other couple. That was reality, and he could cope with it fine.

What he *couldn't* cope with was the constant worry that if they had a spat now, she wouldn't feel committed enough to stick around and work it out. Every day he loved her more and put a bigger chunk of his heart at risk. He knew damn well she loved him, so why wouldn't she just come right out and *say* so?

He'd been miserable enough when Nancy had left him. If Maggie left him, too... God, he could hardly stand to think about it. But he couldn't *not* think about it, either. In fact, the longer she refused to discuss the future, the less he could think about anything else.

"Well, nephew, what do you think of our Little Fed now?" Frank said. "Looks to me like you two are gettin' mighty close."

"Yeah." Shoving his hands into his pockets, Jackson sat on the edge of the reception desk.

"You're in love with her."

"Yeah."

Rolling his eyes in exasperation, Frank muttered something in Cheyenne. "So? What are you gonna do about it?"

"I've done everything I *can* do about it, uncle. Maggie's the one draggin' her feet."

"You've already asked her to marry you?"

"Sort of."

"What the hell does that mean?"

Jackson briefly explained the situation, then added, "She's really tied to the white world, through Baldwin and her father. I don't know if I've got enough to offer her to convince her to stay."

Frank came over and gave Jackson's shoulder a sympathetic squeeze. "It's a big decision for her. You're wise to give her time to think it over."

"Yeah, well, it's drivin' me nuts," Jackson grumbled.

"Maybe if I offered her a job coordinating our social programs—"

"I already did that," Jackson admitted, with a sheepish grin. "I figured you'd go along with it."

"After today, there's no question the tribal council would agree," Frank said. "Be patient a little longer. I believe this will work out."

"I hope you're right. But something's eatin' at her, you know? I wish I knew what it was."

Frank nudged Jackson with his elbow and waggled his eyebrows. "You take her home and love her up good. She'll forget about it, whatever it is."

Before Jackson could reply, Frank's office door opened and Maggie hurried into the reception area.

"It's a good thing we had the meeting today," she said. "Congressman Baldwin wants the report on his desk by Tuesday morning. I'll have just enough time to revise it and get it there by express mail."

Frank reached out and grasped both of her hands. "Before you go, I want to say thank-you. We all appreciate your work very much."

"You're welcome. It's been a wonderful experience for me," Maggie said.

"We don't want you to leave, Maggie. When you're all done, you come talk to me about a job with the tribe."

Pulling her hands away, she shot Jackson an accusing look. "You promised—"

"I didn't bring it up," Jackson said. "Uncle Frank thought of it himself."

Frank nodded vigorously. "You handled yourself so well today, and the things you wrote were so helpful, I'd have to be crazy not to offer you a job. You think about it, Maggie. The offer stands, whether you marry this guy or not."

"Oh, you talked about that, too?" she asked, shooting another accusing look in Jackson's direction.

"A reservation's like any other small town," Frank said with a chuckle. "Everybody minds everybody else's business, but there's no harm intended. It's easy for those of us who know

Jackson to see he's a man in love. You should put him out of his misery.''

"Come on, Maggie. Let's go home," Jackson said, silently adding, *Before Mr. Big Mouth gets me in big trouble.*

But it seemed that he already had. Maggie accompanied him out to the pickup without saying another word. Jackson allowed the silence to continue for five long miles. Then he said, "I'm sorry if Uncle Frank made you feel uncomfortable, Maggie. He didn't mean to—"

"Oh, I'm sure he didn't." She scowled at him, then looked straight ahead again. "I just don't appreciate being discussed when my back is turned."

"I understand, but he's right. Now that you're living with me, it's obvious to everyone something's going on. My uncle asked how things stood between us, and I told him."

"You agreed we wouldn't discuss this until I'd finished my report."

"I agreed I wouldn't bring it up with you," he said. "I didn't promise not to talk to anyone else. Uncle Frank cares about both of us, and you're damn near done with the report, so what's the big problem?"

"Oh, never mind," she muttered, folding her arms over her midriff.

"Damn it, Maggie, don't sulk. I've really stuck my neck out here, and you've kept me danglin' for two weeks. Surely by now you've got *some* idea of what you want to do."

"Don't push me, Jackson. When I'm ready to talk about this, you'll be the first to know."

Though her words reeked of defiance, Jackson heard a hint of strain in them, too. Aw, nuts. This was hardly the way to get her to open up to him. He didn't want to fight with her or spoil what should be an occasion to celebrate. Forcing himself to take deep, calming breaths, he turned into his driveway.

"All right," he said. "I won't mention it again."

"I'm not trying to make you miserable, Jackson. Please, believe that."

"Do you love me at all, Maggie?"

"Oh, yes," she said, her voice soft and husky. "Quite a lot, actually."

Though he wanted to whoop with delight, Jackson forced himself to maintain his dignity, for fear of scaring her off completely. He reached across the seat and squeezed her hand. "Then that's all I need to know. For now."

Parking next to the house, he jumped out and ran around the front of the pickup. She had her door open by the time he reached the passenger side, making it easy to scoop her off the seat and kiss the daylights out of her. Using his foot to shut the door, he carried her into the house.

"Jackson, I should work," she said when he headed up the stairs to his bedroom.

"Later." He paused and gave her another soul-melting kiss. "I can wait to talk, but I can't wait for this."

He climbed the rest of the stairs and set her on her feet beside the bed. She looked up at him with such aching tenderness in her eyes, it was tempting to crush her against him and beg her to stay. He couldn't do that, of course, but there were ways to communicate without words.

Sliding his fingers into her hair, above her ears, he kissed her eyelids, her cheeks, the tip of her nose, her stubborn little chin. She sighed and let her head fall back, raising her lips in a silent demand for attention there. He kissed the underside of her chin instead, then followed the graceful curve of her neck until he reached the top button of her blouse.

Freeing the buttons one by one, he kissed his way down to the waistband of her skirt. Since he was already in the neighborhood, he undid that button, too, and slowly lowered the zipper while he kissed his way back up to her mouth. Her lips parted eagerly for his tongue, and while he dipped inside for a taste, he stripped away her blouse and dispensed with her bra.

Oh, this was what he loved, filling his hands with her soft, warm skin, drinking in her sweet moans with kiss after kiss, inhaling her light, floral scent until he made himself dizzy with it. She reached for the pearl snaps on his white Western shirt, but he captured her hands and pushed them down to her sides.

He wasn't gonna let her get all impatient and distract him into losing his head this time. Since she wouldn't give him a commitment, there might well come a day when memories would be all he had left of her. So this time, he was gonna

store up as many memories as he could, like a squirrel getting
ready for a long, cold winter.

It only took a little push to make her skirt slide over her hips,
but the panty hose she wore underneath called for more ag-
gressive tactics. Sneaking his thumbs under the elastic, he lei-
surely kissed his way down her neck again and across the swell
of her breasts while he peeled the panty hose down her legs,
managing to snag her lacy little scrap of panties along with
them. He went down on one knee, lifting her left foot, then her
right, leaving her as naked as *Maheo* had made her.

She was exquisite.

He sat back on his heel and let his eyes feast on her beauty.
And when his eyes were finally satisfied, he raised his hands
to fondle and caress and memorize the curves and indentations
that so delighted him. Then his lips demanded their turn. Holding her hips, he rubbed his face over her skin, letting her gasps
and moans guide him.

Her breasts were luscious, her nipples like sweet berries that
begged for his tongue. Her belly was shy and ticklish, but he
wouldn't allow it to shrink from his touch. No, he nuzzled it
and kissed it all over, following it down and down, to the soft
folds where her legs came together.

She grasped the sides of his head, holding it tightly, as if she
didn't know whether to pull him to her or push him away. He
warmed her with his breath. Smoothed his hands over her hips
and down her thighs, stroking them, gently coaxing them to
part.

As if of their own accord, her hips tilted forward to meet his
eager mouth. He loved and nibbled and drank in her sweetness
until her knees quivered uncontrollably and her ragged breaths
and cries filled the room. Lifting her onto the bed, he kissed
her mouth, letting her taste herself on his lips and tongue. When
he tried to pull back, she grabbed his braids and refused to let
go.

He kissed her again, slowly, hungrily. Stroked his hands over
her breasts and sides. Fondled the plump, moist flesh between
her thighs.

She yanked the ties off the ends of his braids and unwound
them, burying her fingers in the wild mass of his hair. Ah, yes.

The lady. had a thing about his long hair. He found her arms with his hands and followed them to her wrists, which he anchored on either side of her head. She huffed in indignation and, he thought, frustration.

Smiling to himself, he knelt beside her and shook his hair down over the top of his head. Then he swept it back and forth, swirling it across her breasts and waist, changed direction, catching her hips and thighs with the next flick of his neck. He rolled her onto her stomach and brushed it over her back and bottom and legs.

She rolled away from him, sat up and, with a mock-ferocious glare, shook her finger at him. "Enough already. Stop it."

He flipped his hair back out of his eyes and gave her a wicked grin. "Come on, you don't really mean that."

"Well, no," she admitted, her tone tinged with exasperation. "But I'm sick and tired of being the only naked person in this room. Now, either you strip, or it's all over."

Sensing there was more behind her request than a desire for shared nudity, he sat back on his heels and studied her for a moment. "I was only trying to give you pleasure."

"You did. You're a wonderful lover."

"Then I don't understand what's wrong."

"Nothing's wrong. It's just that I like to give pleasure, as well as receive it. You've hardly let me touch you. For heaven's sake, you've still got your boots on."

"I was plannin' to take 'em off before—"

She cut him off with one word. "Now."

"But—"

"Now. I mean it. Strip, or I'm outta here."

He scrambled backward off the bed. In an attempt to lighten the atmosphere, he held his hands out at his sides and said, "What? Don't I even get any music?"

Her lips twitched, but she yanked a pillow in front of her breasts, quickly repressing the smile. "Now."

Gripping the front plackets of his shirt, he popped open the snaps with one quick yank and tossed the shirt onto the floor. Then he unbuckled his belt, unzipped his jeans, sat on the edge of the bed and yanked off his boots and socks. Standing again, he shucked off his jeans and shorts and kicked them aside.

Approaching the bed again, he said, "Okay, I'm naked. Are you happy now?"

"I would be, if you weren't glaring at me like that. This isn't like you at all, Jackson. What's going on?"

"I thought I was doing something really special for you." He sat down beside her and tugged the other pillow over his lap. "But somehow, the mood seems to have gone somewhere else."

"Jackson." She took his hand and folded her palms around it. "I'm sorry if I spoiled your fun, but what was happening didn't feel right to me. It felt like you were...I don't know, using sex as a weapon. Like you were punishing me for not wanting to talk before."

"Aw, Maggie, that's not what I was tryin' to do at all."

"Well, what *were* you trying to do?"

There was no other human being on the planet who could have drugged this admission out of him, but for Maggie, he would try to explain. "When you get your hot little hands all over me, sometimes I forget I'm supposed to hold back, and...well, hell, I just plain go nuts. So I thought if I left my clothes on, maybe I could make it last longer, and really satisfy you." He looked down at the pillow on his lap. "And...I wanted to give myself a special memory of you. In case you decide to go back to Washington."

He felt her fingers under his chin, but he didn't want to look at her if she was mad at him again. Or, worse yet, if she felt sorry for him because of what he'd admitted. Her fingers tugged harder. When he finally raised his head, she got right in his face, and her eyes were all misty, as if she might burst into tears.

"That's the sweetest thing anyone has ever said to me, Jackson. But, as for satisfying me, believe me when I tell you I have no complaints whatsoever. Haven't you noticed when you get your hot little hands on me, I just plain go nuts, too?"

"Well, yeah, but I don't ever want to disappoint you."

"Disappoint me? You crazy man! Half of my pleasure is seeing your pleasure. When you go nuts like that, I feel like the sexiest woman alive."

"You are the sexiest woman alive."

She tossed her pillow aside and looped her arms around his neck. "Is that so?"

He tossed his pillow aside and leaned forward, gently tipping her onto her back. "Damn straight it is."

Ah, God, there was that gorgeous smile of hers, the one that never failed to make his heart beat a little faster. He dipped his head and kissed her inviting lips.

She nibbled down the side of his neck, raising goose bumps with each soft nip of her teeth. "Do you think the mood might come back anytime soon?"

"I think it's back already. How 'bout you?"

She narrowed her eyes in a thoughtful pose. "I think it might be possible."

"What do you s'pose it would take to be sure, honey?"

Her eyes glinting with mischief, she spread-eagled herself on the bed. "That thing you did with your hair was quite a turn-on. Why don't you start there, and we'll see what happens?"

Jackson threw back his head and laughed. Then he swirled his hair over her again and did everything else he'd done before. But this time she was with him, matching touch for touch, kiss for kiss, stroke for stroke. It was better than ever before, and they both went totally, joyously nuts at the same moment.

Holding her in his arms when the storm had ended, he realized it wasn't the particular sexual acts or how long they lasted that made a memory special. It was this feeling of oneness, of wholeness and complete acceptance, that came afterward. He kissed her brow and caressed her back, and silently promised her they would always have this together.

If only she would stay.

But she was like a wild bird. The harder he tried to cage her, the harder she would struggle to fly away from him. Which left him with nothing to do but hope, and pray, and wait.

God, how he hated waiting.

Thirteen

On Monday morning, Maggie entered the final revisions on her laptop, copied the report onto a diskette, then drove to the Indian school and printed a copy on the laser printer her father had donated. She proofread it one last time. Confident she had caught as many typos as possible, she made another copy for her own files and one for Frank's, tossed them in the back seat of her car and headed for Whitehorn.

Traffic was light, allowing her to relax and enjoy the sunshine and Montana's big blue sky overhead. She'd been so wrapped up in her work and Jackson lately, she'd barely noticed the passage of time. But it was already the twenty-fifth of April. The calves in the pastures were much larger than when she had arrived.

Thank heaven the report was finally finished. She could have mailed it from the reservation's post office, but she needed some time alone to take stock of her feelings for Jackson. And since she hadn't left the res for several weeks, she also felt a need to reconnect with the outside world.

As Sara had pointed out, she had agreed to give up her Indian heritage without understanding the extent of the sacrifice her mother had asked her to make. She didn't intend to make that mistake a second time. For Jackson's sake, as well as her own, she had to be absolutely certain of the decision now facing her.

The usual assortment of cars and trucks lined the streets of Whitehorn's business district when Maggie arrived. She stopped at a traffic light, thinking the little town looked familiar and oddly strange at the same time, almost like alien territory. Goodness, had she been out on the res that long?

An ambulance roared by, lights flashing and siren blaring. She watched it pass, feeling a moment's sympathy for whoever needed emergency medical aid on such a beautiful day. Then

she drove on to the post office and mailed her report, enjoying a deep sense of accomplishment.

If Mr. Baldwin used half of the information she had provided, and Congress enacted half of the recommendations she had drafted, life at the Laughing Horse Reservation, and perhaps on other reservations, as well, would change for the better. Her people would have better medical facilities, better educational and job-training opportunities, and a solid foot up on the ladder of economic independence. And she, little Maggie Schaeffer, would have been instrumental in laying the foundation for all of it.

The thought brought with it a heady sense of power and pride. This was legislation with implications for the entire nation, and only a job such as the one she had in Washington could put her in a position to wield the behind-the-scenes influence she now enjoyed. If she gave it all up in order to be with Jackson and work for the tribe, she would still have opportunities for achievement, but on a much smaller scale.

Would she be satisfied with that? Or would she eventually resent both Jackson and the tribe for her loss of power and prestige? Could she willingly subordinate her own, perhaps selfish, interests for the good of the tribe, as so many others had done on Saturday afternoon?

On the other hand, the power and influence her present job afforded her was secondhand at best. All she really did was provide information in a concise, coherent manner. The elected officials were the ones who actually voted on the issues, and she had virtually no control over their final decisions.

Seen in that light, the alleged glamour of her career faded abruptly. Was she willing to give up the only man she had ever loved for it? Or the dreams she had started to have of the children they would raise together? The new friends and relatives she had also come to love? Give up all of that for a job of questionable influence and a lonely apartment in a crime-ridden city?

With those questions echoing in her mind, Maggie went back to her car and slowly cruised the streets. The contrast between these smug, well-kept homes and prosperous businesses and the unrelenting poverty at the reservation offended her. Compared

to Whitehorn, the res looked like a Third World country. Granted, many of her people would never choose to live as the white society did, but the differences didn't have to be so vast.

Driving past the high school, she remembered the day Wanda and Nina had told her they weren't allowed to check out library books. She passed the school district's administration building, and felt a fierce surge of satisfaction at the memory of her confrontation with Edward Reese.

She thought of the many pitiful stories she had heard of people who had surrendered to despair, but she also recalled the ones who had not—the ones who fought in the trenches for social change every single day.

Jackson and Frank, who worked side by side, up to their ears in legal documents and law books, demanding the return of the tribe's land.

Sweet old Earnest Running Bull, who had lost a wife and three children to the ravages of alcohol and drug abuse, and ran the rehab center so that others wouldn't lose their loved ones.

Sara Lewis, who was the artifacts curater at the Native American Museum in Whitehorn and then helped out at the school with the younger children and even at the clinic at the reservation.

Dr. Kane Hunter, who devoted a large share of his time and energy and passed up untold extra income he could have earned in Whitehorn, while he treated sick and hurt tribal members with modern medicine and still managed to respect his patients' traditional beliefs.

The elders, including her own grandmother, who drove over ungodly roads in rattletrap vehicles to pass on beautiful Cheyenne stories and songs to the tykes at the day-care center, maintaining an oral tradition centuries old. The ones who taught the traditional dances to the children.

These people were heroes. All of them. Without their efforts, Laughing Horse would be a miserable, hellish place, with no hope at all.

Maggie pulled into the parking lot of a fast-food restaurant, shut off the car's engine and remembered the traditional Cheyenne saying Sara had stitched in needlepoint and framed on her living room wall. It said:

A Nation is not conquered
Until the hearts of its women
Are on the ground.
Then it is done, no matter
How brave its warriors
Nor how strong its weapons.

Those few short lines had embedded themselves in her memory at first reading. Maggie had thought of them often, but they had never struck her more powerfully than they did at this moment.

Her mother had left Laughing Horse with her heart on the ground. She had run away from the hurt and shame inflicted on her because she belonged to a conquered nation. She had sacrificed everything and fought with all her determination to shield her only child from ever knowing that hurt and shame.

Maggie was grateful for the opportunities she had been given as a result of her mother's sacrifice. She admired her mother for having had such strength and courage.

But she also admired the strength and courage of the unsung heroes and heroines who had stayed on the res, struggled for justice and insisted the Northern Cheyenne could rise above their status as a conquered nation. Despite incredible odds, their hearts were not on the ground, and they never would be.

Margaret Speaks Softly Schaeffer could make a significant contribution to their struggle. These people were her people, their fight was her fight. Her background and education gave her a unique perspective and unique skills to build bridges between the res and the white world, instead of walls. She desperately wanted to do so.

The question was, could she do it without feeling she had betrayed her mother's dying request?

Maggie was ninety-nine-percent certain she'd already made her decision, but there was one person she wanted to talk to before sharing it with Jackson. Spotting a phone booth on the other side of the parking lot, she got out of her car and hurried across the pavement. Using her credit card, she placed the call, smiling when she heard her father's voice.

"Maggie, I was just thinking about you," he said.

"That's probably because I've been thinking about you," she replied. "I need some advice, Daddy."

"Uh-oh, there's that *daddy* word again. What's up?"

And there, in a grungy phone booth in the middle of a funky little Montana cow town, Maggie poured out her heart. Her father was silent for a moment after she'd finished.

Then he said, "What happened to your mother happened a long time ago, honey. Nothing you do or don't do can change it. If I were you, I think I'd try to respect the intent behind the promise Bev demanded of you, and not worry so much about the actual words."

"I'm not sure I understand what you mean," she said.

"All she ever really wanted was for you to be safe and happy. If you feel safe and happy with this Jackson Hawk fellow, well, I don't see why your mother would object. Even if she would, it's *your* life, Maggie."

"Thanks, Daddy. That's what I needed to hear."

"When do I get to meet this guy? Maybe I should fly up there tomorrow and check him out."

Maggie laughed. "Give me a little more time than that. We still have some things to work out."

"You really love him, huh?"

"Oh, yes, Daddy. Almost as much as I love you."

"Aw, you're just saying that to protect my ego."

"Nope. It's a different kind of love, that's all. I'll always be your little girl."

"Good. Now, you'd better find Jackson and start working out those things you mentioned. And don't forget to keep me informed of your progress."

Feeling as if an elephant had been lifted from her shoulders, Maggie bought a burger and a soda in the restaurant, then stopped at the congressman's office to use the WATS line to call Washington. The second she stepped through the door, Bonnie Jenkins, the executive secretary who ran the operation, heaved a melodramatic sigh of relief.

Bonnie was a heavyset woman in her mid-forties. She wore her fading red hair in a curly do that always looked a little frazzled. She had run the congressman's Whitehorn office for

fifteen years. Though extremely efficient, she was a friendly soul, and Maggie had enjoyed getting acquainted with her.

"Oh, thank goodness you're here. I've been trying to reach you all morning," Bonnie said.

"Why? Is something wrong?" Maggie asked.

"Haven't you heard the news?" Bonnie rushed on before Maggie could even shake her head. "Jeremiah Kincaid died today. Mr. Baldwin can't get away from Washington for the funeral, and he wants you to act as his personal representative."

"I was planning to ask for two weeks of vacation," Maggie said, grimacing at the thought of doing funeral duty instead of being with Jackson.

"You can probably take it after the funeral," Bonnie said. "Oh, please do this, Maggie. There's a family visitation thing tomorrow at the mortuary, and you already know Mary Jo Kincaid better than I do. Mr. Baldwin asked for you specifically. You're supposed to call him right away."

"I will, but what happened to Mr. Kincaid?"

Bonnie's voice dropped to a confidential murmur, as if she feared being overheard. Maggie glanced toward the inner office the congressman used when he was in town, but didn't see anyone.

"Well, they say he fell in the shower, hit his head, and then drowned in the bathwater," Bonnie said.

"But you don't believe that?" Maggie asked.

"Oh, I suppose I do. He was getting on in years, and sometimes, he was a little absentminded. But you know, it just doesn't seem like Jeremiah to be so careless. He was always such a powerful man around these parts, it's not going to be the same without him."

"What about his son?" Maggie said. "Won't he take over?"

"Dugin?" Bonnie rolled her eyes, then let out a derisive laugh. "He's not half the man Jeremiah was. Back when we were in high school, he was nothing but a spoiled-rotten rich kid, and he hasn't improved one bit with age. Please, say you'll do it, Maggie. You don't know Dugin well enough to hate him, but I'd have to bite my tongue bloody to be nice to him for five seconds."

"I'll call Mr. Baldwin," Maggie said.

"You go right on back and use his office. I'll even bring you a fresh cup of coffee."

"Bribery, Bonnie?" Maggie asked with a grin.

Bonnie winked at her. "Whatever works, hon. Don't you know that's the first rule of politics?"

Five minutes later, Maggie found herself ensconced behind Baldwin's big desk, a steaming cup of coffee at hand and the phone's receiver clamped to her ear.

"Maggie, it's good to hear from you," her boss said, using the hearty politician's voice he usually reserved for constituents. "How are you?"

"Fine, Mr. Baldwin. I sent my report by express mail this morning. You should receive it tomorrow."

"Excellent. We'll be glad to have you back in the office. Do you mind staying on for Jeremiah Kincaid's funeral? Bonnie filled you in, didn't she?"

"Yes, sir. Actually, I was hoping to take my vacation now," Maggie said.

"I thought you'd requested time in August."

Maggie considered telling him of her intention to resign, but an odd flash of intuition made her opt for caution. "That's right, but I've gotten involved with some things at the reservation I'd like to finish before I leave."

"Couldn't you represent me at the funeral and still do those things at the reservation? You can take your vacation then, and I'll throw in an extra three days off. I really would appreciate this, Maggie."

"All right, sir," Maggie said.

"Great. Stay in touch these next few days. The new president of the Whitehorn Ranchers' Association will probably want to talk to you at the funeral."

"About the Northern Cheyennes' grazing leases?"

"What do you know about that?" Baldwin asked, his tone suddenly sharp.

Maggie raised her eyebrows at the receiver, then said, "Only that the tribe doesn't intend to renew them. Is there something else I should know, sir?"

"No, no. Nothing important." His voice was hearty again.

A shade too hearty. "If anyone says anything to you, just tell them everything's under control."

"Mr. Baldwin, I hope you'll read my report before you take any action on that issue," Maggie said. "I've discussed it at length with the tribal leaders, and I think you'll see they've developed some impressive plans."

"I'll read it as soon as it hits my desk. I've got to run now. Give Jeremiah's family my condolences, and why don't you send a bouquet of flowers to the funeral home? Bonnie can take care of the bill for you."

Maggie hung up the phone and sat at the desk for another moment, feeling uneasy about the conversation with her boss, but unable to pinpoint the exact cause. Then she shook her head, told herself Jackson's paranoia had probably started to rub off on her, and went out to tell Bonnie she wouldn't have to bite her tongue bloody. Leaving the smiling secretary typing at top speed, she got into her car and headed for the res.

It was time to talk to Jackson.

Jackson paced from the kitchen into the living room, glared out the window for a moment, then paced back to the kitchen again. Damn it, where *was* she? He looked at the kitchen clock, swore under his breath and made another trip to the living room window.

He should be at the office, but Uncle Frank had thrown him out two hours ago, telling him not to come back until he stopped feeling so damn irritable and distracted. He'd come home and started pacing, and he'd been pacing ever since. He knew he was acting like an idiot. He also knew he wouldn't be able to stop until Maggie came home from Whitehorn.

Damn it, where *was* she?

And why was he so afraid she wasn't coming back? Her laptop was still on the kitchen table. Her clothes were still in his bedroom. Her makeup was still in his bathroom. She wouldn't just go off and leave all that stuff behind. Irrational though it was, however, his fear persisted.

It was all because of that damn report, of course. Knowing she'd gone to Whitehorn to mail it, that she would no longer be able to use it as an excuse to avoid discussing the future,

had his gut tied in knots and a battalion of ants crawling around under his skin. She'd told him she loved him—"quite a lot, actually"—and he'd tried to content himself with those words. But he had too much lawyer in his soul to settle for anything less than a legal commitment.

Just as he reached the kitchen again, a car door slammed out front. His heart lurched, then started to race as he rushed to the window. Oh, God, she'd come back. And she was smiling. That was a good sign, wasn't it? Of course it was.

He ran to the front door, threw it open and charged down the steps. He didn't stop until he had her in his arms, whirled her around in a giddy circle and planted a kiss on her lips that stole his breath and hers. When he finally let her up for air, she looked up at him with a startled laugh.

"What was that all about?" she asked.

"Nothin' special." He grabbed her hand and practically dragged her into the house. "I'm just damn glad to see you. Maggie, we've really gotta talk."

She turned to him with a smile that made his poor heart hammer even faster. "I know, Jackson, it's time. But there's some news you should hear first."

He opened his mouth to tell her he didn't give a damn about any kind of news, but she didn't give him a chance.

"Jeremiah Kincaid is dead," she said, looking at him expectantly.

"What? Are you sure?"

She nodded. "Evidently he had an accident in the shower this morning. Will this affect your case for the leases?"

Jackson thought about it, then shook his head. "Not really. The suit was filed by the Whitehorn Ranchers' Association, not Jeremiah personally. A guy named Bob Myers will probably take over. He's damn near as rotten as Jeremiah."

"Jackson, the man is dead."

"Doesn't change what he was, Maggie. I'm glad the old coot's dead. In fact, I hope he's already startin' to sizzle."

"That's a terrible thing to say." She shot him an appalled look, then walked into the kitchen and started a pot of coffee.

"It's the truth." Jackson followed her into the kitchen, put his arms around her waist from behind and pulled her back

against him. "Jeremiah Kincaid doesn't matter anymore. You mailed the report, didn't you?"

"Uh-huh." She tipped her head back and grinned up at him. "It's gone."

"Good." He leaned forward and gave her an upside-down kiss that made her laugh. "So, Ms. Schaeffer, what are your plans?"

She turned to face him, laying her palms flat on his chest. "Well, I have a few things to do for Mr. Baldwin in Whitehorn for the next three days, and then I'm going to take my vacation. I know you're going to be busy in court, but I'd like to spend whatever time you can spare with you. Preferably alone."

Oh, the smile she was giving him now made him think of hot sex and rumpled sheets. "What about after your vacation?"

"What do you want me to do after that, Jackson?"

"As if you didn't know," he said reproachfully.

"Well, a woman can't be too careful these days, and you're one of those tricky lawyers." She wrinkled her nose at him. "Maybe I'd like to hear you spell it out."

He put his hands on her waist, picked her up and plunked her little tush down on the work island, which put her at eye level with him. Then he said, "I want you to stay here, Maggie. For good."

"Here, as in Laughing Horse? Or here, in your house?"

"Both. If I had my way, I'd never let you out of my bed."

"And why should I agree to this proposition, Mr. Hawk?"

"Oh, honey, it's not a proposition. It's a proposal."

"Of marriage?"

"Sure is. I'll even give your grandmother both of my horses. I love you, Maggie."

"I love you, too, Jackson."

"So, is that a yes?"

"It's a definite maybe." Looping her arms around his neck, she rested her forehead against his. "It's an awfully big step. Maybe you should carry me upstairs and show me why I should put up with you for the next forty or fifty years."

He looked deeply into her teasing eyes. So, she wanted to play, did she? No problem. Crouching down, he grasped her right wrist and gave it a good yank, pulling her over his shoul-

der in a fireman's carry. Then he put his left hand on her bottom to hold her steady and headed for the stairs.

Shrieking with laughter, she pounded on his back, complaining that this wasn't what she'd had in mind at all. Jackson dumped her unceremoniously in the middle of his bed, and followed her down, kissing her whole face while he stripped her of her clothes. She giggled and wiggled and attacked his clothing with equal fervor.

When the loving was done, he held her in his arms, content at last. She still hadn't given him a straight answer to his proposal, but she had given herself to him freely and completely, and he hadn't seen that worried, haunted look in her eyes even once. Sooner or later, he was confident, she would accept him. If he had anything to say about it, it would be sooner.

Fourteen

After a long, delicious night of lovemaking, Maggie groaned when the sun rose the next morning, assaulting her with bright, obnoxious rays at what had to be an ungodly hour. Raising her head, she squinted at the clock, then groaned again and yanked the covers over her head. When she went into Whitehorn today, she was going to buy blackout shades for the bedroom windows.

She heard Jackson chuckle and felt a hand give her fanny an affectionate pat through the sheet and blanket. Then the mattress dipped, she heard his big bare feet hit the floor, and a second later the mattress shifted again. Smiling to herself, she imagined his every move from the sounds he made.

Now he was at the window, no doubt stretching his magnificent body while he made a visual check on the world outside. A zipper rasped. Okay, he had his jeans on. And he was whistling. Before coffee, no less! Did she really want to marry one of those disgusting morning people?

Several silent minutes passed. Then she heard water running downstairs and the lovely grating whir of an electric coffee grinder. The nice thing about those disgusting morning people was that they sometimes got up and made coffee for nonmorning folks. Chuckling, she rolled onto her back and pulled the covers off her face.

On second look, the sunbeams were actually rather pretty. If she got up right away, they could share a shower and breakfast before Jackson had to leave for the office. She'd go into Whitehorn after that, order the flowers and, if she was lucky, finish her duty call on the Kincaids by noon. Then she could buy the shades, hit the grocery store on the way home, take a nap and still have time to cook a romantic dinner.

"Sounds like a plan," she said, forcing herself to crawl out of bed.

The first part of her plan worked well enough. Jackson was standing near the bottom of the stairs when she streaked from the bedroom to the bathroom. Never one to pass up an opportunity for fun in the shower, he was hot on her heels, and as naked as she was before she could turn the water on. The trouble didn't start until they returned to the bedroom and he saw her take one of her business suits from the closet.

His eyebrows swooped into a scowl, and he crossed the room, zipping up a fresh pair of jeans on the way. "Why so formal today?" he asked, eyeing her intended outfit with distaste.

Maggie sat on the bed and gathered up one leg of her panty hose. "I told you yesterday, Jackson. I have some things to do for Mr. Baldwin in Whitehorn, and I need to dress for the office."

"What things?"

She poked her toe into the toe of the hose, pulled the stocking to her thigh and gathered up the second leg. "He can't come out here for Mr. Kincaid's funeral. I'm going to act as his official representative."

"No."

Maggie glanced up and felt her heart sink. Jackson had folded his arms across his bare chest. His feet were spread apart in a classic fighting stance. The expression on his face could only be called implacable. She didn't like it one bit.

"I beg your pardon?" she said, pulling up the other leg of her hose.

"No. You're not gonna have anything to do with Kincaid's funeral."

She stood and pulled the waistband up where it belonged. Then she calmly walked over to the dresser, took out a bra and put it on. She reached for the pink silk blouse next.

"Did you hear what I said?" he demanded.

"Yes, I did." She whipped the blouse around her shoulders and poked her arms into the sleeves, ignoring his ominous glare as best she could while she buttoned herself up. "I'm hoping

you'll realize how absurd you sound before I have to point it out to you.''

"Maggie, you can't do this."

"It's just a courtesy thing, Jackson." She took her skirt off the hanger and stepped into it. "Don't make a big deal out of it. All right?"

"No, it's not all right." He put his hands on his hips, making his chest look even broader, his frown more intimidating. "Jeremiah Kincaid was an enemy of this tribe."

"Well, he may have been, but this is part of my job." She dragged her pumps out of the closet and slid her feet into them. "I'm still on Mr. Baldwin's payroll, and I don't think this is an unreasonable request. Therefore, I'm going to do it, and you can't stop me."

Stepping around him, she opened her jewelry pouch and dug out a pair of gold earrings. Leaning toward the mirror, she inserted the posts into the holes in her earlobes.

Jackson grasped her shoulder with one hand and turned her around to face him again. "You don't understand what you're doing here. If you go to that funeral, the people on this reservation will see it as a betrayal."

"That's ridiculous."

"No, it's not," he insisted. "Sometimes you can't straddle the fence between the white world and ours. If you want to maintain your credibility, you're gonna have to choose a side, and it had damn well better be the tribe's."

"Has it ever occurred to you that if you did less choosing sides around here, you wouldn't have so many problems with the white community?"

"I'm sure there are some occasions when that's absolutely true. But, honey, trust me, this isn't one of 'em. Go call Baldwin and tell him you can't have anything to do with this."

"What about Mary Jo?" Maggie asked, putting on her watch. "She's been coming out here every day for weeks to tutor the kids. Don't you think it's appropriate for someone from the tribe to show her an act of friendship when there's been a death in her family?"

"Send her a card. Hell, send her flowers." He rolled his eyes and snorted, as if the thought of doing even that much disgusted

him. "But don't go there. Jeremiah Kincaid was a symbol of the white oppression these people have suffered. They won't understand why you're doing this. Much as they've come to respect you, you've got so many ties to the white world, they're gonna think you're sleepin' with the enemy."

Maggie stepped back, as hurt as if he'd slapped her. "I see. If I want to be accepted, I have to turn my back on my boss, and on a woman who has befriended this tribe because she picked the wrong father-in-law. I suppose I should turn my back on my father, too, while I'm at it."

Jackson didn't seem to notice the sarcasm dripping from her last remark. "Until this case with the grazing leases is resolved, it might be a good idea not to draw any extra attention to him."

Unable to believe he could be serious, Maggie gaped at him. "Do you honestly mean that?"

"It's just for a few weeks. Maggie, I don't think you understand how ugly this thing with the leases is liable to get. Even if the court rules in our favor, we may have to call in federal officers or even troops to enforce the decision."

"I don't care how ugly it gets or what anyone has to do, I won't treat my father like some dirty little secret."

"That's not what I meant," Jackson protested.

"That's exactly what you meant. We're in a war with the whites. They're all our enemies, even the ones who've never done anything mean to an Indian. If they're white, they're bad. Isn't that what you're trying to tell me?"

"You're exaggerating what I said, and you're overreacting," Jackson said. "I don't think all white people are bad, Maggie. All I'm saying is, this is going to be a very emotional time for the tribe. When emotions run that high, people don't always think straight, and appearances become very important. For a while, you'll have to be careful to make it absolutely clear your loyalty rests with us."

"What if I think the tribe is wrong, Jackson? Am I supposed to just swallow it down and blindly follow along?"

"For a few weeks—"

"I can't do that." She fiercely shook her head. "This tribe needs *more* communication with the white community, not *less*.

I can facilitate that. But if I stay here, the people are going to have to accept me the way I am.''

"Maggie, be reasonable.''

"No, *you* be reasonable. I don't turn my back on people because it happens to be convenient. If I have too many ties to the white world, that's tough. Nobody chooses who I will or will not associate with but *me*. And nobody owns me or controls me.''

"I'm not trying to control you.''

"Baloney!'' She grabbed her jacket off its hanger, draped it over her arm and picked up her purse from the dresser. "I was planning to accept your proposal this morning, but perhaps we'd better rethink this whole relationship. When you come right down to it, I still may not be Indian enough to suit you.''

"You're overreacting again.''

She walked to the doorway, then looked back over her shoulder at him. "I think not. And I also think the real question isn't whether the people will trust in my loyalty as much as it is whether *you* will trust in it.''

"Honey, if I didn't trust you one hell of a lot, we wouldn't be here right now.''

"Try to remember that today, while I'm at work. I'll see you tonight. Unless, of course, you want me to move out.''

His answer was gruff, but reassuringly automatic. "No, damn it. I just wish you'd think about what you're doing. Jeremiah Kincaid isn't worth the grief this will cause you, and neither is Baldwin.''

"That's for me to decide, Jackson.''

With that, she left, feeling as if her heart were hovering perilously close to the ground. This must be love, or arguing with him wouldn't hurt so darn much. She climbed into her car and looked up at the bedroom window. Jackson waved and blew her a kiss. She blew one back and, feeling a little better, drove away from the house.

To be honest, she had no real desire to attend any of the functions connected to the burial of Jeremiah Kincaid. She really hadn't liked the man the one time she met him. And, while she appreciated Mary Jo's efforts with the kids, she had to admit it was pretty difficult to warm up to the woman. Bonnie's

remarks about Dugin didn't sound very encouraging, either. So why the heck was she willing to fight Jackson so hard in order to do any of this?

It was the principle of the thing.

The issue really had nothing to do with any of the Kincaids. If she let Jackson tell her what to do before they were married, he would expect to go on doing so. That wasn't the kind of marriage she intended to have. Her mother had drilled the importance of maintaining her independence so thoroughly into her head, Maggie felt uneasy enough about committing herself to a man for a lifetime.

She might have viewed the situation differently if he had asked her not to go. But he hadn't asked. He'd *ordered,* and she couldn't tolerate that. She would never be able to go through with a wedding unless he understood and accepted her need to be treated as an equal, as well as her need to live by her own set of principles.

Keeping that thought firmly in mind, Maggie drove on into Whitehorn and went about her business. After checking in with Bonnie, she ordered flowers for the funeral, drove out to the Kincaid ranch and made a brief sympathy call on Mary Jo, who appeared to be grieving, but holding up well under the circumstances. She also met Dugin Kincaid, who appeared to have every intention of staying drunk for the foreseeable future.

Needless to say, Maggie was not impressed with the man. Nor was she impressed with the gorgeous Kincaid house. It was actually a mansion, by Whitehorn standards, with expensive furnishings and meticulously landscaped grounds. But the whole place had a cold, dismal atmosphere that Maggie was more than happy to escape.

The atmosphere back at Jackson's house was better than she had expected it to be. To his credit, he'd adopted a let's-agree-to-disagree attitude, which Maggie found encouraging. She had made no effort to hide her visit to the Kincaids or her attendance at Jeremiah's wake on Tuesday. When the word got out on the res, she began to receive angry phone calls. While Jackson wasn't exactly sympathetic whenever she had to handle one, he refrained from saying, "I told you so." He also re-

mained affectionate with her, which Maggie also found encouraging.

By Thursday, the day of the funeral, she was eager to be finished with the entire mess. Just one more day, and they would have weathered the worst of this particular storm. Perhaps they could even go away for a romantic weekend together.

Maggie felt painfully out of place at the funeral service. She had often been the only nonwhite person attending an event, but she'd never before experienced the subtle waves of hostility she sensed coming from some of the members of the congregation. She didn't understand it until the pallbearers wheeled the casket down the center aisle of the church and cowboy hats started blooming in every pew.

Of course, she thought, calmly returning the cold glances she received from the men who wore those hats. It only made sense that the members of the Whitehorn Ranchers' Association would be among Jeremiah's closest friends. With the grazing leases set to expire in a month, they were bound to see any Indian they encountered as "the enemy." So why had Mr. Baldwin asked her to represent him?

That question plagued her during the graveside ceremony, but she couldn't come up with a satisfactory answer. When the mourners dispersed, Mary Jo approached her with an obviously inebriated Dugin in tow.

"Thank you for coming, Maggie," she said, daintily dabbing at her eyes with a lacy handkerchief. "You're coming to the reception, aren't you?"

"Oh, I wouldn't want to intrude, Mary Jo," Maggie said.

"Nonsense, ya gotta be there," Dugin said, his voice loud, his words slurred. "We're gonna have us a party to send the old man off in style. If you don' show, I'll have to call that bastard Baldwin and tell him you were a bad girl."

Mary Jo elbowed him in the ribs, then gave Maggie a pleading look. "Please come. Most of these people are Jeremiah's friends. I'd like to have some of my own there this afternoon."

Unable to help feeling sorry for the poor woman, Maggie agreed. "All right. But just for a little while."

Dabbing at her eyes again, Mary Jo nodded and dragged Dugin off to the funeral home's limousine. Maggie returned to

her rental car and drove to the Kincaid house again. A uniformed maid answered the door and directed her to the dining room, where a lavish buffet had been set out.

Maggie served herself a cup of coffee, then carried it into the adjoining living room, hoping to find an out-of-the-way place to sit. The sofa and matching love seats grouped in front of the massive stone fireplace were occupied, but she spotted an empty pair of wing chairs tucked into a corner. Carefully making her way through the clusters of chatting guests, Maggie claimed one of the chairs with a quiet sigh of relief.

Trying to be as unobtrusive as possible, she sipped her coffee and listened to the general buzz of conversation, mentally planning the romantic weekend with Jackson that she'd been considering all day. Then a tall, gray-haired man wearing a Western-cut suit broke away from a group standing near the grand piano and headed straight toward her. Half expecting a verbal assault, Maggie braced herself while she plastered on a polite smile.

Without waiting for an invitation, the man sat in the other wing chair and looked her over with an expression that was barely short of insulting. "You work for Baldwin?"

"That's right. I'm Maggie Schaeffer. And your name is?" she asked, declining to offer her hand.

"Robert Myers. I'm the new president of the Whitehorn Ranchers' Association."

Maggie studied him for a moment. Myers wasn't nearly as handsome as Jeremiah had been, but he had the same arrogant bearing she remembered. "Is there something you need from Mr. Baldwin?"

"Yeah. You tell him he's not off the hook, just because Jeremiah's dead. We still expect results, and he'd better produce 'em, if he knows what's good for him."

"Results in regard to what?" Maggie asked, struggling to maintain a neutral tone of voice.

Myers looked her over again, and this time he made no bones about being insulting. Then he leaned closer, giving her a predatory smile that chilled her blood. "I don't think I have to spell it out to you, honey. Just tell him what I said. And you can

also tell him he's got one hell of a warped sense of humor to use you as his messenger.''

Then Myers walked back to his companions. Her stomach knotted with fear that Jackson had been right about her boss all along, Maggie got up and left the room. She had to find Mary Jo and say goodbye as quickly as possible. And then she had to talk to Jackson.

Mary Jo Kincaid stood in the entryway, warmly greeting guests as they entered and left, silently cursing her idiot husband. Dugin should be the one listening to all this phony sympathy. But no, he was too busy celebrating the death of the old son of a bitch who'd sired him. Still, she had to admit it *was* fun to flaunt her wealth in front of all these self-righteous prigs.

Dugin was a wimp, but as Jeremiah's sole surviving heir, he was now a filthy-stinking-rich one. God, it was wonderfully ironic. Here she was, wearing designer clothes, playing lady of the manor, with the town's leading citizens sucking up to her like she'd always been one of them. Hah!

If only they could have seen her the day she was standing on a street corner with her boobs practically falling out of a tank top and a short, tight skirt barely covering her ass, trying to pick up her first trick. It seemed like it was only yesterday, but it wasn't. She was a different person now. Completely different.

''Mary Jo?''

The sound of her name startled Mary Jo out of her memories. Turning, she saw Maggie Schaeffer staring at her with concern and sympathy. Dear, sweet Maggie. If it wasn't for her, those other damn Indians wouldn't have allowed a Kincaid onto the reservation at all.

''Hello, dear.'' Mary Jo clasped Maggie's outstretched hand between both of hers. ''I'm so glad you could come. Do you really have to leave so soon?''

''I'm afraid so,'' Maggie said with a smile.

''Well, then, I'll walk you out to your car. I could use a breath of fresh air.''

Mary Jo brushed past the maid and opened the door herself. An old lady dressed in a ratty-looking black polyester pantsuit

stood on the porch, her hand raised, as if she'd been about to ring the bell.

"I'm Winona Cobb," she said. "I've come to pay my respects to Jeremiah's kin."

Mary Jo shook Winona's hand. She'd much rather chat with Maggie, but she could hardly neglect her duties as a hostess. The old woman's eyes widened, then rolled back in their sockets. A second later, she slumped to the floor in a dead faint. Maggie dropped to her knees beside Winona.

"She's breathing, but you'd better call an ambulance, Mary Jo," she said.

"When there's three doctors in my living room?" Mary Jo ordered the maid to fetch one, then knelt down on the other side of Winona. "Winona. Yoo-hoo. Winona, can you hear me?"

The old woman frowned, but didn't open her eyes. "No need to shout," she muttered. "I'm psychic, not hard of hearing."

Mary Jo barely repressed a snort of laughter. "Are you having a vision, Winona?"

Winona opened her eyes, but only to scowl fiercely at Mary Jo. Before she could say anything, however, Dr. Wilson arrived. Mary Jo and Maggie stepped out of the way while he examined the old woman. Five minutes later, he came over to talk to them.

"I think she'll be fine, but I'd better get her over to the hospital for tests. Would you mind calling an ambulance, Mrs. Kincaid?"

"Not at all," Mary Jo said, giving him her sweetest smile.

Maggie reached over and squeezed Mary Jo's hand. "I really do need to leave now. Thanks for inviting me."

"You're welcome. I'll be back out to the reservation next week," Mary Jo said. "I'll probably see you then."

She watched Maggie walk out to the long, curved drive, and, for a moment, wished she could go with her. Even the reservation was a happier place than this big old house, with only Dugin for company. Shaking her head at her own foolishness, she went inside to call an ambulance for that weird old bat on her front porch. A psychic. Hah!

*   *   *

Maggie took one last glance at the Kincaid house, then heaved a sigh of relief and drove away. She ought to demand combat pay for this day's work. Thank heaven it was finally over. It would feel wonderful to get back to the res.

When she passed the city limits, she reviewed her conversation with Robert Myers. The longer she thought about it, the more worried she became. If Myers felt confident enough to pass on such a direct threat to a U.S. congressman, something was definitely going on, and it had to involve the grazing leases.

She wanted to call Mr. Baldwin and demand an explanation, but she no longer trusted him enough to do so. No matter how hard she tried to rationalize the message from Myers, it smacked of dirty political deals between Baldwin and the ranchers.

Damn it, much as she would love a romantic weekend with Jackson, her instincts said she should head back to D.C. and see what she could learn from other sources. Gripping the steering wheel more tightly, she mashed the accelerator to the floorboards. She had to talk to Jackson and Frank.

Jackson shook his head, unwilling to believe what his old friend Bennie Gonzales had just told him. "Say that again, Bennie."

"I wouldn't kid about something like this, Jackson. I know it's a disaster for your people. Do you have any idea what Schaeffer put in that report?"

"Yeah. She read it in front of the whole tribe, and spent two full days revising it. It was great."

"Did you read the final version?"

"Well, no, but—"

"It's too damn big to fax, but I'll send out a copy by express mail tonight. This thing is so damning of the tribal leadership, she must have pulled a switch on you. I'll get off the phone now, so you can start calling around for support. You're gonna need a lot of it, pal."

Feeling as if he'd been kicked in the face, Jackson hung up the phone and stared into space. God, no. Maggie wouldn't have betrayed him like that. She wouldn't have betrayed the tribe. She wouldn't—

His throat slammed shut. A burning ache pierced his chest. A bitter taste filled his mouth. He was a lawyer. He believed in facts and evidence. And the evidence in this case pointed toward Maggie.

She had never promised to marry him. She hadn't said she would accept a job with the tribe. She'd insisted on representing Baldwin at Kincaid's funeral. She hadn't shown him or Frank the final report.

Hearing a car door slam outside, he turned to the window and gripped the padded arms of his chair so hard, it was a wonder they didn't crumple. The Little Fed had arrived. Well, wasn't this just as convenient as hell? Taking deep breaths, he forced himself to release the chair arms, sat back and waited. He didn't have to wait long.

"Jackson? Frank?" she called from the reception area. "I need to talk to both of you."

"Frank's gone home for the day," Jackson answered. "Come on in my office."

She rushed into the room a second later and perched on the chair she always used, her forehead wrinkled with worry. "I had a strange conversation with Robert Myers after the funeral today, Jackson. I think I'd better go back to Washington right away, so I can find out what's going on."

Jackson shook his head in feigned admiration. "You're good, Ms. Schaeffer. Damn good. But you can save the theatrics. I already know what's going on."

"What are you talking about?" she asked, staring at him as if he'd suddenly started to speak in Chinese.

"You're not the only one with contacts in Washington. I went to law school there, and some of my old classmates work on the Hill. One of them called me a few minutes ago and spilled the beans."

"What beans?" she demanded. "Jackson, start at the beginning."

"Now, why should I do that? You probably know more about what's going on than I do. I've gotta hand it to you, Maggie. You fooled me, and everybody else on this reservation. I never dreamed you could be involved in something so vicious."

"For God's sake, what are you accusing me of?"

Damn it she really was good, he thought. In fact, she probably had Academy Award potential, if she ever took her act to Hollywood. Well, enough of this bull.

"Your beloved boss introduced some legislation today. According to Bennie, he quoted extensively from your report."

"So?" she asked. "What parts did he quote?"

"The parts where you recommended the termination of this reservation. And the parts where you recommended that all of the people here be relocated to the Northern Cheyenne reservation at Lame Deer, because our tribal leadership is too weak to adequately serve them. Besides, that way we won't clutter up so much of Montana's valuable land."

"What?" She came off the chair as if a nail had suddenly poked through the seat and into her rump. "I didn't recommend anything of the sort. There's got to be some mistake."

"Yeah, and I'm the one who made it. At the very least, the court will extend those damned leases until Baldwin's legislation is passed or defeated. It could take months to settle this mess. Maybe even years. I can't believe how easily you suckered me in."

"I didn't sucker you, or anyone else! I read that report in front of the entire tribe. The only changes I made were the ones everyone agreed to."

"Then why haven't I seen the final copy? Why hasn't Frank? We've both asked you about it."

She rolled her eyes as if she were exasperated beyond endurance. "It's in the back seat of the car, where I tossed it when I was on my way to the post office to mail Mr. Baldwin's copy. I just forgot to bring it in."

"Yeah, that's what you said before."

"Well, I'll go get it, then." She pivoted on one heel and stomped toward the doorway. Jackson called her back.

"Don't bother. It's easy to fake a document with all the computer equipment your daddy donated. How would I know if what you show me now was what you actually sent to Baldwin?"

She turned back to face him again, her shoulders rigid, her chin lifted, her eyes flashing with fury. "You could trust me."

"You don't know how much I wish I could, Maggie. But I'm afraid it's too late."

"I see. Then I'll, uh..." She paused and cleared her throat before continuing. "I'll go pack my things and get out of your house. Goodbye, Jackson."

He sat there, rigid as a chunk of petrified wood, until he heard her car door slam and the sound of the engine faded into silence. Then he rubbed his burning eyes and reached for the phone. He couldn't allow his emotions to get the better of him. He had to call Uncle Frank and tell him the bad news. Maggie wasn't the only one who'd been sleepin' with the enemy. Jackson Hawk had, too.

Fifteen

"Then is it your testimony, Ms. Schaeffer, that Congressman Baldwin has grossly misrepresented the facts cited in your report, in order to pay off illegal campaign contributions from the Whitehorn Ranchers' Association?"

"That is correct, Mr. Chairman. The proof of my charges is contained in these documents."

Sitting off to the left, where he could see the side of Maggie's face, Jackson watched her pass a thick stack of papers to a congressional page, who then delivered them to Congressman Ralph McPhearson of Minnesota, chairman of the House Subcommittee on Native American Affairs. She looked so small, sitting there by herself in this big, ornate hearing room, but she faced the fifteen members of the subcommittee with a quiet dignity that lent credence to her every word.

Three weeks had passed since he'd last seen her. Twenty-one endless days and nights to miss her and regret his hasty accusations. In those same twenty-one days, she had been fighting for the tribe with astonishing ferocity. The woman obviously had plenty of her own connections in Washington, particularly with the press corps; from the size of the stink she'd raised, Jackson figured she'd used them all.

Baldwin had pulled every trick in the book to discredit her, claiming her membership in the tribe created a conflict of interest, hinting she was only acting out of vengeance because he'd spurned her sexual advances, suggesting he'd been about to fire her for shoddy work. Too many of his fellow committee members had seen Maggie's previous work to believe that last charge, however. As a result, they hadn't believed his other charges, either.

Maggie had been interviewed on the morning news programs of all three major networks, as well as the prime-time magazine

programs. In fact, the press had been having such a field day with the scandal, the Whitehorn Ranchers' Association had dropped their lawsuit over the grazing leases, and several embarrassed members had agreed to testify against Baldwin. Baldwin, who hadn't had the nerve to show up for this hearing, had already announced he would not seek reelection.

The publicity had brought about some other positive changes for the tribe. A group of Hollywood stars who owned homes in Montana had hosted a benefit for the tribe to pay the expenses of fighting the legislation and buy stock for the land that had been returned to the tribe's control.

Outraged at being portrayed as a bunch of rednecked racists, white citizens from every part of the state were contacting all of Montana's Indian tribes, opening up the kind of communication Maggie had hoped to facilitate.

They still had a long way to go, but the people of the Laughing Horse Reservation were slowly starting to find hope again. Forty percent of the tribe's high school seniors had graduated in caps and gowns. Ten new people had enrolled themselves at the alcohol and drug rehab center. Participation in all the programs at the Indian school had increased.

All because of one stubborn, feisty, compassionate little woman who wasn't afraid to stand up for her principles. A woman he had woefully misjudged. Thank God she didn't believe in "blaming a whole group of innocent people because of the actions of one rude jerk," as she had put it the first day he met her.

The committee members finished flipping through the papers the chairman had passed on to them. Congressman McPhearson gaveled the room back to order and invited the other committee members to question the witness.

Frank nudged Jackson in the ribs, then leaned over and whispered, "You watch. The Little Fed's gonna take care of everything. We won't even have to testify."

Jackson nodded in agreement. After watching Maggie's performances on television, he would be amazed if she didn't have the entire committee eating out of her dainty little hand in damn short order. Sure enough, though the members fired question

after question at her, she answered them clearly and directly, without resorting to rhetoric or defensiveness.

By the time the chairman invited her to make a closing statement, Jackson felt like he'd been dragged through ten miles of brush by a runaway horse. Maggie looked as chipper as if she'd simply had a friendly chat with a group of close friends. She sipped from her water glass, set aside the stack of papers in front of her, then began to speak.

"Thank you, Mr. Chairman. I would also like to thank the other members of the committee for your time and attention this afternoon. And, lastly, I would like to thank Congressman Baldwin."

She smiled at the surprised looks she received from the committee members.

"Whatever his motives for giving me this assignment, my life has been tremendously enriched by the opportunity to become acquainted with the people of the Laughing Horse Reservation."

Maggie talked from her heart then, telling the committee, and the rest of the nation through the television cameras broadcasting the hearing live, about her background. She spoke of her feelings of alienation from her own people and the difficulties she'd encountered on the res because she was an apple. She told of her initial reactions to the poverty and despair she had witnessed. She informed them about the discrimination the high school kids had faced, and the involuntary sterilization of Indian women.

Then she really cut loose. "Ladies and gentleman, since the arrival of the Pilgrims at Plymouth Rock, our two cultures have shared this continent. Our history together has often been marred by hatred and violence. We all need to know the truth of our mutual history and understand it. However, I would submit to you, to the Northern Cheyenne, and to all the other citizens of this country, that it is time to look to the future.

"Yes, I found terrible problems at Laughing Horse. But I also found an incredible amount of untapped potential. Instead of deploring the plight of these poor, conquered people, I suggest it's time for both sides to get to work.

"Let's stop blaming and finger-pointing and fearing each

other. Native Americans have much to learn from the white society. They also have much to teach.

"Honor the treaties this government has made with them. As conquered nations, grant them as much compassion and economic development assistance as this government gave to the Germans and the Japanese after World War II. Give them a fighting chance to achieve their potential and contribute their unique talents and perspectives to this society, as the Irish, the Poles, the Italians and every other ethnic group has done.

"Passing the legislation I drafted in my original report is only the first step in this process. But, ladies and gentleman, the time to take that first step is now, and only you can take it. Please, give it your consideration and support. Thank you."

Applause thundered through the chamber. Congressman McPhearson banged his gavel again, repeatedly calling for order.

"Thank you, Ms. Schaeffer." He leaned forward, bracing one elbow on the desk in front of him. After glancing at his colleagues, he directed a charming smile at Maggie. "By the way, if you're ever interested in a position on my staff, I'd be delighted to hear from you."

Two other committee members grabbed their microphones.

"Same goes for me, Ms. Schaeffer."

"Talk to me before you make any decisions."

Maggie chuckled and shook her head. "Thank you. I'll keep that in mind."

McPhearson's gaze searched the room until he located Frank. "Mr. Many Horses, are you prepared to testify now?"

Frank stood and waited for quiet. Then he spoke in a loud voice that needed no help from a microphone. "I would be happy to do that, Congressman, but I think Maggie's already said it all, except for one thing."

"What's that, Mr. Many Horses?"

"Maggie doesn't need a job on any of your staffs. She belongs with her people, and we want her to come home very much. If you folks need help here, though, we can find you plenty of other talented Northern Cheyenne young people who do need jobs."

Maggie looked over at him with a warm smile that never reached as far as the chair Jackson occupied. He stared at her,

willing her to look at him, but the effort proved futile. His heart sank. A jagged lump formed in his throat, but he told himself her refusal to acknowledge him was only what he deserved.

Frank sat down. McPhearson adjourned the hearing, and journalists swarmed around Maggie.

"Are you going back to the reservation, Maggie?"

"Is it true you've been offered a million-dollar advance to write a book about your experiences on the reservation?"

"Will you run for Baldwin's seat in the House, Ms. Schaeffer?"

Smiling, Maggie shook her head. "I haven't made any decisions about the future. Thank you all so much for the help you've given us. We really appreciate it."

Frank elbowed Jackson in the ribs again. "See? It's not hopeless. If you'll make peace with her, she'll come home."

"She hates me, Uncle Frank," Jackson replied. "And I don't blame her."

"Nonsense. She's a forgiving soul, but you must ask for that forgiveness. What have you got to lose by trying?"

What indeed? Jackson wondered. His uncle was right, of course. Without Maggie, the rest of his life stretched before him like a thousand miles of bad road.

Fear clawing at his vitals, he left the hearing room. He felt like an idiot, waiting in the hallway in the three-piece suit and wing tips he'd dug from the back of his closet for the occasion. He'd even thought about cutting his hair, but had decided the suit was enough of a gesture to gain acceptance.

Suddenly, she was there in the doorway, reporters still swarming, shouting questions at her like a pack of yapping dogs. Her eyes widened when she spotted him, and she came to an abrupt halt, forcing the journalists to crash into each other or run her down. Luckily, they chose the former option.

Jackson's voice deserted him. His muscles locked up. All it seemed he could do was stand there and gaze into her big, dark eyes—and hurt. A wary expression passed over her face, followed a second later by one that was utterly blank.

Then she turned, and would have walked off without so much as a greeting. Seeing what was probably his last chance to make amends slipping away spurred him to action.

"Maggie, wait. Please."

She froze. Looked over her shoulder at him. Raised her eyebrows at him as if to say, "What could you possibly want from me now, you slimeball?"

"I, uh, really need to talk to you, if you can spare a minute," he said, hating the desperation he could hear in his voice, but feeling helpless to erase it.

The reporters pivoted toward him as a group, their noses practically twitching with the scent of a new story. Jackson ignored them.

"Please, Maggie. It's important."

"Hey, Chief," one of the reporters called. "What's your name, and whaddaya want with Maggie?"

"No comment." Jackson shot the man a mind-your-own-damn-business glance, then returned his attention to Maggie. "You want me to beg in front of these people?"

Shaking her head, she stepped away from the crowd. When she reached Jackson's side, she turned to the journalists. "Come on, folks, I've been answering your questions for weeks. Give me a little break, okay? If there's any real news, I'll be sure to let you all know."

They grumbled a little, but gradually moved off down the hallway. She waited until the last straggler rounded the corner, then turned back to Jackson. Standing this close, he could see exhaustion in her face and feel tension quivering inside her like a guitar string pulled so tight it would snap at the slightest touch. He desperately wanted to pull her into his arms and offer her his strength and comfort. She'd probably kick him in the nuts. Just to play it safe, he shoved his hands into his trouser pockets.

"All right, Jackson," she said. "What is it?"

"You did a magnificent job for the tribe, Maggie. Thank you."

"I don't want thanks, from you or anyone else. They're my people, too."

"I know. And I'm sorry for what I said. I should have trusted you."

He saw her work down a hard swallow, and felt the lump in her throat as if it were his own.

"Yes, you should have," she said.

"Will you forgive me?"

"I did that a long time ago." She smiled at him, but it was a smile tinged with sadness and resignation. "Hating you was taking more energy than I could spare."

"God, if you only knew how much I've regretted losing my temper like that. It was a stupid, knee-jerk reaction. When Bennie used the word, *termination,* I went nuts. I knew I was wrong an hour later, but when I got to the house, you were already gone."

"It doesn't matter anymore, Jackson."

How could four little words, so quietly spoken, strike such terror into a grown man's heart? Jackson wondered, staring at her in dismay.

"Doesn't matter?" He yanked his hands out of his pockets and reached for her shoulders, ignoring the inner voice that warned him to stop and think. He was long past the ability to think rationally, anyhow. "Of course it matters."

When she tried to pull out of his grasp, he gave her a little shake. "No. I love you, Maggie. You've got to believe me."

"I believe you loved me as much as you could," she said slowly. "And I honestly don't blame you for the way you reacted."

"Then come back. If you'll give me another chance, I promise I'll never doubt you again."

She glared at him until he let go of her. "Don't make promises you can't keep."

"But I *can* keep it," he insisted. "I've learned so much in the last month... Hell, Maggie, you'd be amazed."

She shook her head and stepped back, holding up one hand as if she feared she would have to fend him off. "No. Jackson, I'm really sorry. I wish I could believe you, but I couldn't handle it if you ever turned on me like that again. It's too late."

Though he'd expected as much, hearing her say those words with such finality hit him like a kidney punch. He inhaled a deep, shuddering breath, let it out, then shoved his hands back into his pockets. "All right. But what about the tribe? They still need you."

"No, they don't. According to what I've heard, the prospects

at Laughing Horse look much better now. You and Frank will lead the people just fine.''

''You're wrong. If it's too uncomfortable for you to come back with me there, I'll leave Laughing Horse.''

She gaped at him as if he'd just offered to commit suicide in front of her. ''That's ridiculous, Jackson. You're their lawyer. You're a vital part of the leadership there. You can't just leave.''

''The people see you as their champion, and it's been too many years since they've had one. There are other Indian lawyers around. There's only one Maggie Schaeffer.''

''Well, it's out of the question, so don't even think about it.''

''What are you gonna do?''

''I'll have to stay here until the legislation passes. After that, I don't know. I need some time to rest and figure it out.''

''You'll let us know if there's anything we can do to help? With the legislation, I mean.''

''Of course. By the way, I hope you've noticed how many white people have stepped forward to help our cause. I never would have gotten this far without them.''

Jackson grinned slightly. ''Yeah, I've noticed. And it's already different when we go into Whitehorn now. I figure, if some of those knotheads can change their attitudes, so can I.''

''Good. Take care of yourself, Jackson.''

''You too, Maggie. If you ever change your mind about trying again, you know where to find me.''

A stiff nod was her only response before she turned and left. Letting her walk away was the hardest thing he'd ever had to do. Frozen in torment, he stood there long after she disappeared around the corner. He started when a big hand descended onto his shoulder.

Looking up, he found himself gazing into his uncle's sympathetic eyes. ''It was a good effort, nephew,'' Frank said.

Jackson laughed, without much humor. ''I suppose you listened to the whole thing.''

Frank nodded. ''I'm sorry it didn't work out. C'mon, I'm tired of this big-city stuff. Let's go home.''

Grateful for his uncle's understanding, Jackson accompanied

him out of the building. By the time they boarded their flight at National Airport, dusk had fallen. Jackson took the window seat, strapped himself in, then sat back and closed his eyes.

He didn't open them again until the plane took off. Hunching forward, he looked out the small window at the lights flashing on all over the city. Maggie was down there somewhere. He didn't want to believe she really intended to end their relationship for good. He couldn't approach her again himself, but he'd be damned if he'd give her up, either. Not just yet.

So what the hell was he gonna do? Wait and pray for Maggie to change her mind? Hah! Well, he wouldn't count that out entirely, but as stubborn as she was, a man could get too old to enjoy sex before she budged a centimeter. Talk about a criminal waste of resources.

Tapping his fingers on the armrest, he struggled to come up with some other options. If he could just find a way to get her back out on the res, so that she could see all the things that were happening... Yeah, that was what he needed to do, all right.

But how? She wouldn't come to see him. Hell, she probably wouldn't want to get within a hundred miles of him. But what about her grandmother? Would Annie Little Deer help him? Well, there was only one way to find out.

Four weeks later, Maggie sat at the dinette table in her apartment, flipping through the stack of job offers she had received. Though some of them were extremely interesting, she was tired of looking at them, and even more tired of being holed up in her apartment. But for the life of her, she couldn't bring herself to make a decision.

She'd managed just fine while the legislation she had proposed was working its way through Congress. Congressman McPhearson and his subcommittee had really gotten behind it. One of Montana's senators had sponsored identical bills in the Senate at the same time, and since no politician wanted to risk being labeled anti-Indian after all the recent publicity, the legislation had been enacted with record speed. The president of the United States had signed the bills last week, and had personally thanked her for her efforts at the ceremony.

The excitement had died down quickly after that. When she first returned to Washington, the danger to the tribe's survival had been too immediate for her to be able to afford the luxury of tears over Jackson's betrayal. The minute she returned from the White House, however, all the pain and rage she'd been forced to repress had hit her like the proverbial ton of bricks.

She'd wept off and on for the better part of three days. Then she'd pulled herself together and spent the next three days going through the mountain of mail she'd received from all over the country. Now it was time to get on with her life.

There would be no melodramatic depression over her failed romance with Jackson Hawk. She refused to sit around whining and feeling sorry for herself. She'd gambled and lost, and she'd acknowledged the hurt. As far as she was concerned, that should be the end of it.

The only problem was, she couldn't stop thinking about Jackson. Couldn't stop dreaming about him at night. Couldn't stop missing the wretched man, though why she would miss someone who had believed such vile things about her, she hadn't a clue. Perhaps she should see a shrink about these masochistic tendencies.

Sighing in disgust, she flipped through the job offers again, setting the most appealing ones to the right. Now wasn't that interesting? All the congressional offers had landed on the left, as had the ones from other government agencies and national Native American organizations that wanted her to become a lobbyist. It must be time to get out of Washington.

Shoving that stack to the edge of the table, she went through the remaining letters more slowly, again setting the most appealing offers to the right. Now she could count out the universities that wanted her to teach Native American studies or public administration courses. Great. She was finally making progress.

Piling the newest rejects on top of the others, she repeated the process. This time it bogged down completely. She hadn't been offered a million-dollar advance for a book about her experiences at Laughing Horse, but the offer she *had* received was certainly respectable. The idea of writing such a book in-

trigued her more than the money involved, anyway. Okay, so she wanted to write the book.

But what would she do after that? It wasn't as if she anticipated a long career as a writer. She could do a credible job with this one project, but she didn't have any other stories screaming to be put on paper.

The other offers were from Indian tribes all over the country. Some wanted her to coordinate social programs. Others wanted her to conduct a needs assessment similar to the one she had done at Laughing Horse. She couldn't even decide what kind of work she wanted to do, much less which tribe she wanted to work for.

The Seminoles in Florida? The Lakota in South Dakota? The Blackfeet in Montana? The Oneida in New York? The Apache in Arizona? The Choctaw in Oklahoma? Perhaps she should hire herself out as a roving consultant and travel from tribe to tribe. Did she want anything to do with Native Americans at all?

Yes. Nothing had ever given her as much personal satisfaction as helping the Northern Cheyenne had. Would she feel the same way about another tribe? Or had knowing she was working for her mother's people, her *own* people, added a special dimension?

Flipping through the stack one last time, she pulled out the letter from Frank Many Horses. Her throat constricted, and a film of tears blurred her vision. Damn it, she wanted to go home. Not to Denver, although she would love to visit her father soon. But somehow, home had come to mean Laughing Horse.

She couldn't go there, of course, because she wasn't ready, might never be ready, to see Jackson. The temptation to try again would be too strong. God, it had been so hard to walk away from him that day after the hearing. So hard not to fling herself into his arms, when he'd apologized so sincerely. Even after all this time, it hurt to remember that conversation. Had she made a mistake?

"No," she said aloud, pushing herself away from the table. "You did what any self-respecting woman would do, so don't

start second-guessing yourself. You're lonely and confused, but you'll get over it.''

The phone rang. Grateful for any form of distraction, Maggie lunged for it.

"*Pave-voona o!* Maggie. This is Rose."

"Good morning to you, too, Aunt Rose," Maggie said with a smile. *"Ne-toneto-mohta-he?"*

"I'm fine," Rose replied. "Your Cheyenne is improvin'."

"Thanks, but you've now heard most of my working vocabulary, so you'd probably better stick with English."

Rose chuckled. "Well, hey, you should come home and get to work on it. That's why I'm callin', Maggie."

"Oh, Aunt Rose," Maggie said, "I haven't decided what I'm going to do yet."

"I didn't mean forever. I'll nag you about that some other time. This time, I just want to make sure you're comin' to Mama's birthday party on Saturday. You got a plane reservation, don't cha?"

"Yes, but—"

"Don't give me no buts," Rose said. "She's gonna be eighty years old, and she wants to hold a giveaway in your honor. Everyone in the family has contributed. You must be there, or you will shame her."

Maggie gulped. Holy smokes, there was no graceful way to get out of this one. According to Northern Cheyenne tradition, you simply did not shame your elders, intentionally or otherwise. Not unless you never intended to see any of your relatives again.

"Well, um," Maggie stammered, "I, uh, I really don't know what to say."

"Say yes," Rose demanded. She was silent for a moment, but when she spoke again, her voice was soft with sympathy. "Maggie, we know you and Jackson broke up. He won't be at the party. You won't have to see him. Losin' Bevy hurt Mama enough. Don't you hurt her, too."

"All right. I'll be there."

"Good. We'll hold a sweat tomorrow night. Someone will meet you at the airport in Billings."

"Fine, but I'd rather rent my own car, Aunt Rose."

"Whatever you want. We'll see you soon."

Maggie hung up the phone, then stood there and stared at it for a moment, trying to convince herself there hadn't been a sneaky undertone to her aunt's voice. Aunt Rose wouldn't lie to her, would she? No, that was silly and paranoid. If Rose said Jackson wouldn't be there, then he wouldn't.

So why did she feel so...alive, all of a sudden? Granted, she was pleased to be wanted at her grandmother's birthday party. And having a traditional giveaway ceremony, a public expression of love and respect from one's family, held in her honor was certainly a thrill.

Deep down inside, however, she knew her excitement had nothing to do with her relatives. No, it had everything to do with the possibility that while she was at Laughing Horse she would somehow manage to run into Jackson.

Cursing under her breath, Maggie whacked her forehead with the heel of her palm, as if she could knock some sense into her own head. Unfortunately, it didn't help. Not even a little.

Sixteen

Maggie was welcomed back to the res like a long-lost daughter. Tipped off by a child posted to watch for her, the aunts, uncles and cousins rushed out of Annie's house as she parked her car. Unbearably touched by all the talking, laughing and hugging, she wiped away happy tears and went inside to greet her grandmother.

Annie wept for joy at the sight of her, kissed her cheeks and demanded to hear all about meeting the president and what it was like to be on TV. When Maggie had finished, her uncle, William Little Deer, told everyone to get ready for the sweat. The experience was similar to the sweat she had shared with Jackson, with a few notable exceptions.

The lodge was large enough to accommodate fifteen people; the number of family members present required three separate ceremonies, two of which had already taken place. Uncle William conducted the ceremony Maggie attended. Her cousin, Mike Weasel Tail, served as the fire keeper, and Uncle Henry Little Deer was the drummer.

The heat and darkness didn't frighten her this time. All of the prayers were offered in Cheyenne, but the spirit of closeness and safety and belonging with these people was the same. It was as if the sacred steam had cleansed them of all harsh thoughts and feelings.

Because the night was warm and Annie's little house had only one bathroom, everyone plunged into a nearby creek to bathe when the sweat was over. Then they all trooped back to the house, changed into dry clothes and gathered in the kitchen for a feast. Listening to the affectionate teasing and bickering, Maggie told herself she owed Jackson a huge debt for helping her reconnect with this family.

Even in the midst of forty-some loving relatives, she found

herself missing him. Wanting him. Loving him. And hating herself for it. For God's sake, she was twenty-seven years old, and she'd never been one of those women who desperately needed a man to make her happy. She should be getting over him by now. Why didn't the nagging ache of longing for him just go away?

She found no answers that night, or the next morning. At noon, the family piled into their vehicles and drove to the Indian school in Laughing Horse for the party. The dining hall quickly filled with people. At first, Maggie flinched inwardly every time a new group arrived. As time passed and Jackson never appeared, however, she began to relax.

Annie received a lovely assortment of gifts from her many friends and relatives. Then, with Uncle Henry announcing an embarrassingly long list of Maggie's accomplishments, Annie gave away an even larger assortment of gifts. It was a lovely ceremony, a way of expressing gratitude to the community for the love and support that had made it possible for her granddaughter to succeed.

Since Maggie and Annie were not allowed to help serve the huge meal the women in the family had prepared, they ate together, chatting and enjoying each other's company. If Maggie had seen Frank Many Horses approaching, she would have made an excuse to leave the room. She was so involved with her grandmother, however, that she didn't notice him until he was only two steps away.

To her dismay, her grandmother invited him to join them, and after a few minutes of polite conversation, Annie excused herself from the table. While Maggie smelled a rat the size of a buffalo in this whole setup, she didn't see any polite way to avoid hearing what he had to say.

"It's good to have you back here again, Maggie," Frank said, giving her a charming smile that reminded her painfully of Jackson.

"Thank you. It's nice to be back."

"Have you considered our job offer?" he asked.

She nodded. "Of course. It's tempting, Frank, but I'm afraid I can't accept it."

"You're refusing because of Jackson."

She started to shake her head, then changed her mind and nodded again. Frank had never been less than honest with her. She believed he deserved the same courtesy. "I think it would be too…uncomfortable for both of us."

"You have accepted another job, then?"

"No. I'm having a hard time deciding."

"I see." Frank clasped his hands together on the table in front of him and gazed down at them for a long moment. "My nephew is sometimes a pigheaded turnip-brain, Maggie."

"Oh, Frank…" Maggie sputtered with laughter and shook her head. "He's not that bad."

Frank smiled, but didn't look up at her. "Yes, sometimes he is. But he has a good heart. He is deeply sorry for the things he said to you, and I know he would tell you so again if you would listen to him. He loves you very much."

"Loving someone means trusting them," Maggie said. "Jackson has never really been able to trust me."

"Trust does not come easy for many of us. It takes a long time to grow, especially if a person's trust has been betrayed before, as Jackson's was. Is it possible you expected too much, too soon?"

"I suppose. I was only here for two months."

"That is not very long. Did you ever really trust him?"

"I moved in with him, Frank."

He shrugged one shoulder in a near-perfect imitation of Jackson. "So, you trusted him with your body. Did you ever trust him with your heart?"

"For a woman, one usually goes along with the other," Maggie said.

"That is not always the case for a man, Maggie. My nephew needed a solid commitment from you. Perhaps if you had given him one, it would have been easier for him to give you his trust."

Maggie thought back to the day Jackson had proposed to her. She had never agreed to marry him, not in so many words. When they argued about Jeremiah Kincaid's funeral, she had suggested rethinking their whole relationship. After the way he'd opened himself up to her, that must have hurt him. And

when he'd accused her of betraying the tribe, she'd run away instead of fighting to convince him he was wrong about her.

"Maybe some of what happened was my fault, Frank. But I still have a problem with his attitude toward whites. Every time we disagreed over something, my background became an issue. He always said or implied I didn't understand because I'm just an apple. I can't live with him if he's going to continually point out I'm not Indian enough."

Chuckling, Frank finally looked up at her, his eyes glinting with deviltry. "And here I thought you were supposed to be such a smart gal."

Maggie raised an eyebrow at him. "You mean I'm not?"

"Sometimes I think you kids with your big college degrees don't know anything about livin'."

"Okay. Explain it to me, then."

"Jackson lived with divided loyalties for years, Maggie. He knows how difficult it can be to make choices when a conflict of cultures occurs. He also knows how seductive the white world can be. If he knew in his heart that your first loyalty was to *him*, I don't think he'd be so afraid that other influences would take you away from him."

"That's where all of these apple remarks come from? He's afraid I'll leave him?"

"Your guess is as good as mine," Frank said, "but if you're as smart as I think you are, you'll ask Jackson that yourself."

Maggie studied him for a moment before giving him a rueful smile. "You sly devil. You set me up like a pro."

"Yeah. But you know I'm right."

"So tell me something. How do you know so much?"

His eyes dancing with glee, he shrugged again. "Aw, it's nothing. I'm just a wise old Indian. Like in the movies."

For the first time in weeks, Maggie threw back her head and laughed, laughed until her sides ached. Frank laughed right along with her. By the time they'd both regained control, she felt as if the black cloud that had been her constant companion for weeks had finally given way to sunshine.

"Do you think my grandmother would be offended if I left for a few hours?" she asked.

"I think she'll be more offended if you don't," he answered. "She went to a lot of trouble to get you out here for this."

"I wondered about that." Maggie dug the keys to her rental car out of her purse, then stood and kissed Frank's cheek. "Where is Jackson today?"

"At his house."

"I'll go see him, but I can't make any promises, Frank."

"Just hear him out, Maggie. That's all any of us will ask of you. I'll tell Annie where you went."

Maggie slipped from the room and hurried out of the building. Her stomach suddenly felt as queasy and nervous as it had the day of the hearing, but she squared her shoulders, climbed into her car and drove toward Jackson's house. At some level, she'd known all along that any visit to Laughing Horse would eventually come to this.

She had to face Jackson one more time, and, hopefully, find a way to resolve their differences. Though she had always seen herself as an independent woman, the truth was, her life wouldn't be any fun at all without him.

Rip, plunk. Rip, rip, plunk. Rip, rip, rip, rip, plunk. Wiping his sweaty forehead with the back of his hand, Jackson glanced at the sun, figured it must be about three o'clock, and went back to pulling weeds. The June heat was bringing his garden to full production. He'd planted so much this year, it wouldn't be easy to keep up with the harvesting.

He usually enjoyed being out in the sunshine and working without a shirt. But today, despite the radio he had blaring on the patio, he couldn't find the right rhythm for pulling these damn weeds. Rip, plunk. Rip, rip, rip, plunk. *Rip.* Aw, hell.

Throwing down the bean plant he'd accidentally yanked out by the roots, he straightened up and brushed the dirt off the scars on his chest from last year's Sun Dance, sucking in deep breaths to calm himself. It didn't help, of course. Knowing Maggie was back on the res made it impossible to feel anything close to calm.

Damn it, he shouldn't have let his hopes get so high. She wasn't gonna come to see him today. By tomorrow she'd be gone again. There wasn't a blessed thing he could do about it,

so he might as well get back to work. The women in charge of the canning project for the reservation's food bank would be glad to get his produce.

Rip, plunk. Rip, rip, plunk. Rip, rip, rip, rip, rip, plunk. Next year, he'd expand his garden to a half acre. It might not be as exciting a way to provide food for the tribe as it had been in the old days, when Cheyenne men hunted buffalo, deer and elk, but it worked. In fact, he was amazed at how much food a person could get out of a little plot of land.

If Maggie was here to coordinate this thing, she'd probably be running the county extension agent ragged, testing everybody's soil and giving classes on how to improve yields. And she'd be infecting everyone with enthusiasm to get involved. But Maggie wasn't here. She wasn't ever gonna be here to do things like that again. He had to find a way to accept it.

"Jackson?"

He paused for an instant, then shook his head and went back to work. Great. It wasn't bad enough he had to see visions of her everywhere? Evidently not. Now he was imagining the sound of her voice, too. Before long, he'd be having full-fledged hallucinations. Rip, rip, plunk. Rip, rip, rip—

"Jackson."

Still bent over the plants, he froze. Oh, God, it had sounded so real that time, he was afraid to look. Forcing his fingers to release the weeds, he listened to them plunk into the bushel basket at his feet. Then he slowly turned his head.

Twenty feet away, two sleek, nylon-covered legs came into view, followed by a full, bright red skirt. Lifting his gaze, he saw a narrow waist cinched by a belt of silver and turquoise conchos. The fitted bodice of a sundress covering full breasts came next. And finally, a graceful neck and Maggie's face. If this was a hallucination, it was so beautiful, he hoped it would stick around a while.

Maintaining eye contact, he straightened to his full height. "Are you real?"

"Of course I'm real." She squinted at him, then raised one hand to shade her eyes. "Jackson, are you all right?"

"If you're really here, I'm fine. If you're not, it's time to call the guys in the white coats to come and get me."

Maggie walked over to the patio and shut off the radio. Then she came back to the garden and carefully made her way between the rows of plants, stopping two feet away from him. "I'm real, and I'm here, Jackson. I need to talk to you."

Turning to face her directly, he slowly raised one hand to touch her, halting in midair when he heard her gasp.

"Good Lord, haven't you been eating anything?" she demanded. "You must have lost twenty pounds!"

Jackson shrugged. "I haven't been very hungry."

Lifting her right hand, she traced his Sun Dance scars with a butterfly-soft touch. Every nerve ending in his body jumped to full alert. God, she *was* real.

"You're not going to have your chest pierced again this year, are you?"

"Yes, I am. It's an act of gratitude and sacrifice for the tribe's continued survival."

"Wasn't it awfully painful?" she asked.

"That's what a sacrifice is all about. It's an old, old tradition for our people and the other Plains tribes. The scars are considered marks of honor."

She gulped, then raised her gaze to meet his. "The tribe means everything to you, doesn't it?"

"The tribe and my family," he agreed. "Since I killed any hope of a future with you, they're all I have left."

"Could we talk for a little while?" she asked.

He studied her, desperately wanting to believe she'd come for a reconciliation, but fearing another failure with equal desperation. "What do you want to talk about?"

Clasping her hands in front of her waist, she looked down at them. "I saw your Uncle Frank at the party. He, um, helped me to see you weren't the only one who made mistakes. I'd like to try to work things out if we can."

"Why, Maggie?"

"Because I miss you." She looked up at him again, hesitating for what seemed like an excruciatingly long time before adding, "And, because I can't seem to stop loving you."

Jackson exhaled his pent-up breath, feeling the same wonderful sense of release he'd felt at the Sun Dance, when the leather thongs, threaded under his skin by the holy man's

skilled hands finally tore loose. That moment had held a promise of freedom from agony, as did this one. Please, *Maheo,* give me the right words this time, he thought. Don't let me screw up again.

He cupped the side of her face with his hand, smiled at the grubby swath his dirty thumb left on her soft cheek, then motioned for her to precede him from the garden. Her skirt swirled around her knees as she turned away from him and hurried toward the grass. His gut knotting with a combination of anxiety and hope, he followed her to a shady patch of grass under the old cottonwood tree.

She sat cross-legged, skirt spread around her, elbows propped on her thighs, fingers tangled in a nervous little ball that dangled between her knees. He sat facing her, with his legs stretched out in front of him and his hands braced on the grass behind him. He wanted to erase the worried wrinkles from her forehead, but he had no idea where to start. So he waited in silence and enjoyed the simple pleasure of looking at her.

Finally, she said, "I lied about something, Jackson."

"What was it?"

"I said I'd already forgiven you, but I really hadn't."

"I don't blame you, Maggie. The things I said were pretty unforgivable."

She nodded. "They hurt me a lot. But your uncle seems to think you might not have said them if I had agreed to marry you. That, um, maybe if I'd given you the commitment you needed, it would have been easier for you to trust me. Is that true?"

"Aw, Maggie..." Jackson sighed. "You're not responsible for my lousy temper. I am."

"I agree. But if you were always afraid I would leave, I can see how my refusal to give you a commitment might have helped confirm your worst fears about trusting me."

"Yeah, it did that, all right," he admitted. "I didn't want to believe you would betray me or the tribe, but when I got that call, I panicked. I could have handled it for myself, but the thought of all those other people paying such a high price for my bad judgment was almost more than I could take."

"I understand that now."

Leaning forward, he raised his knees and propped his elbows on them. "You know, one thing you said has haunted me. It was something about your not being Indian enough to suit me."

"I remember," she said. "It frustrated me half to death. You didn't trust me because I grew up off the reservation. Since I couldn't change that, I couldn't figure out what it would take to win your trust."

"You want to hear something funny? One of my big worries about getting involved with you was the fear that I might be *too* Indian to suit you."

She rolled her eyes in exasperation. "Oh, Jackson..."

"I'm serious. You grew up in the same society my ex-wife did. Nancy liked me just fine, as long as I was a yuppie Indian. But when she saw how my family lived and I stopped pretending I was as white as the next guy, she didn't want me anymore."

"But I'm not like that," Maggie protested. "I may not always understand your traditions and beliefs, but I respect them. Your willingness to share them with me was one of the things I loved most about you."

He smiled at that.

"Hey, intellectually, I know you're nothing like Nancy. Emotionally, it was a whole different story. When someone you love sees who you really are inside, and decides she can't love you anymore because of that..."

"It's pretty hard to trust anyone else," Maggie said. "I didn't trust you, either. And my reasons weren't any more rational than yours."

"Yeah? What were they?"

"If you think you denied you were Indian, you should have seen my mother. The only way I could win her approval was to be what you'd call an apple, but I always knew I really wasn't white. I guess, like you, I never believed the real me was very lovable. And then there was all that stuff with my biological father."

"What did that have to do with not trusting me?" Jackson asked.

She smiled. "He was a man. You're a man. My mother's

attitude about men was, don't count on them, you can never trust them to be there when you need them the most.''

"I thought she had a happy marriage with Cal Schaeffer."

"She did. But she always insisted I should never forget Cal was the exception to the rule. It's made it difficult for me to go beyond casual friendships with men."

"That's understandable."

"I suppose it is. Daniel Speaks Softly let her down when she was as vulnerable as any woman can get. That hurt never healed for her, and I accepted her ideas without questioning them."

"You were just a kid, Maggie. That's what kids do."

"Unfortunately, that's also how nasty things like racism and sexism get carried on from one generation to the next."

She shook her head and laughed without humor. "While I was accusing you of bigotry for lumping all white people together, I was equally guilty of lumping you with every man in the world who ever let a woman down. I'm sorry, Jackson. I should have known better, and I've hurt you because of it."

"It's not your fault."

He took one of her hands in his so that she'd stop torturing her poor fingers. They sat there, enjoying a peaceful moment of silence. She turned her hand over and clasped his, palm to palm. A deep sense of contentment bloomed in his chest. With it came a feeling of confidence that, at long last, they finally understood and accepted each other.

"Well, we've got some learning to do," he said, smiling because he simply couldn't help it. "But it sounds to me like we've been carryin' around a lot of baggage that belongs to other people, and it's been gettin' in our way. What do you think we should do with it?"

Maggie's eyes glinted with the playfulness he loved as much as he loved her tender heart. She tipped her head to one side and scrunched her face up, as if she were taking his question quite seriously. "We could bury it in the garden."

Jackson shook his head. "It'd kill off all the plants. We're dealin' with poisonous stuff here."

"Yeah, it's like toxic waste," she said. "We can't hurt Mother Earth. How the heck do we get rid of it, then?"

"It's not easy. But this wise old Indian I know told me that if you love somebody enough, just the way they are, and you keep on tryin' to work problems out, even when it's really tough, sometimes this kind of toxic waste will evaporate."

He noticed a subtle quivering around her chin, and her voice dropped to a whisper. "How much love is enough, Jackson?"

"I don't know." He squeezed her hand. "It's one of those spiritual things, you know? Where you just have to close your eyes and take what they call a leap of faith."

A fat tear rolled down her cheek, and her smile looked pretty crooked, but there was suddenly a light in her eyes he'd never seen before. She cleared her throat, as if it felt as tight and scratchy as his own did.

Then she said, "You know, I've always wanted to take one of those leaps, but I always needed a best friend to jump with me."

"I'll jump with you, Maggie. Anytime. Anyplace. You just tell me, and I'll be there."

One second she was sitting in front of him. The next she was a red blur. And, finally, she was in his arms, laughing and crying, kissing him with so much enthusiasm, she literally bowled him over. Flat on his back, he pulled her on top of him and held her sweet face between his palms.

"I love you, Maggie. Don't ever doubt that."

"I won't. Not even when you're being a pigheaded turnip-brain."

Jackson groaned, then had to laugh with her. "You and Uncle Frank must have had one hell of a talk."

She wrinkled her nose at him. "Oh, we did. I guess I'd better do what he told me to, or he'll call me something even worse."

"What did he tell you to do?"

"Give you a commitment, of course." She leaned down and kissed him. When she pulled away, the expression in her eyes was warm, but serious. "I love you, Jackson Hawk. Don't ever doubt that. Will you please marry me?"

"Anytime. Anyplace, honey."

"A week from today, at my grandmother's house. I want my father to be here."

"June 25 it is. And you won't ever have to worry about

choosing your father or me. I'll get along with him if it kills me.''

"You'll do much better than that," she scolded, poking his chest with her index finger. "Dad's going to love you, and you're going to love him."

"We'll see. But I guess any guy who had a hand in raising you can't be all bad."

"Thank you." She gave him a playful smooch. Then her eyes took on a dreamy, wistful expression that somehow managed to be sexy as hell. "Will you give me those pretty babies my grandmother said you would?''

"We've gotta do our part to keep the tribe alive, don't we? In fact, why don't we get started on those babies right now?''

Wrapping one arm around her waist, he rolled over, reversing their positions. She linked her hands behind his neck and pulled him down for a kiss that was hotter than the sun overhead.

Her eyes held a lusty gleam, her voice was a sultry purr, and her hips moved under his with an unmistakable promise. "You should know I'll expect you to share the child-rearing, Mr. Hawk. I'm going to be very busy with my new job."

"You're gonna work for the tribe?''

"Uh-huh. It's what I've wanted all along. Do you know, this is the first place I've ever really felt that I belonged?''

"At Laughing Horse?''

Her eyes misted over. "At Laughing Horse, and with you. I feel incredibly...safe here. As if I've finally come home.''

"You have, Maggie. No matter where we go or what we do, if we're together, we'll always be home.''

He kissed her. Gently. Tenderly. Reverently. And then there were no more words. Because, as a wise old Indian had once told him, there was a time for talk and a time for action. Jackson Hawk, tribal attorney, was smart enough to know the difference.

*   *   *   *   *

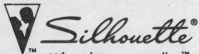

Celebrate Silhouette's 20th Anniversary

With beloved authors, exciting new miniseries and special keepsake collections, **plus** the chance to enter our 20th anniversary contest, in which one lucky reader wins the trip of a lifetime!

Take a look at who's celebrating with us:

DIANA PALMER

April 2000: SOLDIERS OF FORTUNE
May 2000 in Silhouette Romance: *Mercenary's Woman*

NORA ROBERTS

May 2000: IRISH HEARTS, the 2-in-1 keepsake collection
June 2000 in Special Edition: *Irish Rebel*

LINDA HOWARD

July 2000: MacKENZIE'S MISSION
August 2000 in Intimate Moments: *A Game of Chance*

ANNETTE BROADRICK

October 2000: a special keepsake collection, plus a brand-new title in
November 2000 in Desire

Available at your favorite retail outlet.

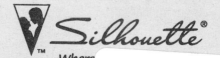

Where